WUTHERING HEIGHTS

Emily Brontë

edited by
Christopher Heywood

broadview literary texts

National Library of Canada Cataloguing in Publication Data

Brontë, Emily, 1818-1848
          Wuthering Heights

(Broadview literary texts)
Includes bibliographical references.
ISBN 1-55111-247-7

I. Heywood, Christopher.   II. Title.   III. Series.
PR4172.W7 2001   823'.8   C00-933207-3

Broadview Press Ltd. is an independent, international publishing house, incorporated in 1985.

North America:
P.O. BOX 1243, Peterborough, Ontario, Canada K9J 7H5
3576 California Road, Orchard Park, NY 14127
TEL: (705) 743-8990; FAX (705) 743-8353;
E-MAIL: customerservice@broadviewpress.com

United Kingdom:
Thomas Lyster Ltd.,
Unit 9, Ormskirk Industrial Park
Old Boundary Way, Burscough Road.,
Ormskirk, Lancashire L39 2YW
TEL: (01695) 575112; FAX: (01695) 570120; E-MAIL: books@tlyster.co.uk

Australia:
St. Clair Press, P.O. BOX 287, Rozelle, NSW 2039
TEL: (02) 818-1942; FAX: (02) 418-1923

www.broadviewpress.com

Broadview Press is grateful to Professors Eugene Benson and L.W. Conolly for advice on editorial matters for the Broadview Literary Texts series.

Broadview Press gratefully acknowledges the financial support of the Ministry of Canadian Heritage through the Book Publishing Industry Development Program.

PRINTED IN CANADA

Contents

Preface

This edition explores new literary ground. The Introduction begins with Emily's landscape, which matches the terrain around the Clergy Daughters' School at Cowan Bridge, at the northern edge of the Yorkshire Dales. In that setting, *Wuthering Heights* emerges as a skilled handling of a main landscape and a group of family histories from the Dales, the mountainous terrain running from Skipton to the region around Ingleborough. That enormous hill, the crown of the Dales, is Yorkshire's most celebrated natural landmark. It dominates the skyline in the views around Tunstall and Cowan Bridge, and in the view from the moorland around Withins Height, the summit of Haworth Moor. A reconstruction shows that Ingleborough occupies a position exactly matching that of Emily Brontë's hill named Wuthering Heights. That relationship between the text and its landscape was recognised by experienced writers on Yorkshire in the 19th century. They take the reader behind and beyond the concealments which Charlotte Brontë maintained in her Preface, and in her communications with Elizabeth Gaskell. This edition works onwards from there.

In its setting, Emily Brontë's novel emerges as a pioneering work in the tradition of English regional realism. Like other writers with knowledge of provincial and colonial life, she adopted and modified the central preoccupations of early Victorian England, the most powerful nation of that age. In its setting, *Wuthering Heights* overturns Charlotte Brontë's presentation of it in her Preface, as a novel with an evil hero. In maturity, it appears, Emily Brontë discovered that the Dales had been a rural summit of English slaveholding and its Parliamentary patronage. The central figure in her story, and the social problem he represents, reflect her knowledge about the black persons whom she cannot have failed to see around the Clergy Daughters' School. She shared the Emancipationist belief that oppression of the workforce, and evil acts of all kinds, originate in human ideas, and can be remedied by human action. The Emancipationists argued that as members of a single species, the pale and dark races are morally and intellectually on the same footing, and mutually dependent on each other for survival. They insisted that slavery corrupts the enslavers who started the violence, as well as the enslaved; that favouritism, and employment founded on slaveholding, result in violence among whites as well as blacks; and that the moral corruption generated by centuries of Atlantic slaveholding would be overcome through education. Their cornerstone was an enlightened view of our species in the history of the globe. Brontë built her story around that framework.

Another difficulty can be traced back to Charlotte Brontë's Preface. Contrary to her presentation of *Wuthering Heights* as a tangled text by an unskilled writer, it is possibly the most skilfully constructed of all novels in English. It reflects Emily Brontë's skill as a poet, painter, musician, and her interest in geometry. In a style borrowed from music and poetry of the Baroque and Metaphysical traditions, the symmetrical halves of this novel are divided into sections which resemble the act and scene divisions of a play, or the wings of a butterfly. Time and ideas are presented in mirrored structures resembling those of a musical canon or fugue. The two symmetrically numbered halves of her novel reverse the ideas about the two Yorkshire landscapes, the limestone north and the moorland south, which had marked the Picturesque movement in art and literature. Through that structure she dramatised the Emancipationist grand design: manufacturing output from the moorland industrial towns was envisaged as a cure for the blight brought on by the remittance economy, founded on slaveholding. Emily Brontë emerges in this light as a pioneering writer in the main stream of social thinking and literary methods of the 1830s and 1840s. These principles are outlined in this edition.

·

Abbreviations

Baines: Edward Baines, *History, Directory & Gazetteer, of the County of York*, 1822

BL: British Library

BST: *Brontë Society Transactions*

Carr: W. Carr, *The Dialect of Craven*, 2 vols., 1828

Craven: T.D. Whitaker, *The History and Antiquities of the Deanery of Craven in the County of York*, 1805

CRO/K: Cumbria Record Office, Kendal

EDD: Joseph Wright, *English Dialect Dictionary*, Oxford: Oxford University Press, 6 vols., 1899-1901

EIC: *Essays in Criticism*

Garnett: Emmeline Garnett, *John Marsden's Will*, London: Hambledon, 1998

Hutton: John Hutton, 'A Tour to the Caves' (1781), Addendum 7 in Thomas West, *Guide to the Lakes* (1812), pp. 238-85

K: *Catalogue of Books at the Keighley Mechanics' Institute*, Keighley, 1844-7 (Keighley Public Library)

K&K: The Keighley and Kendal Turnpike Trust, and Road

LRO: Lancashire Record Office, Preston

MLR: *Modern Language Review*

NCF: *Nineteenth-Century Fiction*

NED: *A New English Dictionary*, ed. James Murray and others, 13 vols, Oxford: Oxford University Press, 1888-1933 ('OED')

N&Q: *Notes and Queries*

P: *Catalogue of Books in the Library of Robert Heaton Esq, of Ponden House*, 1897 (Bradford City Archive)

Paterson: *Paterson's Roads in England and Wales*, 18th edn., ed. Edward Mogg, 1829

Smith: A.H. Smith, *The Place-Names of the West Riding of Yorkshire*, 8 Parts [vols.], Cambridge: Cambridge University Press, 1961-63

WYA/W: West Yorkshire Archive, Wakefield

Note: To avoid confusion, and for brevity, in this edition the names 'Emily' and 'Charlotte' refer to Emily Brontë and Charlotte Brontë in their domestic setting, in their literary handlling of texts and Yorkshire story material, and in their authorial relationship to the reader. Other members of Emily Brontë's household are similarly referred to as Anne, Branwell, and Patrick. The name 'Brontë' is reserved the the discussion of Emily Brontë's work where she cannot be mistaken for any other authors who are generally known by their father's names, for example, Donne, Goethe, Shakespeare, Wordsworth, and others. The name 'Emily Brontë signifies the individual of that name.

References to *Wuthering Heights* are generally to *WH*. The abbreviations (*K*) and (*P*) indicate works available to the Brontës in the libraries of Keighley and Ponden House.

Acknowledgements

Numerous contacts have made this edition possible. My students, colleagues and friends at the University of Sheffield, and in Japan, where I worked in several Universities, have been patient audiences. For insights into Africa, I am indebted to my colleagues and friends during two instructive years of work at the University of Ife, Nigeria. Among others who are too numerous to list in full, I thank especially the following, and in some instances, their unfading memory: Harry Armytage and Frances Armytage; Clyde Binfield; Louis and Nancy Carus; Alan Cass; John Figueroa and Dorothy Figueroa; Annemarie Heywood; Colin Holmes; Ron Hollett and Christopher Hollett; Eldred Jones; Bernth Lindfors; Eric Mackerness; Janet Nelson; Maurice Schofield; Margaret Sutton; Lance Tufnell; Maja-Lisa von Sneidern; Richard Westall; John Widdowson; and Vandy Wilkinson. My inquiries about pictures of the Clifford family were generously assisted by Lord Sackville, and by the staff of the Abbot Hall Gallery at Kendal and the National Portrait Gallery. My inquiries about the Brontës' Irish stories were assisted by Sir John Biggs-Davison, Kathleen Cann, Ronald Crossland, Elizabeth Diamond, Hazel Douglas, Patrick Humphries, Mary Lusk, Roger Lusk, Frank Pierce, and David Rankin. During my work as external examiner at Edge Hill College, Geraldine Wilby drew my attention to the article by Kim Lyon on the Sills of Dent; by sharing her research in response to an inquiry, Kim Lyon gave new impetus to my reading into the literary tradition associated with William Wilberforce and his circle. My exploration of Lunesdale would not have been possible without tireless help and encouragement from Ann Binder. Welcome assistance and hospitality have come from Hena Maes-Jelinek and Jeanne Delbaere-Garant. Helpful suggestions about the typescript have been made by Aveek Sen. The arguments presented here took root in a conversation with my Head of Department at the University of Sheffield, Sir William Empson. My childhood and education in and around Stellenbosch have contributed to my understanding of this novel, which I first read there. The reading embodied in this edition has been generously encouraged by John Bayley, Dennis Burden, John Buxton, and Lord David Cecil, my teachers at Oxford. Some are no longer with us; all are warmly thanked.

Among Libraries and Archives too numerous to list in full, and whose staff have given the tireless assistance which has made this edition possible, I thank especially the following: Aberdeen City Libraries; Banbridge Public Library; Bradford City Libraries and Bradford City Archive; the British Library and the outlying Newspaper Library at Colindale; the Bibliothèque Royale Albert Ier, Brussels; Cambridge University Library, and the Bible Society Archive before and after its incorporation into Cambridge University Library; the Adam Sedgwick Museum, Cambridge; Cradock Public Library; the Cumbria Record Office at Kendal and Carlisle; University College Library, Dublin; the John G. Wolbach Library of Harvard College Observatory; Haverford College Library and the Quaker Collection, Haverford College; the Brontë Parsonage Museum, Haworth; the Island Record Office at Spanish Town, and the National Library of Jamaica at Kingston, Jamaica; Kendal Public Library; the Lancashire Record Office, Preston; Lancaster University Library; Lancaster City Libraries and St George's Quayside Museum, Lancaster; the Brotherton Library and the Brotherton Collection of Leeds University; Leeds City Libraries; Liverpool City Libraries; the Public Record Office, London; the Pierpont Morgan Library, New York; the Bodleian Library, Oxford, and its outlying Libraries at Rhodes House and the Taylor Institution; the John Carter Brown Library at Brown University, Providence; Sheffield City Archive and Sheffield City Libraries; Sheffield Galleries and Museums Trust; Sheffield University Libraries and the Centre for English Language and Tradition (CECTAL) at Sheffield University; Skipton Public Library; the Humanities Research Center and the University Library at the University of Texas at Austin; the Victoria and Albert Museum; the West Yorkshire Archive at Wakefield, Leeds, and Bradford; the West Yorkshire County Library, Wakefield; and the Borthwick Institute, York. An inquiry into firearms was illumined by the staff of the Musée de l'Armée, Paris, the Musée de l'Armée, Liège, and Sheffield City Museum. In the final stages of preparing the illustrations I received invaluable assistance from Colourbox Techunique, of Oxford. A research and travel grant from Sheffield University enabled me to consult sites and documents in Jamaica; the hospitality of Professor John Figueroa and his family contributed to the welcome I found there. The authorities of Okayama University and Seto College/Kobe Women's University provided funding and study leave enabling me to pursue research during several happy years in Japan. All these are warmly thanked.

Wherever possible, studies of *WH* are acknowledged in the notes and Bibliography. In addition, I have drawn silently at many points on the researches and criticism of the following: David Cecil; Stevie Davies; Winifred Gérin; Q.D. Leavis; John Lock and W.T. Dixon; K.M. Petyt; C.P. Sanger; Joseph Wright; the *Wellesley Index of Victorian Periodicals*, and the editions of *Wuthering Heights* published by W.W. Norton (the Norton edition), and Oxford University Press (World's Classics, and the Clarendon edition).

The following are thanked for permission to reproduce pictorial and visual material in their keeping: the Trustees of the British Library; Greenwood Publishing Group, New York; Mary Farnell; Ann Binder; the Brontë Society; Sheffield City Museum Trust; the Victoria and Albert Museum, London; the Brotherton Collection, Leeds University Library; the National Portrait Gallery, London; Nottingham County Libraries; Hull City Museums; Manchester City Galleries; Huddersfield City Libraries.

For listening to my early presentations of this reading I thank the Departments of English at the University of Cape Town, the Jagiellonski University at Krakow, the University of Lodz, the University of Michigan at Ann Arbor, Okayama University, Rhodes University, the University of Texas at Austin, Texas Tech University, the University of the West Indies at Mona, Jamaica, and Witwatersrand University; also, the Barnsley Literary and Philosophical Society, the Librarian's Seminar at the John Carter Brown Library of Brown University, the organisers and sponsors of the Grahamstown Festival, the Brontë Scholars' Conference of Leeds University, the Adam Sedgwick Bicentenary Conference at Sedbergh, the Victorian Society at Sheffield, the Modern Studies Seminar of the University of Sheffield, the British Studies Association of the Humanities Research Center at the University of Texas at Austin, and the Katsu Yamamoto Memorial lecture, sponsored by John Jerwood at Hitotsubashi University, Tokyo.

For first publishing my articles setting out material and arguments which are incorporated in this edition, I thank the editors of *Brontë Society Transactions*, *Comparative Criticism*, *Durham University Journal*, *Essays in Criticism*, *Hitotsubashi Journal of Arts and Sciences*, *Lore and Language*, *Modern Language Review*, *Okayama University Journal of Arts and Sciences*, *Quarto* (Kendal), *The Review of English Studies*, *The Sedbergh Historian*, *The Sheffield Art Review*, *Romanticism and Wild Places*. *Essays in Honour of Paul Edwards*, edited by Paul Hullah, and *Litera IV. Essays in Honour of Yozo Muroya*, edited by Shigetake Morokawa.

Lastly, I warmly thank Broadview Press for the invitation to produce this edition. Also, all the opinions offered here, and any errors and omissions, are my own.

Okayama, Seto, Gargrave, Oxford

List of Illustrations

Emily Brontë: A Brief Chronology

1818   31 July: Emily Jane Brontë born at the parsonage of the
        Church of St James, Thornton, a chapelry of Bradford
        parish;

1820   On her father Patrick's appointment as Perpetual
        Curate of the Church of St Michael and All Angels at
        Haworth, a neighbouring chapelry of Bradford par-
        ish, Emily and her family move to the Parsonage at
        Haworth;

1821   Death of Maria Brontë, *née* Branwell (1783-1821),
        mother of the Brontë children, and entry of her sister,
        Elizabeth Branwell, into residence at Haworth Parson-
        age, after the rejection of Patrick's offer of marriage to
        Mary Burder, who had cherished hopes of such an
        offer in their youth;

1824   25 November: Emily is registered at the Clergy Daugh-
        ters' School, Cowan Bridge; spends the Christmas/New
        Year break at the home of the Principal, the Revd
        William Carus Wilson; in the spring and summer of
        1825, her two eldest sisters die from illnesses contracted
        at the School;

1825   1 June: returns home with with Charlotte;

1826   Patrick initiates his children's story-telling 'game' about
        historical personages;

1833   June: with Branwell, Anne and Charlotte, Emily makes
        a day trip in the Haworth pony cart, driven by Bran-
        well, to Bolton Bridge in Wharfedale, a round trip of
        38 miles; there meets Ellen Nussey, Charlotte's school
        friend at Roe Head School, and her mill-owning fam-
        ily;

1834   Begins writing the 'Gondal Poems' about love and war-
        fare between Gondal, a north Pacific island kingdom,
        and Gaaldine, an island to the south;

1835	Attends Roe Head School near Huddersfield;
1837-38	Employed for six months as teacher in Miss Patchett's school at Southowram, Halifax;
1842	January: escorted by Patrick, departs with Charlotte for Brussels; enters the Pensionnat (academy for young ladies) run by Constantin Heger and his wife; composes *devoirs* (essays) in French, and is appointed piano teacher at the Pensionnat;
1842	November: on the death of her aunt Elizabeth Branwell, returns to Haworth;
1842-48	As her father's housekeeper at Haworth Parsonage, witnesses family crises; in a nominal collaboration with her younger sister Anne, composes Gondal Poems and other poems; writes diary fragments addressed to Anne; holds nocturnal discussions with Charlotte and Anne on their writings, after 9 p.m., Patrick's bed-time; publishes a selection of her poems under the pseudonym Ellis Bell in *Poems* (1846) by Ellis, Acton and Currer Bell; publishes *Wuthering Heights* (1847); during this period, performs from her manuscript in the family circle at Haworth;
1848	23 December: aged thirty, dies of tuberculosis.

Introduction

1. The Wuthering Heights landscape

Recognition

In the Preface to the 1850 edition of *Wuthering Heights*, Charlotte hinted that 'the locality where the scenes of the story are laid', and 'the inhabitants, the customs, the natural characteristics of the outlying hills and hamlets in the West-Riding of Yorkshire' (Appendix B), are to be found in the vicinity of Haworth. However, the high, westward facing crags and western seaboard plain in Emily Brontë's novel do not match Haworth's low moorland hills, with their shallow gradients inclined north-east. In addition, Charlotte concealed Emily's studies, her teaching career, and her reading. For this she used selectively her reading resource of some 3,000 volumes at the Mechanics' Institute Library and at Ponden House, and other private collections which have remained unlisted. Charlotte's picture of Emily as a 'home-bred, country girl', a 'native and nursling of the moors' who 'rarely crossed the threshold of home', has deflected attention from the penetration and breadth of reading behind her sister's novel.

The difficulty of discovering the original for Emily's Yorkshire landscape was noted in *The Brontë Country* (1888), by J. Erskine Stuart, who observed that the Haworth region does not match the novel. In its gritstone southern Pennine moorland setting,[1] on a tributary of the eastward-flowing river Aire, Haworth had been a populous shearing and weaving town since Tudor times.[2] In contrast, *WH* portrays high crags facing westward across the seaboard plain, enclosing a secluded and thinly populated valley, which runs south-west. Narrowly missing a solution to that disparity, Stuart recognised the atmosphere of *WH* in the region of Ingleborough and Cowan Bridge, but made no further investigations.[3] Unknown to himself, his journey to Cowan Bridge took him into the heart of the celebrated landscape which stood as a model for the Brontë sisters' portrait of a Yorkshire region. By the time Stuart wrote, recognition of her Yorkshire original had appeared in a book which he appears not to have read, *Chronicles and Stories of the Craven Dales* (1881), by G.H. Dixon, who observed:

> Let the reader turn to *Wuthering Heights*, and if he know anything of Craven or its scenery, he will find in that wonderful novel some truly graphic sketching. Long before we knew anything of the author, we said 'This is Craven!' and we knew where to find the bleak and barren moorland solitudes, where the misanthropic hero had his crazy dwelling. Perhaps, we could have pointed out the misanthrope himself.[4]

Under a readily penetrated disguise, *WH* portrays the region around Ingleborough, where the Brontë sisters first went to school. The same Craven landscape is transparently portrayed as the setting of the Lowood Institute in *Jane Eyre*. Against that background, *WH* emerges as the work of a versatile and informed mind, at work on the parts of Yorkshire the Brontës had seen.

Numerous difficulties disappear when the landscape and Emily's technique of enigmatic presentation have been identified. In the first half of *WH*, she created a limestone landscape based on the Cowan Bridge region. Her story, constructed and presented with incomparable skill, turns out to have been based on prominent family histories from the same region, the Yorkshire Dales or Craven highlands, which run northwards from Skipton to Cowan Bridge. In the second half of the novel, however, the limestone landscape of the northern West Riding is anomalously clad with a moor, patterned on the southern moorland which reaches southwards from Skipton to Hathersage. After the pause in the story at chapter 17, the moorland is laid like a magic carpet over the landscape which she experienced in her school year at Cowan Bridge.

Another writer on Yorkshire identified several of Emily Brontë's historical originals from the Dales, and their links with Caribbean and English slaveholding. In *Wooers and Winners* (1880), Isabella Banks, a writer equipped with extensive experience of

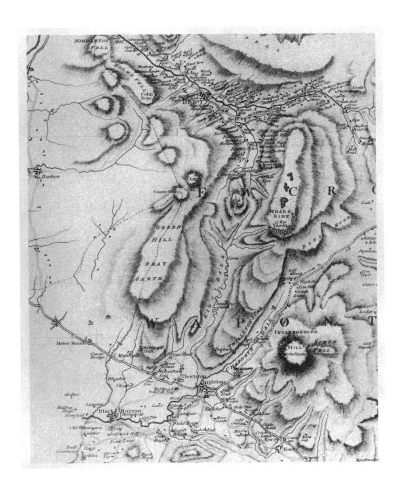

Plate 1 – Thomas Jefferys, *Map of the County of York* (detail).
Reproduced by permission of the British Library, London.

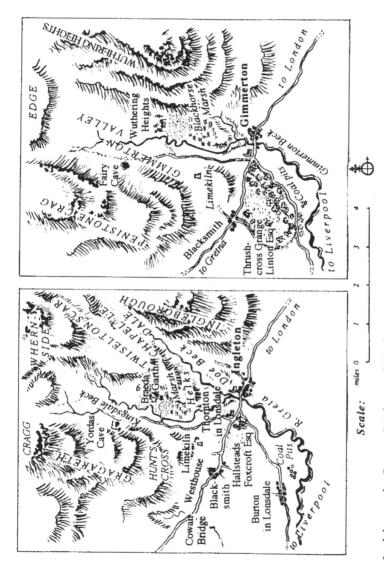

Plate 2 – Ingleborough, Cowan Bridge, and Wuthering Heights. Sources: John Tuke, *Map of the County of York* (1818); Thomas Jefferys, *Map of the County of York* (1771); Ordnance Survey 1" and 6" maps (1840) (West Yorkshire Archive, Wakefield); Emily Brontë, *Wuthering Heights*. Maps drawn by C. Heywood.

Yorkshire and its inhabitants, identified the story material and landscape in *WH* (Appendix C). Set in a neighbouring part of the Ingleborough region, *Wooers and Winners*, a thinly veiled *roman à clef*, identifies the historical and topographical originals in *WH*. Her compass bearings, limestone hills, valley, farmhouse, Fairy Cave, crossroads, kirk, beck, village, and back gates of the Grange park, are matched around Ingleborough (Plate 1). Along the old K&K, Thornton in Lonsdale and Ingleton were the coach's last stops before Cowan Bridge.[5] The old crossing of the Greta, in the chasm between Ingleton and Thornton in Lonsdale, was circumvented by the present main road (A65), opened shortly after the Brontës' journey home in the summer of 1825.[6]

Light concealment was part of Emily Brontë's intention. Her fictional landscape is defined in three brief asides which are made by Nelly Dean in the course of her narration (chs. 10, 11, 15, 18). These scattered clues have baffled readers who are accustomed to direct description in novels. Michael Irwin has observed: 'The reader can never establish quite where Gimmerton is situated in relation to Thrushcross Grange or Wuthering Heights'.[7] The presentation in *WH* anticipates the puzzle pictures which have emerged with the *Gestalt* movement in literature, art and psychology. In *Gestalt* pictures drawn by Gaetano Kanizsa, a church springs to view when outlines which are present from the start, among what look like random lines, are slightly thickened (Plate 3).[8] Similarly, the landscape definitions are lightly veiled by casual presentation as riddles and asides. Nevertheless, they accurately define the setting around Ingleborough which the Brontë's had seen.

Memory

Emily's puzzle picture is complicated by her combination of the two landscapes of the old West Riding, the limestone north and the moorland south. The sudden appearance of the moorland in the second half of her text (chs. 18-34) creates the dreamlike impression that it has been there from the start of the novel. It is named in the first half of the novel, but not described (ch. 3). The moorland and limestone landscapes of Yorkshire are sharply divided, however, by geographical, geological, botanical and social

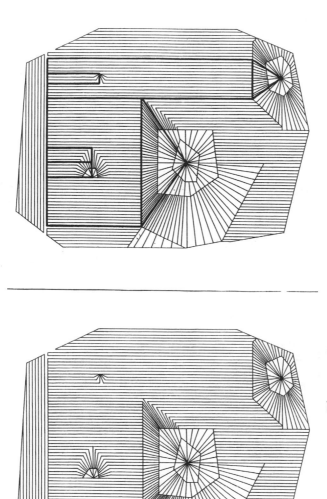

Plate 3 – Gaetano Kanizsa, *Gestalt* drawings.
From Gaetano Kanizsa, *Organization in Vision*, New York: Praeger, 1969, pp. 34–35.
Reproduced with permission of Greenwood Publishing Group, Inc., Westport, CT.

differences.[9] The division is implied in *A Springtime Saunter* (1911), by Whiteley Turner, who refers to lime from the north passing across Haworth Moor as though from fairyland, on trains of the Dalesman's sure-footed pony, the galloway: 'Old people tell us it was no uncommon sight when they were children to see twenty or thirty galloways [...] with tinkling bells, and panniers laden with lime, file down the moor'.[10] The gulf separating the two landscapes is recognised in *Goodbye to Yorkshire*, by Roy Hattersley, another writer from Yorkshire's industrialised moorland south, who recalls his first experience of the Dales landscape: 'It was almost twenty years before—in remembering it—I realized how beautiful it was'.[11]

With experience of the borders between picture making, illusion, dreaming, memory, and reality, Emily reconstructed her landscape from memory, books, and maps. Her powers of observation at the approach to her seventh birthday were remembered by her teachers at Cowan Bridge: 'a darling child [...] quite the pet nursling of the school', who 'reads prettily'.[12] Her watchfulness at the age of fourteen, when she observed the Dales landscape around Bolton Abbey in Yorkshire, was recalled by Ellen Nussey. In a memoir based on Ellen Nussey's documents, T. Wemyss Reid wrote: 'Emily Brontë does not talk so much as the rest of the party, but her wonderful eyes, brilliant and unfathomable as the pool at the foot of a waterfall, but radiant also with a wealth of tenderness and warmth, show how her soul is expanding, under the influences of the scene'.[13] She retained perfect memory of a landscape seen in childhood. Her first description of Wuthering Heights hill invokes the view of Ingleborough in the view from Cowan Bridge on the night of Tuesday 31st May, 1825.[14] On the next day, Wednesday 1 June, the sisters took the daily Royal Union coach from Kendal to Keighley. The halt at Thornton in Lonsdale was scheduled for 9.30 a.m.[15] A view of Ingleborough by moonlight and morning light, rising above the ground mist which swathes the vale at its foot, was created by the cold and cloudless weather of that week. A thunderstorm on the previous Thursday night produced two and a half inches of rain (63 mm) at Kendal.[16] Cold weather during that week, and the clear skies which would have caused it, obliged Robert Southey, on his journey from Keswick to London that week, to buy extra underwear at Brough.[17] These conditions create a counterpart, visible from the windows of the Clergy Daughters' School and along the homeward route, of Nelly Dean's view of Wuthering Heights hill by the light of the harvest moon:

> [...] the valley of Gimmerton, with a long line of mist winding nearly to its top (for very soon after you pass the chapel, as you may have noticed, the sough that runs from the marshes joins a beck which follows the bend of the glen). Wuthering Heights rose above this silvery vapour; but our old house was invisible—it rather dips down on the other side (ch. 10).

Other features show Emily's dependence on exact memory. No counterpart appears in *WH* for Whernside, Yorkshire's highest hill, and its flanking dale, Chapel le Dale, at the foot of Ingleborough. Her acute visual memory explains the absence of counterparts for these features in *WH*: Whernside and Chapel le Dale are invisible from the K&K. The novel follows her memory of the view from Thornton in Lonsdale, at the foot of Kingsdale, with research and reading as sources for Kingsdale features which are invisible from the road. For her description of Gimmerton valley, the counterpart of Kingsdale, she borrowed and improved phrases in *A Tour to the Caves* (1781) (*P*),[18] by the Revd John Hutton, Vicar of Burton in Lonsdale (Appendix D). At the time, Burton or Black Burton was a coal mining township or division, equivalent to a chapelry under ancient ecclesiastical administration, in the parish of Thornton in Lonsdale. Hutton's *Tour* was available to Emily among books at Ponden House, the home of Robert Heaton, Patrick's senior lay patron at Haworth. Other sources which she appears to have consulted were *Paterson* and the *Map of the County of York* (1771), by John Tuke, in the 1818 edition.

Accurate observation appears in every detail in *WH*. The 1818 edition of Tuke's *Map* shows the drainage channel or sough, installed around 1817 to drain a tract of marshy ground in Kingsdale. The marsh is hinted in earlier editions of Tuke's *Map*, which shows the meandering course of Kingsdale Beck before the construction of the sough. The sough, the marsh and the bend in the Twiss, as it joins the Doe to form the Greta in its celebrated glen, appear with speaking accuracy in Nelly Dean's description of the invisible part of Gimmerton valley: 'the sough that runs from the marshes joins a beck which follows the bend of the glen' (ch. 10). More exactly, Kingsdale beck continues beyond its sough into the glen, where it joins the other beck, which the text omits. At this point, Emily used one of her numerous double frames of reference. She retained the marsh, together with the sough or ditch which drained it, and she kept the confluence, despite having omitted the second beck and Chapel le Dale. The works of reference she evidently consulted would have formed part of the collection of books at the vicarage of the Revd Theodore Dury, Vicar of Keighley from 1819 until 1840, a Trustee of the Mechanics' Institute Library at Keighley, and of the K&K as well as of the Clergy Daughters' School.[19] In their capacity as Patrick Brontë's senior clergy neighbours and patrons, Dury and his wife, Anne Greenwood, appear to have encouraged Emily Brontë's reading into the Yorkshire literary and topographical tradition.

Riddles

Many of the scattered landscape clues in *WH* appear as riddles. The Ingleborough region matches Nelly Dean's reference to her 'parish where two or three miles was the ordinary distance between cottage and cottage' (ch. 9). Her first glimpse of Wuthering Heights hill identifies the position of the farmhouse in relation to the foothills, the Grange, and the beck (ch. 10). In a second aside she gives the compass bearings and the position of the crossroads in relation to the village and Grange park (ch. 11). Next she defines the positions of the Grange and the farmhouse in relation to the beck (ch. 15). The fourth and final glimpse (ch. 18) returns to the distant view of Ingleborough between Cowan Bridge and Thornton in Lonsdale. From there until Lockwood's return (ch. 32) the landscape is dominated by the moorland.

Besides omitting Chapel le Dale, Emily made minor alterations to the Yorkshire map. Her *kirk*, northern English for parish church,[20] has its Yorkshire counterpart in St Oswald's Church,

Thornton in Lonsdale. London, Lancaster, Kendal, and Dent are linked by the scattered crossroads around that parish church. By straightening the crossroads, and moving the church closer to Gimmerton, Emily removed the parish boundary which separates the two villages. This, too, reflects her accurate observation. Ingleton, the Yorkshire counterpart of Gimmerton, still serves Thornton in Lonsdale, the tiny hamlet of the neighbouring parish, as its village. This alteration required moving Thornton in Lonsdale church about three hundred yards eastwards. In doing so, Emily constructed a match for a feature of several Dales parishes, notably Tunstall, Leck, Rylston, and Linton. The first two were known to her; others are described in the writings on the Dales by T.D. Whitaker. In these parishes, the church stands at distances of half a mile or less away from the village. In a seemingly trifling action, Nelly Dean confirms the position of the modified crossroads in relation to the village and the back gates of the Grange park. Emerging from the park, she heads for Gimmerton, which lies beyond the church, reads the guidestone, then changes her mind, and turns left to proceed northwards up the dale (ch. 11). That seemingly irrational action explains Emily's minor alteration to the crossroads at Thornton in Lonsdale. Gimmerton must lie to the right of the park gates, with the church in the north-east corner of the crossroads, and the rough road up the dale leads off northwards, to the left. This means that the counterpart for St Oswald's Church at Thornton in Lonsdale has moved over a little to the east, and stands nearer to Gimmerton than its counterpart does to Ingleton. The layout is confirmed in reverse when Lockwood makes his last tour down the hill (ch. 34), and when Isabella stares at the midwinter sunset, across the Grange (ch. 13). Her glance confirms that Thrushcross Grange is to the south-west of the revised crossroads, in a position matching that of Hallsteads, its counterpart at Thornton in Lonsdale (Plate 2).

Another alteration re-positioned the fictional manor or Grange two miles further from the crossroads than its Dales counterpart. Though the Grange park is incomparably bigger than its topographical original, it retained the compass bearings, gates, architectural scale and tree-lined appearance of Hallsteads. The name Grange points to the barnlike form of that house, which is glimpsed behind trees in the view from the old K&K. The enormous Grange park in *WH*, two miles across, is on a scale rarely found except among the demesne parks of dukes and a few other expansive landowners, for example at Castle Howard, Chatsworth, Blenheim, and Woburn. Its size enables the younger Catherine to grow up in seclusion until her thirteenth birthday (ch. 18). No model for a park of that size appears around Ingleborough and Lunesdale, where the terrain is too uneven, and the local economy too fragmented, for a park on the grand scale.

Emily recognised the difficulty created by her superimposition of a two-mile park on the relatively modest setting around Ingleborough. The only description is Nelly Dean's 'wild green park' around Thrushcross Grange, and the trees which screen the music of the beck in summer (ch. 15). Surrounding clues identify the two-mile park of Harewood House, in Wharfedale, which the Brontës did not visit but evidently knew from maps, as the probable model for the Grange park (see below, 'Africa and Yorkshire unchained'). It appears in the 1818 edition of Tuke's *Map*, prominently marked in green, and similarly in Thomas Jefferys' *Map of the County of York* (1767). By placing a park of Harewood's dimensions on the site of Hallsteads, Emily created the double frame of reference which has been noted in the critical repertoire.[21] As in the view from Hallsteads, the parish church in *WH* appears near to the Grange when Isabella gazes at the sunset, and again when Edgar Linton emerges with the congregation on the day of Heathcliff's last visit. However, Edgar Linton's walk across Thrushcross Grange park takes half an hour, as it would at Harewood (ch. 15). The vast park reappears on Lockwood's last visit, when he leaves his servant at the village, and makes his way for some distance on horseback, down the valley to the Grange (ch. 32). Underlining Harewood's eminence in the Dales, it appears, Emily parcelled out the name between Hareton and Lockwood.

Emily's reason for concealing several of her clues in riddles appears to have been her wish to avoid easy recognition of the model for her Yorkshire landscape. Gretna Green, the unnamed site for the clandestine marriages (chs. 12, 27), appears indirectly through the distance of 300 miles to London, which is given once (ch. 20). That seemingly unrelated clue places Gimmerton for the time being at Cockermouth, 305 miles from London (*Paterson*) and close enough to the Scottish border to foil pursuit of the runaways (ch. 12). Probably with a copy of *Paterson* in her hand, Emily used that distance as a makeshift to lend credibility to the two Scottish marriages in *WH*. For the rest of her story she remained within the framework of the Ingleborough region, 220 miles from London. Further clues confirm that Gimmerton occupies a position matching that of Ingleton, at the foot of Ingleborough. The distance to Liverpool from Ingleton (about 68 miles) cannot be found in *Paterson*, where distances are noted from London. Probably Emily guessed her 60 miles from Gimmerton to Liverpool (ch. 4), or borrowed the 60 miles from Haworth. In contrast, the distances between Gimmerton and three unnamed market towns in *WH* are matched by the distances from Kingsdale to corresponding market towns in *Paterson*. One of these appears to the south when Lockwood arrives for his second shooting trip (ch. 32). Two clues identify it as the counterpart of Settle, 14 miles south-east from Kingsdale along the K&K. On arriving, Lockwood observes the name Gimmerton on a wagon marketing a late harvest of oats: it must come from the north.[22] The second clue is given by the local resident who explains to Lockwood that Gimmerton is 'Happen [maybe] fourteen mile o'er th' hills, and a rough road' (ch. 32). That matches the fourteen miles to Kingsdale, northwards from Settle (*Paterson*), a large market town near the southern foot of Ingleborough. That sector of the old K&K gave the Brontës first-hand experience of a 'rough road'. The town with a grammar school 20 miles from Gimmerton, where Heathcliff finds a Latin teacher for his son (ch. 20), matches Kendal, the K&K terminus, 20 miles north of Ingleton, or Lancaster, the same distance to the south-west (*Paterson*). Another market town appears on the occasion of the 'justice-meeting at the next town' (ch. 10) which Edgar Linton attends. This matches Kirby Lonsdale, the magistrature a few miles beyond Thornton in Lonsdale and Cowan Bridge (*Paterson*).

Emily avoided naming a distance from the crossroads to a farmhouse which can be easily found on the maps of Kingsdale. That distance identifies Braeda Garth, the farmhouse in Kingsdale which is marked in both maps, as the topographical counterpart of the fictional farmhouse. Braeda Garth cannot have been seen by the Brontës. Emily veiled the two miles under two readily solved riddles. The first appears in Lockwood's journal, when he silently gives the two miles from the farmhouse to the crossroads and the back gate of the Grange: the reader is invited to subtract the size of the park, two miles, from the distance between the Grange and the farmhouse, four miles (ch. 3). In a second and slightly more difficult riddle, solved in two steps, Emily confirmed the distances between the farmhouse, the crossroads, and the Grange. When the younger Catherine is 'two miles nearer Wuthering Heights than her own home' (ch. 21), she is a mile from the farmhouse. Given the frequently repeated distance of four miles between the farmhouse and the Grange, the two miles are arrived at by subtracting one mile from three. Since they disclose the locality Emily had in mind, the two miles from the farmhouse to the crossroads are playfully concealed and yet named in both riddles.

Through puzzles in ascending ranks of difficulty, Emily drew her readers into the gulf separating reality from appearances and dreaming. The riddles which perplex Lockwood at the farmhouse and in his dreams (chs. 2, 3) stream out across the novel as a whole. The reader is invited to tussle with them, as Lockwood does, until final meanings are reached. The direction of Gimmerton dale is given first in reverse: 'the north wind, blowing over the edge' (ch. 1), must blow southwards down the dale. Another riddle locates Wuthering Heights, the eponymous hill, in the position of Ingleborough. The reader is invited to travel in imagination to the south-west from the crossroads, along the road to Thrushcross Grange (ch. 11), as Lockwood does on his second visit (ch. 32). On looking back in imagination along the park and its flanking road, and beyond the church (ch. 15), the reader will find the hill named Wuthering Heights in the position observed through the window by Nelly and the younger Catherine (chs. 10, 18), to the north-east. This gives an exact match for the position of Ingleborough in relation to Hallsteads and the crossroads at Thornton in Lonsdale. Nelly confirms the compass bearing during Catherine's delirium: 'We were in the middle of winter, the wind blew strong from the north-east' (ch. 11). An adjacent limestone hill of huge size in *WH* is named Penistone Crag, after a similarly named gritstone quarrying mound on low ground near Haworth. Since the beck runs between the hills, past the farmhouse and down past the Grange (ch. 15), that hill can only lie to the left in the view from the Grange, in a position matching that of Gragareth, the limestone hill facing Ingleborough across Kingsdale. In Jefferys' *Map of the County of York* (1767) its summit is marked 'Crag'. Another local detail confirms Emily's use of one or both of the standard Yorkshire maps. The direction on the guidestone at the Gimmerton crossroads points east to the village (ch. 11). This matches the three-quarter mile between Thornton in Lonsdale and Ingleton along the old K&K, which runs east at this point. The missing fourth direction cannot easily be defined, since the direction of the K&K at that point is westwards to Far Westhouse, then north-west to Cowan Bridge and onwards to Kendal and Cockermouth, with Gretna beyond. Emily silently filled in that gap on the guidestone by placing a blacksmith's shop two miles from Gimmerton (ch. 12). This matches the blacksmiths' works at Westhouses, two miles from Ingleton in the direction of Cowan Bridge.[23]

These riddles bridge the gulf between the text and its subject material. They dramatise a recurrent theme in *WH*: illusion is corrected through experience, observation, memory, conversation, and works of reference. It appears in the contrast between the innocent younger Catherine's first impressions of the limestone landscape of the Dales, and Nelly Dean's knowledge of it. The experienced Nelly Dean knows that the pale grey limestone appears golden in the sunlight at sunset. Pausing at the crossroads to read the guidepost, which would be a limestone pillar or *stoop* with hands showing the directions (Plate 13), she observes: 'The sun shone yellow on its grey head' (ch. 11). Like others in *WH*, this seemingly trifling clue appears once only, correcting the child's misreading of her own sense impressions. Inexperience causes the child to confuse appearance and reality when she gazes at the west-facing crags in the sunset: the younger Catherine imagines she is seeing 'golden rocks' (ch. 18). In another instance, however, the child's innocent eye seizes an obvious truth. The celebrated brow-like outline of Ingleborough, the commanding Pennine feature, appears unequivocally when the younger Catherine refers to

Plate 4 – (a) Mary Farnell, Ingleborough from Keasden (etching reproduced by kind permission of the artist) (b) Ann Binder, Ingleborough from Kingsdale (photograph reproduced by kind permission of the photographer).

'the brow of that tallest point' in her view of the crags (Plate 4). The portrayal of a limestone dale in the first half of *WH* is confirmed by the white building materials around Gimmerton (chs. 1, 3, 6) and Joseph's activity, 'loading lime' (ch. 7), not spreading or delivering it, at the foot of Penistone Crag.

In the second half of *WH*, the limestone district in the first half is suddenly clad in a moorland mantle. The result is the topographical anomaly which has perplexed readers of Charlotte's Preface from Matthew Arnold onwards (Appendix B). In the Dales, green pasture surrounds the villages. Above that, woods, now largely removed, reach to the crags, and moorland appears only on their wild gritstone caps and plateaux. Early writers on the Dales explained the puzzling oceanic fossil life in the limestone uplands with the notion that as proof of his power, their creator had placed fossils in the sky. The answer appeared in the 1830s and 1840s. The limestone district was created by volcanic pressure which up-ended the underlying slate beds, thrusting skywards the deep layer of limestone and its upper mantle of gritstone. Next, the limestone crags and their oceanic fossils were exposed to view by the glaciers which scrubbed off the gritstone upper layer from the valleys and slopes, leaving behind only the isolated gritstone caps on the summits. A less powerful upthrust produced the low-lying southern moorland hills. Among the relatively low-lying gritstone *edges* around Haworth, Halifax, Huddersfield and Hathersage, the gritstone mantle has remained, fractured and dislocated, but not removed from its underlying limestone bed.[24] As a result, the heather-clad southern Pennine moorland, which thrives in the gritstone environment, runs down from the shallow *edges* to the town walls. That Pennine peculiarity exactly matches Emily's description of the grave of the elder Catherine: 'It was dug on a green slope, in a corner of the kirkyard, where the wall is so low that heath and bilberry plants have climbed over it from the moor; and peat mould almost buries it' (ch. 16). Nelly invisibly joins the two landscapes at this point.

Emily's novel grew, it appears, out of her contemplation of the view which appears northwards from Withins Height, the summit of Haworth Moor, in the clear conditions created by light north-easterly breezes. Withins Height lies four miles out from the village, over rough ground. Some twelve miles northwards in that view, the dark moorland ridges give way to the limestone hills of the Craven highlands, rising like a pale fairyland to the skyline some thirty miles away. The geological rift known as the Craven Fault runs along to the left, crowned by Ingleborough, which sails beyond, screening off the invisible K&K and Cowan Bridge. Whernside, a long, whale-backed or quern-shaped hill, is to the right, a scarcely noticeable shade higher than its neighbours, Ingleborough, Cam Fell, Penyghent, and Grassington Edge. These lead the eye to the lower ridges concealing the vast southern Pennine industrial towns to the north, east, south and west: Keighley, Bradford, Leeds, Sheffield, Huddersfield, and Manchester. That inspiring amphitheatre, it appears, suggested the masterly novel which grew out of the astonishing powers of observation, memory, reading and imagination which Emily Brontë brought to bear on the landscape of her heart.

2. The story: symmetry

WH begins and ends with Lockwood, a diarist who writes down a story which he is told by the housekeeper Nelly Dean. The story she tells is written in two winglike sections of seventeen chapters each. Like the landscape, this symmetrical presentation can only have been conceived in a single sweep of the imagination. Recognition of its symmetrical structure is left to the reader, who is invited to assemble and recognise the scattered clues. The first steps were taken by C.P. Sanger in his essay, *The Structure of Wuthering Heights* (1926). He first deciphered the chronology, showed the symmetry between the Earnshaw and Linton family trees, sketched the topography, and in defining property law, suggested that it guided Brontë's handling of ownership and inheritance. He demonstrated the mirrored configuration of the family trees which provide the story: each has three generations; two sets of parents have four children in matching pairs of brothers and sisters, and each in due course has a single child (Appendix B). Heathcliff and Nelly Dean are poised uneasily between the families: she has no children, his child dies, and the surviving pair of cousins will continue the family line.

The principle of symmetry reappears in the chapter numbering. Pauses in the narrative subdivide each half of the story into matching sets of eight and nine chapters. These chapter divisions form a symmetrical four-part figure: 9+8 = 8+9. Probably Emily guided her writing by drawing up a chapter plan, a pair of family trees, a sketch map and a chronological table, executed with the precision, firmness, and economy of her surviving drawings.[25] The divisions in her story, effaced in editions hitherto, would have appeared in her manuscript (see below, 'Note on the Text'). They run:

[*First half*]

(a) [Part 1] (chs. 1-9): The diarist Lockwood introduces himself and the farmhouse, and learns the story of Heathcliff's arrival as a dark-skinned orphan among the Earnshaws, his adoption as a foundling from Liverpool, his fondness for his adoptive sister Catherine, and the rivalry for the father's affection. The childhood sweethearts are torn apart by sexual jealousy and by Catherine's preference for Edgar Linton, the blue-eyed boy from Thrushcross Grange, the nearest house four miles away. Her preference precipitates Heathcliff's flight from the farm.

(b) [Part 2] (chs. 10-17): Heathcliff returns after three years, and explains his harsh behaviour as a consequence of his having been treated 'infernally' (ch. 11). In a heartless marriage to Isabella Linton, he attempts to usurp the Linton estate; gambling and mortgaging lead to his gaining control of the Earnshaw land (chs. 11-17).[26] The closing chapters bring the deaths of the elder Catherine and her brother Hindley Earnshaw, the birth of her daughter Catherine (ch. 16), the fight at the farmhouse, Isabella's flight to London (chs. 16, 17), and a semblance of triumph for Heathcliff's designs on the properties.

[*Second half*]

(c) [Part 3] (chs. 18-25): Nelly Dean announces an interval of twelve years, 'the happiest of my life' (ch. 18). A fertile moorland is laid over the destructive limestone landscape of the preceding eight chapters. The younger Catherine discovers her cousins, Hareton

Earnshaw and Linton Heathcliff, experiencing childhood love and then adolescent love for Linton. Heathcliff ensnares her into visiting the farmhouse and caring for his ailing son. She attains independence from her father, who feels the approach of death. This section closes with the chapter which begins with her words: 'These things happened last winter, sir' (ch. 25). Past and present converge from here onwards.

(d) [Part 4] (chs. 26-34): Catherine nurses Linton Heathcliff in an illness which is silently diagnosed as tuberculosis, and Heathcliff tricks her into a forced marriage which takes place across the silently present Scottish border nearby. He forces his dying son to bequeath the property to himself. Lockwood leaves Gimmerton, and on his return in the autumn, he hears about how Catherine taught Hareton Earnshaw to read, and redesigned Joseph's garden with him, thus paving the way for Heathcliff's depression and death, and their future marriage. That event holds a promise of regeneration for a blighted society (ch. 34).

Symmetry persists in the matching roles of the main characters. The narrator and the diarist both confess their mismanagement of people and events in the past. Similarly, Heathcliff and the elder Catherine confess their misreadings of each other. Nelly confesses her recognition of Heathcliff as a tragic fellow human being (chs. 9, 12, 29, 34). A further symmetry emerges through the narrators who present the story in concentric narratives. These mirror and enclose each other in rings or spirals. Parts of the story which cannot be witnessed by Nelly Dean, the housekeeper and principal narrator, appear at the centre. These are the elder Catherine's diary and the confession by her ghost (ch. 3), the letter and narrative from Isabella (chs. 13, 17), and the story told by Zillah, the new housekeeper at the farmhouse (ch. 30). This inner ring is encircled by Nelly Dean's narrative. In turn, her narrative is encircled by the written account in Lockwood's diary. A final enclosing ring appears invisibly: Emily refers the entire series to her reader, who is invited to solve her riddles, recognise her landscape, and re-assemble the questions and probable answers which appear silently in her text.

Emily's emotional presence in her text appears through two symmetrically and enigmatically presented voices or streams of ideas. Each is related to the double chronology which she constructed around the adjacent years 1778 and 1779: (i) the discourse of legislation in the age of William Wilberforce, Patrick's patron at Cambridge.[27] This stream originates in the year 1766, the birth year of Ann Sill of Dent, a key figure among the Dales family histories from which Emily drew her story material, and the silently identified birth year of Catherine Earnshaw in the '1779' chronology (see below, Appendices A and C); (ii) a world of dreams, ghosts, traditional literature, the calendar and its seasons, associated with several mother figures. This stream originates in the year 1783, the year of Emily Brontë's mother's birth and the silently identified crisis year for Catherine Earnshaw in the '1778' chronology (Appendices A and B).

These are perhaps the most difficult riddles or Hieroglyphs (Appendix B) in Emily's text. The dreamlike and visionary impact of her novel, and its elusive social message, arise from her enigmatic handling of this double system of reference.

The symmetrical structure of Emily's novel resembles the figures in her Geometrical Drawings, signed 'E.J. Brontë' and dated 1837, shortly after her nineteenth birthday (Plate 5). Her exceptional command of time and space was noticed by Constantin Heger, her teacher in Brussels, who wrote: 'She should have been a man—a great navigator. Her powerful reason would have deduced new spheres of discovery from the knowledge of the old; and her strong, imperious will would never have been daunted by opposition or difficulty; never have given way but with life'.[28] Charlotte's caricature of the 'home-bred, country girl' who constructed a novel which is 'moorish and wild, and knotty as the root of heath', 'in a wild workshop, with simple tools, out of homely materials', is considerably modified by these drawings and Constantin Heger's impressions. *Wuthering Heights* is better compared to the poetry and plays written in the circle of John Dee (1527-1608), the Tudor *magus* and mathematician who exercised a wide influence in the north-west of England and whose London circle included William Shakespeare, Christopher Marlowe, and John Donne.[29]

Plate 5 – Emily Brontë, Geometrical Drawings.
Brontë Parsonage Museum, Haworth.
Reproduced by courtesy of the Brontë Society.

3. The marriage prohibition

A case of incest has been proposed by Eric Solomon as the source of tension between the childhood sweethearts in *WH*.[30] To justify his impression that a hidden prohibition lurked within the text, he created a scenario in which old Mr Earnshaw maintains a black lady partner in Liverpool over the years, brings home the child whom she has returned to him in exasperation, and shrouds all this activity under an impenetrable cloak of lies which he takes with him to the grave. That would be another novel. In *WH*, old Mr Earnshaw's visit to Liverpool is his first and last. If his visit formed part of the chain of contacts required for a paternity case of seven years' standing and more, he would not announce the distance, and he would anticipate and conceal the fatigue it entailed (ch. 4). Contrary to Charlotte's suggestion in the Preface that Emily lost control of her story—'having formed these beings, she did not know what she had done'—and that 'she had scarcely more practical knowledge of the peasantry amongst whom she lived, than a nun has of the country people who sometimes pass her convent gates', Emily maintained rigorous control of every detail in her presentation of landscape, social reality, illusion, concealment, confession, probability, and procreation.

None the less, Eric Solomon's article raises a leading problem in Emily's story. A marriage prohibition appears silently in *WH*, akin to, but not identical with, cases of incest in classical tragedy, mythology, and the Bible. Emily installed a range of resonances around the problem. The legend of Lot (*Genesis* 19-22), a case of procreation among prohibited blood relations, is invoked by Joseph during the storm marking Heathcliff's flight from the farm (ch. 9). It has no visible bearing on the story, however, since the paternal relationship required for that transgression has been removed from the farmhouse by the death of old Mr. Earnshaw. Another prohibition in *Leviticus* appears when Joseph observes about the effeminate, blonde and blue-eyed Linton Heathcliff, Heathcliff's son: '"Sure-ly," said Joseph after a grave inspection, "he's swopped wi'ye, maister, an' yon's his lass!"' ['It looks as though your wife's betrayed you with her brother, sir, and that's his daughter'] (ch. 20).[31] His idea is blocked by the action: in the crucial months, the sister is infatuated with the future father of her child, the brother is preoccupied with his wife and inflamed with jealousy over Heathcliff, and he excludes his sister from the family house when she elopes (ch. 12). The resolution begins to appear when the younger Catherine plays nurse and mother to her cousin, Linton Heathcliff. Approaching maturity, she expresses the natural impulse of a lonely child: 'Pretty Linton! I wish you were my brother!'. Unwittingly prophesying his end, he responds: 'And then you would like me as well as your father?' (ch. 23).

As with her landscape and her symmetries, it turns out, Emily wrote variations on problem features of English marriage law. She constructed her story around the marriage prohibitions affecting cousins and *affines*, or siblings by adoption and marriage. She can hardly have remained ignorant of the marriage law relating to her Aunt Branwell, the *affine* who lived upstairs at the parsonage. The barrier which prohibited Patrick from offering marriage, had he wished, was removed by a campaign lasting several decades, culminating in the Deceased Wife's Sister Act (1908). This prohibition is at the root of the ballad 'Fair Annie,' to which Emily refers towards the close of the story (ch. 32). This pressure is reflected in the proliferation of marriage prohibitions in novels by the female Brontës; *WH* is constructed around variations on that problem. Early canon law required a dispensation for any marriage of cousins nearer than the seventh degree, or sixth cousins. Under pressure from the labour entailed in checking the kinship network, the prohibited range was later reduced to the fourth degree or third cousins. This was removed in England by Statute 38 of 1540, repealed under Queen Mary, reintroduced in the reign of Queen Elizabeth I, and still in position. It states: '[…] no Reservation or Prohibition […] shall trouble or impeach [prohibit] any Marriage without [not listed in] the Levitical Degrees'.[32] Cousins do not appear among prohibited marriage degrees in *Leviticus* and are similarly absent from the Table of Kindred and Affinity in the English *Book of Common Prayer*. That framework is maintained in *WH*, where two cousin marriages bring the second half of the story to a close.

Besides permitting cousin marriages and prohibiting marriage among siblings, and parents and children, English marriage law prohibits marriage between siblings through affinity by adoption, of whom the younger has been adopted under the age of eighteen. Foster children are exempt from the prohibition. The prohibition affecting these *affines* is defined by Rupert Bursell: 'the marriage of any person to another within certain degrees of affinity is void [...] except if both have reached the age of twenty-one and the younger of the two has at no time before reaching the age of eighteen been a child of the family in relation to the other'. He clarifies: 'a child of the family in relation to a marriage means a child of both parties to the marriage (including an illegitimate or adopted child), or any other child, not being a foster child who has been placed with these parties as foster parents by a local authority of voluntary organisation, who has been treated by them as a child of their family'.[33] Short of delivering an explanatory interjection of the type she never offered, Emily could not have introduced this prohibition more explicitly. In giving their foundling from Liverpool the name of their child who had died (ch. 4), the Earnshaws debar him from marrying into their family. The entire story results from the prohibition. Catherine's initiative signals the rescue: 'I've found out, Hareton, that I want—that I'm glad—that I should like you to be my cousin, now, if you had not grown so cross to me, and so rough' (ch. 32).

As with her presentation of the landscape, Emily signals to her reader the things which the participants in her drama do not explain or understand. In a full sense she was an *eiron*, a Greek ironist or dissembler, with the talkative, remorseful and truthful Nelly Dean as her chorus. The narrator and diarist do not understand the full import of their story: the reader is her court of appeal. As with lacework or *pointilliste* painting, her picture is complete, with spaces which the reader is invited to fill in. Nelly Dean's colloquy with Catherine about marriage prospects, and her confession of having concealed the moment of Heathcliff's running away (ch. 9), does not include her probable knowledge that these children were victims of a marriage prohibition which did not apply to herself, since non-consanguineous foster children are able to marry into the family they enter. Hindley, her childhood sweetheart (ch. 11), marries Frances, an unknown person whom Nelly Dean welcomes without visible jealousy to the house (ch. 6), and whose child she cares for as her own. She retains her father's name, knows her parents, and is fostered and employed as a servant by the Earnshaws. At Hindley's death, she crosses the partition between foster children and *affines*, and weeps for him 'as for a blood relation' (ch. 17). Two Yorkshire novels, *Hope On, Hope Ever!* (1840) (*K*), by Mary Howitt, and *Wooers and Winners* (1880), by Isabella Banks, form the immediate social and literary context bracketing *WH* (Appendices B, C). In each, pairs of orphans in positions matching that of Heathcliff and the elder Catherine are able to marry, since they are visibly non-consanguineous, and they are foster children, not *affines*, within their protectors' households.

As a child of Africa from the world's largest slave port, Heathcliff is at the furthest available point from consanguinity with his childhood playmate, the elder Catherine. As a dark orphan he is cast in the role of the chained and pleading slave in the medallion by Josiah Wedgwood, celebrating the work of Wilberforce's Anti-Slavery Society. The legend, 'Am I not a Man and a Brother?' (Plate 10), explains the ambiguity which forbids marriage and leads to his death. Subject to the slave's or ex-slave's expectation of violent death or separation, as a slave he would be free to marry Catherine; as an adoptive sibling he is forbidden. The hidden cause of their tragedy remains unknown to them. As children, Heathcliff and Catherine experience innocent love, but are separated by his being deprived of educational opportunities, consignment to field work, and flogging by Joseph under orders from an adoptive brother who views him as a child of the devil and treats him as a slave.

Against all this, Heathcliff pits the series of obsessive actions which release the Earnshaws from their blight. Without knowing what he is doing, through his life and death he purifies a poisoned society. Heathcliff's actions precipitate three marriages in the first seventeen chapters, and two in the next; as best they can, the released ghosts dispense with a third marriage by walking on the moor. The younger Catherine is shielded against the threat of affinity through adoption by what appears to be a maze of seemingly haphazard circumstances. They are consequences of Heathcliff's character and actions, and they resemble a ladder or spiral rather than a maze. In an ascending series, each step brings the

Earnshaws nearer to release from bondage. With increasing vigour, each step reflects a rise in Heathcliff's social dominance, his moral decline, and by a spiral or contrary motion, his rise to fulfilment. The first step in that series is the jealous rivalry with his adoptive brother, the underlying cause which precipitates the first marriage in the story. The alienated and wilful Hindley Earnshaw marries the stranger named Frances. She is proved to be exempt from the threat of affinity by the delight she finds in the strange farmhouse (ch. 6). Paving the way for the second marriage in the series, Heathcliff's leadership brings Catherine to the Grange, where she finds the family into which she later marries. She comes dangerously close to being adopted by the Lintons, but by nursing her during her convalescence, returning her to the farm, and dying, they leave her free to enter their alien and demonstrably non-consanguineous family through marriage, not adoption (chs. 4, 6, 9, 10, 25). The next marriage, between Heathcliff and Isabella, is spectacularly exempt from any threat of adoption, since she discovers the farmhouse in Joseph's comic tour, on her return from the wedding journey (ch. 13). Hindley's Frances finds a bright haven at the farmhouse, and dies there. Mirrored in reverse, Isabella discovers a hell, and escapes while pregnant, before dying (ch. 17). The elder Catherine's incarceration at the Grange is enlivened by Heathcliff's return. That event precipitates the short-lived reconciliation with her husband which leads to her pregnancy and death (chs. 10, 16).

The cousin marriages in the second half of the story are further consequences of Heathcliff's actions. Driven by dogged possessiveness, evidently without knowing the framework which justifies his actions, he rescues both boys from the threat of adoption by Edgar Linton. Any hint of adoption would blight the marriage chances of the younger Catherine. By keeping Hareton at the farmhouse after the death of his mother (ch. 9), and more forcefully, of his father (chs. 17, 20), Heathcliff shields the boy against becoming the younger Catherine's *affine*. Both cousins are strangers to the younger Catherine, and both are delightful to her, though she rejects the rough-mannered Hareton when she discovers that he is her cousin and not a servant (ch. 18). Heathcliff repeats his move when his son arrives from London (ch. 20). His rough-handling leaves both boys free to marry their cousin. Catherine's foiled childhood affection grows into her thwarted teenage infatuation for her cousin Linton Heathcliff. Next she rediscovers him in her maturing capacity as sick-visitor (chs. 22-4). They fall apart, and then marriage is forced on this cousin by Heathcliff, his violent and seemingly perverse father (chs. 27, 28). This step rescues Catherine Linton from any possible threat of adoption; she is still under eighteen. She arrives under the same roof as Hareton through marriage to her mother's nephew by marriage. At this point she is shielded from the triple threat of adoption, adultery and sexual consummation: her dying boy-husband locks her into their room, and seeks Hareton's company: 'he begged to sleep with Hareton, and his petition was granted for once' (ch. 28). As a widow, still under eighteen when Lockwood arrives at the farmhouse, the younger Catherine is in another prohibited affinity in relation to Heathcliff (son's wife). This leaves her free to marry her elder cousin.

Lockwood, the unsuspecting male egotist, cannot read the picture he finds. Nelly Dean explains the relationships, but she, too, leaves their underground meaning unexplained. That task is referred to the reader, who must unravel a riddle lying across the length of the story. Lockwood arrives at the farmhouse, precipitates Heathcliff's reconciliation with the past, and finds the cousins poised for reconciliation and marriage. On his second visit he learns how the past horrors have been resolved by the combination of violence, innocence, and experience which his first visit had unleashed. The estates are united, and prosperity has some chance of returning through the marriage of Hareton and Catherine, who will inherit both properties. All this follows from Heathcliff's actions. Contrary to supposition within the critical repertoire from Charlotte's Preface onwards, and contrary to the surface action described by Nelly Dean, the slave and tyrant of the Earnshaws turns out to be a guardian angel who secures their release and survival. His success finds recognition in Nelly Dean's exclamation over the forthcoming cousin marriage: 'There won't be a happier woman than myself in England!' (ch. 32).

The lives of both male Earnshaws are preserved by acts of impulsive generosity which subvert Heathcliff's declared, but hollow, drive towards revenge. In the chapter marking the main pause in the action, his overriding generosity leads to a brief respite in

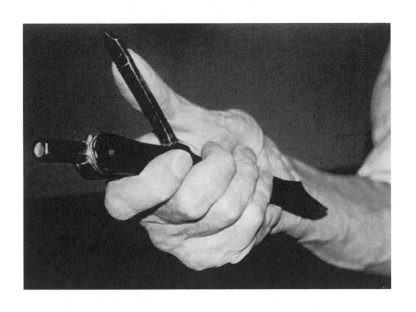

Plate 6 – Lacroix Pistol Knife.
Photograph by C. Heywood,
reproduced by courtesy of the
Sheffield Museums and Galleries Trust.

Hindley's suicidal course. The pocket weapon which Hindley shows to Isabella (ch. 13) appears to have been the Lacroix muzzle-loading version (around 1835) of a widely manufactured weapon, the Saloon Pistol Knife. Later versions mounted the blade in the bayonet position. With the Lacroix model, however, the blade must be snapped shut when the weapon is used as a firearm, since the blade, if left open, is directed into the user's wrist. The bullet is discharged when a percussion cap, inserted above the muzzle, is fired by snapping down the spring-loaded lever (Plate 6).[34] Only a very drunk man would leave the blade open or half shut when offering to use the weapon as a firearm. In breaking the window pane and grasping the weapon by the front end, Heathcliff snaps down the firing lever, deflecting the barrel and causing the bullet to miss its intended victim: neither murder nor suicide takes place. Heathcliff drags away the half-closed weapon, causing the blade to gash Hindley's wrist. He breaks the window frame with a stone and succumbs for a while to his declared passion for revenge, which causes him to batter his would-be assassin on the floor. At this point, however, he yields to an overriding impulse towards generosity. He jolts Joseph out of useless prayer into administering health care in the form of spirits, then helps the fallen Hindley, and binds up the wound (ch. 17). The pressure towards a vengeful murder is suppressed by this parody of care for a fallen enemy by the outcast from Samaria (*Luke*, 10:30–34). Unlike that Samaritan, however, Heathcliff is on both sides of a division among the races, and indeed the fallen man is his adoptive brother. Perhaps over-kindly but with reason, Q.D. Leavis has observed: 'The worst and almost the only genuine wounds received in *Wuthering Heights* are given by the tongue'.[35]

Heathcliff's mental hostility is overwhelmed by his impulsive acts of generosity: he is a modern divided character. Though they are scarcely recognisable, in Emily's hands, his actions are acts of love. In an essay which was available to her, Hartley Coleridge wrote about the appearance in the modern world of things unsuspected by William Shakespeare: 'The world of thought, the mysterious substratum of our affections, sympathies, antipathies, undefined anticipations, and reminiscences, and the dread secret of the hidden will, of which the conscious volition is only an abortive issue, a fleeting phenomenon, were to him a world unknown'.[36] He seems to have revised that idea in his essay on Hamlet. In Emily's hands, Heathcliff's impulsive will achieves the Earnshaws' survival. Driven by that life-saving impulse on another occasion, with lightning speed he catches the falling infant Hareton, who would otherwise have died (ch. 9). His subsequent rage against that impulsive act of generosity results from his declared wish to devastate Hindley, the father, by letting the child die. His craze for revenge, in Hartley Coleridge's words his 'conscious volition […] is only an abortive issue, a fleeting phenomenon'. Native generosity, his deeper drive, Hartley Coleridge's 'secret of the hidden will', has the upper hand. This secures the life of Hareton Earnshaw for his later preservation of the garden, the estate, and his family line.

Heathcliff's harsh actions unlock the chain and lock which the Earnshaws laid on him at his arrival. They take him into the family and classify him as a son of Ham and child of the devil. A modern Hamlet without knowing it, and yet without murder, he is cruel to be kind, but he makes no hypocritical pretences. He resembles the modern character identified by Hartley Coleridge in his essay on Shakespeare (p. 147), victim of 'an inward contradiction, a schism in the soul, jarring impulses, and all the harmony of thoughts and feelings like sweet bells jangled, out of tune and harsh'. In appearance violent and destructive, he knows only the painful truthfulness which drives him to take perverse joy in his enemies' discomfiture. And yet, the final wedding is a consequence of seemingly venomous actions which are, without his knowing why or how, life-preserving in practice. By a contrary or spiral motion, the seemingly benevolent and self-evidently forgivable old Mr Earnshaw unwittingly exercises the malignant influence which Heathcliff expiates. Besides giving Heathcliff his Earnshaw family name, and classifying him as a child of the Devil, old Mr Earnshaw thinks his son Hindley is 'a naught' and that he 'would never thrive as where he wandered' (ch. 5). The enigmatic phrase admits two readings, both negative: wherever he may wander, Hindley's nothingness will prevent him from thriving; or, he will thrive only if he wanders, and come to nothing. Torn to the centre by what amounts to a father's curse, the son dies where he was born, at the farmhouse, crushed but not murdered by his adoptive brother. His release comes through Hareton, the bearer of an ancient name and child of the dying but sprightly girl he finds on his wanderings.

Heathcliff's designs on the properties collapse, yet he has ensured their survival. His marriage does not confer the heiress's property on him, and since it is entailed in the female line, it passes to her son. With encouragement from her father, the younger Catherine is forced by Heathcliff to marry his son, who is under the property owning age. The childish Linton Heathcliff scoffs that her toys are his: 'All her nice books are mine—she offered to give me them, and her pretty birds, and her pony Minny, if I would get the key of our room, and let her out: but I told her she had nothing to give, and they were all, all mine' (ch. 28). He scoffs in vain, since his forced marriage is unconsummated and void, and since it is Scottish, it lacks validity for the transmission of property or legitimacy in England. He dies before his father, but Heathcliff has lost his ambition. His hollow plan, founded on Scottish marriages, collapses. Lord Brougham explained in 1838:

> By the law of England no marriage is valid which is not solemnised according to the provision of the Marriage Act [of 1837]. By the Scotch law, any parties of the legal age— that is, fourteen and twelve respectively—may contract a valid marriage by [...] promising to intermarry, and then cohabiting [...] This state of the law has often been lamented by those who considered it as mischievous in tendency and grossly inconsistent, that the same party who, until he attains twenty-one, is incapable of affecting in any manner the most inconsiderable portion of his landed property, or binding himself in almost any way, should be suffered, by an improvident marriage hastily contracted, to incur the most important of all obligations, and to bestow upon his issue by a designing, and possibly a profligate, woman, the inheritance of the highest honours and the most ample possessions.[37]

Brontë probably knew this tract. Evidently she knew its arguments. In her story she reversed Brougham's provocative handling of the sexes, and effaced his explicit references to his native Scotland, but silently retained their effects. For good measure she added a few years to the ages of the parties, and further loaded her picture with the brutal coercion exercised by the groom's father, the tepid encouragement brought by the father of the bride, and an emasculated bridegroom. Perhaps her sense of fun overreached itself at this point: but Brougham invited the onslaught. None the less, she retained his reforming drive, adding her own message: there is a chance of survival for property passing through female hands. The deaths of Edgar Linton, the enfeebled Linton Heathcliff, and Heathcliff himself (chs. 28, 29, 34) allow Heathcliff's hollow plan to be repositioned in a female line of succession. The removal of the male chain brings both properties to the younger Catherine, who will bestow them on Hareton at their marriage. That event is a culmination of the slow progress which began in the Fairy Cave (ch. 18): Brontë's novel is a fairy tale, that is, a tale founded on actions of the ancient fates, lost gods, and marriage prohibitions.[38]

With the skill of Sophocles and Shakespeare, augmented by a probing, humorous and secretive female mind, Brontë's story outlines the cures which Wilberforce and his circle advocated for a society which had been corrupted by slaveholding. Lord Brougham dedicated a half-century of Parliamentary labour and a stream of articles in the *Edinburgh Review* (K) to the reform of marriage law, education, and slaveholding. Partly sympathising with and partly straining against his effort, Emily Brontë constructed Heathcliff's character as a single arc. His compulsive actions cure the malaise of his society. Self-evidently a victim of slaveholding society, his hidden role was to expiate or redeem the father's unwittingly imposed twofold curse which accompanied his adoption among the Earnshaws.

4. Lockwood's Wilberforcean dreams

In a letter to her publisher, Charlotte Brontë remarked: 'Nor can I take up a philanthropic scheme, though I honour philanthropy; and voluntarily and sincerely veil my face before such a mighty subject as that handled in Mrs Beecher Stowe's work, *Uncle Tom's Cabin*'.[39] Despite this disclaimer, *Jane Eyre* and *Wuthering Heights* were constructed around crises in slaveholding society.

Like Nelly Dean, who cannot understand the story she tells, and Heathcliff, whose actions are unintelligible to himself, Lockwood cannot read his dreams. His apprenticeship in distinguishing reality from illusion begins when he doubles the distance across the snow-covered Thrushcross Grange park: 'The distance from the gate to the Grange is two miles' (ch. 3). The enormous park and its name are pointers to Emily's knowledge about the work of William Wilberforce, her father's patron during his studies at Cambridge. Following a line drawn south-eastwards from Thornton in Lonsdale or Cowan Bridge, the crow would fly over Thruscross, now submerged in a reservoir and at that time a village not far from Bolton Abbey in upper Wharfedale, where the Brontës made a day tour in 1833. Harewood, spelt thus by Tuke and Harwood by Thoresby,[40] and locally pronounced both ways, lies in lower Wharfedale, a few degrees to the right along an almost straight line beyond Thruscross. A candidate at the Yorkshire election of 1807 was the Hon. Henry Lascelles, heir to Harewood's two-mile demesne park and extensive estates in Wharfedale and Barbados. At the election for a second Member of Parliament for the county of Yorkshire, he stood against William Wilberforce's candidate, Charles William Wentworth (1786-1857) of Wentworth Woodhouse, near Sheffield, then titled Lord Milton and later 3rd Earl Fitzwilliam. Lord Milton's narrow majority ensured the arrival of the Abolition of the Slave Trade Act (1807) and the Emancipation of Slaves Act (1833). He was championed by Edward Baines (1784-1848), founder and editor of the *Leeds Mercury* and publisher of Wilberforce's manifesto, *Yorkshire Election* (1807). That work abounds in gibes against Harewood and the Lascelles family's plantation interests in Barbados. A mock advertisement offered spoiled sugar cane, 'tinctured with a few *red* spots resembling drops of African blood, recently imported from Barbadoes'. Expenses, the advertisement noted, would be paid out of 'the Harewood poor-box'.

Baines warned in his mock advertisement: 'No Clothier, Methodist, Quaker, or any other *honest* elector need apply'.[41] He pointed to the origin of the Emancipation movement among Quakers and Methodists, first in America and later England. The movement began with the journey to England of John Woolman

(1720–1772), whose mission from the Philadelphia Quaker Meeting brought him to London in 1772, and on foot along the K&K, to Settle and onwards through Preston Patrick to Kendal. That route took him along the K&K through Ingleton and Thornton in Lonsdale, and across Leckbeck, the *coln, cowen* or stream named after Leck, a township of Tunstall parish, with Cowan Bridge as its hamlet. His journey ended in York, where he fell ill, died, and is buried in the Quaker graveyard at the Retreat. Emily's novel is foreshadowed in his journal. He meditated on Quakers' participation in slavery, the plight of the poor, the voice of an angel in his dream telling him he was dead, his coughing blood, his relief in watching animals and birds in nature, his distress over luxuries among slaveholding Quakers, and the hope 'that Friends [Quakers] may dig deep, may carefully cast forth the loose matter and get down to the rock, the sure foundation' (Appendix D).[42] His walk from London to York took place in the period portrayed in the novel, through the landscape and family histories which appear in *WH*.

The Quaker presence in Emily's story material and its chain of transmission, and Woolman's prefigurings of her themes at numerous points, suggest that she drew inspiration from his *Journal*. The appearance of her female protagonist, the younger Catherine, with 'her yellow curls combed back behind her ears, as plain as a quaker, she couldn't comb them out' (ch. 30), points to the Brontës' knowledge of the Quaker origins of the Emancipationist movement. Before arriving in England, the *Journal* reports, Woolman encountered a Biblical authority for the most determined opposition to Emancipation: 'Negroes were understood to be the offspring of Cain, their blackness being the mark God set upon him after he murdered Abel his brother [...] One of them said that after the flood Ham went to the land of Nod and took a wife, that Nod was a land far distant, inhabited by Cain's race'.[43] Woolman overturned that doctrine by invoking the mother Eve, through whom we are all of 'one blood',[44] or branches of one *species*, the term he insisted on using, in preference to *race*.

Brontë attacked the obstacles which Woolman had found. Without recognising what he finds, Lockwood encounters the tradition about Cain and Ham at the farmhouse. His landlord, 'a dark skinned gypsy, in aspect, in dress, and manners, a gentleman' (ch. 1),[45] is classified in popular superstition as a son of Ham. The second housekeeper at the farmhouse, the 'lusty dame' (ch. 1), is named after Zillah, wife of Lamech, a descendant of Cain. As the mother of 'an instructor of every artificer in brass and iron' (*Genesis* 4:22), however, the Biblical Zillah is a maternal ancestor of the Mechanics' Institutes at Keighley and elsewhere. Armed with pan and bellows, she appears in *WH* as a peacemaker, firemaker, and guide. She is the reliable reporter and angel or *angelos* who speaks without irony or deception (chs. 2, 3, 28). Under the leadership of Lord Brougham and his fellow Emancipationists, Mechanics' Institutes were planned to foster the ideas and techniques that would liberate England from dependence on wealth from slave-holding plantations. The Birkbeck family, Quaker bankers at Settle, were among the founders of these institutions, which led to the modern University and Public Library systems in England. Cain's line of descent continues through Adah, co-wife of Lamech with Zillah. Adah's son Tubal Cain, a teacher of music and patron of 'all such as handle the harp and organ' (*Genesis* 4:21), had the Brontës among his following.

The moral ideals behind the Emancipation movement were outlined by William Wilberforce (1750-1833) in his book *A Practical View of* […] *Real Christianity* (1797) (*P*). Writing shortly after the defeat of his first Bill for the abolition of slavery (1793), he argued that the evils of modern society resulted from the Parliamentary electors' enslavement to the passions, which he defined as the old sins in modern dress: avarice, envy, gluttony, lust, wrath or rage, suicidal despair or sloth, and their chief, pride. Echoing Hamlet, he urged the electors in the unreformed Parliament to reform the ideas which had led to his defeat: 'How do anger, and envy, and hatred, and revenge, spring up in his [the elector's] wretched bosom! How is he a slave to the meanest of his appetites! What fatal propensities does he discover to evil! What inaptitude to good!' (pp. 28-9). Adapting Hamlet's ironic outburst, 'What a piece of work is man! […]' and his plea, 'Give me that man / That is not passion's slave, and I will wear him / In my heart's core, ay, in my heart of heart',[46] Wilberforce proposed that freedom is attained when the soul adopts invisible chains as a slave of God. He followed the arguments of Jakob Arminius (Jakob Hermanus, 1560-1609), from whom the Arminianism of Wesley and Wilberforce took its name. In his inaugural lecture as Professor of theology at the University of Leiden in 1603, translated from the Latin as *A Discourse on the Priesthood of Christ* (1815), Arminius outlined his belief that evil in the world is remediable. He emphasised the universal availability of grace and forgiveness for the human species, notwithstanding its being, in his phrase, 'enslaved by sin and Satan'. The redeemer, he argued, took up his cross as a slave of slaves to the passions. His supreme sacrifice was the choice to 'annihilate himself, assume the form of a slave'.[47] As a secular character outside the ministry, Heathcliff dispenses with the redeemer's faith, but still embodies his destiny. Misread as a Gypsy, Lascar, castaway, and prince of India and China, he is judged by all who meet him to be a son of Ham, child of the devil, a useful labourer and slave. He fades away when a cure for their disease is found, and he is free to recognise his true position as a slave of love.

Within that moral mainstream, Brontë developed the Romantic technique of omitting the judgments, and yet dramatising and modifying the ideas of the Biblical tradition. Viewed in the light of the principal sins, her characters are overwhelmed by lust, avarice, envy, wrath, gluttonous despair in the form of blind drunkenness, and pride: yet all are understood and forgiven. The teenage Edgar Linton and his sister Isabella are slaves of animal appetite or lust; the elder Catherine succumbs to pride, and Linton Heathcliff and his father Heathcliff drift into sloth or despair, the modern terms for the lethal *accidie* and its sequel, death. As with her landscape, Emily's moral ideas are ironically veiled, yet her diagnostic categories are instantly recognisable. Heathcliff makes a pilgrimage towards his tragic self-recognition or *anagnorisis* as a slave, not of the explicitly identified God and Redeemer of the sacred texts, but of love, the enigmatic presence haunting the Gospels and Epistles, *Hamlet*, the Sonnets, and modernism in general. At a late stage in the story, he enlightens Nelly by relating his experience of being led home by Catherine's ghost from her grave, and finding himself 'incomparably consoled' (ch. 29).

Lockwood's enigmatic dreams are curtain-raisers to an Arminian story. Like Nelly's landscape descriptions, his dreams introduce three thinly veiled and instantly recognisable historical characters who lay close to the Brontë circle and their Emancipationist patrons. Under scantily disguised names, his first dream warns against hypocrisy about slavery among the Yorkshire clergy. The name of the Revd Jabez Bunting (1779-1858), Patrick's colleague as examiner at Woodhouse Grove School, appears in Lockwood's preacher, the Revd Jabes Branderham. However, the travesty of *Matthew* 18:22 at the Chapel of Gimmerden Sough (ch. 3), and the uproar it provokes, bear little or no resemblance to any of the silver-tongued Bunting's sermons. His main activity in Yorkshire lay in furthering Methodist Separatism, the severance of ties between the followers of Wesley and the Anglican establishment. This movement represented a threat to Patrick's position as a follower of Wesley within the established church. It forms the hidden target of Emily's satirical attack in *WH* on the dream preacher's list of 491 ineradicable sins. The number refers to the text in *Matthew* which requires forgiveness for wrongdoings or trespasses to a total of 'seventy times seven', a proverbial phrase for innumerable. The resulting uproar echoes the rampage at St Michael and All Angels, Haworth, against the Revd Samuel Redhead, Patrick's rejected precursor as Perpetual Curate.[48] In the dream sermon and its consequences, Emily dramatised the alarm sounded by Henry Nelson Coleridge, cousin of the poet, in his book *Six Months in the West Indies* (1826), one of several books and articles on colonial affairs which she appears to have read. Foreshadowing Lockwood's dream, Henry Nelson Coleridge attacked the disruptive influence of Methodist Separatism in colonial society: 'parent and child are watches on each other, sister is set against sister and brother against brother; each is on his guard against all, and all against each'.[49]

Through Lockwood's dream, Brontë attacked Jabez Bunting's anti-Arminian support for slavery. According to the tract *Methodism As It Is* (1863), he supported the electioneering campaign of Lord Sandon, an anti-Emancipationist candidate at the 1835 Liverpool election. This action provoked a suppressed pamphlet lamenting that 'the page of Methodism, on which his name is inscribed, is disgraced with tyranny'.[50] Arminianism, the ideological mainstay of the Emancipation movement, was repudiated by the Revd Joseph Benson, a principal Methodist preacher on the Leeds circuit and supporter of the Revd Bunting's Separatist campaign. Joseph Benson proclaimed the indelible imprint of sin, and wrongfully mocked Arminianism as a 'hypothesis, that man is now the holy and happy being he was when he came out of the hands of his Creator'.[51] Foreshadowing the character of Emily's Joseph in his oration at Joseph Benson's funeral, Jabez Bunting observed that his friend had been 'mighty in the Scriptures', but tended 'to indulge in views of men and things more gloomy than just or accurate'.[52] Emily presents Benson virtually undisguised in the character of Joseph, who leads the way to the dream chapel at Gimmerden Sough, scolds and sermonizes instead of teaching and amusing the children (ch. 3), upbraids Nelly Dean for doing just that (ch. 32), and bursts into prayer instead of helping the fallen Hindley (ch. 17). Joseph's interminable sermons parody Benson's custom of overwhelming his congregation for hours in this style: 'Have you not been long enough unholy and unhappy, a robber of God, and a murderer of your soul?'.[53]

Notwithstanding Joseph's unchanging belief that Heathcliff is a child of the devil (ch. 34), Brontë viewed him from an Arminian stance. On finding his garden ravaged by the younger generation, Joseph complains that he would rather work on the roads than be deprived of his heritage (ch. 34). His attachment to his garden affirms Woolman's Arminian theme: our species began in a garden, and hence, Joseph and Heathcliff are of one blood. Contrary to appearances, Joseph, too, is a divided character, driven without knowing it into affirming the attainability of survival through innocence. His idea that road mending represented the deepest imaginable degradation reflects Emily Brontë's knowledge that Hugh Brontë III, her uncle and literary admirer, worked as a road mender, and her grandfather worked as a slave for his sons and daughters (Appendix D).

After the travesty of *Matthew*, Jabes Branderham hurls at Lockwood the charge brought by the prophet Nathan against the hypocritical King David, who professes horror over the rich man who slaughters a poor man's pet lamb rather than one of his own vast flock. The king himself is that wicked man: 'Thou Art The Man!' (2 *Samuel* 12:7) (ch. 3). The next dream declares the author's moral intention in *WH*. Lockwood's dream conscience accuses him, it appears, of complicity in a notorious blot on slaveholding society. The Brontës' friends, the Greenwoods of Keighley, were related by marriage to John Bolton, a millionaire Liverpool slave trader and professing philanthropist who retired to Storrs Hall, near Rydal.[54] Like Jabez Bunting, this man was attacked in a suppressed pamphlet which cannot have escaped the notice of his Keighley relations, and through them, the Brontës. In addition, he was known to his neighbour, Hartley Coleridge, whom Branwell visited for the day on 1 April 1840. The pamphlet relates how Bolton amassed a fortune by crushing the friends who had helped him when he arrived destitute in Jamaica. On his departure for England, the story continues, he abandoned the black lady who had borne their children. Swimming after his boat, she grasped the gunwale, then sank and drowned when his nod directed a mariner's cutlass to sever her wrist.[55] Through the nightmare of the ghost whose wrist he slashes on the broken window-pane (ch. 3), Lockwood's dream conscience accuses him of complicity in a crime committed by a hypocritical philanthropist. Like John Bolton, Lockwood negated the love of the girl he courted and who returned his love. Unlike Bolton, however, he acts brutally only in a dream. Through dreams and encounters at Gimmerton, he acts as a lightning-conductor for Heathcliff's emotional storm, and beyond the story, for the Arminian campaign of Woolman, Wilberforce, and their innumerable retinue in the modern world.

5. Africa and Yorkshire unchained

The arms of the Iveson family display a rebus or verbal sign for their manor, Blackbank, near Leeds, in the form of three heads of blacks in profile surrounding a *bank*, the northern term for hill, shown as a chevron or peak (Plate 7).[56] The name Heathcliff is a similar rebus or puzzle representation of the two West Riding landscapes, the dark, heather-clad southern moorland and the white crags of the Craven highlands. It reflects Emily's interest in word games and puzzle pictures,[57] and it embodies the public debates of the 1830s and 1840s about Atlantic slavery and Yorkshire slavery. The name is implied in the view from Withins Height. The dark moorlands and their mill towns were viewed in

Plate 7 – Arms of Iveson of Blackbank.
From T.D. Whitaker, *Loidis and Elmete* (1816), vol. 2, p. 103.

the Emancipationist campaigns of the 1820s and 1830s as the source of a cure for the slaveholding economy, which was epitomised by vast landowning and slaveholding properties in the west country, the Midlands, the Dales and Cumberland. Industrial exports from the despised moorland region, the argument ran, would replace the remittance economy of the seemingly grandiose landowning estates. Despite its long working hours, the machine age was destined to set right the loss of revenue from the slaveholders' plantations. The underlying proposition was that by removing the slave's chains, the slaveholder frees himself or herself.

By a contrary motion, the proposition seemed to have the result of perpetuating poverty, violence, and servitude. In the formative period portrayed in *WH*, wealth came from Yorkshire cotton manufactures[58] as well as the sugar plantations in the Caribbean. Both were based on produce of slave plantations, and both were in decline by the 1830s. Moreover, the old fortunes of private plantation proprietors reappeared in the vast fortunes of the new mill owners, built, it appeared, on an enslaved workforce. An expanded Emancipationist attack included the plight of the industrial working class, the importing of indentured cheap labour from Asia to the Caribbean, and the imposition of colonial rule by industrial nations. The new mood appeared in a leading article of 1838 by William Byles, editor by the *Bradford Observer*, on the young W.E. Gladstone's proposal to import Asiatic labour to the Caribbean. The article 'The New Slave Trade and its Patron, Mr. Gladstone', reflects the mood of the decade:

> Had a council of demons been held in the court of Lucifer, a more fraudulent, bloody and infernal plot could not have been hatched, to destroy the spirit of the emancipationist, and to cast hopeless despair upon the objects for whose redemption this nation has made such splendid sacrifices.[59]

The cost of liberating African slaves on the plantations was seen as a threat to the improvement of working conditions in the early factories. The strained relationship between the slaveholding economy and poverty at home made an early appearance in

Baines' reference to the 'Harewood poor-box' as the source of the Hon. Henry Lascelles' funding for his 1807 election campaign.[60] The Brontës' poverty in Ireland, and the famine years of the 1840s, contributed to the formation of *Wuthering Heights*.[61] The emerging view was that the slaveholding habits of the plantation economy died hard, that slavery had reasserted itself in the factories of the 1820s, 1830s and 1840s, and that the ultimate causes of enslavement lay in an outrageous system of materials, distribution, wages, capital, and profit. Emancipationists adhered to the staple of history none the less: whatever signs of prosperity may have been found among black survivors, white victims of poverty were never bought and sold, lynched, thrown to the sharks, and subjected to other irreparable horrors of Atlantic slavery.

The new revolutionary mood foreshadowed the modern world of perpetual economic change, exploitation, and protest. It appears in Emily's handling of Heathcliff's relationships with his adoptive brother Hindley. The pronouncement by Arnold Kettle, 'Heathcliff was born not in the pages of Byron, but in a Liverpool slum',[62] applies to Hindley and his equivalents in the Yorkshire moorland towns, as well as to Heathcliff, his adoptive brother of African stock. Under the heading 'Slavery in Yorkshire', in 'the language connected with the bottomless pit', or 'brimstone rhetoric', as the editor phrased his outbursts, Richard Oastler reminded readers of the *Leeds Mercury* of the appalling conditions imposed on factory workers in the Yorkshire woollen industry (Appendix D). His campaign for the Ten Hours Bill led him to explain to a meeting in Keighley in 1846: 'I should like, if that were possible, to communicate in a very few words the reason why you are slaves. Why you are, perhaps, worse here than in any other part of the country'.[63] The onslaught continued for the remainder of the century and beyond. In *Darkest England And The Way Out* (1891), Charles Booth invoked the problem in the language of the imperial decades: 'England emancipated her negroes sixty years ago, at a cost of £40,000,000, and has never ceased boasting about it since. But at our own doors, from "Plymouth to Peterhead," stretches this waste Continent of humanity—three million human beings who are enslaved—some of them to taskmasters as merciless as any West Indian overseer, all of them to destitution and despair'.[64]

The violence produced by slavery invaded the whole of society, the Emancipationist argument ran, attacking marriage as well as factories, mines, land transport and ships. Isabella's plight reflects that development. In 1843, William Howitt exhorted the Anti-Slavery Society to remember that slavery did not cease with Emancipation: 'The lurid mountains of slavery tower above your heads, and there your enemies, armed with the whip, and the manacles, and with insolence, the pincers with which they tear already broken hearts,—stand and laugh at you!'[65] His phrasing reappears in Isabella's defiance of Heathcliff: 'Pulling out the nerves with red hot pincers, requires more coolness than knocking on the head' (ch. 17). The alliance between slavery, marriage, sugar and female subjugation is dramatised in *WH* when Linton Heathcliff sits idly licking sugar while congratulating himself on locking his wife into their room, and appropriating her treasures (ch. 28). Her plight had been prophetically summarised in *Vindication of the Rights of Woman* (1792), by Mary Wollstonecraft: 'Is sugar always to be produced by vital blood? Is one half of the human species, like the poor African slaves, to be subject to prejudices that brutalize them, when principles would be a surer guard, only to sweeten the cup of man?'[66]

Adhering to the image of slaveholding society which emerged through the Emancipation movement, Emily presented Heathcliff's life in four phases, from enslavement to release, in the four parts of her story:

(a) chs. 1-9: as a dark child from Liverpool, he is viewed by old Mr Earnshaw as a chattel, 'a gift of God; though it's as dark almost as if it came from the devil' (ch. 4). This flawed attitude imposes a curse on the house of Earnshaw which Heathcliff is destined to suffer and expiate. He moves through the stereotyped roles which slaveholding society imposed on ancient African civilization:[67] a chattel who is seen as a child of the devil; the favoured protégé of his white patron; the vagabond who peeps through the windows of the great house, where he is pursued by their hounds; the prince from India and China; the violent child who is insulted about the colour of his hair, eyes, and skin, and when he resists, is locked up, relegated to field labour, flogged, deprived of education, and alienated from his white playmate. He becomes the rejected lover of the girl who prefers a rich, blonde boy, and as a runaway servant, echoes the plight of Thomas Anson, the runaway slave from Dent (Appendix C) (chs. 4-9). The rival claims of English workmen and Caribbean slaves appear in Hindley's rejection of Heathcliff on the grounds of old Mr Earnshaw's favoritism: 'the young master had learnt to regard his father as an oppressor rather than a friend, and Heathcliff as a usurper of his parent's affections, and his privileges, and he grew bitter with brooding over these injuries' (ch. 4).[68]

(b) Chs. 10-17: on his return, Heathcliff has undergone a moral deline, the inverse of his social rise. Lockwood speculates about how he obtained his wealth: 'Did he finish his education on the Continent, and come back a gentleman? Or did he get a sizer's place at college? Or escape to America, and earn honours by drawing blood from his foster country? Or make a fortune more promptly, on the English highways?' (ch. 10). Lockwood's hasty conclusions spring from mistaken ideas. As *WH* stands, all these avenues to wealth are closed to Heathcliff. Through his wealth, military bearing, and the experience of slavery arising from his residence in the rural hinterland of Lancaster and Liverpool, England's leading slave ports, Emily points silently to his only option: re-entering the Atlantic slave economy. From experience he rebukes the elder Catherine about her participation in slaveholding society: 'I want you to be aware that I *know* you have treated me infernally—infernally! Do you hear?' He adds: 'I seek no revenge on you [...] That's not the plan—the tyrant grinds down his slaves and they don't turn against him, they crush those beneath them' (ch. 11). His designs lead to his social downfall, and by a contrary motion, to his moral rise and the restoration of the Earnshaws.

(c) Chs. 18-25: hope of curing the tainted social fabric emerges with the younger Catherine's apprenticeship in love, nature, and the Fairy Cave. This part of the story invokes the rise of Anne Clifford of Skipton, the legendary benefactor, patron and landowner of the Dales, and redeemer of a family history which had been tainted by profligacy and slave raiding (Appendix C) (Plate 8).

(d) Chs. 26-34: as a new recruit into Wilberforce's prime social target, the voting class who withheld their power to abolish slav-

Plate 8 – 'Anne Clifford'.
From Hartley Coleridge, *Worthies of Yorkshire and Lancashire*
(1836), p. 241.

ery until 1807 and 1832, Heathcliff practises the techniques associated with slaveholding society: fraud, intimidation, violence, and imprisonment (ch. 27). He recalls his action at the time of the elder Catherine's death (ch. 29), which invokes Hamlet's leap into the grave of his childhood love. He undergoes a metamorphosis or rite of passage[69] which he cannot resist or understand: 'Nelly, there is a strange change approaching—I'm in its shadow at present' (ch. 33). He loses control of himself as well as of other people. His decline and death accompany Hareton's rise to maturity and prospects of retrieving, through marriage to the younger Catherine, his father's lost estate. The echoes from the story of Anne Clifford are augmented by echoes from the story of Henry Clifford, the Shepherd Lord, who rose from illiteracy to regain the estate which his family had forfeited during the rule of the House of York (Appendix C).

Through these steps, Emily created a tragic hero of the age of Emancipation and Reform. His work is achieved when the younger Catherine teaches Hareton to read, and they re-order the garden together at Easter. For a while, Nelly Dean yields to the belief that Heathcliff is a devil: 'Is he a ghoul, or a vampire?' (ch. 34), and then continues: 'And then, I set myself to reflect, how I had tended him in infancy; and watched him grow to youth; and followed him almost through his whole course; and what absurd nonsense it was to yield to that sense of horror' (ch. 34). Arminian daylight replaces the superstition which overtook her during her vigil: '"where did he come from, the little dark thing, harboured by a good man to his bane?" muttered superstition, as I dozed into unconsciousness. [...] Dawn restored me to common sense' (ch. 34). She re-states Woolman's theme: the legends of Cain and Ham are replaced by the argument from the blood-line of Eve.

Through Heathcliff's plantation attitudes,[70] Emily dramatised the arguments in *England Enslaved by her Slave Colonies* (1826), by James Stephen (1789-1859), a disciple of William Wilberforce. In an early tract, James Stephen referred to slavery in ancient Egypt and the 'scriptural characteristic of those crimes, by which the penal doom of nations has been sealed'.[71] Emily appears to have read his work, which argued against public expenditure on the military force which was required to quell slave protest and resistance in the Caribbean. Through subjection to the plantation owning oligarchy, the British public was reduced, he argued:

> to the condition of their own slave-drivers, except that we are implicitly to enforce their despotic behests, not with the cart-whip, but with the sword. In other words, we are to be reduced to the situation defined by the title of this work—we are to be the SLAVES OF OUR OWN SLAVE-COLONIES.[72]

Heathcliff follows that pattern: he adopts the slaveholding practices which the Earnshaws had introduced into their rural parish. Old Mr Earnshaw's mixture of benevolence and negrophobia is intensified by Heathcliff's reappearance, on his return from abroad, equipped with the techniques of slaveholding society: violence, gambling, seduction, abduction, imprisonment, and the withholding of education (chs. 10-17).

Images of slaveholding society were familiar to the Brontës. In the cartoon 'Alas! Poor Caunt', Branwell portrayed plantation society's most notorious character type, the Europeanised, slave-driving oppressor or *buckraman* (linen-trousered man) who insults his recruit. In the spirit of Wilberforce and Stephen, Branwell used these stereotypes as masks for the white pugilists Caunt and Bendigo. In his picture they are metamorphosed into slaves of the betting public's avarice. Like Emily, Branwell detected a sting in the motto on Wedgwood's celebratory medal, the Kneeling Slave, 'Am I Not A Man And A Brother?' (Plate 9d).[73] Another violent incident was widely reported in newspapers of the Emancipation decade. Heathcliff's embrace of the pregnant Catherine, which precipitates the birth of her child and her death (chs. 15, 22), re-enacts an event which was reported at a public meeting of 1838, in which a slave driver brutalised a female field labourer. The woman was 'far advanced in pregnancy', the report ran, and her distress hastened the birth, producing severe hardship: 'in five hours she was delivered and [...] she remained for three hours more without food, or even light! (great sensation, and general cries of "shame!")'.[74] Heathcliff plans revenge on his social superiors by exploiting Isabella, whom he treats as a chattel and ex-

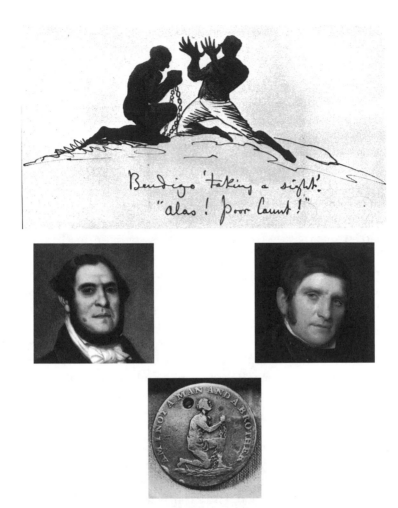

Plate 9 – (a) Branwell Brontë, 'Bendigo "taking a sight". Alas! Poor Caunt!'. Reproduced by courtesy of the Brotherton Collection, Leeds University. (b) Ben Caunt (detail; artist unknown), from J.H. Beardsmore, *The History of Hucknall Torkard* (1909). Reproduced by courtesy of Nottinghamshire County Library. (c) 'Bendigo' (William Thompson), detail of portrait by Thomas Earl, National Portrait Gallery, London. Reproduced by courtesy of the National Portrait Gallery. (d) Josiah Wedgwood, 'Am I not a Man and a Brother', Anti-Slavery Society Commemoration Medal. Reproduced by courtesy of Wilberforce House, Kingston upon Hull City Museums and Art Gallery, UK.

ploits as a slave. She thinks Heathcliff is not human. Through Emancipationist lenses, however, he impersonates the brutality imposed on slaveholding society by the slaveholders' beliefs and malpractices.

Slavery was buttressed by theories about the gulf between the races of our species. *WH* plays on the the two main meanings of *race*: family heritage or blood line; and peculiarities of dress, language, colour, diet, and the like, among inhabitants of the five continents. As families the Lintons are fair and the Earnshaws are dark; the exotic Heathcliff is a pale black, a black among whites and a white among blacks. In another of the riddles in Emily's brief, Nelly Dean confirms Lockwood's first impression of the 'dark-skinned gypsy' (ch. 1) when she discovers in the bathtub that his skin does not wash white and that he is pale dark all over. She proposes: 'A good heart will help you to a bonny face, my lad, [...] if you were a regular black' (ch. 7). Later events define his position in the Spanish theoretical circuit which ran from whiteness through blackness and back to white in seven steps. The stages were termed mulatto, quadroon, octoroon, mustee, mustefino, and white. In that circuit of seven generations, all partners except the first must be white: from mulatto onwards, a black partner yields the sambo child who must start again. Presumably the seven steps were devised to justify early Creole society, since a black partner and a white could under no circumstances encounter the prohibition against marrying cousins nearer than the seventh degree. The system is explained in a work which Emily appears to have read, the *Journal of a West Indian Proprietor*, by M.G. Lewis. In this classification, Heathcliff is ranked as mustefino or child of a mustee: 'the child of a mustee by a white man is called a mustee-fino, and the children [of a mustefino] rank as white persons to all intents and purposes'.[75] As the father of a blonde girl's white child, Heathcliff occupies the rank of *mustefino*, the last black position in that Creole circuit.

This system underwent revision in North America. Until the recent past, the legendary sons of Ham (*Genesis* 9:25) were invoked there to define black persons and their descendants, regardless of tint, as black and therefore slaves in perpetuity. This idea is satirised in *Not Without Laughter*, by Langston Hughes, a novel playing symphonically, with prophetic enlightenment, on the colours and the races:

> Sandy's playmate was a small ivory-white Negro child with straight golden hair, which his mother made him wear in curls. His eyes were blue and doll-like and he in no way resembled a colored youngster; but he was colored. Sandy himself was the shade of a nicely browned piece of toast, with dark, brown-black eyes and a head of rather kinky, sandy hair that would lie smooth only after a rigorous application of vaseline and water.[76]

Another strand in the Emancipationist argument showed that the horrors of slavery fell with equal severity on royalty and the village inhabitant. In a horrific early exposure of slavery and the Christian enslavers' hypocrisy, the prince Oroonoko, the black hero of Aphra Behn's *The Royal Slave* (around 1690), is renamed Caesar by his professedly Christian patrons, who bring him to a Surinam plantation with false promises of hospitality. He foments a slave revolt with a harangue to his fellow slaves about 'the miseries and ignominies of slavery', goes mad, kills his pregnant beloved, and suffers a ferociously cruel death by slow dismemberment at the hands of bottomlessly perfidious whites.[77] Purged of its Jacobeanisms, re-ordered to accommodate Emancipationist views of mind and society, and recast in a modern style, Aphra Behn's novel appears to have contributed substantially to the inner structure of *WH* (Appendix B). During the washing which exposes his blackness, Nelly Dean asks Heathcliff: 'Who knows, but your father was Emperor of China, and your mother an Indian queen, each of them able to buy up, with one week's income, Wuthering Heights and Thrushcross Grange together? And you were kidnapped by wicked sailors, and brought to England' (ch. 7). By omitting the vital continent, Nelly Dean's proposal lightly veils the African origin of the Lunesdale black presence on which Emily founded her novel. It does not ward off his humiliation and imprisonment on Christmas day.

Heathcliff's presence is explained in rural Lunesdale. This was a main hinterland for the Liverpool and Lancaster black community, which came in that period from Africa: 'By the 1780s there were always at least 50 African schoolchildren, girls as well as boys, in Liverpool and the villages around'.[78] Heathcliff's plight foreshadows the dilemma outlined by Frantz Fanon in his book *Black Skin, White Masks* (*Peau noir, masques blancs*, 1952). Tracing the disorder to its origin in white superstition, Fanon wrote of the black man: 'this automatic manner of classifying him, imprisoning him, primitivizing him, decivilizing him, that makes him angry'.[79] Fanon exemplified a global tension. Pausing in his castigation of Europe for its demonization of blacks, Fanon, a pale Antillean African of the same complexion as Heathcliff, recognised his complicity in the betrayal: 'I too am guilty, here I am talking of Apollo! There is no help for it: I am a white man. For unconsciously I distrust what is black in me, that is, the whole of my being'.[80] Heathcliff follows the example of Othello, a stereotype identified by Fanon as the black man with an appetite for the blonde female: he marries without love into the blonde slaveholding class. In a further step, Heathcliff exercises the oppression he has adopted when he forces marriage on the younger Catherine. The psychological burden kills him, but he paves the way for the restoration of order in Gimmerton society. In a confession to Nelly Dean, he recognises his true role as a pilgrim of love (ch. 29). A modern Hamlet, he dies as a martyr and hero of social change.

Suggestions for aspects of Heathcliff's character probably came from the performance in the title role of *Othello*, at Bradford in 1841, by Ira Aldridge, a celebrated American actor (Appendix B and Plate 10).[81] In *WH*, Othello's seduction of the pallid Desdemona is mirrored in reverse: the blonde Isabella flings herself at her sister-in-law's pale black friend. Reversing Shakespeare's stereotype with characteristic decisiveness, Brontë gave her female protagonist the courage to escape and live on after the birth of her child. Heathcliff, in turn, lives on, not by founding a dynasty, but by recognising the true metal in the boy he had brutalised and enslaved: 'gold put to the use of paving stones' (ch. 21). Emily appears to have felt that as in the stories of Hamlet, Othello, and Oroonoko, Heathcliff is caught between two worlds. In a universally used literary configuration he dies heroically and sacrificially, leaving a world shattered but purged of slavery.

Plate 10 – 'Othello, the Moor of Venice': portrait of Ira Aldridge, by J.W. Northcote, R.A., © Manchester City Art Galleries.

The circumstances of Mellany Hayne, aged seventeen, a senior student who befriended Charlotte Brontë at the Clergy Daughters' School, explain the supposition advanced by Elizabeth Gaskell, that she and her sister Charlotte Hayne, aged twenty-two, were from the West Indies. Through experience shared with a clergy daughter from a neighbouring vicarage in Bedfordshire, the Hayne sisters appear to have acted as interpreters to the Brontës of plantation society, and to have become mistaken for West Indians as a result by Mrs Gaskell, and possibly by Charlotte Brontë. The home of the orphaned Hayne sisters, who registered at the School in 1824, was care of their mother and brother, the Revd William Burgess Hayne, Vicar of Henlow in Bedfordshire. The address in England of Eliza Rawlins Walwyn, daughter of Anne Walwyn and her husband, the Revd John Walwyn, Rector of St Paul's Church on the Island of St Kitts, is given in the School Registration Book as care of Mrs Houston, of Ansley Vicarage, Biggleswade, Bedfordshire. Eliza Walwyn entered the School on 22 July 1825, shortly after the departure of the Brontës on 1 June. Probably, in anticipation of Eliza's arrival, the Brontës were told about the Walwyns by the Haynes. In the process the Brontës would have found explanations for the presence in England of blacks, creoles, plantation proprietors, and slave traders. That social system, which forms the nucleus of *WH* and *Jane Eyre*, was absent from the Brontës' industrialised parish of Bradford.[82]

Others have noticed the mixed social presence in Lunesdale. In Turner's picture of Hornby, a few miles downstream from Cowan Bridge, the girl and the boy who is scolding her about spilt milk are African. In Radclyffe's engraving of Turner's picture, the dark-skinned boy is Asiatic (Plate 11).[83] Along similar lines, Emily highlighted the confusion in the minds of the minor characters who classify Heathcliff as American, Spanish, Lascar, Indian, Chinese, and Gypsy. Heathcliff's dates and locality define him as an enigmatically presented pale African, possibly embodying elements from Edward Guy of Leck, and partly modelled on Thomas Anson, the runaway slave of the Sills of Dent. His position in society is the starting point for an assessment of his character. He re-enacts the origin of our species. Reviewing the African origin and outward emigration of our species in their book *African Exodus*, Chris

Stringer and Robert McKie conclude: 'We are indeed all Africans under our skin'; and: 'Africa is no worse, and no better, than any other global arena, for the simple reason that human cruelty is universal and knows no geographical boundaries'.[84]

6. Signs of fertility

In the second half of her novel, Emily presented the younger generation's discovery of each other in a fertile moorland south, overlaid upon the barren limestone north. That contrast reverses the symbolic handling of landscape in a painting by William Gilpin (1724-1804), founder of the Picturesque movement in England. Gilpin painted the same configuration of hills under two aspects, the fertile Picturesque limestone and the barren Non-Picturesque moorland (Plate 12).[85] Possibly Emily saw his picture; certainly she overturned its ideas. The Picturesque tradition contrasted the pastoral uprightness of the limestone landscape with the Non-Picturesque moorland, which was presented as the symbol of barrenness, industry, crime, overpopulation, and death. Overturning that system of ideas, *WH* presents the limestone landscape in the first half of the story as the setting for betrayal, violence, and death, and the moorland in the second half as the setting for regeneration.

Love of her childhood environment helped Emily to overturn the view of Haworth in T.D. Whitaker's *Loidis and Elmete* ('Leeds and Bradford'), where her home is presented as the summit of the Non-Picturesque: 'On the whole, Haworth is to Bradford as Heptenstall to Halifax—almost at the extremity of population, high, bleak, dirty, and difficult of access'.[86] For her portrayal of the Ingleborough landscape, it appears, she drew on *A Tour to the Caves* (1781), by the Revd John Hutton. This work is printed as an Addendum to Thomas West's *Guide to the Lakes* (1780) (P) (Appendix D). The discovery of Yorkshire reality is symbolised by Lockwood's journey into a perilous fairyland, from a stormy opening to the tranquil ending which he finds on his second visit. Emily retained the Picturesque principle that the Sublime affects the mind through terror as well as calm. The infernal storm and idyllic calm in *Wuthering Heights* match Gilpin's definition of the Sublime experience:

Plate 11 – (a) 'Hornby Castle from Tatham Church', engraving by
W. Radclyffe from the painting by J.M.W. Turner, R.A., in T.D.
Whitaker, *Richmondshire* (1823), vol. 2, p. 263. (b) J.M.W. Turner,
'Hornby Castle from Tatham Church' (detail). Victoria & Albert
Museum, London © V & A Picture Library. (c) Detail from (a).

Plate 12 – W. Gilpin,
'Picturesque and Non-Picturesque Landscapes'.
From W. Gilpin, *Three Essays* (1792), p. 19.

> If the imagination be thus fired by these romantic scenes even in their *common* state, how much more may we suppose it wrought on, when they strike us under some *extraordinary* circumstance of beauty, or terror—in the tranquillity of a calm, or the agitation of a storm?[87]

Lockwood experiences Sublime moments of both types at the terror-laden beginning and in the churchyard at the end of the story.

Emily's modification of Picturesque principles followed the new geological definition of the Pennine landscape. She appears to have found it in writings by Adam Sedgwick (1785-1873), Professor of Geology at Cambridge University and a main contributor to her handling of Dales family histories (Appendix C) as well as her ideas. In his 'Letters to Wordsworth', printed as an Appendix to the 1842 edition of William Wordsworth's *Guide to the Lakes* (1810), Sedgwick explained that the earlier view of the earth which had been propagated in the eighteenth century by A.G. Werner had been superseded. Floods and volcanic activity, the Wernerian argument ran, were afterthoughts sent as punishments for delinquent towns and cities, and the earth was the product of crystallisation out of relatively tranquil oceans, with a time span of a few thousand years. The new view presented the earth as the result of turbulence over thousands of millions of years, with volcanic activity, oceanic surges, deluges, and glacial erosion as the natural forces which produced it (Appendix D). Besides offering corrections to William Wordsworth, his friend and an adherent of the Wernerian theory of the earth, Sedgwick explained the classification of rocks as three main types emerging from that turmoil: sedimentary (slate, shale, sandstone, chalk, flint), igneous (granite), and metamorphic (limestone).[88]

Adam Sedgwick's discoveries depended on diagrams which linked fragments scattered over the vast distances which he covered on foot, driven by love of his native Dent and its hills, streams, and valleys, and ancient farming community. The Ingleborough region, he explained, 'was the home of my boyhood, and is still the home of my heart'.[89] His system of ideas appears to have been used by Emily as a central metaphor for her story. His rock classification foreshadows the sequence of generations in *WH*, where the calm old Earnshaws and Lintons are convulsed by the volcanic energy of the second generation. In turn, the fiery middle generation collapses, yielding to a third, which has been metamorphosed and toughened by experience. Like Sedgwick's image of the earth as a book to be read by linking distant parts, scattered over large areas, Brontë presented her landscape in scattered fragments. In his fourth Letter, Sedgwick defined the geologist as a reader of the earth's secrets:

> We must, in imagination, sweep off the drifted matter that clogs the surface of the ground; we must suppose all the covering of moss and heath and wood to be torn away from the sides of the mountains, and the green mantle that lies near their feet to be lifted up; we may then see the muscular integuments, and sinews, and bones of our mother Earth, and so judge of the part played by each of them during those old convulsive movements whereby her limbs were contorted and drawn up into their present posture.[90]

The elder Catherine uses those terms to describe her experience of love:

> 'My love for Linton is like the foliage in the woods. Time will change it, I'm well aware, as winter changes the trees. My love for Heathcliff resembles the eternal rocks beneath—a source of little visible delight, but necessary. Nelly, I *am* Heathcliff—he's always, always in my mind—not as a pleasure, any more than I am always a pleasure to myself—but as my own being' (ch. 9).

Unaware that her parish history recapitulates Sedgwick's drama of the earth's history, Nelly Dean outlines matching epochs of tranquillity and upheaval in the life of the Earnshaws. Sedgwick's alternating stages of violence and calm in the formation of the earth are re-enacted in the crises at the endings of the four parts of *WH*: Heathcliff's disappearance in a thunderstorm (ch. 9); the violent deaths of Hindley and his sister Catherine (chs. 16-17); the triumph of the younger Catherine over her father (ch. 25); and the defeat of Heathcliff after her collaboration with Hareton in the garden at Easter (ch. 34).

Geological images, permeated by Sedgwick's declared Emancipationist sympathies, reappear in Brontë's symbols of fertility and procreation in *WH*: the fertile earth became her symbol for survival. Haworth farming cannot have failed to offer abundant opportunities for observing procreation and managing the procreative activity of cattle and other beasts of all sizes. Activities such as penning, castration, and marking the breasts of rams with red earth paint, or reddle, so that ewes or gimmers with red backs can be sent off, to give the unmarked ones a chance, are the substance of pastoral life. Explanations about sex among sheep, fish and pigs occur sporadically in Whitaker's *Deanery of Craven* and in Carr's *Dialect of Craven*, two books which Emily Brontë evidently ransacked. The role of the male sheep appears a few pages after Whitaker's praise for Lady Anne Clifford: 'Tupps are rams; which I should not have thought it necessary to observe, had not Shakespeare's commentators stumbled at an indelicate passage in Othello, where the word is used as a verb—A sensible north-country farmer would often explain our old poets better than their learned editors'.[91]

No less expert with dogs and other animals than the farmers round about, Emily Brontë used her entire landscape and its names as a rebus or puzzle picture, emblazoning Adam Sedgwick's image of the geologist's function, to 'see the muscular integuments, and sinews, and bones of our mother Earth, and so judge of the part played by each of them during those old convulsive movements whereby her limbs were contorted and drawn up'. The suffix *-den*, from *Dean* and *Dene*, refers to a valley or dean. Around Haworth Moor it appears in names such as Denholm, Crimsworth Dean, and Todmorden Dean, in Emily's replacement of -ton with -den in Gimmerden Sough (ch. 3), and her use of *den* for valley (ch. 32). Through early spellings, Whitaker explained Dent as Dene-town or Denton: 'Denton is the town of the dene or valley'.[92] A *gimmer* is a young female sheep awaiting a first impregnation, or a ewe, or a sharp-tongued elder human female, and when pronounced *jimmer*, a hinge.[93] The ancient wapontakes or military districts of Craven, around Ingleborough, termed Ewecross and Staincliff or stone-cliff, are thus marked in Tuke's *Map*. In Emily's winged novel, Zillah, the Catherines and Nelly Dean play all these animal types. Gimmerton is the maturing young female sheep's town, as in Skipton, explained by Whitaker: 'Skipton, then, is the town of sheep'.[94]

As in Lockwood's dreams, dreamlike transformations of Dales maps, names, activities, stories and memories appear in *WH*. The names *Dean*, *Gimmerton*, *Penistone*, and *Wuthering* embody Emily Brontë's symbols of procreation in individuals and society. Through the word *wuthering* or *whithering*, 'shaking', 'to throw with violence', and 'giant', as in Carr's example, 'he's a girt *withering* tyke,'[95] from the Norse *hvithra*, 'shake', 'tremble', she linked the excited male and female body, the weather, and the earth. Her life in Yorkshire encompassed Haworth and Halifax, her two Thorntons, and Bolton Bridge in Wharfedale, the site of her visit in 1833. Hallsteads, the counterpart of Thrushcross Grange at Thornton in Lonsdale, was linked with Harewood by their having been properties in Plantagenet and Tudor times of the Redmayne (Redman) family (Appendix C).[96] The owners of Hallsteads at the time of the Brontës' journeys were the Foxcrofts, former partners in Welsh & Co., Liverpool's biggest slave traders.[97] Harewood and the Lascelles family attracted Emancipationist lampoons at the 1807 Parliamentary election. The place names around Thornton, near Bradford, Emily's birthplace, include Throstle Nest, Thornton Hall and Thornton Heights.[98] These Yorkshire words contributed to her inspired feat of imagination, at work on this web of names and their localities.

Emily's knowledge of the suffixes *-ton* and *-tone*, 'enclosure' or 'township', appears in her spelling of Penistone Crag on one occasion as 'Pennistone' (ch. 8).[99] As with her naming of London, Liverpool, and Yorkshire, this seemingly erratic spelling occurs once only, signalling her emphasis on the phonetic value of that name. This implies her recognition of the difference between the short *e* in the pronunciation of the Yorkshire place name, and the long *e* of the Latin root, which refers to the male organ of generation, and metaphorically to pens, pencils, feathers, and the Pennines and Appennines. An inverse mirroring of castration is generally installed by the youthful hands that remove the suffix *-tone* from signs which name Penistone (Plate 13). As in her handling of the

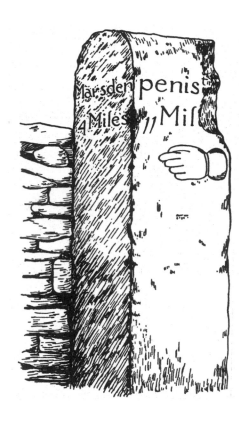

Plate 13 – Guide Stoops.
From W.B. Crump, *Huddersfield Highways Down the Ages* (1949),
p. 148. Reproduced by courtesy of Kirklees Cultural Services,
Huddersfield.

double chronology (Appendix A), Emily's symbolic argument grew around events leading to her birth. Dates associated with that event are closely observed in her presentation of the chronology of her novel. Through an ironically controlled, dreamlike symbolism, *WH* is a tale told by a person whose name, Dean or valley, represents the female body, with a geological equivalent of a male procreative organ and its female counterpart, a magical cave, occupying a single space at the far end. Gimmerton, the female village, lies downstream at the foot of a quaking or *wuthering* mountain. In the rural vernacular, the term for the reproductive act, a rhyme with clucking, unprintable until 1960 and subsequently printed out of usefulness, fills the social and metrical gap behind the dash used by Emily for Heathcliff's word, which Hareton parrots but is evidently too young to understand: 'I was told the curate should have his—teeth dashed down his—throat, if he stepped over the threshold—Heathcliff had promised that!' (ch. 11).

The procreative theme persists throughout the story. A female child achieves release for her society through courage, humour, and literacy. The date set for her wedding, 1 January (ch. 34), does not appear among wedding dates of the decade 1835-1845 at Haworth, which disappear around Christmas and start again at the end of January.[100] Emily's date refers rather, it seems, to the position of 1st January in her copy of the Prayer Book and in modern diaries as a celebration of the Circumcision. Patrick's sermon on this topic, given at Hartshead on the eve of his marriage to Maria Branwell, expounds the view taken by St Paul in *Romans* 2:29: 'circumcision is that of the heart, in the spirit, and not in the letter'.[101] The idea found an illustration, available to Emily, in the uncircumcised *manneken-pis* in Brussels, a probable part model for her 'shameless little boys' (ch. 1). A female counterpart appears in the concentric structure of *WH*, which resembles an onion or Russian doll. For children's amusement, this toy parodies the female body's capacity to contain likenesses of itself. The concentric narrative structure of *Wuthering Heights* is foreshadowed in *Indiana* (1831), by George Sand, and *Frankenstein* (1818), by Mary Shelley.[102] The transition from the militarism which sustained slavery, to the modern ideal of equality of esteem at the workplace and hearth for women and blacks, appears symbolically in these paradigms of Romantic and post-Romantic fiction by female writers.[103] Both tell stories of oppression and release through a concentric series of narratives and confessions. Besides contributing to the tradition of social realism (Appendix B), Emily Brontë foreshadowed the Symbolist movement in modern literature.

7. Note on the text

Structure

Since the manuscript and proofs of *WH* have not survived, the publishing history of the first edition can only be surmised. Clues can be found, but no full picture. Possibly Anna and Emily presented their manuscripts in a form suggesting publication as a novel in three volumes. Charlotte's manuscript of *The Professor* appears to have been thought of as a separate work: 'Currer Bell also wrote a narrative in one volume', she noted in her 'Biographical notice of Ellis and Acton Bell' (1850 Preface). The fragmentary publication history begins there.

Newby's anomalous three-decker, *Wuthering Heights* and *Agnes Grey*, by two authors named Bell, has a bulky Volume II flanked by two thinner volumes of similar length. In setting up his volumes, Newby appears to have started from the end, with Anne's *Agnes Grey* (363 pages), a work of presentable length for Volume III of a book with a market as a three-decker novel about Yorkshire, by two authors named Bell. Emily's manuscript, the obvious candidate for Volume I and Volume II of a Yorkshire novel, presented a problem. Newby's division at the end of chapter 14 rested, it appears, on the need to preserve symmetry in the thicknesses of the volumes. Dividing at the end of Emily's chapter 17 would have produced a bulky Volume I (423 pages), with two relatively slender volumes of approximately equal length tagged on as Volumes II and III. To achieve a semblance of symmetry, evidently Newby ignored Emily's chapter numbering after building his Volume I (348 pages) out of her chapters 1–14, tacking her next three chapters on to the seventeen chapters which formed the second half of her manuscript, and renumbering his job lot as chapters 1–20 of his Volume II. That step obliterated the probable layout of a manuscript which undoubtedly presented its 34 chapters in two parts, each numbered 1 to 17. Emily's second set of seventeen chapters emerged from this rough-handling as his chapters 4-20. These steps yielded a seemingly symmetrical 1847 edition, but with Emily's symmetry effaced.

Winifred Gérin's observation about the long delay in production, and Newby's handling of the proofs—'none of their corrections on the proof-sheets were made'—[104] suggests that the proof-sheets, if returned, presented problems which Newby could not resolve, or ignored. For whatever reason, whether because Emily tried to restore her chapter divisions, or abandoned the whole procedure under the combined impact of illness and despondency over Newby's mangling, he evidently set aside any corrected proofs she may have returned. Probably, with one eye on the Christmas market and the other on the success of another Yorkshire novel by a Bell, he merely ran off his first typesetting. None the less, the accurate rendering of the Haworth dialect in his edition[105] suggests that Emily wrote those parts in a script resembling print. Also, her punctuation marks, and her short paragraphs, laid like pearls, survived more or less intact. By whatever series of steps his mangled chapter sequence was arrived at, the impression of confusion in *WH* can be traced back to his numbering of Emily's chapters after ch. 14. Undoubtedly the misprints, the removal of the pause between her two sets of seventeen chapters, and the numbering from her fifteenth chapter onwards, were Newby's work. In obliterating the symmetry she clearly intended, he deadened the redemptive impact of the second half of the story. The damage was obscured by Charlotte's continuously renumbered 1850 edition, where the damage was compounded by dissolving and resetting Emily's brief paragraphs into slabs.

Until the discovery of symmetry by C.P. Sanger and David Cecil (Appendix B), Charlotte's Preface and edition ensured oblivion for her sister's intention. Newby's mangled chapter plan probably contributed to Charlotte's idea of *WH* as 'wild, and knotty as the root of heath'.[106] Emily unfolded her story, however, in groups of chapters in the scheme *abba* or *abccba*, not unlike the rhyme schemes in some of her poems, where she generally adopted the scheme *abab*, probably for its wave-like, lyrical movement, and simplicity. Her chapters appear in the figure 9+8=8+9, or more exactly, 3+6+8=8+6+3. Suggestions for a plan of this type can be found within her reading resources. The *Divine Poems* (1664) (*K*) and the *Divine Fancies* (1671) (*P*), by Francis Quarles, and poems by George Herbert, have winged or Hieroglyphic patterning of this type. She is likely to have read both these devotional poets.[107] Her uneven chapter lengths resulted from the priority she evidently gave to her numerical patterning. Her first seventeen chapters were overbalanced by her crowded chapters 9 and 17. At the cost of extreme length, these first and second turning points secured loose ends in her story, but by overburdening the word and page count, drove Newby into what appears to have been his renumbering of her second set.

WH is divided along lines resembling the divisions in *Indiana*, by George Sand, and Frederika Bremer's *The Bondmaid* (1844), two novels she had probably read (Appendix B). In a numbering system of the type they used, the four parts of *WH* would appear thus: Part I, chs. 1–9; Part II, chs 1–8; Part III, chs. 1–8; Part IV, chs. 1–9. Since they function like act and scene divisions in a play, these numbers appear in brackets in Appendix A, supplementing the consecutive chapter numbers 1–34, which appear in most editions since 1850 and which this edition follows in its references.

Language

Notoriously, Newby's edition abounds in misprints and misspellings. None the less, it brings us as close as possible to Emily's lost manuscript, and from there to her spoken performance. Caution is enjoined over correcting suspected errors by the assurance emerging from the intensive study by K.M. Petyt. He has demonstrated that Newby's text reliably reflects Emily's sustained rendering of Haworth English.[108] Glaring printing errors are, however, silently corrected in this text. Occasional archaic phonetic spellings in the 1847 edition, for example, *wont* for 'won't', and *eat* for 'ate', have been silently modernised. As in other modern editions, too, *up stairs* and *up-stairs* are standardised to 'upstairs', notwithstanding the distinction in Yorkshire English, which Emily Brontë preserved, between *up stairs* (up the staircase) and *up-stairs* (on the first/second floor). Occasional alterations are explained in the notes, for example, the reading 'hand-pillar' for 'sand-pillar' (ch. 11).

Besides reflecting the author's command of Haworth English, Newby's text retains spoken forms which point to his having printed his edition from the manuscript which Emily Brontë used for performance in the family circle at Haworth. In this edition the dialect passages are translated in full, idiomatically as far as possible, in the notes. In that form, possibly, they suggest the eloquence and humour which were intended as part of Joseph's character, and which would have been rendered flawlessly, uproariously, and intelligibly at the oral performance. Her punctuation in the remainder of the text is spoken rather than grammatical: her novel is an oral text. Silent reading may obscure Nelly Dean's expressive use of northern standard English for a narrative which Emily read aloud. By the time she wrote, Yorkshire English had been described by William Carr in his *Dialect of Craven* (1828) as having been 'the language of crowned heads, of the court, and of the most eminent English historians, divines, and poets, of former ages'. A modernised version of that language is spoken by Nelly Dean: her clarity rescues Lockwood from southern affectation. Emily's performing style appears in her use of the dash [—], a pause mark of variable depth between comma [,], semi-colon [;] and full stop/period [.]. This mark appears in the speeches of Lord Brougham, and essays by William Hazlitt, Hartley Coleridge, and others. Emily Brontë's spoken style produced the effortless, terse and expressive prose of a novel which has become one of the world's treasures.

Another feature of Yorkshire English, Emily Brontë's rendering of the expressively accented form 'But, [...]' is generally retained here, for example: 'But, Mr. Heathcliff forms a singular contrast to his abode and style of living' (ch. 1). Deference to the author's probable spoken style accounts for the retention here of Newby's punctuation at other points, for example:

> The apartment, and furniture would have been nothing extraordinary as belonging to a homely, northern farmer with a stubborn countenance, and stalwart limbs, set out to advantage in knee-breeches, and gaiters (ch. 1).

The graphic quality of standard Yorkshire English vanishes if this is repunctuated into its grammatical parts:

> The apartment and furniture would have been nothing extraordinary as belonging to a homely northern farmer with a stubborn countenance, and stalwart limbs set out to advantage in knee-breeches and gaiters.

Similarly, Isabella cries out in standard Yorkshire English: 'You asked, what has driven me to flight at last? I was compelled to attempt it, because, I had succeeded in rousing his rage a pitch above his malignity' (ch. 17). Her emphasis fades if her 'because' is merged into its phrase by the removal of the comma.

Brontë's incomparably deft handling of setting, atmosphere and mood, and the original use of such words as 'crackly', 'liker', 'snoozled', 'sparely', 'spatters', and many others, appear on every page of *WH*. The spellings, many of them standard in the transitional phase of spelling, are silently retained in this edition where possible: 'ecstacy', 'gallopped', 'ribband', 'skurrying', 'staunchily', 'visiter', and others. Spoken punctuation emphasises the flow of ideas in *WH*. Lockwood's phrasing enacts a man's shock on encountering a shattering narrative: 'She would not hear of staying a second longer—in truth, I felt rather disposed to defer the sequel of her narrative, myself: and now, that she is vanished to her rest, and I have meditated for another hour or two, I shall summon courage to go, also, in spite of aching laziness of head and limbs' (ch. 9). In passages like this, Emily Brontë's prose approaches the mimetic, thought-patterned prose of James Joyce and Virginia Woolf.

1 P.F. Kendall and H.E. Wroot, *Geology of Yorkshire*, 2 vols (1924), vol. 1, pp. 108-124.

2 John James, *History of Bradford* (1841), pp. 346-353; also, Nora Carus-Wilson, 'The Woollen Industry', in *The Cambridge Economic History of Europe* (1952), ed. M. Postain and E.E. Rich, ch. 6, pp. 355-428.

3 J. Erskine Stuart, *The Brontë Country* (1888), pp. 69-70, 98.

4 J.G. Dixon, *Chronicles and Stories of the Craven Dales* (1881), p. 18.

5 *Paterson*, p. 246.

6 *Paterson*, 'London to Whitehaven', pp. 244-8; also, WYA/W: RT.50 (K&K Minutes, 1821-5).

7 Michael Irwin, *Picturing. Description and Illusion in the 19th Century Novel* (1979), p. 138; see also, Gaetano Kanizsa, *Organization in Vision. Essays on Gestalt Perception* (1979), pp. 31-33, and throughout. An analogy with the related form of *trompe-l'oeuil* painting has been identified by Stevie Davies, who observes in *Emily Brontë: Heretic* (1994), p. 181: 'Few readers emerge aware of how little the moorland has been described in the first half of the novel'.

8 Gaetano Kanizsa, *Organization in Vision*, pp. 34-7.

9 P.F. Kendall and H.E. Wroot, *Geology of Yorkshire*, 2 vols (1924), vol. 1, pp. 43-82 (limestone), and pp. 108-124 (millstone grit).

10 Whiteley Turner, *A Spring-time Saunter Round and About Brontë Land* (1911), p. 69. W. Youatt, *The Horse* (1831), pp. 57-8, notes the galloway: 'a beatiful breed of little horses once found in the south of Scotland', valued for its 'speed, stoutness, and sure-footedness in a very rugged and mountainous country'; also, Adam Sedgwick, in his *Memorial of the Trustees of Cowgill Chapel* (1868), p. 75, observed: 'Dent was famous for its Galloway ponies'.

11 Roy Hattersley, *Goodbye to Yorkshire* (1978), p. 49.

12 Mrs Ellis H. Chadwick, *In the Footsteps of the Brontës* (1914), pp. 75-6.

13 T. Wemyss Reid, *Charlotte Brontë. A Memoir* (1877), p. 31.

14 *The Nautical Almanac and Astronomical Ephemeris for the year 1825* (1822), p. 61.

15 CRO/K: Casterton School WD S/38: Clergy Daughters' School Register 1824-5; also, Baines, p. 620; and *Paterson*, pp. 244-8.

16 *Westmorland Gazette*, 12 June 1825.

17 Letter of Friday 3 June 1825, in *New Letters of Robert Southey*, ed. K. Curry, 2 vols. (1965), vol. 2, p. 281.

18 West's *Guide*, with Hutton as Addendum, bound with *Curiosities of Malham*, by Thomas Hurtley, appears in P (1300) as: *Lakes, a Guide to, in Cumberland, Westmorland, and Lancashire, and Natural Curiosities of Malham-in-Craven*, 1 vol., 1789; see also, Peter Bicknell, *The Picturesque Scenery of the Lake District 1752-1855* (1990), pp. 33-40; and Malcolm Andrews, *The Search for the Picturesque. Landscape Aesthetics and Tourism in Britain, 1760-1800* (1989).

19 CRO/K: Casterton School, W D S/38: Clergy Daughters' School Register 1824-5; WYA/W: RT.50. K&K (Minute Book).

20 In Carr, vol. 2, p. 311, Farmer Giles complains: 't' reason why they [Methodists] dunnot gang tot' kirk is, [th]at kirk parsons dunnot preeach t' gospel'.

21 In her book *A Strange Way of Killing* (1987), p. 50, Meg Harris Williams observes: 'the boundaries of the Grange [park] are fluid'; see also, W.H. Stevenson, '*Wuthering Heights*: the Facts', *EIC*, 35 (1985), pp. 149-166 (p. 155).

22 In her diary of a tour through the region, *Through England on a Side Saddle* (1888), p. 158, Cclia Ficnnes observes: 'In these Northern Countryes they have only the summer Graine, as barley, oates, peas, beans, and Lentils, not wheate or Rhye for they are so cold and Late in their yeare they cannot venture at that sort of tillage'.

23 See below, pp. 226-27, note 1.

24 P.F. Kendall and H.E. Wroot, *Geology of Yorkshire*, 2 vols (1924), vol. 1, p. 9; also chapters. 6-10, pp. 43-82 (limestone), and chapters 14-15, pp. 108-124 (millstone grit).

25 See Christine Alexander and Jane Sellars, *The Art of the Brontës* (1995), pp. 370-93.

26 See Maja-Lisa von Sneidern, '*Wuthering Heights* and the Liverpool Slave Trade', *ELH* 62 (1995), 171-96.

27 Bodleian MS Wilberforce d. 14 fol. 16, 17; also, John Lock and W.T. Dixon, *A Man of Sorrow* (1965, reprint, 1979), pp. 18-20.

28 Cited in Winifred Gérin, *Emily Brontë* (1979), p. 127.

29 See Peter J. French, *John Dee. The World of an Elizabethan Magus* (1984), throughout.

30 Eric Solomon, 'The Incest Theme in *Wuthering Heights*', *Nineteenth-Century Fiction*, 14 (1959). Solomon's proposal is silently adopted in Q.D. Leavis, 'A Fresh Approach to *Wuthering Heights*', in F.R. Leavis and Q.D. Leavis, *Essays in America* (1969), pp. 85-142 (p. 89).

31 Emily's copy of the *Book of Common Prayer*) (BPM) lists the prohibition (*Catalogue of the Bonnell Collection*, 1932, ed. C.W. Hatfield, item 53, p. 21).

32 Henry VIII [1540], cap. 38, in *The Statutes at Large* (1786), vol. 2, p. 287; also, *Leviticus* 18:6-25 and 20:10-21.

33 Rupert D.G. Bursell, *Liturgy, Order and the Law* (1996), p. 160. The prohibition is not indicated in James T. Hamick, *The Marriage Law of England* (1873), pp. 30-43; modern elucidations, it appears, including the Marriage Act (1949), from which Bursell's clarification is taken, explain or elaborate upon customary practice. See also, Sybil Wolfram, *In-Laws and Outlaws* (1987), throughout; and Otto Rank, *The Incest Theme in Literature and Legend* (1992; first pbd. 1912).

34 Lacroix Pistol Knife (around 1835), by courtesy of Sheffield City Museums Trust; see also, Pierre Jarlier, *Répertoire d'arquebusiers et de fourbisseurs français* (St-Julien-du-Sault: F.-P. Lobies, no date), pp. 154-55; and Lewis Winant, *Firearms Curiosa* (New York, 1955), pp. 122-33.

35 Q.D. Leavis, 'A Fresh Approach to *Wuthering Heights*', in F.R. Leavis and Q.D. Leavis, *Essays in America* (1969), p. 142.

36 'Shakespeare a Tory and a Gentleman', *Blackwood's Magazine*, 24, Nov. 1828, 570-583 (*K*); reprinted in Hartley Coleridge, *Essays*, 1851, 2 vols., vol. 1, pp. 113-147 (p. 140).

37 Henry Brougham (Lord Brougham), 'Discourse on the Law of Marriage, Divorce, and Legitimacy', in *Speeches of Henry Lord Brougham*, 4 vols. (1838), pp. 429-71 (pp. 460-61).

38 The widespread view that fairy tales retain survivals from lost religions appeared in *The Fairy Mythology: Illustrative of the Romance and Superstition of Various Countries*, 2 vols. (1833), by Thomas Keighley.

39 Elizabeth Gaskell, *The Life of Charlotte Brontë* (1985), p. 483.

40 Ralph Thoresby, *Ducatus Leodensis* (Duchy of Leeds) (1715) (*K*), 2nd edn., published as vol. 2 of T.D. Whitaker, *Loidis and Elmete* [Leeds and Bradford] (1816), p. 134; also, Smith, 4, p. 181: 'There is a measure of ambiguity in the interpretation of this name. It is probably from OE *haer* "rock, heap of stones" (gen. pl. *hara*), but it could be "hare wood" from OE *hara* and *wudu*'.

41 Edward Baines, *Yorkshire Election* (Leeds, 1807), p. 42 and throughout.

42 *The Journal and Major Essays of John Woolman*, ed. Phillips P. Moulton (1971), pp. 182-87 (p. 184).

43 *Equiano's Travels* (1789), ed. Paul Edwards (1977), pp. 72, 158; also, Ruth Cowhig, 'Blacks in English Renaissance drama and the role of Shakespeare's Othello', in *The Black Presence in English Literature* (1985), ed. David Dabydeen, pp. 1-25; 'The Bodies of Men', ch. 6 of Winthrop D. Jordan, *White Over Black. American Attitudes to the Negro, 1550-1812* (1969), pp. 216-65; Jean R. Soderlund, *Quakers and Slavery. A Divided Spirit* (1988), p. 8.

44 *The Journal and Major Essays of John Woolman*, p. 200; also, Henry J. Cadbury, *John Woolman in England 1772. A Documentary Supplement* (1971); and Jean R. Soderlund, *Quakers & Slavery. A Divided Spirit*, throughout.

45 Emily's unambiguous reference to Heathcliff's dark skin is obliterated by Charlotte's repunctuation: 'a dark-skinned gypsy in aspect, in dress and manners a gentleman' (1850 edition, and others).

46 William Wilberforce, *A Practical View of the Prevailing Religious System of Professed Christians, in the Higher and Middle Classes in this Country, Contrasted with Real Christianity* (1797), pp. 19, 28-9; also, William Shakespeare, *Hamlet*, 2.2.295-312; 3.2.69-70.

47 Jakob Hermanus (James Arminius), *A Discourse on the Priesthood of Christ* (1603), trs. Miles Martindale (1815), pp. 20, 31.

48 John Lock and W.T. Dixon, *A Man of Sorrow* (1965; reprint, 1979), pp. 192-4.

49 Henry Nelson Coleridge, *Six Months in the West Indies* (1826), p. 179.

50 *Methodism as it Is*, 2 (1863), p. 193.

51 James MacDonald, *Memoirs of the Rev. Joseph Benson* (London: T. Blanshard, 1822), p. 51.

52 James MacDonald, *Memoirs of the Rev. Joseph Benson* (1822), pp. 530, 533; also, *Early Victorian Methodism. The Correspondence of Jabez Bunting 1830-1858*, ed. W.R. Ward (1976); and G. Elsie Harrison, *The Clue to the Brontës* (1948), throughout. The idea of murdering the soul reappears in Heathcliff's rebuke to Catherine: 'I love *my* murderer—but *yours*! how can I?' (ch. 15).

53 James MacDonald, *Memoirs of the Rev. Joseph Benson*, pp. 66, 382.

54 See Sarah Fermi and Robin Greenwood, '*Jane Eyre* and the Greenwood Family', *BST* 22 (1997), 44-53.

55 CRO/K: WDX.783, 'Colonel Bolton'; also, Clement Jones, *John Bolton of Storrs* (1959), p. v.

56 Ralph Thoresby, *Ducatus Leodensis* (1715) (*K*), 2nd edn. (1816), p. 103, reads: '*Argent*, a Chevron *Sable*, between three Negroes Heads couped proper' ('a black chevron on a silver ground, surrounded by three African heads, severed and painted in their own colour').

57 See 'Enigmatic Puzzles and Wafers', *Sixteen Treasures*, Haworth: BPM (1988), item 43; for rebus names in English, see 'Rebus, or Name-Devises', in William Camden, *Remains Concerning Britain* (1872 reprint), pp. 171-181; also, 'The Rebus', in Tony Augarde, *The Oxford Guide to Word Games* (1986), pp. 84-91. A verbal rebus for Ingleton appears in *The Lonsdale Magazine*, vol. 3 (1822), pp. 238, 318, a journal which the Brontës appear to have read: 'What's useful in Scotland, when it is cold weather, / And the name of a weight, when they're joined together, / a Small town in Yorkshire, to you will display, / which near the foot of a mountain does lay'.

58 See George Ingle, *Yorkshire Cotton. The Yorkshire Cotton Industry* (1997), throughout.

59 *The Bradford Observer*, 12 April 1838, p. 1; also, David James, 'William Byles and the *Bradford Observer*', in *Victorian Bradford. Essays in Honour of Jack Reynolds*, ed. D.G. Wright and J.A. Jowitt (1982), pp. 115-36.

60 Edward Baines, *Yorkshire Election* (Leeds, 1807), p. 42.

61 Winifred Gérin, *Emily Brontë. A Biography* (1979), pp. 225-26; Terry Eagleton, *Heathcliff and the Great Hunger* (1995), pp. 1-26; and below, Appendix B.

62 Arnold Kettle, 'Emily Brontë: *Wuthering Heights* (1847)', in his *An Introduction to the English Novel*, 2 vols. (1951), cited in McNees, vol. 2, pp. 188-200 (p. 188).

63 *The Leeds Intelligencer*, 21 Nov. 1846, p. 8; also, 'Slavery in Yorkshire', *The Leeds Mercury*, 19 March 1831, p. 4 (Appendix B); and J.T. Ward, *Slavery in Yorkshire*, Bradford: *The Journal*, Bradford Textile Society (1960-61).

64 Charles Booth ('General Booth'), *In Darkest England And The Way Out* (1891), p. 23; see also R.H. Sherard, *The White Slaves of England* (1893).

65 William Howitt, *A Serious Address to the Members of the Anti-Slavery Society on the Present Position and Prospects* (1843), p. 5.

66 Mary Wollstonecraft, *Vindication of the Rights of Woman* (1985), p. 257.
67 See J.R. Rogers, *Sex and Race*, 3 vols. (New York, 1941); Cheikh Anta Diop, *The African Origin of Civilization*, trs. Mercer Cook (Chicago, 1974); M.W. Debrunner, *Presence and Prestige. Africans in Europe before 1918* (Basel, 1979); Martin Bernal, *Black Athena* (1989); Hugh Honour, Part IV of *The Image of the Black in Western Art*, ed. Ladislas Bugner, Parts I-IV (1989); Basil Davidson, *Africa in History* (1995): all throughout; *Afrocentrism* (1999), a hostile study by Stephen Howe, ends with the inexplicable view that its subject is 'all unutterably sad' (p. 285).
68 See Maja-Lisa von Sneidern, '*Wuthering Heights* and the Liverpool Slave Trade', *ELH* 62 (1995), 171-96.
69 See Arnold van Gennep, *The Rites of Passage* (1960) (*Les rites de passage*, 1909); also, Joseph O. Campbell, *The Hero with a Thousand Faces* (1973), both throughout; and Stevie Davies, *Emily Brontë. The Artist as a Free Woman* (1983), ch. 7, 'In at the Window. Rites of Passage', pp. 114-128, and throughout.
70 See Maja-Lisa von Sneidern, '*Wuthering Heights* and the Liverpool Slave Trade', *ELH*, 62 (1995), 171-96.
71 James Stephen, *New Reasons for Abolishing the Slave Trade* (1807), p. 45.
72 James Stephen, *England Enslaved by her Slave Colonies* (1826), p. 181.
73 C. Heywood, '"Alas! Poor Caunt": Branwell Brontë's Emancipationist Cartoon', *BST*, 21 (1995), 177-85.
74 *Bradford Observer*, 26 April 1838, p. 4.
75 M.G. Lewis, *Journal of a West Indian Proprietor* (1834), p. 55.
76 Langston Hughes, *Not Without Laughter* (1930), p. 17. In his book *The Black People and Whence they Came* (Pietermaritzburg: University of Natal Press, 1979), p. 52, Mangena M. Fuze observes that the descendants of white traders in Natal 'are distinguished by being white, but they are black in all other respects'.
77 *The Novels of Mrs Aphra Behn*, ed. Ernest A. Baker (1913), p. 63.
78 Peter Fryer, *Staying Power. The History of Black People in Britain* (1984), p. 60.
79 Frantz Fanon, *Black Skin, White Masks* (1967), p. 32.
80 Fanon, *Black Skin*, p. 191.
81 With thanks to Bernth Lindfors for references.
82 CRO/K:WDS/38/3: Clergy Daughters' School Entrance Book, entries 37, 38 (Hayne) and 58 (Walwyn); see also, Elizabeth Gaskell, *The Life of Charlotte Brontë*, ed. Alan Shelston (London: Penguin, 1985), p. 108; J.A. Venn, *Alumni Cantabrigienses*, Part 2, vol. 3 (Cambridge: Cambridge University Press, 1947), p. 302 ('Hayne'), and J. Foster, *Alumni Oxonienses 1715-1886*, Vol. 4 (Oxford: Parker, 1888), p. 1495 ('Walwyn'); with special thanks for documents supplied by Victoria Borg O'Flaherty, Archivist of the National Archives of St Kitts and Nevis. For the possibility that the Brontës returned to the Clergy Daughters' School after the summer of 1825, see Sarah Fermi, 'The Brontës at the Clergy Daughters' School: When Did They Leave?', *BST* 21 (1996), 219-31.

83 V&A Picture Library; T.D. Whitaker, *Richmondshire*, 2 vols (1822), vol. 2, p. 263; David Hess, *In Turner's Footsteps* (1993), plate 18 [p. 123].

84 Chris Stringer and Robert McKie, *African Exodus* (1996), pp. 170-83 (p. 171), and throughout; also, Charles Darwin, *The Descent of Man* (1873), and Charles Pickering, *The Races of Man* (1850), both throughout.

85 W. Gilpin, 'Picturesque and Non-Picturesque Mountain Landscapes', in W. Gilpin, *Three Essays* (1792), pp. 18-19; also, C. Heywood, 'Yorkshire Landscapes in *Wuthering Heights*', *EIC* 48 (1998), 13-34; *Wuthering Heights* is omitted in Alexander M. Ross, *The Imprint of the Picturesque on Nineteenth-Century British Fiction* (1986).

86 T.D. Whitaker, *Loidis and Elmete* [Leeds and Bradford] (1816), p. 356.

87 William Gilpin, *Observations on* [...] *the Mountains and Lakes of Cumberland and Westmoreland*, 2 vols. (1808), vol. 1, p. 131.

88 See Colin Speakman, *Adam Sedgwick. Geologist and Dalesman* (1982); A. Hallam, *Great Geological Controversies* (1983).

89 Adam Sedgwick, *Memorial of the Trustees of Cowgill Chapel* (1868), p. vi.

90 Sedgwick, 'Letters to Wordsworth', in W. Wordsworth, *Guide to the Lakes* (1842), p. 180.

91 *Craven*, p. 293.

92 T.D. Whitaker, *Richmondshire* (1822), vol. 2, p. 362.

93 Carr, vol. 1, p. 183; also, *EDD*.

94 *Craven*, p. 210.

95 Carr, vol. 2, p. 259.

96 W. Greenwood, *The Redmans of Levens and Harewood* (1905), throughout.

97 C. Heywood, 'Yorkshire Slavery in *Wuthering Heights*', *RES* 38 (1987), 148-97.

98 Smith, 3, p. 273.

99 See below, page 161, note 2.

100 Bradford City Archive: Haworth Parish Registers, 1823-47.

101 Patrick Brontë, Sermon at Hartshead (typescript transcription), Leeds: Brotherton Collection.

102 For a discussion of a related concentric narrative, see Chris Baldick, *In Frankenstein's Shadow* (1987), throughout.

103 See Eva Figes, *Sex and Subterfuge* (1982), throughout.

104 See Winifred Gérin, *Emily Brontë* (1979), pp. 209-10; also, 'Biographical Notice of Ellis and Acton Bell', in *Wuthering Heights* (1894), ed. Charlotte Brontë, p. viii.

105 K.M. Petyt, *Wuthering Heights and the Haworth Dialect* (Menston: Yorkshire Dialect Society, 1970).

106 For a pioneering re-evaluation of the 1850 Preface, see David Cecil, 'Emily Brontë and *Wuthering Heights*', in his *Early Victorian Novelists* (1934) (McNees, pp. 102-126; and below, Appendix B).

107 See Michael Bath, *Speaking Pictures* (1994), throughout.

108 K.M. Petyt, *Wuthering Heights and the Haworth Dialect* (1970), throughout.

WUTHERING HEIGHTS

1801—I have just returned from a visit to my landlord—the solitary neighbour that I shall be troubled with. This is certainly, a beautiful country![1] In all England, I do not believe that I could have fixed on a situation so completely removed from the stir of society. A perfect misanthropist's Heaven—and Mr. Heathcliff and I are such a suitable pair to divide the desolation between us. A capital fellow! He little imagined how my heart warmed towards him when I beheld his black eyes withdraw so suspiciously under their brows, as I rode up, and when his fingers sheltered themselves, with a jealous resolution, still further in his waistcoat, as I announced my name.

"Mr. Heathcliff?" I said.

A nod was the answer.

"Mr. Lockwood your new tenant, sir—I do myself the honour of calling as soon as possible, after my arrival, to express the hope that I have not inconvenienced you by my perseverance in soliciting the occupation of Thrushcross Grange: I heard, yesterday, you had some thoughts—"

"Thrushcross Grange is my own, sir," he interrupted wincing, "I should not allow any one to inconvenience me, if I could hinder it—walk in!"

The "walk in," was uttered with closed teeth and expressed the sentiment, "Go to the Deuce!" Even the gate over which he leant manifested no sympathizing movement to the words; and I think that circumstance determined me to accept the invitation: I felt interested in a man who seemed more exaggeratedly reserved than myself.

When he saw my horse's breast fairly pushing the barrier, he did pull out his hand to unchain it, and then sullenly preceded me up the causeway, calling, as we entered the court:

"Joseph, take Mr. Lockwood's horse; and bring up some wine."

---

1   Country: region, as in 'this beautiful country', W. Wordsworth, *Guide to the Lakes* (1853), p. 145.

"Here we have the whole establishment of domestics, I suppose," was the reflection, suggested by this compound order, "No
wonder the grass grows up between the flags, and cattle are the
only hedge-cutters."

Joseph was an elderly, nay, an old man, very old, perhaps,
though hale and sinewy.

"The Lord help us!" he soliloquised in an undertone of peevish displeasure, while relieving me of my horse: looking, meantime,
in my face so sourly that I charitably conjectured he must have
need of divine aid to digest his dinner, and his pious ejaculation
had no reference to my unexpected advent.

Wuthering Heights is the name of Mr. Heathcliff's dwelling,
"wuthering" being a significant provincial adjective, descriptive of
the atmospheric tumult to which its station is exposed, in stormy
weather. Pure, bracing ventilation they must have up there, at all
times, indeed: one may guess the power of the north wind, blowing over the edge, by the excessive slant of a few, stunted firs at the
end of the house; and by a range of gaunt thorns all stretching their
limbs one way, as if craving alms of the sun. Happily, the architect
had foresight to build it strong: the narrow windows are deeply set
in the wall; and the corners defended with large jutting stones.

Before passing the threshold, I paused to admire a quantity of
grotesque carving lavished over the front, and especially about the
principal door, above which, among a wilderness of crumbling
griffins, and shameless little boys, I detected the date "1500,"[1] and

---

1   Several architectural features are present here. Stone building materials
    entered domestic use only after about 1600; accordingly the date 1500
    invokes the Tudor family histories of Hornby Castle and Skipton Castle
    (Appendix C). A datestone on Ponden House, near Haworth, is dated
    1801 and inscribed with the name of the owner, Robert Heaton; the
    crumbling griffins resemble the sculptures on the façade of High Sunder-
    land Hall, Halifax, now demolished; the 'shameless little boys' resemble
    the draped and averted *putti* on the Maison Royale (1696), flanking the
    Town Hall on the Grand Place in Brussels, recast as 'shameless' to match
    the celebrated monument by Dequesnoy nearby, the *Manneken-pis* (1619)
    or fountain simulating an older boy as a urinating *putto*; see André Vanrie,
    Brussel in oude gravures (Brussels, 1978), pp. 85, 110-11; and George-Henri
    Dumont, *Belgique et Luxembourg* (Brussels, 1980), pp. 145-49; also, Emme-
    line Garnett, *The Dated Buildings of South Lonsdale* (1994).

the name "Hareton Earnshaw." I would have made a few comments, and requested a short history of the place, from the surly owner, but his attitude at the door appeared to demand my speedy entrance, or complete departure, and I had no desire to aggravate his impatience, previous to inspecting the penetralium.[1]

One step brought us into the family sitting-room, without any introductory lobby, or passage: they call it here "the house" preeminently. It includes kitchen, and parlor, generally, but I believe at Wuthering Heights, the kitchen is forced to retreat altogether, into another quarter, at least I distinguished a chatter of tongues, and a clatter of culinary utensils, deep within; and I observed no signs of roasting, boiling, or baking, about the huge fire-place, nor any glitter of copper saucepans and tin cullenders on the walls. One end, indeed, reflected splendidly both light and heat, from ranks of immense pewter dishes; interspersed with silver jugs, and tankards, towering row after row, in a vast oak dresser, to the very roof. The latter had never been underdrawn,[2] its entire anatomy lay bare to an inquiring eye, except where a frame of wood laden with oatcakes, and clusters of legs of beef, mutton and ham, concealed it. Above the chimney were sundry villainous old guns, and a couple of horse-pistols, and, by way of ornament, three gaudily painted canisters disposed along its ledge. The floor was of smooth, white stone:[3] the chairs high-backed, primitive structures, painted green: one or two heavy black ones lurking in the shade. In an arch, under the dresser, reposed a huge, liver-coloured bitch pointer surrounded by a swarm of squealing puppies, and other dogs haunted other recesses.

The apartment, and furniture would have been nothing extraordinary as belonging to a homely, northern farmer with a stubborn countenance, and stalwart limbs, set out to advantage in knee-breeches, and gaiters. Such an individual, seated in his armchair, his mug of ale frothing on the round table before him, is to be seen in any circuit of five or six miles among these hills, if you go at the right time, after dinner. But, Mr. Heathcliff forms a sin-

---

1 *penetralium*: ostentatious Latinism for interior.
2 *underdrawn*: equipped with a ceiling.
3 *white stone*: a first indication of the limestone region.

gular contrast to his abode and style of living. He is a dark skinned gypsy, in aspect, in dress, and manners, a gentleman, that is, as much a gentleman as many a country squire: rather slovenly, perhaps, yet not looking amiss, with his negligence, because he has an erect and handsome figure—rather morose—possibly, some people might suspect him of a degree of under-bred pride—I have a sympathetic chord within that tells me it is nothing of the sort; I know, by instinct, his reserve springs from an aversion to showy displays of feeling—to manifestations of mutual kindliness. He'll love and hate, equally under cover, and esteem it a species of impertinence, to be loved or hated again—No, I'm running on too fast—I bestow my own attributes over liberally on him. Mr. Heathcliff may have entirely dissimilar reasons for keeping his hand out of the way, when he meets a would-be acquaintance, to those which actuate me. Let me hope my constitution is almost peculiar: my dear mother used to say I should never have a comfortable home, and only last summer, I proved myself perfectly unworthy of one.

While enjoying a month of fine weather at the sea-coast, I was thrown into the company of a most fascinating creature, a real goddess, in my eyes, as long as she took no notice of me. I "never told my love"[1] vocally; still, if looks have language, the merest idiot might have guessed I was over head and ears: she understood me, at last, and looked a return—the sweetest of all imaginable looks—and what did I do? I confess it with shame—shrunk icily into myself, like a snail, at every glance retired colder and farther; till, finally, the poor innocent was led to doubt her own senses, and, overwhelmed with confusion at her supposed mistake, persuaded her mamma to decamp.

By this curious turn of disposition I have gained the reputation of deliberate heartlessness, how undeserved, I alone can appreciate.

I took a seat at the end of the hearthstone opposite that towards which my landlord advanced, and filled up an interval of

---

1   From Shakespeare, *Twelfth Night*, 2.4.110: Viola tells of the lady who pined away in silence, but Lockwood is a male egotist who causes havoc by concealing his feelings.

silence by attempting to caress the canine mother, who had left her nursery, and was sneaking wolfishly to the back of my legs, her lip curled up, and her white teeth watering for a snatch.

My caress provoked a long, guttural gnarl.[1]

"You'd better let the dog alone," growled Mr. Heathcliff, in unison, checking fiercer demonstrations with a punch of his foot. "She's not accustomed to be spoiled—not kept for a pet."

Then, striding to a side-door, he shouted again,

"Joseph!"

Joseph mumbled indistinctly in the depths of the cellar; but, gave no intimation of ascending; so, his master dived down to him, leaving me *vis-à-vis* the ruffianly bitch, and a pair of grim, shaggy sheep dogs, who shared with her a jealous guardianship over all my movements.

Not anxious to come in contact with their fangs, I sat still—but, imagining they would scarcely understand tacit insults, I unfortunately indulged in winking and making faces at the trio, and some turn of my physiognomy so irritated madam, that she suddenly broke into a fury, and leapt on my knees. I flung her back, and hastened to interpose the table between us. This proceeding roused the whole hive. Half-a-dozen four-footed fiends, of various sizes, and ages, issued from hidden dens to the common centre. I felt my heels and coat-laps peculiar subjects of assault; and, parrying off the larger combatants, as effectually as I could, with the poker, I was constrained to demand, aloud, assistance from some of the household, in re-establishing peace.

Mr. Heathcliff and his man climbed the cellar steps with vexatious phlegm. I don't think they moved one second faster than usual, though the hearth was an absolute tempest of worrying and yelping.

Happily, an inhabitant of the kitchen made more dispatch; a lusty dame, with tucked up gown, bare arms, and fire-flushed cheeks, rushed into the midst of us flourishing a frying-pan; and used that weapon and her tongue to such a purpose, that the

---

1 As a verb, a standard archaism in Shakespeare, *2 Henry VI* 3.1.192: 'wolves are gnarling who shall gnaw thee first'; as a noun, peculiar to *WH* (*NED*); also, *gnar*, 'to growl, to snarl', Carr I, p. 189.

storm subsided magically, and she only remained, heaving like a sea after a high wind, when her master entered on the scene.

"What the devil is the matter?" he asked, eyeing me in a manner that I could ill endure after this inhospitable treatment.

"What the devil, indeed!" I muttered. "The herd of possessed swine[1] could have had no worse spirits in them than those animals of yours, sir. You might as well leave a stranger with a brood of tigers!"

"They won't meddle with persons who touch nothing," he remarked, putting the bottle before me, and restoring the displaced table. "The dogs do right to be vigilant. Take a glass of wine?"

"No, thank you."

"Not bitten, are you?"

"If I had been, I would have set my signet on the biter."

Heathcliff's countenance relaxed into a grin.

"Come, come," he said, "you are flurried, Mr. Lockwood. Here, take a little wine. Guests are so exceedingly rare in this house that I and my dogs, I am willing to own, hardly know how to receive them. Your health, sir!"

I bowed and returned the pledge; beginning to perceive that it would be foolish to sit sulking for the misbehaviour of a pack of curs: besides, I felt loath to yield the fellow further amusement, at my expense; since his humour took that turn.

He—probably swayed by prudential considerations of the folly of offending a good tenant—relaxed, a little, in the laconic style of chipping of his pronouns, and auxiliary verbs; and introduced, what he supposed would be a subject of interest to me, a discourse on the advantages and disadvantages of my present place of retirement.

I found him very intelligent on the topics we touched; and, before I went home, I was encouraged so far as to volunteer another visit, to-morrow.

He evidently wished no repetition of my intrusion. I shall go, notwithstanding. It is astonishing how sociable I feel myself compared with him.

---

8   *Luke* 8:27-36 tells of a man whose devils leave him, enter a herd of pigs, and are drowned when they rush into the lake; Lockwood hints that Heathcliff's demons have left him.

CHAPTER 2

Yesterday afternoon set in misty and cold. I had half a mind to spend it by my study fire, instead of wading through heath and mud to Wuthering Heights.

On coming up from dinner, however (N.B. I dine between twelve and one o'clock; the housekeeper, a matronly lady taken as a fixture along with the house, could not, or would not comprehend my request that I might be served at five)[1] —on mounting the stairs with this lazy intention, and stepping into the room, I saw a servant-girl on her knees, surrounded by brushes, and coalscuttles; and raising an infernal dust as she extinguished the flames with heaps of cinders. This spectacle drove me back immediately; I took my hat, and, after a four miles walk,[2] arrived at Heathcliff's garden gate just in time to escape the first feathery flakes of a snow shower.

On that bleak hill top the earth was hard with a black frost, and the air made me shiver through every limb. Being unable to remove the chain, I jumped over, and, running up the flagged causeway bordered with straggling gooseberry bushes,[3] knocked vainly for admittance, till my knuckles tingled, and the dogs howled.

"Wretched inmates!" I ejaculated, mentally, "you deserve perpetual isolation from your species for your churlish inhospitability. At least, I would not keep my doors barred in the day time—I don't care—I will get in!"

So resolved, I grasped the latch, and shook it vehemently. Vinegar-faced Joseph projected his head from a round window of the barn.

---

1   Northern districts retained the Tudor noonday dinner hour, which moved to late afternoon in eighteenth-century southern England, and into the evening during the nineteenth century; see Arnold Palmer, *Movable Feasts* (1952). Lockwood's confusion survives in England.

2   In doubling the distance between the Thornton in Lonsdale counterparts, Brontë appears to invoke the walk from Haworth to Withins Height.

3   Details found around Ponden House, near Haworth.

"Whet are ye for?" he shouted. "T' maisters dahn i' t' fowld. Goa rahnd by th'end ut' laith, if yah went tuh spake tull him."[1]

"Is there nobody inside to open the door?" I hallooed, responsively.

"They's nobbut t' missis; and shoo'll nut oppen't an ye mak yer flaysome dins till neeght."[2]

"Why cannot you tell her who I am, eh, Joseph?"

"Nor-ne me! Aw'll hae noa hend wi't,"[3] muttered the head vanishing.

The snow began to drive thickly. I seized the handle to essay another trial; when a young man, without coat, and shouldering a pitchfork, appeared in the yard behind. He hailed me to follow him, and, after marching through a wash-house, and a paved area containing a coal-shed, pump, and pigeon-cote, we at length arrived in the large, warm, cheerful apartment, where I was formerly received.

It glowed delightfully in the radiance of an immense fire, compounded of coal, peat, and wood: and near the table, laid for a plentiful evening meal, I was pleased to observe the "missis," an individual whose existence I had never previously suspected.

I bowed and waited, thinking she would bid me take a seat. She looked at me, leaning back in her chair, and remained motionless and mute.

"Rough weather!" I remarked. "I'm afraid, Mrs. Heathcliff, the floor must bear the consequences of your servants' leisurely[4] attendance: I had hard work to make them hear me!"

---

1   *Whet are ye for?*: 'What do you want? The master's down in the field. Go round by the end of the barn, if you want to speak to him.'

2   *They's nobbut*: 'There's no one here except the lady; and she'll not open the door if you make this wretched noise until nightfall.'

3   *Nor-ne me!*: 'No, not me, I'll have no hand in it'.

4   *WH* (1847), vol. 1, p. 17, has 'servant's leisure attendance': combining hypocrisy with faulty understanding, Lockwood pretends Joseph is slow and hard of hearing, when he heard clearly and refused entry; he mistakes Hareton for another servant; and after muddying the floor with his boots, blames others. The rudeness and ineptitude of southerners is similarly satirised in the dialogues of Bridget and Farmer Giles, appended to W. Carr, *The Dialect of Craven* (1828).

She never opened her mouth. I stared—she stared also. At any rate, she kept her eyes on me, in a cool, regardless manner, exceedingly embarrassing and disagreeable.

"Sit down," said the young man, gruffly. "He'll be in soon."

I obeyed; and hemmed, and called the villain Juno, who deigned, at this second interview, to move the extreme tip of her tail, in token of owning my acquaintance.

"A beautiful animal!" I commenced again. "Do you intend parting with the little ones, madam?"

"They are not mine," said the amiable hostess more repellingly than Heathcliff himself could have replied.

"Ah, your favourites are among these!" I continued, turning to an obscure cushion full of something like cats.

"A strange choice of favourites," she observed scornfully.

Unluckily, it was a heap of dead rabbits—I hemmed once more, and drew closer to the hearth, repeating my comment on the wildness of the evening.

"You should not have come out," she said, rising and reaching from the chimney piece two of the painted canisters.

Her position before was sheltered from the light: now, I had a distinct view of her whole figure and countenance. She was slender, and apparently scarcely past girlhood: an admirable form, and the most exquisite little face that I have ever had the pleasure of beholding: small features, very fair; flaxen ringlets, or rather golden, hanging loose on her delicate neck; and eyes—had they been agreeable in expression, they would have been irresistible—fortunately for my susceptible heart, the only sentiment they evinced hovered between scorn and a kind of desperation, singularly unnatural to be detected there.

The canisters were almost out of her reach; I made a motion to aid her; she turned upon me as a miser might turn, if any one attempted to assist him in counting his gold.

"I don't want your help," she snapped, "I can get them for myself."

"I beg your pardon," I hastened to reply.

"Were you asked to tea?" she demanded, tying an apron over her neat black frock, and standing with a spoonful of the leaf poised over the pot.

"I shall be glad to have a cup," I answered.

"Were you asked?" she repeated.

"No," I said, half smiling. "You are the proper person to ask me."

She flung the tea back, spoon and all; and resumed her chair in a pet, her forehead corrugated, and her red under-lip pushed out, like a child's, ready to cry.

Meanwhile, the young man had slung onto his person a decidedly shabby upper garment, and, erecting himself before the blaze, looked down on me, from the corner of his eyes, for all the world as if there were some mortal feud unavenged between us. I began to doubt whether he were a servant or not; his dress and speech were both rude, entirely devoid of the superiority observable in Mr. and Mrs. Heathcliff; his thick, brown curls were rough and uncultivated, his whiskers encroached bearishly over his cheeks, and his hands were embrowned like those of a common labourer, still his bearing was free, almost haughty; and he showed none of a domestic's assiduity in attending on the lady of the house.

In the absence of clear proofs of his condition, I deemed it best to abstain from noticing his curious conduct, and, five minutes afterwards, the entrance of Heathcliff relieved me, in some measure, from my uncomfortable state.

"You see, sir, I am come according to promise!" I exclaimed, assuming the cheerful—"and I fear I shall be weather-bound for half an hour, if you can afford me shelter during that space."

"Half an hour?" he said, shaking the white flakes from his clothes; "I wonder you should select the thick of a snow-storm to ramble about in. Do you know that you run a risk of being lost in the marshes? People familiar with these moors often miss their road on such evenings, and I can tell you, there is no chance of a change at present."

"Perhaps I can get a guide among your lads, and he might stay at the Grange till morning—could you spare me one?"

"No, I could not."

"Oh, indeed! Well then, I must trust to my own sagacity."

"Umph."

"Are you going to mak th' tea?" demanded he of the shabby coat, shifting his ferocious gaze from me to the young lady.

"Is *he* to have any?" she asked, appealing to Heathcliff.

"Get it ready, will you?" was the answer, uttered so savagely that I started. The tone in which the words were said, revealed a genuine bad nature. I no longer felt inclined to call Heathcliff a capital fellow.

When the preparations were finished, he invited me with—

"Now, sir, bring forward your chair." And we all, including the rustic youth, drew round the table, an austere silence prevailing while we discussed our meal.

I thought, if I had caused the cloud, it was my duty to make an effort to dispel it. They could not every day sit so grim and taciturn, and it was impossible, however ill-tempered they might be, that the universal scowl they wore was their every day countenance.

"It is strange," I began in the interval of swallowing one cup of tea, and receiving another, "it is strange how custom can mould our tastes and ideas; many could not imagine the existence of happiness in a life of such complete exile from the world as you spend, Mr. Heathcliff; yet, I'll venture to say, that, surrounded by your family, and with your amiable lady as the presiding genius over your home and heart—"

"My amiable lady!" he interrupted, with an almost diabolical sneer on his face. "Where is she—my amiable lady?"

"Mrs. Heathcliff, your wife, I mean."

"'Well, yes—Oh! you would intimate that her spirit has taken the post of ministering angel and guards the fortunes of Wuthering Heights, even when her body is gone. Is that it?"

Perceiving myself in a blunder, I attempted to correct it. I might have seen there was too great a disparity between the ages of the parties to make it likely that they were man and wife. One was about forty; a period of mental vigour at which men seldom cherish the delusion of being married for love, by girls: that dream is reserved for the solace of our declining years. The other did not look seventeen.

Then it flashed upon me; "the clown at my elbow, who is drinking his tea out of a basin, and eating his bread with unwashed hands, may be her husband. Heathcliff, junior, of course. Here is the consequence of being buried alive: she has thrown herself away upon that boor, from sheer ignorance that better individuals existed! A sad pity—I must beware how I cause her to regret her choice."

The last reflection may seem conceited; it was not. My neighbour struck me as bordering on repulsive. I knew, through experience, that I was tolerably attractive.

"Mrs. Heathcliff is my daughter-in-law," said Heathcliff, corroborating my surmise. He turned, as he spoke, a peculiar look in her direction, a look of hatred—unless he has a most perverse set of facial muscles that will not, like those of other people, interpret the language of his soul.

"Ah, certainly—I see now; you are the favoured possessor of the beneficent fairy," I remarked, turning to my neighbour.

This was worse than before: the youth grew crimson, and clenched his fist with every appearance of a meditated assault. But he seemed to recollect himself, presently; and smothered the storm in a brutal curse, muttered on my behalf, which, however, I took care not to notice.

"Unhappy in your conjectures, sir!" observed my host; "we neither of us have the privilege of owning your good fairy; her mate is dead. I said she was my daughter-in-law, therefore, she must have married my son."

"And this young man is—"

"Not my son, assuredly!"

Heathcliff smiled again, as if it were rather too bold a jest to attribute the paternity of that bear to him.

"My name is Hareton Earnshaw," growled the other; "and I'd counsel you to respect it!"

"I've shown no disrespect," was my reply, laughing internally at the dignity with which he announced himself.

He fixed his eye on me longer than I cared to return the stare, for fear I might be tempted either to box his ears, or render my hilarity audible. I began to feel unmistakably out of place in that pleasant family circle. The dismal spiritual atmosphere overcame, and more than neutralized the glowing physical comforts round me; and I resolved to be cautious how I ventured under those rafters a third time.

The business of eating being concluded, and no one uttering a word of sociable conversation, I approached a window to examine the weather.

A sorrowful sight I saw; dark night coming down prematurely, and sky and hills mingled in one bitter whirl of wind and suffocating snow.

"I don't think it possible for me to get home now, without a guide," I could not help exclaiming. "The roads will be buried already; and, if they were bare, I could scarcely distinguish a foot in advance."

"Hareton, drive those dozen sheep into the barn porch. They'll be covered if left in the fold all night; and put a plank before them," said Heathcliff.

"How must I do?" I continued, with rising irritation.

There was no reply to my question; and, on looking round, I saw only Joseph bringing in a pail of porridge for the dogs; and Mrs. Heathcliff leaning over the fire, diverting herself with burning a bundle of matches which had fallen from the chimney-piece as she restored the tea-canister to its place.

The former, when he had deposited his burden, took a critical survey of the room; and, in cracked tones, grated out:

"Aw woonder hagh yah can faishion tuh stand thear i'idleness and war, when all on 'em's goan aght! Bud yah're a nowt, and it's noa use talking—yah'll niver mend uh yer ill ways; bud, goa raight tuh t' divil, like yer mother afore ye!"[1]

I imagined, for a moment, that this piece of eloquence was addressed to me; and, sufficiently enraged, stepped towards the aged rascal with an intention of kicking him out of the door.

Mrs. Heathcliff, however, checked me by her answer.

"You scandalous old hypocrite!" she replied. "Are you not afraid of being carried away bodily, whenever you mention the devil's name? I warn you to refrain from provoking me, or I'll ask your abduction as a special favour. Stop, look here, Joseph," she continued, taking a long, dark book from a shelf. "I'll show you

---

1 'I wonder how you can manage to stand there in idleness and worse, when they have all gone out! But you're a nobody, and it's no use talking—you'll never improve your bad ways, but go to the devil, like your mother before you!'

how far I've progressed in the Black Art—I shall soon be competent to make a clear house of it. The red cow didn't die by chance; and your rheumatism can hardly be reckoned among providential visitations!"

"Oh, wicked, wicked!" gasped the elder, "may the Lord deliver us from evil!"

"No, reprobate! you are a castaway—be off, or I'll hurt you seriously! I'll have you all modelled in wax and clay; and the first who passes the limits I fix, shall—I'll not say what he shall be done to—but, you'll see! Go, I'm looking at you!"

The little witch put a mock malignity into her beautiful eyes, and Joseph, trembling with sincere horror, hurried out praying and ejaculating "wicked" as he went.

I thought her conduct must be prompted by a species of dreary fun; and, now that we were alone, I endeavoured to interest her in my distress.

"Mrs. Heathcliff," I said, earnestly, "you must excuse me for troubling you—I presume, because, with that face, I'm sure you cannot help being good-hearted. Do point out some landmarks by which I may know my way home—I have no more idea how to get there than you would have how to get to London!"

"Take the road you came," she answered, ensconcing herself in a chair, with a candle, and the long book open before her. "It is brief advice: but, as sound as I can give."

"Then, if you hear of me being discovered dead in a bog, or a pit full of snow, your conscience won't whisper that it is partly your fault?"

"How so? I cannot escort you. They wouldn't let me go to the end of the garden-wall."

"*You*! I should be sorry to ask you to cross the threshold, for my convenience, on such a night," I cried. "I want you to *tell* me my way, not to *show* it; or else to persuade Mr. Heathcliff to give me a guide."

"Who? There is himself, Earnshaw, Zillah, Joseph, and I. Which would you have?"

"Are there no boys at the farm?"

"No, those are all."

"Then, it follows that I am compelled to stay."

"That you may settle with your host. I have nothing to do with it."

"I hope it will be a lesson to you, to make no more rash journeys on these hills," cried Heathcliff's stern voice from the kitchen entrance. "As to staying here, I don't keep accommodations for visitors; you must share a bed with Hareton, or Joseph, if you do."

"I can sleep on a chair in this room," I replied.

"No, no! A stranger is a stranger, be he rich or poor—it will not suit me to permit any one in the range of the place while I am off guard!" said the unmannerly wretch.

With this insult my patience was at an end. I uttered an expression of disgust, and pushed past him into the yard, running against Earnshaw in my haste. It was so dark that I could not see the means of exit, and, as I wandered round, I heard another specimen of their civil behaviour amongst each other.

At first, the young man appeared about to befriend me.

"I'll go with him as far as the park," he said.

"You'll go with him to hell!" exclaimed his master, or whatever relation he bore. "And who is to look after the horses, eh?"

"A man's life is of more consequence than one evening's neglect of the horses; somebody must go," murmured Mrs. Heathcliff, more kindly than I expected.

"Not at your command!" retorted Hareton. "If you set store on him, you'd better be quiet."

"Then I hope his ghost will haunt you; and I hope Mr. Heathcliff will never get another tenant, till the Grange is a ruin!" she answered sharply.

"Hearken, hearken, shoo's cursing on me!" muttered Joseph, towards whom I had been steering.

He sat within earshot, milking the cows, by the aid of a lantern which I seized unceremoniously, and calling out that I would send it back on the morrow, rushed to the nearest postern.

"Maister, maister, he's staling t' lantern!" shouted the ancient, pursuing my retreat. "Hey, Gnasher! Hey, dog! Hey, Wolf, holld him, holld him!"

On opening the little door, two hairy monsters flew at my throat, bearing me down, and extinguishing the light, while a mingled guffaw, from Heathcliff and Hareton, put the copestone on my rage and humiliation.

Fortunately, the beasts seemed more bent on stretching their paws, and yawning, and flourishing their tails, than devouring me alive; but, they would suffer no resurrection, and I was forced to lie till their malignant masters pleased to deliver me: then hatless, and trembling with wrath, I ordered the miscreants to let me out—on their peril to keep me one minute longer—with several incoherent threats of retaliation, that in their indefinite depth of virulency, smacked of King Lear.

The vehemence of my agitation brought on a copious bleeding at the nose, and still Heathcliff laughed and still I scolded. I don't know what would have concluded the scene had there not been one person at hand rather more rational than myself, and more benevolent than my entertainer. This was Zillah,[1] the stout housewife; who at length issued forth to inquire into the nature of the uproar. She thought that some of them had been laying violent hands on me; and, not daring to attack her master, she turned her vocal artillery against the younger scoundrel.

"Well, Mr. Earnshaw," she cried, "I wonder what you'll have agait[2] next! Are we going to murder folk on our very doorstones? I see this house will never do for me—look at t' poor lad, he's fair choking! Wisht, wisht! you mun'n't go on so—come in, and I'll cure that. There now, hold ye still."

With these words she suddenly splashed a pint of icy water down my neck, and pulled me into the kitchen. Mr. Heathcliff followed, his accidental merriment expiring quickly in his habitual moroseness.

I was sick exceedingly, and dizzy and faint; and thus compelled, perforce, to accept lodgings under his roof. He told Zillah to give me a glass of brandy, and then passed on to the inner room, while she condoled with me on my sorry predicament, and having obeyed his orders, whereby I was somewhat revived, ushered me to bed.

---

1 Named after Zillah, wife of Lamech, son of Cain (*Genesis* 4:22).
2 *have agait*: be getting up to.

CHAPTER 3

While leading the way upstairs, she recommended that I should hide the candle, and not make a noise, for her master had an odd notion about the chamber she would put me in; and never let anybody lodge there willingly.

I asked the reason.

She did not know, she answered; she had only lived there a year or two; and they had so many queer goings on, she could not begin to be curious.

Too stupefied to be curious myself, I fastened my door and glanced round for the bed. The whole furniture consisted of a chair, a clothes-press, and a large oak case, with squares cut out near the top, resembling coach windows.[1]

Having approached this structure, I looked inside, and per-ceived it to be a singular sort of old-fashioned couch, very conve-niently designed to obviate the necessity for every member of the family having a room to himself. In fact, it formed a little closet, and the ledge of a window, which it enclosed, served as a table.

I slid back the panelled sides, got in with my light, pulled them together again, and felt secure against the vigilance of Heathcliff, and every one else.

The ledge, where I placed my candle, had a few mildewed books piled up in one corner; and it was covered with writing scratched on the paint. This writing, however, was nothing but a name repeated in all kinds of characters, large and small—*Cather-ine Earnshaw*; here and there varied to *Catherine Heathcliff*, and then again to *Catherine Linton*.

In vapid listlessness I leant my head against the window, and continued spelling over Catherine Earnshaw—Heathcliff—Lin-ton, till my eyes closed; but they had not rested five minutes when

---

1 Box beds are noted in J.C. Loudon, *Encyclopedia of Cottage, Farmhouse and Villa Architecture and Furniture* (1838), pp. 332-3, with shelves and locks 'so that a person going to bed, may have all his treasures round him', but without the coach windows, which evoke the Brontë's coach journeys to and from Cowan Bridge.

a glare of white letters started from the dark, as vivid as spectres—the air swarmed with Catherines; and rousing myself to dispel the obtrusive name, I discovered my candle wick reclining on one of the antique volumes, and perfuming the place with an odour of roasted calf-skin.

I snuffed it off, and, very ill at ease, under the influence of cold and lingering nausea, sat up, and spread open the injured tome on my knee. It was a Testament, in lean type, and smelling dreadfully musty: a fly-leaf bore the inscription—"Catherine Earnshaw, her book," and a date some quarter of a century back.

I shut it, and took up another, and another, till I had examined all. Catherine's library was select; and its state of dilapidation proved it to have been well used, though not altogether for a legitimate purpose; scarcely one chapter had escaped a pen and ink commentary, at least, the appearance of one, covering every morsel of blank that the printer had left.

Some were detached sentences; other parts took the form of a regular diary, scrawled in an unformed, childish hand. At the top of an extra page, quite a treasure probably when first lighted on, I was greatly amused to behold an excellent caricature of my friend Joseph, rudely yet powerfully sketched.

An immediate interest kindled within me for the unknown Catherine, and I began, forthwith, to decipher her faded hiero-glyphics.[1]

"An awful Sunday!" commenced the paragraph beneath. "I wish my father were back again. Hindley is a detestable substitute—his conduct to Heathcliff is atrocious—H. and I are going to rebel—

---

1   The article 'Marquis Spineto on Hieroglyphics', *Blackwood's Magazine*, 24 (Sep. 1828), 313-26 (*K*), by Mary Margaret Bush, reports a lecture series in which Spineto emphasised the principle of symmetry underlying the ancient writer-artists' compositions. Besides supporting his view that civilization fanned out from Egypt after moving downstream from Ethiopia, she proposed the existence of links between the ancient Egypt-ian and ancient Indian civilizations, and noted that earlier failed attempts at decipherment resulted from the difficulty that 'men's eyes, blinded by prejudice, could not discern the truth presented to them' (p. 316). See also Maurice Pope, *The Story of Decipherment. From Egyptian Hieroglyphs to Maya Script* (1999), pp. 60-84 and throughout; and above, p. 89, note 67.

we took our initiatory step this evening.

"All day had been flooding with rain; we could not go to church, so Joseph must needs get up a congregation in the garret; and, while Hindley and his wife basked down stairs before a comfortable fire, doing anything but reading their Bibles, I'll answer for it; Heathcliff, myself, and the unhappy plough-boy, were commanded to take our Prayer-books, and mount—we were ranged in a row, on a sack of corn, groaning and shivering, and hoping that Joseph would shiver too, so that he might give us a short homily for his own sake. A vain idea! The service lasted precisely three hours; and yet my brother had the face to exclaim, when he saw us descending,

"'What, done already?'

"On Sunday evenings we used to be permitted to play, if we did not make much noise; now a mere titter is sufficient to send us into corners!

"'You forget you have a master here,' says the tyrant. 'I'll demolish the first who puts me out of temper! I insist on perfect sobriety and silence. Oh, boy! was that you? Frances, darling, pull his hair as you go by; I heard him snap his fingers.'

"Frances pulled his hair heartily; and then went and seated herself on her husband's knee, and there they were, like two babies, kissing and talking nonsense by the hour—foolish palaver[1] that we should be ashamed of.

"We made ourselves as snug as our means allowed in the arch of the dresser. I had just fastened our pinafores together, and hung them up for a curtain, when in comes Joseph, on an errand from the stables. He tears down my handywork, boxes my ears, and croaks:

"'T' maister nobbut just buried, and Sabbath nut oe'red, und t' sahnd uh't gospel still i' yer lugs, and yah darr be laiking! shame on ye! sit ye dahn, ill childer! they's good books eneugh if ye'll read 'em; sit ye dahn, and think uh yer sowls!'[2]

---

1   Walter Scott, *St Ronan's Well* (1824) (*K*), ch. 6, has 'a solemn palaver (as the natives of Madagascar call their national convention)' (*NED*).

2   'Here we are with the master hardly buried, and with Sunday not over, you can still hear the sound of the gospel in your ears, yet you dare to be playing! Shame on you, sit down, you wicked children! There are enough good books for you to read; sit down, and think of your souls.'

"Saying this, he compelled us so to square our positions that we might receive, from the far-off fire, a dull ray to show us the text of the lumber he thrust upon us.

"I could not bear the employment. I took my dingy volume by the scroop,[1] and hurled it into the dog-kennel, vowing I hated a good book.

"Heathcliff kicked his to the same place.

"Then there was a hubbub!

"'Maister Hindley!' shouted our chaplain, 'Maister, coom hither! Miss Cathy's riven th' back off 'Th' Helmet uh Salvation,' un Heathcliff's pawsed his fit intuh t' first part uh 'T' Brooad Way to Destruction!' It's fair flaysome ut yah let 'em goa on this gait. Ech! th'owd man ud uh laced 'em properly—bud he's goan!'[2]

"Hindley hurried up from his paradise on the hearth, and seizing one of us by the collar, and the other by the arm, hurled both into the back-kitchen; where, Joseph asseverated, "owd Nick"[3] would fetch us as sure as we were living; and, so comforted, we each sought a separate nook to await his advent.

---

1   *scroop*: obscure; usually, 'grating noise'; *NED* suggests a 'mistake for scruff'; possibly, however, a printer's misreading of her phonetic *scroof* (scruff); or, possibly, a slip reflecting interest in Shakespeare, *Richard II* 3.2.190–99: Heathcliff's tormenting tactics are anticipated in the announcement of national disaster by Sir Stephen Scrope (Scroop), member of a powerful family in Ireland and northern England, with the aside, 'I play the torturer by small and small / To lengthen out the worst that must be spoken' (see below, p. 247, note 2). For Lord Scroop and the Clifford family, see Hartley Coleridge, *Worthies of Yorkshire and Lancashire* (1836). p. 256.

2   'Master Hindley, come here! Miss Cathy's torn the back off 'The Helmet of Salvation', and Heathcliff's thrust his feet into the first part of 'The Broad Way to Destruction'! It's truly dreadful that you let them go on in this way. Oh! the old man would have lashed them properly, but he's gone!' The reference to Mr Earnshaw's death dates the diary to the year 1777–78 (Appendix A). For the Brontës' opposition to the ideas professed by Joseph, see Elsie Harrison, *The Clue to the Brontës* (1948), throughout.

3   'Old Nick': the devil. Carr, vol. 2, p. 8, offers a derivation from *nicken*, 'deity of the waters, worshipped by the ancient Danes and Germans'. This is denounced by *NED*, which finds no origin for the name; see, however, German *nickel*: demon, dwarf, deceiver.

"I reached this book, and a pot of ink from a shelf, and pushed the house-door ajar to give me light, and I have got the time on with writing for twenty minutes; but my companion is impatient and proposes that we should appropriate the dairy woman's cloak, and have a scamper on the moors, under its shelter. A pleasant suggestion—and then if the surly old man come in, he may believe his prophesy verified—we cannot be damper, or colder, in the rain than we are here."

★   ★   ★   ★   ★

I suppose Catherine fulfilled her project, for the next sentence took up another subject; she waxed lachrymose.

"How little did I dream that Hindley would ever make me cry so!" she wrote. "My head aches, till I cannot keep it on the pillow; and still I can't give over. Poor Heathcliff! Hindley calls him a vagabond, and won't let him sit with us, he says, and he and I must not play together, and threatens to turn him out of the house if we break his order.

"He has been blaming our father (how dared he?)[1] for treating H. too liberally; and swears he will reduce him to his right place—"

★   ★   ★   ★   ★

I began to nod drowsily over the dim page; my eye wandered from manuscript to print. I saw a red ornamented title... "Seventy Times Seven, and the First of the Seventy First.[2] A Pious Discourse delivered by the Reverend Jabes Branderham, in the Chapel of Gimmerden Sough."[3] And while I was, half consciously, worrying

---

1   A prohibition against criticising parents occurs in *Leviticus* 20:9.

2   *Matthew* 18:21-22, reads: 'Then came Peter to him, and said, Lord, How oft shall my brother sin against me, and I forgive him? Till seven times? Jesus saith unto him, I say not unto thee, Until seven times: but, Until seventy times seven'.

3   The Revd Jabez Bunting (1779-1858) is here satirised as a sulphurous revivalist, nicknamed after *brand* or faggot in a fire: see *Early Victorian Methodism: The Correspondence of Jabez Bunting 1830-1858* (1976), ed. W.R. Ward; for *Gimmerden*, see above, Introduction, 'Signs of Fertility', pp. 71-80.

my brain to guess what Jabes Branderham would make of his subject, I sank back in bed, and fell asleep.

Alas, for the effects of bad tea and bad temper! what else could it be that made me pass such a terrible night? I don't remember another that I can at all compare with it since I was capable of suffering.

I began to dream, almost before I ceased to be sensible of my locality. I thought it was morning; and I had set out on my way home, with Joseph for a guide. The snow lay yards deep in our road; and, as we floundered on, my companion wearied me with constant reproaches that I had not brought a pilgrim's staff: telling me I could never get into the house without one, and boastfully flourishing a heavy-headed cudgel, which I understood to be so denominated.[1]

For a moment I considered it absurd that I should need such a weapon to gain admittance into my own residence. Then, a new idea flashed across me. I was not going there; we were journeying to hear the famous Jabes Branderham preach from the text— "Seventy Times Seven;" and either Joseph, the preacher, or I had committed the "First of the Seventy First," and were to be publicly exposed and excommunicated.

We came to the chapel—I have passed it really in my walks, twice or thrice: it lies in a hollow, between two hills—an elevated hollow—near a swamp,[2] whose peaty moisture is said to answer all the purposes of embalming on the few corpses deposited there. The roof has been kept whole hitherto, but, as the clergyman's stipend is only twenty pounds per annum, and a house with two rooms, threatening speedily to determine into one,[3] no clergyman will undertake the duties of pastor, especially, as it is currently reported that his flock would rather let him starve[4] than increase the

---

1 Probably a satirical reference to Patrick's shillelagh.
2 This matches Kingsdale, the locality around Thornton in Lonsdale. The drainage system in Kingsdale appears in John Tuke, *Map of the County of York* (1818).
3 *determine into one*: be reduced to one; a possible reference to Patrick's one-roomed birthplace at Drumballyroney.
4 *starve*: here, 'die of hunger'; frequently, the northern 'freezing'; occasionally both.

living by one penny from their own pockets. However, in my dream, Jabes had a full and attentive congregation: and he preached—good God—what a sermon! Divided into *four hundred and ninety* parts[1]—each fully equal to an ordinary address from the pulpit—and each discussing a separate sin! Where he searched for them, I cannot tell; he had his private manner of interpreting the phrase, and it seemed necessary the brother should sin different sins on every occasion.

They were of the most curious character—odd transgressions that I never imagined previously.

Oh, how weary I grew. How I writhed, and yawned, and nodded, and revived! How I pinched and pricked myself, and rubbed my eyes, and stood up, and sat down again, and nudged Joseph to inform me if he would *ever* have done!

I was condemned to hear all out—finally, he reached the *"First of the Seventy-First."* At that crisis, a sudden inspiration descended on me; I was moved to rise and denounce Jabes Branderham as the sinner of the sin that no Christian need pardon.[2]

"Sir," I exclaimed, "sitting here, within these four walls, at one stretch, I have endured and forgiven the four hundred and ninety heads of your discourse. Seventy times seven times have I plucked up my hat, and been about to depart—Seventy times seven times have you preposterously forced me to resume my seat. The four hundred and ninety-first is too much. Fellow martyrs, have at him! Drag him down, and crush him to atoms, that the place which knows him may know him no more!"[3]

"Thou art the Man!"[4] cried Jabes, after a solemn pause, leaning over his cushion. "Seventy times seven times didst thou gapingly

---

1   the equivalent of 'seventy times seven' (Matthew 18: 22), a proverbial phrase for 'limitless' (A.S. Peake, *A Commentary on the Bible*, London: T.C. and E.C. Jack, 1919, p. 716).

2   *the sin*: not identified; possibly, attributing hypocrisy to others, and hence, the sign of pride.

3   *Job* 7:10, 'neither shall his place know him any more': the prophetic hero laments being lost.

4   The prophet Nathan's words in *2 Samuel* 12:7 accuse King David of hypocrisy; self-confessedly a hypocritical lover, Lockwood's dream conscience accuses him of complicity in a national crime.

contort thy visage—seventy times seven did I take counsel with my soul!—Lo, this is human weakness; this also may be absolved! The First of the Seventy-First is come. Brethren, execute upon him the judgment written![1] such honour have all His saints!"

With that concluding word, the whole assembly, exalting their pilgrim's staves, rushed round me in a body, and I, having no weapon to raise in self-defence, commenced grappling with Joseph, my nearest and most ferocious assailant, for his. In the confluence of the multitude, several clubs crossed; blows, aimed at me, fell on other sconces. Presently the whole chapel resounded with rappings and counter-rappings. Every man's hand was against his neighbour;[2] and Branderham, unwilling to remain idle, poured forth his zeal in a shower of loud taps on the boards of the pulpit which responded so smartly, that, at last, to my unspeakable relief, they woke me.

And what was it that had suggested the tremendous tumult; what had played Jabes' part in the row? Merely, the branch of a fir-tree that touched my lattice, as the blast wailed by, and rattled its dry cones against the panes!

I listened doubtingly an instant; detected the disturber, then turned and dozed, and dreamt again; if possible, still more disagreeably than before.

This time, I remembered I was lying in the oak closet, and I heard distinctly the gusty wind, and the driving of the snow; I heard also, the fir-bough repeat its teasing sound, and ascribed it to the right cause: but, it annoyed me so much, that I resolved to silence it, if possible; and, I thought, I rose and endeavoured to unhasp the casement. The hook was soldered into the staple, a circumstance observed by me, when awake, but forgotten.

"I must stop it, nevertheless!" I muttered, knocking my knuckles through the glass, and stretching an arm out to seize the im-

---

1   Psalm 149:9 undertakes to punish tyrants with enslavement: 'To bind their kings with chains, and their nobles with fetters of iron'.

2   Hagar, wife of the eighty-six-year-old Abraham, conceives her son Ishmael extra-maritally, with the result that he has 'every man's hand against him' (*Genesis* 16:12), and the further result that civil strife arises in Egypt: 'the Egyptians [...] shall fight every man against his brother, and every one against his neighbour' (*Isaiah* 19: 2).

portunate branch; instead of which, my fingers closed on the fingers of a little, ice-cold hand!

The intense horror of nightmare came over me; I tried to draw back my arm, but, the hand clung to it, and a most melancholy voice sobbed,

"Let me in—let me in!"[1]

"Who are you?" I asked, struggling, meanwhile, to disengage myself.

"Catherine Linton," it replied, shiveringly (why did I think of *Linton*? I had read *Earnshaw*, twenty times for Linton) "I'm come home, I'd lost my way on the moor!"

As it spoke, I discerned, obscurely, a child's face looking through the window—Terror made me cruel; and, finding it useless to attempt shaking the creature off, I pulled its wrist on to the broken pane, and rubbed it to and fro till the blood ran down and soaked the bed-clothes: still it wailed, "Let me in!" and maintained its tenacious gripe, almost maddening me with fear.[2]

"How can I?" I said at length. "Let me go, if you want me to let you in!"

The fingers relaxed, I snatched mine through the hole, hurriedly piled the books up in a pyramid against it, and stopped my ears to exclude the lamentable prayer.

I seemed to keep them closed above a quarter of an hour, yet, the instant I listened again, there was the doleful cry moaning on!

"Begone!" I shouted, "I'll never let you in, not if you beg for twenty years!"

"It's twenty years," mourned the voice, "twenty years, I've been a waif for twenty years!"[3]

Thereat began a feeble scratching outside, and the pile of books moved as if thrust forward.

---

1   See Appendix B, 'The Helks Lady'; also, C. Heywood, '"The Helks Lady" and other Legends Surrounding *Wuthering Heights*', *Lore and Language* 11 (1992–3), 127–42.

2   See Introduction, 'Lockwood's Wilberforcean Dreams', pp. 49–56; also, Clement Jones, *John Bolton of Storrs* (1959), p. v; and 'Colonel Bolton', CRO/K:WDX.783.

3   A first reference to the double chronology in *WH* (Appendix A).

I tried to jump up; but, could not stir a limb; and so, yelled aloud, in a frenzy of fright.

To my confusion, I discovered the yell was not ideal.[1] Hasty footsteps approached my chamber door: somebody pushed it open, with a vigorous hand, and a light glimmered through the squares at the top of the bed. I sat shuddering, yet, and wiping the perspiration from my forehead: the intruder appeared to hesitate and muttered to himself.

At last, he said in a half-whisper, plainly not expecting an answer,

"Is any one here?"

I considered it best to confess my presence, for I knew Heathcliff's accents, and feared he might search further, if I kept quiet.

With this intention, I turned and opened the panels—I shall not soon forget the effect my action produced.

Heathcliff stood near the entrance, in his shirt and trousers; with a candle dripping over his fingers, and his face as white as the wall behind him. The first creak of the oak startled him like an electric shock: the light leaped from his hold to a distance of some feet, and his agitation was so extreme, that he could hardly pick it up.

"It is only your guest, sir," I called out, desirous to spare him the humiliation of exposing his cowardice further. "I had the misfortune to scream in my sleep, owing to a frightful nightmare. I'm sorry I disturbed you."

"Oh God confound you, Mr. Lockwood! I wish you were at the—" commenced my host setting the candle on a chair, because he found it impossible to hold it steady.

"And who showed you up to this room?" he continued, crushing his nails into his palms, and grinding his teeth to subdue the maxillary convulsions. "Who was it? I've a good mind to turn them out of the house, this moment!"

"It was your servant, Zillah," I replied, flinging myself on to the floor, and rapidly resuming my garments. "I should not care if you did, Mr. Heathcliff; she richly deserves it. I suppose that she wanted to get another proof that the place was haunted, at my

---

1   *ideal*: imaginary.

expense—Well, it is—swarming with ghosts and goblins! You have reason in shutting it up, I assure you. No one will thank you for a doze in such a den!"

"What do you mean?" asked Heathcliff, "and what are you doing? Lie down and finish out the night, since you *are* here; but, for Heaven's sake! don't repeat that horrid noise—Nothing could excuse it, unless you were having your throat cut!"

"If the little fiend had got in at the window, she probably would have strangled me!" I returned. "I'm not going to endure the persecutions of your hospitable ancestors, again—Was not the Reverend Jabes Branderham akin to you on the mother's side? And that minx,[1] Catherine Linton, or Earnshaw, or however she was called—she must have been a changeling—wicked little soul! She told me she had been walking the earth these twenty years: a just punishment for her mortal transgressions, I've no doubt!"

Scarcely were these words uttered, when I recollected the association of Heathcliff's with Catherine's name in the book, which had completely slipped from my memory till thus awakened. I blushed at my inconsideration; but without showing further consciousness of the offence, I hastened to add,

"The truth is, sir, I passed the first part of the night in—" Here, I stopped afresh—I was about to say "perusing those old volumes," then it would have revealed my knowledge of their written, as well as their printed contents; so correcting myself,[2] I went on,

"In spelling over the name scratched on that window-ledge. A monotonous occupation, calculated to set me asleep, like counting, or—"

"What *can* you mean, by talking in this way to *me!*" thundered Heathcliff with savage vehemence. "How—how *dare* you, under my roof—God! he's mad to speak so!" And he struck his forehead with rage.

I did not know whether to resent this language, or pursue my explanation; but he seemed so powerfully affected that I took pity and proceeded with my dreams; affirming I had never heard the

---

1 *minx*: a lapdog or small pet; derogatory when referring to women.
2 A trail of deceptions in *WH* begins here.

appellation of "Catherine Linton," before, but, reading it often over produced an impression which personified itself when I had no longer my imagination under control.

Heathcliff gradually fell back into the shelter of the bed, as I spoke, finally, sitting down almost concealed behind it. I guessed, however, by his irregular and intercepted breathing, that he struggled to vanquish an access of violent emotion.

Not liking to show him that I heard the conflict, I continued my toilette rather noisily, looked at my watch, and soliloquised on the length of the night:

"Not three o'clock, yet! I could have taken oath it had been six—time stagnates here—we must surely have retired to rest at eight!"

"Always at nine in winter, and always rise at four," said my host, suppressing a groan; and, as I fancied, by the motion of his shadow's arm, dashing a tear from his eyes.

"Mr. Lockwood," he added, "you may go into my room; you'll only be in the way, coming down stairs so early: and your childish outcry has sent sleep to the devil for me."

"And for me too," I replied. "I'll walk in the yard till daylight, and then I'll be off; and you need not dread a repetition of my intrusion. I am now quite cured of seeking pleasure in society, be it country or town. A sensible man ought to find sufficient company in himself."

"Delightful company!" muttered Heathcliff, "Take the candle, and go to where you please. I shall join you directly. Keep out of the yard though—the dogs are unchained; and the house—Juno mounts sentinel there—and—nay, you can only ramble about the steps and passages—but, away with you! I'll come in two minutes."

I obeyed, so far as to quit the chamber; when, ignorant where the narrow lobbies led, I stood still, and was witness, involuntarily, to a piece of superstition on the part of my landlord, which belied, oddly, his apparent sense.

He got on to the bed, and wrenched open the lattice, bursting, as he pulled at it, into an uncontrollable passion of tears.

"Come in! come in!" he sobbed. "Cathy, do come. Oh do— once more! Oh! my heart's darling, hear me this time—Catherine, at last!"

The spectre showed a spectre's ordinary caprice; it gave no sign of being; but the snow and wind whirled wildly through, even reaching my station, and blowing out the light.

There was such anguish in the gush of grief that accompanied this raving, that my compassion made me overlook its folly, and I drew off, half angry to have listened at all, and vexed at having related my ridiculous nightmare, since it produced that agony; though *why*, was beyond my comprehension.

I descended cautiously to the lower regions and landed in the back-kitchen, where a gleam of fire, raked compactly together, enabled me to rekindle my candle.

Nothing was stirring except a brindled, grey cat, which crept from the ashes, and saluted me with a querulous mew.

Two benches, shaped in sections of a circle, nearly enclosed the hearth; on one of these I stretched myself, and Grimalkin[1] mounted the other. We were both of us nodding, ere any one invaded our retreat; and then it was Joseph shuffling down a wooden ladder that vanished in the roof, through a trap, the ascent to his garret, I suppose.

He cast a sinister look at the little flame which I had enticed to play between the ribs, swept the cat from its elevation, and bestowing himself in the vacancy, commenced the operation of stuffing a three-inch pipe with tobacco; my presence in his sanctum was evidently esteemed a piece of impudence too shameful for remark. He silently applied the tube to his lips, folded his arms, and puffed away.

I let him enjoy the luxury, unannoyed; and after sucking out the last wreath, and heaving a profound sigh, he got up, and departed as solemnly as he came.

A more elastic footstep entered next, and now I opened my mouth for a "good morning," but closed it again, the salutation unachieved; for Hareton Earnshaw was performing his orisons,[2]

---

1   *Grimalkin*: the witch's cat in *Macbeth*, 1.1.9: 'Grimalkin calls'; as 'jealous or imperious old woman' (*NED*), a sign of Lockwood's misogyny.

2   *orisons*: prayers; in *Hamlet* 3.1.90-91, 'nymph, in thy orisons, be all my sins remembered', the words are followed by his archetypal outburst against women.

sotto voce, in a series of curses directed against every object he touched, while he rummaged a corner, for a spade or shovel to dig through the drifts. He glanced over the back of the bench dilating his nostrils, and thought as little of exchanging civilities with me, as with my companion, the cat.

I guessed by his preparations that egress was allowed, and leaving my hard couch, made a movement to follow him. He noticed this, and thrust at an inner door with the end of his spade, intimating by an inarticulate sound, that there was the place where I must go, if I changed my locality.

It opened into the house, where the females were already astir, Zillah urging flakes of flame up the chimney with a colossal bellows; and Mrs. Heathcliff, kneeling on the hearth, reading a book by the aid of the blaze.

She held her hand interposed between the furnace-heat and her eyes; and seemed absorbed in her occupation: desisting from it only to chide the servant for covering her with sparks, or to push away a dog, now and then, that snoozled[1] its nose over forwardly into her face.

I was surprised to see Heathcliff there also. He stood by the fire, his back towards me, just finishing a stormy scene to poor Zillah, who ever and anon interrupted her labour to pluck up the corner of her apron, and heave an indignant groan.

"And you, you worthless—" he broke out as I entered, turning to his daughter-in-law, and employing an epithet as harmless as duck, or sheep, but generally represented by a dash.

"There you are at your idle tricks again! The rest of them do earn their bread—you live on my charity! Put your trash away, and find something to do. You shall pay me for the plague of having you eternally in my sight—do you hear, damnable jade?"

"I'll put my trash away, because you can make me, if I refuse," answered the young lady, closing her book, and throwing it on a chair. "But I'll not do anything, though you should swear your tongue out, except what I please!"

Heathcliff lifted his hand, and the speaker sprang to a safer dis-

---

1   Hutton (1781 edn.), p. 96, has *snuzzle*, 'to hide the face in the bosom as children'.

tance, obviously acquainted with its weight.

Having no desire to be entertained by a cat and dog combat, I stepped forward briskly, as if eager to partake the warmth of the hearth, and innocent of any knowledge of the interrupted dispute. Each had enough decorum to suspend further hostilities; Heathcliff placed his fists, out of temptation, in his pockets: Mrs. Heathcliff curled her lip, and walked to a seat far off; where she kept her word by playing the part of a statue during the remainder of my stay.

That was not long. I declined joining their breakfast, and, at the first gleam of dawn, took an opportunity of escaping into the free air, now clear, and still, and cold as impalpable ice.

My landlord hallooed for me to stop ere I reached the bottom of the garden, and offered to accompany me across the moor. It was well he did, for the whole hill-back was one billowy, white ocean; the swells and falls not indicating corresponding rises and depressions in the ground—many pits, at least, were filled to a level; and entire ranges of mounds, the refuse of the quarries, blotted from the chart which my yesterday's walk left pictured in my mind.

I had remarked on one side of the road, at intervals of six or seven yards, a line of upright stones, continued through the whole length of the barren: these were erected, and daubed with lime, on purpose to serve as guides in the dark, and also, when a fall, like the present, confounded the deep swamps on either hand with the firmer path; but, excepting a dirty dot pointing up, here and there, all traces of their existence had vanished; and my companion found it necessary to warn me frequently to steer to the right, or left, when I imagined I was following, correctly, the windings of the road.

We exchanged little conversation, and he halted at the entrance of Thrushcross park, saying, I could make no error there. Our adieux were limited to a hasty bow, and then I pushed forward, trusting to my own resources, for the porter's lodge is untenanted as yet.

The distance from the gate to the Grange is two miles:[1] I

---

1   Yorkshire demesne parks of this size at Castle Howard and Harewood are marked green in John Tuke, *Map of the County of York* (1818), and in Thomas Jefferys, *Map of the County of York* (1771).

believe I managed to make it four; what with losing myself among the trees, and sinking up to the neck in snow, a predicament which only those who have experienced it can appreciate. At any rate, whatever were my wanderings, the clock chimed twelve as I entered the house; and that gave exactly an hour for every mile of the usual way from Wuthering Heights.[1]

My human fixture and her satellites rushed to welcome me; exclaiming, tumultuously, they had completely given me up; everybody conjectured that I perished last night; and they were wondering how they must set about the search for my remains.

I bid them be quiet, now that they saw me returned, and, benumbed to my very heart, I dragged upstairs, whence, after putting on dry clothes, and pacing to and fro, thirty or forty minutes, to restore the animal heat, I am adjourned to my study, feeble as a kitten, almost too much so to enjoy the cheerful fire, and smoking coffee which the servant has prepared for my refreshment.

---

1 The riddle has two parts: (i) Lockwood walks at one mile per hour, since twice two miles, equal to the four miles between the Grange and the farmhouse, take four hours; (ii) since it is four miles from the farmhouse to the Grange, it is two miles from the farmhouse to the park gate. Lockwood's walk dramatises Emily main alteration to the Kingsdale topography: see above, Plate 2, and Introduction. 'The Wuthering Heights landscape', pp. 18-34.

CHAPTER 4

What vain weather-cocks we are! I, who had determined to hold myself independent of all social intercourse, and thanked my stars that, at length, I had lighted on a spot where it was next to impracticable, I, weak wretch, after maintaining till dusk a struggle with low spirits, and solitude, was finally compelled to strike my colours;[1] and, under the pretence of gaining information concerning the necessities of my establishment, I desired Mrs. Dean, when she brought in supper, to sit down while I ate it, hoping sincerely she would prove a regular gossip, and either rouse me to animation, or lull me to sleep by her talk.

"You have lived here a considerable time," I commenced; "did you not say sixteen years?"

"Eighteen,[2] sir; I came, when the mistress was married, to wait on her; after she died, the master retained me for his house-keeper."

"Indeed."

There ensued a pause. She was not a gossip, I feared, unless about her own affairs, and those could hardly interest me.

However, having studied for an interval, with a fist on either knee, and a cloud of meditation over her ruddy countenance, she ejaculated—

"Ah, times are greatly changed since then!"

"Yes," I remarked, "you've seen a good many alterations, I suppose?"

"I have: and troubles too," she said.

"Oh, I'll turn the talk on my landlord's family!" I thought to myself. "A good subject to start—and that pretty girl-widow, I should like to know her history; whether she be a native of the country, or, as is more probable, an exotic that the surly indigenae will not recognise for kin."

With this intention I asked Mrs. Dean why Heathcliff let Thrushcross Grange, and preferred living in a situation and residence so much inferior.

---

1   *strike my colours*: take down the flags, surrender.
2   A second reference to the double chronology (Appendix A).

"Is he not rich enough to keep the estate in good order?" I enquired.

"Rich sir!" she returned. "He has, nobody knows what money, and every year it increases.[1] Yes, yes, he's rich enough to live in a finer house than this; but he's very near—close-handed; and, if he had meant to flit to Thrushcross Grange, as soon as he heard of a good tenant, he could not have borne to miss the chance of getting a few hundreds more. It is strange people should be so greedy, when they are alone in the world!"

"He had a son, it seems?"

"Yes, he had one—he is dead."

"And that young lady, Mrs. Heathcliff, is his widow?"

"Yes."

"Where did she come from originally?"

"Why, sir, she is my late master's daughter; Catherine Linton was her maiden name. I nursed her, poor thing! I did wish Mr. Heathcliff would remove here, and then we might have been together again."

"What, Catherine Linton!" I exclaimed, astonished. But a minute's reflection convinced me that it was not my ghostly Catherine. "Then," I continued, "my predecessor's name was Linton?"

"It was."

"And who is that Earnshaw, Hareton Earnshaw, who lives with Mr. Heathcliff? are they relations?"

"No; he is the late Mrs. Linton's nephew."

"The young lady's cousin then?"

"Yes; and her husband was her cousin also—one, on the mother's—the other, on the father's side—Heathcliff married Mr. Linton's sister."

"I see the house at Wuthering Heights has 'Earnshaw' carved over the front door. Are they an old family?"

"Very old, sir; and Hareton is the last of them, as our Miss Cathy is of us—I mean, of the Lintons. Have you been to Wuthering Heights? I beg pardon for asking; but I should like to hear how she is!"

---

[1] A reference to the falsely rumoured wealth of Richard Sutton, who raised a mortgage to purchase West House in Dent (Appendix C).

"Mrs. Heathcliff? she looked very well and very handsome; yet, I think, not very happy."

"Oh dear, I don't wonder! And how did you like the master?"

"A rough fellow, rather, Mrs. Dean. Is not that his character?"

"Rough as a saw-edge, and hard as whinstone!¹ The less you meddle with him the better."

"He must have had some ups and downs in life to make him such a churl. Do you know anything of his history?"

"It's a cuckoo's; sir—I know all about it; except where he was born, and who were his parents and how he got his money, at first—and Hareton has been cast out like an unfledged dunnock.² The unfortunate lad is the only one, in all this parish, that does not guess how he has been cheated!"

"Well, Mrs. Dean, it will be a charitable deed to tell me something of my neighbours—I feel I shall not rest, if I go to bed; so be good enough to sit, and chat an hour."

"Oh, certainly, sir! I'll just fetch a little sewing, and then I'll sit as long as you please—but you've caught cold, I saw you shivering, and you must have some gruel to drive it out."

The worthy woman bustled off; and I crouched nearer the fire: my head felt hot, and the rest of me chill: moreover I was excited, almost to a pitch of foolishness through my nerves and brain. This caused me to feel, not uncomfortable, but rather fearful, as I am still, of serious effects from the incidents of today and yesterday.

She returned presently, bringing a smoking basin, and a basket of work; and, having placed the former on the hob, drew in her seat, evidently pleased to find me so companionable.

"Before I came to live here," she commenced, waiting no further invitation to her story, "I was almost always at Wuthering Heights; because, my mother had nursed Mr. Hindley Earnshaw,

---

1 *whinstone*: volcanic rock from the Whin Sill outcrop in Durham and Yorkshire; see J. Phillips, 'the origin of the whin-sill', *Encyclopedia Metropolitana*, 1845 (*NED*).

2 *dunnock*: the 'hedge-sparrow', *prunella modularis occidentalis* (not *passer* or sparrow); noted in Edmund Sandars, *A Bird Book for the Pocket* (1934), p. 32: '*Manners*: Excitable, fidgety, "Shufflewing." Mock combats in courtship. Hardy'. The story and the animal overturn Nelly Dean's analogy.

that was Hareton's father, and I got used to playing with the children—I ran errands too, and helped to make hay, and hung about the farm ready for anything that anybody would set me to.

"One fine summer morning—it was the beginning of harvest, I remember—Mr. Earnshaw, the old master, came down stairs, dressed for a journey; and, after he had told Joseph what was to be done during the day, he turned to Hindley, and Cathy, and me— for I sat eating my porridge, with them, and he said, speaking to his son,

"Now my bonny man, I'm going to Liverpool, to-day...What shall I bring you? You may choose what you like; only let it be little, for I shall walk there and back; sixty miles each way, that is a long spell!"

Hindley named a fiddle, and then he asked Miss Cathy; she was hardly six years old, but she could ride any horse in the stable, and she chose a whip.

He did not forget me, for, he had a kind heart, though he was rather severe, sometimes. He promised to bring me a pocketful of apples, and pears, and then he kissed his children good by, and set off.

It seemed a long while to us all—the three days of his absence—and often did little Cathy ask when he would be home: Mrs. Earnshaw, expected him by supper-time, on the third evening; and she put the meal off hour after hour; there were no signs of his coming, however; and at last the children got tired of running down to the gate to look—Then it grew dark, she would have had them to bed, but they begged sadly to be allowed to stay up; and, just about eleven o'clock, the door-latch was raised quietly and in stept the master. He threw himself into a chair, laughing and groaning, and bid them all stand off, for he was nearly killed—he would not have such another walk for the three kingdoms.[1]

"And at the end of it, to be flighted[2] to death!" he said opening his great coat, which he held bundled up in his arms. "See

---

1   *three kingdoms*: the realms claimed by Plantagenet and later monarchs were England, France, and Ireland.
2   *flighted*: NED adopts this instance to illustrate 'to frighten, scare'.

here, wife; I was never so beaten with anything in my life; but you must e'en take it as a gift of God; though it's as dark almost as if it came from the devil."

We crowded round, and, over Miss Cathy's head, I had a peep at a dirty, ragged, black-haired child; big enough both to walk and talk—indeed, its face looked older than Catherine's—yet, when it was set on its feet, it[1] only stared round, and repeated over and over again, some gibberish that nobody could understand. I was frightened, and Mrs. Earnshaw was ready to fling it out of doors: she did fly up—asking how he could fashion to bring that gipsy brat into the house, when they had their own bairns to feed, and fend for? What he meant to do with it, and whether he were mad?

The master tried to explain the matter; but, he was really half dead with fatigue, and all that I could make out, amongst her scolding, was a tale of his seeing it starving,[2] and houseless, and as good as dumb in the streets of Liverpool where he picked it up and inquired for its owner.[3] Not a soul knew to whom it belonged, he said, and his money and time, being both limited, he thought it better, to take it home with him, at once, than run into vain expenses there; because he was determined he would not leave it as he found it.

Well, the conclusion was that my mistress grumbled herself calm; and Mr. Earnshaw told me to wash it, and give it clean things, and let it sleep with the children.

Hindley and Cathy contented themselves with looking and listening till peace was restored: then both began searching their father's pockets for the presents he had promised them. The former was a boy of fourteen, but when he drew out, what had been a fiddle crushed to morsels in the great coat, he blubbered aloud, and Cathy, when she learnt the master had lost her whip in attending on the stranger, showed her humour by grinning and

---

1   *it*: babies and ghosts appear in *WH* as *it*, but Heathcliff is seven; *WH* underlines the chattel status conferred by Nelly on a part African child, speaking the Liverpool dialect.

2   *starving*: freezing and dying of hunger; both meanings are present.

3   *owner*: explicit reference to chattel status.

spitting at the stupid little thing, earning for her pains, a sound blow from her father to teach her cleaner manners.

They entirely refused to have it in bed with them, or even in their room, and I had no more sense, so, I put it on the landing of the stairs, hoping it might be gone on the morrow. By chance, or else attracted by hearing his voice, it crept to Mr. Earnshaw's door and there he found it on quitting his chamber. Inquiries were made as to how it got there; I was obliged to confess, and in recompense for my cowardice and inhumanity was sent out of the house.

This was Heathcliff's first introduction to the family: on coming back a few days afterwards, for I did not consider my banishment perpetual, I found they had christened him "Heathcliff;" it was the name of a son who died in childhood, and it has served him ever since, both for Christian and surname.[1]

Miss Cathy and he were now very thick;[2] but Hindley hated him, and to say the truth I did the same; and we plagued and went on with him shamefully, for I wasn't reasonable enough to feel my injustice, and the mistress never put in a word on his behalf, when she saw him wronged.

He seemed a sullen, patient child; hardened, perhaps, to ill-treatment: he would stand Hindley's blows without winking or shedding a tear, and my pinches moved him only to draw in a breath, and open his eyes as if he had hurt himself by accident, and nobody was to blame.

This endurance made old Earnshaw furious when he discovered his son persecuting the poor, fatherless child, as he called him. He took to Heathcliff strangely, believing all he said (for that matter, he said precious little, and generally the truth) and petting

---

1   The parish register of St George's Church, Leck, across the road from the Clergy Daughters' School, notes the baptism on 11 Aug. 1807 of Edward Guy, aged twenty-five, a (presumably) freed slave identified as the son of 'Guy born in Africa' (LRO PR.3323/1/1, Leck Parish Register). Naming Heathcliff with a family name signals adoption into the Earnshaw family, debarring legal marriage among them; see above, Introduction, 'The Marriage Prohibition', pp. 39–49. Like Edward Guy, Linton Heathcliff adopts his father's given name as a surname or slave name.

2   *thick*: 'intimate, familiar' (*NED*).

him up far above Cathy, who was too mischievous and wayward for a favourite.

So, from the very beginning, he bred bad feeling in the house; and at Mrs. Earnshaw's death, which happened in less than two years after, the young master had learnt to regard his father as an oppressor rather than a friend, and Heathcliff as a usurper of his parent's affections, and his privileges, and he grew bitter with brooding over these injuries.

I sympathised awhile, but, when the children fell ill of the measles and I had to tend them, and take on me the cares of a woman, at once, I changed my ideas. Heathcliff was dangerously sick, and while he lay at the worst he would have me constantly by his pillow; I suppose he felt I did a good deal for him, and he hadn't wit to guess that I was compelled to do it. However, I will say this, he was the quietest child that ever nurse watched over. The difference between him and the others forced me to be less partial: Cathy and her brother harassed me terribly: *he* was as uncomplaining as a lamb; though hardness, not gentleness, made him give little trouble.

He got through, and the doctor affirmed it was in a great measure owing to me, and praised me for my care. I was vain of his commendations, and softened towards the being by whose means, I earned them, and thus Hindley lost his last ally; still I couldn't dote on Heathcliff, and I wondered often what my master saw to admire so much in the sullen boy who never, to my recollection, repaid his indulgence by any sign of gratitude. He was not insolent to his benefactor; he was simply insensible, though knowing perfectly the hold he had on his heart, and conscious he had only to speak and all the house would be obliged to bend to his wishes.

As an instance, I remember Mr. Earnshaw once bought a couple of colts at the parish fair, and gave the lads each one. Heathcliff took the handsomest, but it soon fell lame, and when he discovered it, he said to Hindley,

"You must exchange horses with me; I don't like mine, and, if you won't I shall tell your father of the three thrashings you've given me this week, and show him my arm which is black to the shoulder."

Hindley put out his tongue, and cuffed him over the ears.

"You'd better do it, at once," he persisted, escaping to the porch (they were in the stable) "you will have to, and, if I speak of these blows, you'll get them again with interest."

"Off dog!" cried Hindley, threatening him with an iron weight, used for weighing potatoes, and hay.

"Throw it," he replied, standing still, "and then I'll tell how you boasted that you would turn me out of doors as soon as he died, and see whether he will not turn you out directly."

Hindley threw it, hitting him on the breast, and down he fell but staggered up, immediately, breathless and white, and had not I prevented it he would have gone just so to the master, and got full revenge by letting his condition plead for him, intimating who had caused it.

"Take my colt, gipsy, then!" said young Earnshaw, "and I pray that he may break your neck, take him, and be damned, you beggarly interloper! and wheedle my father out of all he has, only, afterwards, show him what you are, imp of Satan[1]—and take that, I hope he'll kick out your brains!"

Heathcliff had gone to loose the beast, and shift it to his own stall—he was passing behind it, when Hindley finished his speech by knocking him under its feet, and without stopping to examine whether his hopes were fulfilled, ran away as fast as he could.

I was surprised to witness how coolly the child gathered himself up, and went on with his intention, exchanging saddles and all; and then sitting down on a bundle of hay to overcome the qualm which the violent blow occasioned, before he entered the house.

I persuaded him easily to let me lay the blame of his bruises on the horse; he minded little what tale was told since he had what he wanted. He complained so seldom, indeed, of such stirs as these, that I really thought him not vindictive—I was deceived, completely, as you will hear.

---

1   *imp of Satan*: Henry Nelson Colerdige, *Six Months in the West Indies* (1826), p. 284, notes: 'A poor white woman […] with her dishevelled hair and young black Flibbertigibbet by her side […] looked as like a real witch and an imp of Satan as attending on her as any thing I ever saw'; generally 'A "child" of the devil, or of hell' (*NED*).

CHAPTER 5

In the course of time, Mr. Earnshaw began to fail. He had been active and healthy, yet his strength left him suddenly; and when he was confined to the chimney-corner he grew grievously irritable. A nothing vexed him, and suspected slights of his authority nearly threw him into fits.

This was especially to be remarked if any one attempted to impose upon, or domineer over his favourite: he was painfully jealous lest a word should be spoken amiss to him, seeming to have got into his head the notion that, because he liked Heathcliff, all hated, and longed to do him an ill-turn.

It was a disadvantage to the lad, for the kinder among us did not wish to fret the master, so we humoured his partiality; and that humouring was rich nourishment to the child's pride and black tempers. Still it became in a manner necessary; twice, or thrice, Hindley's manifestations of scorn, while his father was near, roused the old man to a fury. He seized his stick to strike him, and shook with rage that he could not do it.

At last, our curate (we had a curate then who made the living answer by teaching the little Lintons and Earnshaws, and farming his bit of land himself)—he advised that the young man should be sent to college, and Mr. Earnshaw agreed, though with a heavy spirit, for he said—

"Hindley was naught, and would never thrive as where[1] he wandered."

I hoped heartily we should have peace now. It hurt me to think the master should be made uncomfortable by his own good deed. I fancied the discontent of age and disease arose from his family disagreements, as he would have it that it did—really, you know, sir, it was in his sinking frame.

We might have got on tolerably, notwithstanding; but for two people, Miss Cathy, and Joseph, the servant; you saw him, I dare say, up yonder. He was, and is yet, most likely, the wearisomest

---

1   *as where*: no matter where, wherever; *NED* cites John Bale, *A Comedy Concerning Three Laws* (1538): 'Where as is no law, can no good order be'.

self-righteous Pharisee[1] that ever ransacked a Bible to rake out the promises to himself, and fling the curses on his neighbours. By his knack of sermonizing and pious discoursing, he contrived to make a great impression on Mr. Earnshaw, and, the more feeble the master became, the more influence he gained.

He was relentless in worrying him about his soul's concerns, and about ruling his children rigidly. He encouraged him to regard Hindley as a reprobate; and, night after night, he regularly grumbled out a long string of tales against Heathcliff and Catherine; always minding to flatter Earnshaw's weakness by heaping the heaviest blame on the last.

Certainly, she had ways with her such as I never saw a child take up before; and she put all of us past our patience fifty times and oftener in a day: from the hour she came down stairs, till the hour she went to bed, we had not a minute's security that she wouldn't be in mischief. Her spirits were always at high-water mark, her tongue always going—singing, laughing, and plaguing everybody who would not do the same. A wild, wick[2] slip she was—but, she had the bonniest eye, and sweetest smile, and lightest foot in the parish; and, after all, I believe she meant no harm; for when once she made you cry in good earnest, it seldom happened that she would not keep you company; and oblige you to be quiet that you might comfort her.

She was much too fond of Heathcliff. The greatest punishment we could invent for her was to keep her separate from him: yet, she got chided more than any of us on his account.

In play, she liked, exceedingly, to act the little mistress; using her hands freely, and commanding her companions: she did so to me, but I would not bear slapping, and ordering; and so I let her know.

---

1   *Pharisee*: 'formalist, hypocrite; an ancient Jewish sect distinguished by their strict observance of the traditional and written law, and by their pretensions to superior sanctity'; from Hebrew *parush*, 'separated, separatist' (*NED*); a reflection of the Brontës' hostility to the Separatist Methodism of the Revd Joseph Needham of Leeds. See above, Introduction, 'Lockwood's Wilberforcean dreams', pp. 49-56; also, G. Elsie Harrison, *The Clue to the Brontës* (1948), chs. 2-4, pp. 10-36, and throughout.

2   *wick*: alive. Carr, vol. 2, notes *wicken* (*royn, rowan*): 'A tree of wonderful efficacy in depriving witches of their infernal power' (p. 83).

Now, Mr. Earnshaw did not understand jokes from his children: he had always been strict and grave with them; and Catherine, on her part, had no idea why her father should be crosser and less patient in his ailing condition, than he was in his prime.

His peevish reproofs wakened in her a naughty delight to provoke him; she was never so happy as when we were all scolding her at once, and she was defying us with her bold, saucy look, and her ready words; turning Joseph's religious curses into ridicule, baiting me, and doing just what her father hated most, showing how her pretended insolence, which he thought real, had more power over Heathcliff than his kindness. How the boy would do *her* bidding in anything, and *his* only when it suited his own inclination.

After behaving as badly as possible all day, she sometimes came fondling to make it up at night.

"Nay, Cathy," the old man would say, "I cannot love thee; thou'rt worse than thy brother. Go, say thy prayers, child, and ask God's pardon. I doubt[1] thy mother and I must rue that we ever reared thee!"

That made her cry, at first; and then, being repulsed continually hardened her, and she laughed if I told her to say she was sorry for her faults, and beg to be forgiven.

But the hour came, at last, that ended Mr. Earnshaw's troubles on earth. He died quietly in his chair one October evening, seated by the fire-side.

A high wind blustered round the house, and roared in the chimney: it sounded wild and stormy, yet it was not cold, and we were all together—I, a little removed from the hearth, busy at my knitting, and Joseph reading his Bible near the table (for the servants generally sat in the house then, after their work was done). Miss Cathy had been sick, and that made her still; she leant against her father's knee, and Heathcliff was lying on the floor with his head in her lap.

I remember the master, before he fell into a doze, stroking her bonny hair—it pleased him rarely to see her gentle—and saying—

"Why canst thou not always be a good lass, Cathy?"

And she turned her face up to his, and laughed, and answered,

---

1   *doubt*: 'fear, anticipate with apprehension' (*NED*).

"Why cannot you always be a good man, father?"

But as soon as she saw him vexed again, she kissed his hand, and said she would sing him to sleep. She began singing very low, till his fingers dropped from hers, and his head sank on his breast. Then I told her to hush, and not stir, for fear she would wake him. We all kept as mute as mice a full half-hour, and should have done longer, only Joseph, having finished his chapter, got up and said that he must rouse the master for prayers and bed. He stepped forward, and called him by name, and touched his shoulder, but he would not move—so he took the candle and looked at him.

I thought there was something wrong as he set down the light; and seizing the children each by an arm, whispered them to "frame[1] upstairs, and make little din—they might pray alone that evening—he had summut to do."

"I shall bid father good-night first," said Catherine, putting her arms round his neck, before we could hinder her.

The poor thing discovered her loss directly—she screamed out—

"Oh, he's dead, Heathcliff! he's dead!"

And they both set up a heart-breaking cry.

I joined my wail to theirs, loud and bitter; but Joseph asked what we could be thinking of to roar in that way over a saint in Heaven.

He told me to put on my cloak and run to Gimmerton for the doctor and the parson. I could not guess the use that either would be of, then. However, I went, through wind and rain, and brought one, the doctor, back with me; the other said he would come in the morning.

Leaving Joseph to explain matters, I ran to the children's room; their door was ajar, I saw they had never laid down, though it was past midnight; but they were calmer, and did not need me to console them. The little souls were comforting each other with better thoughts than I could have hit on; no parson in the world ever pictured Heaven so beautifully as they did, in their innocent talk; and, while I sobbed, and listened, I could not help wishing we were all there safe together.

---

1   *frame*: contrive [to go].

CHAPTER 6

Mr. Hindley came home to the funeral; and—a thing that amazed us, and set the neighbours gossiping right and left—he brought a wife with him.

What she was, and where she was born he never informed us; probably, she had neither money nor name to recommend her, or he would scarcely have kept the union from his father.

She was not one that would have disturbed the house much on her own account. Every object she saw, the moment she crossed the threshold, appeared to delight her; and every circumstance that took place about her, except the preparing for the burial, and the presence of the mourners.

I thought she was half silly from her behaviour while that went on; she ran into her chamber, and made me come with her, though I should have been dressing the children; and there she sat shivering and clasping her hands, and asking repeatedly—

"Are they gone yet?"

Then she began describing with hysterical emotion the effect it produced on her to see black; and started and trembled, and, at last, fell a-weeping—and when I asked what was the matter? answered, she didn't know; but she felt so afraid of dying!

I imagined her as little likely to die as myself. She was rather thin, but young, and fresh complexioned, and her eyes sparkled as bright as diamonds. I did remark, to be sure, that mounting the stairs made her breathe very quick, that the least sudden noise set her all in a quiver, and that she coughed troublesomely sometimes: but, I knew nothing of what these symptoms portended, and had no impulse to sympathize with her. We don't in general take to foreigners here, Mr. Lockwood, unless they take to us first.

Young Earnshaw was altered considerably in the three years of his absence. He had grown sparer, and lost his colour, and spoke and dressed quite differently: and, on the very day of his return, he told Joseph and me we must thenceforth quarter ourselves in the back-kitchen, and leave the house for him. Indeed he would have carpeted and papered a small spare room for a parlour; but his wife expressed such pleasure at the white floor,[1] and huge glowing fire-place, at the pewter dishes, and delf-cast, and dog-kennel, and the wide space there was to move about in, where they usually sat, that he thought it unnecessary to her comfort, and so dropped the intention.

She expressed pleasure, too, at finding a sister among her new acquaintance, and she prattled to Catherine, and kissed her, and ran about with her, and gave her quantities of presents, at the beginning. Her affection tired very soon, however, and when she grew peevish, Hindley became tyrannical. A few words from her, evincing a dislike to Heathcliff, were enough to rouse in him all his old hatred of the boy. He drove him from their company to the servants, deprived him of the instructions of the curate, and insisted that he should labour out of doors instead, compelling him to do so, as hard as any other lad on the farm.

He bore his degradation pretty well at first, because Cathy taught him what she learnt, and worked or played with him in the fields. They both promised fair to grow up as rude as savages, the young master being entirely negligent how they behaved, and what they did, so they kept clear of him. He would not even have seen after their going to church on Sundays, only Joseph and the curate reprimanded his carelessness when they absented themselves, and that reminded him to order Heathcliff a flogging, and Catherine a fast from dinner or supper.

But it was one of their chief amusements to run away to the moors in the morning and remain there all day, and the after punishment grew a mere thing to laugh at. The curate might set as many chapters as he pleased for Catherine to get by heart, and Joseph might thrash Heathcliff till his arm ached; they forgot everything the minute they were together again, at least the minute they had contrived some naughty plan of revenge, and many a time I've cried to myself to watch them growing more reckless daily, and I not daring to speak a syllable for fear of losing the small power I still retained over the unfriended creatures.

One Sunday evening, it chanced that they were banished from the sitting-room, for making a noise, or a light offence of the kind,

---

1   A reference to building materials in a limestone region.

and when I went to call them to supper, I could discover them nowhere.

We searched the house, above and below, and the yard, and stables. They were invisible; and at last, Hindley in a passion told us to bolt the doors, and swore nobody should let them in that night.

The household went to bed; and I, too anxious to lie down, opened my lattice and put my head out to hearken, though it rained, determined to admit them in spite of the prohibition, should they return.

In a while, I distinguished steps coming up the road, and the light of a lantern glimmered through the gate.

I threw a shawl over my head and ran to prevent them from waking Mr. Earnshaw by knocking. There was Heathcliff, by himself; it gave me a start to see him alone.

"Where is Miss Catherine?" I cried hurriedly. "No accident, I hope?"

"At Thrushcross Grange," he answered, "and I would have been there too but they had not the manners to ask me to stay."

"Well, you will catch it!" I said, "you'll never be content till you're sent about your business. What in the world led you wandering to Thrushcross Grange?"

"Let me get off my wet clothes, and I'll tell you all about it, Nelly," he replied.

I bid him beware of rousing the master, and while he undressed, and I waited to put out the candle, he continued—

"Cathy and I escaped from the wash-house to have a ramble at liberty, and getting a glimpse of the Grange lights, we thought we would just go and see whether the Lintons passed their Sunday evenings standing shivering in corners, while their father and mother sat eating and drinking, and singing and laughing, and burning their eyes out before the fire. Do you think they do? Or reading sermons, and being catechised by their man-servant, and set to learn a column of Scripture names, if they don't answer properly?"

"Probably not," I responded. "They are good children, no doubt, and don't deserve the treatment you receive, for your bad conduct."

"Don't you cant, Nelly," he said. "Nonsense! We ran from the top of the Heights[1] to the park, without stopping—Catherine completely beaten in the race, because she was barefoot. You'll have to seek for her shoes in the bog to-morrow. We crept through a broken hedge, groped our way up the path, and planted ourselves on a flower-plot under the drawing-room window. The light came from thence; they had not put up the shutters, and the curtains were only half closed. Both of us were able to look in by standing on the basement, and clinging to the ledge, and we saw—ah! it was beautiful—a splendid place carpeted with crimson, and crimson-covered chairs and tables, and a pure white ceiling bordered by gold, a shower of glass-drops hanging in silver chains from the centre, and shimmering with little soft tapers. Old Mr. and Mrs. Linton were not there. Edgar and his sister had it entirely to themselves; shouldn't they have been happy? We should have thought ourselves in heaven! And now, guess what your good children were doing? Isabella, I believe she is eleven, a year younger than Cathy, lay screaming at the farther end of the room, shrieking as if witches were running red hot needles into her. Edgar stood on the hearth weeping silently, and in the middle of the table sat a little dog shaking its paw and yelping, which, from their mutual accusations, we understood they had nearly pulled in two between them. The idiots! That was their pleasure! to quarrel who should hold a heap of warm hair, and each began to cry because both, after struggling to get it, refused to take it. We laughed outright at the petted things, we did despise them! When would you catch me wishing to have what Catherine wanted? or find us by ourselves, seeking entertainment in yelling, and sobbing, and rolling on the ground, divided by the whole room? I'd not exchange, for a thousand lives, my condition here, for Edgar Linton's at Thrushcross Grange—not if I might have the privilege of flinging Joseph off the highest gable, and painting the house-front with Hindley's blood!"

"Hush, hush!" I interrupted. "Still you have not told me, Heathcliff, how Catherine is left behind?"

---

1   The first reference to the hill from which the farmhouse and the novel take their name.

"I told you we laughed," he answered "The Lintons heard us, and with one accord, they shot like arrows to the door; there was silence, and then a cry, 'Oh, mamma, mamma! Oh, papa! Oh, mamma, come here. Oh papa, oh!' They really did howl out, something in that way. We made frightful noises to terrify them still more, and then we dropped off the ledge, because somebody was drawing the bars, and we felt we had better flee. I had Cathy by the hand, and was urging her on, when all at once she fell down.

"'Run, Heathcliff, run!' she whispered. 'They have let the bull-dog loose, and he holds me!'

"The devil had seized her ankle, Nelly; I heard his abominable snorting. She did not yell out—no! She would have scorned to do it, if she had been spitted on the horns of a mad cow. I did, though, I vociferated curses enough to annihilate any fiend in Christendom, and I got a stone and thrust it between his jaws, and tried with all my might to cram it down his throat. A beast of a servant came up with a lantern, at last, shouting—

"'Keep fast, Skulker, keep fast!'

"He changed his note, however, when he saw Skulker's game. The dog was throttled off, his huge, purple tongue hanging half a foot out of his mouth, and his pendant lips streaming with bloody slaver.

"The man took Cathy up; she was sick; not from fear, I'm certain, but from pain. He carried her in; I followed grumbling execrations and vengeance.

"'What prey, Robert?' hallooed Linton from the entrance.

"'Skulker has caught a little girl, sir,' he replied, 'and there's a lad here,' he added, making a clutch at me, 'who looks an out-and-outer! Very like, the robbers were for putting them through the window, to open the doors to the gang, after all were asleep, that they might murder us at their ease. Hold your tongue, you foul-mouthed thief, you! you shall go to the gallows for this. Mr. Linton, sir, don't lay by your gun!'

"'No, no, Robert!', said the old fool. 'The rascals knew that yesterday was my rent day; they thought to have me cleverly. Come in; I'll furnish them a reception. There, John, fasten the chain. Give Skulker some water, Jenny. To beard a magistrate in his strong-hold, and on the Sabbath, too! where will their inso-lence stop? Oh, my dear Mary, look here! Don't be afraid, it is but a boy—yet, the villain scowls so plainly in his face, would it not be a kindness to the country to hang him at once, before he shows his nature in acts, as well as features?'

"He pulled me under the chandelier, and Mrs. Linton placed her spectacles on her nose and raised her hands in horror. The cowardly children crept nearer also, Isabella lisping—

"'Frightful thing! Put him in the cellar, papa. He's exactly like the son of the fortune-teller, that stole my tame pheasant. Isn't he, Edgar?'

"While they examined me, Cathy came round; she heard the last speech, and laughed. Edgar Linton, after an inquisitive stare, collected sufficient wit to recognise her. They see us at church, you know, though we seldom meet them elsewhere.

"'That's Miss Earnshaw!' he whispered to his mother, 'and look how Skulker has bitten her—how her foot bleeds!'

"'Miss Earnshaw? Nonsense!' cried the dame, 'Miss Earnshaw scouring the country with a gipsy!¹ And yet, my dear, the child is in mourning—surely it is—and she may be lamed for life!'

"'What culpable carelessness in her brother!' exclaimed Mr. Linton, turning from me to Catherine. 'I've understood from Shielders (that was the curate sir) that he lets her grow up in absolute heathenism. But who is this? Where did she pick up this companion? Oho! I declare he is that strange acquisition my late neighbour made in his journey to Liverpool—a little Lascar,² or an American or Spanish castaway.'

"'A wicked boy, at all events,' remarked the old lady, 'and quite unfit for a decent house! Did you notice his language, Linton? I'm shocked that my children should have heard it.'

---

1   Romany ('gipsy') caravans used and still use the K&K to and from fairs at Brough.

2   *Lascar.* in *Hobson-Jobson. A Glossary of Colloquial Anglo-Indian Words* (1886; 1990 reprint), pp. 507-8, Henry Yule notes 'sailor', through Portuguese from the Hindi/Persian *lashkar*: soldiers, sailors (generally servile); see also, Rozina Vizram, *Ayahs, Lascars and Princes. Indians in Britain 1700-1947* (1986), p. 231, and ch. 3, pp. 34-54, 'The Sailors who Filled the Gap: the Lascars'.

"I recommenced cursing—don't be angry Nelly—and so Robert was ordered to take me off—I refused to go without Cathy—he dragged me into the garden, pushed the lantern into my hand, assured me that Mr. Earnshaw should be informed of my behaviour, and bidding me march, directly, secured the door again.

"The curtains were still looped up at one corner; and I resumed my station as spy, because, if Catherine had wished to return, I intended shattering their great glass panes to a million fragments, unless they let her out.

"She sat on the sofa quietly, Mrs. Linton took off the grey cloak of the dairy maid which we had borrowed for our excursion; shaking her head, and expostulating with her, I suppose; she was a young lady and they made a distinction between her treatment, and mine. Then the woman servant brought a basin of warm water, and washed her feet; and Mr. Linton mixed a tumbler of negus,[1] and Isabella emptied a plateful of cakes into her lap, and Edgar stood gaping at a distance. Afterwards, they dried and combed her beautiful hair, and gave her a pair of enormous slippers, and wheeled her to the fire, and I left her, as merry as she could be, dividing her food between the little dog and Skulker, whose nose she pinched as he ate; and kindling a spark of spirit in the vacant blue eyes of the Lintons—a dim reflection from her own enchanting face—I saw they were full of stupid admiration; she was so immeasurably superior to them—to everybody on earth; is she not, Nelly?"

"There will more come of this business than you reckon on," I answered covering him up and extinguishing the light, "You are incurable, Heathcliff, and Mr. Hindley will have to proceed to extremities, see if he won't."

My words came truer than I desired. The luckless adventure made Earnshaw furious. And then, Mr. Linton, to mend matters, paid us a visit himself, on the morrow; and read the young master such a lecture on the road he guided his family, that he was stirred to look about him, in earnest.

---

1   *negus*: a soothing drink of sweetened water and wine (port or sherry), reputedly named after Colonel Francis Negus in the time of Queen Anne (*NED*).

Heathcliff received no flogging, but he was told that the first word he spoke to Miss Catherine should ensure a dismissal; and Mrs. Earnshaw undertook to keep her sister-in-law in due restraint when she returned home, employing art, not force—with force she would have found it impossible.

CHAPTER 7

Cathy stayed at Thrushcross Grange five weeks, till Christmas. By that time her ankle was thoroughly cured, and her manners much improved. The mistress visited her often, in the interval, and commenced her plan of reform, by trying to raise her self-respect with fine clothes, and flattery, which she took readily: so that, instead of a wild, hatless little savage jumping into the house, and rushing to squeeze us all breathless, there lighted from a handsome black pony a very dignified person with brown ringlets falling from the cover of a feathered beaver, and a long cloth habit which she was obliged to hold up with both hands that she might sail in.

Hindley lifted her from her horse exclaiming delightedly,

"Why, Cathy, you are quite a beauty! I should scarcely have known you—you look like a lady now—Isabella Linton is not to be compared with her, is she Frances?"

"Isabella has not her natural advantages," replied his wife, "but she must mind and not grow wild again here. Ellen, help Miss Catherine off with her things—stay, dear, you will disarrange your curls—let me untie your hat."

I removed the habit, and there shone forth, beneath a grand plaid silk frock, white trousers, and burnished shoes; and, while her eyes sparkled joyfully when the dogs came bounding up to welcome her, she dared hardly touch them lest they should fawn upon her splendid garments.

She kissed me gently; I was all flour making the Christmas cake, and it would not have done to give me a hug; and, then, she looked round for Heathcliff. Mr. and Mrs. Earnshaw watched anxiously their meeting, thinking it would enable them to judge, in some measure, what grounds they had for hoping to succeed in separating the two friends.

Heathcliff was hard to discover, at first—if he were careless, and uncared for, before Catherine's absence, he has been ten times more so, since.

Nobody but I even did him the kindness to call him a dirty boy, and bid him wash himself, once a week; and children of his age seldom have a natural pleasure in soap and water. Therefore, not to mention his clothes, which had seen three month's service in mire and dust, and his thick uncombed hair; the surface of his face and hands was dismally beclouded. He might well skulk behind the settle, on beholding such a bright, graceful damsel enter the house, instead of a rough-headed counterpart to himself, as he expected.

"Is Heathcliff not here?" she demanded, pulling off her gloves, and displaying fingers wonderfully whitened with doing nothing, and staying indoors.

"Heathcliff, you may come forward," cried Mr. Hindley, enjoying his discomfiture and gratified to see what a forbidding young blackguard he would be compelled to present himself as. "You may come and wish Miss Catherine welcome, like the other servants."

Cathy, catching a glimpse of her friend in his concealment, flew to embrace him; she bestowed seven or eight kisses on his cheek within the second, and, then, stopped, and drawing back, burst into a laugh, exclaiming,

"Why, how very black and cross you look! and how—how funny and grim. But that's because I'm used to Edgar, and Isabella Linton. Well, Heathcliff, have you forgotten me?"

She had some reason to put the question, for shame, and pride threw double gloom over his countenance, and kept him immoveable.

"Shake hands, Heathcliff," said Mr. Earnshaw, condescendingly; "once in a way, that is permitted."

"I shall not!" replied the boy, finding his tongue at last, "I shall not stand to be laughed at, I shall not bear it!"

And he would have broken from the circle, but Miss Cathy seized him again.

"I did not mean to laugh at you," she said, "I could not hinder myself, Heathcliff; shake hands, at least! What are you sulky for? It was only that you looked odd—if you wash your face, and brush your hair it will be all right. But you are so dirty!"

She gazed concernedly at the dusky fingers she held in her own, and also at her dress which she feared had gained no embellishment from its contact with his.

"You needn't have touched me!" he answered, following her eye and snatching away his hand. "I shall be as dirty as I please, and I like to be dirty, and I will be dirty."

With that he dashed head foremost out of the room, amid the merriment of the master and mistress, and to the serious disturbance of Catherine who could not comprehend how her remarks should have produced such an exhibition of bad temper.

After playing lady's maid to the new comer, and putting my cakes in the oven, and making the house and kitchen cheerful with great fires befitting Christmas eve, I prepared to sit down and amuse myself by singing carols, all alone; regardless of Joseph's affirmations that he considered the merry tunes I chose as next door to songs.

He had retired to private prayer in his chamber, and Mr. and Mrs. Earnshaw were engaging Missy's attention by sundry gay trifles bought for her to present to the little Lintons, as an acknowledgment of their kindness.

They had invited them to spend the morrow at Wuthering Heights, and the invitation had been accepted, on one condition, Mrs. Linton begged that her darlings might be kept carefully apart from that "naughty, swearing boy."

Under these circumstances I remained solitary. I smelt the rich scent of the heating spices; and admired the shining kitchen utensils, the polished clock, decked in holly, the silver mugs ranged on a tray ready to be filled with mulled ale for supper; and above all, the speckless purity of my particular care—the scoured and well-swept floor.

I gave due inward applause to every object and, then, I remembered how old Earnshaw used to come in when all was tidied, and call me a cant lass,[1] and slip a shilling into my hand, as a Christmas box: and, from that, I went on to think of his fondness for Heathcliff, and his dread lest he should suffer neglect after death had removed him; and that naturally led me to consider the poor lad's situation now, and from singing I changed my mind to crying. It struck me soon, however, there would be more sense in endeavouring to repair some of his wrongs than shedding tears over them—I got up and walked into the court to seek him.

He was not far. I found him smoothing the glossy coat of the new pony in the stable, and feeding the other beasts, according to custom.

---

1 *cant*: 'lively' (Carr).

"Make haste, Heathcliff!" I said, "the kitchen is so comfortable—and Joseph is upstairs: make haste, and let me dress you smart before Miss Cathy comes out—and then you can sit together, with the whole hearth to yourselves, and have a long chatter till bedtime."

He proceeded with his task and never turned his head towards me.

"Come—are you coming?" I continued, "there's a little cake for each of you, nearly enough; and you'll need half an hour's donning."

I waited five minutes, but getting no answer left him. Catherine supped with her brother and sister-in-law: Joseph and I joined at an unsociable meal seasoned with reproofs on one side, and sauciness on the other. His cake and cheese remained on the table all night, for the fairies. He managed to continue work till nine o'clock, and, then, marched dumb and dour, to his chamber.

Cathy sat up late; having a world of things to order for the reception of her new friends: she came into the kitchen, once, to speak to her old one, but he was gone, and she only staid to ask what was the matter with him, and then went back.

In the morning, he rose early; and, as it was a holiday, carried his ill-humour on to the moors: not re-appearing till the family were departed for church. Fasting, and reflection seemed to have brought him to a better spirit. He hung about me, for a while, and having screwed up his courage, exclaimed abruptly,

"Nelly, make me decent, I'm going to be good."

"High time, Heathcliff," I said, "you *have* grieved Catherine; she's sorry she ever came home, I dare say! It looks as if you envied her, because she is more thought of than you."

The notion of *envying* Catherine was incomprehensible to him, but the notion of grieving her, he understood clearly enough.

"Did she say she was grieved?" he inquired, looking very serious.

"She cried when I told her you were off again this morning."

"Well, *I* cried last night," he returned, "and I had more reason to cry than she."

"Yes, you had the reason of going to bed, with a proud heart, and an empty stomach," said I; "proud people breed sad sorrows for themselves—but, if you be ashamed of your touchiness, you must ask pardon, mind, when she comes in. You must go up, and offer to kiss her, and say—you know best what to say, only, do it heartily,[1] and not as if you thought her converted into a stranger by her grand dress. And now, though I have dinner to get ready, I'll steal time to arrange you so that Edgar Linton shall look quite a doll beside you: and that he does—you are younger, and yet, I'll be bound, you are taller and twice as broad across the shoulders— you could knock him down in a twinkling; don't you feel that you could?"

Heathcliff's face brightened a moment; then, it was overcast afresh, and he sighed.

"But, Nelly, if I knocked him down twenty times, that wouldn't make him less handsome, or me more so. I wish I had light hair and a fair skin, and was dressed, and behaved as well, and had a chance of being as rich as he will be!"

"And cried for mamma, at every turn," I added, "and trembled if a country lad heaved his fist against you, and sat at home all day for a shower of rain. O, Heathcliff, you are showing a poor spirit! come to the glass, and I'll let you see what you should wish. Do you mark those two lines between your eyes, and those thick brows, that instead of rising arched, sink in the middle, and that couple of black fiends, so deeply buried, who never open their windows boldly, but lurk glinting under them, like devil's spies? Wish and learn to smooth away the surly wrinkles, to raise your lids frankly, and change the fiends to confident, innocent angels, suspecting and doubting nothing, and always seeing friends where they are not sure of foes—don't get the expression of a vicious cur that appears to know the kicks it gets are its desert, and yet, hates all the world, as well as the kicker, for what it suffers."

"In other words, I must wish for Edgar Linton's great blue eyes, and even forehead," he replied. "I do—and that won't help me to them."

---

1   *heartily*: from the heart.

"A good heart will help you to a bonny face my lad," I continued, "if you were a regular black;[1] and a bad one will turn the bonniest into something worse than ugly. And now we've done washing, and combing, and sulking—tell me whether you don't think yourself rather handsome? I'll tell you, I do. You're fit for a prince in disguise. Who knows, but your father was Emperor of China, and your mother an Indian queen, each of them able to buy up, with one week's income, Wuthering Heights and Thrushcross Grange together? And you were kidnapped by wicked sailors, and brought to England. Were I in your place, I would frame high notions of my birth; and the thoughts of what I was should give me courage and dignity to support the oppressions of a little farmer!"

So I chattered on; and Heathcliff gradually lost his frown, and began to look quite pleasant; when, all at once, our conversation was interrupted by a rumbling sound moving up the road and entering the court. He ran to the window, and I to the door, just in time to behold the two Lintons descend from the family carriage, smothered in cloaks and furs, and the Earnshaws dismount from their horses—they often rode to church in winter. Catherine took a hand of each of the children, and brought them into the house, and set them before the fire which quickly put colour into their white faces.

I urged my companion to hasten now, and show his amiable humour; and he willingly obeyed; but ill luck would have it, that as he opened the door leading from the kitchen on one side, Hindley opened it on the other; they met, and the master, irritated

---

1   *regular black*: after washing him, Nelly observes that he is a pale black, probably a *mustefino*, that is, dark all over, and not black; see above, Introduction p. 66, and note 75. She plays on a conventional jest from the era of racism, about soap and black skins: Thomas Hood, in his *Whimsicalities*, 2 vols. (1844), 'A Black Job', vol. 1, pp. 215-24 (p. 216) satirises a Philanthropic Society which encouraged the consumption of soap 'To see each Crow, or Jim, or John / Go in a raven and come out a swan!'. Hood distanced himself some way from the racism of his era, though not far enough, in *Hood's Own; or Laughter from Year to Year* (1839) (*K*), 'The Black and White Question' (pp. 145-52), where he notes the advantages of a black skin, 'which wears well, washes well, does not fly, and moreover hides the dirt' (p. 146).

at seeing him clean and cheerful, or, perhaps, eager to keep his promise to Mrs. Linton, shoved him back with a sudden thrust, and angrily bade Joseph "keep the fellow out of the room—send him into the garret till dinner is over. He'll be cramming his fingers in the tarts, and stealing the fruit, if left alone with them a minute."

"Nay, sir," I could not avoid answering, "he'll touch nothing, not he—and, I suppose, he must have his share of the dainties as well as we."

"He shall have his share of my hand, if I catch him down-stairs again till dark," cried Hindley. "Begone, you vagabond! What, you are attempting the coxcomb, are you? Wait till I get hold of those elegant locks—see if I won't pull them a bit longer!"

"They are long enough already," observed Master Linton, peeping from the door-way, "I wonder they don't make his head ache. It's like a colt's mane over his eyes!"

He ventured this remark without any intention to insult; but, Heathcliff's violent nature was not prepared to endure the appearance of impertinence from one whom he seemed to hate, even then, as a rival. He seized a tureen of hot apple-sauce, the first thing that came under his gripe, and dashed it full against the speaker's face and neck—who instantly commenced a lament that brought Isabella and Catherine hurrying to the place.

Mr. Earnshaw snatched up the culprit directly and conveyed him to his chamber, where, doubtless, he administered a rough remedy to cool the fit of passion, for he reappeared red and breathless. I got the dish-cloth, and rather spitefully, scrubbed Edgar's nose and mouth, affirming, it served him right for meddling. His sister began weeping to go home, and Cathy stood by confounded, blushing for all.

"You should not have spoken to him!" she expostulated with Master Linton. "He was in a bad temper, and now you've spoilt your visit, and he'll be flogged—I hate him to be flogged! I can't eat my dinner. Why did you speak to him, Edgar?"

"I didn't," sobbed the youth, escaping from my hands, and finishing the remainder of the purification with his cambric pocket-handkerchief. "I promised mamma that I wouldn't say one word to him, and I didn't!"

"Well, don't cry!" replied Catherine, contemptuously. "You're not killed—don't make more mischief—my brother is coming—be quiet! Give over, Isabella! Has anybody hurt *you*?"

"There, there, children—to your seats!" cried Hindley, bustling in. "That brute of a lad has warmed me nicely. Next time, Master Edgar, take the law into your own fists—it will give you an appetite!"

The little party recovered its equanimity at sight of the fragrant feast. They were hungry, after their ride, and easily consoled, since no real harm had befallen them.

Mr. Earnshaw carved bountiful platefuls; and the mistress made them merry with lively talk. I waited behind her chair, and was pained to behold Catherine, with dry eyes and an indifferent air, commence cutting up the wing of a goose before her.

"An unfeeling child," I thought to myself, "how lightly she dismisses her old playmate's troubles. I could not have imagined her to be so selfish."

She lifted a mouthful to her lips; then, she set it down again: her cheeks flushed, and the tears gushed over them. She slipped her fork to the floor, and hastily dived under the cloth to conceal her emotion. I did not call her unfeeling long, for, I perceived she was in purgatory throughout the day, and searching to find an opportunity of getting by herself, or paying a visit to Heathcliff, who had been locked up by the master, as I discovered, on endeavouring to introduce to him a private mess of victuals.

In the evening we had a dance. Cathy begged that she might be liberated then, as Isabella Linton had no partner; her entreaties were vain and I was appointed to supply the deficiency.

We got rid of all gloom in the excitement of the exercise, and our pleasure was increased by the arrival of the Gimmerton band, mustering fifteen strong; a trumpet, a trombone, clarionets, bassoons, French horns, and a bass viol, besides singers. They go the rounds of all the respectable houses, and receive contributions every Christmas, and we esteemed it a first-rate treat to hear them.

After the usual carols had been sung we set them to songs and glees. Mrs. Earnshaw loved the music, and, so, they gave us plenty.

Catherine loved it too; but she said it sounded sweetest at the top of the steps, and she went up in the dark: I followed. They shut the house door below, never noting our absence, it was so full of people. She made no stay at the stairs' head, but mounted farther, to the garret where Heathcliff was confined; and called him. He stubbornly declined answering for a while—she persevered, and finally persuaded him to hold communion with her through the boards.

I let the poor things converse unmolested, till I supposed the songs were going to cease, and the singers to get some refreshment: then, I clambered up the ladder to warn her.

Instead of finding her outside, I heard her voice within. The little monkey had crept by the skylight out of one garret, along the roof, into the skylight of the other, and it was with the utmost difficulty I could coax her out again.

When she did come, Heathcliff came with her; and she insisted that I should take him into the kitchen, as my fellow-servant had gone to a neighbour's to be removed from the sound of our "devil's psalmody," as it pleased him to call it.

I told them I intended, by no means, to encourage their tricks; but as the prisoner had never broken his fast since yesterday's dinner, I would wink at his cheating Mr. Hindley that once.

He went down; I set him a stool by the fire, and offered him a quantity of good things; but, he was sick and could eat little: and my attempts to entertain him were thrown away. He leant his two elbows on his knees, and his chin on his hands, and remained wrapt in dumb meditation. On my inquiring the subject of his thoughts, he answered gravely—

"I'm trying to settle how I shall pay Hindley back. I don't care how long I wait, if I can only do it, at last. I hope he will not die before I do!"

"For shame, Heathcliff!" said I. "It is for God to punish wicked people; we should learn to forgive."

"No, God won't have the satisfaction that I shall," he returned. "I only wish I knew the best way! Let me alone, and I'll plan it out: while I'm thinking of that, I don't feel pain."

"But, Mr. Lockwood, I forget these tales cannot divert you. I'm annoyed how I should dream of chattering on at such a rate; and your gruel cold, and you nodding for bed! I could have told Heathcliff's history, all that you need hear, in half-a-dozen words."

Thus interrupting herself, the housekeeper rose, and proceeded to lay aside her sewing; but I felt incapable of moving from the hearth, and I was very far from nodding.

"Sit still, Mrs. Dean," I cried, "do sit still, another half hour! You've done just right to tell the story leisurely. That is the method I like; and you must finish in the same style. I am interested in every character you have mentioned, more or less."

"The clock is on the stroke of eleven, sir."

"No matter—I'm not accustomed to go to bed in the long hours. One or two is early enough for a person who lies till ten."

"You shouldn't lie till ten. There's the very prime of the morning gone long before that time. A person who has not done one half his day's work by ten o'clock, runs a chance of leaving the other half undone."

"Nevertheless, Mrs. Dean, resume your chair; because to-morrow I intend lengthening the night till afternoon. I prognosticate for myself an obstinate cold at least."

"I hope not, sir. Well, you must allow me to leap over some three years, during that space, Mrs. Earnshaw—"

"No, no, I'll allow nothing of the sort! Are you acquainted with the mood of mind in which, if you are seated alone, and the cat licking its kitten on the rug before you, you would watch the operation so intently that puss's neglect of one ear would put you seriously out of temper?"

"A terribly lazy mood, I should say."

"On the contrary, a tiresomely active one. It is mine, at present, and, therefore, continue minutely. I perceive that people in these regions acquire over people in towns the value that a spider in a dungeon does over a spider in a cottage, to their various occupants; and yet the deepened attraction is not entirely owing to the situation of the looker-on. They *do* live more in earnest, more in themselves, and less in surface change, and frivolous external things. I could fancy a love for life here almost possible; and I was a fixed unbeliever in any love of a year's standing—one state resembles setting a hungry man down to a single dish on which he may concentrate his entire appetite, and do it justice—the other, introducing him to a table laid out by French cooks; he can perhaps extract as much enjoyment from the whole; but each part is a mere atom in his regard and remembrance."

"Oh! here we are the same as anywhere else, when you get to know us," observed Mrs. Dean, somewhat puzzled at my speech.

"Excuse me," I responded; "you, my good friend, are a striking evidence against that assertion. Excepting a few provincialisms of slight consequence, you have no marks of the manners that I am habituated to consider as peculiar to your class. I am sure you have thought a great deal more than the generality of servants think. You have been compelled to cultivate your reflective faculties, for want of occasions for frittering your life away in silly trifles."

Mrs. Dean laughed.

"I certainly esteem myself a steady, reasonable kind of body," she said, "not exactly from living among the hills, and seeing one set of faces, and one series of actions, from year's end to year's end: but I have undergone sharp discipline which has taught me wisdom; and than, I have read more than you would fancy, Mr. Lockwood. You could not open a book in the library that I have not looked into, and got something out of also; unless it be that range of Greek and Latin, and that of French—and those I know one from another, it is as much as you can expect of a poor man's daughter.

"However, if I am to follow my story in true gossip's fashion, I had better go on; and instead of leaping three years, I will be content to pass to the next summer—the summer of 1778, that is nearly twenty-three[1] years ago."

---

[1] *twenty-three*: no error need be assumed in this reference to 1779; see below, Appendix A.

CHAPTER 8

On the morning of a fine June day, my first bonny little nursling, and the last of the ancient Earnshaw stock was born.

We were all busy with the hay in a far away field, when the girl that usually brought our breakfasts came running, an hour too soon, across the meadow and up the lane, calling me as she ran.

"Oh, such a grand bairn!" she panted out. "The finest lad that ever breathed! but the doctor says missis must go; he says she's been in a consumption[1] these many months. I heard him tell Mr. Hindley—and now she has nothing to keep her, and she'll be dead before winter. You must come home directly. You're to nurse it, Nelly—to feed it with sugar and milk, and take care of it, day and night—I wish I were you, because it will be all yours when there is no missis!"

"But is she very ill?" I asked, flinging down my rake, and tying my bonnet.

"I guess she is; yet she looks bravely," replied the girl, "and she talks as if she thought of living to see it grow a man. She's out of her head for joy, it's such a beauty! If I were her I'm certain I should not die. I should get better at the bare sight of it, in spite of Kenneth. I was fairly mad at him. Dame Archer brought the cherub down to master, in the house, and his face just began to light up, then the old croaker steps forward, and, says he: 'Earnshaw, it's a blessing your wife has been spared to leave you this son. When she came, I felt convinced we shouldn't keep her long; and now, I must tell you, the winter will probably finish her. Don't take on, and fret about it too much, it can't be helped. And besides, you should have known better than to choose such a rush of a lass!'"

"And what did the master answer?" I enquired.

"I think he swore—but, I didn't mind him, I was straining to see the bairn," and she began again to describe it rapturously. I, as zealous as herself, hurried eagerly home to admire, on my part, though I was very sad for Hindley's sake; he had room in his heart

---

1 *consumption*: tuberculosis.

only for two idols—his wife and himself—he doted on both, and adored one, and I couldn't conceive how he would bear the loss.

When we got to Wuthering Heights, there he stood at the front door; and, as I passed in, I asked, how was the baby?

"Nearly ready to run about, Nell!" he replied, putting on a cheerful smile.

"And the mistress?" I ventured to inquire, "the doctor says she's—"

"Damn the doctor!" he interrupted, reddening. "Frances is quite right—she'll be perfectly well by this time next week. Are you going upstairs? will you tell her that I'll come, if she'll promise not to talk. I left her because she would not hold her tongue; and she must—tell her Mr. Kenneth says she must be quiet."

I delivered the message to Mrs. Earnshaw; she seemed in flighty spirits, and replied merrily—

"I hardly spoke a word, Ellen, and there he has gone out twice, crying. Well, say I promise I won't speak; but that does not bid me not to laugh at him!"

Poor soul! Till within a week of her death that gay heart never failed her; and her husband persisted doggedly, nay, furiously, in affirming her health improved every day. When Kenneth warned him that his medicines were useless at that stage of the malady, and he needn't put him to further expense by attending her, he retorted—

"I know you need not—she's well—she does not want any more attendance from you! She never was in a consumption. It was a fever; and it is gone—her pulse is as slow as mine now, and her cheek as cool."

He told his wife the same story, and she seemed to believe him; but one night, while leaning on his shoulder, in the act of saying she thought she should be able to get up tomorrow, a fit of coughing took her—a very slight one—he raised her in his arms; she put her two hands about his neck, her face changed, and she was dead.

As the girl had anticipated, the child Hareton, fell wholly into my hands. Mr. Earnshaw, provided he saw him healthy, and never heard him cry, was contented, as far as regarded him. For himself, he grew desperate; his sorrow was of that kind that will not lament, he neither wept nor prayed—he cursed and defied—execrated God and man, and gave himself up to reckless dissipation.

The servants could not bear his tyrannical and evil conduct long: Joseph and I were the only two that would stay. I had not the heart to leave my charge; and besides, you know, I had been his foster sister,[1] and excused his behaviour more readily than a stranger would.

Joseph remained to hector over tenants and labourers; and because it was his vocation to be where he had plenty of wickedness to reprove.

The master's bad ways and bad companions formed a pretty example for Catherine and Heathcliff. His treatment of the latter was enough to make a fiend of a saint. And, truly, it appeared as if the lad *were* possessed of something diabolical at that period. He delighted to witness Hindley degrading himself past redemption; and became daily more notable for savage sullenness and ferocity.

I could not half tell what an infernal house we had. The curate dropped calling, and nobody decent came near us, at last; unless, Edgar Linton's visits to Miss Cathy might be an exception. At fifteen she was the queen of the country-side; she had no peer: and she did turn out a haughty, headstrong creature! I own I did not like her, after her infancy was past; and I vexed her frequently by trying to bring down her arrogance; she never took an aversion to me though. She had a wondrous constancy to old attachments; even Heathcliff kept his hold on her affections unalterably, and young Linton, with all his superiority, found it difficult to make an equally deep impression.

He was my late master; that is his portrait over the fireplace. It used to hang on one side, and his wife's on the other; but hers has been removed, or else you might see something of what she was. Can you make that out?

Mrs. Dean raised the candle, and I discerned a soft-featured face, exceedingly resembling the young lady at the Heights, but more pensive and amiable in expression. It formed a sweet picture. The long light hair curled slightly on the temples; the eyes

---

1 *foster sister*: this status exempts Nelly from the marriage prohibition; see above, Introduction, 'The Marriage Prohibition', pp. 39-49.

were large and serious; the figure almost too graceful. I did not marvel how Catherine Earnshaw could forget her first friend for such an individual. I marvelled much how he, with a mind to correspond with his person, could fancy my idea of Catherine Earnshaw.

"A very agreeable portrait," I observed to the housekeeper. "Is it like?"

"Yes," she answered; "but he looked better when he was animated, that is his every day countenance; he wanted spirit in general."

Catherine had kept up her acquaintance with the Lintons since her five weeks' residence among them; and as she had no temptation to show her rough side in their company, and had the sense to be ashamed of being rude where she experienced such invariable courtesy, she imposed unwittingly on the old lady and gentleman, by her ingenious cordiality; gained the admiration of Isabella, and the heart and soul of her brother—acquisitions that flattered her from the first, for she was full of ambition—and led her to adopt a double character without exactly intending to deceive anyone.

In the place where she heard Heathcliff termed a "vulgar young ruffian," and "worse than a brute," she took care not to act like him; but at home she had small inclination to practise politeness that would only be laughed at and restrain an unruly nature when it would bring her neither credit, nor praise.

Mr. Edgar seldom mustered courage to visit Wuthering Heights openly. He had a terror of Earnshaw's reputation, and shrunk from encountering him, and yet, he was always received with our best attempts at civility: the master himself, avoided offending him— knowing why he came, and if he could not be gracious, kept out of the way. I rather think his appearance there was distasteful to Catherine; she was not artful, never played the coquette, and had evidently an objection to her two friends meeting at all: for when Heathcliff expressed contempt of Linton, in his presence, she could not half coincide, as she did in his absence; and when Linton evinced disgust, and antipathy to Heathcliff, she dare not treat his sentiments with indifference, as if depreciation of her playmate were of scarcely any consequence to her.

I've had many a laugh at her perplexities, and untold troubles, which she vainly strove to hide from my mockery. That sounds ill-natured—but she was so proud, it became really impossible to pity her distresses, till she should be chastened into more humility.

She did bring herself, finally, to confess, and confide in me. There was not a soul else that she might fashion into an adviser.

Mr. Hindley had gone from home, one afternoon; and Heathcliff presumed to give himself a holiday, on the strength of it. He had reached the age of sixteen then, I think, and without having bad features or being deficient in intellect, he contrived to convey an impression of inward and outward repulsiveness that his present aspect retains no traces of.

In the first place, he had, by that time, lost the benefit of his early education: continual hard work, begun soon and concluded late, had extinguished any curiosity he once possessed in pursuit of knowledge, and any love for books, or learning. His childhood's sense of superiority, instilled into him by the favours of old Mr. Earnshaw, was faded away. He struggled long to keep up an equality with Catherine in her studies and yielded with poignant though silent regret: but, he yielded completely; and there was no prevailing on him to take a step in the way of moving upward, when he found he must, necessarily, sink beneath his former level. Then personal appearance sympathised with mental deterioration; he acquired a slouching gait, and ignoble look; his naturally reserved disposition was exaggerated into an almost idiotic excess of unsociable moroseness; and he took a grim pleasure, apparently, in exciting the aversion rather than the esteem of his few acquaintances.

Catherine and he were constant companions still, at his seasons of respite from labour; but, he had ceased to express his fondness for her in words, and recoiled with angry suspicion from her girlish caresses, as if conscious there could be no gratification in lavishing such marks of affection on him. On the before-named occasion he came into the house to announce his intention of doing nothing, while I was assisting Miss Cathy to arrange her dress—she had not reckoned on his taking it into his head to be idle, and imagining she would have the whole place to herself, she managed, by some means, to inform Mr. Edgar of her brother's absence, and was then preparing to receive him.

"Cathy, are you busy, this afternoon?" asked Heathcliff. "Are you going anywhere?"

"No, it is raining," she answered.

"Why have you that silk frock on, then?" he said, "nobody coming here I hope?"

"Not that I know of," stammered Miss, "but you should be in the field now, Heathcliff. It is an hour past dinner time; I thought you were gone."

"Hindley does not often free us from his accursed presence," observed the boy, "I'll not work any more to-day, I'll stay with you."

"Oh, but Joseph will tell," she suggested, "you'd better go!"

"Joseph is loading lime[1] on the farther side of Penniston[2] Crag, it will take him till dark, and he'll never know."

So saying he lounged to the fire, and sat down. Catherine reflected an instant, with knitted brows—she found it needful to smooth the way for an intrusion.

"Isabella and Edgar Linton talked of calling this afternoon," she said at the conclusion of a minute's silence. "As it rains, I hardly expect them; but, they may come, and if they do, you run the risk of being scolded for no good."

"Order Ellen to say you are engaged, Cathy," he persisted, "Don't turn me out for those pitiful, silly friends of yours! I'm on the point sometimes, of complaining that they—but I'll not—"

"That they what?" cried Catherine, gazing at him with a troubled countenance. "Oh Nelly!" she added petulantly jerking her head away from my hands, "you've combed my hair quite out of curl! That's enough, let me alone. What are you on the point of complaining about, Heathcliff?"

---

1 *loading lime*: production, not distribution; a conclusive reference to the limestone region.

2 *Penniston*: *WH* (1847) and subsequent edns. have 'Pennistow'. Here, Penistone appears to have been spelt phonetically in the MS. For the possibility of a printer's misreading of -on / -one as -ow, see 'crimson', 'lone', 'alone', 'now', 'low', fols. 9r, 1or, 9v. of E. Brontë, 'Gondal Poems', BL. Add. MS 43, 483. See Introduction above, and Plate 13, pp. 76-78.

"Nothing—only look at the almanack, on that wall," he pointed to a framed sheet hanging near the window, and continued,

"The crosses are for the evenings you have spent with the Lintons, and dots for those spent with me—do you see I've marked every day!"

"Yes—very foolish; as if I took notice!" replied Catherine in a peevish tone. "And where is the sense of that?"

"To show that I *do* take notice," said Heathcliff.

"And should I always be sitting with you," she demanded, growing more irritated. "What good do I get—what do you talk about? you might be dumb or a baby for anything you say to amuse me, or for anything you do, either!"

"You never told me, before, that I talked too little, or that you disliked my company, Cathy!" exclaimed Heathcliff in much agitation.

"It is no company at all, when people know nothing and say nothing," she muttered.

Her companion rose up, but he hadn't time to express his feelings further, for a horse's feet were heard on the flags, and, having knocked gently, young Linton entered, his face brilliant with delight at the unexpected summons he had received.

Doubtless Catherine marked the difference between her friends as one came in, and the other went out. The contrast resembled what you see in exchanging a bleak, hilly, coal country, for a beautiful fertile valley; and his voice, and greeting were as opposite as his aspect—he had a sweet, low manner of speaking, and pronounced his words as you do, that's less gruff than we talk here and softer.

"I'm not come too soon, am I?" he said, casting a look at me, I had begun to wipe the plate, and tidy some drawers at the far end in the dresser.

"No," answered Catherine. "What are you doing there, Nelly?"

"My work, Miss," I replied. (Mr. Hindley had given me directions to make a third party in any private visits Linton chose to pay.)

She stepped behind me and whispered crossly, "Take yourself and your dusters off! When company are in the house, servants don't commence scouring and cleaning in the room where they are!"

"It's a good opportunity, now that master is away," I answered aloud, "he hates me to be fidgetting over these things in his presence—I'm sure Mr. Edgar will excuse me."

"I hate you to be fidgetting in *my* presence," exclaimed the young lady imperiously, not allowing her guest time to speak—she had failed to recover her equanimity since the little dispute with Heathcliff.

"I'm sorry for it Miss Catherine!" was my response; and I proceeded assiduously with my occupation.

She, supposing Edgar could not see her, snatched the cloth from my hand, and pinched me, with a prolonged wrench, very spitefully on the arm.

I've said I did not love her; and rather relished mortifying her vanity, now and then; besides, she hurt me extremely, so I started up from my knees, and screamed out.

"O, Miss, that's a nasty trick! You have no right to nip me, and I'm not going to bear it!"

"I didn't touch you, you lying creature!" cried she, her fingers tingling to repeat the act, and her ears red with rage. She never had power to conceal her passion, it always set her whole complexion in a blaze.

"What's that then?" I retorted, showing a decided purple witness to refute her.

She stamped her foot, wavered a moment, and then, irresistibly impelled by the naughty spirit within her, slapped me on the cheek a stinging blow that filled both eyes with water.

"Catherine, love! Catherine!" interposed Linton, greatly shocked at the double fault of falsehood, and violence, which his idol had committed.

"Leave the room, Ellen!" she repeated, trembling all over.

Little Hareton, who followed me everywhere, and was sitting near me on the floor, at seeing my tears commenced crying himself, and sobbed out complaints against "wicked aunt Cathy," which drew her fury on to his unlucky head: she seized his shoulders, and shook him till the poor child waxed livid, and Edgar thoughtlessly laid hold of her hands to deliver him. In an instant one was wrung free, and the astonished young man felt it applied over his own ear in a way that could not be mistaken for jest.

He drew back in consternation—I lifted Hareton in my arms, and walked off to the kitchen with him; leaving the door of communication open, for I was curious to watch how they would settle their disagreement.

The insulted visitor moved to the spot where he had laid his hat, pale and with a quivering lip.

"That's right!" I said to myself, "Take warning and begone! It's a kindness to let you have a glimpse of her genuine disposition."

"Where are you going?" demanded Catherine, advancing to the door.

He swerved aside and attempted to pass.

"You must not go!" she exclaimed energetically.

"I must and shall!" he replied in a subdued voice.

"No," she persisted, grasping the handle; "not yet, Edgar Linton—sit down, you shall not leave me in that temper. I should be miserable all night, and I won't be miserable for you!"

"Can I stay after you have struck me?" asked Linton.

Catherine was mute.

"You've made me afraid, and ashamed of you," he continued; "I'll not come here again!"

Her eyes began to glisten and her lids to twinkle.

"And you told a deliberate untruth!" he said.

"I didn't!" she cried, recovering her speech, "I did nothing deliberately—well, go, if you please—get away! And now I'll cry—I'll cry myself sick!"

She dropped down on her knees by a chair and set to weeping in serious earnest.

Edgar persevered in his resolution as far as the court; there, he lingered. I resolved to encourage him.

"Miss is dreadfully wayward, sir!" I called out. "As bad as any marred child—you'd better be riding home, or else she will be sick, only to grieve us."

The soft thing looked askance through the window—he possessed the power to depart, as much as a cat possesses the power to leave a mouse half killed, or a bird half eaten[1]—

Ah, I thought; there will be no saving him—he's doomed, and flies to his fate!

And, so it was; he turned abruptly, hastened into the house again, shut the door behind him; and, when I went in a while after to inform them that Earnshaw had come home rabid drunk, ready to pull the old place about our ears (his ordinary frame of mind in that condition) I saw the quarrel had merely effected a closer intimacy—had broken the outworks of youthful timidity, and enabled them to forsake the disguise of friendship, and confess themselves lovers.

Intelligence of Mr. Hindley's arrival drove Linton speedily to his horse, and Catherine to her chamber. I went to hide little Hareton, and to take the shot out of the master's fowling piece, which he was fond of playing with in his insane excitement, to the hazard of the lives of any who provoked, or even, attracted his notice too much; and I had hit upon the plan of removing it, that he might do less mischief, if he did go to the length of firing the gun.

---

1 *bird half eaten*: in more forthright French, Emily Brontë invokes a cat with a half-eaten rat's tail hanging from its mouth to symbolise parental approval of a boy's wanton cruelty in her essay 'Le chat'; see Charlotte Brontë and Emily Brontë, *The Belgian Essays* (1996), ed. Sue Lonoff, pp. 56–59.

CHAPTER 9

He entered, vociferating oaths dreadful to hear; and caught me in the act of stowing his son away in the kitchen cupboard. Hareton was impressed with a wholesome terror of encountering either his wild-beast's fondness, or his madman's rage—for in one he ran a chance of being squeezed and kissed to death, and in the other of being flung into the fire, or dashed against the wall—and the poor thing remained perfectly quiet wherever I chose to put him.

"There, I've found it out at last!" cried Hindley, pulling me back by the skin of the neck, like a dog. "By Heaven and Hell, you've sworn between you to murder that child! I know how it is, now, that he is always out of my way. But, with the help of Satan, I shall make you swallow the carving knife, Nelly! You needn't laugh; for I've just crammed Kenneth head-downmost, in the Blackhorse marsh;[1] and two is the same as one—and I want to kill some of you, I shall have no rest till I do!"

"But I don't like the carving knife, Mr. Hindley," I answered, "it has been cutting red herrings—I'd rather be shot if you please."

"You'd rather be damned!" he said, "and so you shall—no law in England can hinder a man from keeping his house decent, and mine's abominable! Open your mouth."

He held the knife in his hand, and pushed its point between my teeth: but, for my part I was never much afraid of his vagaries. I spat out, and affirmed it tasted detestable—I would not take it on any account.

"Oh!" said he, releasing me, "I see that hideous little villain is not Hareton—I beg your pardon, Nell—if it be, he deserves flaying alive for not running to welcome me, and for screaming as if I were a goblin. Unnatural cub, come hither! I'll teach thee to impose on a good-hearted, deluded father—now, don't you think the lad would be handsomer cropped? It makes a dog fiercer, and I love something fierce—get me a scissors—something fierce and trim! Besides, it's infernal affectation—devilish conceit, it is, to

---

1   Baines, pp. 407, 522, notes public houses named Black Horse along the K&K at Skipton ('post chaises') and Hellifield; still open.

cherish our ears—we're asses enough without them. Hush, child, hush! Well then, it is my darling! wisht, dry thy eyes—there's a joy; kiss me; what, it won't? Kiss me, Hareton! Damn thee, kiss me! By God, as if I would rear such a monster! As sure as I'm living, I'll break the brat's neck!"

Poor Hareton was squalling and kicking in his father's arms with all his might, and redoubled his yells when he carried him up-stairs and lifted him over the bannister. I cried out that he would frighten the child into fits, and ran to rescue him.

As I reached them, Hindley leant forward on the rails to listen to a noise below; almost forgetting what he had in his hands.

"Who is that?" he asked, hearing some one approaching the stair's-foot.

I leant forward, also, for the purpose of signing to Heathcliff, whose step I recognized, not to come further; and, at the instant when my eye quitted Hareton, he gave a sudden spring, delivered himself from the careless grasp that held him, and fell.

There was scarcely time to experience a thrill of horror before we saw that the little wretch was safe. Heathcliff arrived underneath just at the critical moment; by a natural impulse, he arrested his descent, and setting him on his feet, looked up to discover the author of the accident.

A miser who has parted with a lucky lottery ticket for five shillings and finds next day he has lost in the bargain five thousand pounds, could not show a blanker countenance than he did on beholding the figure of Mr. Earnshaw above—it expressed, plainer than words could do, the intensest anguish at having made himself the instrument of thwarting his own revenge. Had it been dark, I dare say, he would have tried to remedy the mistake by smashing Hareton's skull on the steps; but, we witnessed his salvation; and I was presently below with my precious charge pressed to my heart.

Hindley descended more leisurely, sobered and abashed.

"It is your fault, Ellen," he said, "you should have kept him out of sight; you should have taken him from me! is he injured anywhere?"

"Injured!" I cried angrily, "if he's not killed he'll be an idiot! Oh! I wonder his mother does not rise from her grave to see how you use him. You're worse than a heathen—treating your own flesh and blood in that manner!"

He attempted to touch the child, who on finding himself with me sobbed off his terror directly. At the first finger his father laid on him, however, he shrieked again louder than before, and struggled as if he would go into convulsions.

"You shall not meddle with him!" I continued, "he hates you—they all hate you—that's the truth! A happy family you have; and a pretty state you're come to!"

"I shall come to a prettier, yet, Nelly!" laughed the misguided man, recovering his hardness. "At present, convey yourself and him away—and, hark you, Heathcliff! clear you too,[1] quite from my reach and hearing. I wouldn't murder you to-night, unless, perhaps I set the house on fire; but that's as my fancy goes—"

While saying this he took a pint bottle of brandy from the dresser, and poured some into a tumbler.

"Nay don't!" I entreated, "Mr. Hindley, do take warning. Have mercy on this unfortunate boy, if you care nothing for yourself!"

"Any one will do better for him, than I shall," he answered.

"Have mercy on your own soul!" I said, endeavouring to snatch the glass from his hand.

"Not I! on the contrary, I shall have great pleasure in sending it to perdition, to punish its maker," exclaimed the blasphemer, "Here's to its hearty damnation!"

He drank the spirits, and impatiently bade us go; terminating his command with a sequel of horrid imprecations, too bad to repeat, or remember.

"It's a pity he cannot kill himself with drink," observed Heathcliff, muttering an echo of curses back when the door was shut. "He's doing his very utmost; but his constitution defies him—Mr. Kenneth says he would wager his mare, that he'll outlive any man on this side Gimmerton, and go to the grave a hoary sinner; unless some happy chance out of the common course befall him."

I went into the kitchen and sat down to lull my little lamb to sleep. Heathcliff, as I thought, walked through to the barn. It turned out, afterwards, that he only got as far as the other side of

---

1   *clear you too…*: 'you, too, get away from me'.

the settle, when he flung himself on a bench by the wall, removed from the fire, and remained silent.

I was rocking Hareton on my knee, and humming a song that began:

> "It was far in the night, and the bairnies grat,
> The mither beneath the mools heard that"[1]

when Miss Cathy who had listened to the hubbub from her room, put her head in, and whispered,

"Are you alone, Nelly?"

"Yes, Miss," I replied.

She entered and approached the hearth. I, supposing she was going to say something, looked up. The expression of her face seemed disturbed and anxious. Her lips were half asunder as if she meant to speak; and she drew a breath, but it escaped in a sigh, instead of a sentence.

I resumed my song: not having forgotten her recent behaviour.

"Where's Heathcliff?" she said, interrupting me.

"About his work in the stable," was my answer.

He did not contradict me; perhaps, he had fallen into a doze.

There followed another long pause, during which I perceived a drop or two trickle from Catherine's cheek to the flags.

Is she sorry for her shameful conduct? I asked myself. That will be a novelty, but, she may come to the point as she will—I shan't help her!

No, she felt small trouble regarding any subject, save her own concerns.

"Oh, dear!" she cried at last, "I'm very unhappy!"

"A pity," observed I, "you're hard to please—so many friends and so few cares, and can't make yourself content!"

"Nelly, will you keep a secret for me?" she pursued, kneeling

---

1 "*It was far...*": 'It was late at night, and the children wept; from under the clods, their mother heard'. From the ballad in *Kempe Viser* (combat manual), translated from Danish in R. Jamieson, *Ballads* (1806) and included in the Notes to Walter Scott, *The Lady of the Lake* (1810) (*K*), p. 376-81.

down by me, and lifting her winsome eyes to my face with that sort of look which turns off bad temper, even, when one has all the right in the world to indulge it.

"Is it worth keeping?" I inquired less sulkily.

"Yes, and it worries me, and I must let it out! I want to know what I should do—today, Edgar Linton has asked me to marry him, and I've given him an answer—now, before I tell you whether it was a consent, or denial—you tell me which it ought to have been."

"Really, Miss Catherine, how can I know?" I replied. "To be sure, considering the exhibition you performed in his presence, this afternoon, I might say it would be wise to refuse him—since he asked you after that, he must either be hopelessly stupid, or a venturesome fool."

"If you talk so, I won't tell you any more," she returned, peevishly, rising to her feet. "I accepted him, Nelly; be quick, and say whether I was wrong!"

"You accepted him? Then, what good is it discussing the matter? You have pledged your word, and cannot retract."

"But, say whether I should have done so—do!" she exclaimed in an irritated tone; chafing her hands together, and frowning.

"There are many things to be considered, before that question can be answered properly," I said sententiously, "First and foremost, do you love Mr. Edgar?"

"Who can help it? of course I do," she answered.

The I put her through the following catechism—for a girl of twenty-two[1] it was not injudicious.

"Why do you love him, Miss Cathy?"

"Nonsense, I do—that's sufficient."

"By no means; you must say why!"

"Well, because he is handsome, and pleasant to be with."

"Bad," was my commentary.

"And because he is young and cheerful."

"Bad, still."

---

1   Nelly's twenty-seventh birthday has occurred when Hindley dies in the autumn of 1784 (ch. 17); her age in the summer of 1780 locates her birthday between summer and autumn, around the harvest moon (Appendix A).

"And, because he loves me."

"Indifferent; coming there."[1]

"And he will be rich, and I shall like to be the greatest woman of the neighbourhood, and I shall be proud of having such a husband."

"Worst of all! And, now, say how you love him?"

"As everybody loves—you're silly, Nelly."

"Not at all—answer."

"I love the ground under his feet, and the air over his head, and everything he touches, and every word he says—I love all his looks, and all his actions, and him entirely, and altogether. There now!"

"And why?"

"Nay—you are making a jest of it; it is exceedingly ill-natured! It's no jest to me!" said the young lady scowling, and turning her face to the fire.

"I'm very far from jesting, Miss Catherine," I replied, "you love Mr. Edgar, because he is handsome, and young, and cheerful, and rich, and loves you. The last, however, goes for nothing—you would love him without that, probably, and with it, you wouldn't unless he possessed the four former attractions."

"No, to be sure not—I should only pity him—hate him, perhaps, if he were ugly, and a clown."

"But, there are several other handsome, rich young men in the world; handsomer, possibly, and richer than he is—what should hinder you from loving them?"

"If there be any, they are out of my way—I've seen none like Edgar."

"You may see some; and he won't always be handsome, and young, and may not always be rich."

"He is now; and I have only to do with the present—I wish you would speak rationally."

"Well, that settles it—if you have only to do with the present, marry Mr. Linton."

"I don't want your permission for that—I *shall* marry him; and yet, you have not told me whether I'm right."

---

1   *Indifferent:* 'not a very good reason, but getting better'.

"Perfectly right; if people be right to marry only for the present. And now let us hear what you are unhappy about. Your brother will be pleased... The old lady and gentleman will not object, I think—you will escape from a disorderly, comfortless home into a wealthy respectable one; and you love Edgar, and Edgar loves you. All seems smooth and easy—where is the obstacle?"

"*Here!* and *here!*" replied Catherine, striking one hand on her forehead, and the other on her breast. "In whichever place the soul lives—in my soul, and in my heart, I'm convinced I'm wrong!"

"That's very strange! I cannot make it out."

"It's my secret; but if you will not mock at me, I'll explain it; I can't do it distinctly—but I'll give you a feeling of how I feel."

She seated herself by me again: her countenance grew sadder and graver, and her clasped hands trembled.

"Nelly do you never dream queer dreams?" she said, suddenly, after some minutes' reflection.

"Yes, now and then," I answered.

"And so do I. I've dreamt in my life dreams that have stayed with me ever after, and changed my ideas; they've gone through and through me, like wine through water, and altered the colour of my mind. And this is one—I'm going to tell it—but take care not to smile at any part of it."

"Oh! don't, Miss Catherine!" I cried. "We're dismal enough without conjuring up ghosts, and visions to perplex us. Come, come, be merry, and like yourself! Look at little Hareton—*he's* dreaming nothing dreary. How sweetly he smiles in his sleep!"

"Yes; and how sweetly his father curses in his solitude! You remember him, I dare say, when he was just such another as that chubby thing—nearly as young and innocent. However, Nelly, I shall oblige you to listen—it's not long; and I've no power to be merry to-night."

"I won't hear it, I won't hear it!" I repeated, hastily.

I was superstitious about dreams then, and am still; and Catherine had an unusual gloom in her aspect, that made me dread something from which I might shape a prophecy, and foresee a fearful catastrophe.

She was vexed, but she did not proceed. Apparently taking up another subject, she re-commenced in a short time.

"If I were in heaven, Nelly, I should be extremely miserable."

"Because you are not fit to go there," I answered. "All sinners would be miserable in heaven."

"But it is not for that. I dreamt, once, that I was there."

"I tell you I won't harken to your dreams, Miss Catherine! I'll go to bed," I interrupted again.

She laughed, and held me down, for I made a motion to leave my chair.

"This is nothing," cried she; "I was only going to say that heaven did not seem to be my home: and I broke my heart with weeping to come back to earth; and the angels were so angry that they flung me out, into the middle of the heath on the top of Wuthering Heights;[1] where I woke sobbing for joy. That will do to explain my secret, as well as the other. I've no more business to marry Edgar Linton than I have to be in heaven; and if the wicked man in there, had not brought Heathcliff so low I shouldn't have thought of it. It would degrade me to marry Heathcliff, now; so he shall never know how I love him; and that, not because he's handsome, Nelly, but because he's more myself than I am. Whatever our souls are made of, his and mine are the same, and Linton's is as different as a moonbeam from lightning, or frost from fire."

Ere this speech ended I became sensible of Heathcliff's presence. Having noticed a slight movement, I turned my head, and saw him rise from the bench, and steal out, noiselessly.[2] He had listened till he heard Catherine say it would degrade her to marry him, and then he staid to hear no farther.

---

1   Wuthering Heights: the first full reference to the eponymous hill; for a similar dream, see John Woolman, *Journal* (Appendix D).
2   Thomas Moore, *Letters and Journals of Lord Byron, with Notices of his Life*, 2 vols (1830), vol. 1, p. 55, notes the boy poet's dismay and running from her house on hearing himself mocked behind his back, but only for his deformity, by Mary Chaworth, the cousin whom he adored but who loved another; he wrote: 'Her sighs were not for him; to her he was / Even as a brother—nothing more'.

My companion, sitting on the ground, was prevented by the back of the settle from remarking his presence or departure; but I started, and bade her hush!

"Why?" she asked, gazing nervously round.

"Joseph is here," I answered, catching opportunely, the roll of his cartwheels up the road; "and Heathcliff will come in with him. I'm not sure whether he were not at the door this moment."

"Oh, he couldn't overhear me at the door!" said she. "Give me Hareton, while you get the supper, and when it is ready ask me to sup with you. I want to cheat my uncomfortable conscience, and be convinced that Heathcliff has no notion of these things—he has not, has he? He does not know what being in love is?"

"I see no reason that he should not know, as well as you," I returned; "and if *you* are his choice, he'll be the most unfortunate creature that ever was born! As soon as you become Mrs. Linton, he loses friend, and love, and all! Have you considered how you'll bear the separation, and how he'll bear to be quite deserted in the world? Because, Miss Catherine—"

"He quite deserted! we separated!" she exclaimed, with an accent of indignation. "Who is to separate us, pray? They'll meet the fate of Milo![1] Not as long as I live, Ellen—for no mortal creature. Every Linton on the face of the earth might melt into nothing, before I could consent to forsake Heathcliff. Oh, that's not what I intend—that's not what I mean! I shouldn't be Mrs. Linton were such a price demanded! He'll be as much to me as he has been all his lifetime. Edgar must shake off his antipathy, and tolerate him, at least. He will when he learns my true feelings towards him. Nelly, I see now, you think me a selfish wretch, but, did it never strike you that, if Heathcliff and I married, we

---

1   *the fate of Milo*: 'if anyone tries to keep us apart, they will punished like the Greek tyrant who was drowned by his subjects'. Ellis Bell appears to have had in mind the reference by Ovid to the Arcadian tyrant Milo, noted in J. Lemprière, *Classical Dictionary* (1792) (*K*): 'A tyrant of Pisa in Elis, thrown into the river Alpheus by his subjects for his oppression'. Alpheus was consecrated to poetry: Brontë suggests that poets such as herself might liberate slaves and victims of the marriage prohibition; see above, Introduction, 'The Marriage Prohibition', pp. 39-49; Lemprière, op. cit., notes two other figures named Milo.

should be beggars?[1] Whereas, if I marry Linton, I can aid Heathcliff to rise, and place him out of my brother's power."

"With your husband's money, Miss Catherine?" I asked. "You'll find him not so pliable as you calculate upon: and, though I'm hardly a judge, I think that's the worst motive you've given yet for being the wife of young Linton."

"It is not," retorted she, "it is the best! The others were the satisfaction of my whims; and for Edgar's sake, too, to satisfy him. This is for the sake of one who comprehends in his person my feelings to Edgar and myself. I cannot express it; but surely you and everybody have a notion that there is, or should be, an existence of yours beyond you. What were the use of my creation if I were entirely contained here? My great miseries in this world have been Heathcliff's miseries, and I watched and felt each from the beginning; my great thought in living is himself. If all else perished, and *he* remained, I should still continue to be; and, if all else remained, and he were annihilated, the Universe would turn to a mighty stranger. I should not seem a part of it. My love for Linton is like the foliage in the woods. Time will change it, I'm well aware, as winter changes the trees—my love for Heathcliff resembles the eternal rocks beneath[2]—a source of little visible delight, but necessary. Nelly, I *am* Heathcliff—he's always, always in my mind—not as a pleasure, any more than I am always a pleasure to myself—but, as my own being—so, don't talk of our separation again—it is impracticable; and—"

She paused, and hid her face in the folds of my gown; but I jerked it forcibly away. I was out of patience with her folly!

"If I can make any sense of your nonsense, Miss," I said, "it only goes to convince me that you are ignorant of the duties you undertake in marrying; or else, that you are a wicked, unprinci-

---

1   Nelly confesses her concealment of Heathcliff's having left before Catherine's declaration of love, but leaves unconfessed her concealment of the marriage prohibition, which does not affect her; see above, Introduction, 'The Marriage Prohibition', pp. 39-49.

2   For the geological metaphor, see above, Introduction, 'Signs of fertility', pp. 71-80; also, Adam Sedgwick, 'Letters to Wordsworth', and John Woolman, *Journal*, both below, Appendix D; also, C. Heywood, 'Yorkshire Landscapes in *Wuthering Heights*', *EIC*, 48 (1998), 13-34.

pled girl. But, trouble me with no more secrets. I'll not promise to keep them."

"You'll keep that?" she asked, eagerly.

"No, I'll not promise," I repeated.

She was about to insist, when the entrance of Joseph finished our conversation; and Catherine removed her seat to a corner, and nursed Hareton, while I made the supper.

After it was cooked, my fellow servant and I began to quarrel who should carry some to Mr. Hindley; and we didn't settle it till all was nearly cold. Then we came to the agreement that we would let him ask, if he wanted any, for we feared particularly to go into his presence when he had been sometime alone.

"Und hah isn't that nowt comed in frough th' field, be this time? What is he abaht? girt eedle seeght!"[1] demanded the old man, looking round for Heathcliff.

"I'll call him," I replied, "He's in the barn, I've no doubt."

I went and called, but got no answer. On returning, I whispered to Catherine that he had heard a good part of what she said, I was sure; and told how I saw him quit the kitchen just as she complained of her brother's conduct regarding him.

She jumped up in a fine fright—flung Hareton onto the settle, and ran to seek for her friend herself, not taking leisure to consider why she was so flurried, or how her talk would have affected him.

She was absent such a while that Joseph proposed we should wait no longer. He cunningly conjectured they were staying away in order to avoid hearing his protracted blessing. They were "ill eneugh for ony fahl manners,"[2] he affirmed. And, on their behalf, he added that night a special prayer to the usual quarter of an hour's supplication before meat, and would have tacked another to the end of the grace, had not his young mistress broken in upon him with a hurried command, that he must run down the road, and, wherever Heathcliff had rambled, find and make him re-enter directly!

---

1   *Und hah*: 'How come that ninny hasn't come in from the field by now? What does he think he's doing, that lubberly spectacle!'
2   *ill eneugh*: 'so bad they would be as rude as they please'.

"I want to speak to him, and I *must*, before I go upstairs," she said, "And the gate is open, he is somewhere out of hearing; for he would not reply, though I shouted at the top of the fold as loud as I could."

Joseph objected at first; she was too much in earnest, however, to suffer contradiction; and, at last, he placed his hat on his head, and walked grumbling forth.

Meantime, Catherine paced up and down the floor, exclaiming—

"I wonder where he is—I wonder where he *can* be! What did I say, Nelly? I've forgotten. Was he vexed at my bad humour this afternoon? Dear! tell me what I've said to grieve him? I do wish he'd come. I do wish he would!"

"What a noise for nothing!" I cried, though rather uneasy myself. "What a trifle scares you! It's surely no great cause of alarm that Heathcliff should take a moonlight saunter on the moors, or even lie too sulky to speak to us, in the hay-loft. I'll engage he's lurking there. See, if I don't ferret him out!"

I departed to renew my search; its result was disappointment, and Joseph's quest ended in the same.

"Yon lad gets war un war!" observed he on re-entering. "He's left th'yate ut t' full swing, and Miss's pony has trodden dahn two rigs uh corn, un plottered through, raight o'er intuh t' meadow! Hahsomdiver, t' maister 'ull play t' divil to-morn, and he'll do weel. He's patience itsseln wi' sich careless, offald craters—patience itsseln he is! Bud he'll nut be soa allus—yah's see, all on ye! Yah munn't drive him aht uf his heed fur nowt!"[1]

"Have you found Heathcliff, you ass?" interrupted Catherine, "Have you been looking for him, as I ordered?"

"Aw sud more likker look for th' horse," he replied. "It'ud be tuh more sense. Bud, aw can look for norther horse, nur man uf

---

1   *Yon lad*:'That boy gets worse and worse! [...] He's left the gate swinging wide open, and Missy's pony has flattened two hayricks, and trampled right across into the meadow! Well, anyway [however], the master will carry on like a devil until tomorrow, and that's the way he should. He puts up with that type of careless, rubbishy people—he's patience itself. But he won't always be like that—you'll all see that! You mustn't drive him mad for no reason!'

a neeght loike this—as black as t' chimbley! und Hathecliff's noan
t' chap tuh coom ut *maw* whistle—happen he'll be less hard uh
hearing wi' *he*!"[1]

It was a very dark evening for summer: the clouds appeared
inclined to thunder, and I said we had better all sit down; the approaching rain would be certain to bring him home without
further trouble.

However, Catherine would not be persuaded into tranquillity. She kept wandering to and fro, from the gate to the door, in
a state of agitation, which permitted no repose: and, at length,
took up a permanent situation on one side of the wall, near the
road; where, heedless of my expostulations, and the growling
thunder, and the great drops that began to plash around her, she
remained calling, at intervals, and then listening, and then crying
outright. She beat Hareton, or any child, at a good, passionate fit
of crying.

About midnight, while we still sat up, the storm came rattling
over the Heights in full fury. There was a violent wind, as well as
thunder, and either one or the other split a tree off at the corner
of the building; a huge bough fell across the roof, and knocked
down a portion of the east chimney-stack, sending a clatter of
stones and soot into the kitchen fire.

We thought a bolt had fallen in the middle of us, and Joseph
swung onto his knees, beseeching the Lord to remember the
patriarchs Noah and Lot; and, as in former times, spare the righteous, though he smote the ungodly. I felt some sentiment that it
must be a judgment on us also. The Jonah,[2] in my mind, was Mr.
Earnshaw, and I shook the handle of his den that I might ascertain
if he were yet living. He replied audibly enough, in a fashion
which made my companion vociferate more clamorously than

---

1   *Aw sud more likker look*: 'I'd do better to look for the horse. It'd make
    more sense. But I can't look for horse or man on a night like this, it's as
    black as the chimney! And Heathcliff's not the chap to come when *I*
    whistle—perhaps he'll be less deaf if *he* [Hindley] calls!'.
2   Joseph invokes figures trapped in national disaster who achieve their com-
    munity's survival through infringements of Mosaic law; see *Genesis* 5-9
    (Noah), 19-22 (Lot); *Jonah* 1-4; and *2 Peter* 2, 5-9 (Noah and Lot); also,
    Matthew 9:13: 'I am not come to call the righteous, but sinners […]'.

before that a wide distinction might be drawn between saints like himself, and sinners like his master. But, the uproar passed away in twenty minutes, leaving us all unharmed, excepting Cathy, who got thoroughly drenched for her obstinacy in refusing to take shelter, and standing bonnetless and shawlless to catch as much water as she could with her hair and clothes.

She came in, and lay down on the settle, all soaked as she was, turning her face to the back, and putting her hands before it.

"Well Miss!" I exclaimed, touching her shoulder, "you are not bent on getting your death, are you? Do you know what o'clock it is? Half-past twelve. Come! come to bed; there's no use waiting longer on that foolish boy—he'll be gone to Gimmerton, and he'll stay there now. He guesses we shouldn't wake for him till this late hour; at least, he guesses that only Mr. Hindley would be up; and he'd rather avoid having the door opened by the master."

"Nay, nay, he's noan at Gimmerton!" said Joseph. "Aw's niver wonder, bud he's at t' bothom uf a bog-hoile. This visitation worn't for nowt, und aw wod hev ye tuh look aht, Miss—yah muh be t' next. Thank Hiven for all! All warks togither for gooid tuh them as is chozzen, and piked aht froo' th' rubbidge! Yah knaw whet t' Scripture ses—"[1]

And he began quoting several texts; referring us to the chapters and verses, where we might find them.

I having vainly begged the wilful girl to rise and remove her wet things, left him preaching, and her shivering, and betook myself to bed with little Hareton; who slept as fast as if every one had been sleeping round him.

I heard Joseph read on a while afterwards; then, I distinguished his slow step on the ladder, and then I dropt asleep.

Coming down somewhat later than usual, I saw, by the sunbeams piercing the chinks of the shutters, Miss Catherine still seated near the fire-place. The house door was ajar, the light entered

---

1 *Nay, nay:* 'No, no, he's not at Gimmerton! I shouldn't wonder if he's at the bottom of a pot-hole. This tribulation isn't for nothing, and I would have you look out, Miss—you might be the next. Thank Heaven for everything! Everything works together for the good of the chosen ones who are picked out from the rubbish! You know what the Bible says—'

from its unclosed windows; Hindley had come out, and stood on the kitchen hearth, haggard and drowsy.

"What ails you, Cathy?" he was saying when I entered; "you look as dismal as a drowned whelp—why are you so damp and pale, child?"

"I've been wet," she answered reluctantly, "and I'm cold, that's all."

"Oh, she is naughty!" I cried, perceiving the master to be tolerably sober; "she got steeped in the shower of yesterday evening, and there she has sat, the night through, and I couldn't prevail on her to stir."

Mr. Earnshaw stared at us in surprise. "The night through," he repeated. "What kept her up, not fear of the thunder, surely? That was over, hours since."

Neither of us wished to mention Heathcliff's absence, as long as we could conceal it; so, I replied, I didn't know how she took it into her head to sit up; and she said nothing.

The morning was fresh and cool; I threw back the lattice, and presently the room filled with sweet scents from the garden: but Catherine called peevishly to me.

"Ellen, shut the window. I'm starving!"[1] And her teeth chattered as she shrunk closer to the almost extinguished embers.

"She's ill—" said Hindley, taking her wrist, "I suppose that's the reason she would not go to bed—Damn it! I don't want to be troubled with more sickness, here—what took you into the rain?"

"Running after t' lads, as usuald!" croaked Joseph, catching an opportunity, from our hesitation, to thrust in his evil tongue.

"If Aw wur yah, maister, Aw'd just slam t' boards i' their faces all on 'em, gentle and simple! Never a day ut yah're off, but yon cat uh Linton comes sneaking hither—and Miss Nelly shoo's a fine lass! shoo sits watching for ye i' t' kitchen; and as yah're in at one door, he's aht at t' other—Und, then, wer grand lady goes a coorting uf hor side! It's bonny behaviour, lurking among t' fields, after twelve ut' night, wi' that fahl, flaysome divil uf a gipsy Heathcliff! They think *Aw'm* blind; but Aw'm noan, nowt ut' soart!

---

1   *starving*: freezing.

Aw seed young Linton, boath coming and going, and Aw seed *yah* (directing his discourse to me) yah gooid fur nowt, slattenly witch! nip up und bolt intuh th' hahs, t' minute yah heard t' maister's horse fit clatter up t' road."[1]

"Silence, eavesdropper!" cried Catherine, "none of your insolence, before me! Edgar Linton came yesterday, by chance, Hindley: and it was *I* who told him to be off: because, I knew you would not like to have met him as you were."

"You lie, Cathy, no doubt," answered her brother, "and you are a confounded simpleton! But, never mind Linton, at present. Tell me, were you not with Heathcliff last night? Speak the truth, now. You need not be afraid of harming him—though I hate him as much as ever, he did me a good turn, a short time since, that will make my conscience tender of breaking his neck. To prevent it, I shall send him about his business, this very morning; and after he's gone, I'd advise you all to look sharp, I shall only have the more humour for you!"

"I never saw Heathcliff last night," answered Catherine, beginning to sob bitterly, "and if you do turn him out of doors, I'll go with him. But, perhaps, you'll never have an opportunity—perhaps, he's gone." Here she burst into uncontrollable grief, and the remainder of her words were inarticulate.

Hindley lavished on her a torrent of scornful abuse, and bid her get to her room immediately, or she shouldn't cry for nothing! I obliged her to obey, and I shall never forget what a scene she acted, when we reached her chamber. It terrified me—I thought she was going mad, and I begged Joseph to run for the doctor.

---

1   *If aw wur yah* [...]: 'If I were you, sir, I'd just slam the shutters in their faces, all of them, polished and rough! Whenever you are away, that tomcat Linton comes sneaking along, and that Miss Nelly, she's a fine lass! She sits watching for you in the kitchen, and as you come in at one door, he's out at the other—And then our grand lady goes courting on her own! It's a fine way to carry on, lurking in the fields after midnight, with that foul, dreadful gipsy devil Heathcliff! They think I'm blind, but I'm not, nothing of the sort! I've seen young Linton, coming and going, and I've seen *you* (addressing myself, Nelly), you good-for-nothing, slatternly witch!—nip along and slip into the house [living room] as soon as you heard the master's [Hindley's] horse's hooves clatter along the road.'

It proved to be the commencement of delirium. Mr. Kenneth, as soon as he saw her, pronounced her dangerously ill; she had a fever.

He bled her, and he told me to let her live on whey, and water gruel; and take care she did not throw herself down stairs, or out of the window; and then he left; for, he had enough to do in the parish where two or three miles was the ordinary distance between cottage and cottage.

Though I cannot say I made a gentle nurse, and Joseph and the master were no better; and, though our patient was as wearisome and headstrong as a patient could be, she weathered it through.

Old Mrs. Linton paid us several visits, to be sure; and set things to rights, and scolded and ordered us all; and when Catherine was convalescent, she insisted on conveying her to Thrushcross Grange; for which deliverance we were very grateful. But, the poor dame had reason to repent of her kindness; she and her husband both took the fever, and died within a few days of each other.

Our young lady returned to us, saucier, and more passionate, and haughtier than ever. Heathcliff had never been heard of since the evening of the thunder-storm, and, one day, I had the misfortune, when she had provoked me exceedingly, to lay the blame of his disappearance on her (where indeed it belonged, as she well knew). From that period for several months, she ceased to hold any communication with me save in the relation of a mere servant. Joseph fell under a ban also; he *would* speak his mind, and lecture her all the same as if she were a little girl; and she esteemed herself a woman, and our mistress; and thought that her recent illness gave her a claim to be treated with consideration. Then the doctor had said that she would not bear crossing much, she ought to have her own way; and it was nothing less than murder, in her eyes, for any one, to presume to stand up and contradict her.

From Mr. Earnshaw and his companions she kept aloof, and tutored by Kenneth, and serious threats of a fit that often attended her rages, her brother allowed her whatever she pleased to demand, and generally avoided aggravating her fiery temper. He was rather *too* indulgent in humouring her caprices; not from affection but from pride; he wished earnestly to see her bring honour to the family by an alliance with the Lintons, and, as long as she let him alone, she might trample us like slaves for ought he cared!

Edgar Linton, as multitudes have been before, and will be after him, was infatuated; and believed himself the happiest man alive on the day he led her to Gimmerton chapel, three years subsequent to his father's death.

Much against my inclination, I was persuaded to leave Wuthering Heights and accompany her here. Little Hareton was nearly five years old, and I had just begun to teach him his letters.

We made a sad parting, but Catherine's tears were more powerful than ours. When I refused to go, and when she found her entreaties did not move me, she went lamenting to her husband, and brother. The former offered me munificent wages; the latter ordered me to pack up—he wanted no woman in the house, he said, now that there was no mistress; and as to Hareton, the curate should take him in hand, by and bye. And so, I had but one choice left, to do as I was ordered—I told my master he got rid of all decent people only to run to ruin a little faster. I kissed Hareton good bye; and since then, he has been a stranger, and it's very queer to think it, but I've no doubt, he has completely forgotten all about Ellen Dean and that he was ever more than all the world to her, and she to him!

At this point of the housekeeper's story she chanced to glance towards the time-piece over the chimney; and was in amazement, on seeing the minute-hand measure half past one. She would not hear of staying a second longer—in truth, I felt rather disposed to defer the sequel of her narrative, myself: and now, that she is vanished to her rest, and I have meditated for another hour or two, I shall summon courage to go, also, in spite of aching laziness of head and limbs.

CHAPTER 10

A charming introduction to a hermit's life! Four weeks' torture, tossing and sickness! Oh, these bleak winds, and bitter northern skies, and
impassable roads, and dilatory country surgeons! And, oh, this dearth
of the human physiognomy, and, worse than all, the terrible intimation of Kenneth that I need not expect to be out of doors till spring!

Mr. Heathcliff has just honoured me with a call. About seven
days ago he sent me a brace of grouse—the last of the season.
Scoundrel! he is not altogether guiltless in this illness of mine; and
that I had a great mind to tell him. But, alas! how could I offend a
man who was charitable enough to sit at my bedside a good hour,
and talk on some other subject than pills, and draughts, blisters, and
leeches?

This is quite an easy interval. I am too weak to read, yet I feel
as if I could enjoy something interesting. Why not have up Mrs.
Dean to finish her tale? I can recollect its chief incidents, as far as
she had gone. Yes, I remember her hero had run off, and never
been heard of for three years: and her heroine was married. I'll
ring; she'll be delighted to find me capable of talking cheerfully.

Mrs. Dean came.

"It wants twenty minutes, sir, to taking the medicine," she
commenced.

"Away, away with it!" I replied; "I desire to have—"

"The doctor says you must drop the powders."

"With all my heart! Don't interrupt me. Come and take your
seat here. Keep your fingers from that bitter phalanx of vials.
Draw your knitting out of your pocket—that will do—now continue the history of Mr. Heathcliff, from where you left off, to the
present day. Did he finish his education on the Continent, and
come back a gentleman? Or did he get a sizer's place at college?
Or escape to America, and earn honours by drawing blood from
his foster country? Or make a fortune more promptly, on the
English highways?"[1]

---

1   *highways*: Heathcliff's entry into gentility and absence are adapted from
    Hope On, Hope Ever! (1840) (K), by Mary Howitt (Appendix B); sup-

"He may have done a little in all these vocations Mr. Lock-wood; but I couldn't give my word for any. I stated before that I didn't know how he gained his money; neither am I aware of the means he took to raise his mind from the savage ignorance into which it was sunk; but, with your leave, I'll proceed in my own fashion, if you think it will amuse, and not weary you. Are you feeling better this morning?"

"Much."

"That's good news. I got Miss Catherine and myself to Thrush-cross Grange: and to my agreeable disappointment, she behaved infinitely better than I dared to expect. She seemed almost over fond of Mr. Linton; and even to his sister, she showed plenty of affection. They were both very attentive to her comfort, certainly. It was not the thorn bending to the honeysuckles, but the honeysuckles embracing the thorn. There were no mutual concessions; one stood erect, and the others yielded; and who *can* be ill-natured, and bad-tempered, when they encounter neither opposition, nor indifference?

"I observed that Mr. Edgar had a deep-rooted fear of ruffling her humour. He concealed it from her; but if ever he heard me answer sharply, or saw any other servant grow cloudy at some imperious order of hers, he would show his trouble by a frown of displeasure that never darkened on his own account. He, many a time, spoke sternly to me about my pertness; and averred that the stab of a knife could not inflict a worse pang than he suffered at seeing his lady vexed.

"Not to grieve a kind master I learnt to be less touchy; and, for the space of half a year, the gunpowder lay as harmless as sand, because no fire came near to explode it. Catherine had seasons of gloom and silence, now and then; they were respected with sympathizing silence by her husband, who ascribed them to an alteration in her constitution, produced by her perilous illness, as she

---

positions about the sources of Heathcliff's wealth appear in *Heathcliff* (1977), by Jeffrey Caine, and Lin Haire-Sargeant, *H. The Story of Heathcliff's Journey Back to Wuthering Heights* (1992). However, the *WH* landscape ties Heathcliff to Liverpool and Lancaster, the neighbouring slave ports.

was never subject to depression of spirits before. The return of sunshine was welcomed by answering sunshine from him. I believe I may assert that they were really in possession of deep and growing happiness.

It ended. Well, we *must* be for ourselves in the long run; the mild and generous are only more justly selfish than the domineering—and it ended when circumstances caused each to feel that the one's interest was not the chief consideration in the other's thoughts.

On a mellow evening in September, I was coming from the garden with a heavy basket of apples which I had been gathering. It had got dusk, and the moon looked over the high wall of the court, causing undefined shadows to lurk in the corners of the numerous projecting portions of the building. I set my burden on the house steps by the kitchen door, and lingered to rest, and draw in a few more breaths of the soft, sweet air; my eyes were on the moon, and my back to the entrance, when I heard a voice behind me say—

"'Nelly, is that you?'

It was a deep voice, and foreign in tone; yet, there was something in the manner of pronouncing my name which made it sound familiar. I turned about to discover who spoke, fearfully, for the doors were shut, and I had seen nobody on approaching the steps.

Something stirred in the porch; and moving nearer, I distinguished a tall man dressed in dark clothes with dark face and hair. He leant against the side and held his fingers on the latch, as if intending to open for himself.

"Who can it be?" I thought. "Mr. Earnshaw? Oh, no! The voice has no resemblance to his."

"I have waited here an hour," he resumed, while I continued staring; "and the whole of that time all round has been as still as death. I dared not enter. You do not know me? Look, I'm not a stranger!"

A ray fell on his features; the cheeks were sallow, and half covered with black whiskers; the brows lowering, the eyes deep set and singular. I remembered the eyes.

"What!" I cried, uncertain whether to regard him as a worldly visitor,[1] and I raised my hands in amazement. "What! you come back? Is it really you? Is it?"

"Yes, Heathcliff," he replied, glancing from me up to the windows which reflected a score of glittering moons, but showed no lights from within. "Are they at home—where is she? Nelly, you are not glad—you needn't be so disturbed. Is she here? Speak! I want to have one word with her—your mistress. Go, and say some person from Gimmerton desires to see her."

"How will she take it?" I exclaimed, "what will she do? The surprise bewilders me—it will put her out of her head! And you *are* Heathcliff? But altered! Nay, there's no comprehending it. Have you been for a soldier?"

"Go, and carry my message," he interrupted impatiently; "I'm in hell till you do!"

He lifted the latch, and I entered; but when I got to the parlour where Mr. and Mrs. Linton were, I could not persuade myself to proceed.

At length, I resolved on making an excuse to ask if they would have the candles lighted, and I opened the door.

They sat together in a window whose lattice lay back against the wall, and displayed beyond the garden trees, and the wild green park, the valley of Gimmerton, with a long line of mist winding nearly to its top (for very soon after you pass the chapel, as you may have noticed, the sough that runs from the marshes joins a beck which follows the bend of the glen). Wuthering Heights rose above this silvery vapour; but our old house was invisible—it rather dips down on the other side.

Both the room and its occupants, and the scene they gazed on, looked wondrously peaceful. I shrank reluctantly from performing my errand: and was actually going away, leaving it unsaid after having put my question about the candles, when a sense of my folly compelled me to return, and mutter:

"A person from Gimmerton wishes to see you ma'am."

"What does he want?" asked Mrs. Linton.

"I did not question him," I answered.

---

1   *worldly visitor*: Nelly thinks he may be a ghost.

"Well, close the curtains, Nelly," she said; "and bring up tea. I'll be back again directly."

She quitted the apartment; Mr. Edgar inquired carelessly, who it was?

"Some one the mistress does not expect," I replied. "That Heathcliff, you recollect him, sir, who used to live at Mr. Earnshaw's."

"What, the gipsy—the plough-boy?" he cried. "Why did you not say so to Catherine?"

"Hush! you must not call him by those names, master," I said. "She'd be sadly grieved to hear you. She was nearly heart-broken when he ran off; I guess his return will make a jubilee to her."

Mr. Linton walked to a window on the other side of the room that overlooked the court. He unfastened it, and leant out. I suppose they were below, for he exclaimed, quickly:—

"Don't stand there love! Bring the person in, if it be any one particular."

Ere long, I hard the click of the latch, and Catherine flew upstairs, breathless and wild, too excited to show gladness; indeed, by her face, you would rather have surmised an awful calamity.

"Oh, Edgar, Edgar!" she panted, flinging her arms round his neck. "Oh, Edgar, darling! Heathcliff's come back—he is!" And she tightened her embrace to a squeeze.

"Well, well," cried her husband, crossly, "don't strangle me for that! He never struck me as such a marvellous treasure. There is no need to be frantic!"

"I know you didn't like him," she answered, repressing a little the intensity of her delight. "Yet for my sake, you must be friends now. Shall I tell him to come up?"

"Here," he said, "into the parlour?"

"Where else?" she asked.

He looked vexed, and suggested the kitchen as a more suitable place for him.

Mrs. Linton eyed him with a droll expression—half angry, half laughing at his fastidiousness.

"No," she added, after a while; "I cannot sit in the kitchen. Set two tables here, Ellen; one for your master and Miss Isabella, being gentry; and the other for Heathcliff and myself, being of the lower orders. Will that please you dear? Or must I have a fire lighted elsewhere? If so, give directions. I'll run down and secure my guest. I'm afraid the joy is too great to be real!"

She was about to dart off again; but Edgar arrested her.

"*You* bid him step up," he said, addressing me; "and, Catherine, try to be glad, without being absurd! The whole household need not witness the sight of your welcoming a runaway servant as a brother."

I descended and found Heathcliff waiting under the porch, evidently anticipating an invitation to enter. He followed my guidance without waste of words, and I ushered him into the presence of the master and mistress, whose flushed cheeks betrayed signs of warm talking. But the lady's glowed with another feeling when her friend appeared at the door; she sprang forward, took both his hands, and led him to Linton; and then she seized Linton's reluctant fingers and crushed them into his.

Now fully revealed by the fire and candle-light, I was amazed, more than ever, to behold the transformation of Heathcliff. He had grown a tall, athletic, well-formed man; beside whom, my master seemed quite slender and youth-like. His upright carriage suggested the idea of his having been in the army. His countenance was much older in expression, and decision of feature than Mr. Linton's; it looked intelligent, and retained no marks of former degradation. A half-civilized ferocity lurked yet in the depressed brows, and eyes full of black fire, but it was subdued; and his manner was even dignified, quite divested of roughness though too stern for grace.

My master's surprise equalled or exceeded mine: he remained for a minute at a loss how to address the ploughboy, as he had called him; Heathcliff dropped his slight hand, and stood looking at him coolly till he chose to speak.

"Sit down, sir," he said, at length. "Mrs. Linton, recalling old times, would have me give you a cordial reception, and, of course, I am gratified when anything occurs to please her."

"And I also," answered Heathcliff, "especially if it be anything in which I have a part. I shall stay an hour or two willingly."

He took a seat opposite Catherine, who kept her gaze fixed on him as if she feared he would vanish were she to remove it. He did not raise his to her, often; a quick glance now and then sufficed; but it flashed back, each time, more confidently, the undisguised delight he drank from hers.

They were too much absorbed in their mutual joy to suffer embarrassment; not so Mr. Edgar; he grew pale with pure annoyance, a feeling that reached its climax when his lady rose—and stepping across the rug, seized Heathcliff's hands again, and laughed like one beside herself.

"I shall think it a dream to-morrow! she cried. "I shall not be able to believe that I have seen, and touched, and spoken to you once more—and yet, cruel Heathcliff! you don't deserve this welcome. To be absent and silent for three years, and never to think of me!"

"A little more than you have thought of me!" he murmured. "I heard of your marriage, Cathy, not long since; and, while waiting in the yard below, I meditated this plan—just to have one glimpse of your face—a stare of surprise, perhaps, and pretended pleasure; afterwards settle my score with Hindley; and then prevent the law by doing execution on myself. Your welcome has put these ideas out of my mind; but beware of meeting me with another aspect next time! Nay, you'll not drive me off again—you were really sorry for me, were you? Well, there was cause. I've fought through a bitter life since I last heard your voice, and you must forgive me, for I struggled only for you!"

"Catherine, unless we are to have cold tea, please come to the table," interrupted Linton, striving to preserve his ordinary tone, and a due measure of politeness. "Mr. Heathcliff will have a long walk, wherever he may lodge to-night, and I'm thirsty."

She took her post before the urn; and Miss Isabella came, summoned by the bell; then, having handed their chairs forward, I left the room.

The meal hardly endured ten minutes—Catherine's cup was never filled, she could neither eat, nor drink. Edgar had made a slop in his saucer, and scarcely swallowed a mouthful.

Their guest did not protract his stay, that evening, above an hour longer. I asked, as he departed, if he went to Gimmerton?

"No, to Wuthering Heights," he answered, "Mr. Earnshaw invited me when I called this morning."

Mr. Earnshaw invited *him*! and *he* called on Mr. Earnshaw! I pondered this sentence painfully, after he was gone. Is he turning out a bit of a hypocrite, and coming into the country to work mischief under a cloak? I mused—I had a presentiment, in the bottom of my heart, that he had better have remained away.[1]

About the middle of the night, I was wakened from my first nap by Mrs. Linton gliding into my chamber, taking a seat on my bed-side, and pulling me by the hair to rouse me.

"I cannot rest, Ellen," she said by way of apology. "And I want some living creature to keep me company in my happiness! Edgar is sulky, because I'm glad of a thing that does not interest him—he refuses to open his mouth, except to utter pettish, silly speeches; and he affirmed I was cruel and selfish for wishing to talk when he was so sick and sleepy. He always contrives to be sick at the least cross! I gave a few sentences of commendation to Heathcliff, and he, either for a headache or a pang of envy, began to cry: so I got up and left him."

"What use is it praising Heathcliff to him?" I answered, "as lads they had an aversion to each other, and Heathcliff would hate just as much to hear him praised—it's human nature. Let Mr. Linton alone about him, unless you would like an open quarrel between them."

"But does it not show great weakness?" pursued she. "I'm not envious—I never feel hurt at the brightness of Isabella's yellow hair, and the whiteness of her skin; at her dainty elegance, and the fondness all the family exhibit for her. Even you Nelly, if we have a dispute sometimes, you back Isabella, at once; and I yield like a foolish mother—I call her a darling, and flatter her into a good temper. It pleases her brother to see us cordial, and that pleases me. But, they are very much alike—they are spoiled children, and fancy the world was made for their accommodation; and, though I humour both, I think a smart chastisement might improve them, all the same."

"You're mistaken, Mrs. Linton," said I, "They humour you—I know what there would be to do if they did not! You can well

---

1   See Appendix C for transformation and censorship of the Hornby story material.

afford to indulge their passing whims, as long as their business is to anticipate all your desires—you may, however fall out, at last, over something of equal consequence to both sides; and, then those you term weak are very capable of being as obstinate as you!"

"And then we shall fight to the death, shan't we, Nelly?" she returned laughing, "No! I tell you, I have such faith in Linton's love that I believe I might kill him and he wouldn't wish to retaliate."

I advised her to value him the more for his affection.

"I do," she answered, "but, he needn't resort to whining for trifles. It is childish; and, instead of melting into tears, because I said that Heathcliff was now worthy of any one's regard, and it would honour the first gentleman in the country to be his friend; he ought to have said it for me, and been delighted from sympathy. He must get accustomed to him, and he may as well like him—considering how Heathcliff has reason to object to him, I'm sure he behaved excellently!"

"What do you think of his going to Wuthering Heights?" I inquired. "He is reformed in every respect, apparently—quite a Christian—offering the right hand of fellowship to his enemies all round!"

"He explained it," she replied. "I wondered as much as you. He said he called to gather information concerning me, from you, supposing you resided there still; and Joseph told Hindley, who came out, and fell to questioning him of what he had been doing, and how he had been living: and finally, desired him to walk in. There were some persons sitting at cards—Heathcliff joined them; my brother lost some money to him; and, finding him plentifully supplied, he requested that he would come again in the evening, to which he consented. Hindley is too reckless to select his acquaintance prudently; he doesn't trouble himself to reflect on the causes he might have for mistrusting one whom he has basely injured. But, Heathcliff affirms his principal reason for resuming a connection with his ancient persecutor is a wish to install himself in quarters at walking distance from the Grange, and an attachment to the house where we lived together, and, likewise a hope that I shall have more opportunities of seeing him there than I could have if he settled in Gimmerton. He means to offer liberal payment for permission to lodge at the Heights; and doubtless my brother's covetousness will prompt him to accept the terms; he was always greedy, though what he grasps with one hand, he flings away with the other."

"It's a nice place for a young man to fix his dwelling in!" said I. "Have you no fear of the consequences, Mrs. Linton?"

"None for my friend," she replied, "his strong head will keep him from danger—a little for Hindley; but, he can't be made morally worse than he is; and I stand between him and bodily harm. The event of this evening has reconciled me to God, and humanity! I had risen in angry rebellion against providence— Oh, I've endured very, very bitter misery. Nelly! If Edgar knew how bitter, he'd be ashamed to cloud its removal with idle petulance. It was kindness for him which induced me to bear it alone: had I expressed the agony I frequently felt, he would have been taught to long for its alleviation as ardently as I. However, it's over, and I'll take no revenge on his folly—I can afford to suffer anything, hereafter! Should the meanest thing alive slap me on the cheek, I'd not only turn the other, but, I'd ask pardon for provoking it—and, as a proof, I'll go make my peace with Edgar instantly. Good-night—I'm an angel!"

In this self-complacent conviction she departed; and the success of her fulfilled resolution was obvious on the morrow. M r. Linton had not only abjured his peevishness (though his spirits seemed still subdued by Catherine's exuberance of vivacity) but he ventured no objection to her taking Isabella with her to Wuthering Heights in the afternoon; and she rewarded him with such a summer of sweetness and affection, in return, as made the house a paradise for several days; both master and servants profiting from the perpetual sunshine.

Heathcliff—Mr. Heathcliff I should say in future—used the liberty of visiting at Thrushcross Grange cautiously, at first: he seemed estimating how far its owner would bear his intrusion. Catherine also, deemed it judicious to moderate her expressions of pleasure in receiving him; and he gradually established his right to be expected.

He retained a great deal of the reserve for which his boyhood was remarkable, and that served to repress all startling demonstrations of feeling. My master's uneasiness experienced a lull, and further circumstances diverted it to another channel for a space.

His new source of trouble sprang from the not anticipated misfortune of Isabella Linton evincing a sudden and irresistible attraction towards the tolerated guest. She was at that time a charming young lady of eighteen;[1] infantile in manners, though possessed of keen wit, keen feelings, and a keen temper, too, if irritated. Her brother, who loved her tenderly, was appalled at this fantastic preference. Leaving aside the degradation of an alliance with a nameless man, and the possible fact that his property, in default of heirs male, might pass into such a one's power, he had sense to comprehend Heathcliff's disposition—to know that, though his exterior was altered, his mind was unchangeable, and unchanged. And he dreaded that mind; it revolted him; he shrank forebodingly from the idea of committing Isabella to its keeping.

He would have recoiled still more had he been aware that her attachment rose unsolicited, and was bestowed where it awakened no reciprocation of sentiment;[2] for the minute he discovered its existence, he laid the blame on Heathcliff's deliberate designing.

We had all remarked, during some time, that Miss Linton fretted and pined over something. She grew cross and wearisome, snapping at and teazing Catherine, continually, at the imminent risk of exhausting her limited patience. We excused her to a certain extent, on the plea of ill health—she was dwindling and fading before our eyes. But, one day when she had been peculiarly wayward, rejecting her breakfast, complaining that the servants did not do what she told them; that the mistress would allow her to be nothing in the house, and Edgar neglected her; that she had caught a cold with the doors being left open, and we let the par-

---

1   For Isabella's age, sixteen at this point, see Appendix A; 'eighteen' lends credibility to her choice.
2   Heathcliff avoids dissembling along the lines of the indifference feigned towards Queen Isabella by Abdelazer in *The Moor's Revenge*, by Aphra Behn, *Plays*, 3rd edn., 4 vols. (1724) (*P*), vol. 2: 'I have dissembled coldness all the while' (Act 1, Scene 1). In the play, the events leading to the lovers' deaths are inaugurated by Abdelazer's false repudiation (see below, Appendix B).

lour fire go out on purpose to vex her; with a hundred yet more frivolous accusations. Mrs. Linton peremptorily insisted that she should get to-bed; and, having scolded her heartily, threatened to send for the doctor.

Mention of Kenneth caused her to exclaim instantly, that her health was perfect, and it was only Catherine's harshness which made her unhappy.

"How can you say I am harsh, you naughty fondling?" cried the mistress, amazed at the unreasonable assertion. "You are surely losing your reason. When have I been harsh, tell me?"

"Yesterday," sobbed Isabella, "and now!"

"Yesterday!" said her sister-in-law. "On what occasion?"

"In our walk along the moor; you told me to ramble where I pleased, while you sauntered on with Mr. Heathcliff!"

"And that's your notion of harshness?" said Catherine, laughing. "It was no hint that your company was superfluous; we didn't care whether you kept with us or not; I merely thought Heathcliff's talk would have nothing entertaining for your ears."

"Oh, no," wept the young lady, "you wished me away, because you knew I looked to be there!"

"Is she sane?" asked Mrs. Linton, appealing to me. "I'll repeat our conversation, word for word, Isabella; and you point out any charm it could have had for you."

"I don't mind the conversation," she answered: "I wanted to be with—"

"Well!" said Catherine, perceiving her hesitate to complete the sentence.

"With him; and I won't be always sent off!" she continued, kindling up. "You are a dog in the manger, Cathy, and desire no one to be loved but yourself!"

"You are an impertinent little monkey!" exclaimed Mrs. Linton, in surprise. "But I'll not believe this idiocy! It is impossible that you can covet the admiration of Heathcliff—that you can consider him an agreeable person! I hope I have misunderstood you, Isabella?"

"No, you have not," said the infatuated girl. "I love him more than ever you loved Edgar; and he might love me if you would let him!"

"I wouldn't be you for a kingdom, then!" Catherine declared, emphatically—and she seemed to speak sincerely. "Nelly, help me to convince her of her madness. Tell her what Heathcliff is—an unreclaimed creature, without refinement—without cultivation; an arid wilderness of furze and whinstone. I'd as soon put that little canary into the park on a winter's day as recommend you to bestow your heart on him! It is deplorable ignorance of his character, child, and nothing else, which makes that dream enter your head. Pray don't imagine that he conceals depths of benevolence and affection beneath a stern exterior! He's not a rough diamond—a pearl-containing oyster of a rustic; he's a fierce, pitiless, wolfish man. I never say to him let this or that enemy alone, because it would be ungenerous or cruel to harm them—I say let them alone, because *I* should hate them to be wronged: and he'd crush you, like a sparrow's egg, Isabella, if he found you a troublesome charge. I know he couldn't love a Linton; and yet, he'd be quite capable of marrying your fortune, and expectations. Avarice is growing with him a besetting sin. There's my picture; and I'm his friend—so much so, that had he thought seriously to catch you, I should, perhaps, have held my tongue, and let you fall into his trap."

Miss Linton regarded her sister-in-law with indignation.

"For shame! for shame!" she repeated, angrily. "You are worse than twenty foes, you poisonous friend!"

"Ah! you won't believe me, then?" said Catherine. "You think I speak from wicked selfishness?"

"I'm certain you do," retorted Isabella; "and I shudder at you!"

"Good!" cried the other. "Try for yourself, if that be your spirit; I have done, and yield the argument to your saucy insolence."

"And I must suffer for her egotism!" she sobbed, as Mrs. Linton left the room. "All, all is against me; she has blighted my single consolation. But she uttered falsehoods, didn't she? Mr. Heathcliff is not a fiend; he has an honourable soul, and a true one, or how could he remember her?"

"Banish him from your thoughts, miss," I said. "He's a bird of bad omen; no mate for you. Mrs. Linton spoke strongly, and yet, I can't contradict her. She is better acquainted with his heart than I, or any one besides; and she never would represent him as worse than he is. Honest people don't hide their deeds. How has he been living? How has he got rich? Why is he staying at Wuthering Heights, the house of a man whom he abhors? They say Mr. Earnshaw is worse and worse since he came. They sit up all night together continually: and Hindley has been borrowing money on his land; and does nothing but play and drink, I heard only a week ago; it was Joseph who told me—I met him at Gimmerton."

"Nelly," he said, "we's hae a Crahnr's 'quest enah, at ahr folks. One on 'em's a'most getten his finger cut off wi'hauding t' other froo' sticking hisseln loik a cawlf. That's maister, yah knaw, ut's soa up uh going tuh t' grand 'sizes. He's noan feard uh t' Bench uh judges, norther Paul, nur Peter, nur John, nor Mathew,[1] nor noan on 'em, nut he! He fair like's he lang tuh set his brazened face agean 'em! And yon bonny lad Heathcliff, yah mind, he's a rare un! He can girn a laugh, as well's onybody at a raight divil's jest. Does he niver say nowt of his fine living amang us, when he goas tuh t' Grange? This is t' way on't—up at sun-dahn; dice, brandy, cloised shutters, und can'le lught till next day, at nooin—then, t' fooil gangs banning un raving tuh his cham'er, makking dacent fowks dig thur fingers i' thur lugs fur varry shaume; un' th' knave, wah! he carn cahnt his brass, un' ate, un' sleep, un' off tuh his neighbour's tuh gossip wi' t' wife. I' course, he tells Dame Catherine hah hor father's goold runs intuh his pocket, and her father's son gallops dahn t' Broad road, while he flees afore tuh oppen t' pikes?"[2]

---

1 Joseph confuses the Apostles, Evangelists, and *Judges*.

2 *pikes*: gates equipped with pikes or spikes (*turnpikes*) discouraged riders from avoiding payment by jumping them with their mounts; hence Turnpike Trusts, including the K&K. Joseph prophesies: "Nelly, we'll have a coroner's inquest, sure enough, amongst us. One of those two [Heathcliff] almost got his finger cut off when preventing the other [Hindley] from stabbing him like a calf. It's the master, you know, and he's so keen on going to the grand Assizes. He has no fear of the Bench or the judges, not Paul, nor Peter, nor John, nor Matthew—not he! He carries on as though he's longing to set his brazen face against them! And that fine lad Heathcliff, you know, he's a rare one! He can laugh with a grin as well as another over a proper devil's joke. When he goes to the Grange, does he ever say anything about how he lords it up here? That's how it goes—up at sunset, gambling and brandy behind closed shutters, and candle light till next day at noon—then the fool [Hindley]

Now, Miss Linton, Joseph is an old rascal, but no liar; and, if his account of Heathcliff's conduct be true, you would never think of desiring such a husband, would you?"

"You are leagued with the rest, Ellen!" she replied. "I'll not listen to your slanders. What malevolence you must have to wish to convince me that there is no happiness in the world!"

Whether she would have got over this fancy if left to herself, or persevered in nursing it perpetually, I cannot say; she had little time to reflect. The day after, there was a justice-meeting at the next town;[1] my master was obliged to attend; and Mr. Heathcliff, aware of his absence, called rather earlier than usual.

Catherine and Isabella were sitting in the library, on hostile terms, but silent. That latter, alarmed at her recent indiscretion, and the disclosure she had made of her secret feelings in a transient fit of passion; the former, on mature consideration, really offended with her companion; and, if she laughed again at her pertness, inclined to make it no laughing matter to *her*.

She did laugh as she saw Heathcliff pass the window. I was sweeping the hearth, and I noticed a mischievous smile on her lips. Isabella, absorbed in her meditations, or a book, remained till the door opened, and it was too late to attempt an escape, which she would gladly have done had it been practicable.

"Come in, that's right!" exclaimed the mistress, gaily, pulling a chair to the fire. "Here are two people sadly in need of a third to thaw the ice between them; and you are the very one we should both of us choose. Heathcliff, I'm proud to show you at last, somebody that dotes on you more than myself. I expect you to feel flattered—nay, it's not Nelly; don't look at her! My poor little sister-in-law is breaking her heart by mere contemplation of your

---

goes shouting and raving to his room, making decent folks dig their fingers into their ears in shame; and the rascal [Heathcliff], huh! he's too rich to count his money, and he eats, sleeps, and runs off to his neighbour to hobnob with his wife. And then—[does he] tell[s] Dame Catherine how her father's gold runs into his pocket, and her father's son gallops down the broad path to damnation, while he rushes ahead to open the gates?'

1 *next town*: counterpart of Kirkby Lonsdale, two and a quarter miles beyond Cowan Bridge (*Paterson*).

physical and moral beauty. It lies in your own power to be Edgar's brother! No, no, Isabella, you shan't run off," she continued, arresting, with feigned playfulness, the confounded girl who had risen indignantly. "We were quarrelling like cats about you, Heathcliff; and I was fairly beaten in protestations of devotion, and admiration; and, moreover, I was informed that if I would but have the manners to stand aside, my rival, as she will have herself to be, would shoot a shaft into your soul that would fix you for ever, and send my image into eternal oblivion!"

"Catherine," said Isabella, calling up her dignity, and disdaining to struggle from the tight grasp that held her, "I'd thank you to adhere to the truth and not slander me, even in joke! Mr. Heathcliff, be kind enough to bid this friend of yours release me—she forgets that you and I are not intimate acquaintances, and what amuses her is painful to me beyond expression."

As the guest answered nothing, but took his seat, and looked thoroughly indifferent what sentiments she cherished concerning him, she turned, and whispered an earnest appeal for liberty to her tormentor.

"By no means!" cried Mrs. Linton in answer. "I won't be named a dog in the manger again. You *shall* stay, now then! Heathcliff, why don't you evince satisfaction at my pleasant news? Isabella swears that the love Edgar has for me, is nothing to that she entertains for you. I'm sure she made some speech of the kind, did she not, Ellen? And she has fasted ever since the day before yesterday's walk, from sorrow and rage that I despatched her out of your society, under the idea of being unacceptable."

"I think you belie her," said Heathcliff, twisting his chair to face them. "She wishes to be out of my society now, at any rate!"

And he stared hard at the object of discourse, as one might do at a strange repulsive animal, a centipede from the Indies,[1] for instance, which curiosity leads one to examine in spite of the aversion it raises.

---

1   *a centipede from the Indies*: the Caribbean millipede, noted as a Galli-wasp in M.G. Lewis, *Journal of a West Indian Proprietor* (1834), p. 113, where an example appears, measuring 18 inches (46 cm): 'an Alligator in miniature, even more dreaded by the negroes than its great relation'.

The poor thing couldn't bear that; she grew white and red in rapid succession, and, while tears beaded her lashes, bent the strength of her small fingers to loosen the firm clutch of Catherine, and perceiving that, as fast as she raised one finger off her arm, another closed down, and she could not remove the whole together, she began to make use of her nails, and their sharpness presently ornamented the detainer's with crescents of red.

"There's a tigress!" exclaimed Mrs. Linton, setting her free, and shaking her hand with pain. "Begone, for God's sake, and hide your vixen face! How foolish to reveal those talons to *him*. Can't you fancy the conclusions he'll draw? Look, Heathcliff! they are instruments that will do execution—you must beware of your eyes."

"I'd wrench them off her fingers, if they ever menaced me," he answered, brutally, when the door had closed after her. "But, what did you mean by teasing the creature in that manner, Cathy? You were not speaking the truth, were you?"

"I assure you I was," she returned. "She has been pining for your sake several weeks; and raving about you this morning, and pouring forth a deluge of abuse, because I represented your failings in a plain light for the purpose of mitigating her adoration. But don't notice it further. I wished to punish her sauciness, that's all—I like her too well, my dear Heathcliff, to let you absolutely seize and devour her up."

"And I like her too ill to attempt it," said he, "except in a very ghoulish fashion. You'd hear of odd things, if I lived alone with that mawkish, waxen face; the most ordinary would be painting on its white the colours of the rainbow, and turning the blue eyes, black, every day or two; they detestably resemble Linton's."

"Delectably," observed Catherine. "They are dove's eyes— angels!"

"She's her brother's heir, is she not?" he asked, after a brief silence.

"I should be sorry to think so," returned his companion. "Half-a-dozen nephews shall erase her title, please Heaven! Abstract your mind from the subject, at present—you are too prone to covet your neighbour's goods: remember *this* neighbour's goods are mine."

"If they were *mine*, they would be none the less that," said Heathcliff, "but though Isabella Linton may be silly, she is scarcely mad; and—in short we'll dismiss the matter as you advise."

From their tongues, they did dismiss it; and Catherine, probably, from her thoughts. The other, I felt certain, recalled it often in the course of the evening; I saw him smile to himself—grin rather—and lapse into ominous musing whenever Mrs. Linton had occasion to be absent from the apartment.

I determined to watch his movements. My heart invariably cleaved to the master's in preference to Catherine's side; with reason, I imagined, for he was kind, and trustful, and honourable: and she—she could not be called the *opposite*, yet, she seemed to allow herself such wide latitude, that I had little faith in her principles, and still less sympathy for her feelings. I wanted something to happen which might have the effect of freeing both Wuthering Heights and the Grange of Mr. Heathcliff, quietly, leaving us as we had been prior to his advent. His visits were a continual nightmare to me; and, I suspected, to my master also. His abode at the Heights was an oppression past explaining. I felt that God had forsaken the stray sheep there to its own wicked wanderings, and an evil beast prowled between it and the fold, waiting his time to spring and destroy.

CHAPTER 11

Sometimes, while meditating on these things in solitude, I've got up in a sudden terror, and put on my bonnet to go see how all was at the farm. I've persuaded my conscience that it was a duty to warn him how people talked regarding his ways; and then I've recollected his confirmed bad habits, and, hopeless of benefiting him, have flinched from re-entering the dismal house, doubting if I could bear to be taken at my word.

One time, I passed the old gate, going out of my way, on a journey to Gimmerton. It was about the period that my narrative has reached—a bright, frosty afternoon; and the ground bare, and the road hard and dry.

I came to a stone where the highway branches off on to the moor at your left hand; a rough hand-pillar,[1] with the letters W.H. cut on its north side, on the east, G., and on the south-west, T.G. It serves as a guide-post to the Grange and Heights, and village.

The sun shone yellow on its grey head[2] reminding me of summer; and I cannot say why, but all at once, a gush of child's sensations flowed into my heart. Hindley and I held it a favourite spot twenty years before.

I gazed long at the weather-worn block; and, stooping down, perceived a hole near the bottom still full of snail-shells and pebbles which we were fond of storing there with more perishable

---

1   *hand-pillar*: *WH* (1847) and all other edns. have *sand-pillar*, however, such an object has not appeared in Yorkshire or further afield. Emily's zigzag formation of the letters *h* and *s* (Emily Brontë, 'Gondal Poems', BL. Add. MS. 43, 483) would account for a printer's misreading of *hand-pillar*, the word probably intended in her manuscript. Patterned on the wooden *finger-post* used in southern counties, *hand-pillar* translates *stoop*, the northern guidestone or stone waymark. To remove ambiguity, hand signs were introduced on stoops around 1700; these required a 90-degree rotation of the early form, which had been planted in the form of labels or modern motor road signs, the names set at right angles to the direction of travel. See Howard Smith and Chris Boulton, *The Guide Stoops of Derbyshire* (Sheffield, 1996); W.B. Crump, *Huddersfield Highways down the Ages* (Huddersfield, 1988); and above, plate 13.

2   *grey head*: the underlying colour of limestone, here altered by sunlight.

things—and, as fresh as reality, it appeared that I beheld my early playmate seated on the withered turf; his dark, square head bent forward, and his little hand scooping out the earth with a piece of slate.

"Poor Hindley!" I exclaimed, involuntarily.

I started—my bodily eye was cheated into a momentary belief that the child lifted its face and stared straight into mine! It vanished in a twinkling; but, immediately, I felt an irresistible yearning to be at the Heights. Superstition urged me to comply with this impulse—supposing he should be dead![1] I thought—or should die soon!—supposing it were a sign of death!

The nearer I got to the house the more agitated I grew: and on catching sight of it, I trembled in every limb. The apparition had outstripped me; it stood looking through the gate. That was my first idea on observing an elf-locked, brown-eyed boy setting his ruddy countenance against the bars. Further reflection suggested this must be Hareton, *my* Hareton, not altered greatly since I left him, ten months since.

"God bless thee, darling!" I cried, forgetting instantaneously my foolish fears. "Hareton, it's Nelly, Nelly, thy nurse."

He retreated out of arm's length, and picked up a large flint.[2]

"I am come to see thy father, Hareton," I added, guessing from the action that Nelly, if she lived in his memory at all, was not recognised as one with me.

He raised his missile to hurl it; I commenced a soothing speech, but could not stay his hand. The stone struck my bonnet, and then ensued, from the stammering lips of the little fellow, a string of curses which, whether he comprehended them or not, were delivered with practised emphasis, and distorted his baby features into a shocking expression of malignity.

---

1   Patterned on Wordsworth's poem beginning 'Strange fits of passion have I known' and ending 'if Lucy should be dead!', Nelly's childhood love for Hindley is a lightly sketched subplot in *WH*. For an enlargement or engrossment along lines borrowed from novels by Henry James and L.P. Hartley, see *Catherine, Her Book* (1974), by John Wheatcroft.

2   *flint*: more probably chert or whinstone, a northern volcanic mineral resembling flint; see P.F. Kendall and H.E. Wroot, *Geology of Yorkshire*, 2 vols. (1924), vol. 1, pp. 253-58.

You may be certain this grieved, more than angered me. Fit to cry, I took an orange from my pocket, and offered it to propitiate him.

He hesitated, and then snatched it from my hold, as if he fancied I only intended to tempt, and disappoint him.

I showed another, keeping it out of his reach.

"Who has taught you those fine words, my barn,"[1] I inquired. "The curate?"

"Damn the curate, and thee! Gie me that," he replied.

"Tell us where you got your lessons, and you shall have it," said I. "Who's your master?"

"Devil daddy," was his answer.

"And what do you learn from Daddy?" I continued.

He jumped at the fruit; I raised it higher. "What does he teach you?" I asked.

"Naught," said he, "but to keep out of his gait—Daddy cannot bide me, because I swear at him."

"Ah! and the devil teaches you to swear at Daddy?" I observed.

"Aye—nay," he drawled.

"Who then?"

"Heathcliff."

I asked if he liked Mr. Heathcliff?

"Aye!" he answered again.

Desiring to have his reasons for liking him, I could only gather the sentences, "I known't—he pays Dad back what he gies to me—he curses Daddy for cursing me—he says I mun do as I will."

"And the curate does not teach you to read and write, then?" I pursued.

"No, I was told the curate should have his —— teeth dashed down his —— throat, if he stepped over the threshold—Heathcliff had promised that!"

I put the orange in his hand; and bade him tell his father that a woman called Nelly Dean was waiting to speak with him, by the garden gate.

---

1   *barn*: child, bairn; in a tale told by Bridget to Giles in Carr, vol. 2, p. 292, a southern tourist asks: 'Good day to you, good woman, have you got a barn?' and she replies, 'Eigh, says I, hauf a dozen'.

He went up the walk, and entered the house; but, instead of Hindley, Heathcliff appeared on the door-stones, and I turned directly and ran down the road as hard as ever I could race, making no halt till I gained the guide-post, and feeling as scared as if I had raised a goblin.

This is not much connected with Miss Isabella's affair; except, that it urged me to resolve further on mounting vigilant guard, and doing my utmost to check the spread of such bad influence at the Grange, even though I should wake a domestic storm, by thwarting Mrs. Linton's pleasure.

The next time Heathcliff came, my young lady chanced to be feeding some pigeons in the court. She had never spoken a word to her sister-in-law, for three days; but, she had likewise dropped her fretful complaining, and we found it a great comfort.

Heathcliff had not the habit of bestowing a single unnecessary civility on Miss Linton, I knew. Now, as soon as he beheld her, his first precaution was to take a sweeping survey of the house-front. I was standing by the kitchen window, but I drew out of sight. He then stept across the pavement to her, and said something: she seemed embarrassed, and desirous of getting away; to prevent it, he laid his hand on her arm: she averted her face; he apparently put some question which she had no mind to answer. There was another rapid glance at the house, and supposing himself unseen, the scoundrel had the impudence to embrace her.

"Judas! Traitor!" I ejaculated, "you are a hypocrite too, are you? A deliberate deceiver."

"Who is, Nelly?" said Catherine's voice at my elbow—I had been over-intent on watching the pair outside to mark her entrance.

"Your worthless friend!" I answered warmly, "the sneaking rascal yonder—Ah, he has caught a glimpse of us—he is coming in! I wonder will he have the art to find a plausible excuse, for making love to Miss, when he told you he hated her?"

Mrs. Linton saw Isabella tear herself free, and run into the garden; and a minute after, Heathcliff opened the door.

I couldn't withhold giving some loose to my indignation; but Catherine angrily insisted on silence, and threatened to order me out of the kitchen, if I dared be so presumptuous as to put in my insolent tongue.

"To hear you, people might think *you* were the mistress!" she cried. "You want setting down in your right place! Heathcliff, what are you about, raising this stir? I said you must let Isabella alone! I beg you will unless you are tired of being received here, and wish Linton to draw the bolts against you!"

"God forbid that he should try!" answered the black villain—I detested him just then. "God keep him meek and patient! Every day I grow madder after sending him to heaven!"

"Hush!" said Catherine, shutting the inner door. "Don't vex me. Why have you disregarded my request? Did she come across you on purpose?"

"What is it to you?" he growled, "I have a right to kiss her, if she chooses, and you have no right to object—I'm not *your* husband! *You* needn't be jealous of me!"

"I'm not jealous of you," replied the mistress, "I'm jealous for you. Clear your face, you shan't scowl at me! If you like Isabella, you shall marry her. But, do you like her, tell the truth, Heathcliff? There, you won't answer. I'm certain you don't!"

"And would Mr. Linton approve of his sister marrying that man?" I inquired.

"Mr. Linton should approve," returned my lady decisively.

"He might spare himself the trouble," said Heathcliff, "I could do as well without his approbation—and, as to you, Catherine, I have a mind to speak a few words, now, while we are at it—I want you to be aware that I *know* you have treated me infernally—infernally! Do you hear? And, if you flatter yourself that I don't perceive it you are a fool—and if you think I can be consoled by sweet words you are an idiot—and if you fancy I'll suffer unrevenged, I'll convince you of the contrary, in a very little while! Meantime, thank you for telling me your sister-in-law's secret—I swear I'll make the most of it, and stand you aside!"

"What new phase of his character is this?" exclaimed Mrs. Linton, in amazement. "I've treated you infernally—and you'll take revenge! How will you take it, ungrateful brute? How have I treated you infernally?"

"I seek no revenge on you," replied Heathcliff less vehemently. "That's not the plan—the tyrant grinds down his slaves and they don't turn against him, they crush those beneath them—you are welcome to torture me to death for your amusement, only, allow me to amuse myself a little in the same style—and refrain from insult, as much as you are able. Having levelled my palace, don't erect a hovel and complacently admire your own charity in giving me that for a home. If I imagined you really wished me to marry Isabella, I'd cut my throat!"

"Oh the evil is that I am *not* jealous, is it?" cried Catherine. "Well, I won't repeat my offer of a wife—it is as bad as offering Satan a lost soul—your bliss lies, like his, in inflicting misery—you prove it—Edgar is restored from the ill-temper he gave way to at your coming; I begin to be secure and tranquil; and, you, restless to know us at peace, appear resolved on exciting a quarrel—quarrel with Edgar if you please, Heathcliff, and deceive his sister; you'll hit on exactly the most efficient method of revenging yourself on me."

The conversation ceased—Mrs. Linton sat down by the fire, flushed and gloomy. The spirit which served her was growing intractable: she could neither lay nor control it. He stood on the hearth, with folded arms brooding on his evil thoughts; and in this position I left them to seek the master, who was wondering what kept Catherine below so long.

"Ellen," said he, when I entered, "have you seen your mistress?"

"Yes, she's in the kitchen, sir," I answered. "She's sadly put out by Mr. Heathcliff's behaviour: and, indeed, I do think it's time to arrange his visits on another footing. There's harm in being too soft, and now it's come to this—." And I related the scene in the court, and, as near as I dared, the whole subsequent dispute. I fancied it could not be very prejudicial to Mrs. Linton, unless she made it so, afterwards, by assuming the defensive for her guest.

Edgar Linton had difficulty in hearing me to the close—his first words revealed that he did not clear his wife of blame.

"This is insufferable!" he exclaimed. "It is disgraceful that she should own him for a friend, and force his company on me! Call me two men out of the hall, Ellen—Catherine shall linger no longer to argue with the low ruffian—I have humoured her enough."

He descended, and, bidding the servants wait in the passage, went, followed by me, to the kitchen. Its occupants had recommenced their angry discussion; Mrs. Linton, at least, was scolding with renewed vigour; Heathcliff had moved to the window, and hung his head somewhat cowed, by her violent rating apparently.

He saw the master first, and made a hasty motion that she should be silent; which she obeyed, abruptly, on discovering the reason of his intimation.

"How is this?" said Linton, addressing her; "what notion of propriety must you have to remain here, after the language which has been held to you by that blackguard? I suppose, because it is his ordinary talk, you think nothing of it—you are habituated to his baseness, and, perhaps, imagine I can get used to it too!"

"Have you been listening at the door, Edgar?" asked the mistress, in a tone particularly calculated to provoke her husband, implying both carelessness and contempt of his irritation.

Heathcliff, who had raised his eyes at the former speech, gave a sneering laugh at the latter, on purpose, it seemed, to draw Mr. Linton's attention to him.

He succeeded; but Edgar did not mean to entertain him with any high flights of passion.

"I have been so far forbearing with you, sir," he said, quietly; "not that I was ignorant of your miserable, degraded character, but, I felt you were only partly responsible for that; and Catherine, wishing to keep up your acquaintance, I acquiesced—foolishly. Your presence is a moral poison that would contaminate the most virtuous—for that cause, and to prevent worse consequences, I shall deny you, hereafter, admission into this house, and give notice, now, that I require your instant departure. Three minutes' delay will render it involuntary and ignominious."

Heathcliff measured the height and breadth of the speaker with an eye full of derision.

"Cathy, this lamb of yours threatens like a bull!" he said. "It is in danger of splitting its skull against my knuckles. By God, Mr. Linton, I'm mortally sorry that you are not worth knocking down!"

My master glanced towards the passage, and signed me to fetch the men—he had no intention of hazarding a personal encounter.

I obeyed the hint; but Mrs. Linton suspecting something, followed, and when I attempted to call them, she pulled me back, slammed the door to, and locked it.

"Fair means!" she said, in answer to her husband's look of angry surprise. "If you have not the courage to attack him, make an apology, or allow yourself to be beaten. It will correct you of feigning more valour than you possess. No, I'll swallow the key before you shall get it! I'm delightfully rewarded for my kindness to each! After constant indulgence of one's weak nature, and the other's bad one, I earn, for thanks, two samples of blind ingratitude, stupid to absurdity! Egad, I was defending you, and yours; and I wish Heathcliff may flog you sick, for daring to think an evil thought of me!"

It did not need the medium of a flogging to produce that effect on the master. He tried to wrest the key from Catherine's grasp; and for safety she flung it into the hottest part of the fire; whereupon Mr. Edgar was taken with a nervous trembling, and his countenance grew deadly pale. For his life he could not avert that access of emotion—mingled anguish and humiliation overcame him completely. He leant on the back of a chair, and covered his face.

"Oh! Heavens! In old days this would win you knighthood!" exclaimed Mrs. Linton. "We are vanquished! We are vanquished! Heathcliff would as soon lift a finger at you as the king would march his army against a colony of mice. Cheer up, you shan't be hurt. Your type is not a lamb, it's a sucking leveret."

"I wish you joy of the milk-blooded coward, Cathy!" said her friend. "I compliment you on your taste: and that is the slavering shivering thing you preferred to me! I would not strike him with my fist, but I'd kick him with my foot, and experience considerable satisfaction. Is he weeping, or is he going to faint for fear?"

The fellow approached and gave the chair on which Linton rested a push. He'd better have kept his distance: my master quickly sprang erect, and struck him full on the throat a blow that would have levelled a slighter man.

It took his breath for a minute; and, while he choked, Mr. Linton walked out by the back door into the yard, and from thence, to the front entrance.

"There! You've done with coming here," cried Catherine. "Get away, now—he'll return with a brace of pistols, and half-a-dozen assistants. If he did overhear us, of course, he'd never forgive you.

You've played me an ill turn, Heathcliff! But, go—make haste! I'd rather see Edgar at bay than you."

"Do you suppose I'm going with that blow burning in my gullet?" he thundered. "By Hell, no! I'll crush his ribs in like a rotten hazel-nut, before I cross the threshold! If I don't floor him now, I shall murder him sometime, so, as you value his existence, let me get at him!"

"He is not coming," I interposed, framing a bit of a lie. "There's the coachman, and the two gardeners; you'll surely not wait to be thrust into the road by them! Each has a bludgeon, and master will, very likely, be watching from the parlour windows to see that they fulfil his orders."

The gardeners and coachman *were* there; but Linton was with them. They had already entered the court. Heathcliff, on second thoughts resolved to avoid a struggle against three underlings; he seized the poker, smashed the lock from the inner door, and made his escape as they tramped in.

Mrs. Linton, who was very much excited, bid me accompany her up stairs. She did not know my share in contributing to the disturbance, and I was anxious to keep her in ignorance.

"I'm nearly distracted, Nelly!" she exclaimed, throwing herself on the sofa. "A thousand smiths' hammers are beating in my head! Tell Isabella to shun me—this uproar is owing to her; and should she or anyone else aggravate my anger at present, I shall get wild. And, Nelly, say to Edgar, if you see him again to-night, that I'm in danger of being seriously ill—I wish it may prove true. He has startled and distressed me shockingly! I want to frighten him. Besides, he might come and begin a string of abuse, or complainings; I'm certain I should recriminate, and God knows where we should end! Will you do so, my good Nelly? You are aware that I am no way blameable in this matter. What possessed him to turn listener? Heathcliff's talk was outrageous, after you left us; but I could soon have diverted him from Isabella, and the rest meant nothing. Now, all is dashed wrong by the fool's-craving to hear evil of self that haunts some people like a demon! Had Edgar never gathered our conversation, he would never have been the worse for it. Really, when he opened on me in that unreasonable tone of displeasure, after I had scolded Heathcliff till I was hoarse for *him*; I did not care, hardly, what they did to each other, especially as I felt that, however the scene closed, we should all be driven asunder for nobody knows how long! Well, if I cannot keep Heathcliff for my friend—if Edgar will be mean and jealous, I'll try to break their hearts by breaking my own. That will be a prompt way of finishing all, when I am pushed to extremity! But it's a deed to be reserved for a forlorn hope[1]—I'd not take Linton by surprise with it. To this point he has been discreet in dreading to provoke me; you must represent the peril of quitting that policy; and remind him of my passionate temper, verging, when kindled, on frenzy—I wish you could dismiss that apathy out of your countenance, and look rather more anxious about me!"

The stolidity with which I received these instructions was, no doubt, rather exasperating; for they were delivered in perfect sincerity, but I believed a person who could plan the turning of her fits of passion to account, beforehand, might, by exerting her will, manage to control herself tolerably even while under their influence; and I did not wish to "frighten" her husband, as she said, and multiply his annoyances for the purpose of serving her selfishness.

Therefore I said nothing when I met the master coming towards the parlour; but I took the liberty of turning back to listen whether they would resume their quarrel together.

He began to speak first.

"Remain where you are, Catherine," he said, without any anger in his voice, but with much sorrowful despondency. "I shall not stay. I am neither come to wrangle, nor be reconciled: but I wish just to learn whether, after this evening's events, you intend to continue your intimacy with—"

"Oh, for mercy's sake," interrupted the mistress, stamping her foot, "for mercy's sake, let us hear no more of it now! Your cold blood cannot be worked into a fever—your veins are full of ice-water—but mine are boiling, and the sight of such chilliness makes them dance."

---

1 *forlorn hope*: 'the soldiers who are sent first to attack, and are therefore doomed to perish', Samuel Johnson, *Dictionary of the English Language* (1756) (Dutch: *verloren*, lost; *hoop*, group of men).

"To get rid of me—answer my question" persevered Mr. Linton. "You *must* answer it; and that violence does not alarm me. I have found that you can be as stoical as any one, when you please. Will you give up Heathcliff hereafter, or will you give up me? It is impossible for you to be *my* friend, and *his* at the same time; and I absolutely *require* to know which you choose."

"I require to be let alone!" exclaimed Catherine, furiously, "I demand it! Don't you see I can scarcely stand? Edgar, you—you leave me!"

She rung the bell till it broke with a twang: I entered leisurely. It was enough to try the temper of a saint, such senseless, wicked rages! There she lay dashing her head against the arm of the sofa, and grinding her teeth, so that you might fancy she would crash them to splinters!

Mr. Linton stood looking at her in sudden compunction and fear. He told me to fetch some water. She had no breath for speaking.

I brought a glass full; and, as she would not drink, I sprinkled it on her face. In a few seconds she stretched herself out stiff, and turned up her eyes, while her cheeks, at once blanched and livid, assumed the aspect of death.

Linton looked terrified.

"There is nothing in the world the matter," I whispered. I did not want him to yield, though I could not help being afraid in my heart.

"She has blood on her lips!" he said, shuddering.

"Never mind!" I answered, tartly. And I told him how she had resolved, previous to his coming, on exhibiting a fit of frenzy.

I incautiously gave the account aloud, and she heard me, for she started up—her hair flying over her shoulders, her eyes flashing, the muscles of her neck and arms standing out preternaturally. I made up my mind for[1] broken bones, at least; but she only glared about her, for an instant, and then rushed from the room.

The master directed me to follow; I did, to her chamber door; she hindered me from going farther by securing it against me.

---

1   *made up my mind for*: began to expect.

As she never offered to descend to breakfast next morning, I went to ask whether she would have some carried up.

"No!" she replied, peremptorily.

The same question was repeated at dinner, and tea; and again on the morrow after, and received the same answer.

Mr. Linton, on his part, spent his time in the library, and did not inquire concerning his wife's occupations. Isabella and he had had an hour's interview, during which he tried to elicit from her some sentiment of proper horror for Heathcliff's advances; but he could make nothing of her evasive replies, and was obliged to close the examination, unsatisfactorily; adding, however, a solemn warning, that if she were so insane as to encourage that worthless suitor, it would dissolve bonds of relationship between herself and him.

CHAPTER 12

While Miss Linton moped about the park and garden, always silent, and almost always in tears; and her brother shut himself up among books that he never opened; wearying, I guessed, with a continual vague expectation that Catherine, repenting her conduct, would come of her own accord to ask pardon, and seek a reconciliation; and *she* fasted pertinaciously, under the idea, probably, that at every meal, Edgar was ready to choke her for her absence, and pride alone held him from running to cast himself at her feet; I went about my household duties, convinced that the Grange had but one sensible soul in its walls, and that lodged in my body.

I wasted no condolences on miss, nor any expostulations on my mistress, nor did I pay attention to the sighs of my master who yearned to hear his lady's name, since he might not hear her voice.

I determined they should come about as they pleased for me; and though it was a tiresomely slow process, I began to rejoice at length in a faint dawn of its progress, as I thought at first.

Mrs. Linton, on the third day, unbarred her door; and having finished the water in her pitcher and decanter, desired a renewed supply, and basin of gruel, for she believed she was dying. That I set down as a speech meant for Edgar's ears, I believed no such thing, so I kept it to myself, and brought her some tea and dry toast.

She ate and drank eagerly; and sank back on her pillow again clenching her hands and groaning.

"Oh, I will die," she exclaimed, "since no one cares anything about me. I wish I had not taken that."

Then a good while after I heard her murmur, "No, I'll not die—he'd be glad—he does not love me at all—he would never miss me!"

"Did you want anything, ma'am?" I enquired, still preserving my external composure, in spite of her ghastly countenance, and strange exaggerated manner.

"What is that apathetic being doing?" she demanded, pushing the thick entangled locks from her wasted face. "Has he fallen into a lethargy, or is he dead?"

"Neither," replied I; "if you mean Mr. Linton. He's tolerably well, I think, though his studies occupy him rather more than they ought; he is continually among his books, since he has no other society."

I should not have spoken so, if I had known her true condition, but I could not get rid of the notion that she acted a part of her disorder.

"Among his books!" she cried, confounded. "And I dying! I on the brink of the grave! My God! does he know how I'm altered?" continued she, staring at her reflection in a mirror, hanging against the opposite wall. "Is that Catherine Linton? He imagines me in a pet—in play, perhaps. Cannot you inform him that it is frightful earnest? Nelly, if it be not too late, as soon as I learn how he feels, I'll choose between these two—either to starve,[1] at once: that would be no punishment unless he had a heart—or to recover and leave the country.[2] Are you speaking the truth about him now? Take care. Is he actually so utterly indifferent for my life?"

"Why, ma'am," I answered, "the master has no idea of your being deranged; and, of course, he does not fear that you will let yourself die of hunger."

"You think not? Cannot you tell him I will?" she returned; "persuade him—speak of your own mind—say you are certain I will!"

"No, you forget, Mrs. Linton," I suggested, "that you have eaten some food with relish this evening, and to-morrow you will perceive its good effects."

"If I were only sure it would kill him," she interrupted, "I'd kill myself directly! These three awful nights, I've never closed my lids—and oh, I've been tormented! I've been haunted, Nelly! But I begin to fancy you don't like me. How strange! I thought, though everybody hated and despised each other, they could not avoid loving me—and they have all turned to enemies in a few hours. *They* have, I'm positive; the people *here*. How dreary to meet death, surrounded by their cold faces! Isabella, terrified and

---

1   *starve*: here, die of hunger.
2   *country*: district.

repelled, afraid to enter the room, it would be so dreadful to watch Catherine go. And Edgar standing solemnly by to see it over; then offering prayers of thanks to God for restoring peace to his house, and going back to his *books*! What in the name of all that feels, has he to do with *books*, when I am dying?"

She could not bear the notion which I had put into her head of Mr. Linton's philosophical resignation. Tossing about, she increased her feverish bewilderment to madness, and tore the pillow with her teeth, then raising herself up all burning, desired that I would open the window. We were in the middle of winter, the wind blew strong from the north-east, and I objected.

Both the expressions flitting over her face, and the changes of her moods, began to alarm me terribly; and brought to my recollection her former illness, and the doctor's injunction that she should not be crossed.

A minute previously she was violent; now, supported on one arm, and not noticing my refusal to obey her, she seemed to find childish diversion in pulling the feathers from the rents she had just made, and ranging them on the sheet according to their different species: her mind had strayed to other associations.

"That's a turkey's," she murmured to herself; "and this is a wild-duck's; and this is a pigeon's. Ah, they put pigeons' feathers[1] in the pillows—no wonder I couldn't die! Let me take care to throw it on the floor when I lie down. And here is a moor-cock's; and this—I should know it among a thousand—it's a lapwing's. Bonny bird; wheeling over our heads in the middle of the moor. It wanted to get to its nest, for the clouds touched the swells, and it felt rain coming. This feather was picked up from the heath, the bird was not shot—we saw its nest in the winter, full of little skeletons. Heathcliff set a trap over it, and the old ones dare not come. I made him promise he'd never shoot a lapwing, after that, and he didn't. Yes, here are more! Did he shoot my lapwings, Nelly? Are they red, any of them? Let me look."

"Give over with that baby-work!" I interrupted, dragging the

---

1   *pigeons' feathers*: R. Blakeborough, in his *Wit, Character, Folklore and Customs of the North Riding of Yorkshire* (1911), p. 116, notes the belief that 'the soul cannot free itself if the dying person has been laid on a bed containing pigeon feathers, or the feathers of wild birds even'.

pillow away, and turning the holes towards the mattress, for she was removing its contents by handfuls. "Lie down and shut your eyes, you're wandering. There's a mess! The down is flying about like snow!"

I went here and there collecting it.

"I see in you, Nelly," she continued, dreamily, "an aged woman—you have grey hair, and bent shoulders. This bed is the fairy cave[1] under Peniston Crag,[2] and you are gathering elf-bolts[3] to hurt our heifers; pretending, while I am near, that they are only locks of wool. That's what you'll come to fifty hears hence; I know you are not so now. I'm not wandering, you're mistaken, or else I should believe you really *were* that withered hag, and I should think I *was* under Penistone Crag, and I'm conscious it's night, and there are two candles on the table making the black press[4] shine like jet."

"The black press? Where is that?" I asked. "You are talking in your sleep!"

"It's against the wall, as it always is," she replied. "It *does* appear odd—I see a face in it!"

"There is no press in the room, and never was," said I, resuming my seat, and looping up the curtain that I might watch her.

"Don't *you* see that face?" she enquired, gazing earnestly at the mirror.

And say what I could, I was incapable of making her comprehend it to be her own; so I rose and covered it with a shawl.

"It's behind there still!" she pursued, anxiously. "And it stirred. Who is it? I hope it will not come out when you are gone! Oh! Nelly, the room is haunted! I'm afraid of being alone!"

---

1   *fairy cave*: Hutton notes Yordas Cave, the Yorkshire counterpart of the Fairy Cave in *WH*, as 'alternately the habitation of giants and fairies, as the different mythology prevailed in the country'; see below, Appendix D.

2   *Peniston Crag*: the name is taken from Penistone Crag, a quarrying site on Haworth Moor.

3   *elf-bolts*: R. Blakeborough, p. 137, notes that he showed flint arrowheads 'to an old fellow who was hedging; without hesitation he pronounced it to be an elf-stone, declaring that elves were evil spirits, who in days past used to throw them at the kie [cows]'.

4   *press*: wardrobe.

I took her hand in mine, and bid her be composed, for a succession of shudders convulsed her frame, and she *would* keep straining her gaze towards the glass.

"There's nobody here!" I insisted. "It was *yourself*, Mrs. Linton; you knew it a while since."

"Myself!" she gasped, "and the clock is striking twelve! It's true then; that's dreadful!"

Her fingers clutched the clothes, and gathered them over her eyes. I attempted to steal to the door with an intention of calling her husband; but I was summoned back by a piercing shriek. The shawl had dropped from the frame.

"Why what *is* the matter?" cried I. "Who is coward now? Wake up! That is the glass—the mirror, Mrs. Linton; and you see yourself in it, and there am I too by your side."

Trembling and bewildered, she held me fast, but the horror gradually passed from her countenance; its paleness gave place to a glow of shame.

"Oh dear! I thought I was at home," she sighed. "I thought I was lying in my chamber at Wuthering Heights. Because I'm weak, my brain got confused, and I screamed unconsciously. Don't say anything; but stay with me. I dread sleeping, my dreams appal me."

"A sound sleep would do you good, ma'am," I answered; "and I hope this suffering will prevent you trying starving again."

"Oh, if I were but in my own bed in the old house!" she went on bitterly, wringing her hands. "And that wind sounding in the firs by the lattice. Do let me feel it—it comes straight down the moor—do let me have one breath!"

To pacify her, I held the casement ajar, a few seconds. A cold blast rushed through, I closed it, and returned to my post.

She lay still, now: her face bathed in tears—exhaustion of body had entirely subdued her spirit; our fiery Catherine was no better than a wailing child!

"How long is it since I shut myself in here?" she asked, suddenly reviving.

"It was Monday evening," I replied, "and this is Thursday night, or rather Friday morning, at present."

"What! of the same week?" she exclaimed. "Only that brief time?"

"Long enough to live on nothing but cold water, and ill-temper," observed I.

"Well, it seems a weary number of hours," she muttered doubtfully, "it must be more—I remember being in the parlour, after they had quarrelled; and Edgar being cruelly provoking, and me running into this room desperate—as soon as ever I had barred the door, utter blackness overwhelmed me, and I fell on the floor. I couldn't explain to Edgar how certain I felt of having a fit, or going raging mad, if he persisted in teasing me! I had no command of tongue, or brain, and he did not guess my agony, perhaps; it barely left me sense to try to escape from him and his voice. Before I recovered, sufficiently to see, and hear, it began to be dawn; and Nelly, I'll tell you what I thought, and what has kept recurring and recurring till I feared for my reason—I thought as I lay there with my head against that table leg, and my eyes dimly discerning the grey square of the window, that I was enclosed in the oak-panelled bed at home; and my heart ached with some great grief which, just waking, I could not recollect—I pondered, and worried myself to discover what it could be; and most strangely, the whole last seven years of my life grew a blank! I did not recall that they had been at all. I was a child; my father was just buried, and my misery arose from the separation that Hindley had ordered between me, and Heathcliff—I was laid alone, for the first time, and rousing from a dismal doze after a night of weeping— I lifted my hand to push the panels aside, it struck the table-top! I swept it along the carpet, and then, memory burst in—my late anguish was swallowed in a paroxysm of despair—I cannot say why I felt so wildly wretched—it must have been temporary derangement for there is scarcely cause—But, supposing at twelve years old, I had been wrenched from the Heights, and every early association, and my all in all, as Heathcliff was at that time, and been converted at a stroke into Mrs. Linton, the lady of Thrushcross Grange, and the wife of a stranger; an exile, and outcast, thenceforth, from what had been my world—you may fancy a glimpse of the abyss where I grovelled! Shake your head, as you will, Nelly, *you* have helped to unsettle me! You should have spoken to Edgar, indeed you should, and compelled him to leave me quiet! Oh, I'm burning! I wish I were out of doors—I wish I were a girl again, half savage and hardy, and free...and laughing at injuries, not maddening under them! Why am I so changed? why does my blood rush into a hell of tumult at a few words? I'm sure I should be myself were I once among the heather on those hills... Open the window again wide, fasten it open! Quick, why don't you move?"

"Because, I won't give you your death of cold," I answered.

"You won't give me a chance of life, you mean," she said sullenly. "However, I'm not helpless yet, I'll open it myself."

And sliding from the bed before I could hinder her, she crossed the room, walking very uncertainly, threw it back, and bent out, careless of the frosty air that cut about her shoulders as keen as a knife.

I entreated, and finally attempted to force her to retire. But I soon found her delirious strength much surpassed mine; (she *was* delirious, I became convinced by her subsequent actions, and ravings.)

There was no moon, and everything beneath lay in misty darkness; not a light gleamed from any house, far or near; all had been extinguished long ago; and those at Wuthering Heights were never visible...still she asserted she caught their shining.

"Look!" she cried eagerly, "that's my room, with the candle in it, and the trees swaying before it...and the other candle is in Joseph's garret...Joseph sits up late, doesn't he? He's waiting till I come home that he may lock the gate...well, he'll wait a while yet. It's a rough journey, and a sad heart to travel it; and we must pass by Gimmerton Kirk,[1] to go that journey! We've braved its ghosts often together, and dared each other to stand among the graves and ask them to come...But Heathcliff, if I dare you now, will you venture? If you do, I'll keep you. I'll not lie there by myself; they may bury me twelve feet deep, and throw the church

---

1   *Kirk*: parish church; also termed chapel; in the discussion between Giles and Bridget in Carr, vol. 2, p. 311, on Methodism and the Anglican church, Bridget observes: 'Our kirk doesn't allow wer Parsons to preeach i'chapels unconsecrated (I think they caw it) bi' th' Bishop'. See also, George Lawton, *Collections Relative to Churches and Chapels within the Diocese of York* (1842); and the map *Yorkshire Ancient Chapelries and Parishes* (Leeds: Yorkshire Archaeological Society, 1973).

down over me; but I won't rest till you are with me...I never will!"

She paused, and resumed with a strange smile, "he's considering...he'd rather I'd come to him! Find a way, then! not through that Kirkyard...you are slow! Be content, you always followed me!"

Perceiving it vain to argue against her insanity, I was planning how I could reach something to wrap about her, without quitting my hold of herself, for I could not trust her alone by the gaping lattice; when to my consternation, I heard the rattle of the door-handle, and Mr. Linton entered. He had only then come from the library, and, in passing through the lobby, had noticed our talking, and been attracted by curiosity, or fear, to examine what it signified at that late hour.

"Oh, sir!" I cried, checking the exclamation risen to his lips at the sight which met him, and the bleak atmosphere of the chamber.

"My poor Mistress is ill, and she quite masters me; I cannot manage her at all, pray, come and persuade her to go to bed. Forget your anger, for she's hard to guide any way but her own."

"Catherine ill?" he said hastening to us. "Shut the window, Ellen! Catherine! why..."

He was silent; the haggardness of Mrs. Linton's appearance smote him speechless, and he could only glance from her to me in horrified astonishment.

"She's been fretting here," I continued, "and eating scarcely anything, and never complaining; she would admit none of us till this evening, and so we couldn't inform you of her state, as we were not aware of it ourselves, but it is nothing."

I felt I uttered my explanations awkwardly; the master frowned. "It is nothing is it, Ellen Dean?" he said sternly. "You shall account more clearly for keeping me ignorant of this!" And he took his wife in his arms, and looked at her with anguish.

At first she gave him no glance of recognition...he was invisible to her abstracted gaze. The delirium was not fixed, however; having weaned her eyes from contemplating the outer darkness, by degrees, she centred her attention on him, and discovered who it was that held her.

"Ah! you are come, are you, Edgar Linton?" she said with angry animation..." You are one of those things that are ever found when least wanted, and when you are wanted never! I suppose we shall have plenty of lamentations, now...I see we shall...but they can't keep me from my narrow home out yonder—my resting place where I'm bound before Spring is over! There it is, not among the Lintons, mind, under the chapel-roof; but in the open air with a head-stone, and you may please yourself, whether you go to them, or come to me!"

"Catherine, what have you done?" commenced the master. "Am I nothing to you, any more? Do you love that wretch, Heath—"

"Hush!" cried Mrs. Linton. "Hush, this moment! You mention that name and I end the matter, instantly, by a spring from the window! What you touch at present, you may have; but my soul will be on that hilltop before you lay hands on me again. I don't want you, Edgar; I'm past wanting you...Return to your books...I'm glad you possess a consolation, for all you had in me is gone."

"Her mind wanders, sir," I interposed. "She has been talking nonsense the whole evening; but, let her have quiet and proper attendance, and she'll rally...Hereafter, we must be cautious how we vex her."

"I desire no further advice from you," answered Mr. Linton. "You know your mistress's nature, and you encouraged me to harass her. And not to give me one hint of how she has been these three days! It was heartless! Months of sickness could not cause such a change!"

I began to defend myself, thinking it too bad to be blamed for another's wicked waywardness!

"I knew Mrs. Linton's nature to be headstrong and domineering," cried I; "but I didn't know that you wished to foster her fierce temper! I didn't know that, to humour her, I should wink at Mr. Heathcliff. I performed the duty of a faithful servant in telling you, and I have got a faithful servant's wages! Well, it will teach me to be careful next time. Next time you may gather intelligence for yourself!"

"The next time you bring a tale to me, you shall quit my service, Ellen Dean," he replied.

"You'd rather hear nothing about it, I suppose, then, Mr. Linton?" said I. "Heathcliff has your permission to come a courting to Miss and to drop in at every opportunity your absence offers, on purpose to poison the mistress against you?"

Confused as Catherine was, her wits were alert at applying our conversation.

"Ah! Nelly has played traitor," she exclaimed, passionately. "Nelly is my hidden enemy—you witch! So you do seek elf-bolts to hurt us! Let me go, and I'll make her rue! I'll make her howl a recantation!"

A maniac's fury kindled under her brows; she struggled desperately to disengage herself from Linton's arms. I felt no inclination to tarry the event; and resolving to seek medical aid on my own responsibility, I quitted the chamber.

In passing the garden to reach the road, at a place where a bridle hook is driven into the wall, I saw something white, moved irregularly evidently by another agent than the wind. Notwithstanding my hurry, I staid to examine it, lest ever after I should have the conviction impressed on my imagination that it was a creature of the other world.

My surprise and perplexity were great to discover, by touch more than vision, Miss Isabella's springer Fanny, suspended to a handkerchief, and nearly at its last gasp.

I quickly released the animal, and lifted it into the garden. I had seen it follow its mistress up-stairs, when she went to bed, and wondered much how it could have got out there, and what mischievous person had treated it so.

While untying the knot round the hook, it seemed to me that I repeatedly caught the beat of horses' feet galloping at some distance; but there were such a number of things to occupy my reflections that I hardly gave the circumstance a thought, though it was a strange sound, in that place, at two o'clock in the morning.

Mr. Kenneth was fortunately just issuing from his house to see a patient in the village as I came up the street; and my account of Catherine Linton's malady induced him to accompany me back immediately.

He was a plain, rough man; and he made no scruple to speak his doubts of her surviving this second attack, unless she were more submissive to his directions than she had shown herself before.

"Nelly Dean," said he, "I can't help fancying there's an extra cause for this. What has there been to do at the Grange? We've odd reports up here. A stout, hearty lass like Catherine does not fall ill for a trifle; and that sort of people should not either. It's hard work bringing them through fevers, and such things. How did it begin?"

"The master will inform you," I answered; "but you are acquainted with the Earnshaws' violent dispositions, and Mrs. Linton caps them all. I may say this; it commenced in a quarrel. She was struck during a tempest of passion with a kind of fit. That's her account, at least; for she flew off in the height of it, and locked herself up. Afterwards, she refused to eat, and now she alternatively raves, and remains in a half dream, knowing those about her, but having her mind filled with all sorts of strange ideas and illusions."

"Mr. Linton will be sorry?" observed Kenneth, interrogatively.

"Sorry? He'll break his heart should anything happen!" I replied. "Don't alarm him more than necessary."

"Well, I told him to beware," said my companion, "and he must bide the consequences of neglecting my warning! Hasn't he been thick[1] with Mr. Heathcliff lately?"

"Heathcliff frequently visits at the Grange," answered I, "though more on the strength of the mistress having known him when a boy, than because the master likes his company. At present, he's discharged from the trouble of calling; owing to some presumptuous aspirations after Miss Linton which he manifested. I hardly think he'll be taken in again."

"And does Miss Linton turn a could shoulder on him?" was the doctor's next question.

"I'm not in her confidence," returned I, reluctant to continue the subject.

"No, she's a sly one," he remarked, shaking his head. "She keeps her own counsel! But she's a real little fool. I have it from good authority, that, last night, and a pretty night it was! she and

---

1   *thick*: close, intimate.

Heathcliff were walking in the plantation at the back of your house, above two hours; and he pressed her not to go in again, but just mount his horse and away with him! My informant said she could only put him off by pledging her word of honour to be prepared on their first meeting after that—when it was to be, he didn't hear, but you urge Mr. Linton to look sharp!"

This news filled me with fresh fears; I outstripped Kenneth, and ran most of the way back. The little dog was yelping in the garden yet. I spared a minute to open the gate for it, but instead of going to the house door, it coursed up and down snuffing the grass, and would have escaped to the road, had I not seized and conveyed it in with me.

On ascending to Isabella's room, my suspicions were confirmed; it was empty. Had I been a few hours sooner, Mrs. Linton's illness might have arrested her rash step. But what could be done now? There was a bare possibility of overtaking them if pursued instantly.[1] I could not pursue them, however, and I dare not rouse the family, and fill the place with confusion; still less unfold the business to my master, absorbed as he was in his present calamity, and having no heart to spare for a second grief!

I saw nothing for it, but to hold my tongue, and suffer matters to take their course: and Kenneth being arrived, I went with a badly composed countenance to announce him.

Catherine lay in a troubled sleep; her husband had succeeded in soothing the access of frenzy; he now hung over her pillow, watching every shade, and every change of her painfully expressive features.

The doctor, on examining the case for himself, spoke hopefully to him of its having a favourable termination, if we could only preserve around her perfect and constant tranquillity. To me, he

---

1   *pursued instantly*: proximity to Gretna Green is secured by the distance of 300 miles to London (ch. 21). Scottish marriages for English couples who lacked parental consent had been encouraged by the Hardwicke Act (1753), but began to disappear after the Marriage and Registry Acts (1837) for which Lord Brougham had campaigned; see *Speeches of Henry Lord Brougham*, 4 vols. (1838), 'Discourse on the Law of Marriage, Divorce, and Legitimacy', vol. 3, pp. 429-471; also, Warren Henry, *Gretna Green Romances* (1926).

signified the threatening danger was, not so much death, as permanent alienation of intellect.

I did not close my eyes that night, nor did Mr. Linton; indeed, we never went to bed: and the servants were all up long before the usual hour, moving through the house with stealthy tread, and exchanging whispers as they encountered each other in their vocations. Every one was active, but Miss Isabella; and they began to remark how sound she slept—her brother too asked if she had risen, and seemed impatient for her presence, and hurt that she showed so little anxiety for her sister-in-law.

I trembled lest he should send me to call her; but I was spared the pain of being the first proclaimant of her flight. One of the maids, a thoughtless girl, who had been on an early errand to Gimmerton, came panting up stairs, open-mouthed, and dashed into the chamber, crying,

"Oh, dear, dear! What mun we have next? Master, master, our young lady—"

"Hold your noise!" cried I hastily, enraged at her clamorous manner.

"Speak lower, Mary—what is the matter?" said Mr. Linton. "What ails your young lady?"

"She's gone, she's gone! Yon' Heathcliff's run off wi' her!" gasped the girl.

"That's not true!" exclaimed Linton, rising in agitation. "It cannot be—how has the idea entered you head? Ellen Dean, go and seek her—it is incredible—it cannot be."

As he spoke he took the servant to the door, and, then, repeated his demand to know her reasons for such an assertion.

"Why, I met on the road a lad that fetches milk here," she stammered, "and he asked whether we wern't in trouble at the Grange—I though he meant for Missis's sickness, so I answered, yes. Then says he, 'they's somebody gone after 'em, I guess?' I stared. He saw I knew naught about it, and he told how a gentleman and lady had stopped to have a horse's shoe fastened at a blacksmith's shop, two miles out of Gimmerton,[1] not very long

---

1   *blacksmith's shop*: Baines, p. 631, lists Alexander Kirkbride and James Lister as blacksmiths serving the K&K at Westhouses, two miles from Ingleton

after midnight. And how the blacksmith's lass had got up to spy who they were: she knew them both directly—and she noticed the man, Heathcliff it was, she felt certain, nob'dy could mistake him, besides—put a sovereign in her father's hand for payment. The lady had a cloak about her face; but having desired a sup of water, while she drank, it fell back, and she saw her very plain— Heathcliff held both bridles as they rode on, and they set their faces from the village, and went as fast as the rough roads would let them. The lass said nothing to her father, but she told it all over Gimmerton this morning."

I ran and peeped, for form's sake, into Isabella's room: con-firming, when I returned, the servant's statement. Mr. Linton had resumed his seat by the bed; on my re-entrance, he raised his eyes, read the meaning of my blank aspect, and dropped them without giving an order, or uttering a word.

"Are we to try any measures for overtaking and bringing her back," I inquired. "How should we do?"

"She went of her own accord," answered the master; "she had a right to go if she pleased. Trouble me no more about her— hereafter she is only my sister in name; not because I disown her, but because she has disowned me."

And that was all he said on the subject; he did not make a sin-gle inquiry further, or mention her in any way, except directing me to send what property she had in the house to her fresh home, wherever it was, when I knew it.

on the way to Cowan Bridge (*Paterson*), in the direction of Gretna Green, where marriages took place in 'the blacksmith's shop at Headlesscross' (Warren Henry, *Gretna Green Romances* [1926], p. 15).

CHAPTER 13

For two months the fugitives remained absent; in those two months, Mrs. Linton encountered and conquered the worst shock of what was denominated a brain fever. No mother could have nursed an only child more devotedly than Edgar tended her. Day and night, he was watching, and patiently enduring all the annoyances that irritable nerves and a shaken reason could inflict. Though Kenneth remarked that what he saved from the grave would only recompense his care by forming the source of constant future anxiety—in fact, that his health and strength were being sacrificed to preserve a mere ruin of humanity—he knew no limits in gratitude and joy, when Catherine's life was declared out of danger. Hour after hour, he would sit beside her, tracing the gradual return to bodily health, and flattering his too sanguine hopes with the illusion that her mind would settle back to its right balance also, and she would soon be entirely her former self.

The first time she left her chamber, was at the commencement of the following March. Mr. Linton had put on her pillow, in the morning, a handful of golden crocuses; her eye, long stranger to any gleam of pleasure, caught them in waking, and shone delighted as she gathered them eagerly together.

"These are the earliest flowers at the Heights!" she exclaimed. "They remind me of soft thaw winds, and warm sunshine, and nearly melted snow—Edgar, is there not a south wind, and is not the snow almost gone?"

"The snow is quite gone, down here, darling!" replied her husband, "and I only see two white spots on the whole range of moors—the sky is blue, and the larks are singing, and the becks and brooks are all brim full. Catherine, last spring at this time, I was longing to have you under this roof—now, I wish you were a mile or two up those hills, the air blows so sweetly, I feel that it would cure you."

"I shall never be there, but once more!" said the invalid; "and then you'll leave me, and I shall remain, for ever. Next spring you'll long again to have me under this roof, and you'll look back and think you were happy to-day."

Linton lavished on her the kindest caresses, and tried to cheer her by the fondest words; but vaguely regarding the flowers, she let the tears collect on her lashes, and stream down her cheeks unheeding.

We knew she was really better, and therefore, decided that long confinement to a single place produced much of this despondency, and it might be partially removed by a change of scene.

The master told me to light a fire in the many-weeks' deserted parlour, and to set an easy-chair in the sunshine by the window; and then he brought her down, and she sat a long while enjoying the genial heat, and, as we expected, was revived by the objects round her, which though familiar, were free from the dreary associations investing her hated sick-chamber. By evening, she seemed greatly exhausted; yet no arguments could persuade her to return to that apartment, and I had to arrange the parlour sofa for her bed, till another room could be prepared.

To obviate the fatigue of mounting and descending the stairs, we fitted up this, where you lie at present; on the same floor with the parlour: and she was soon strong enough to move from one to the other, leaning on Edgar's arm.

Ah, I thought to myself, she might recover, so waited on as she was. And there was double cause to desire it, for on her existence depended that of another;[1] we cherished the hope that in a little while, Mr. Linton's heart would be gladdened, and his lands secured from a stranger's gripe, by the birth of an heir.

I should mention that Isabella sent to her brother, some six weeks from her departure, a short note, announcing her marriage with Heathcliff. It appeared dry and cold; but at the bottom, was dotted in with pencil, an obscure apology, and an entreaty for kind remembrance, and reconciliation, if her proceeding had offended him; asserting that she could not help it then, and being done, she had now no power to repeal it.

Linton did not reply to this I believe; and, in a fortnight more, I got a long letter which I considered odd coming from the pen of a bride just out of the honeymoon. I'll read it, for I keep it yet. Any relic of the dead is precious, if they were valued living.

---

1 *another*: a first explicit reference to Catherine's pregnancy.

"DEAR ELLEN," it begins:

I came, last night, to Wuthering Heights, and heard, for the first time, that Catherine has been, and is yet, very ill. I must not write to her I suppose, and my brother is either too angry, or too distressed to answer what I send him. Still, I must write to somebody, and the only choice left me is you.

Inform Edgar that I'd give the world to see his face again—that my heart returned to Thrushcross Grange in twenty-four hours after I left it, and is there at this moment, full of warm feelings for him, and Catherine! *I can't follow it through*—(those words are underlined) they need not expect me, and they may draw what conclusions they please; taking care however, to lay nothing at the door of my weak will, or deficient affection.

The remainder of the letter is for yourself, alone. I want to ask you two questions: the first is,

How did you contrive to preserve the common sympathies of human nature when you resided here? I cannot recognise any sentiment which those around, share with me.

The second question, I have great interest in; it is this—

Is Mr. Heathcliff a man? If so, is he mad? And if not, is he a devil? I shan't tell my reasons for making this inquiry; but, I beseech you to explain, if you can, what I have married—that is, when you call to see me; and you must call, Ellen, very soon. Don't write, but come, and bring me something from Edgar.

Now, you shall hear how I have been received in my new home, as I am led to imagine the Heights will be. It is to amuse myself that I dwell on such subjects as the lack of external comforts; they never occupy my thoughts, except at the moment when I miss them—I should laugh and dance for joy, if I found their absence was the total of my miseries, and the rest was an unnatural dream!

The sun set behind the Grange,[1] as we turned on to the moors; by that, I judged it to be six o'clock; and my companion halted half-an-hour, to inspect the park, and the gardens, and, probably, the place itself, as well as he could; so it was dark when

---

1   *behind the Grange*: Isabella confirms that the Grange lies to the south-west from the crossroads.

we dismounted in the paved yard of the farm-house, and your old fellow-servant, Joseph, issued out to receive us by the light of a dip candle. He did it with a courtesy that redounded to his credit. His first act was to elevate his torch to a level with my face, squint malignantly, project his under lip, and turn away.

Then he took the two horses, and led them into the stables; reappearing for the purpose of locking the outer gate, as if we lived in an ancient castle.

Heathcliff stayed to speak to him, and I entered the kitchen— a dingy, untidy hole; I dare say you would not know it, it is so changed since it was in your charge.

By the fire stood a ruffianly child, strong in limb, and dirty in garb, with a look of Catherine in his eyes, and about his mouth.

"This is Edgar's legal nephew," I reflected—"mine in a manner; I must shake hands, and—yes—I must kiss him. It is right to establish a good understanding at the beginning."

I approached, and, attempting to take his chubby fist, said—

"How do you do, my dear?"

He replied in a jargon I did not comprehend.

"Shall you and I be friends, Hareton?" was my next essay at conversation.

An oath, and a threat to set Throttler on me if I did not "frame off" rewarded my perseverance.

"Hey, Throttler, lad!" whispered the little wretch, rousing a half-bred bull-dog from its lair in a corner. "Now, wilt tuh be ganging?" he asked authoritatively.

Love for my life urged a compliance; I stepped over the threshold to wait till the others should enter. Mr. Heathcliff was nowhere visible; and Joseph, whom I followed to the stables, and requested to accompany me in, after staring and muttering to himself, screwed up his nose and replied—

"Mim! mim! mim! Did iver Christian body hear owt like it? Minching un' munching! Hah can Aw tell whet ye say?"[1]

"I say, I wish you to come with me into the house!" I cried, thinking him deaf, yet highly disgusted at his rudeness.

---

[1] 'Mim! Mim! Mim! Did any Christian ever hear anything like this? Mincing and mouthing! How can I tell what you are saying?'

"Nor nuh me! Aw getten summut else to do,"¹ he answered, and continued his work, moving his lantern jaws meanwhile, and surveying my dress and countenance (the former a great deal too fine, but the latter, I'm sure as sad as he could desire) with sovereign contempt.

I walked round the yard, and through a wicket, to another door, at which I took the liberty of knocking, in hopes some more civil servant might show himself.

After a short suspense it was opened by a tall, gaunt man, without neckerchief, and otherwise extremely slovenly; his features were lost in masses of shaggy hair that hung on his shoulders; and *his* eyes, too, were like a ghostly Catherine's, with all their beauty annihilated.

"What's your business here?" he demanded, grimly. "Who are you?"

"My name *was* Isabella Linton," I replied. "You've seen me before, sir. I'm lately married to Mr. Heathcliff; and he has brought me here—I suppose by your permission."

"Is he come back, then?" asked the hermit, glaring like a hungry wolf.

"Yes—we came just now," I said; "but he left me by the kitchen door; and when I would have gone in, your little boy played sentinel over the place, and frightened me off by the help of a bull-dog."

"It's well the hellish villain has kept his word!" growled my future host, searching the darkness beyond me in expectation of discovering Heathcliff, and then he indulged in a soliloquy of execrations, and threats of what he would have done had the "fiend" deceived him.

I repented having tried this second entrance; and was almost inclined to slip away before he finished cursing, but ere I could execute that intention, he ordered me in, and shut and re-fastened the door.

There was a great fire, and that was all the light in the huge apartment, whose floor had grown a uniform grey; and the once

---

1   *Nor nuh me!:* 'Not me! I've got something else to do.'

brilliant pewter dishes which used to attract my gaze when I was a girl partook of a similar obscurity, created by tarnish and dust.

I inquired whether I might call the maid, and be conducted to a bed-room? Mr. Earnshaw vouchsafed no answer. He walked up and down, with his hands in his pockets, apparently quite forgetting my presence; and his abstraction was evidently so deep, and his whole aspect so misanthropical, that I shrank from disturbing him again.

You'll not be surprised, Ellen, at my feeling particularly cheerless, seated in worse than solitude, on that inhospitable hearth, and remembering that four miles distant lay my delightful home, containing the only people I loved on earth: and there might as well be the Atlantic[1] to part us, instead of those four miles—I could not overpass them!

I questioned with myself—where must I turn for comfort? And—mind you don't tell Edgar, or Catherine—above every sorrow beside, this rose pre-eminent—despair at finding nobody who could or would be my ally against Heathcliff!

I had sought shelter at Wuthering Heights, almost gladly, because I was secured by that arrangement from living alone with him; but he knew the people we were coming amongst, and he did not fear their intermeddling.

I sat and thought a doleful time; the clock struck eight, and nine, and still my companion paced to and fro, his head bent on his breast, and perfectly silent, unless a groan, or a bitter ejaculation forced itself out at intervals.

I listened to detect a woman's voice in the house, and filled the interim with wild regrets, and dismal anticipations, which, at last, spoke audibly in irrepressible sighing, and weeping.

I was not aware how openly I grieved, till Earnshaw halted opposite, in his measured walk, and gave me a stare of newly awakened surprise. Taking advantage of his recovered attention, I exclaimed—

"I'm tired with my journey, and I want to go to bed! Where is the maid-servant? Direct me to her, as she won't come to me!"

---

1   the Atlantic: In 'Yamba's Lament' (Appendix D) the enslaved Yamba is 'Parted many a thousand mile, / Never, never to return' to Africa.

"We have none," he answered; "you must wait on yourself!"[1]

"Where must I sleep, then?" I sobbed—I was beyond regarding self-respect, weighed down by fatigue and wretchedness.

"Joseph will show you Heathcliff's chamber," said he; "open that door—he's in there."

I was going to obey, but he suddenly arrested me, and adding in the strangest tone—

"Be so good as to turn your lock, and draw your bolt—don't omit it!"

"Well!" I said, "But why, Mr. Earnshaw?" I did not relish the notion of deliberately fastening myself in with Heathcliff.

"Look here!" he replied, pulling from his waistcoat a curiously constructed pistol, having a double edged spring knife attached to the barrel.[2] "That's a great tempter to a desperate man, is it not? I cannot resist going up with this, every night, and trying his door. If once I find it open he's done for! I do it invariably, even though the minute before I have been recalling a hundred reasons that should make me refrain—it is some devil that urges me to thwart my own schemes by killing him—you fight against that devil, for love, or as long as you may; when the time comes, not all the angels in heaven shall save him!"

I surveyed the weapon inquisitively; a hideous notion struck me. How powerful I should be possessing such an instrument! I took it from his hand, and touched the blade. He looked astonished at the expression my face assumed during a brief second. It was not horror, it was covetousness. He snatched the pistol back, jealously; shut the knife, and returned it to its concealment.

"I don't care if you tell him" said he. Put him on his guard, and watch for him. You know the terms we are on, I see; his danger does not shock you."

"What has Heathcliff done to you?" I asked. "In what has he wronged you to warrant this appalling hatred? Wouldn't it be wiser to bid him quit the house?"

"No," thundered Earnshaw, "should he offer to leave me, he's a dead man, persuade him to attempt it, and you are a murderess!

---

1   Zillah has not yet been appointed as the new housekeeper.
2   See above, Plate 6, Lacroix Pistol Knife.

Am I to lose *all*, without a chance of retrieval? Is Hareton to be a beggar? Oh, damnation! I *will* have it back; and I'll have *his* gold too; and then his blood; and hell shall have his soul! It will be ten times blacker with that guest than ever it was before!"

You've acquainted me, Ellen, with your old master's habits. He is clearly on the verge of madness—he was so last night, at least. I shuddered to be near him, and thought on the servant's ill-bred moroseness as comparatively agreeable.

He now recommenced his moody walk, and I raised the latch, and escaped into the kitchen.

Joseph was bending over the fire, peering into a large pan that swung above it; and a wooden bowl of oatmeal stood on the settle close by. The contents of the pan began to boil, and he turned to plunge his hand into the bowl; I conjectured that this preparation was probably for our supper, and, being hungry, I resolved it should be eatable—so crying out, sharply—"*I'll* make the porridge!" I removed the vessel out of his reach, and proceeded to take off my hat and riding habit. "Mr. Earnshaw," I continued, "directs me to wait on myself—I will—I'm not going to act the lady among you, for fear I should starve."[1]

"Gooid Lord!" he muttered, sitting down, and stroking his ribbed stockings from the knee to the ankle. "If they's tuh be fresh ortherings—just when Aw getten used tuh two maisters, if aw mun hev a *mistress* set o'er my heead, it's loike time tuh be flitting. Aw niver *did* think tuh say t' day ut aw mud lave th' owld place—but aw daht it's nigh at hend!"[2]

This lamentation drew no notice from me; I went briskly to work; sighing to remember a period when it would have been all merry fun; but compelled speedily to drive off the remembrance. It racked me to recall past happiness, and the greater peril there was of conjuring up its apparition, the quicker the thible[3] ran round, and the faster the handfuls of meal fell into the water.

---

1   *starve*: die of hunger.
2   'Good Lord! [...] If there are going to be new orders, just when I was getting used to two masters—if I have to have a *mistress* set up over my head, it's about time to be moving off. I never thought I would see the day when I would have to leave the old place, but I'm afraid it's near to hand!'
3   *thible*: 'a wooden spatula to stir pottage' (Carr).

Joseph beheld my style of cookery with growing indignation.

"Thear!" he ejaculated. "Hareton, thah willut sup thy porridge tuh neeght; they'll be nowt bud lumps as big as maw nave. Thear, agean! Aw'd fling in bowl un all, if aw were yah! Thear, pale t' guilp off, un' then yah'll hae done wi't. Bang, bang. It's a marcy t' bothom isn't deaved aht!"[1]

It *was* rather a rough mess, I own, when poured into the basins; four had been provided, and a gallon pitcher of new milk was brought from the dairy, which Hareton seized and commenced drinking and spilling from the expansive lip.

I expostulated, and desired that he should have his in a mug; affirming that I could not taste the liquid treated so dirtily. The old cynic chose to be vastly offended at this nicety; assuring me, repeatedly, that "the barn[2] was every bit as gooid" as I, "and every bit as wollsome,"[3] and wondering how I could fashion to be so conceited; meanwhile, the infant ruffian continued sucking; and glowered up at me defyingly, as he slavered into the jug.

"I shall have my supper in another room," I said. "Have you no place you call a parlour?"

"*Parlour!*" he echoed, sneeringly, "*parlour!* Nay, we've noa *parlours.* If yah dunnut loike wer company, they's maister's; un' if yah dunnot loike maister, they's us."[4]

"Then I shall go up-stairs", I answered; "show me a chamber!"

I put my basin on a tray, and went myself to fetch some more milk.

---

1 Joseph deplores Isabella's cooking style: *pale*, 'strip off, peel'; and (as noun) 'a flat, spade-shaped tool used by bakers, to take dishes out of the oven' (*NED*): 'There! Hareton, you won't have porridge for supper tonight; it'll have nothing but lumps as big as my fist. There she goes again! If I were you [Isabella], I'd fling in the bowl as well! Go on, scoop off the crust, and there'll be nothing left. Bang, bang. It's lucky you haven't knocked out the bottom [of the pan]'.
2 *barn*: child.
3 *wollsome*: healthy, presentable.
4 *Parlour!*: '*Parlour!* No, we don't have *parlours* here. If you don't like our company, there's the master's; and if you don't like the master, there's us.'

With great grumblings, the fellow rose, and preceded me in my ascent: we mounted to the garrets; he opening a door, now and then, to look into the apartments we passed.

"Here's a rahm," he said, at last, flinging back a crank board on hinges. "It's weel eneugh tuh ate a few porridge in. They's a pack uh corn i' t' corner, theear, meeterly clane; if yah're feared uh muckying yer grand silk cloes, spread yer hankerchir ut t' top on't."[1]

The "rahm" was a kind of lumber-hole smelling strong of malt and grain; various sacks of which articles were piled around leaving a wide, bare space in the middle.

"Why, man!" I exclaimed, facing him angrily, "this is not a place to sleep in. I wish to see my bed-room."

"*Bed-rume!*" he repeated, in a tone of mockery. "Yah's see all t' *bed-rumes* thear is—yon's mine."

He pointed into the second garret, only differing from the first in being more naked about the walls, and having a large, low, curtainless bed, with an indigo-coloured quilt, at one end.

"What do I want with yours?" I retorted. "I suppose Mr. Heathcliff does not lodge at the top of the house, does he?"

"Oh! it's Maister *Hathecliff's* yah're wenting?" cried he, as if making a new discovery. "Couldn't ye uh said soa, at onst? un then, aw mud uh telled ye, baht all this wark, ut that's just one yah cannut sea—he allas keeps it locked, un' nob'dy iver mells on't but hisseln."[2]

"You've a nice house, Joseph," I could not refrain from observing, "and pleasant inmates; and I think the concentrated essence of all the madness in the world took up its abode in my brain the day I linked my fate with theirs! However that is not to the present purpose—there are other rooms. For heaven's sake, be quick, and let me settle somewhere!"

---

1 *Here's a rahm*: 'Here's a room. It's good enough to eat a bit of porridge in. There's a sack of corn in the corner over there, more or less clean; if you're scared of dirtying your grand silk clothes, spread your handkerchief on top of it.'

2 'Oh! you're wanting *Heathcliff's* room? Why didn't you say so at first? I'd have told you then, without all this trouble, that that's just the one you can't see—he always keeps it locked, and nobody ever meddles with it except himself.'

He made no reply to this adjuration; only plodding doggedly down the wooden steps, and halting before an apartment which, from that halt, and the superior quality of its furniture, I conjectured to be the best one.

There was a carpet, a good one; but the pattern was obliterated by dust; a fire-place hung with cut paper dropping to pieces; a handsome oak-bedstead with ample crimson curtains of rather expensive material, and modern make. But they had evidently experienced rough usage, and valances hung in festoons, wrenched from their rings; and the iron rod supporting them was bent in an arc, on one side, causing the drapery to trail upon the floor. The chairs were also damaged, many of them severely; and deep indentations deformed the panels of the walls.

I was endeavouring to gather resolution for entering, and taking possession, when my fool of a guide announced—

"This here is t' maister's."

My supper by this time was cold, my appetite gone, and my patience exhausted. I insisted on being provided instantly with a place of refuge, and means of repose.

"Whear the divil," began the religious elder. "The Lord bless us! The Lord forgie us! Whear the *hell*, wold ye gang? Ye marred, wearisome nowt! Yah seen all bud Hareton's bit uf a cham'er. They's nut another hoile tuh lig dahn in i' th' hahse!"[1]

I was so vexed, I flung my tray and its contents to the ground; and then seated myself at the stairs-head, hid my face in my hands, and cried.

"Ech! ech!" exclaimed Joseph. "Weel done, Miss Cathy! weel done, Miss Cathy! Hahsiver, t' maister sall just tum'le o'er them broken pots; un' then we's hear summut; we's hear hah it's tuh be. Gooid-fur-nowt madling! yah desarve pining froo this tuh Churstmas, flinging t' precious gifts uh God under fooit i' yer flaysome rages! Bud, aw'm mista'en if yah shew yer sperrit lang. Will Hathecliff bide sich bonny ways, think ye? Aw nob-

---

1   *Whear the divil:* 'Where the devil—The Lord bless us! the Lord forgive us! Where the *hell*, d'you want to go? You spoilt, boring ne'er-do-well! You've seen everything except Hareton's corner of a room. This house hasn't got another hole to lie down in!'

but wish he muh cotch ye i' that plisky.[1] Aw nobbut wish he may."[1]

And so he went scolding to his den beneath, taking the candle with him, and I remained in the dark.

The period of reflection succeeding this silly action, compelled me to admit the necessity of smothering my pride, and choking my wrath, and bestirring myself to remove its effects.

An unexpected aid presently appeared in the shape of Throttler, whom I now recognised as a son of our old Skulker; it had spent its whelphood at the Grange, and was given by my father to Mr. Hindley. I fancy it knew me—it pushed its nose against mine by way of salute, and then hastened to devour the porridge, while I groped from step to step, collecting the shattered earthenware, and drying the spatters of milk from the bannister with my pocket-handkerchief.

Our labours were scarcely over when I heard Earnshaw's tread in the passage; my assistant tucked in his tail, and pressed to the wall; I stole into the nearest doorway. The dog's endeavour to avoid him was unsuccessful; as I guessed by a scutter down stairs, and a prolonged, piteous yelping. I had better luck. He passed on, entered his chamber, and shut the door.

Directly after, Joseph came up with Hareton, to put him to bed. I had found shelter in Hareton's room, and the old man on seeing me, said—

"They's rahm fur boath yah, un yer pride, nah, aw sud think i' th' hahse. It's empty; yah my hev it all tuh yerseln, un Him as allas maks a third, i' sich ill company!"[2]

---

1 *plisky*: plight, sorry state (*NED*); 'Ech! ech! Miss Cathy has trained you well! Well done, Miss Cathy! However, soon enough the master'll stumble over the smashed crockery, and then we'll hear something—we'll hear what's what. Worthless loony! you deserve to be in misery from now till Christmas, flinging the precious gifts of God underfoot in your nasty tantrums! But I'd be surprised if you keep up your temper for long. Do you think Heathcliff will put up with your fancy ways? I just about hope he might catch you in this state. I just wish he would.'

2 'Well, now, there's room for you as well as your pride, I shouldn't wonder, in the living room downstairs. It's empty, and you can have it all to yourself, with the devil, who always makes a trio with such bad company.'

Gladly did I take advantage of this intimation; and the minute I flung myself into a chair, by the fire, I nodded, and slept.

My slumber was deep, and sweet, though over far too soon. Mr. Heathcliff awoke me; he had just come in, and demanded, in his loving manner, what I was doing there?

I told him the cause of my staying up so late—that he had the key of our room in his pocket.

The adjective *our* gave mortal offence. He swore it was not, nor ever should be mine; and he'd—but I'll not repeat his language, nor describe his habitual conduct; he is ingenious and unresting in seeking to gain my abhorrence! I sometimes wonder at him with an intensity that deadens my fear: yet, I assure you, a tiger, or a venomous serpent could not rouse terror in me equal to that which he wakens. He told me of Catherine's illness, and accused my brother of causing it; promising that I should be Edgar's proxy in suffering, till he could get a hold of him.

I do hate him—I am wretched—I have been a fool! Beware of uttering one breath of this to any one at the Grange. I shall expect you every day—don't disappoint me!

ISABELLA

As soon as I had perused this epistle, I went to the master, and informed him that his sister had arrived at the Heights, and sent me a letter expressing her sorrow for Mrs. Linton's situation and her ardent desire to see him; with a wish that he would transmit to her, as early as possible, some token of forgiveness by me.

"Forgiveness?" said Linton, "I have nothing to forgive her, Ellen—you may call at Wuthering Heights this afternoon, if you like, and say that I am not *angry*, but I'm *sorry* to have lost her: especially as I can never think she'll be happy. It is out of the question my going to see her, however; we are eternally divided; and should she really wish to oblige me, let her persuade the villain she has married to leave the country."

"And you won't write her a little note, sir?" I asked, imploringly.

"No," he answered. "It is needless. My communication with Heathcliff's family shall be as sparing as his with mine. It shall not exist!"

Mr. Edgar's coldness depressed me exceedingly; and all the way from the Grange, I puzzled my brains how to put more heart into what he said, when I repeated it; and how to soften his refusal of even a few lines to console Isabella.

I dare say she had been on the watch for me since morning: I saw her looking through the lattice, as I came up the garden causeway and I nodded to her; but she drew back, as if afraid of being observed.

I entered without knocking. There never was such a dreary, dismal scene as the formerly cheerful house presented! I must confess that, if I had been in the young lady's place, I would, at least, have swept the hearth, and wiped the tables with a duster. But she already partook of the pervading spirit of neglect which encompassed her. Her pretty face was wan and listless; her hair uncurled; some locks hanging lankly down, and some carelessly twisted round her head. Probably she had not touched her dress since yester evening.

Hindley was not there. Mr. Heathcliff sat at a table running over some papers in his pocket-book; but he rose when I appeared, asked me how I did, quite friendly, and offered me a chair.

He was the only thing there that seemed decent, and I thought he never looked better. So much had circumstances altered their positions, that he would certainly have struck a stranger as a born and bred gentleman, and his wife as a thorough little slattern!

She came forward eagerly to greet me; and held out one hand to take the expected letter.

I shook my head. She wouldn't understand the hint, but followed me to a side-board, where I went to lay my bonnet, and importuned me in a whisper to give her directly what I had brought.

Heathcliff guessed the meaning of her manoeuvres, and said—

"If you have got anything for Isabella, as no doubt you have, Nelly, give it to her. You needn't make a secret of it; we have no secrets between us."

"Oh, I have nothing," I replied thinking it best to speak the truth at once. "My master bid me tell his sister that she must not expect either a letter or a visit from him at present. He sends his love, ma'am, and his wishes for your happiness, and his pardon for the grief you have occasioned; but he thinks that after this time, his household, and the household here, should drop intercommunication; as nothing good could come of keeping it up."

Mrs. Heathcliff's lip quivered slightly, and she returned to her seat in the window. Her husband took his stand on the hearth-stone, near me, and began to put questions concerning Catherine.

I told him as much as I thought proper of her illness, and he extorted from me, by cross-examination, most of the facts connected with its origin.

I blamed her, as she deserved, for bringing it all on herself; and ended by hoping that he would follow Mr. Linton's example, and avoid future interference with his family, for good or evil.

"Mrs. Linton is now just recovering" I said, "she'll never be like she was, but her life is spared, and if you really have a regard for her, you'll shun crossing her way again. Nay you'll move out of this country[1] entirely; and that you may not regret it, I'll inform you Catherine Linton is as different now, from your old friend Catherine Earnshaw, as that young lady is different from me! Her appearance is changed greatly, her character much more so; and the person, who is compelled, of necessity, to be her companion, will only sustain his affection hereafter, by the remembrance of what she once was, by common humanity, and a sense of duty!"

"That is quite possible," remarked Heathcliff, forcing himself to seem calm, "quite possible that your master should have nothing but common humanity, and a sense of duty to fall back on. But do you imagine that I shall leave Catherine to his *duty* and *humanity*? And can you compare my feelings respecting Catherine, to his? Before you leave this house, I must exact a promise from you, that you'll get me an interview with her—consent, or refuse, I *will* see her! What do you say?"

"I say, Mr. Heathcliff," I replied, "you must not—you never shall through my means. Another encounter between you and the master, would kill her altogether!"

"With your aid that may be avoided," he continued, "and should there be danger of such an event—should he be the cause of adding a single trouble more to her existence—why, I think I shall be justified in going to extremes! I wish you had sincerity enough to tell me whether Catherine would suffer greatly from his loss. The fear that she would, restrains me: and there you see the distinction between our feelings—had he been in my place, and I in his, though I hated him with a hatred that turned my life to gall, I never would have raised a hand against him. You may look incredulous, if you please! I never would have banished him from her society, as long as she desired his. The moment her regard ceased, I would have torn his heart out, and drunk his blood! But, till then, if you don't believe me, you don't know me—till then, I would have died by inches before I touched a single hair of his head!"

"And yet," I interrupted, "you have no scruples in completely ruining all hopes of her perfect restoration, by thrusting yourself

---

1   *country*: district.

into her remembrance, now, when she has nearly forgotten you, and involving her in a new tumult of discord, and distress."

"You suppose she has nearly forgotten me?" he said. "Oh Nelly! You know she has not! You know as well as I do, that for every thought she spends on Linton, she spends a thousand on me! At a most miserable period of my life, I had a notion of the kind, it haunted me on my return to the neighbourhood, last summer, but only her own assurance, could make me admit the horrible idea again. And then, Linton would be nothing, nor Hindley, nor all the dreams that ever I dreamt. Two words would comprehend my future: *death* and *hell*—existence, after losing her, would be hell.

"Yet I was a fool to fancy for a moment that she valued Edgar Linton's attachment more than mine—if he loved with all the powers of his puny being, he couldn't love as much in eighty years, as I could in a day. And Catherine has a heart as deep as I have; the sea could be as readily contained in that horse-trough, as her whole affection be monopolized by him. Tush! he is scarcely a degree dearer to her than her dog, or her horse—it is not in him to be loved like me, how can she love in him what he has not?"

"Catherine and Edgar are as fond of each other, as any two people can be!" cried Isabella with sudden vivacity. "No one has a right to talk in that manner, and I won't hear my brother depreciated in silence!"

"Your brother is wondrous fond of you too, isn't he?" observed Heathcliff scornfully. "He turns you adrift on the world with surprising alacrity."

"He is not aware of what I suffer," she replied. "I didn't tell him that."

"You have been telling him something, then—you have written, have you?"

"To say that I was married, I did write—you saw the note."

"And nothing since?"

"No."

"My young lady is looking sadly the worse, for her change of condition," I remarked. "Somebody's love comes short in her case, obviously—whose I may guess; but, perhaps, I shouldn't say."

"I should guess it was her own," said Heathcliff. "She degenerates into a mere slut! She is tired of trying to please me, uncommonly early—you'd hardly credit it, but the very morrow of our wedding, she was weeping to go home. However, she'll suit this house so much the better for not being over nice, and I'll take care she does not disgrace me by rambling abroad."

"Well, sir," returned I, "I hope you'll consider that Mrs. Heathcliff is accustomed to be looked after, and waited on; and that she has been brought up like an only daughter whom every one was ready to serve—you must let her have a maid to keep things tidy about her, and you must treat her kindly. Whatever be your notion of Mr. Edgar, you cannot doubt that she has a capacity for strong attachments, or she wouldn't have abandoned the elegancies, and comforts, and friends of her former home, to fix contentedly, in such a wilderness as this, with you."

"She abandoned them under a delusion," he answered, "picturing in me a hero of romance, and expecting unlimited indulgences from my chivalrous devotion. I can hardly regard her in the light of a rational creature, so obstinately has she persisted in forming a fabulous notion of my character, and acting on the false impressions she cherished. But at last, I think she begins to know me—I don't perceive the silly smiles and grimaces that provoked me, at first; and the senseless incapability of discerning that I was in earnest when I gave her my opinion of her infatuation, and herself—it was a marvellous effort of perspicacity to discover that I did not love her.[1] I believed at one time, no lessons could teach her that! And yet it is poorly learnt; for this morning she announced, as a piece of appalling intelligence, that I had actually succeeded in making her hate me! A positive labour of Hercules, I assure you! If it be achieved, I have cause to return thanks—can I trust your assertion, Isabella, are you sure you hate me? If I let you alone for half-a-day, won't you come sighing and wheedling to me again? I dare say she would rather I had seemed all tender-

---

1   In *Abdelazer, or, the Moor's Revenge*, by Aphra Behn (*Plays*, 3rd edn., 4 vols., vol. 2) (P), the eponymous hero feigns indifference to Isabella, Queen of Spain, with whom he is having a clandestine affair; see below, Appendix B.

ness before you; it wounds her vanity to have the truth exposed. But, I don't care who knows that the passion was wholly on one side, and I never told her a lie about it. She cannot accuse me of showing a bit of deceitful softness. The first thing she saw me do, on coming out of the Grange, was to hang up her little dog, and when she pleaded for it, the first words I uttered were a wish that I had the hanging of every being belonging to her, except one: possibly she took that exception for herself—but no brutality disgusted her—I suppose, she has an innate admiration of it, if only her precious person were secure from injury! Now, was it not the depth of absurdity—of genuine idiocy—for that pitiful, slavish, mean-minded brach[1] to dream that I could love her? Tell your master, Nelly, that I never, in all my life, met with such an abject thing as she is—she even disgraces the name of Linton; and I've sometimes relented, from pure lack of invention, in my experiments on what she could endure, and still creep shamefully cringing back! But tell him also to set his fraternal and magisterial heart at ease, that I keep strictly within the limits of the law— I have avoided, up to this period, giving her the slightest right to claim a separation; and what's more, she'd thank nobody for dividing us—if she desired to go she might—the nuisance of her presence outweighs the gratification to be derived from tormenting her!"

"Mr. Heathcliff," said I, "this is the talk of a madman, and your wife most likely is convinced you are mad; and, for that reason, she has borne with you hitherto: but now that you say she may go, she'll doubtless avail herself of the permission—you are not so bewitched ma'am, are you, as to remain with him, of your own accord?"

"Take care, Ellen!" answered Isabella, her eyes sparkling irefully—there was no misdoubting by their expression, the full success of her partner's endeavours to make himself detested. "Don't put faith in a single word he speaks. He's a lying fiend, a monster, and not a human being! I've been told I might leave him before; and I've made the attempt, but I dare not repeat it! Only Ellen, promise you'll not mention a syllable of his infamous conversation to my

---

1   *brach*: unclassified hunting dog; mongrel.

brother or Catherine—whatever he may pretend, he wishes to provoke Edgar to desperation—he says he has married me on purpose to obtain power over him; and he shan't obtain it—I'll die first! I just hope, I pray that he may forget his diabolical prudence, and kill me! The single pleasure I can imagine is to die, or to see him dead!"

"There—that will do for the present!" said Heathcliff. "If you are called upon in a court of law, you'll remember her language, Nelly! And take a good look at that countenance—she's near the point which would suit me. No, you're not fit to be your own guardian, Isabella, now; and I, being your legal protector, must retain you in my custody, however distasteful the obligation may be—go upstairs; I have something to say to Ellen Dean, in private. That's not the way—upstairs, I tell you! Why this is the road[1] upstairs, child!"

He seized, and thrust her from the room; and returned muttering:

"I have no pity! I have no pity! The more the[2] worms writhe, the more I yearn to crush out their entrails! It is a moral teething, and I grind with greater energy, in proportion to the increase of pain."

"Do you understand what the word pity means?" I said hastening to resume my bonnet. "Did you ever feel a touch of it in your life?"

"Put that down!" he interrupted, perceiving my intention to depart. "You are not going yet. Come here now, Nelly—I must either persuade, or compel you to aid me in fulfilling my determination to see Catherine, and that without delay—I swear that I meditate no harm; I don't desire to cause any disturbance, or to exasperate, or insult Mr. Linton; I only wish to hear from herself how she is, and why she has been ill; and to ask, if anything that I could do would be of use to her. Last night, I was in the Grange garden six hours, and I'll return there to-night; and every night

---

1   *road*: way.
2   Heathcliff's comparison is elliptically expressed in *WH* (1847), where 'more the' is lacking, possibly the printer's miscopying; possibly, however, Brontë avoided an over-emphatically grammatical form.

I'll haunt the place, and every day, till I find an opportunity of entering. If Edgar Linton meets me, I shall not hesitate to knock him down, and give him enough to ensure his quiescence while I stay. If his servants oppose me, I shall threaten them off with these pistols. But wouldn't it be better to prevent my coming in contact with them or their master? And you could do it so easily! I'd warn you when I came, and then you might let me in unobserved, as soon as she was alone, and watch till I departed—your conscience quite calm; you would be hindering mischief."

I protested against playing that treacherous part in my employer's house; and besides, I urged the cruelty and selfishness of his destroying Mrs. Linton's tranquillity, for his satisfaction.

"The commonest occurrence startles her painfully," I said. "She's all nerves, and she couldn't bear the surprise, I'm positive—don't persist, sir!—or else, I shall be obliged to inform my master of your designs, and he'll take measures to secure his house and its inmates from any such unwarrantable intrusions!"

"In that case, I'll take measures to secure you, woman!" exclaimed Heathcliff; "you shall not leave Wuthering Heights till tomorrow morning. It is a foolish story to assert that Catherine could not bear to see me; and as to surprising her, I don't desire it, you must prepare her—ask her if I may come. You say she never mentions my name, and that I am never mentioned to her. To whom should she mention me if I am a forbidden topic in the house? She thinks you are all spies for her husband—oh, I've no doubt she's in hell among you! I guess, by her silence as much as anything, what she feels. You say she is often restless, and anxious looking—is that a proof of tranquillity? You talk of her mind, being unsettled—how the devil could it be otherwise, in her frightful isolation? And that insipid, paltry creature attending her from *duty* and *humanity*! From *pity* and *charity*. He might as well plant an oak in a flower-pot, and expect it to thrive, as imagine he can restore her to vigour in the soil of his shallow cares! Let us settle it at once; will you stay here, and am I to fight my way to Catherine over Linton, and his footmen? Or will you be my friend, as you have been hitherto, and do what I request? Decide! Because there is no reason for my lingering another minute, if you persist in your stubborn ill-nature."

Well, Mr. Lockwood, I argued, and complained, and flatly refused him fifty times; but in the long run he forced me to an agreement—I engaged to carry a letter from him to my mistress; and should she consent, I promised to let him have intelligence of Linton's next absence from home, when he might come, and get in as he was able—I wouldn't be there, and my fellow servants should be equally out of the way.

Was it right, or wrong? I fear it was wrong, though expedient. I thought I prevented another explosion by my compliance; and I thought too, it might create a favourable crisis in Catherine's mental illness: and then I remembered Mr. Edgar's stern rebuke of my carrying tales; and I tried to smooth away all disquietude on the subject, by affirming, with frequent iteration, that that betrayal of trust, if it merited so harsh an appellation, should be the last.

Notwithstanding, my journey homeward was sadder than my journey thither; and many misgivings I had, ere I could prevail on myself to put the missive into Mrs. Linton's hand.

But here is Kenneth—I'll go down, and tell him how much better you are. My history is *dree*, as we say, and will serve to while away another morning.

Dree, and dreary!¹ I reflected as the good woman descended to receive the doctor; and not exactly of the kind which I should have chosen to amuse me; but never mind! I'll extract wholesome medicines from Mrs. Dean's bitter herbs; and firstly let me beware of the fascination that lurks in Catherine Heathcliff's brilliant eyes. I should be in a curious taking if I surrendered my heart to that young person, and the daughter turned out a second edition of the mother!

---

1 She quotes Carr, vol. 1, where '*dree*: tedious; to undergo with difficulty', and '*drearisome*: dreary, solitary' are juxtaposed.

CHAPTER 15

Another week over—and I am so many days nearer health, and spring! I have now heard all my neighbour's history, at different sittings, as the housekeeper could spare time from more important occupations. I'll continue it in her own words, only a little condensed. She is, on the whole, a very fair narrator and I don't think I could improve her style.

"In the evening," she said, "the evening of my visit to the Heights, I knew as well as if I saw him, that Mr. Heathcliff was about the place; and I shunned going out, because I still carried his letter in my pocket, and I didn't want to be threatened, or teased any more.

I had made up my mind not to give it till my master went somewhere; as I could not guess how its receipt would affect Catherine. The consequence was, that it did not reach her before the lapse of three days. The fourth was Sunday, and I brought it into her room, after the family were gone to church.

There was a man servant left to keep the house with me, and we generally made a practice of locking the doors during the hours of service; but on that occasion, the weather was so warm and pleasant that I set them wide open; and to fulfil my engagement, as I knew who would be coming, I told my companion that the mistress wished very much for some oranges, and he must run over to the village, and get a few, to be paid for on the morrow. He departed, and I went up-stairs.

Mrs. Linton sat in a loose, white dress, with a light shawl over her shoulder, in the recess of the open window, as usual. Her thick, long hair had been partly removed at the beginning of her illness: and now, she wore it simply combed in its natural tresses over her temples and neck. Her appearance was altered, as I had told Heathcliff, but when she was calm, there seemed unearthly beauty in the change.

The flash of her eyes had been succeeded by a dreamy and melancholy softness: they no longer gave the impression of looking at the objects around her; they appeared always to gaze beyond, and far beyond—you would have said out of this world.

Then, the paleness of her face, its haggard aspect having vanished, she recovered flesh, and the peculiar expression arising from her mental state, though painfully suggestive of their causes,[1] added to the touching interest, which she wakened—and invariably to me, I know, and to any person who saw her, I should think, refuted more tangible proofs of convalescence and stamped her as one doomed to decay.

A book lay spread on the sill before her, and the scarcely perceptible wind fluttered its leaves at intervals. I believe Linton had laid it there, for she never endeavoured to divert herself with reading, or occupation of any kind; and he would spend many an hour in trying to entice her attention to some subject which had formerly been her amusement.

She was conscious of his aim, and in her better moods, endured his efforts placidly; only showing their uselessness by now and then suppressing a wearied sigh, and checking him at last, with the saddest of smiles and kisses. At other times, she would turn petulantly away, and hide her face in her hands, or even push him off angrily; and then he took care to let her alone, for he was certain of doing no good.

Gimmerton chapel bells were still ringing; and the full, mellow flow of the beck in the valley, came soothingly on the ear. It was a sweet substitute for the yet absent murmur of the summer foliage which drowned that music about the Grange, when the trees were in leaf. At Wuthering Heights it always sounded on quiet days, following a great thaw, or a season of steady rain—and, of Wuthering Heights, Catherine was thinking as she listened; that is, if she thought, or listened at all; but she had the vague, distant look, I mentioned before, which expressed no recognition of material things either by ear or eye.

"There's a letter for you, Mrs. Linton," I said, gently inserting it in one hand that rested on her knee. "You must read it immediately, because it wants an answer. Shall I break the seal?"

"Yes," she answered, without altering the direction of her eyes.

I opened it—it was very short.

---

1   *causes*: alienation, conflict, and pregnancy.

"Now," I continued, "read it."

She drew away her hand, and let it fall. I replaced it in her lap, and stood waiting till it should please her to glance down; but that movement was so long delayed that at last I resumed—

"Must I read it, ma'am? It is from Mr. Heathcliff."

There was a start, and a troubled gleam of recollection, and a struggle to arrange her ideas. She lifted the letter, and seemed to peruse it; and when she came to the signature she sighed; yet still I found she had not gathered its import; for upon my desiring to hear her reply she merely pointed to the name, and gazed at me with mournful and questioning eagerness.

"Well, he wishes to see you," said I, guessing her need of an interpreter. "He's in the garden by this time, and impatient to know what answer I shall bring."

As I spoke, I observed a large dog lying on the sunny grass beneath, raise its ears, as if about to bark; and then smoothing them back, announce by a wag of the tail that some one approached whom it did not consider a stranger.

Mrs. Linton bent forward, and listened breathlessly. The minute after a step traversed the hall; the open house was too tempting for Heathcliff to resist walking in: most likely he supposed that I was inclined to shirk my promise, and so resolved to trust to his own audacity.

With straining eagerness Catherine gazed towards the entrance of her chamber. He did not hit the right room directly; she motioned me to admit him; but he found it out, ere I could reach the door, in a stride or two was at her side, and had grasped her in his arms.

He neither spoke, nor loosed his hold, for some five minutes, during which period he bestowed more kisses than ever he gave in his life before, I dare say; but then my mistress had kissed him first, and I plainly saw that he could hardly bear, for downright agony, to look into her face! The same conviction had stricken him as me, from the instant he beheld her, that there was no prospect of ultimate recovery there—she was fated, sure to die.

"Oh, Cathy! Oh my life! how can I bear it?" was the first sentence he uttered, in a tone that did not seek to disguise his despair.

And now he stared at her so earnestly that I thought the very intensity of his gaze would bring tears into his eyes; but they burned with anguish, they did not melt.

"What now?" said Catherine, leaning back, and returning his look with a suddenly clouded brow—her humour was a mere vane for constantly varying caprices. "You and Edgar have broken my heart, Heathcliff! And you both come to bewail the deed to me, as if you were the people to be pitied! I shall not pity you, not I. You have killed me—and thriven on it, I think. How strong you are! How many years do you mean to live after I am gone?"

Heathcliff had knelt on one knee to embrace her; he attempted to rise, but she seized his hair, and kept him down.

"I wish I could hold you," she continued, bitterly, "till we were both dead! I shouldn't care what you suffered. I care nothing for your sufferings. Why shouldn't you suffer? I do! Will you forget me—will you be happy when I am in the earth? Will you say twenty years hence, 'That's the grave of Catherine Earnshaw. I loved her long ago, and was wretched to lose her; but it is past. I've loved many others since—my children are dearer to me than she was, and, at death, I shall not rejoice that I am going to her, I shall be sorry that I must leave them!' Will you say so, Heathcliff?"

"Don't torture me till I'm as mad as yourself," cried he, wrenching his head free, and grinding his teeth.

The two, to a cool spectator, made a strange and fearful picture. Well might Catherine deem that Heaven would be a land of exile to her, unless, with her mortal body, she cast away her mortal character also. Her present countenance had a wild vindictiveness in its white cheek, and a bloodless lip, and scintillating eye; and she retained, in her closed fingers, a portion of the locks she had been grasping. As to her companion, while raising himself with one hand, he had taken her arm with the other; and so inadequate was his stock of gentleness to the requirements of her condition, that on his letting go, I saw four distinct impressions left blue in the colourless skin.

"Are you possessed with a devil," he pursued, savagely, "to talk in that manner to me, when you are dying? Do you reflect that all those words will be branded in my memory, and eating deeper eternally, after you have left me? You know you lie to say I have killed you; and, Catherine, you know that I could as soon forget you, as my existence! Is it not sufficient for your infernal selfishness, that while you are at peace I shall writhe in the torments of hell?"

"I shall not be at peace," moaned Catherine, recalled to a sense of physical weakness by the violent, unequal throbbing of her heart, which beat visibly, and audibly under this excess of agitation.

She said nothing further till the paroxysm was over; then she continued, more kindly—

"I'm not wishing you greater torment than I have, Heathcliff! I only wish us never to be parted—and should a word of mine distress you hereafter, think I feel the same distress underground, and for my own sake, forgive me! Come here and kneel down again! You never harmed me in your life. Nay, if you nurse anger, that will be worse to remember than my harsh words! Won't you come here again? Do!"

Heathcliff went to the back of her chair, and leant over, but not so far as to let her see his face, which was livid with emotion. She bent round to look at him; he would not permit it; turning abruptly, he walked to the fire-place, where he stood, silent, with his back towards us.

Mrs. Linton's glance followed him suspiciously: every movement woke a new sentiment in her. After a pause, and a prolonged gaze, she resumed, addressing me in accents of indignant disappointment.

"Oh, you see, Nelly! he would not relent a moment, to keep me out of the grave! *That* is how I'm loved! Well, never mind! That is not *my* Heathcliff. I shall love mine yet; and take him with me—he's in my soul. And," added she, musingly, "the thing that irks me most is this shattered prison, after all. I'm tired, tired of being enclosed here. I'm wearying to escape into that glorious world, and to be always there; not seeing it dimly through tears, and yearning for it through the walls of an aching heart; but really with it, and in it. Nelly, you think you are better and more fortunate than I; in full health and strength—you are sorry for me —very soon that will be altered. I shall be sorry for *you*. I shall be incomparably beyond and above you all. I *wonder* he won't be near me!" she went on to herself. "I thought he wished it. Heathcliff dear! you should not be sullen now. Do come to me, Heathcliff."

In her eagerness she rose, and supported herself on the arm of the chair. At that earnest appeal, he turned to her, looking absolutely desperate. His eyes wide, and wet, at last, flashed fiercely on her; his breast heaved convulsively. An instant they held asunder; and then how they met I hardly saw, but Catherine made a spring, and he caught her, and they were locked in an embrace from which I thought my mistress would never be released alive. In fact, to my eyes, she seemed directly insensible. He flung himself into the nearest seat, and on my approaching hurriedly to ascertain if she had fainted, he gnashed at me, and foamed like a mad dog, and gathered her to him with greedy jealousy. I did not feel as if I were in the company of a creature of my own species; it appeared that he would not understand, though I spoke to him; so, I stood off, and held my tongue, in great perplexity.

A movement of Catherine's relieved me a little presently: she put up her hand to clasp his neck, and bring her cheek to his, as he held her: while he, in return, covering her with frantic caresses, said wildly—

"You teach me now how cruel you've been—cruel and false. *Why* did you despise me? *Why* did you betray your own heart, Cathy? I have not one word of comfort—you deserve this. You have killed yourself. Yes, you may kiss me, and cry; and wring out my kisses and tears. They'll blight you—they'll damn you. You love me— then what *right* had you to leave me? What right— answer me—for the poor fancy you felt for Linton? Because misery, and degradation, and death, and nothing that God or satan could inflict would have parted us, *you*, of your own will, did it. I have not broken your heart—*you* have broken it—and in breaking it, you have broken mine. So much the worse for me, that I am strong. Do I want to live? What kind of living will it be when you—oh God! would *you* like to live with your soul in the grave?"

"Let me alone. Let me alone," sobbed Catherine. "If I've done wrong, I'm dying for it. It is enough! You left me too; but I won't upbraid you! I forgive you. Forgive me!"

"It is hard to forgive, and to look at those eyes, and feel those wasted hands," he answered. "Kiss me again; and don't let me see your eyes! I forgive what you have done to me. I love *my* murderer—but *yours*! how can I?"

They were silent—their faces hid against each other, and washed by each other's tears. At least, I suppose the weeping was on both sides; as it seemed Heathcliff *could* weep on a great occasion like this.

I grew very uncomfortable, meanwhile; for the afternoon wore fast away, the man whom I had sent off returned from his errand, and I could distinguish, by the shine of the westering sun up the valley, a concourse thickening outside Gimmerton chapel porch.

"Service is over," I announced. "My master will be here in half-an-hour."[1]

Heathcliff groaned a curse, and strained Catherine closer—she never moved.

Ere long I perceived a group of the servants passing up the road towards the kitchen wing. Mr. Linton was not far behind; he opened the gate himself, and sauntered slowly up, probably enjoying the lovely afternoon that breathed as soft as summer.

"Now he is here," I exclaimed. "For Heaven's sake, hurry down! You'll not meet any one on the front stairs. Do be quick; and stay among the trees till he is fairly in."

"I must go, Cathy," said Heathcliff, seeking to extricate himself from his companion's arms. "But, if I live, I'll see you again before you are asleep. I won't stray five yards from your window."

"You must not go!" she answered, holding him as firmly as her strength allowed. "You shall not, I tell you."

"For one hour," he pleaded, earnestly.

"Not for one minute," she replied.

"I *must*—Linton will be up immediately," persisted the alarmed intruder.

---

1   The two-mile walk is imagined; the view is based on the proximity of the Yorkshire originals, St Oswald's Church and Hallsteads, at Thornton in Lonsdale; see above, Plate 2 and Introduction, 'The Wuthering Heights landscape', pp. 18-34.

He would have risen, and unfixed her fingers by the act—she clung fast gasping; there was mad resolution in her face.

"No!" she shrieked. "Oh, don't, don't go. It is the last time! Edgar will not hurt us. Heathcliff, I shall die! I shall die!"

"Damn the fool. There he is," cried Heathcliff, sinking back into his seat. "Hush, my darling! Hush, hush, Catherine! I'll stay. If he shot me so, I'd expire with a blessing on my lips."

And there they were fast again. I heard my master mounting the stairs—the cold sweat ran from my forehead; I was horrified.

"Are you going to listen to her ravings?" I said, passionately. "She does not know what she says. Will you ruin her, because she has not wit to help herself? Get up! You could be free instantly. That is the most diabolical deed that ever you did. We are all done for—master, mistress, and servant."

I wrung my hands, and cried out; and Mr. Linton hastened his step at the noise. In the midst of my agitation, I was sincerely glad to observe that Catherine's arms had fallen relaxed, and her head hung down.

"She's fainted or dead," I thought, "so much the better. Far better that she should be dead, than lingering a burden, and a misery-maker to all about her."

Edgar sprang to his unbidden guest, blanched with astonishment and rage. What he meant to do, I cannot tell; however, the other stopped all demonstrations, at once, by placing the lifeless-looking form in his arms.

"Look there," he said, "unless you be a fiend, help her first—then you shall speak to me!"

He walked into the parlour, and sat down. Mr. Linton summoned me, and, with great difficulty, and after resorting to many means, we managed to restore her to sensation; but she was all bewildered; she sighed, and moaned, and knew nobody. Edgar, in his anxiety for her, forgot her hated friend. I did not. I went, at the earliest opportunity, and besought him to depart, affirming that Catherine was better, and he should hear from me in the morning, how she passed the night.

"I shall not refuse to go out of doors," he answered; "but I shall stay in the garden; and, Nelly, mind you keep your word to-morrow. I shall be under those larch trees, mind! or I pay another visit, whether Linton be in or not."

He sent a rapid glance through the half-open door of the chamber, and ascertaining that what I stated was apparently true, delivered the house of his luckless presence.

CHAPTER 16

About twelve o'clock, that night, was born the Catherine you saw at Wuthering Heights, a puny, seven months' child; and two hours after the mother died, having never recovered sufficient consciousness to miss Heathcliff, or know Edgar.

The latter's distraction at his bereavement is a subject too painful to be dwelt on; its after effects showed how deep the sorrow sunk.

A great addition, in my eyes, was his being left without an heir. I bemoaned that, as I gazed on the feeble orphan; and I mentally abused old Linton for, what was only natural partiality, the securing his estate to his own daughter, instead of his son's.[1]

An unwelcomed infant it was, poor thing! It might have wailed out of life, and nobody cared a morsel, during those first hours of existence. We redeemed the neglect afterwards; but its beginning was as friendless as its end is likely to be.

Next morning—bright and cheerful out of doors—stole softened in through the blinds of the silent room, and suffused the couch and its occupant with a mellow, tender glow.

Edgar Linton had his head laid on the pillow, and his eyes shut. His young and fair features were almost as death-like as those of the form beside him, and almost as fixed; but *his* was the hush of exhausted anguish, and *hers* of perfect peace. Her brow smooth, her lids closed, and her lips wearing the expression of a smile; no angel in heaven could be more beautiful than she appeared; and I partook of the infinite calm in which she lay. My mind was never in a holier frame, than while I gazed on that untroubled image of Divine rest. I instinctively echoed the words she had uttered, a few hours before. "Incomparably beyond, and above us all! Whether still on earth or now in Heaven her spirit is at home with God!"

I don't know if it be a peculiarity in me, but I am seldom otherwise than happy while watching in the chamber of death, should

---

1   Old Mr Linton bequeaths the estate to Isabella and her children; Heathcliff's machinations will result in its passing to Hareton Earnshaw through his marriage to the widow of Isabella's son.

no frenzied or despairing mourner share the duty with me. I see a repose that neither earth nor hell can break; and I feel an assurance of the endless and shadowless hereafter—the Eternity they have entered—where life is boundless in its duration, and love in its sympathy, and joy in its fulness. I noticed on that occasion how much selfishness there is even in a love like Mr. Linton's, when he so regretted Catherine's blessed release! To be sure one might have doubted, after the wayward and impatient existence she had led, whether she merited a haven of peace at last. One might doubt in seasons of cold reflection, but not then, in the presence of her corpse. It asserted its own tranquillity, which seemed a pledge of equal quiet to its former inhabitants.

"Do you believe such people *are* happy in the other world, sir? I'd give a great deal to know."

I declined answering Mrs. Dean's question, which struck me as something heterodox. She proceeded:

"Retracing the course of Catherine Linton I fear we have no right to think she is: but we'll leave her with her Maker."

The master looked asleep, and I ventured soon after sunrise to quit the room and steal out to the pure, refreshing air. The servants thought me gone to shake off the drowsiness of my protracted watch; in reality my chief motive was seeing Mr. Heathcliff. If he had remained among the larches all night he would have heard nothing of the stir at the Grange, unless, perhaps, he might catch the gallop of the messenger going to Gimmerton. If he had come nearer he would probably be aware, from the lights flitting to and fro, and the opening and shutting of the outer doors, that all was not right within.

I wished yet feared to find him. I felt the terrible news must be told, and I longed to get it over, but *how* to do it I did not know.

He was there—at least a few yards further in the park; leant against an old ash tree, his hat off, and his hair soaked with the dew that had gathered on the budded branches, and fell pattering round him. He had been standing a long time in that position, for I saw a pair of ousels passing and repassing, scarcely three feet from him, busy in building their nest, and regarding his proximity no more than that of a piece of timber. They flew off at my approach, and he raised his eyes and spoke:

"She's dead!" he said; "I've not waited for you to learn that. Put your handkerchief away—don't snivel before me. Damn you all! she wants none of *your* tears!"

I was weeping as much for him as her: we do sometimes pity creatures that have none of the feeling either for themselves or others; and when I first looked into his face I perceived that he had got intelligence of the catastrophe; and a foolish notion struck me that his heart was quelled, and he prayed, because his lips moved, and his gaze was bent on the ground.

"Yes, she's dead!" I answered, checking my sobs, and drying my cheeks. "Gone to heaven, I hope, where we may, everyone, join her, if we take due warning, and leave our evil ways to follow good!"

"Did *she* take due warning, then?" asked Heathcliff, attempting a sneer. "Did she die like a saint? Come, give me a true history of the event. How did—"

He endeavoured to pronounce the name, but could not manage it; and compressing his mouth, he held a silent combat with his inward agony, defying, meanwhile, my sympathy with an unflinching, ferocious stare.

"How did she die?" he resumed, at last—fain, notwithstanding his hardihood, to have a support behind him, for, after the struggle, he trembled, in spite of himself, to his very finger-ends.

"Poor wretch!" I thought; "you have a heart and nerves the same as your brother men! Why should you be so anxious to conceal them? Your pride cannot blind God! You tempt him to wring them till he forces a cry of humiliation!"

"Quietly as a lamb!" I answered, aloud. "She drew a sigh, and stretched herself, like a child reviving, and sinking again to sleep; and five minutes after I felt one little pulse at her heart, and nothing more!"

"And—and did she ever mention me?" he asked, hesitating, as if he dreaded the answer to his question would introduce details that he could not bear to hear.

"Her senses never returned—she recognised nobody from the time you left her," I said. "She lies with a sweet smile on her face; and her latest ideas wandered back to pleasant early days. Her life closed in a gentle dream—may she wake as kindly in the other world!"

"May she wake in torment!" he cried, with frightful vehemence, stamping his foot, and groaning in a sudden paroxysm of ungovernable passion. "Why, she's a liar to the end! Where is she? Not *there*—not in heaven—not perished—where? Oh! you said you cared nothing for my sufferings! And I pray one prayer—I repeat it till my tongue stiffens—Catherine Earnshaw, may you not rest, as long as I am living! You said I killed you—haunt me then! The murdered *do* haunt their murderers. I believe—I know that ghosts *have* wandered on earth. Be with me always—take any form—drive me mad! only *do* not leave me in this abyss, where I cannot find you! Oh, God! it is unutterable! I *cannot* live without my life! I *cannot* live without my soul!"

He dashed his head against the knotted trunk; and, lifting up his eyes, howled, not like a man, but like a savage beast getting goaded to death with knives and spears.

I observed several splashes of blood about the bark of the tree, and his hand and forehead were both stained; probably the scene I witnessed was a repetition of others acted during the night. It hardly moved my compassion—it appalled me; still I felt reluctant to quit him so. But the moment he recollected himself enough to notice me watching, he thundered a command for me to go, and I obeyed. He was beyond my skill to quiet or console!

Mrs. Linton's funeral was appointed to take place on the Friday following her decease; and till then her coffin remained uncovered, and strewn with flowers and scented leaves, in the great drawing-room. Linton spent his days and nights there, a sleepless guardian; and—a circumstance concealed from all but me—Heathcliff spent his nights, at least, outside, equally a stranger to repose.

I held no communication with him; still I was conscious of his design to enter, if he could; and on the Tuesday, a little after dark, when my master from sheer fatigue, had been compelled to retire a couple of hours, I went and opened one of the windows, moved by his perseverance to give him a chance of bestowing on the fading image of his idol one final adieu.

He did not omit to avail himself of the opportunity, cautiously and briefly; too cautiously to betray his presence by the slightest noise; indeed, I shouldn't have discovered that he had been there, except for the disarrangement of the drapery about the corpse's face, and for observing on the floor a curl of light hair, fastened with a silver thread, which, on examination, I ascertained to have been taken from a locket hung round Catherine's neck. Heathcliff had opened the trinket, and cast out its contents, replacing them by a black lock of his own. I twisted the two, and enclosed them together.

Mr. Earnshaw was, of course, invited to attend the remains of his sister to the grave; and he sent no excuse, but he never came; so that besides her husband, the mourners were wholly composed of tenants and servants. Isabella was not asked.

The place of Catherine's interment, to the surprise of the villagers, was neither in the chapel, under the carven monument of the Lintons, nor yet by the tombs of her own relations, outside. It was dug on a green slope, in a corner of the kirkyard, where the wall is so low that heath and bilberry plants have climbed over it from the moor;[1] and peat mould almost buries it. Her husband lies in the same spot, now; and they have each a simple headstone, above, and a plain grey block at their feet, to mark the graves.

---

1   *climbed over it from the moor*: a speaking likeness of Haworth churchyard's west wall.

CHAPTER 17

That Friday made the last of our fine days, for a month. In the evening, the weather broke; the wind shifted from south to northeast, and brought rain, first, and then sleet, and snow.

On the morrow one could hardly imagine that there had been three weeks of summer: the primroses and crocuses were hidden under wintry drifts: the larks were silent, the young leaves of the early trees smitten and blackened—And dreary, and chill, and dismal that morrow did creep over! My master kept his room—I took possession of the lonely parlour, converting it into a nursery; and there I was sitting, with the moaning doll of a child laid on my knee; rocking it to and fro, and watching, meanwhile the still driving flakes build up the uncurtained window, when the door opened, and some person entered out of breath, and laughing!

My anger was greater than my astonishment for a minute; I supposed it one of the maids, and I cried,

"Have done! How dare you show your giddiness, here? What would Mr. Linton say if he heard you?"

"Excuse me!" answered a familiar voice, "but I know Edgar is in bed, and I cannot stop myself."

With that, the speaker came forward to the fire, panting and holding her hand to her side.

"I have run the whole way from Wuthering Heights!" she continued, after a pause. "Except where I've flown—I couldn't count the number of falls I've had—Oh, I'm aching all over! Don't be alarmed—There shall be an explanation as soon as I can give it—only just have the goodness to step out, and order the carriage to take me on to Gimmerton, and tell a servant to seek up a few clothes in my wardrobe."

The intruder was Mrs. Heathcliff—she certainly seemed in no laughing predicament: her hair streamed on her shoulders dripping with snow and water; she was dressed in the girlish dress she commonly wore, befitting her age more than her position; with a low frock, with short sleeves, and nothing on either head, or neck. The frock was of light silk, and clung to her with wet; and her feet were protected merely by thin slippers; add to this a deep cut under one ear, which only the cold prevented from bleeding profusely, a white face scratched and bruised, and a frame hardly able to support itself through fatigue, and you may fancy my first fright was not much allayed when I had leisure to examine her.

"My dear young lady," I exclaimed "I'll stir nowhere, and hear nothing, till you have removed every article of your clothes, and put on dry things; and certainly you shall not go to Gimmerton to-night; so it is needless to order the carriage."

"Certainly, I shall;" she said; "walking or riding—yet I've no objection to dress myself decently; and—ah, see how it flows down my neck now! the fire does make it smart."

She insisted on my fulfilling her directions, before she would let me touch her; and not till after the coachman had been instructed to get ready, and a maid set to pack up some necessary attire, did I obtain her consent for binding the wound, and helping to change her garments.

"Now Ellen," she said when my task was finished, and she was seated in an easy chair on the hearth, with a cup of tea before her, "You sit down opposite me, and put poor Catherine's baby away—I don't like to see it! You mustn't think I care little for Catherine, because I behaved so foolishly on entering—I've cried too, bitterly—yes, more than any one else has reason to cry—we parted unreconciled, you remember, and I shan't forgive myself. But for all that, I was not going to sympathise with him—the brute beast! O give me the poker! This is the last thing of his I have about me," she slipped the gold ring from her third finger, and threw it on the floor. "I'll smash it!" she continued, striking with childish spite. "And then I'll burn it!" and she took and dropped the misused article among the coals. "There! he shall buy another, if he gets me back again. He'd be capable of coming to seek me, to tease Edgar—I dare not stay, lest that notion should possess his wicked head! And besides, Edgar has not been kind, has he? And I won't come suing for his assistance; nor will I bring him into more trouble—Necessity compelled me to seek shelter here; though if I had not learnt he was out of the way, I'd have halted at the kitchen, washed my face, warmed myself, got you to bring what I wanted, and departed again to anywhere out of the reach of my accursed—of that incarnate goblin! Ah, he was in such a fury—if he had caught me! It's a pity, Earnshaw is not his match in strength—I wouldn't have run, till I'd seen him all but demolished, had Hindley been able to do it!"

"Well, don't talk so fast, Miss!" I interrupted, "you'll disorder the handkerchief I have tied round your face, and make the cut bleed again—Drink your tea, and take breath and give over[1] laughing—Laughter is sadly out of place under this roof, and in your condition!"

"An undeniable truth," she replied, "Listen to that child! It maintains a constant wail—send it out of my hearing for an hour; I shan't stay any longer."

I rang the bell, and committed it to a servant's care; and then I inquired what had urged her to escape from Wuthering Heights in such an unlikely plight—and where she meant to go, as she refused remaining with us?

"I ought, and I wish to remain;" answered she; "to cheer Edgar, and take care of the baby, for two things, and because the Grange is my right home—but I tell you, he wouldn't let me! Do you think he could bear to see me grow fat, and merry; and could bear to think that we were tranquil, and not resolve on poisoning our comfort? Now, I have the satisfaction of being sure that he detests me to the point of its annoying him seriously to have me within ear-shot, or eye-sight—I notice, when I enter his presence, the muscles of his countenance are involuntarily distorted into an expression of hatred; partly arising from his knowledge of the good causes I have to feel that sentiment for him, and partly from original aversion—It is strong enough to make me feel pretty certain that he would not chase me over England, sup-posing I contrived a clear escape; and therefore I must get quite away. I've recovered from my first desire to be killed by him. I'd rather he'd kill himself! He has extinguished my love effectually, and so I'm at my ease. I can recollect yet how I loved him; and can dimly imagine that I could still be loving him, if—No, no! Even, if he had doted on me, the devilish nature would have re-vealed its existence, somehow. Catherine had an awfully perverted taste to esteem him so dearly, knowing him so well—Monster!

---

1 *give over*: stop.

would that he could be blotted out of creation, and out of my memory!"

"Hush, hush! He's a human being," I said. "Be more charitable; there are worse men than he is yet!"

"He's not a human being," she retorted; "and he has no claim on my charity—I gave him my heart, and he took and pinched it to death; and flung it back to me—people feel with their hearts, Ellen, and since he has destroyed mine, I have not power to feel for him, and I would not, though he groaned from this, to his dying day; and wept tears of blood for Catherine! No, indeed, I wouldn't!" And here Isabella began to cry; but, immediately dashing the water from her lashes, she recommenced.

"You asked, what has driven me to flight at last? I was compelled to attempt it, because, I had succeeded in rousing his rage a pitch above his malignity. Pulling out the nerves with red hot pincers, requires more coolness than knocking on the head.[1] He was worked up to forgetting the fiendish prudence he boasted of, and proceeding to murderous violence: I experienced pleasure in being able to exasperate him: the sense of pleasure woke my instinct of self-preservation; so, I fairly broke free, and if ever I come into his hands again he is welcome to a signal revenge.

"Yesterday, you know, Mr. Earnshaw should have been at the funeral. He kept himself sober, for the purpose—tolerably sober; not going to bed mad at six o'clock, and getting up drunk, at twelve. Consequently, he rose, in suicidal low spirits; as fit for the church, as for a dance; and instead, he sat down by the fire, and swallowed gin or brandy by tumblerfuls.

"Heathcliff—I shudder to name him! has been a stranger in the house from last Sunday till to-day—Whether the angels have fed him, or his kin beneath, I cannot tell; but, he has not eaten a meal with us for nearly a week—He has just come home at dawn, and gone upstairs to his chamber; locking himself in—as if anybody dreamt of coveting his company! There he has continued, praying like a methodist; only the deity he implored is senseless

---

1   For matching phrases in *A Serious Address to the Members of the Anti-Slavery Society on the Present Position and Prospects* (1843), by William Howitt, see above, Introduction, 'Africa and Yorkshire unchained', pp. 56-71.

dust and ashes; and God, when addressed, was curiously confounded with his own black father![1] After concluding these precious orisons—and they lasted generally till he grew hoarse, and his voice was strangled in his throat—he would be off again; always straight down to the Grange! I wonder Edgar did not send for a constable, and give him into custody! For me, grieved as I was about Catherine, it was impossible to avoid regarding this season of deliverance from degrading oppression as a holiday.

"I recovered spirits sufficient to hear Joseph's eternal lectures without weeping; and to move up and down the house, less with the foot of a frightened thief, than formerly. You wouldn't think that I should cry at anything Joseph could say, but he and Hareton are detestable companions. I'd rather sit with Hindley, and hear his awful talk, than with 't' little maister,' and his staunch supporter, that odious old man!

"When Heathcliff is in, I'm often obliged to seek the kitchen, and their society, or starve[2] among the damp, uninhabited chambers; when he is not, as was the case this week, I establish a table, and chair, at one corner of the house fire, and never mind how Mr. Earnshaw may occupy himself; and he does not interfere with my arrangements: he is quieter, now, than he used to be, if no one provokes him; more sullen and depressed, and less furious. Joseph affirms he's sure he's an altered man; that the Lord has touched his heart, and he is saved 'so as by fire.' I'm puzzled to detect signs of the favourable change, but it is not my business.

"Yester-evening, I sat in my nook reading some old books, till late on towards twelve. It seemed so dismal to go upstairs, with the wild snow blowing outside, and my thoughts continually reverting to the kirkyard, and the new made grave! I dared hardly lift my eyes from the page before me, that melancholy scene so instantly usurped its place.

---

1   *black father*: in thinking of Heathcliff as a child of the devil, Isabella unwittingly exposes and condemns her own and the popular ideology. In a lampoon, 'A Whiter Indian', *The Lonsdale Magazine*, 1 (1820), 397-400, Yamaboo, a traveller who visits England from Ethiopia, describes the prayers of the natives of the British Isles to a God named the devil, who is black.

2   *starve*: freeze.

"Hindley sat opposite; his head leant on his hand, perhaps meditating on the same subject. He had ceased drinking at a point below irrationality, and had neither stirred, nor spoken during two or three hours. There was no sound through the house, but the moaning wind which shook the windows every now and then: the faint crackling of the coals; and the click of my snuffers as I removed at intervals the long wick of the candle. Hareton and Joseph were probably fast asleep in bed. It was very, very sad, and while I read, I sighed, for it seemed as if all joy had vanished from the world, never to be restored.

The doleful silence was broken, at length, by the sound of the kitchen latch—Heathcliff had returned from his watch earlier than usual, owing, I suppose, to the sudden storm. That entrance was fastened; and we heard him coming round to get in by the other. I rose with an irrepressible expression of what I felt on my lips, which induced my companion, who had been staring towards the door, to turn and look at me.

"I'll keep him out five minutes," he exclaimed. "You won't object?"

"No, you may keep him out the whole night, for me," I answered. "Do! put the key in the lock, and draw the bolts."

Earnshaw accomplished this, ere his guest reached the front; he then came, and brought his chair to the other side of my table; leaning over it, and searching in my eyes, a sympathy with the burning hate that gleamed from his: as he both looked, and felt like an assassin, he couldn't exactly find that; but he discovered enough to encourage him to speak.

"You, and I," he said, "have each a great debt to settle with the man out yonder. If we were neither of us cowards, we might combine to discharge it. Are you as soft as your brother? Are you willing to endure to the last, and not once attempt a repayment?"

"I'm weary of enduring now," I replied, "and I'd be glad of a retaliation that wouldn't recoil on myself; but treachery, and violence, are spears pointed at both ends—they wound those who resort to them, worse than their enemies."

"Treachery and violence are a just return for treachery and violence!" cried Hindley. "Mrs. Heathcliff, I'll ask you to do nothing, but sit still, and be dumb—Tell me now, can you? I'm sure you would have as much pleasure as I, in witnessing the conclusion of the fiend's existence: he'll be *your* death unless you overreach him—and he'll be *my* ruin—Damn the hellish villain! He knocks at the door, as if he were master here, already! Promise to hold your tongue, and before that clock strikes—it wants three minutes of one[1]—you're a free woman!"

He took the implements which I described to you in my letter from his breast, and would have turned down the candle— I snatched it away, however, and seized his arm.

"I'll not hold my tongue!" I said, "You mustn't touch him... Let the door remain shut and be quiet!"

"No! I've formed my resolution, and by God, I'll execute it!" cried the desperate being, "I'll do you a kindness, in spite of yourself, and Hareton justice! And you needn't trouble your head to screen me, Catherine is gone—Nobody alive would regret me, or be ashamed though I cut my throat, this minute—and it's time to make an end!"

I might as well have struggled with a bear; or reasoned with a lunatic. The only resource left me was to run to a lattice, and warn his intended victim of the fate which awaited him.

"You'd better seek shelter somewhere else to-night!" I exclaimed in a rather triumphant tone. "Mr. Earnshaw has a mind to shoot you, if you persist in endeavouring to enter."

"You'd better open the door, you—" he answered, addressing me by some elegant term[2] that I don't care to repeat.

"I shall not meddle in the matter," I retorted again. "Come in, and get shot,[3] if you please! I've done my duty."

With that I shut the window, and returned to my place by the fire; having too small a stock of hypocrisy at my command to pretend any anxiety for the danger that menaced him.

Earnshaw swore passionately at me; affirming that I loved the villain yet: and calling me all sorts of names for the base spirit I evinced. And I, in my secret heart (and conscience never re-

---

1   *three minutes of one*: it's three minutes to one.
2   *elegant term*: derogatory term for female person, rhyming with door (whore).
3   *get shot*: Hindley may shoot.

proached me) thought what a blessing it would be for *him*, should Heathcliff put him out of misery: and what a blessing for *me*, should he send Heathcliff to his right abode! As I sat nursing these reflections, the casement behind me, was banged on to the floor by a blow from the latter individual; and his black countenance looked blightingly through. The stanchions stood too close to suffer his shoulders to follow; and I smiled, exulting in my fancied security. His hair and clothes were whitened with snow, and his sharp cannibal teeth,[1] revealed by cold and wrath, gleamed through the dark.

"Isabella let me in, or I'll make you repent!" he 'girned',[2] as Joseph calls it.

"I cannot commit murder;" I replied "Mr. Hindley stands sentinel with a knife, and loaded pistol."

"Let me in by the kitchen door!" he said.

"Hindley will be there before me," I answered. "And that's a poor love of yours, that cannot bear a shower of snow! We were left at peace in our beds, as long as the summer moon shone, but the moment a blast of winter returns, you must run for shelter! Heathcliff, if I were you, I'd go stretch myself over her grave, and die like a faithful dog...The world is surely not worth living in now, is it? You had distinctly impressed on me, the idea that Catherine was the whole joy of your life—I can't imagine how you think of surviving her loss."

"He's there...is he?" exclaimed my companion, rushing to the gap. "If I can get my arm out I can hit him!"

"I'm afraid Ellen, you'll set me down as really wicked—but you don't know all, so don't judge! I wouldn't have aided or abet-

---

1   For contacts between Africa and Liverpool merchants in the 1830s, and references to cannibalism and filed teeth, see *Tramp Royal* (Johannesburg, 1992), by Tim Couzens (pp. 91-105). Northern hemisphere cannibalism appears in *Memoir of Ireland* (1843), by D. O'Connell: 'in the county of Cork, [...] a malefactor was executed to death, and his body left upon the gallows, certain poor people did secretly come, took him down, and did eat him' (p. 88); he cites Edmund Spenser's view of poverty in Ireland: 'by this hard restraint they would quietly consume themselves, and devour one another' (p. 79).

2   *girn*: 'grin' (Carr); 'show the teeth in rage, snarl (*NED*).

ted an attempt on even *his* life, for anything—Wish that he were dead, I must; and therefore, I was fearfully disappointed, and unnerved by terror for the consequences of my taunting speech when he flung himself on Earnshaw's weapon and wrenched it from his grasp.

The charge exploded, and the knife, in springing back, closed into its owner's wrist. Heathcliff pulled it away by main force, slitting up the flesh as it passed on,[1] and thrust it dripping into his pocket. He then took a stone, struck down the division between two windows and sprung in. His adversary had fallen senseless with excessive pain, and the flow of blood that gushed from an artery, or a large vein.

The ruffian kicked and trampled on him, and dashed his head repeatedly against the flags;[2] holding me with one hand, meantime, to prevent me summoning Joseph.

He exerted preter-human self-denial in abstaining from finishing him, completely; but getting out of breath, he finally desisted, and dragged the apparently inanimate body onto the settle.

There he tore off the sleeve of Earnshaw's coat, and bound up the wound with brutal roughness, spitting and cursing, during the operation, as energetically as he had kicked before.

Being at liberty, I lost no time in seeking the old servant; who, having gathered by degrees the purport of my hasty tale, hurried below, gasping, as he descended the steps two at once.

"Whet is thur tuh do, nah? Whet is thur tuh do, nah?"

"There's this to do," thundered Heathcliff, "that your master's mad; and should he last another month, I'll have him in an asylum. And how the devil did you come to fasten me out, you toothless hound? Don't stand muttering and mumbling there. Come, I'm not going to nurse him. Wash that stuff away; and mind the sparks of your candle—it is more than half brandy!"

"Und soa, yah been murthering on him?" exclaimed Joseph, lifting his hands and eyes in horror. "If iver Aw seed a seeght loike this! May the Lord—"

Heathcliff gave him a push onto his knees, in the middle of the

---

1   See above, Introduction, pp. 45-46, and Plate 6, and note.
2   *flags*: flagstones.

blood; and flung a towel to him; but instead of proceeding to dry it up, he joined his hands, and began a prayer which excited my laughter from its odd phraseology. I was in the condition of mind to be shocked at nothing; in fact, I was as reckless as some male-factors show themselves at the foot of the gallows.

"Oh, I forgot you," said the tyrant, "you shall do that. Down with you. And you conspire with him against me, do you, viper? There, that is work fit for you!"

He shook me till my teeth rattled, and pitched me beside Joseph, who steadily concluded his supplications, and then rose, vowing he would set off for the Grange directly. Mr. Linton was a magistrate, and though he had fifty wives dead, he should in-quire into this.

He was so obstinate in his resolution that Heathcliff deemed it expedient to compel, from my lips, a recapitulation of what had taken place; standing over me, heaving with malevolence, as I re-luctantly delivered the account in answer to his questions.

It required a great deal of labour to satisfy the old man that he was not the aggressor; especially with my hardly wrung replies. However, Mr. Earnshaw soon convinced him that he was alive still; he hastened to administer a dose of spirits, and by their suc-cour his master presently regained motion and consciousness.

Heathcliff, aware that he was ignorant of the treatment re-ceived while insensible, called him deliriously intoxicated; and said he should not notice his atrocious conduct further; but advised him to get to bed. To my joy, he left us after giving this judicious counsel,[1] and Hindley stretched himself on the hearth-stone. I de-parted to my own room, marvelling that I had escaped so easily.

This morning, when I came down, about half-an-hour before noon, Mr. Earnshaw was sitting by the fire, deadly sick; his evil genius almost as gaunt and ghastly, leant against the chimney. Nei-

---

1   *He, him, his*: Joseph thinks Heathcliff has murdered Hindley, but accepts
     Isabella's narrative, which proves the contrary; Hindley shows signs of life,
     and is dosed with spirits by Joseph; Heathcliff, who knows that Hindley
     was unconscious while the dosage was administered, accuses Hindley of
     being drunk and delirious, forgives him, prescribes rest for Hindley,
     and goes off; Hindley stretches himself before the fire.

ther appeared inclined to dine;[1] and having waited till all was cold on the table, I commenced alone.

Nothing hindered me from eating heartily; and I experienced a certain sense of satisfaction and superiority as, at intervals, I cast a look towards my silent companions, and felt the comfort of a quiet conscience within me.

After I had done, I ventured on the unusual liberty of drawing near the fire; going round Earnshaw's seat, and kneeling in the corner beside him.

Heathcliff did not glance my way, and I gazed up, and contemplated his features, almost as confidently as if they had been turned to stone. His forehead, that I once thought so manly, and that I now think so diabolical, was shaded with a heavy cloud; his basilisk eyes were nearly quenched by sleeplessness—and weeping, perhaps, for the lashes were wet then: his lips devoid of their ferocious sneer, and sealed in an expression of unspeakable sadness. Had it been another, I would have covered my face, in the presence of such grief. In *his* case, I was gratified: and ignoble as it seems to insult a fallen enemy, I couldn't miss this chance of sticking in a dart; his weakness was the only time when I could taste the delight of paying wrong for wrong.

"Fie, fie, Miss!" I interrupted. "One might suppose you had never opened a Bible in your life. If God afflict your enemies, surely that ought to suffice you. It is both mean and presumptuous to add your torture to his!"

"In general, I'll allow that it would be, Ellen," she continued. "But what misery laid on Heathcliff could content me, unless I have a hand in it? I'd rather he suffered *less*, if I might cause his sufferings, and he might *know* that I was the cause. Oh, I owe him so much. On only one condition can I hope to forgive him. It is, if I may take an eye for an eye, a tooth for a tooth,[2] for every wrench of agony, return a wrench, reduce him to my level. As he was the first to injure, make him the first to implore pardon;

---

1   For the dinner hour, see above, p. 99, note 1.
2   *a tooth for a tooth*: 'Eye for eye, tooth for tooth' (*Exodus* 21:24); also, 'whosoever shall smite thee on thy right cheek, turn to him the other also' (*Matthew* 5:37-38).

and then—why then, Ellen, I might show you some generosity. But it is utterly impossible I can ever be revenged, and therefore I cannot forgive him. Hindley wanted some water, and I handed him a glass, and asked him how he was."

"Not as ill as I wish," he replied. "But leaving out my arm, every inch of me is as sore as if I had been fighting with a legion of imps!"

"Yes, no wonder," was my next remark. "Catherine used to boast that she stood between you and bodily harm—she meant that certain persons would not hurt you, for fear of offending her. It's well people don't *really* rise from their grave, or, last night, she might have witnessed a repulsive scene! Are not you bruised, and cut over your chest and shoulders?"

"I can't say," he answered; "but what do you mean? Did he dare to strike me when I was down?"

"He trampled on, and kicked you, and dashed you on the ground," I whispered. "And his mouth watered to tear you with his teeth; because, he's only half a man—not so much."

Mr. Earnshaw looked up, like me, to the countenance of our mutual foe; who, absorbed in his anguish, seemed insensible to anything around him; the longer he stood, the plainer his reflections revealed their blackness through his features.

"Oh, if God would but give me strength to strangle him in my last agony, I'd go to hell with joy," groaned the impatient man writhing to rise, and sinking back in despair, convinced of his inadequacy for the struggle.

"Nay, it's enough that he has murdered one of you," I observed aloud. "At the Grange, every one knows your sister would have been living now, had it not been for Mr. Heathcliff. After all, it is preferable to be hated, than loved by him. When I recollect how happy we were—how happy Catherine was before he came—I'm fit to curse the day."

Most likely, Heathcliff noticed more the truth of what was said, than the spirit of the person who said it. His attention was roused, I saw, for his eyes rained down tears among the ashes, and he drew his breath in suffocating sighs.

I stared full at him, and laughed scornfully. The clouded windows of hell flashed, a moment towards me; the fiend which usually looked out, however, was so dimmed and drowned that I did not fear to hazard another sound of derision.

"Get up, and begone out of my sight," said the mourner.

I guessed he uttered those words, at least, though his voice was hardly intelligible.

"I beg your pardon," I replied. "But I loved Catherine too; and her brother requires attendance which, for her sake, I shall supply. Now that she's dead, I see her in Hindley; Hindley has exactly her eyes, if you had not tried to gouge them out, and made them black and red, and her—"

"Get up, wretched idiot, before I stamp you to death!" he cried, making a movement that caused me to make one also.

"But then," I continued, holding myself ready to flee; "if poor Catherine had trusted you, and assumed the ridiculous, con-temptible, degrading title of Mrs. Heathcliff, she would soon have presented a similar picture! *She* wouldn't have borne your abom-inable behaviour quietly; her detestation and disgust must have found voice."

The back of the settle, and Earnshaw's person interposed between me and him; so instead of endeavouring to reach me, he snatched a dinner knife from the table, and flung it at my head. It struck beneath my ear, and stopped the sentence I was uttering; but pulling it out, I sprang to the door, and delivered another[1] which I hope went a little deeper than his missile.

The last glimpse I caught of him was a furious rush, on his part, checked by the embrace of his host; and both fell locked together on the hearth.

In my flight through the kitchen I bid Joseph speed to his master; I knocked over Hareton, who was hanging a litter of pup-pies from a chair back in the doorway; and, blest as a soul escaped from purgatory, I bounded, leaped, and flew down the steep road: then, quitting its windings, shot direct across the moor, rolling over banks, and wading through marshes; precipitating myself, in fact, towards the beacon light of the Grange. And far rather would I be condemned to a perpetual dwelling in the infernal regions, than even for one night abide beneath the roof of Wuthering

---

1   *another*: a racist and/or sexist provocation.

Heights again."

Isabella ceased speaking, and took a drink of tea; then she rose, and bidding me put on her bonnet, and a great shawl I had brought, and turning a deaf ear to my entreaties for her to remain another hour, she stepped onto a chair, kissed Edgar's and Catherine's portraits, bestowed a similar salute on me, and descended to the carriage accompanied by Fanny, who yelped wild with joy at recovering her mistress. She was driven away, never to revisit this neighbourhood; but a regular correspondence was established between her and my master when things were more settled.

I believe her new abode was in the south, near London; there she had a son born, a few months subsequent to her escape. He was christened Linton, and from the first, she reported him to be an ailing, peevish creature.

Mr. Heathcliff, meeting me one day in the village, inquired where she lived. I refused to tell. He remarked that it was not of any moment, only she must beware of coming to her brother; she should not be with him, if he had to keep her himself.

Though I would give no information, he discovered, through some of the other servants, both her place of residence, and the existence of the child. Still he didn't molest her; for which forbearance she might thank his aversion, I suppose.

He often asked about the infant, when he saw me; and on hearing its name, smiled grimly, and observed:

"They wish me to hate it too, don't they?"

"I don't think they wish you to know any thing about it," I answered.

"But I'll have it," he said, "when I want it. They may reckon on that!"

Fortunately, its mother died before the time arrived, some thirteen years after the decease of Catherine, when Linton was twelve, or a little more.

On the day succeeding Isabella's unexpected visit, I had no opportunity of speaking to my master: he shunned conversation, and was fit for discussing nothing. When I could get him to listen, I saw it pleased him that his sister had left her husband, whom he abhorred with an intensity which the mildness of his nature would scarcely seem to allow. So deep and sensitive was his aversion, that he refrained from going anywhere where he was likely to see or hear of Heathcliff. Grief, and that together, transformed him into a complete hermit: he threw up his office of magistrate, ceased even to attend church, avoided the village on all occasions, and spent a life of entire seclusion within the limits of his park and grounds: only varied by solitary rambles on the moors, and visits to the grave of his wife, mostly at evening, or early morning, before other wanderers were abroad.

But he was too good to be thoroughly unhappy long. *He* didn't pray for Catherine's soul to haunt him: time brought resignation, and a melancholy sweeter than common joy. He recalled her memory with ardent, tender love, and hopeful aspiring to the better world, where, he doubted not she was gone.

And he had earthly consolation and affections, also. For a few days, I said, he seemed regardless of the puny successor to the departed: that coldness melted as fast as snow in April, and ere the tiny thing could stammer a word or totter a step, it wielded a despot's sceptre in his heart.

It was named Catherine, but he never called it the name in full, as he had never called the first Catherine short, probably because Heathcliff, had a habit of doing so. The little one was always Cathy, it formed to him a distinction from the mother, and yet, a connection with her; and his attachment sprang from its relation to her, far more than from its being his own.

I used to draw a comparison between him, and Hindley Earnshaw, and perplex myself to explain satisfactorily, why their conduct was so opposite in similar circumstances. They had both been fond husbands, and were both attached to their children; and I could not see how they shouldn't both have taken the same road, for good or evil. But, I thought in my mind, Hindley with apparently the stronger head, has shown himself sadly the worse and the weaker man. When his ship struck, the captain abandoned his post; and the crew, instead of trying to save her, rushed into riot, and confusion, leaving no hope for their luckless vessel. Linton, on the contrary, displayed the true courage of a loyal and faithful soul: he trusted God; and God comforted him. One hoped, and the other despaired: they chose their own lots, and were righteously doomed to endure them.

But you'll not want to hear my moralizing, Mr. Lockwood: you'll judge as well as I can, all these things; at least, you'll think you will and that's the same.

The end of Earnshaw was what might have been expected: it followed fast on his sister's, there was scarcely six months between them. We, at the Grange, never got a very succinct account of his state preceding it; all that I did learn, was on occasion of going to aid in the preparations for the funeral. Mr. Kenneth came to announce the event to my master.

"Well, Nelly;" said he, riding into the yard, one morning, too early not to alarm me with an instant presentiment of bad news. "It's your and my turn to go into mourning at present. Who's given us the slip, now do you think?"

"Who?" I asked in a flurry.

"Why, guess!" he returned, dismounting, and slinging his bridle on a hook by the door. "And nip up the corner of your apron; I'm certain you'll need it."

"Not Mr. Heathcliff, surely?" I exclaimed.

"What! would you have tears for him?" said the doctor. "No, Heathcliff's a tough young fellow; he looks blooming to-day—I've just seen him. He's rapidly regaining flesh since he lost his better half."

"Who is it, then Mr. Kenneth?" I repeated impatiently.

"Hindley Earnshaw! Your old friend Hindley—" he replied. "And my wicked gossip; though he's been too wild for me this long while. There! I said we should draw water—But cheer up! He died true to his character, drunk as a lord—poor lad; I'm sorry too. One can't help missing an old companion; though he had the worst tricks with him that ever man imagined; and has done me many a rascally turn—he's barely twenty-seven, it seems; that's your own age; who would have thought you were born in one year!"

I confess the blow was greater to me than the shock of Mrs. Linton's death: ancient associations lingered round my heart; I sat down in the porch, and wept as for a blood relation, desiring Kenneth to get another servant to introduce him to the master.

I could not hinder myself from pondering on the question—"Had he had fair play?" Whatever I did that idea would bother me: it was so tiresomely pertinacious that I resolved on requesting leave to go to Wuthering Heights, and assist in the last duties to the dead. Mr. Linton was extremely reluctant to consent, but I pleaded eloquently for the friendless condition in which he lay; and I said my old master, and foster brother had a claim on my services as strong as his own. Besides, I reminded him that the child, Hareton, was his wife's nephew; and, in the absence of nearer kin, he ought to act as its guardian; and he ought to and must inquire how the property was left, and look over the concerns of his brother-in-law.

He was unfit for attending to such matters then, but he bid me speak to his lawyer; and at length, permitted me to go. His lawyer had been Earnshaw's also: I called at the village, and asked him to accompany me. He shook his head, and advised that Heathcliff should be let alone; affirming, if the truth were known, Hareton would be found little else than a beggar.

"His father died in debt;" he said, "the whole property is mortgaged, and the sole chance for the natural heir is to allow him an opportunity of creating some interest in the creditor's heart, that he may be inclined to deal leniently towards him."

When I reached the Heights, I explained that I had come to see everything carried on decently; and Joseph, who appeared in sufficient distress, expressed satisfaction at my presence. Mr. Heathcliff said he did not perceive that I was wanted, but I might stay and order the arrangements for the funeral, if I chose.

"Correctly," he remarked, "that fool's body should be buried at the cross-roads,[1] without ceremony of any kind—I happened to leave him ten minutes, yesterday afternoon; and, in that interval, he fastened the two doors of the house against me, and he has spent the night in drinking himself to death deliberately! We broke in this morning, for we heard him snorting like a horse; and there he was, laid over the settle—flaying and scalping would not have wakened him—I sent for Kenneth, and he came; but not till the beast had changed into carrion—he was both dead and cold, and stark; and so you'll allow, it was useless making more stir about him!"

---

1   *cross-roads*: customary site for burial of suicides and witches.

The old servant confirmed this statement, but muttered,

"Aw'd rayther he'd goan hisseln for t' doctor! Aw sud uh taen tent uh t' maister better nur him—un he warn't deead when Aw left, nowt uh t' soart!"[1]

I insisted on the funeral being respectable—Mr. Heathcliff said I might have my own way there too; only, he desired me to remember, that the money for the whole affair came out of his pocket.

He maintained a hard, careless deportment, indicative of neither joy nor sorrow; if anything, it expressed a flinty gratification at a piece of difficult work, successfully executed. I observed once, indeed, something like exultation in his aspect. It was just when the people were bearing the coffin from the house; he had the hypocrisy to represent a mourner; and previous to following with Hareton he lifted the unfortunate child on to the table, and muttered with peculiar gusto,

"Now my bonny lad you are *mine*! And we'll see if one tree won't grow as crooked as another, with the same wind to twist it!"

The unsuspecting thing was pleased at this speech; he played with Heathcliff's whiskers, and stroked his cheek, but I divined its meaning and observed tartly,

"That boy must go back with me to Thrushcross Grange, Sir —There is nothing in the world less yours than he is!"

"Does Linton say so?" he demanded.

"Of course—he has ordered me to take him," I replied.

"Well," said the scoundrel, "We'll not argue the subject now; but I have a fancy to try my hand at rearing a young one, so intimate to your master, that I must supply the place of this with my own, if he attempt to remove it;[2] I don't engage to let Hareton go,

---

1 *Aw'd rayther*: 'I'd rather he'd gone himself for the doctor! I'd have taken better care of the master than him, and he wasn't dead when I left, nothing of the sort!' For a proposal that Heathcliff murdered Hindley, see John Sutherland, *Is Heathcliff a Murderer?* (1996); the action, however, upholds the denunciation by Woolman, Brougham, and others, of the stigma wrongfully fixed on the alleged posterity of Cain. In line with Isabella's the night before, Heathcliff's testimony is upheld by Joseph.

2 *I must supply*: 'I will bring my own child here in place of this one, if he tries to take him away'.

undisputed; but, I'll be pretty sure to make the other come! Remember to tell him."

This hint was enough to bind our hands. I repeated its substance, on my return, and Edgar Linton, little interested at the commencement, spoke no more of interfering. I'm not aware that he could have done it to any purpose, had he been ever so willing.

The guest was now the master of Wuthering Heights: he held firm possession, and proved to the attorney, who, in his turn, proved it to Mr. Linton, that Earnshaw had mortgaged every yard of land he owned for cash to supply his mania for gaming: and he, Heathcliff, was the mortgagee.

In that manner, Hareton, who should now be the first gentleman in the neighbourhood, was reduced to a state of complete dependence on his father's inveterate enemy; and lives in his own house as a servant deprived of the advantage of wages, and quite unable to right himself, because of his friendlessness, and his ignorance that he has been wronged.

CHAPTER 18

"The twelve years," continued Mrs. Dean, "following that dismal period, were the happiest of my life: my greatest trouble, in their passage, rose from our little lady's trifling illnesses which she had to experience in common with all children, rich and poor."

For the rest, after the first six months, she grew like a larch; and could walk and talk too, in her own way, before the heath blossomed a second time over Mrs. Linton's dust.

She was the most winning thing that ever brought sunshine into a desolate house—a real beauty, in face—with the Earnshaw's handsome dark eyes, but the Lintons' fair skin, and small features, and yellow curling hair. Her spirit was high, though not rough, and qualified by a heart, sensitive and lively to excess in its affections. That capacity for intense attachments reminded me of her mother; still she did not resemble her; for she could be soft and mild as a dove, and she had a gentle voice, and pensive expression: her anger was never furious; her love never fierce; it was deep and tender.

However, it must be acknowledged, she had faults to foil her gifts. A propensity to be saucy was one; and a perverse will that indulged children invariably acquire, whether they be good tempered or cross. If a servant chanced to vex her, it was always: "I shall tell papa!" And if he reproved her, even by a look, you would have thought it a heart-breaking business: I don't believe he ever did speak a harsh word to her.

He took her education entirely on himself, and made it an amusement: fortunately, curiosity, and a quick intellect urged her into an apt scholar; and she learnt rapidly and eagerly, and did honour to his teaching.

Till she reached the age of thirteen, she had not once been beyond the range of the park by herself. Mr. Linton would take her with him, a mile or so outside, on rare occasions; but he trusted her to no one else. Gimmerton was an unsubstantial name in her ears; the chapel, the only building she had approached, or entered, except her own home; Wuthering Heights and Mr. Heathcliff did not exist for her; she was a perfect recluse; and, apparently, perfectly contented. Sometimes, indeed, while surveying the country from her nursery window, she would observe—

"Ellen, how long will it be before I can walk to the top of those hills? I wonder what lies on the other side—is it the sea?"

"No, Miss Cathy," I would answer, "it is hills again just like these."

"And what are those golden rocks like, when you stand under them?" she once asked.

The abrupt descent of Penistone Craggs particularly attracted her notice, especially when the setting sun shone on it, and the topmost Heights; and the whole extent of landscape besides lay in shadow.

I explained that they were bare masses of stone, with hardly enough earth in their clefts[1] to nourish a stunted tree.

"And why are they bright so long after it is evening here?" she pursued.

"Because they are a great deal higher up than we are," replied I; "you could not climb them, they are too high and steep. In winter the frost is always there before it comes to us; and, deep into summer, I have found snow under that black hollow on the north-east side!"

"Oh, you have been on them!" she cried, gleefully. "Then I can go, too, when I am a woman. Has papa been, Ellen?"

"Papa would tell you, Miss," I answered, testily, "that they are not worth the trouble of visiting. The moors, where you ramble with him, are much nicer; and Thrushcross park is the finest place in the world.

"But I know the park, and I don't know those," she murmured to herself. "And I should delight to look round me, from the brow of that tallest point[2]—my little pony, Minny, shall take

---

1   *clefts*: Gordale Scar appears in T.D. Whitaker, *The Deanery of Craven*, p. 194: 'Wherever a cleft in the rock, or a lodgement of earth appears, the yew-tree […] contrasts its deep and glossy green with the pale grey of the limestone'; also, Frederic Montagu, *Gleanings in Craven* (1838), p. 102: '[in] the clefts in the rocks' sides, or wherever a lodgment of earth appears, the deep and glossy green of the yew refreshes the eye in its wandering over the pale grey of the vast rock'.

2   *tallest point*: see above, Introduction, 'The Wuthering Heights landscape', pp. 18-34, and Plate 4.

me sometime."

One of the maids mentioning the Fairy cave,[1] quite turned her head with a desire to fulfil this project; she teased Mr. Linton about it; and he promised she should have the journey when she got older: but Miss Catherine measured her age by months, and—

"Now, am I old enough to go to Penistone Craggs?" was the constant question in her mouth.

The road thither wound close by Wuthering Heights. Edgar had not the heart to pass it; so she received as constantly the answer:

"Not yet, love, not yet."

I said Mrs. Heathcliff lived above a dozen years after quitting her husband. Her family were of a delicate constitution: she and Edgar both lacked the ruddy health that you will generally meet in these parts. What her last illness was, I am not certain; I con-jecture, they died of the same thing, a kind of fever, slow at its commencement, but incurable, and rapidly consuming life to-wards the close.[2]

She wrote to inform her brother of the probable conclusion of a four months' indisposition, under which she had suffered; and entreated him to come to her, if possible, for she had much to settle, and she wished to bid him adieu, and deliver Linton safely into his hands. Her hope was, that Linton might be left with him, as he had been with her; his father, she would fain convince her-self, had no desire to assume the burden of his maintenance or education.

My master hesitated not a moment in complying with her request; reluctant as he was to leave home at ordinary calls, he flew to answer this; commending Catherine to my peculiar vigilance, in his absence; with reiterated orders that she must not wander out of the park, even under my escort; he did not calculate on her going unaccompanied.

He was away three weeks: the first day or two, my charge sat in a corner of the library, too sad for either reading or playing: in that quiet state she caused me little trouble; but it was succeeded

---

1   *Fairy cave*: see above, Introduction, 'The Wuthering Heights landscape', pp. 18-34 and Plate 2.
2   Like Frances and Linton Heathcliff, the Lintons die of tuberculosis.

by an interval of impatient, fretful weariness; and being too busy, and too old then, to run up and down amusing her, I hit on a method by which she might entertain herself.

I used to send her on her travels round the grounds—now on foot, and now on a pony; indulging her with a patient audience of all her real and imaginary adventures, when she returned.

The summer shone in full prime; and she took such a taste for this solitary rambling that she often contrived to remain out from breakfast till tea; and then the evenings were spent in recounting her fanciful tales. I did not fear her breaking bounds, because the gates were generally locked, and I thought she would scarcely venture forth alone, if they had stood wide open.

Unluckily, my confidence proved misplaced. Catherine came to me, one morning, at eight o'clock, and said she was that day an Arabian merchant, going to cross the Desert with his caravan; and I must give her plenty of provision for herself, and beasts, a horse, and three camels, personated by a large hound, and a couple of pointers.

I got together good store of dainties, and slung them in a basket on one side of the saddle; and she sprang up as gay as a fairy, sheltered by her wide-brimmed hat and gauze veil from the July sun, and trotted off with a merry laugh, mocking my cautious counsel to avoid galloping, and come back early.

The naughty thing never made her appearance at tea. One traveller, the hound, being an old dog, and fond of its ease, returned; but neither Cathy, nor the pony, nor the two pointers were visible in any direction; and I despatched emissaries down this path, and that path, and, at last, went wandering in search of her myself.

There was a labourer working at a fence round a plantation, on the borders of the grounds. I enquired of him if he had seen our young lady?

"I saw her at morn," he replied, "she would have me to cut her a hazel switch; and then she leapt her galloway[1] over the hedge yonder, where it is lowest, and gallopped out of sight."

You may guess how I felt at hearing this news. It struck me directly she must have started for Penistone Craggs.

---

1   See above, p. 85, note 10.

"What will become of her?" I ejaculated, pushing through a gap which the man was repairing, and making straight to the high road.

I walked as if for a wager, mile after mile, till a turn brought me in view of the Heights, but no Catherine could I detect, far or near.

The Craggs lie about a mile and a half beyond Mr. Heathcliff's place, and that is four from the Grange, so I began to fear night would fall ere I could reach them.

"And what if she should have slipped in clambering among them," I reflected, "and been killed, or broken some of her bones?"

My suspense was truly painful; and, at first, it gave me delightful relief to observe, in hurrying by the farm-house, Charlie, the fiercest of the pointers, lying under a window, with swelled head, and bleeding ear.

I opened the wicket, and ran to the door, knocking vehemently for admittance. A woman whom I knew, and who formerly lived at Gimmerton, answered—she had been servant since the death of Mr. Earnshaw.

"Ah," said she, "you are come a-seeking your little mistress! don't be frightened. She's here safe—but I'm glad it isn't the master."

"He is not at home then, is he?" I panted, quite breathless with quick walking and alarm.

"No, no," she replied, "both he and Joseph are off, and I think they won't return this hour or more. Step in and rest you a bit."

I entered, and beheld my stray lamb, seated on the hearth, rocking herself in a little chair that had been her mother's, when a child. Her hat was hung against the wall, and she seemed perfectly at home, laughing and chattering, in the best spirits imaginable, to Hareton, now a great, strong lad of eighteen, who stared at her with considerable curiosity and astonishment; comprehending precious little of the fluent succession of remarks and questions which her tongue never ceased pouring forth.

"Very well, Miss," I exclaimed, concealing my joy under an angry countenance. "This is your last ride, till papa comes back. I'll not trust you over the threshold again, you naughty, naughty girl."

"Aha, Ellen!" she cried, gaily, jumping up, and running to my side. "I shall have a pretty story to tell to-night—so you've found me out. Have you ever been here in your life before?"

"Put that hat on, and come home at once," said I. I'm dreadfully grieved at you, Miss Cathy, you've done extremely wrong! It's no use pouting and crying; that won't repay the trouble I've had, scouring the country after you. To think how Mr. Linton charged me to keep you in; and you stealing off so; it shows you are a cunning little fox, and nobody will put faith in you any more."

"What have I done?" sobbed she, instantly checked. "Papa charged[1] me nothing—he'll not scold me, Ellen—he's never cross, like you!"

"Come, come!" I repeated. "I'll tie the riband. Now, let us have no petulance. Oh, for shame. You thirteen years old, and such a baby!"

This exclamation was caused by her pushing the hat from her head, and retreating to the chimney out of my reach.

"Nay," said the servant, "don't be hard on the bonny lass, Mrs. Dean. We made her stop—she'd fain have ridden forwards, afeard you should be uneasy. But Hareton offered to go with her, and I thought he should. It's a wild road over the hills."

Hareton, during the discussion, stood with his hands in his pockets, too awkward to speak, though he looked as if he did not relish my intrusion.

"How long am I to wait?" I continued, disregarding the woman's interference. "It will be dark in ten minutes. Where is the pony, Miss Cathy? And where is Phenix? I shall leave you, unless you be quick, so please yourself."

"The pony is in the yard," she replied, "and Phenix is shut in there. He's bitten—and so is Charlie. I was going to tell you all about it; but you are in a bad temper, and don't deserve to hear."

I picked up her hat, and approached to reinstate it; but perceiving that the people of the house took her part, she commenced capering round the room; and, on my giving chase, ran

---

1   *charged*: ordered.

like a mouse, over and under, and behind the furniture, rendering it ridiculous for me to pursue.

Hareton and the woman laughed; and she joined them, and waxed more impertinent still; till I cried, in great irritation,

"Well, Miss Cathy, if you were aware whose house this is, you'd be glad enough to get out."

"It's your father's, isn't it?" said she, turning to Hareton.

"Nay," he replied, looking down, and blushing bashfully.

He could not stand a steady gaze from her eyes, though they were just his own.

"Whose then—your master's?" she asked.

He coloured deeper, with a different feeling, muttered an oath, and turned away.

"Who is his master?" continued the tiresome girl, appealing to me. "He talked about 'our house,' and 'our folk.' I thought he had been the owner's son. And he never said, Miss; he should have done, shouldn't he, if he's a servant?"

Hareton grew black as a thunder-cloud, at this childish speech. I silently shook my questioner, and, at last, succeeded in equipping her for departure.

"Now, get my horse," she said, addressing her unknown kinsman as she would one of the stable-boys at the Grange. "And you may come with me. I want to see where the goblin hunter[1] rises in the marsh, and to hear about the *farishes*, as you call them—but, make haste! What's the matter? Get my horse, I say."

"I'll see thee damned, before I be *thy* servant!" growled the lad.

"You'll see me *what*?" asked Catherine in surprise.

"Damned—thou saucy witch!" he replied.

"There, Miss Cathy! you see you have got into pretty company," I interposed. "Nice words to be used to a young lady! Pray don't begin to dispute with him—Come, let us seek for Minny ourselves, and begone."

---

1 *goblin hunter*: Hunter's Cross (also Hunt's Cross), a legendary feature at the summit of Gragareth, the counterpart of Penistone Crag; see R.R. & M. Balderston, *Ingleton: Bygone & Present* (undated: around 1888); also, R. Balderston Cragg, *Legendary Rambles. Ingleton and Lonsdale* (undated; around 1900), p. 24.

"But Ellen," cried she, staring, fixed in astonishment. "How dare he speak so to me? Mustn't he be made to do as I ask him? You wicked creature, I shall tell papa what you said—Now then!"

Hareton did not appear to feel this threat; so the tears sprung into her eyes with indignation. "You bring the pony," she exclaimed, turning to the woman, "and let my dog free this moment!"

"Softly, Miss," answered the addressed. "You'll lose nothing, by being civil. Though Mr. Hareton, there, be not the master's son, he's your cousin; and I was never hired to serve you."

"*He* my cousin!" cried Cathy with a scornful laugh.

"Yes, indeed," responded her reprover.

"Oh, Ellen! don't let them say such things," she pursued in great trouble. "Papa is gone to fetch my cousin from London—my cousin is a gentleman's son—*That* my—" she stopped, and wept outright; upset at the bare notion of relationship with such a clown.

"Hush, hush!" I whispered, "people can have many cousins and of all sorts, Miss Cathy, without being any the worse for it; only they needn't keep their company, if they be disagreeable, and bad."

"He's not, he's not my cousin, Ellen!" she went on, gathering fresh grief from reflection, and flinging herself into my arms for refuge from the idea.

I was much vexed at her and the servant for their mutual revelations; having no doubt of Linton's approaching arrival, communicated by the former, being reported to Mr. Heathcliff; and feeling as confident that Catherine's first thought on her father's return, would be to seek an explanation of the latter's assertion, concerning her rude-bred kindred.

Hareton, recovering from his disgust at being taken for a servant, seemed moved by her distress; and, having fetched the pony round to the door, he took, to propitiate her, a fine crooked-legged terrier whelp from the kennel; and putting it into her hand, bid her *wisht* for he meant naught.

Pausing in her lamentations, she surveyed him with a glance of awe, and horror, then burst forth anew.

I could scarcely refrain from smiling at this antipathy to the poor fellow; who was a well-made, athletic youth, good looking in features, and stout and healthy, but attired in garments befitting his daily occupations of working on the farm, and lounging among the moors after rabbits and game. Still, I thought I could detect in his physiognomy a mind owning better qualities than his father ever possessed. Good things lost amid a wilderness of weeds, to be sure, whose rankness far over-topped their neglected growth; yet notwithstanding, evidence of a wealthy soil that might yield luxuriant crops, under other and favourable circumstances. Mr. Heathcliff, I believe, had not treated him physically ill; thanks to his fearless nature which offered no temptation to that course of oppression; it had none of the timid susceptibility that would have given zest to ill-treatment, in Heathcliff's judgment. He appeared to have bent his malevolence on making him a brute: he was never taught to read or write; ever rebuked for any bad habit which did not annoy his keeper; never led a single step towards virtue, or guarded by a single precept against vice. And from what I heard, Joseph contributed much to his deterioration by a narrow minded partiality which prompted him to flatter, and pet him, as a boy, because he was the head of the old family. And as he had been in the habit of accusing Catherine Earnshaw, and Heathcliff, when children, of putting the master past his patience, and compelling him to seek solace in drink, by what he termed, their 'offalld ways,' so at present, he laid the whole burden of Hareton's faults on the shoulders of the usurper of his property.

If the lad swore he wouldn't correct him; nor however culpably he behaved. It gave Joseph satisfaction, apparently, to watch him go the worst lengths. He allowed that he was ruined; that his soul was abandoned to perdition; but then, he reflected that Heathcliff must answer for it. Hareton's blood would be required at his hands; and there lay immense consolation in that thought.

Joseph had instilled into him a pride of name, and of his lineage; he would had he dared, have fostered hate between him and the present owner of the Heights, but his dread of that owner amounted to superstition; and he confined his feelings, regarding him, to muttered inuendos and private comminations.

I don't pretend to be intimately acquainted with the mode of living customary in those days, at Wuthering Heights. I only speak from hearsay; for I saw little. The villagers affirmed Mr. Heathcliff was *near*, and a cruel hard landlord to his tenants; but the house, inside, had regained its ancient aspect of comfort under female management; and the scenes of riot common in Hindley's time, were not now enacted within its walls. The master was too gloomy to seek companionship with any people, good or bad, and he is yet—

This, however, is not making progress with my story. Miss Cathy rejected the peace-offering of the terrier, and demanded her own dogs, Charlie and Phenix. They came limping, and hanging their heads; and we set out for home, sadly out of sorts, every one of us.

I could not wring from my little lady how she had spent the day; except that, as I supposed, the goal of her pilgrimage was Penistone Crags; and she arrived without adventure to the gate of the farmhouse, when Hareton happened to issue forth, attended by some canine followers who attacked her train.

They had a smart battle, before their owners could separate them: that formed an introduction. Catherine told Hareton who she was, and where she was going; and asked him to show her the way; finally, beguiling him to accompany her.

He opened the mysteries of the Fairy cave, and twenty other queer places; but being in disgrace, I was not favoured with a description of the interesting objects she saw.

I could gather however, that her guide had been a favourite till she hurt his feelings by addressing him as a servant, and Heathcliff's housekeeper hurt hers, by calling him her cousin.

Then the language he had held to her rankled in her heart; she who was always "love," and "darling," and "queen," and "angel," with everybody at the Grange; to be insulted so shockingly by a stranger! She did not comprehend it; and hard work I had, to obtain a promise that she would not lay the grievance before her father.

I explained how he objected to the whole household at the Heights, and how sorry he would be to find she had been there; but, I insisted most on the fact, that if she revealed my negligence of his orders, he would perhaps, be so angry that I should have to leave; and Cathy couldn't bear that prospect: she pledged her word, and kept it, for my sake—after all, she was a sweet little girl.

CHAPTER 19

A letter, edged with black, announced the day of my master's return. Isabella was dead; and he wrote to bid me get mourning for his daughter, and arrange a room, and other accommodations, for his youthful nephew.

Catherine ran wild with joy at the idea of welcoming her father back: and indulged most sanguine anticipations of the innumerable excellencies of her "real" cousin.

The evening of their expected arrival came. Since early morning, she had been busy, ordering her own small affairs; and now, attired in her new black frock—poor thing! her aunt's death impressed her with no definite sorrow—she obliged me, by constant worrying, to walk with her, down through the grounds, to meet them.

"Linton is just six months younger than I am," she chattered as we strolled leisurely over the swells and hollows of mossy turf, under the shadow of the trees. "How delightful it will be to have him for a playfellow! Aunt Isabella sent papa a beautiful lock of his hair; it was lighter than mine—more flaxen, and quite as fine. I have it carefully preserved in a little glass box; and I've often thought what pleasure it would be to see its owner—Oh! I am happy—and papa, dear, dear papa! come, Ellen, let us run! come run!"

She ran, and returned and ran again, many times before my sober footsteps reached the gate, and then she seated herself on the grassy bank beside the path, and tried to wait patiently; but that was impossible; she couldn't be still a minute.

"How long they are!" she exclaimed. "Ah, I see some dust on the road—they are coming! No! When will they be here? May we not go a little way—half a mile, Ellen, only just half a mile? Do say yes, to that clump of birches at the turn!"

I refused staunchily: and, at length, her suspense was ended: the travelling carriage rolled in sight.

Miss Cathy shrieked, and stretched out her arms, as soon as she caught her father's face, looking from the window. He descended, nearly as eager as herself; and a considerable interval elapsed, ere they had a thought to spare for any but themselves.

While they exchanged caresses, I took a peep in to see after Linton. He was asleep, in a corner, wrapped in a warm, fur-lined cloak, as if it had been winter—A pale, delicate, effeminate boy, who might have been taken for my master's younger brother, so strong was the resemblance, but there was a sickly peevishness in his aspect, that Edgar Linton never had.

The latter saw me looking; and having shaken hands, advised me to close the door, and leave him undisturbed; for the journey had fatigued him.

Cathy would fain have taken one glance; but her father told her to come on, and they walked together up the park, while I hastened before, to prepare the servants.

"Now, darling," said Mr. Linton, addressing his daughter, as they halted at the bottom of the front steps. "Your cousin is not so strong, or so merry as you are, and he has lost his mother, remember, a very short time since, therefore, don't expect him to play, and run about with you directly. And don't harass him much by talking—let him be quiet this evening, at least, will you?"

"Yes, yes, papa," answered Catherine; "but I do want to see him; and he hasn't once looked out."

The carriage stopped; and the sleeper, being roused, was lifted to the ground by his uncle.

"This is your cousin Cathy, Linton," he said, putting their little hands together. "She's fond of you already; and mind you don't grieve her by crying to-night. Try to be cheerful now; the travelling is at an end, and you have nothing to do but rest and amuse yourself as you please."

"Let me go to bed then," answered the boy, shrinking from Catherine's salute; and he put his fingers to his eyes to remove incipient tears.

"Come, come, there's a good child," I whispered, leading him in. "You'll make her weep too—see how sorry she is for you!"

I do not know whether it were sorrow for him, but his cousin put on as sad a countenance as himself, and returned to her father. All three entered, and mounted to the library where tea was laid ready.

I proceeded to remove Linton's cap, and mantle, and placed him on a chair by the table; but he was no sooner seated than he began to cry afresh. My master inquired what was the matter.

"I can't sit on a chair," sobbed the boy.

"Go to the sofa then; and Ellen shall bring you some tea," answered his uncle, patiently.

He had been greatly tried during the journey, I felt convinced, by his fretful, ailing charge.

Linton slowly trailed himself off, and lay down. Cathy carried a foot-stool and her cup to his side.

At first she sat silent; but that could not last; she had resolved to make a pet of her little cousin, as she would have him to be; and she commenced stroking his curls, and kissing his cheek, and offering him tea in her saucer, like a baby. This pleased him, for he was not much better; he dried his eyes, and lightened into a faint smile.

"Oh, he'll do very well," said the master to me, after watching them a minute. "Very well, if we can keep him, Ellen. The company of a child of his own age will instil new spirit into him soon: and by wishing for strength he'll gain it."

Aye, if we can keep him! I mused to myself; and sore misgivings came over me that there was slight hope of that. And then, I thought, however will that weakling live at Wuthering Heights, between his father and Hareton? what playmates and instructors they'll be.

Our doubts were presently decided; even earlier than I expected. I had just taken the children upstairs, after tea was finished; and seen Linton asleep—he would not suffer me to leave him, till that was the case—I had come down, and was standing by the table in the hall, lighting a bed-room candle for Mr. Edgar, when a maid stepped out of the kitchen, and informed me that Mr. Heathcliff's servant, Joseph, was at the door, and wished to speak with the master.

"I shall ask him what he wants first," I said, in considerable trepidation. "A very unlikely hour to be troubling people, and the instant they have returned from a long journey. I don't think the master can see him."

Joseph had advanced through the kitchen, as I uttered these

words, and now presented himself in the hall. He was donned in his Sunday garments, with his most sanctimonious and sourest face; and holding his hat in one hand, and his stick in the other, he proceeded to clean his shoes on the mat.

"Good evening, Joseph," I said, coldly. "What business brings you here to-night?"

"It's Maister Linton Aw mun spake tull,"[1] he answered, waving me disdainfully aside.

"Mr. Linton is going to bed; unless you have something particular to say, I'm sure he won't hear it now," I continued. "You had better sit down in there, and entrust your message to me."

"Which is his rahm?"[2] pursued the fellow, surveying the range of closed doors.

I perceived he was bent on refusing my mediation; so very reluctantly, I went up to the library, and announced the unseasonable visiter; advising that he should be dismissed till next day.

Mr. Linton had no time to empower me to do so, for he mounted close at my heels, and pushing into the apartment, planted himself at the far side of the table, with his two fists clapped on the head of his stick, and began in an elevated tone, as if anticipating opposition.

"Hathecliff has send me for his lad, un Aw munn't goa back 'baht him."[3]

Edgar Linton was silent a minute; an expression of exceeding sorrow overcast his features; he would have pitied the child on his own account; but, recalling Isabella's hopes and fears, and anxious wishes for her son, and her commendations of him to his care, he grieved bitterly at the prospect of yielding him up, and searched in his heart how it might be avoided. No plan offered itself: the very exhibition of any desire to keep him would have rendered the claimant more peremptory: there was nothing left but to resign him. However, he was not going to rouse him from his sleep.

"Tell Mr. Heathcliff," he answered, calmly, "that his son shall come to Wuthering Heights to-morrow. He is in bed, and too

---

1   *It's Maister*: 'I have to speak to Mr. Linton'.
2   'Which room is his?'
3   'Heathcliff has sent me for his boy, and I mustn't go back without him'.

tired to go the distance now. You may also tell him that the mother of Linton desired him to remain under my guardianship; and, at present, his health is very precarious."

"Noa!" said Joseph, giving a thud with his prop on the floor, and assuming an authoritative air. "Noa! that manes nowt—Hathecliff maks noa 'cahnt uh t' mother, nur yah norther—bud he'll hev his lad; and Aw mun tak him—soa nah yah knaw!"[1]

"You shall not to-night!" answered Linton, decisively. "Walk down stairs at once, and repeat to your master what I have said. Ellen, show him down. Go—"

And, aiding the indignant elder with a lift by the arm, he rid the room of him, and closed the door.

"Varrah weel!" shouted Joseph, as he slowly drew off. "Tuh morn, he's come hisseln, un' thrust *him* aht, if yar darr!"[2]

---

1   *Noa:* 'No, that means nothing—Heathcliff takes no account of the mother, nor of you—but he'll have his boy, and I must take him—so now you know!'

2   *Varrah weel:* 'Very well! Tomorrow, he'll come himself, and push *him* out if you dare!'

To obviate the danger of this threat being fulfilled, Mr. Linton commissioned me to take the boy home early, on Catherine's pony, and, said he—

"As we shall now have no influence over his destiny, good or bad, you must say nothing of where he is gone to my daughter; she cannot associate with him hereafter; and it is better for her to remain in ignorance of his proximity, lest she should be restless, and anxious to visit the Heights—merely tell her, his father sent for him suddenly, and he has been obliged to leave us."

Linton was very reluctant to be roused from his bed, at five o'clock, and astonished to be informed that he must prepare for further travelling: but I softened off the matter by stating that he was going to spend some time with his father, Mr. Heathcliff, who wished to see him so much, he did not like to defer the pleasure till he should recover from his late journey.

"My father?" he cried, in strange perplexity. "Mamma never told me I had a father. Where does he live? I'd rather stay with uncle."

"He lives a little distance from the Grange," I replied, "just beyond those hills—not so far, but you may walk over here, when you get hearty. And you should be glad to go home, and to see him. You must try to love him, as you did your mother, and then he will love you."

"But why have I not heard of him before?" asked Linton; "why didn't mamma and he, live together as other people do?"

"He had business to keep him in the north," I answered; "and your mother's health required her to reside in the south."

"And why didn't mamma speak to me about him?" persevered the child. "She often talked of uncle, and I learnt to love him long ago. How am I to love papa? I don't know him."

"Oh, all children love their parents," I said. "Your mother, perhaps, thought you would want to be with him, if she mentioned him often to you. Let us make haste. An early ride on such a beautiful morning is much preferable to an hour's more sleep."

CHAPTER 21

We had sad work with little Cathy that day: she rose in high glee, eager to join her cousin; and such passionate tears and lamentations followed the news of his departure, that Edgar, himself, was obliged to sooth her, by affirming he should come back soon; he added, however, "if I can get him;" and there were no hopes of that.

This promise poorly pacified her; but time was more potent; and though still, at intervals, she inquired of her father, when Linton would return; before she did see him again, his features had waxed so dim in her memory that she did not recognise him.

When I chanced to encounter the housekeeper of Wuthering Heights, in paying business-visits to Gimmerton, I used to ask how the young master got on; for he lived almost as secluded as Catherine herself, and was never to be seen. I could gather from her that he continued in weak health, and was a tiresome inmate. She said Mr. Heathcliff seemed to dislike him even longer and worse, though he took some trouble to conceal it. He had an antipathy to the sound of his voice, and could not do at all with his sitting in the same room with him many minutes together.

There seldom passed much talk between them; Linton learnt his lessons, and spent his evenings in a small apartment, they called the parlour; or else lay in bed all day; for he was constantly getting coughs, and colds, and aches, and pains of some sort.

"And I never knew such a faint-hearted creature," added the woman; "nor one so careful of hisseln. He *will* go on, if I leave the window open, a bit late in the evening. Oh! it's killing, a breath of night air! And he must have a fire in the middle of summer; and Joseph's 'bacca pipe is poison; and he must always have sweets and dainties, and always milk, milk for ever—heeding naught how the rest of us are pinched in winter—and there he'll sit, wrapped in his furred cloak in his chair by the fire, and some toast and water, or other slop on the hob to sip at; and if Hareton, for pity, comes to amuse him—Hareton is not bad-natured, though he's rough—they're sure to part, one swearing, and the other crying. I believe the master would relish Earnshaw's thrashing him to a mummy, if he were not his son: and, I'm certain, he would be fit to turn him out of doors, if he knew half the nursing he gives hisseln.[1] But then, he won't go into danger of temptation; he never enters the parlour, and should Linton show those ways in the house where he is, he sends him upstairs directly."

I divined, from this account, that utter lack of sympathy had rendered young Heathcliff selfish and disagreeable, if he were not so originally; and my interest in him, consequently, decayed; though still I was moved with a sense of grief at his lot, and a wish that he had been left with us.

Mr. Edgar encouraged me to gain information; he thought a great deal about him, I fancy, and would have run some risk to see him; and he told me once to ask the housekeeper whether he ever came into the village?

She said she had only been twice, on horse-back, accompanying his father: and both times he pretended to be quite knocked up for three or four days afterwards.

That housekeeper left, if I recollect rightly, two years after he came; and another, whom I did not know, was her successor: she lives there still.

Time wore on at the Grange in its former pleasant way, till Miss Cathy reached sixteen. On the anniversary of her birth we never manifested any signs of rejoicing, because it was, also, the anniversary of my late mistress's death. Her father invariably spent that day alone in the library; and walked, at dusk, as far as Gimmerton kirkyard, where he would frequently prolong his stay beyond midnight. Therefore Catherine was thrown on her own resources for amusement.

This twentieth of March was a beautiful spring day, and when her father had retired, my young lady came down dressed for going out, and said she had asked to have a ramble on the edge of the moors with me; and Mr. Linton had given her leave, if we went only a short distance, and were back within the hour.

---

1   *hisseln*: himself; 'if Heathcliff knew half of what there is to know about how his son nurses himself [how sickly he is], he would turn him out of doors'.

"So make haste Ellen!" she cried, "I know where I wish to go; where a colony of moor game[1] are settled; I want to see whether they have made their nests yet."

"That must be a good distance up," I answered; they don't breed on the edge of the moor."

"No, it's not," she said, "I've gone very near with papa."

I put on my bonnet, and sallied out; thinking nothing more of the matter. She bounded before me, and returned to my side, and was off again like a young greyhound; and, at first, I found plenty of entertainment in listening to the larks singing far and near; and enjoying the sweet, warm sunshine; and watching her, my pet, and my delight, with her golden ringlets flying loose behind, and her bright cheek, as soft and pure in its bloom, as a wild rose, and her eyes radiant with cloudless pleasure. She was a happy creature, and an angel, in those days. It's a pity she could not be content.

"Well," said I, "where are your moor-game, Miss Cathy? We should be at them—the Grange park-fence is a great way off now."

"Oh, a little further—only a little further, Ellen," was her answer, continually. "Climb to that hillock, pass that bank, and by the time you reach the other side, I shall have raised the birds."

But there were so many hillocks and banks to climb and pass, that, at length, I began to be weary, and told her we must halt, and retrace our steps.

I shouted to her, as she had outstripped me, a long way; she either did not hear, or did not regard, for she still sprang on, and I was compelled to follow. Finally, she dived into a hollow; and before I came in sight of her again, she was two miles nearer Wuthering Heights than her own home;[2] and I beheld a couple of persons arrest her, one of whom I felt convinced was Mr. Heathcliff himself.

Cathy had been caught in the fact of plundering, or, at least, hunting out the nests of the grouse.

The Heights were Heathcliff's land, and he was reproving the poacher.

"I've neither taken any nor found any," she said, as I toiled to

---

1   *moor game*: grouse, patridge, etc.
2   *two miles nearer*: see above, Introduction, 'Riddles', pp. 26-34.

them, expanding her hands in corroboration of the statement. "I didn't mean to take them; but papa told me there were quantities up here, and I wished to see the eggs."

Heathcliff glanced at me with an ill-meaning smile, expressing his acquaintance with the party, and, consequently, his malevolence towards it, and demanded who "papa" was?

"Mr. Linton of Thrushcross Grange," she replied. "I thought you did not know me, or you wouldn't have spoken in that way."

"You suppose papa highly esteemed and respected them?" he said, sarcastically.

"And what are you?" inquired Catherine, gazing curiously on the speaker. "That man I've seen before. Is he your son?"

She pointed to Hareton, the other individual; who had gained nothing but increased bulk and strength by the addition of two years[1] to his age: he seemed as awkward and rough as ever.

"Miss Cathy," I interrupted, "it will be three hours instead of one, that we were out, presently. We really must go back."

"No, that man is not my son," answered Heathcliff, pushing me aside. "But I have one, and you have seen him before too; and, though your nurse is in a hurry, I think both you and she would be the better for a little rest. Will you just turn this nab[2] of heath, and walk into my house? You'll get home earlier for the ease; and you shall receive a kind welcome."

I whispered to Catherine, that she mustn't, on any account, accede to the proposal; it was entirely out of the question.

"Why?" she asked, aloud, "I'm tired of running, and the ground is dewy—I can't sit here. Let us go, Ellen! Besides, he says I have seen his son. He's mistaken, I think; but I guess where he lives, at the farm-house I visited in coming from Penistone Craggs. Don't you?"

"I do. Come, Nelly, hold your tongue—it will be a treat for her to look in on us. Hareton, get forwards with the lass. You shall walk with me, Nelly."

"No, she's not going to any such place," I cried, struggling to release my arm which he had seized; but she was almost at the

---

1 *two years*: for dates, birthdays, seasons and ages, see below, Appendix A.
2 *nab*: 'the summit of a hill' (Carr).

door-stones already, scampering round the brow at full speed. Her appointed companion did not pretend to escort her; he shyed off by the road side, and vanished.

"Mr. Heathcliff, it's very wrong," I continued, "you know you mean no good; and there she'll see Linton, and all will be told, as soon as ever we return; and I shall have the blame."

"I want her to see Linton," he answered: he's looking better these few days; it's not often he's fit to be seen. And we'll soon persuade her to keep the visit secret—where is the harm of it?"

"The harm of it is, that her father would hate me, if he found I suffered her to enter your house; and I am convinced you have a bad design in encouraging her to do so," I replied.

"My design is as honest as possible. I'll inform you of its whole scope," he said. "That the two cousins may fall in love, and get married. I'm acting generously to your master; his young chit has no expectations, and should she second my wishes, she'll be provided for at once, as joint successor with Linton."

"If Linton died," I answered, "and his life is quite uncertain, Catherine would be the heir."

"No, she would not," he said. "There is no clause in the will to secure it so; his property would go to me; but, to prevent dispute, I desire their union, and am resolved to bring it about."

"And I'm resolved she shall never approach your house with me again," I returned, as we reached the gate, where Miss Cathy waited our coming.

Heathcliff bid me be quiet; and preceding us up the path, hastened to open the door. My young lady gave him several looks, as if she could not exactly make up her mind what to think of him; but now he smiled when he met her eye, and softened his voice in addressing her, and I was foolish enough to imagine the memory of her mother might disarm him from desiring her injury.

Linton stood on the hearth. He had been out, walking in the fields; for his cap was on, and he was calling to Joseph to bring him dry shoes.

He had grown tall of his age, still wanting some months of sixteen. His features were pretty yet, and his eye and complexion brighter than I remembered them, though with merely temporary lustre borrowed from the salubrious air and genial sun.

"Now, who is that?" asked Mr. Heathcliff, turning to Cathy. "Can you tell?"

"Your son?" she said, having doubtfully surveyed, first one, and then the other.

"Yes, yes," answered he; "but is this the only time you have beheld him? Think! Ah! you have a short memory. Linton, don't you recall your cousin, that you used to tease us so, with wishing to see?"

"What, Linton!" cried Cathy, kindling into joyful surprise at the name. "Is that little Linton? He's taller than I am! Are you Linton?"

The youth stepped forward, and acknowledged himself: she kissed him fervently, and they gazed with wonder at the change time had wrought in the appearance of each.

Catherine had reached her full height; her figure was both plump and slender, elastic as steel, and her whole aspect sparkling with health and spirits. Linton's looks and movements were very languid, and his form extremely slight; but there was a grace in his manner that mitigated these defects, and rendered him not unpleasing.

After exchanging numerous marks of fondness with him, his cousin went to Mr. Heathcliff, who lingered by the door, dividing his attention between the objects inside, and those that lay without, pretending, that is, to observe the latter, and really noting the former alone.

"And you are my uncle, then!" she cried, reaching up to salute him. I thought I liked you, though you were cross, at first. Why don't you visit at the Grange with Linton? To live all these years such close neighbours, and never see us, is odd; what have you done so for?"

"I visited it once or twice too often before you were born," he answered. "There—damn it! If you have any kisses to spare, give them to Linton—they are thrown away on me."

"Naughty Ellen!" exclaimed Catherine, flying to attack me next with her lavish caresses. "Wicked Ellen! to try to hinder me from entering. But, I'll take this walk every morning in future—may I, uncle—and sometimes bring papa? Won't you be glad to see us?"

"Of course!" replied the uncle, with a hardly suppressed grimace, resulting from his deep aversion to both the proposed visiters. "But stay," he continued, turning towards the young lady. "Now I think of it, I'd better tell you. Mr. Linton has a prejudice against me; we quarrelled at one time of our lives, with unchristian ferocity; and, if you mention coming here to him, he'll put a veto on your visits altogether. Therefore, you must not mention it, unless you be careless of seeing your cousin hereafter—you may come, if you will, but you must not mention it."

"Why did you quarrel?" asked Catherine, considerably crestfallen.

"He thought me too poor to wed his sister," answered Heathcliff, "and was grieved that I got her—his pride was hurt, and he'll never forgive it."

"That's wrong!" said the young lady; "sometime, I'll tell him so; but Linton and I have no share in your quarrel. I'll not come here, then; he shall come to the Grange."

"It will be too far for me," murmured her cousin, "to walk four miles[1] would kill me. No, come here, Miss Catherine, now and then, not every morning, but once or twice a week."

The father launched towards his son a glance of bitter contempt.

"I am afraid, Nelly, I shall lose my labour," he muttered to me. "Miss Catherine, as the ninny calls her, will discover his value, and send him to the devil. Now, if it had been Hareton—do you know that, twenty times a day, I covet Hareton, with all his degradation? I'd have loved the lad had he been some one else. But I think he's safe from *her* love. I'll pit him against that paltry creature, unless it bestir itself briskly. We calculate it will scarcely last till it is eighteen. Oh, confound the vapid thing. He's absorbed in drying his feet, and never looks at her—Linton!"

"Yes, father," answered the boy.

"Have you nothing to show your cousin, anywhere about; not even a rabbit, or a weasel's nest? Take her into the garden,

---

1   *four miles*: repetition of the fictional distance masks the Kingsdale setting; see above, Plate 2 and Introduction, 'The Wuthering Heights Landscape' pp. 18–34; also above, p. 307, note 2.

before you change your shoes; and into the stable to see your horse."

"Wouldn't you rather sit here?" asked Linton, addressing Cathy in a tone which expressed reluctance to move again.

"I don't know," she replied, casting a longing look to the door, and evidently eager to be active.

He kept his seat, and shrank closer to the fire.

Heathcliff rose, and went into the kitchen, and from thence to the yard, calling out for Hareton.

Hareton responded, and presently the two re-entered. The young man had been washing himself, as was visible by the glow on his cheeks, and his wetted hair.

"Oh, I'll ask *you*, uncle;" cried Miss Cathy, recollecting the housekeeper's assertion. "That's not my cousin, is he?"

"Yes," he replied, "your mother's nephew. Don't you like him?"

Catherine looked queer.

"Is he not a handsome lad?" he continued.

The uncivil little thing stood on tiptoe, and whispered a sentence in Heathcliff's ear.

He laughed; Hareton darkened; I perceived he was very sensitive to suspected slights, and had obviously a dim notion of his inferiority. But his master or guardian chased the frown by exclaiming—

"You'll be the favourite among us, Hareton! She says you are a—What was it?[1] Well, something very flattering—Here! you go with her round the farm. And behave like a gentleman, mind! Don't use any bad words; and don't stare, when the young lady is not looking at you, and be ready to hide your face when she is; and, when you speak, say your words slowly, and keep your hands out of your pockets. Be off, and entertain her as nicely as you can."

He watched the couple walking past the window. Earnshaw had his countenance completely averted from his companion. He seemed studying the familiar landscape with a stranger's, and an artist's interest.

Catherine took a sly look at him, expressing small admiration. She then turned her attention to seeking out objects of amuse-

---

1   *What was it?*: probably boor; or a derogatory reference to his parents.

ment for herself, and tripped merrily on, lilting a tune to supply the lack of conversation.

"I've tied his tongue," observed Heathcliff. "He'll not venture a single syllable, all the time! Nelly, you recollect me at his age—nay, some years younger—Did I ever look so stupid, so 'gaumless',[1] as Joseph calls it."

"Worse," I replied, "because more sullen with it."

"I've a pleasure in him!" he continued reflecting aloud. "He has satisfied my expectations—If he were a born fool I should not enjoy it half so much—But he's no fool; and I can sympathise with all his feelings, having felt them myself—I know what he suffers now, for instance, exactly—it is merely a beginning of what he shall suffer, though. And he'll never be able to emerge from his bathos[2] of coarseness, and ignorance. I've got him faster than his scoundrel of a father secured me, and lower; for he takes a pride in his brutishness. I've taught him to scorn everything extra-animal, as silly and weak—Don't you think Hindley would be proud of his son, if he could see him? Almost as proud as I am of mine—But there's this difference, one is gold put to the use of paving stones; and the other is tin polished to ape a service of silver—*mine* has nothing valuable about it; yet I shall have the merit, of making it go as far as such poor stuff can go. *His* had first-rate qualities, and they are lost—rendered worse than un-availing—I have nothing to regret; he would have more than any, but I, are aware of—And the best of it is, Hareton is damnably fond of me! You'll own that I've out-matched Hindley there—If the dead villain could rise from his grave to abuse me for his off-spring's wrongs, I should have the fun of seeing the said offspring fight him back again, indignant that he should dare to rail at the one friend he has in the world!"

Heathcliff chuckled a fiendish laugh at the idea; I made no reply, because I saw that he expected none.

Meantime, our young companion, who sat too removed from us to hear what was said, began to evince symptoms of uneasiness:

---

1 *gaumless*: 'ignorant, vacant, thoughtless, inattentive' (Carr).
2 *bathos*: J.M. Marryat, *Joseph Rushbrook, or, the Poacher* (1841), has: 'It was rather a bathos…to sink from a gentleman's son to an under usher' (*NED*).

probably repenting that he had denied himself the treat of Catherine's society, for fear of a little fatigue.

His father remarked the restless glances wandering to the window, and the hand irresolutely extended towards his cap.

"Get up, you idle boy!" he exclaimed with assumed heartiness. "Away after them...they are just at the corner, by the stand of hives."

Linton gathered his energies, and left the hearth. The lattice was open and, as he stepped out, I heard Cathy inquiring of her unsociable attendant, what was that inscription over the door?

Hareton stared up, and scratched his head like a true clown.[1]

"It's some damnable writing;" he answered. "I cannot read it."

"Can't read it?" cried Catherine, "I can read it...It's English... but I want to know, why it is there."

Linton giggled—the first appearance of mirth he had exhibited.

"He does not know his letters," he said to his cousin. "Could you believe in the existence of such a colossal dunce?"

"Is he all as he should be?" asked Miss Cathy seriously, "or is he simple...not right? I've questioned him twice now, and each time he looked so stupid, I think he does not understand me; I can hardly understand *him* I'm sure!"

Linton repeated his laugh, and glanced at Hareton tauntingly, who certainly, did not seem quite clear of comprehension at that moment.

"There's nothing the matter, but laziness, is there, Earnshaw?" he said. "My cousin fancies you are an idiot...There you experience the consequence of scorning 'book-learning,' as you would say...Have you noticed, Catherine, his frightful Yorkshire[2] pronunciation?"

"Why, where the devil is the use on't?" growled Hareton, more ready in answering his daily companion. He was about to enlarge further, but the two youngsters broke into a noisy fit of merriment; my giddy Miss being delighted to discover that she might turn his strange talk to matter of amusement.

---

1   *clown*: peasant.

2   *Yorkshire*: the sole naming of the county.

"Where is the use of the devil in that sentence?" tittered Linton. "Papa told you not to say any bad words, and you can't open your mouth without one...Do try to behave like a gentleman, now do!"

"If thou wern't more a lass than a lad, I'd fell thee this minute, I would; pitiful lath of a crater!"[1] retorted the angry boor retreating, while his face burnt with mingled rage, and mortification; for he was conscious of being insulted, and embarrassed how to resent[2] it.

Mr. Heathcliff having overheard the conversation, as well as I, smiled when he saw him go, but immediately afterwards, cast a look of singular aversion on the flippant pair, who remained chattering in the doorway. The boy finding animation enough while discussing Hareton's faults, and deficiencies, and relating anecdotes of his goings on; and the girl relishing his pert and spiteful sayings, without considering the ill-nature they evinced: but I began to dislike, more than to compassionate, Linton, and to excuse his father, in some measure, for holding him cheap.

We staid till afternoon: I could not tear Miss Cathy away, before: but happily my master had not quitted his apartment, and remained ignorant of our prolonged absence.

As we walked home, I would fain have enlightened my charge on the characters of the people we had quitted; but she got it into her head that I was prejudiced against them.

"Aha!" she cried, "you take papa's side, Ellen—you are partial...I know, or else you wouldn't have cheated me so many years, into the notion that Linton lived a long way from here. I'm really extremely angry, only, I'm so pleased, I can't show it! But you must hold your tongue about my uncle...he's *my* uncle remember, and I'll scold papa for quarrelling with him."

And so she ran on, till I dropped endeavouring to convince her of her mistake.

She did not mention the visit that night, because she did not see Mr. Linton. Next day it all came out, sadly to my chagrin; and

---

1 *lath of a crater*: twig of a creature.
2 *resent*: 'Fr., to be sensible of, or to stomach an action, or affront' (N. Bailey, *Etymological Dictionary*, 1721); a Gallicism is a rarity in Emily's writing.

still I was not altogether sorry: I thought the burden of directing and warning would be more efficiently borne by him than me, but he was too timid in giving satisfactory reason for his wish that she would shun connection with the household of the Heights, and Catherine liked good reasons for every restraint that harassed her petted will.

"Papa!" she exclaimed after the morning's salutations, "guess whom I saw yesterday, in my walk on the moors...Ah, papa, you started! you've not done right, have you, now? I saw—But listen, and you shall hear how I found you out, and Ellen, who is in league with you, and yet pretended to pity me so, when I kept hoping, and was always disappointed about Linton's coming back!"

She gave a faithful account of her excursion and its consequences; and my master, though he cast more than one reproachful look at me, said nothing, till she had concluded. Then he drew her to him, and asked if she knew why he had concealed Linton's near neighbourhood from her? Could she think it was to deny her a pleasure that she might harmlessly enjoy?

"It was because you disliked Mr. Heathcliff," she answered.

"Then you believe I care more for my own feelings than yours, Cathy?" he said. "No, it was not because I disliked Mr. Heathcliff; but because Mr. Heathcliff dislikes me; and is a most diabolical man, delighting to wrong and ruin those he hates, if they give him the slightest opportunity. I knew that you could not keep up an acquaintance with your cousin, without being brought into contact with him; and I knew he would detest you, on my account; so, for your own good, and nothing else, I took precautions that you should not see Linton again—I meant to explain this, sometime as you grew older, and I'm sorry I delayed it!"

"But Mr. Heathcliff was quite cordial, papa," observed Catherine, not at all convinced; "and *he* didn't object to our seeing each other; he said I might come to his house, when I pleased, only I must not tell you, because you had quarrelled with him, and would not forgive him for marrying aunt Isabella. And you won't—*you* are the one to be blamed—he is willing to let *us* be friends, at least; Linton and I—and you are not."

My master, perceiving that she would not take his word for her uncle-in-law's evil disposition, gave a hasty sketch of his conduct to Isabella, and the manner in which Wuthering Heights became his property. He could not bear to discourse long upon the topic, for though he spoke little of it, he still felt the same horror, and detestation of his ancient enemy that had occupied his heart ever since Mrs. Linton's death. "She might have been living yet, if it had not been for him!" was his constant bitter reflection; and, in his eyes, Heathcliff seemed a murderer.

Miss Cathy, conversant with no bad deeds except her own slight acts of disobedience, injustice and passion, rising from hot temper, and thoughtlessness, and repented of on the day they were committed, was amazed at the blackness of spirit that could brood on, and covet revenge for years; and deliberately prosecute its plans, without a visitation of remorse. She appeared so deeply impressed and shocked at this new view of human nature— excluded from all her studies and all her ideas till now—that Mr. Edgar deemed it unnecessary to pursue the subject. He merely added,

"You will know hereafter, darling, why I wish you to avoid his house and family—now, return to your old employments and amusements, and think no more about them!"

Catherine kissed her father, and sat down quietly to her lessons for a couple of hours, according to custom: then she accompanied him into the grounds, and the whole day passed as usual: but in the evening, when she had retired to her room, and I went to help her to undress, I found her crying, on her knees by the bedside.

"Oh fie, silly child!" I exclaimed. "If you had any real griefs, you'd be ashamed to waste a tear on this little contrariety. You never had one shadow of substantial sorrow, Miss Catherine. Suppose, for a minute, that master and I were dead, and you were by yourself in the world—how would you feel, then? Compare the present occasion with such an affliction as that, and be thankful for the friends you have, instead of coveting more."

"I'm not crying for myself, Ellen," she answered, "it's for him —He expected to see me again, to-morrow, and there, he'll be so disappointed—and he'll wait for me, and I shan't come!"

"Nonsense!" said I, "do you imagine he has thought as much of you, as you have of him? Hasn't he Hareton, for a companion? Not one in a hundred would weep at losing a relation they had just seen twice, for two afternoons—Linton will conjecture how it is, and trouble himself no further about you."

"But may I not write a note to tell him why I cannot come?" she asked rising to her feet. "And just send those books, I promised to lend him—his books are not as nice as mine, and he wanted to have them extremely, when I told him how interesting they were —May I not, Ellen?"

"No indeed, no indeed!" replied I with decision. "Then he would write to you, and there'd never be an end of it—No, Miss Catherine, the acquaintance must be dropped entirely—so papa expects, and I shall see that it is done!"

"But how can one little note—" she recommenced, putting on an imploring countenance.

"Silence!" I interrupted. "We'll not begin with your little notes—Get into bed!"

She threw at me a very naughty look, so naughty that I would not kiss her goodnight at first: I covered her up, and shut her door, in great displeasure—but, repenting half-way, I returned softly, and lo! there was Miss, standing at the table with a bit of blank paper before her, and a pencil in her hand, which she slipped out of sight, on my re-entrance.

"You'll get nobody to take that, Catherine," I said, "if you write it; and at present I shall put out your candle."

I set the extinguisher on the flame, receiving as I did so, a slap on my hand, and a petulant "cross thing!" I then quitted her again, and she drew the bolt in one of her worst, most peevish humours.

The letter was finished and forwarded to its destination by a milk-fetcher who came from the village, but that I didn't learn till some time afterwards. Weeks passed on, and Cathy recovered her temper, though she grew wondrous fond of stealing off to corners by herself, and often, if I came near her suddenly while reading she would start, and bend over the book, evidently de-sirous to hide it; and I detected edges of loose paper sticking out beyond the leaves.

She also got a trick of coming down early in the morning, and lingering about the kitchen, as if she were expecting the arrival of something; and she had a small drawer in a cabinet in the library which she would trifle over for hours, and whose key she took special care to remove when she left it.

One day, as she inspected this drawer, I observed that the play-things, and trinkets which recently formed its contents, were transmuted into bits of folded paper.

My curiosity and suspicions were roused; I determined to take a peep at her mysterious treasures; so, at night, as soon as she and my master were safe up stairs, I searched and readily found among my house keys, one that would fit the lock. Having opened, I emptied the whole contents into my apron, and took them with me to examine at leisure in my own chamber.

Though I could not but suspect, I was still surprised to discover that they were a mass of correspondence, daily almost, it must have been, from Linton Heathcliff, answers to documents forwarded by her. The earlier dated were embarrassed and short; gradually however they expanded into copious love letters, foolish as the age of the writer rendered natural, yet with touches, here and there, which I thought were borrowed from a more experienced source.

Some of them struck me as singularly odd compounds of ardour, and flatness; commencing in strong feeling, and concluding in the affected, wordy way that a school-boy might use to a fancied, incorporeal sweetheart.

Whether they satisfied Cathy, I don't know, but they appeared very worthless trash to me.

After turning over as many as I thought proper, I tied them in a handkerchief, and set them aside, re-locking the vacant drawer.

Following her habit, my young lady descended early, and visited the kitchen: I watched her go to the door, on the arrival of a certain little boy; and, while the dairy maid filled his can, she tucked something into his jacket pocket, and plucked something out.

I went round by the garden, and laid wait for the messenger; who fought valorously to defend his trust, and we spilt the milk between us; but I succeeded in abstracting the epistle; and threatening serious consequences if he did not look sharp home, I remained under the wall, and perused Miss Cathy's affectionate composition. It was more simple and more eloquent than her cousin's, very pretty and very silly. I shook my head, and went meditating into the house.

The day being wet, she could not divert herself with rambling about the park; so, at the conclusion of her morning studies, she resorted to the solace of the drawer. Her father sat reading at the table; and I, on purpose, had sought a bit of work in some unripped fringes of the window curtain, keeping my eye steadily fixed on her proceedings.

Never did any bird flying back to a plundered nest which it had left brimful of chirping young ones, express more complete despair in its anguished cries, and flutterings, than she by her single "Oh!" And the change that transfigured her late happy countenance. Mr. Linton looked up.

"What is the matter, love? Have you hurt yourself?" he said.

His tone and look, assured her *he* had not been the discoverer of the hoard.

"No papa—" she gasped, "Ellen! Ellen! come upstairs—I'm sick!"

I obeyed her summons, and accompanied her out.

"Oh, Ellen! you have got them," she commenced immediately dropping on her knees, when we were enclosed alone. "O, give them to me, and I'll never never do so again! Don't tell papa—you have not told papa, Ellen say you have not! I've been exceedingly naughty, but I won't do it any more!"

With grave severity in my manner, I bid her stand up.

"So," I exclaimed, "Miss Catherine, you are tolerably far on, it seems—you may well be ashamed of them! A fine bundle of trash you study in your leisure hours, to be sure—'Why it's good enough to be printed! And what do you suppose the master will think, when I display it before him? I haven't shown it yet, but you needn't imagine I shall keep your ridiculous secrets—For shame! And you must have led the way in writing such absurdities, he would not have thought of beginning, I'm certain."

"I didn't! I didn't!" sobbed Cathy, fit to break her heart. "I didn't once think of loving him till—"

"*Loving!*" cried I, as scornfully as I could utter the word. "*Loving!* Did anybody ever hear the like! I might just as well talk of loving the miller who comes once a year to buy our corn. Pretty loving, indeed, and both times together you have seen Linton hardly four hours, in your life! Now here is the babyish trash. I'm going with it to the library; and we'll see what your father says to such *loving.*"

She sprang at her precious epistles, but I held them above my head; and then she poured out further frantic entreaties that I would burn them—do anything rather than show them. And being really fully as inclined to laugh as scold, for I esteemed it all girlish vanity, I at length, relented in a measure, and asked,

"If I consent to burn them, will you promise faithfully, neither to send, nor receive a letter again, nor a book, for I perceive you have sent him books, nor locks of hair, nor rings, nor playthings?"

"We don't send playthings!" cried Catherine, her pride overcoming her shame.

"Nor anything at all, then, my lady!" I said. "Unless you will, here I go."

"I promise, Ellen!" she cried catching my dress. "Oh put them in the fire, do, do!"

But when I proceeded to open a place with the poker, the sacrifice was too painful to be borne—She earnestly supplicated that I would spare her one or two.

"One or two, Ellen, to keep for Linton's sake!"

I unknotted the handkerchief, and commenced dropping them in from an angle, and the flame curled up the chimney.

"I will have one, you cruel wretch!" she screamed, darting her hand into the fire, and drawing forth some half consumed fragments, at the expense of her fingers.

"Very well—And I will have some to exhibit to papa!" I answered shaking back the rest into the bundle, and turning anew to the door.

She emptied her blackened pieces into the flames, and motioned me to finish the immolation. It was done; I stirred up the ashes, and interred them under a shovel full of coals; and she mutely, and with a sense of intense injury, retired to her private apartment. I descended to tell my master that the young lady's qualm of sickness was almost gone, but I judged it best for her to lie down a while.

She wouldn't dine; but she reappeared at tea, pale and red about the eyes, and marvellously subdued in outward aspect.

Next morning I answered the letter by a slip of paper inscribed, "Master Heathcliff is requested to send no more notes to Miss Linton as she will not receive them." And, thenceforth the little boy came with vacant pockets.

CHAPTER 22

Summer drew to an end, and early Autumn—it was past Michael-
mas, but the harvest was late that year, and a few of our fields were
still uncleared.

Mr. Linton and his daughter would frequently walk out
among the reapers: at the carrying of the last sheaves, they stayed
till dusk, and the evening happening to be chill and damp, my master caught a bad cold, that settling obstinately on his lungs, confined him indoors throughout the whole of the winter, nearly
without intermission.

Poor Cathy, frightened from her little romance, had been considerably sadder and duller since its abandonment: and her father
insisted on her reading less, and taking more exercise. She had his
companionship no longer; I esteemed it a duty to supply its lack,
as much as possible, with mine; an inefficient substitute, for I
could only spare two or three hours, from my numerous diurnal
occupations, to follow her footsteps, and then, my society was
obviously less desirable than his.

On an afternoon in October, or the beginning of November,
a fresh watery afternoon, when the turf and paths were rustling
with moist, withered leaves, and the cold, blue sky was half hidden
by clouds, dark grey streamers, rapidly mounting from the west,
and boding abundant rain; I requested my young lady to forego
her ramble because I was certain of showers. She refused; and I unwillingly donned a cloak, and took my umbrella to accompany
her on a stroll to the bottom of the park; a formal walk which
she generally affected if low-spirited; and that she invariably was
when Mr. Edgar had been worse than ordinary; a thing never
known from his confession, but guessed both by her and me from
his increased silence, and the melancholy of his countenance.

She went sadly on; there was no running or bounding now;
though the chill wind might well have tempted her to a race. And
often, from the side of my eye, I could detect her raising a hand,
and brushing something off her cheek.

I gazed round for a means of diverting her thoughts. On one
side of the road rose a high, rough bank, where hazels and stunted

oaks, with their roots half exposed, held uncertain tenour:[1] the soil was too loose for the latter; and strong winds had blown some nearly horizontal. In summer Miss Catherine delighted to climb along these trunks, and sit in the branches, swinging twenty feet above the ground; and I pleased with her agility, and her light, childish heart, still considered it proper to scold every time I caught her at such an elevation; but so that she knew there was no necessity for descending. From dinner to tea she would lie in her breeze-rocked cradle, doing nothing except singing old songs— my nursery lore—to herself, or watching the birds, joint tenants, feed and entice their young ones to fly, or nestling with closed lids, half thinking, half dreaming, happier than words can express.

"Look, Miss!" I exclaimed, pointing to a nook under the roots of one twisted tree. "Winter is not here yet. There's a little flower, up yonder, the last bud from the multitude of blue-bells that clouded those turf steps in July with a lilac mist. Will you clamber up, and pluck it to show to papa?"

Cathy stared a long time at the lonely blossom trembling in its earthy shelter, and replied, at length—

"No, I'll not touch it—but it looks melancholy, does it not, Ellen?"

"Yes," I observed, "about as starved and sackless[2] as you—your cheeks are bloodless; let us take hold of hands and run. You're so low, I dare say I shall keep up with you."

"No," she repeated, and continued sauntering on, pausing, at intervals, to muse over a bit of moss, or a tuft of blanched grass, or a fungus spreading its bright orange among the heaps of brown foliage; and, ever and anon, her hand was lifted to her averted face.

"Catherine, why are you crying, love?" I asked, approaching and putting my arm over her shoulder. "You mustn't cry, because papa has a cold; be thankful it is nothing worse."

She now put no further restraint on her tears; her breath was stifled by sobs.

"Oh, it *will* be something worse," she said.

---

1   *tenour*: grip, tenure; usually, progress, procedure: Thomas Gray, 'Elegy', 'the noiseless tenour of their way' (*NED*).
2   *starved*: chilled; *sackless*, 'innocent, guiltless, forlorn, dispirited' (Carr).

"And what shall I do when papa and you leave me, and I am by myself? I can't forget your words, Ellen, they are always in my ear. How life will be changed, how dreary the world will be, when papa and you are dead."

"None can tell, whether you won't die before us," I replied. "It's wrong to anticipate evil—we'll hope there are years and years to come before any of us go—master is young, and I am strong, and hardly forty-five.[1] My mother lived till eighty, a canty[2] dame to the last. And suppose Mr. Linton were spared till he saw sixty, that would be more years than you have counted, Miss. And would it not be foolish to mourn a calamity above twenty years beforehand?"

"But Aunt Isabella was younger than papa," she remarked, gazing up with timid hope to seek further consolation.

"Aunt Isabella had not you and me to nurse her," I replied. "She wasn't as happy as master; she hadn't as much to live for. All you need do, is to wait well on your father, and cheer him by letting him see you cheerful; and avoid giving him anxiety on any subject—mind that, Cathy! I'll not disguise, but you might kill him, if you were wild and reckless, and cherished a foolish, fanciful affection for the son of a person who would be glad to have him in his grave—and allowed him to discover that you fretted over the separation, he has judged it expedient to make."

"I fret about nothing on earth except papa's illness," answered my companion, "I care for nothing in comparison with papa. And I'll never—never—oh, never, while I have my senses, do an act, or say a word to vex him. I love him better than myself, Ellen; and I know it by this—I pray every night that I may live after him; because I would rather be miserable than that he should be—that proves I love him better than myself."

"Good words," I replied. "But deeds must prove it also; and after he is well, remember you don't forget resolutions formed in the hour of fear."

---

1 *hardly*: not quite; 1801/02 is Nelly's forty-fifth year; see below, Appendix A.

2 *canty*: 'lively' (Carr); W. Dickinson, *Glossary of Words and Phrases of Cumberland* (1859), has 'merry, lively, cheerful'.

As we talked, we neared a door that opened on the road: and my young lady, lightening into sunshine again, climbed up, and seated herself on the top of the wall, reaching over to gather some hips that bloomed scarlet on the summit branches of the wild rose trees, shadowing the highway side; the lower fruit had disappeared, but only birds could touch the upper, except from Cathy's present station.

In stretching to pull them, her hat fell off; and as the door was locked, she proposed scrambling down to recover it. I bid her be cautious lest she got a fall, and she nimbly disappeared.

But the return was no such easy matter; the stones were smooth and neatly cemented, and the rosebushes, and blackberry stragglers could yield no assistance in re-ascending. I, like a fool, didn't recollect that till I heard her laughing, and exclaiming—

"Ellen! You'll have to fetch the key, or else I must run round to the porter's lodge. I can't scale the ramparts on this side!"

"Stay where you are," I answered, "I have my bundle of keys in my pocket; perhaps I may manage to open it, if not, I'll go."

Catherine amused herself with dancing to and fro before the door, while I tried all the large keys in succession. I had applied the last, and found that none would do; so, repeating my desire that she would remain there, I was about to hurry home as fast as I could, when an approaching sound arrested me. It was the trot of a horse; Cathy's dance stopped; and in a minute the horse stopped also.

"Who is that?" I whispered.

"Ellen, I wish you could open the door," whispered back my companion, anxiously.

"Ho, Miss Linton!" cried a deep voice (the rider's), "I'm glad to meet you. Don't be in haste to enter, for I have an explanation to ask and obtain."

"I shan't speak to you, Mr. Heathcliff!" answered Catherine. "Papa says you are a wicked man, and you hate both him and me; and Ellen says the same."

"That is nothing to the purpose," said Heathcliff. (He it was.) "I don't hate my son, I suppose, and it is concerning him, that I demand your attention. Yes! you have cause to blush. Two or three months since, were you not in the habit of writing to Linton?—

making love in play, eh? You deserved, both of you, flogging for that! you especially, the elder, and less sensitive, as it turns out. I've got your letters, and if you give me any pertness, I'll send them to your father. I presume you grew weary of the amusement, and dropped it, didn't you? Well, you dropped Linton with it, into a Slough of Despond.[1] He was in earnest—in love—really. As true as I live, he's dying for you—breaking his heart at your fickleness, not figuratively, but actually. Though Hareton has made him a standing jest for six weeks, and I have used more serious measures, and attempted to frighten him out of his idiocy, he gets worse daily, and he'll be under the sod before summer, unless you restore him!"

"How can you lie so glaringly to the poor child!" I called from the inside. "Pray ride on! How can you deliberately get up such paltry falsehoods? Miss Cathy, I'll knock the lock with a stone, you won't believe that vile nonsense. You can feel in yourself, it is impossible that a person should die for love of a stranger."

"I was not aware there were eaves-droppers," muttered the detected villain. "Worthy Mrs. Dean, I like you, but I don't like your double dealing," he added aloud. "How could you lie so glaringly, as to affirm I hated the 'poor child?' And invent bugbear stories to terrify her from my door-stones? Catherine Linton (the very name warms me), my bonny lass, I shall be from home all this week, go and see if I have not spoken truth; do, there's a darling! Just imagine your father in my place, and Linton in yours; then think how you would value your careless lover, if he refused to stir a step to comfort you, when your father, himself, entreated him; and don't from pure stupidity, fall into the same error. I swear, on my salvation, he's going to his grave, and none but you can save him!"

The lock gave way, and I issued out.

"I swear Linton is dying," repeated Heathcliff, looking hard at me. "And grief and disappointment are hastening his death. Nelly, if you won't let her go, you can walk over yourself. But I shall not return till this time next week; and I think your master himself would scarcely object to her visiting her cousin!"

---

1 *Slough of Despond*: symbol of despair in *Pilgrim's Progress* (1678–84), by John Bunyan.

"Come in," said I, taking Cathy by the arm and half forcing her to re-enter, for she lingered viewing, with troubled eyes, the features of the speaker, too stern to express his inward deceit.

He pushed his horse close, and, bending down, observed—

"Miss Catherine, I'll own to you that I have little patience with Linton—and Hareton and Joseph have less. I'll own that he's with a harsh set. He pines for kindness, as well as love; and a kind word from you would be his best medicine. Don't mind Mrs. Dean's cruel cautions, but be generous, and contrive to see him. He dreams of you day and night, and cannot be persuaded that you don't hate him, since you neither write nor call."

I closed the door, and rolled a stone to assist the loosened lock in holding it; and spreading my umbrella, I drew my charge underneath, for the rain began to drive through the moaning branches of the trees, and warned us to avoid delay.

Our hurry prevented any comment on the encounter with Heathcliff, as we stretched towards home; but I divined instinctively that Catherine's heart was clouded now in double darkness. Her features were so sad, they did not seem hers: she evidently regarded what she had heard as every syllable true.

The master had retired to rest before we came in. Cathy stole to his room to inquire how he was; he had fallen asleep. She returned, and asked me to sit with her in the library. We took our tea together; and afterwards she lay down on the rug, and told me not to talk for she was weary.

I got a book, and pretended to read. As soon as she supposed me absorbed in my occupation, she recommenced her silent weeping: it appeared, at present, her favourite diversion. I suffered her to enjoy it a while; then, I expostulated; deriding and ridiculing all Mr. Heathcliff's assertions about his son; as if I were certain she would coincide. Alas! I hadn't skill to counteract the effect his account had produced; it was just what he intended.

"You may be right, Ellen," she answered, "but I shall never feel at ease till I know—and I must tell Linton it is not my fault that I don't write; and convince him that I shall not change."

What use were anger and protestations against her silly credulity? We parted that night hostile—but next day beheld me on the road to Wuthering Heights, by the side of my wilful young mistress's pony. I couldn't bear to witness her sorrow, to see her pale, dejected countenance, and heavy eyes; and I yielded in the faint hope that Linton himself might prove by his reception of us, how little of the tale was founded on fact.

CHAPTER 23

The rainy night had ushered in a misty morning—half frost, half drizzle—and temporary brooks crossed our path, gurgling from the uplands. My feet were thoroughly wetted; I was cross and low, exactly the humour suited for making the most of these disagreeable things.

We entered the farm-house by the kitchen way to ascertain whether Mr. Heathcliff were really absent; because I put slight faith in his own affirmation.

Joseph seemed sitting in a sort of elysium alone, beside a roaring fire; a quart of ale on the table near him, bristling with large pieces of toasted oat cake; and his black, short pipe in his mouth.

Catherine ran to the hearth to warm herself. I asked if the master were in?

My question remained so long unanswered, that I thought the old man had grown deaf, and repeated it louder.

"Na—ay!" he snarled, or rather screamed through his nose. "Na—ay! yah muh goa back whear yah coom frough."[1]

"Joseph," cried a peevish voice, simultaneously with me, from the inner room. "How often am I to call you? There are only a few red ashes now. Joseph! come this moment."

Vigorous puffs, and a resolute stare into the grate declared he had no ear for this appeal. The housekeeper and Hareton were invisible; one gone on an errand, and the other at his work, probably. We knew Linton's tones and entered.

"Oh, I hope you'll die in a garret! starved[2] to death," said the boy, mistaking our approach for that of his negligent attendant.

He stopped, on observing his error; his cousin flew to him.

"Is that you, Miss Linton?" he said, raising his head from the arm of the great chair, in which he reclined. "No—don't kiss me. It takes my breath—dear me! Papa said you would call," continued he, after recovering a little from Catherine's embrace; while

---

1   'No, you can go back where you came from'; the younger Catherine echoes his phrase (ch. 2).
2   *starved*: chilled; Linton has acquired a Yorkshire word.

she stood by looking very contrite. "Will you shut the door, if you please? you left it open—and those—those *destestable* creatures won't bring coals to the fire. It's so cold!"

I stirred up the cinders, and fetched a scuttle full myself. The invalid complained of being covered with ashes; but he had a tiresome cough, and looked feverish and ill, so I did not rebuke his temper.

"Well, Linton," murmured Catherine, when his corrugated brow relaxed. "Are you glad to see me? Can I do you any good?"

"Why didn't you come before?" he said. "You should have come, instead of writing. It tired me dreadfully, writing those long letters. I'd far rather have talked to you. Now, I can neither bear to talk, nor anything else. I wonder where Zillah is! will you (looking at me) step into the kitchen and see?"

I had received no thanks for my other service; and being unwilling to run to and fro at his behest, I replied—

"Nobody is out there but Joseph."

"I want to drink," he exclaimed, fretfully, turning away. "Zillah is constantly gadding off to Gimmerton since papa went. It's miserable! And I'm obliged to come down here—they resolved never to hear me upstairs."[1]

"Is your father attentive to you, Master Heathcliff?" I asked, perceiving Catherine to be checked in her friendly advances.

"Attentive? He makes *them* a little more attentive, at least," he cried. "The wretches! Do you know, Miss Linton, that brute Hareton laughs at me—I hate him—indeed, I hate them all—they are odious beings."

Cathy began searching for some water; she lighted on a pitcher in the dresser; filled a tumbler, and brought it. He bid her add a spoonful of wine from a bottle on the table; and having swallowed a small portion, appeared more tranquil, and said she was very kind.

"And are you glad to see me?" asked she, reiterating her former question, and pleased to detect the faint dawn of a smile.

"Yes, I am—It's something new to hear a voice like yours!" he replied, "but I *have* been vexed, because you wouldn't come—And

---

1 'When I call from upstairs, they won't listen.'

papa swore it was owing to me; he called me a pitiful, shuffling, worthless thing; and said you despised me; and if he had been in my place, he would be more the master of the Grange than your father, by this time. But you don't despise me do you Miss—"

"I wish you would say Catherine, or Cathy!" interrupted my young lady. "Despise you? No! Next to papa, and Ellen, I love you better than anybody living. I don't love Mr. Heathcliff, though; and I dare not come when he returns; will he stay away many days?"

"Not many:" answered Linton, "but he goes onto the moors frequently, since the shooting season commenced, and you might spend an hour or two with me, in his absence—Do! say you will! I think I should not be peevish with you; you'd not provoke me, and you'd always be ready to help me, wouldn't you?"

"Yes," said Catherine stroking his long soft hair, "if I could only get papa's consent, I'd spend half my time with you—Pretty Linton! I wish you were my brother!"

"And then you would like me as well as your father?" observed he more cheerfully. "But papa says you would love me better than him, and all the world, if you were my wife—so I'd rather you were that!"

"No! I should never love anybody better than papa," she returned gravely. "And people hate their wives, sometimes; but not their sisters and brothers, and if you were the latter, you would live with us, and papa would be as fond of you, as he is of me."

Linton denied that people ever hated their wives; but Cathy affirmed they did and in her wisdom, instanced his own father's aversion to her aunt.

I endeavoured to stop her thoughtless tongue—I couldn't succeed, till everything she knew was out. Master Heathcliff, much irritated, asserted her relation was false.

"Papa told me; and papa does not tell falsehoods!" she answered pertly.

"*My* papa scorns yours!" cried Linton. "He calls him a sneaking fool!"

"Yours is a wicked man," retorted Catherine, and you are very naughty to dare to repeat what he says—He must be wicked, to have made aunt Isabella leave him as she did!"

"She didn't leave him," said the boy. "you shan't contradict me!"

"She did!" cried my young lady.

"Well I'll tell you *something*!" said Linton. "Your mother hated your father, now then."

"Oh!" exclaimed Catherine, too enraged to continue.

"And she loved mine!" added he.

"You little liar! I hate you now," she panted, and her face grew red with passion.

"She did! she did!" sang Linton sinking into the recess of his chair, and leaning back his head to enjoy the agitation of the other disputant who stood behind.

"Hush, Master Heathcliff!" I said, "that's your father's tale too, I suppose."

"It isn't—you hold your tongue!" he answered, "she did, she did, Catherine, she did, she did!"

Cathy, beside herself, gave the chair a violent push, and caused him to fall against one arm. He was immediately seized by a suffocating cough that soon ended his triumph.

It lasted so long, that it frightened even me. As to his cousin, she wept with all her might, aghast at the mischief she had done, though she said nothing.

I held him, till the fit exhausted itself. Then he thrust me away; and leant his head down, silently—Catherine quelled her lamentations also, took a seat opposite, and looked solemnly into the fire.

"How do you feel now, Master Heathcliff," I inquired after waiting ten minutes.

"I wish *she* felt as I do," he replied, "spiteful, cruel thing! Hareton never touches me, he never struck me in his life—And I was better to-day—and there—" his voice died in a whimper.

"*I* didn't strike you!" muttered Cathy, chewing her lip to prevent another burst of emotion.

He sighed and moaned like one under great suffering; and kept it up for a quarter of an hour, on purpose to distress his cousin, apparently, for whenever he caught a stifled sob from her, he put renewed pain and pathos into the inflexions of his voice.

"I'm sorry I hurt you, Linton!" she said at length, racked beyond endurance. "But *I* couldn't have been hurt by that little push; and I had no idea that you could, either—you're not much, are you, Linton? Don't let me go home, thinking I've done you harm! answer, speak to me."

"I can't speak to you," he murmured, "You've hurt me so, that I shall lie awake all night, choking with this cough! If you had it you'd know what it was—but *you'll* be comfortably asleep, while I'm in agony—and nobody near me! I wonder how you would like to pass those fearful nights!" And he began to wail aloud for very pity of himself.

"Since you are in the habit of passing dreadful nights," I said, "it won't be Miss who spoils your case; you'd be the same, had she never come—However, she shall not disturb you, again—and perhaps, you'll get quieter when we leave you."

"Must I go?" asked Catherine dolefully, bending over him. "Do you want me to go, Linton?"

"You can't alter what you've done," he replied pettishly, shrinking from her, "unless you alter it for the worse, by teasing me into a fever!"

"Well, then I must go? she repeated.

"Let me alone, at least," said he; "I can't bear your talking!"

She lingered, and resisted my persuasions to departure, a tiresome while, but as he neither looked up, nor spoke, she finally made a movement to the door and I followed.

We were recalled by a scream—Linton had slid from his seat on to the hearthstone, and lay writhing in the mere perverseness of an indulged plague of a child, determined to be as grievous and harassing as it can.

I thoroughly gauged his disposition from his behaviour, and saw at once it would be folly to attempt humouring him. Not so my companion, she ran back in terror, knelt down, and cried, and soothed, and entreated, till he grew quiet from lack of breath, by no means from compunction at distressing her.

"I shall lift him on to the settle," I said, "and he may roll about as he pleases; we can't stop to watch him—I hope you are satisfied, Miss Cathy that *you* are not the person to benefit him, and that his condition of health is not occasioned by attachment to you. Now then, there he is! Come away, as soon as he knows there is nobody by to care for his nonsense, he'll be glad to lie still!"

She placed a cushion under his head, and offered him some water, he rejected the latter, and tossed uneasily on the former, as if it were a stone, or a block of wood.

She tried to put it more comfortably.

"I can't do with that," he said, "it's not high enough!"

Catherine brought another to lay above it.

"That's *too* high!" murmured the provoking thing.

"How must I arrange it, then?" she asked despairingly.

He twined himself up to her, as she half knelt by the settle, and converted her shoulder into a support.

"No, that won't do!" I said. "You'll be content with the cushion, Master Heathcliff! Miss has wasted too much time on you, already; we cannot remain five minutes longer."

"Yes, yes, we can!" replied Cathy. "He's good and patient, now —He's beginning to think I shall have far greater misery than he will, to-night, if I believe he is the worse for my visit; and then, I dare not come again—Tell the truth about it, Linton—for I mustn't come, if I have hurt you."

"You must come, to cure me," he answered. "You ought to come because you have hurt me—You know you have, extremely! I was not as ill, when you entered, as I am at present—was I?"

"But you've made yourself ill by crying, and being in a passion."

"I didn't do it all," said his cousin, "However, we'll be friends now. And you want me—you would wish to see me sometimes, really?"

"I told you, I did!" he replied impatiently.

"Sit on the settle and let me lean on your knee—That's as mama used to do, whole afternoons together—Sit quite still, and don't talk, but you may sing a song if you can sing, or you may say a nice, long interesting ballad—one of those you promised to teach me, or a story—I'd rather have a ballad though—begin."

Catherine repeated the longest she could remember. The employment pleased both mightily. Linton would have another, and after that another; notwithstanding my strenuous objections; and so, they went on, until the clock struck twelve, and we heard Hareton in the court, returning for his dinner.

"And to-morrow, Catherine, will you be here to-morrow?" asked the young Heathcliff, holding her frock, as she rose reluctantly.

"No!" I answered, "nor next day neither." She however, gave a different response, evidently, for his forehead cleared, as she stooped, and whispered in his ear.

"You won't go to-morrow, recollect, Miss!" I commenced when we were out of the house. "You are not dreaming of it, are you?"

She smiled.

"Oh, I'll take good care!" I continued, "I'll have that lock mended, and you can escape by no way else."

"I can get over the wall," she said laughing. "The Grange is not a prison, Ellen, and you are not my jailer. And besides I'm almost seventeen. I'm a woman—and I'm certain Linton would recover quickly if he had me to look after him—I'm older than he is, you know, and wiser, less childish, am I not? And he'll soon do as I direct him with some slight coaxing—He's a pretty little darling when he's good. I'd make such a pet of him, if he were mine—We should never quarrel, should we, after we were used to each other? Don't you like him, Ellen?"

"Like him?" I exclaimed. "The worst tempered bit of a sickly slip that ever struggled into its teens! Happily, as Mr. Heathcliff conjectured, he'll not win twenty! I doubt whether he'll see spring indeed, and small loss to his family, whenever he drops off; and lucky it is for us that his father took him—The kinder he was treated, the more tedious and selfish he'd be! I'm glad you have no chance of having him for a husband, Miss Catherine!"

My companion waxed serious at hearing this speech—To speak of his death so regardlessly wounded her feelings.

"He's younger than I," she answered, after a protracted pause of meditation, "and he ought to live the longest, he will—he must live as long as I do. He's as strong now as when he first came into the North, I'm positive of that! It's only a cold that ails him, the same as papa has—you say papa will get better, and why shouldn't he?"

"Well, well," I cried, "after all, we needn't trouble ourselves; for listen, Miss, and mind, I'll keep my word—If you attempt going to Wuthering Heights again, with, or without me, I shall inform Mr. Linton, and unless he allow it, the intimacy with your cousin must not be revived."

"It has been revived!" muttered Cathy sulkily.

"Must not be continued, then!" I said.

"We'll see!" was her reply, and she set off at a gallop, leaving me to toil in the rear.

We both reached home before our dinner-time: my master supposed we had been wandering through the park, and therefore, he demanded no explanation of our absence. As soon as I entered, I hastened to change my soaked shoes, and stockings; but sitting such a while at the Heights, had done the mischief. On the succeeding morning, I was laid up; and during three weeks I remained incapacitated for attending to my duties—a calamity never experienced prior to that period, and never, I am thankful to say, since.

My little mistress behaved like an angel in coming to wait on me, and cheer my solitude: the confinement brought me exceedingly low—It is wearisome, to a stirring active body—but few have slighter reasons for complaint than I had. The moment Catherine left Mr. Linton's room, she appeared at my bed-side. Her day was divided between us; no amusement usurped a minute: she neglected her meals, her studies, and her play; and she was the fondest nurse that ever watched: she must have had a warm heart, when she loved her father so, to give so much to me!

I said her days were divided between us; but the master retired early, and I generally needed nothing after six o'clock, thus the evening was her own.

Poor thing, I never considered what she did with herself after tea. And though frequently, when she looked in to bid me good night I remarked a fresh colour in her cheeks, and a pinkness over her slender fingers; instead of fancying the hue borrowed from a cold ride across the moors, I laid it to the charge of a hot fire in the library.

CHAPTER 24

At the close of three weeks, I was able to quit my chamber, and move about the house. And on the first occasion of my sitting up in the evening, I asked Catherine to read to me, because my eyes were weak. We were in the library, the master having gone to bed: she consented, rather unwillingly, I fancied; and imagining my sort of books did not suit her, I bid her please herself in the choice of what she perused.

She selected one of her own favourites, and got forward steadily about an hour; then came frequent questions.

"Ellen, are not you tired? Hadn't you better lie down now? You'll be sick, keeping up so long, Ellen."

"No, no, dear, I'm not tired," I returned, continually.

Perceiving me immovable, she essayed another method of showing her disrelish[1] for her occupation. It changed to yawning, and stretching, and—

"Ellen, I'm tired."

"Give over then and talk," I answered.

That was worse; she fretted and sighed, and looked at her watch till eight; and finally went to her room, completely overdone with sleep, judging by her peevish, heavy look, and the constant rubbing she inflicted on her eyes.

The following night she seemed more impatient still; and on the third from recovering my company, she complained of a headache, and left me.

I thought her conduct odd; and having remained alone a long while, I resolved on going, and inquiring whether she were better, and asking her to come and lie on the sofa, instead of upstairs, in the dark.

No Catherine could I discover upstairs, and none below. The servants affirmed they had not seen her. I listened at Mr. Edgar's door—all was silence. I returned to her apartment, extinguished my candle, and seated myself in the window.

---

1   *disrelish*: *Othello* 2.1.236 has: 'disrelish and abhor the Moor'.

The moon shone bright; a sprinkling of snow covered the ground, and I reflected that she might, possibly, have taken it into her head to walk about the garden, for refreshment. I did detect a figure creeping along the inner fence of the park; but it was not my young mistress; on its emerging into the light, I recognised one of the grooms.

He stood a considerable period, viewing the carriage road through the grounds; then started off at a brisk pace, as if he had detected something, and reappeared, presently, leading Miss's pony; and there she was, just dismounted, and walking by its side.

The man took his charge stealthily across the grass towards the stable. Cathy entered by the casement-window of the drawing-room, and glided noiselessly up to where I awaited her.

She put the door gently to, slipped off her snowy shoes, untied her hat, and was proceeding, unconscious of my espionage, to lay aside her mantle, when I suddenly rose, and revealed myself. The surprise petrified her an instant: she uttered an inarticulate exclamation, and stood fixed.

"My dear Miss Catherine," I began, too vividly impressed by her recent kindness to break into a scold, "where have you been riding out at this hour? And why should you try to deceive me, by telling a tale. Where have you been? Speak!"

"To the bottom of the park," she stammered. "I didn't tell a tale."

"And no where else?" I demanded.

"No," was the muttered reply.

"Oh, Catherine," I cried, sorrowfully. "You know you have been doing wrong, or you wouldn't be driven to uttering an untruth to me. That does grieve me. I'd rather be three months ill, than hear you frame a deliberate lie."

She sprang forward, and bursting into tears, threw her arms round my neck.

"Well Ellen, I'm so afraid of you being angry," she said. "Promise not to be angry, and you shall know the very truth. I hate to hide it."

We sat down in the window-seat; I assured her I would not scold, whatever her secret might be, and I guessed it, of course, so she commenced—

"I've been to Wuthering Heights, Ellen, and I've never missed going a day since you fell ill; except thrice before, and twice after you left your room. I gave Michael books and pictures to prepare Minny every evening, and to put her back in the stable; you mustn't scold *him* either, mind. I was at the Heights by half-past six, and generally stayed till half-past eight, and then galloped home. It was not to amuse myself that I went; I was often wretched all the time. Now and then, I was happy, once in a week perhaps. At first, I expected there would be sad work persuading you to let me keep my word to Linton, for I had engaged to call again next day, when we quitted him; but, as you stayed upstairs on the morrow, I escaped that trouble; and while Michael was refastening the lock of the park door in the afternoon, I got possession of the key, and told him how my cousin wished me to visit him, because he was sick, and couldn't come to the Grange: and how papa would object to my going. And then I negotiated with him about the pony. He is fond of reading, and he thinks of leaving soon to get married, so he offered, if I would lend him books out of the library, to do what I wished; but I preferred giving him my own, and that satisfied him better.

"On my second visit, Linton seemed in lively spirits; and Zillah, that is their housekeeper, made us a clean room, and a good fire, and told us that as Joseph was out at a prayer-meeting, and Hareton Earnshaw was off with his dogs, robbing our woods of pheasants, as I heard afterwards, we might do what we like.

"She brought me some warm wine and gingerbread; and appeared exceedingly good-natured; and Linton sat in the armchair, and I in the little rocking chair, on the hearthstone, and we laughed and talked so merrily, and found so much to say; we planned where we would go, and what we would do in summer. I needn't repeat that, because you would call it silly.

"One time, however, we were near quarrelling. He said the pleasantest manner of spending a hot July day was lying from morning till evening on a bank of heath in the middle of the moors, with the bees humming dreamily about among the bloom, and the larks singing high up over head, and the blue sky, and bright sun shining steadily and cloudlessly. That was his most perfect idea of heaven's happiness—mine was rocking in a rustling green tree, with a west wind blowing, and bright, white clouds flitting rapidly above; and not only larks, but throstles, and blackbirds, and linnets, and cuckoos pouring out music on every side, and the moors seen at a distance, broken into cool dusky dells; but close by great swells of long grass undulating in waves to the breeze; and woods and sounding water, and the whole world awake and wild with joy. He wanted all to lie in an ecstacy of peace; I wanted all to sparkle, and dance in a glorious jubilee.

"I said his heaven would be only half alive, and he said mine would be drunk; I said I should fall asleep in his, and he said he could not breathe in mine, and began to grow very snappish. At last, we agreed to try both as soon as the right weather came; and then we kissed each other and were friends. After sitting still an hour, I looked at the great room with its smooth, uncarpeted floor; and thought how nice it would be to play in, if we removed the table; and I asked Linton to call Zillah in to help us—and we'd have a game at blind-man's buff—she should try to catch us—you used to, you know, Ellen. He wouldn't; there was no pleasure in it, he said; but he consented to play at ball with me. We found two, in a cupboard, among a heap of old toys; tops, and hoops, and battledoors, and shuttle-cocks. One was marked C., and the other H; I wished to have the C., because that stood for Catherine, and the H. might be for Heathcliff, his name; but the bran came out of H., and Linton didn't like it.

"I beat him constantly; and he got cross again, and coughed, and returned to his chair: that night, though, he easily recovered his good humour; he was charmed with two or three pretty songs —*your* songs, Ellen; and when I was obliged to go, he begged and entreated me to come the following evening, and I promised.

"Minny and I went flying home as light as air: and I dreamt of Wuthering Heights, and my sweet, darling cousin, till morning.

"On the morrow, I was sad; partly because you were poorly, and partly that I wished my father knew, and approved of my excursions: but it was beautiful moonlight after tea; and, as I rode on, the gloom cleared.

"I shall have another happy evening, I thought to myself, and what delights me more, my pretty Linton will.

"I trotted up their garden, and was turning round to the back, when that fellow Earnshaw met me, took my bridle, and bid me go in by the front entrance. He patted Minny's neck, and said she was a bonny beast, and appeared as if he wanted me to speak to him. I only told him to leave my horse alone, or else it would kick him.

"He answered in his vulgar accent:

"'It wouldn't do mitch hurt if it did,' and surveyed its legs with a smile.

"I was half inclined to make it try; however, he moved off to open the door, and, as he raised the latch, he looked up to the inscription above, and said, with a stupid mixture of awkwardness, and elation:

"'Miss Catherine! I can read yon, nah.'

"'Wonderful,' I exclaimed, 'Pray let us hear you—you *are* grown clever!'

"He spelt, and drawled over by syllables, the name—

"'Hareton Earnshaw.'

"'And the figures?' I cried, encouragingly, perceiving that he came to a dead halt.

"'I cannot tell them yet,' he answered.

"'Oh, you dunce!' I said, laughing heartily at his failure.

The fool stared, with a grin hovering about his lips, and a scowl gathering over his eyes, as if uncertain whether he might not join in my mirth; whether it were not pleasant familiarity, or what it really was, contempt.

I settled his doubts by suddenly retrieving my gravity, and desiring him to walk away, for I came to see Linton not him.

He reddened—I saw that by the moonlight—dropped his hand from the latch, and skulked off, a picture of mortified vanity. He imagined himself to be as accomplished as Linton, I suppose, because he could spell his own name; and was marvellously discomfited that I didn't think the same.

"Stop, Miss Catherine, dear!" I interrupted. "I shall not scold, but I don't like your conduct there. If you had remembered that Hareton was your cousin, as much as Master Heathcliff, you would have felt how improper it was to behave in that way. At least, it was praiseworthy ambition, for him to desire to be as accomplished as

Linton: and probably he did not learn merely to show off; you had made him ashamed of his ignorance, before, I have no doubt; and he wished to remedy it and please you. To sneer at his imperfect attempt was very bad breeding—had *you* been brought up in his circumstances, would you be less rude? he was as quick and as intelligent a child as ever you were, and I'm hurt that he should be despised now, because that base Heathcliff has treated him so unjustly."

"Well, Ellen, you won't cry about it, will you?" she exclaimed, surprised at my earnestness. "But wait, and you shall hear if he conned his a b c, to please me; and if it were worth while being civil to the brute." I entered; Linton was lying on the settle and half got up to welcome me.

"I'm ill to-night Catherine, love;" he said, "and you must have all the talk, and let me listen. Come, and sit by me—I was sure you wouldn't break your word, and I'll make you promise again, before you go."

"I knew now that I mustn't tease him, as he was ill; and I spoke softly and put no questions, and avoided irritating him in any way. I had brought some of my nicest books for him; he asked me to read a little of one, and I was about to comply, when Earnshaw burst the door open, having gathered venom with reflection. He advanced direct to us; seized Linton by the arm, and swung him off the seat.

"Get to thy own room!" he said in a voice almost inarticulate with passion, and his face looked swelled and furious. "Take her there if she comes to see thee—thou shalln't keep me out of this. Begone, wi' ye both!"

He swore at us, and left Linton no time to answer, nearly throwing him into the kitchen; and he clenched his fist, as I followed, seemingly longing to knock me down. I was afraid, for a moment, and I let one volume fall; he kicked it after me, and shut us out.

I heard a malignant, crackly laugh by the fire, and turning beheld that odious Joseph, standing rubbing his bony hands, and quivering.

"Aw wer sure he's sarve ye aht! He's a grand lad! He's getten t' raight sperrit in him! *He* knaws—Aye, he knaws, as weel as Aw do, who sud be t' maister yonder—Ech, ech, ech! He made ye skift properly! Ech, ech, ech!"[1]

"Where must we go?" I said to my cousin, disregarding the old wretch's mockery.

"Linton was white and trembling. He was not pretty then—Ellen, Oh! no, he looked frightful! for his thin face, and large eyes were wrought into an expression of frantic, powerless fury. He grasped the handle of the door, and shook it—it was fastened inside.

"'If you don't let me in I'll kill you; If you don't let me in I'll kill you!' he rather shrieked than said. 'Devil! devil! I'll kill you, I'll kill you!'

"Joseph uttered his croaking laugh again.

"'Thear that's t' father!' he cried. 'That's father! We've allas summut uh orther side in us—Niver heed, Hareton, lad—dunnut be 'feard—he cannot get at thee!'[2]

"I took hold of Linton's hands, and tried to pull him away; but he shrieked so shockingly that I dared not proceed. At last, his cries were choked by a dreadful fit of coughing; blood gushed from his mouth,[3] and he fell on the ground.

"I ran into the yard, sick with terror; and called for Zillah, as loud as I could. She soon heard me; she was milking the cows in a shed behind the barn; and hurrying from her work, she inquired what there was to do?

"I hadn't breath to explain; dragging her in, I looked about for Linton; Earnshaw had come out to examine the mischief he had caused, and he was then conveying the poor thing upstairs. Zillah and I ascended after him; but, he stopped me, at the top of the steps, and said, I shouldn't go in, I must go home.

---

1   'I was sure he'll serve you right [out]! He's a fine fellow! He's getting the right spirit in him! *He* knows—yes, he knows, as well as I do, who should be master over there—ech, ech, ech! He made you move properly! Ech, ech, ech!'

2   *Thear that's t' father!*: 'There, he's like his father! That's his father again! We've always got something from the other parent's side in us—Don't worry, Hareton my boy, don't be scared—he can't get at you!'

3   Tuberculosis kills Frances Earnshaw, the elder Lintons, and probably all Patrick's children.

344   EMILY BRONTË

"I exclaimed that he had killed Linton and I *would* enter.

"Joseph locked the door, and declared I should do 'no sich stuff,' and asked me whether I were 'bahn to be as mad as him.'[1]

"I stood crying, till the housekeeper reappeared; she affirmed he would be better in a bit; but he couldn't do with that shrieking, and din, and she took me, and nearly carried me into the house.

"Ellen, I was ready to tear my hair off my head! I sobbed and wept so that my eyes were almost blind: and the ruffian you have such sympathy with, stood opposite; presuming every now and then, to bid me 'wisht,' and denying that it was his fault; and finally, frightened by my assertions that I would tell papa, and that he should be put in prison, and hanged, he commenced blubbering himself, and hurried out to hide his cowardly agitation.

"Still, I was not rid of him: when at length they compelled me to depart, and I had got some hundred yards off the premises, he suddenly issued from the shadow of the road-side, and checked Minny and took hold of me.

"'Miss Catherine, I'm ill grieved,' he began, 'but it's rayther too bad—'

"I gave him a cut with my whip, thinking, perhaps he would murder me—He let go, thundering one of his horrid curses, and I galloped home more than half out of my senses.

"I didn't bid you good-night, that evening; and I didn't go to Wuthering Heights, the next—I wished to, exceedingly; but I was strangely excited, and dreaded to hear that Linton was dead, sometimes; and sometimes shuddered at the thought of encountering Hareton.

"On the third day I took courage; at least, I couldn't bear longer suspense and stole off, once more. I went at five o'clock, and walked, fancying I might manage to creep into the house, and up to Linton's room, unobserved. However, the dogs gave notice of my approach: Zillah received me, and saying 'the lad was mending nicely,' showed me into a small, tidy, carpeted apartment,

---

1   *no sich*: 'no such thing...going to be as angry as him'; *mad*: angry: 'In many dialects in Great Britain and the U.S. the ordinary word for "angry"'; for example, 'how deuced mad she'll be', *A simple Narrative; or a Visit to the Newton Family* (novel) (1806) (*NED*).

where, to my inexpressible joy, I beheld Linton laid on a little sofa, reading one of my books. But he would neither speak to me, nor look at me, through a whole hour, Ellen—He has such an unhappy temper—and what quite confounded me, when he did open his mouth it was to utter the falsehood, that I had occasioned the uproar, and Hareton was not to blame!

"Unable to reply, except passionately, I got up, and walked from the room. He sent after me a faint 'Catherine!' He did not reckon on being answered so—but I wouldn't turn back; and the morrow was the second day on which I stayed at home, nearly determined to visit him no more.

"But it was so miserable going to bed, and getting up, and never hearing anything about him, that my resolution melted into air, before it was properly formed. It *had* appeared wrong to take the journey once; now it seemed wrong to refrain. Michael came to ask if he must saddle Minny; I said 'yes,' and considered myself doing a duty as she bore me over the hills.

"I was forced to pass the front windows to get to the court; it was no use trying to conceal my presence.

"'Young master is in the house,' said Zillah as she saw me making for the parlour.

"I went in, Earnshaw was there also, but he quitted the room directly. Linton sat in the great arm chair half asleep; walking up to the fire, I began in a serious tone, partly meaning it to be true,

"As you don't like me Linton, as you think I come on purpose to hurt you, and pretend that I do so every time, this is our last meeting—let us say good bye; and tell Mr. Heathcliff that you have no wish to see me, and that he mustn't invent any more falsehoods on the subject.

"'Sit down and take your hat off, Catherine,' he answered. 'You are so much happier than I am, you ought to be better. Papa talks enough of my defects, and shows enough scorn of me, to make it natural I should doubt myself—I doubt whether I am not[1] altogether as worthless as he calls me, frequently; and then I feel so cross and bitter, I hate everybody! I *am* worthless, and bad in temper, and bad in spirit, almost always—and if you choose, you *may*

---

1   *I doubt whether I am not*: I fear that I may be.

say good-bye—you'll get rid of an annoyance—Only, Catherine, do me this justice; believe that if I might be as sweet, and as kind, and as good as you are, I would be, as willingly, and more so, than as happy and as healthy.[1] And, believe that your kindness has made me love you deeper than if I deserved your love, and though I couldn't and cannot help showing my nature to you, I regret it, and repent it, and shall regret, and repent it, till I die!"

"I felt he spoke the truth; and I felt I must forgive him; and, though he should quarrel the next moment, I must forgive him again.[2] We were reconciled, but we cried, both of us, the whole time I stayed. Not entirely for sorrow, yet I *was* sorry Linton had that distorted nature. He'll never let his friends be at ease, and he'll never be at ease himself!

"I have always gone to his little parlour, since that night; because his father returned the day after. About three times, I think, we have been merry, and hopeful, as we were the first evening; the rest of my visits were dreary and troubled—now, with his selfishness and spite; and now with his sufferings: but I've learnt to endure the former with nearly as little resentment as the latter.

"Mr. Heathcliff purposely avoids me. I have hardly seen him at all. Last Sunday, indeed, coming earlier than usual, I heard him abusing poor Linton, cruelly, for his conduct of the night before. I can't tell how he knew of it, unless he listened. Linton had certainly behaved provokingly; however, it was the business of nobody but me; and I interrupted Mr. Heathcliff's lecture, by entering, and telling him so. He burst into a laugh, and went away, saying he was glad I took that view of the matter. Since then, I've told Linton he must whisper his bitter things.

"Now, Ellen, you have heard all; and I can't be prevented from going to Wuthering Heights, except by inflicting misery on two people—whereas, if you'll only not tell papa, my going need disturb the tranquillity of none. You'll not tell, will you? It will be very heartless if you do."

---

1 *as healthy*: 'I would be happy to be as happy and healthy as you are, but it would make me even happier to be sweet, kind and good, like you'.

2 Like Heathcliff (ch. 17), she practises the virtue which the Revd Jabes Branderham failed to preach (ch. 3).

"I'll make up my mind on that point by tomorrow, Miss Catherine," I replied. "It requires some study; and so I'll leave you to your rest, and go think it over."

I thought it over aloud, in my master's presence; walking straight from her room to his, and relating the whole story, with the exception of her conversations with her cousin, and any mention of Hareton.

Mr. Linton was alarmed and distressed more than he would acknowledge to me. In the morning, Catherine learnt of my betrayal of her confidence, and she learnt also that her secret visits were to end.

In vain she wept and writhed against the interdict; and implored her father to have pity on Linton: all she got to comfort her was a promise that he would write, and give him leave to come to the Grange when he pleased; but explaining that he must no longer expect to see Catherine at Wuthering Heights. Perhaps, had he been aware of his nephew's disposition and state of health, he would have seen fit to withhold even that slight consolation.

CHAPTER 25

"These things happened last winter, sir," said Mrs. Dean; "hardly more than a year ago. Last winter, I did not think, at another twelve months' end, I should be amusing a stranger to the family with relating them! Yet, who knows how long you'll be a stranger? You're too young to rest always contented, living by yourself; and I some way fancy, no one could see Catherine Linton, and not love her. You smile; but why do you look so lively and interested, when I talk about her—and why have you asked me to hang her picture over your fireplace? and why—"

"Stop, my good friend!" I cried. "It may be very possible that *I* should love her; but would she love me? I doubt it too much to venture my tranquillity, by running into temptation; and then my home is not here. I'm of the busy world, and to its arms I must return. Go on. Was Catherine obedient to her father's commands?"

"She was," continued the housekeeper. "Her affection for him was still the chief sentiment in her heart; and he spoke without anger; he spoke in the deep tenderness of one about to leave his treasure amid perils and foes, and where his remembered words would be the only aid that he could bequeath to guide her.

He said to me, a few days afterwards,

"I wish my nephew would write, Ellen, or call. Tell me, sincerely, what you think of him—is he changed for the better, or is there a prospect of improvement, as he grows a man?"

"He's very delicate, sir," I replied; "and scarcely likely to reach manhood; but this I can say, he does not resemble his father; and if Miss Catherine had the misfortune to marry him, he would not be beyond her control, unless she were extremely and foolishly indulgent. However, master, you'll have plenty of time to get acquainted with him, and see whether he would suit her—it wants four years and more to his being of age."

Edgar sighed; and, walking to the window, looked out towards Gimmerton Kirk. It was a misty afternoon, but the February sun shone dimly, and we could just distinguish the two fir trees in the yard, and the sparely[1] scattered gravestones.

"I've prayed often," he half soliloquized, "for the approach of what is coming; and now I begin to shrink, and fear it. I thought the memory of the hour I came down that glen a bridegroom, would be less sweet than the anticipation that I was soon, in a few months, or, possibly, weeks, to be carried up, and laid in its lonely hollow! Ellen, I've been very happy with my little Cathy. Through winter nights and summer days she was a living hope at my side— but I've been as happy musing by myself among those stones, under that old church—lying through the long June evenings, on the green mound of her mother's grave, and wishing, yearning for the time when I might lie beneath it. What can I do for Cathy? How must I quit her? I'd not care one moment for Linton being Heathcliff's son; nor for his taking her from me, if he could console her for my loss. I'd not care that Heathcliff gained his ends, and triumphed in robbing me of my last blessing! But should Linton be unworthy—only a feeble tool to his father—I cannot abandon her to him! And, hard though it be to crush her buoyant spirit, I must persevere in making her sad while I live, and leaving her solitary when I die. Darling! I'd rather resign her to God, and lay her in the earth before me."

"Resign her to God, as it is, sir," I answered, "and if we should lose you—which may He forbid—under His providence, I'll stand her friend and counsellor to the last. Miss Catherine is a good girl; I don't fear that she will go wilfully wrong; and people who do their duty are always finally rewarded."

Spring advanced; yet my master gathered no real strength, though he resumed his walks in the grounds, with his daughter. To her inexperienced notions, this itself was a sign of convalescence; and then his cheek was often flushed, and his eyes were bright; she felt sure of his recovering.

On her seventeenth birthday, he did not visit the churchyard, it was raining, and I observed—

"You'll surely not go out to-night, sir?"

He answered—

---

1   *sparely*: sparsely.

"No, I'll defer it, this year, a little longer."

He wrote again to Linton, expressing his great desire to see him; and, had the invalid been presentable, I've no doubt his father would have permitted him to come. As it was, being instructed, he returned an answer, intimating that Mr. Heathcliff objected to his calling at the Grange; but his uncle's kind remembrance delighted him, and he hoped to meet him, sometimes, in his rambles, and personally to petition that his cousin and he might not remain long so utterly divided.

That part of his letter was simple, and, probably his own. Heathcliff knew he could plead eloquently enough for Catherine's company, then—

"I do not ask," he said, "that she may visit here; but, am I never to see her, because my father forbids me to go to her home, and you forbid her to come to mine? Do, now and then, ride with her towards the Heights; and let us exchange a few words, in your presence! we have done nothing to deserve this separation; and you are not angry with me—you have no reason to dislike me— you allow yourself. Dear uncle! send us a kind note to-morrow; and leave to join you anywhere you please, except at Thrushcross Grange. I believe an interview would convince you that my father's character is not mine; he affirms I am more your nephew than his son; and though I have faults which render me unworthy of Catherine, she has excused them, and for her sake, you should also. You inquire after my health—it is better; but while I remain cut off from all hope, and doomed to solitude, or the society of those who never did, and never will like me, how can I be cheerful and well?"

Edgar, though he felt for the boy, could not consent to grant his request; because he could not accompany Catherine.

He said, in summer, perhaps, they might meet: meantime, he wished him to continue writing at intervals, and engaged to give him what advice and comfort he was able to by letter; being well aware of his hard position in his family.

Linton complied; and had he been unrestrained, would probably have spoiled all by filling his epistles with complaints and lamentations; but his father kept a sharp watch over him; and, of course, insisted on every line that my master sent being shown; so, instead of penning his peculiar personal sufferings, and distresses, the themes constantly uppermost in his thoughts, he harped on the cruel obligation of being held asunder from his friend and love; and gently intimated that Mr. Linton must allow an interview soon, or he should fear he was purposely deceiving him with empty promises.

Cathy was a powerful ally at home: and, between them, they, at length, persuaded my master to acquiesce in their having a ride or a walk together, about once a week, under my guardianship, and on the moors nearest the Grange; for June found him still declining; and, though he had set aside, yearly, a portion of his income for my young lady's fortune, he had a natural desire that she might retain, or, at least, return, in a short time, to the house of her ancestors; and he considered her only prospect of doing that was by a union with his heir:[1] he had no idea that the latter was failing almost as fast as himself; nor had any one, I believe; no doctor visited the Heights, and no one saw Master Heathcliff to make report of his condition, among us.

I, for my part, began to fancy my forebodings were false, and that he must be actually rallying, when he mentioned riding and walking on the moors, and seemed so earnest in pursuing his object.

I could not picture a father treating a dying child as tyrannically and wickedly as I afterwards learnt Heathcliff had treated him, to compel this apparent eagerness; his efforts redoubling the more imminently his avaricious and unfeeling plans were threatened with defeat by death.

---

1   *his heir*: by the terms of old Mr Linton's will (ch. 17), Linton Heathcliff, Isabella's heir.

CHAPTER 26

Summer was already past its prime, when Edgar reluctantly yield-ed his assent to their entreaties, and Catherine and I set out on our first ride to join her cousin.

It was a close, sultry day; devoid of sunshine, but with a sky too dappled and hazy to threaten rain; and our place of meeting had been fixed at the guidestone, by the crossroads. On arriving there, however, a little herd-boy, despatched as a messenger, told us that—

"Maister Linton were just ut this side th' Heights: and he'd be mitch obleeged to us to gang on a bit further."

"Then Master Linton has forgot the first injunction of his uncle," I observed: "he bid us keep on the Grange land, and here we are, off at once."

"Well, we'll turn our horses' heads round, when we reach him," answered my companion, "our excursion shall lie towards home."

But when we reached him, and that was scarcely a quarter of a mile from his own door, we found he had no horse, and we were forced to dismount, and leave ours to graze.

He lay on the heath, awaiting our approach, and did not rise till we came within a few yards. Then, he walked so feebly, and looked so pale, that I immediately exclaimed—

"Why, Master Heathcliff, you are not fit for enjoying a ram-ble, this morning. How ill you do look!"

Catherine surveyed him with grief and astonishment; and changed the ejaculation of joy on her lips, to one of alarm; and the congratulation on their long postponed meeting, to an anxi-ous inquiry, whether he were worse than usual?

"No—better—better!" he panted, trembling, and retaining her hand as if he needed its support, while his large blue eyes wandered timidly over her; the hollowness round them, trans-forming to haggard wildness, the languid expression they once possessed.

"But you have been worse," persisted his cousin, "worse than when I saw you last—you are thinner, and—"

"I'm tired," he interrupted, hurriedly. "It is too hot for walking, let us rest here. And, in the morning, I often feel sick—papa says I grow so fast."

Badly satisfied, Cathy sat down, and he reclined beside her.

"This is something like your paradise," said she, making an effort at cheerfulness. "You recollect the two days we agreed to spend, in the place and way, each thought pleasantest? This is nearly yours, only there are clouds; but then, they are so soft and mellow, it is nicer than sunshine. Next week, if you can, we'll ride down to the Grange Park, and try mine."

Linton did not appear to remember what she talked of; and he had evidently great difficulty in sustaining any kind of conversation. His lack of interest in the subjects she started, and his equal incapacity to contribute to her entertainment were so obvious, that she could not conceal her disappointment. An indefinite alteration had come over his whole person and manner. The pettishness that might be caressed into fondness, had yielded to a listless apathy; there was less of the peevish temper of a child which frets and teases on purpose to be soothed, and more of the self-absorbed moroseness of a confirmed invalid, repelling consolation, and ready to regard the good-humoured mirth of others, as an insult.

Catherine perceived, as well as I did, that he held it rather a punishment, than a gratification, to endure our company; and she made no scruple of proposing, presently, to depart.

That proposal, unexpectedly, roused Linton from his lethargy, and threw him into a strange state of agitation. He glanced fearfully towards the Heights, begging she would remain another half-hour, at least.

"But, I think," said Cathy, "you'd be more comfortable at home than sitting here; and I cannot amuse you to-day, I see, by my tales, and songs, and chatter; you have grown wiser than I, in these six months; you have little taste for my diversions now; or else, if I could amuse you, I'd willingly stay."

"Stay to rest yourself," he replied. "And, Catherine, don't think, or say that I'm *very* unwell—it is the heavy weather, the heat that make me dull; and I walked about, before you came, a great deal, for me. Tell uncle, I'm in tolerable health, will you?"

"I'll tell him that *you* say so, Linton, I couldn't affirm that you are," observed my young lady, wondering at his pertinacious assertion of what was evidently an untruth.

"And be here again next Thursday," continued he, shunning her puzzled gaze. "And give him my thanks for permitting you to come—my best thanks, Catherine. And—and, if you *did* meet my father, and he asked you about me, don't lead him to suppose that I've been extremely silent and stupid—don't look sad and downcast, as you *are* doing—he'll be angry."

"I care nothing for his anger," exclaimed Cathy, imagining she would be its object.

"But I do," said her cousin, shuddering. "*Don't* provoke him against me, Catherine, for he is very hard."

"Is he severe to you, Master Heathcliff?" I inquired. "Has he grown weary of indulgence, and passed from passive, to active hatred?"

Linton looked at me, but did not answer; and, after keeping her seat by his side, another ten minutes, during which his head fell drowsily on his breast, and he uttered nothing except suppressed moans of exhaustion, or pain, Cathy began to seek solace in looking for bilberries, and sharing the produce of her researches with me: she did not offer them to him, for she saw further notice would only weary and annoy.

"Is it half an hour now, Ellen?" she whispered in my ear, at last. "I can't tell why we should stay. He's asleep, and papa will be wanting us back."

"Well, we must not leave him asleep," I answered; "wait till he wakes and be patient. You were mighty eager to set off, but your longing to see poor Linton has soon evaporated!"

"Why did *he* wish to see me?" returned Catherine. "In his crossest humours, formerly, I liked him better than I do in his present curious mood. It's just as if it were a task he was compelled to perform—this interview—for fear his father should scold him. But, I'm hardly going to come to give Mr. Heathcliff pleasure; whatever reason he may have for ordering Linton to undergo this penance. And, though I'm glad he's better in health, I'm sorry he's so much less pleasant, and so much less affectionate to me."

"You think he *is* better in health, then?" I said.

"Yes," she answered; "because he always made such a great deal of his sufferings, you know. He is not tolerably well, as he told me to tell papa, but he's better, very likely."

"There you differ with me, Miss Cathy," I remarked; "I should conjecture him to be far worse."

Linton here started from his slumber in bewildered terror, and asked if any one had called his name.

"No," said Catherine; "unless in dreams. I cannot conceive how you manage to doze, out of doors, in the morning."

"I thought I heard my father," he gasped, glancing up to the frowning nab[1] above us. "You are sure nobody spoke?"

"Quite sure," replied his cousin. "Only Ellen and I were disputing concerning your health. Are you truly stronger, Linton, than when we separated in winter? If you be, I'm certain one thing is not stronger—your regard for me—speak, are you?"

The tears gushed from Linton's eyes as he answered—

"Yes, yes, I am!"

And, still under the spell of the imaginary voice, his gaze wandered up and down to detect its owner.

Cathy rose.

"For to-day we must part," she said. "And I won't conceal that I have been sadly disappointed with our meeting, though I'll mention it to nobody but you—not that I stand in awe of Mr. Heathcliff!"

"Hush," murmured Linton; "for God's sake, hush! He's coming." And he clung to Catherine's arm, striving to detain her; but, at that announcement, she hastily disengaged herself, and whistled to Minny, who obeyed her like a dog.

"I'll be here next Thursday," she cried, springing to the saddle. "Good-bye. Quick, Ellen!"

And so we left him, scarcely conscious of our departure, so absorbed was he in anticipating his father's approach.

Before we reached home, Catherine's displeasure softened into a perplexed sensation of pity and regret largely blended with vague, uneasy doubts about Linton's actual circumstances, physical

---

1   *nab*: summit of a hill.

and social; in which I partook, though I counselled her not to say much, for a second journey would make us better judges.

My master requested an account of our on-goings: his nephew's offering of thanks was duly delivered, Miss Cathy gently touching on the rest: I also, threw little light on his inquiries, for I hardly knew what to hide, and what to reveal.

CHAPTER 27

Seven days glided away, every one marking its course by the henceforth rapid alteration of Edgar Linton's state. The havoc that months had previously wrought, was now emulated by the inroads of hours.

Catherine, we would fain have deluded, yet, but her own quick spirit refused to delude her. It divined, in secret, and brooded on the dreadful probability, gradually ripening into certainty.

She had not the heart to mention her ride, when Thursday came round; I mentioned it for her; and obtained permission to order her out of doors; for the library, where her father stopped a short time daily—the brief period he could bear to sit up, and his chamber had become her whole world. She grudged each moment that did not find her bending over his pillow, or seated by his side. Her countenance grew wan with watching and sorrow, and my master gladly dismissed her to what he flattered himself would be a happy change of scene and society, drawing comfort from the hope that she would not now be left entirely alone after his death.

He had a fixed idea, I guessed by several observations he let fall, that as his nephew resembled him in person, he would resemble him in mind; for Linton's letters bore few, or no indications of his defective character. And I through pardonable weakness refrained from correcting the error; asking myself what good there would be in disturbing his last moments with information that he had neither power nor opportunity to turn to account.

We deferred our excursion till the afternoon; a golden afternoon of August—every breath from the hills so full of life, that it seemed whoever respired it, though dying, might revive.

Catherine's face was just like the landscape—shadows and sunshine flitting over it, in rapid succession; but the shadows rested longer and the sunshine was more transient, and her poor little heart reproached itself for even that passing forgetfulness of its cares.

We discerned Linton watching at the same spot he had selected before. My young mistress alighted, and told me that as she was resolved to stay a very little while, I had better hold the pony and remain on horseback; but I dissented, I wouldn't risk losing sight of the charge committed to me a minute; so we climbed the slope of heath, together.

Master Heathcliff received us with greater animation on this occasion; not the animation of high spirits though, nor yet of joy; it looked more like fear.

"It is late!" he said, speaking short, and with difficulty. "Is not your father very ill? I thought you wouldn't come."

"*Why* won't you be candid?" cried Catherine, swallowing her greeting. "Why cannot you say at once, you don't want me? It is strange Linton, that for the second time, you have brought me here on purpose, apparently, to distress us both, and for no reason besides!"

Linton shivered, and glanced at her, half supplicating, half ashamed, but his cousin's patience was not sufficient to endure this enigmatical behaviour.

"My father *is* very ill," she said, "and why am I called from his bedside—why didn't you send to absolve me from my promise, when you wished I wouldn't keep it? Come! I desire an explanation—playing and trifling are completely banished out of my mind: and I can't dance attendance on your affectations, now!"

"My affections!" he murmured, "what are they? For Heaven's sake Catherine, don't look so angry! Despise me as much as you please; I am a worthless, cowardly wretch—I can't be scorned enough! but I'm too mean for your anger—hate my father, and spare me, for contempt!"

"Nonsense!" cried Catherine in a passion. "Foolish, silly boy! And there! he trembles, as if I were really going to touch him! You needn't bespeak contempt, Linton; anybody will have it spontaneously, at your service. Get off! I shall return home—it is folly dragging you from the hearth-stone, and pretending—what do we pretend? Let go my frock—if I pitied you for crying, and looking so very frightened, you should spurn such pity. Ellen, tell him how disgraceful this conduct is. Rise, and don't degrade yourself into an abject reptile—*don't*."

With streaming face and an expression of agony, Linton had thrown his nerveless frame along the ground; he seemed convulsed with exquisite terror.

"Oh!" he sobbed, "I cannot bear it! Catherine, Catherine, I'm a traitor too, and I dare not tell you! But leave me and I shall be killed! *Dear* Catherine, my life is in your hands; and you have said you loved me—and if you did, it wouldn't harm you. You'll not go, then? kind, sweet, good Catherine! And perhaps you *will* consent—and he'll let me die with you!"

My young lady, on witnessing his intense anguish, stooped to raise him. The old feeling of indulgent tenderness overcame her vexation, and she grew thoroughly moved and alarmed.

"Consent to what?" she asked, "To stay? Tell me the meaning of this strange talk, and I will. You contradict your own words, and distract me! Be calm and frank, and confess at once, all that weighs on your heart. You wouldn't injure me, Linton, would you? You wouldn't let any enemy hurt me, if you could prevent it? I'll believe you are a coward, for yourself, but not a cowardly betrayer of your best friend."

"But my father threatened me," gasped the boy, clasping his attenuated fingers, "and I dread him—I dread him! I *dare* not tell!"

"Oh well!" said Catherine, with scornful compassion, "keep your secret, *I'm* no coward—save yourself, I'm not afraid!"

Her magnanimity provoked his tears; he wept wildly, kissing her supporting hands, and yet could not summon courage to speak out.

I was cogitating what the mystery might be, and determined Catherine should never suffer to benefit him or any one else, by my good will. When hearing a rustle among the ling,[1] I looked up, and saw Mr. Heathcliff almost close upon us, descending the Heights. He didn't cast a glance towards my companions, though they were sufficiently near for Linton's sobs to be audible; but hailing me in the almost hearty[2] tone he assumed to none besides, and the sincerity of which, I couldn't avoid doubting, he said.

"It is something to see you so near to my house, Nelly! How are you at the Grange? Let us hear! The rumour goes," he added

---

1   *ling*: heather (also ling, a fish).
2   *hearty*: from the heart, sincere (not falsely jovial).

in a lower tone, "that Edgar Linton is on his death-bed—perhaps they exaggerate his illness?"

"No; my master is dying," I replied, "it is true enough. A sad thing it will be for us all, but a blessing for him!"

"How long will he last, do you think?" he asked.

"I don't know," I said.

"Because," he continued, looking at the two young people, who were fixed under his eye—Linton appeared as if he could not venture to stir, or raise his head, and Catherine could not move, on his account—"Because that lad yonder, seems determined to beat me—and I'd thank his uncle to be quick, and go before him[1]—Hallo! Has the whelp been playing that game long? I *did* give him some lessons about snivelling. Is he pretty lively with Miss Linton generally?"

"Lively? no—he has shown the greatest distress;" I answered. "To see him, I should say, that instead of rambling with his sweetheart on the hills, he ought to be in bed, under the hands of a doctor."

"He shall be, in a day or two," muttered Heathcliff. "But first —get up, Linton! Get up!" he shouted. "Don't grovel on the ground, there—up this moment!"

Linton had sunk prostrate again in another paroxysm of helpless fear, caused by his father's glance towards him, I suppose; there was nothing else to produce such humiliation. He made several efforts to obey, but his little strength was annihilated, for the time, and he fell back again with a moan.

Mr. Heathcliff advanced, and lifted him to lean against a ridge of turf.

"Now," said he with curbed ferocity, "I'm getting angry—and if you don't command that paltry spirit of yours—*Damn* you! Get up, directly!"

"I will, father!" he panted. "Only, let me alone, or I shall faint![2] I've done as you wished—I'm sure. Catherine will tell you that I—that I—have been cheerful. Ah! keep by me, Catherine; give

---

1   *beat me…*: 'my son seems likely to die before me, and I wish his uncle would hurry and die first'.

2   The symptoms of advanced tuberculosis are closely observed.

me your hand."

"Take mine," said his father, "stand on your feet! There now —she'll lend you her arm...that's right, look at *her*. You would imagine I was the devil himself, Miss Linton, to excite such horror. Be so kind as to walk home with him, will you? He shudders, if I touch him."

"Linton, dear!" whispered Catherine, "I can't go to Wuthering Heights...papa has forbidden me...He'll not harm you, why are you so afraid?"

"I can never re-enter that house," he answered. "I am *not* to re-enter it without you!"

"Stop..." cried his father. "We'll respect Catherine's filial scruples. Nelly, take him in, and I'll follow your advice concerning the doctor, without delay."

"You'll do well," replied I, "but I must remain with my mistress. To mind your son is not my business."

"You are very stiff!" said Heathcliff, "I know that—but you'll force me to pinch the baby, and make it scream before it moves your charity. Come then, my hero. Are you willing to return, escorted by me?"

He approached once more, and made as if he would seize the fragile being; but shrinking back, Linton clung to his cousin, and implored her to accompany him with a frantic importunity that admitted no denial.

However I disapproved, I couldn't hinder her; indeed how could she have refused him herself? What was filling him with dread, we had no means of discerning, but there he was, powerless under its gripe, and any addition seemed capable of shocking him into idiocy.

We reached the threshold; Catherine walked in; and I stood waiting till she had conducted the invalid to a chair, expecting her out, immediately; when Mr. Heathcliff pushing me forward, exclaimed—

"My house is not stricken with the plague, Nelly; and I have a mind to be hospitable today; sit down, and allow me to shut the door."

He shut and locked it also; I started.

"You shall have tea, before you go home," he added. "I am by myself. Hareton is gone with some cattle to the Lees[1]—and Zillah and Joseph are off on a journey of pleasure. And, though I'm used to being alone, I'd rather have some interesting company, if I can get it. Miss Linton, take your seat by *him*. I give you what I have; the present is hardly worth accepting; but, I have nothing else to offer. It is Linton, I mean. How she does stare! It's odd what a savage feeling I have to anything that seems afraid of me! Had I been born where laws are less strict, and tastes less dainty, I should treat myself to a slow vivisection[2] of those two, as an evening's amusement."

He drew in his breath, struck the table, and swore to himself. "By hell! I hate them."

"I'm not afraid of you!" exclaimed Catherine, who could not hear the latter part of his speech.

She stepped close up; her black eyes flashing with passion and resolution.

"Give me that key—I will have it!" she said. "I wouldn't eat or drink here, if I were starving."[3]

Heathcliff had the key in his hand that remained on the table. He looked up, seized with a sort of surprise at her boldness, or, possibly, reminded by her voice and glance, of the person from whom she inherited it.

She snatched at the instrument, and half succeeded in getting it out of his loosened fingers; but her action recalled him to the present; he recovered it speedily.

"Now, Catherine Linton," he said, "stand off, or I shall knock you down; and that will make Mrs. Dean mad."[4]

---

1   *lees*: fields.
2   *vivisection*: the Vivisection Act (1876) followed agitation against the use of decapitated turtles at public demonstrations in the 1830s of reflex nervous action; see G. Jefferson, 'Marshall Hall, the Grasp Reflex and the Diastaltic Spinal Cord', in *Science, Medicine and History. Essays in Honour of Charles Singer* (1953), ed. E. Ashworth Underwood, pp. 303-20; the violence in *WH* dramatises the convulsive mechanisms defined in Hall's pioneering researches and demonstrations.
3   *starving*: here, 'dying of hunger'.
4   See above, p, 345, note 1.

Regardless of this warning, she captured his closed hand, and its contents again.

"We *will* go!" she repeated, exerting her utmost efforts to cause the iron muscles to relax; and finding that her nails made no impression, she applied her teeth pretty sharply.

Heathcliff glanced at me a glance that kept me from interfering a moment. Catherine was too intent on his fingers to notice his face. He opened them, suddenly, and resigned the object of dispute; but, ere she had well secured it, he seized her with the liberated hand, and, pulling her on his knee, administered, with the other a shower of terrific slaps on both sides of the head, each sufficient to have fulfilled his threat, had she been able to fall.

At this diabolical violence, I rushed on him furiously.

"You villain!" I began to cry, "you villain!"

A touch on the chest silenced me; I am stout, and soon put out of breath; and, what with that and the rage, I staggered dizzily back, and felt ready to suffocate, or to burst a blood-vessel.

The scene was over in two minutes; Catherine, released, put her two hands to her temples, and looked just as if she were not sure whether her ears were off or on. She trembled like a reed, poor thing, and leant against the table perfectly bewildered.

"I know how to chastise children, you see," said the scoundrel, grimly, as he stooped to repossess himself of the key, which had dropped to the floor. "Go to Linton now, as I told you; and cry at your ease! I shall be your father to-morrow—all the father you'll have in a few days—and you shall have plenty of that—you can bear plenty—you're no weakling—you shall have a daily taste, if I catch such a devil of a temper in your eyes again!"

Cathy ran to me instead of Linton, and knelt down, and put her burning cheek on my lap, weeping aloud. Her cousin had shrunk into a corner of the settle, as quiet as a mouse, congratulating himself, I dare say, that the correction had lighted on another than him.

Mr. Heathcliff, perceiving us all confounded, rose, and expeditiously made the tea himself. The cups and saucers were laid ready. He poured it out, and handed me a cup.

"Wash away your spleen," he said. "And help your own naughty pet and mine. It is not poisoned, though I prepared it. I'm going out to seek your horses."

Our first thought, on his departure, was to force an exit some-where. We tried the kitchen door, but that was fastened outside; we looked at the windows—they were too narrow for even Cathy's little figure.

"Master Linton," I cried, seeing we were regularly imprisoned, "You know what your diabolical father is after, and you shall tell us, or I'll box your ears, as he has done your cousin's."

"Yes, Linton you must tell," said Catherine. "It was for your sake I came; and it will be wickedly ungrateful if you refuse."

"Give me some tea, I'm thirsty, and then I'll tell you," he answered. "Mrs. Dean, go away. I don't like you standing over me. Now, Catherine, you are letting your tears fall into my cup! I won't drink that. Give me another."

Catherine pushed another to him, and wiped her face. I felt disgusted at the little wretch's composure, since he was no longer in terror for himself. The anguish he had exhibited on the moor subsided as soon as ever he entered Wuthering Heights; so, I guessed he had been menaced with an awful visitation of wrath, if he failed in decoying us there; and, that accomplished, he had no further immediate fears.

"Papa wants us to be married," he continued, after sipping some of the liquid. "And he knows your papa wouldn't let us marry now; and he's afraid of my dying, if we wait; so we are to be married in the morning, and you are to stay here all night; and, if you do as he wishes, you shall return home next day, and take me with you."

"Take you with her, pitiful changeling?" I exclaimed. "*You* marry? Why, the man is mad, or he thinks us fools, every one. And, do you imagine that beautiful young lady, that healthy, hearty girl, will tie herself to a little perishing monkey like you? Are you cherishing the notion that *anybody*, let alone Miss Catherine Linton, would have you for a husband? You want whipping for bringing us in here at all, with your dastardly, puling tricks; and—don't look so silly now! I've a very good mind to shake you severely, for your contemptible treachery, and your imbecile conceit."

I did give him a slight shaking, but it brought on the cough, and he took to his ordinary resource of moaning and weeping, and Catherine rebuked me.

"Stay all night? No!" she said, looking slowly round. "Ellen, I'll burn that door down, but I'll get out."

And she would have commenced the execution of her threat directly, but Linton was up in alarm, for his dear self, again. He clasped her in his two feeble arms, sobbing—

"Won't you have me, and save me—not let me come to the Grange? Oh! darling Catherine! you mustn't go, and leave me, after all. You must obey my father, you *must!*"

"I must obey my own," she replied, "and relieve him from this cruel suspense. The whole night! What would he think? he'll be distressed already. I'll either break or burn a way out of the house. Be quiet! You're in no danger—but, if you hinder me—Linton, I love papa better than you!"

The mortal terror he felt of Mr. Heathcliff's anger, restored to the boy his coward's eloquence. Catherine was near distraught—still, she persisted that she must go home, and tried entreaty, in her turn, persuading him to subdue his selfish agony.

While they were thus occupied, our jailer re-entered.

"Your beasts have trotted off," he said, "and—Now, Linton! snivelling again? What has she been doing to you? Come, come —have done, and get to bed. In a month or two, my lad, you'll be able to pay her back her present tyrannies, with a vigorous hand—you're pining for pure love, are you not? nothing else in the world—and she shall have you! There, to bed! Zillah won't be here to-night; you must undress yourself. Hush! hold your noise! Once in your own room, I'll not come near you, you needn't fear. By chance, you've managed tolerably. I'll look to the rest."

He spoke these words, holding the door open for his son to pass; and the latter achieved his exit exactly as a spaniel might which suspected the person who attended on it of designing a spiteful squeeze.

The lock was re-secured. Heathcliff approached the fire, where my mistress and I stood silent. Catherine looked op, and instinctively raised her hand to her cheek—his neighbourhood revived a painful sensation. Any-body else would have been incapable of regarding the childish act with sternness, but he scowled on her, and muttered—

"Oh, you are not afraid of me? Your courage is well disguised—you *seem* damnably afraid!"

"I *am* afraid now," she replied; "because if I stay, papa will be miserable; and how can I endure making him miserable—when he—when he—Mr. Heathcliff, *let* me go home! I promise to marry Linton—papa would like me to, and I love him—and why should you wish to force me to do what I'll willingly do of myself?"

"Let him dare to force you!" I cried. "There's law in the land, thank God, there is! though we *be* in an out-of-the-way place. I'd inform, if he were my own son, and it's felony without benefit of clergy!"

"Silence!" said the ruffian, "to the devil with your clamour! I don't want *you* to speak. Miss Linton, I shall enjoy myself remarkably in thinking your father will be miserable; I shall not sleep for satisfaction. You could have hit on no surer way of fixing your residence under my roof, for the next twenty-four hours, than informing me that such an event would follow. As to your promise to marry Linton; I'll take care you shall keep it, for you shall not quit the place till it is fulfilled."

"Send Ellen then, to let papa know I'm safe!" exclaimed Catherine, weeping bitterly. "Or marry me now. Poor papa! Ellen, he'll think we're lost. What shall we do?"

"Not he! He'll think you are tired of waiting on him, and run off, for a little amusement," answered Heathcliff. "You cannot deny that you entered my house of your own accord, in contempt of his injunctions to the contrary. And it is quite natural that you should desire amusement at your age; and that you should weary of nursing a sick man, and that man, *only* your father. Catherine, his happiest days were over when your days began. He cursed you, I dare say, for coming into the world (I did, at least). And it would just do if he cursed you as *he* went out of it. I'd join him. I don't love you! How should I? Weep away. As far as I can see, it will be your chief diversion hereafter: unless Linton make amends for other losses; and your provident parent appears to fancy he may. His letters of advice and consolation entertained me vastly. In his last, he recommended my jewel to be careful of his; and kind to her when he got her. Careful and kind—that's paternal!

But Linton requires his whole stock of care and kindness for himself. Linton can play the little tyrant well. He'll undertake to torture any number of cats if their teeth be drawn, and their claws pared. You'll be able to tell his uncle fine tales of his *kindness*, when you get home again, I assure you."

"You're right there!" I said, "explain your son's character. Show his resemblance to yourself; and then, I hope, Miss Cathy will think twice, before she takes the cockatrice!"[1]

"I don't much mind speaking of his amiable qualities now," he answered, "because she must either accept him, or remain a prisoner, and you along with her, till your master dies. I can detain you both, quite concealed, here. If you doubt, encourage her to retract her word, and you'll have an opportunity of judging!"

"I'll not retract my word," said Catherine, "I'll marry him, within this hour, if I may go to Thrushcross Grange afterwards. Mr. Heathcliff, you're a cruel man, but you're not a fiend; and you won't from *mere* malice, destroy, irrevocably, all my happiness. If papa thought I had left him, on purpose; and if he died before I returned, could I bear to live? I've given over crying; but I'm going to kneel here, at your knee; and I'll not get up, and I'll not take my eyes from your face, till you look back at me! No, don't turn away! *do* look! You'll see nothing to provoke you. I don't hate you. I'm not angry that you struck me. Have you never loved *anybody*, in all your life, uncle? *never*? Ah! you must look once— I'm so wretched—you can't help being sorry and pitying me."

"Keep your eft's[2] fingers off; and move, or I'll kick you!" cried Heathcliff, brutally repulsing her. "I'd rather be hugged by a snake. How the devil can you dream of fawning on me? I *detest* you!"

He shrugged his shoulders—shook himself, indeed, as if his flesh crept with aversion; and thrust back his chair: while I got up, and opened my mouth, to commence a downright torrent of abuse; but I was rendered dumb in the middle of the first sen-

---

1 *cockatrice*: traitor, usurper: S.T. Coleridge, '[Robespierre] the crowned cockatrice whose foul venom infects all Europe'; originally a profusion of mainly reptile and mythical animal species (*NED*).

2 *eft*: newt (from 'an eft, ewt'): James Hurdis, *The Favourite Village* (1800): 'wriggles the viper and the basking eft' (*NED*).

tence, by a threat that I should be shown into a room by myself, the very next syllable I uttered.

It was growing dark—we heard a sound of voices at the garden gate. Our host hurried out, instantly; *he* had his wits about him; *we* had not. There was a talk of two or three minutes, and he returned alone.

"I thought it had been your cousin Hareton," I observed to Catherine. "I wish he would arrive! Who knows but he might take our part?"

"It was three servants sent to seek you from the Grange," said Heathcliff, overhearing me. "You should have opened a lattice, and called out; but I could swear that chit[1] is glad you didn't. She's glad to be obliged to stay, I'm certain."

At learning the chance we had missed, we both gave vent to our grief without control; and he allowed us to wail on till nine o'clock; then he bid us to go upstairs through the kitchen, to Zillah's chamber; and I whispered my companion to obey; perhaps, we might contrive to get through the window there, or into a garret, and out by its skylight.

The window, however, was narrow like those below, and the garret trap was safe from our attempts; for we were fastened in as before. We neither of us lay down: Catherine took her station by the lattice, and watched anxiously for morning—a deep sigh being the only answer I could obtain to my frequent entreaties that she would try to rest.

I seated myself in a chair, and rocked, to and fro, passing harsh judgment on my many derelictions of duty, from which, it struck me then, all the misfortunes of all my employers sprang. It was not the case, in reality, I am aware; but it was, in my imagination, that dismal night, and I thought Heathcliff himself less guilty than I.

At seven o'clock he came, and inquired if Miss Linton had risen.

She ran to the door immediately, and answered—

"Yes."

---

1   *chit*: 'a person considered as no better than a child'; Thackeray, *Paris Sketch Book* (1840): 'To be in love with a young chit of fourteen' (*NED*).

"Here then," he said, opening it, and pulling her out. I rose to follow, but he turned the lock again. I demanded my release.

"Be patient," he replied; "I'll send up your breakfast in a while."

I thumped on the panels, and rattled the latch angrily; and Catherine asked why I was still shut up? He answered, I must try to endure it another hour, and they went away.

I endured it two or three hours; at length, I heard a footstep, not Heathcliff's.

"I've brought you something to eat," said a voice; "oppen t' door!"

Complying eagerly, I beheld Hareton, laden with food enough to last me all day.

"Tak it!" he added, thrusting the tray into my hand.

"Stay one minute," I began.

"Nay!" cried he, and retired, regardless of any prayers I could pour forth to detain him.

And there I remained enclosed, the whole day, and the whole of the next night; and another, and another. Five nights and four days I remained, altogether, seeing nobody but Hareton, once every morning, and he was a model of a jailer—surly, and dumb, and deaf to every attempt at moving his sense of justice or compassion.

CHAPTER 28

On the fifth morning, or rather afternoon, a different step approached—lighter and shorter—and, this time, the person entered the room. It was Zillah; donned in her scarlet shawl, with a black silk bonnet on her head, and a willow basket swung to her arm.

"Eh, dear! Mrs. Dean," she exclaimed. "Well! there is a talk about you at Gimmerton. I never thought, but you were sunk in the Blackhorse marsh, and Missy with you, till master told me you'd been found, and he'd lodged you here! What, and you must have got on an island, sure? And how long were you in the hole? Did master save you, Mrs. Dean? But you're not so thin—you've not been so poorly, have you?"

"Your master is a true scoundrel!" I replied. "But he shall answer for it. He needn't have raised that tale—it shall all be laid bare!"

"What do you mean?" asked Zillah. "It's not his tale—they tell that in the village—about your being lost in the marsh; and I calls to Earnshaw, when I come in—

"'Eh, they's queer things, Mr. Hareton, happened since I went off. It's a sad pity of that likely young lass, and cant[1] Nelly Dean.'

"He stared. I thought he had not heard aught, so I told him the rumour.

"The master listened, and he just smiled to himself, and said —'If they have been in the marsh, they are out now, Zillah. Nelly Dean is lodged, at this minute, in your room. You can tell her to flit, when you go up; here is the key. The bog-water got into her head, and she would have run home, quite flighty, but I fixed her, till she came round to her senses. You can bid her go to the Grange, at once, if she be able, and carry a message from me, that her young lady will follow in time to attend the Squire's funeral.'

"Mr. Edgar is not dead?" I gasped. "Oh, Zillah, Zillah!"

---

1   *cant*: see above, p. 325, note 2.

"Not, no—sit you down, my good mistress," she replied, "you're right sickly yet. He's not dead: Doctor Kenneth thinks he may last another day—I met him on the road and asked."

Instead of sitting down, I snatched my outdoor things, and hastened below, for the way was free.

On entering the house, I looked about for some one to give information of Catherine.

The place was filled with sunshine, and the door stood wide open, but nobody seemed at hand.

As I hesitated whether to go off at once, or return and seek my mistress, a slight cough drew my attention to the hearth.

Linton lay on the settle, sole tenant, sucking a stick of sugar-candy,[1] and pursuing my movements with apathetic eyes.

"Where is Miss Catherine?" I demanded, sternly, supposing I could frighten him into giving intelligence, by catching him thus, alone.

He sucked on like an innocent.

---

1 Sugar: a key topic, mentioned once only, like London, Liverpool, and Yorkshire. In *The History of Sugar*, 2 vols (1949-50), vol. 2, p. 74, Noell Deerr notes 'the ruthless and bloody approach, the curse of organised slavery that for 400 years tainted the New World [sugar] production'; the *Sheffield Register* observed in 1791 that 'an abstinence from the use of sugar has taken place in several families in this town, and also Manchester, Derby, etc.' (cited in E.M. Hunt, *The North of England Agitation for the Abolition of the Slave Trade 1780-1800*, Manchester University: unpublished MA dissertation, 1959), p. 107; T.W. Blanshard, *The Life of Samuel Bradburn, the Methodist Demosthenes* (1870), p. 146, cites a letter by Samuel Bradburn in 1791: 'Mr Clarke and I have given up the use of sugar [...] and this we shall continue till the slave trade is abolished'; in *Vindication of the Rights of Woman*, 1792 (1985), p. 257, Mary Wollstonecraft wrote: 'Is sugar always to be produced by vital blood? Is one half of the human species, like the poor African slaves, to be subject to prejudices that brutalize them, when principles would be a surer guard, only to sweeten the cup of man?'; Thomas Hood, *Hood's Own; or Laughter from Year to Year* (1839) (*K*) has: 'Sugar, [...] an abomination, to indulge in which / Would convert a professing Christian into a practical Cannibal' (p. 45). See also, Joan Baum, *Mind-Forg'd Manacles. Slavery and the English Romantic Poets* (New York, 1994); and N.B. Lewis, 'The Abolitionist Movement in Sheffield, 1823-1833: with letters from Southey, Wordsworth, and Others', *Bulletin of the John Rylands Library*, 18 (1934), 3-18.

"Is she gone?" I said.

"No," he replied; "she's upstairs—she's not to go; we won't let her."

"You won't let her, little idiot!" I exclaimed. "Direct me to her room immediately, or I'll make you sing out sharply."

"Papa would make you sing out, if you attempted to get there," he answered. "He says I'm not to be soft with Catherine— she's my wife, and it's shameful that she should wish to leave me! He says, she hates me, and wants me to die, that she may have my money, but she shan't have it; and she shan't go home! she never shall! she may cry, and be sick as much as she pleases!"

He resumed his former occupation, closing his lids, as if he meant to drop asleep.

"Master Heathcliff," I resumed, "have you forgotten all Catherine's kindness to you, last winter, when you affirmed you loved her, and when she brought you books, and sung you songs, and came many a time through wind and snow to see you? She wept to miss one evening, because you would be disappointed; and you felt then, that she was a hundred times too good to you; and now you believe the lies your father tells, though you know he detests you both! And you join him against her. That's fine gratitude, is it not?"

The corner of Linton's mouth fell, and he took the sugar-candy from his lips.

"Did she come to Wuthering Heights, because she hated you?" I continued. "Think for yourself! As to your money, she does not even know that you will have any. And you say she's sick; and yet, you leave her alone, up there in a strange house! *You*, who have felt what it is to be so neglected! You could pity your own sufferings, and she pitied them, too, but you won't pity hers! I shed tears Master Heathcliff, you see—an elderly woman, and a servant merely—and you, after pretending such affection, and having reason to worship her, almost, store every tear you have for yourself, and lie there quite at ease. Ah! you're a heartless, selfish boy!"

"I can't stay with her," he answered crossly. "I'll not stay, by myself. She cries so I can't bear it. And she won't give over, though I say I'll call my father—I did call him once; and he threatened to strangle her, if she was not quiet, but she began again, the instant he left the room; moaning and grieving, all night long, though I screamed for vexation that I couldn't sleep."

"Is Mr. Heathcliff out," I inquired, perceiving that the wretched creature had no power to sympathise with his cousin's mental tortures.

"He's in the court," he replied, "talking to Doctor Kenneth who says uncle is dying, truly, at last—I'm glad for I shall be master of the Grange after him—and Catherine always spoke of it, as *her* house. It isn't hers! It's mine—papa says everything she has is mine. All her nice books are mine—she offered to give me them, and her pretty birds, and her pony Minny, if I would get the key of our room, and let her out: but I told her she had nothing to give, and they were all, all mine. And then she cried, and took a little picture from her neck, and said I should have that—two pictures in a gold case—on one side her mother, and on the other, uncle, when they were young. That was yesterday—I said *they* were mine, too; and tried to get them from her. The spiteful thing wouldn't let me; she pushed me off, and hurt me. I shrieked out—that frightens her—she heard papa coming, and she broke the hinges, and divided the case and gave me her mother's portrait; the other she attempted to hide; but papa asked what was the matter and I explained it. He took the one I had away; and ordered her to resign hers to me; she refused, and he—he struck her down, and wrenched it off the chain, and crushed it with his foot."

"And were you pleased to see her struck?" I asked: having my designs in encouraging his talk.

"I winked," he answered. "I wink to see my father strike a dog, or a horse, he does it so hard—yet I was glad at first—she deserved punishing for pushing me: but when papa was gone, she made me come to the window and showed me her cheek cut on the inside, against her teeth, and her mouth filling with blood: and then she gathered up the bits of the picture, and went and sat down with her face to the wall, and she has never spoken to me since; and I sometimes think she can't speak for pain. I don't like to think so! but she's a naughty thing for crying continually; and she looks so pale and wild, I'm afraid of her!"

"And you can get the key if you choose?" I said.

"Yes, when I am upstairs," he answered "but I can't walk up-stairs now."

"In what apartment is it?" I asked.

"Oh," he cried, "I shan't tell *you* where it is! It is our secret. Nobody, neither Hareton, nor Zillah are to know. There! you've tired me—go away!" And he turned his face onto his arm, and shut his eyes, again.

I considered it best to depart without seeing Mr. Heathcliff; and bring a rescue for my young lady, from the Grange.

On reaching it the astonishment of my fellow servants to see me, and their joy also, was intense; and when they heard that their little mistress was safe, two or three were about to hurry up, and shout the news at Mr. Edgar's door: but I bespoke the announce-ment of it, myself.

How changed I found him, even in those few days! He lay an image of sadness, and resignation, waiting his death. Very young he looked: though his actual age was thirty-nine; one would have called him ten yours younger, at least. He thought of Catherine for he murmured her name. I touched his hand, and spoke.

"Catherine is coming, dear master!" I whispered, "she is alive, and well; and will be here I hope to-night."

I trembled at the first effects of this intelligence: he half rose up, looked eagerly round the apartment, and then sunk back in a swoon.

As soon as he recovered, I related our compulsory visit, and de-tention at the Heights: I said Heathcliff forced me to go in, which was not quite true; I uttered as little as possible against Linton; nor did I describe all his father's brutal conduct—my intentions being to add no bitterness, if I could help it, to his already overflowing cup.

He divined that one of his enemy's purposes was to secure the personal property, as well as the estate to his son, or rather himself; yet why he did not wait till his decease,[1] was a puzzle to my mas-ter; because ignorant how nearly he, and his nephew would quit the world together.

---

1   *his decease*: Edgar Linton is unaware of Linton Heathcliff's impending death.

However he felt his will had better be altered—instead of leaving Catherine's fortune at her own disposal, he determined to put it in the hands of trustees for her use during life; and for her children, if she had any, after her. By that means, it could not fall to Mr. Heathcliff should Linton die.

Having received his order, I despatched a man to fetch the attorney, and four more, provided with serviceable weapons, to demand my young lady of her jailer. Both parties were delayed very late. The single servant returned first.

He said Mr. Green, the lawyer, was out when he arrived at his house, and he had to wait two hours for his re-entrance: and then Mr. Green told him he had a little business in the village, that must be done, but he would be at Thrushcross Grange before morning.

The four men came back unaccompanied, also. They brought word that Catherine was ill, too ill to quit her room, and Heathcliff would not suffer them to see her.

I scolded the stupid fellows well, for listening to that tale, which I would not carry to my master; resolving to take the whole bevy up to the Heights, at daylight, and storm it, literally, unless the prisoner were quietly surrendered to us.

Her father *shall* see her, I vowed, and vowed again, if that devil be killed on his own door-stones, in trying to prevent it!

Happily, I was spared the journey, and the trouble.

I had gone downstairs at three o'clock to fetch a jug of water; and was passing through the hall, with it in my hand, when a sharp knock, at the front door, made me jump.

"Oh! it is Green"—I said recollecting myself—"only Green," and I went on, intending to send somebody else to open it; but the knock was repeated, not loud, and still importunately.

I put the jug on the bannister, and hastened to admit him, myself.

The harvest moon shone clear outside. It was not the attorney. My own sweet little mistress sprung on my neck sobbing,

"Ellen! Ellen! Is papa alive?"

"Yes!" I cried, "yes my angel he is! God be thanked, you are safe with us again!"

She wanted to run, breathless as she was, upstairs to Mr. Linton's room; but I compelled her to sit down on a chair, and made her drink, and washed her pale face, chafing it into a faint colour with my apron. Then I said I must go first, and tell of her arrival; imploring her to say, she should be happy, with young Heathcliff. She stared, but soon comprehending why I counselled her to utter the falsehood, she assured me she would not complain.

I couldn't abide to be present at their meeting. I stood outside the chamber-door, a quarter of an hour, and hardly ventured near the bed, then.

All was composed, however; Catherine's despair was as silent as her father's joy. She supported him calmly, in appearance; and he fixed on her features his raised eyes that seemed dilating with ecstasy.

He died blissfully, Mr. Lockwood; he died so, kissing her cheek, he murmured,

"I am going to her, and you darling child shall come to us;" and never stirred or spoke again, but continued that rapt, radiant gaze, till his pulse imperceptibly stopped, and his soul departed. None could have noticed the exact minute of his death, it was so entirely without a struggle.[1]

Whether Catherine had spent her tears, or whether the grief were too weighty to let them flow, she sat there dry-eyed till the sun rose—she sat till noon, and would still have remained, brooding over that death-bed, but I insisted on her coming away, and taking some repose.

It was well I succeeded in removing her, for at dinner-time appeared the lawyer, having called at Wuthering Heights to get his instructions how to behave. He had sold himself to Mr. Heathcliff, and that was the cause of his delay in obeying my master's summons. Fortunately, no thought of worldly affairs crossed the latter's mind, to disturb him, after his daughter's arrival.

Mr. Green took upon himself to order everything and everybody about the place. He gave all the servants but me, notice to

---

1   Besides contributing to the revival of 'hierglyphic' literary form, Emily Brontë appears to have had in mind the themes of John Donne, George Herbert, Francis Quarles, and other Emblem or Hieroglyphic writers: see 'As virtuous men pass mildly away...', in John Donne, 'A Valediction: forbidding mourning'; also, 'As when a sick man very near to death...', in Robert Browning, 'Childe Roland to the Dark Tower Came', stanza 5.

quit. He would have carried his delegated authority to the point of insisting that Edgar Linton should not be buried beside his wife, but in the chapel, with his family. There was the will however, to hinder that, and my loud protestations against any infringement of its direction.

The funeral was hurried over; Catherine, Mrs. Linton Heathcliff now, was suffered to stay at the Grange, till her father's corpse had quitted it.

She told me that her anguish had at last spurred Linton to incur the risk of liberating her. She heard the men I sent, disputing at the door, and she gathered the sense of Heathcliff's answer. It drove her desperate—Linton, who had been conveyed up to the little parlour soon after I left, was terrified into fetching the key before his father re-ascended.

He had the cunning to unlock, and re-lock the door, without shutting it; and when he should have gone to bed, he begged to sleep with Hareton, and his petition was granted for once.

Catherine stole out before break of day. She dare not try the doors, lest the dogs should raise an alarm; she visited the empty chambers, and examined their windows; and, luckily, lighting on her mother's she got easily out of its lattice, and onto the ground, by means of the fir tree, close by. Her accomplice suffered for his share in her escape, notwithstanding his timid contrivances.

CHAPTER 29

The evening after the funeral, my young lady and I were seated in the library; now musing mournfully, one of us despairingly, on our loss; now venturing conjectures as to the gloomy future.

We had just agreed the best destiny which could await Catherine, would be a permission to continue resident at the Grange, at least, during Linton's life: he being allowed to join her there, and I to remain as housekeeper. That seemed rather too favourable an arrangement to be hoped for, and yet I did hope, and began to cheer up under the prospect of retaining my home, and my employment, and, above all, my beloved young mistress, when a servant—one of the discarded ones, not yet departed—rushed hastily in, and said, "that devil Heathcliff" was coming through the court, should he fasten the door in his face?

If we had been mad enough to order that proceeding, we had not time. He made no ceremony of knocking, or announcing his name; he was master, and availed himself of the master's privilege to walk straight in, without saying a word.

The sound of our informant's voice directed him to the library: he entered; and motioning him out, shut the door.

It was the same room into which he had been ushered, as a guest, eighteen years before; the same moon shone through the window; and the same autumn landscape lay outside. We had not yet lighted a candle, but all the apartment was visible, even to the portraits on the wall—the splendid head of Mrs. Linton, and the graceful one of her husband.

Heathcliff advanced to the hearth. Time had little altered his person either. There was the same man; his dark face rather sallower, and more composed, his frame a stone or two heavier, perhaps, and no other difference.

Catherine had risen with an impulse to dash out, when she saw him.

"Stop!" he said, arresting her by the arm. "No more runnings away! Where would you go? I'm come to fetch you home; and I hope you'll be a dutiful daughter, and not encourage my son to further disobedience. I was embarrassed how to punish him when

I discovered his part in the business—he's such a cobweb, a pinch would annihilate him—but, you'll see by his look that he has received his due! I brought him down one evening, the day before yesterday, and just set him in a chair, and never touched him afterwards. I sent Hareton out, and we had the room to ourselves. In two hours, I called Joseph to carry him up again; and, since then, my presence is as potent on his nerves, as a ghost; and I fancy he sees me often, though I am not near. Hareton says he wakes and shrieks in the night by the hour together; and calls you to protect him from me; and, whether you like your precious mate or not, you must come—he's your concern now; I yield all my interest in him to you."

"Why not let Catherine continue here?" I pleaded, "and send Master Linton to her. As you hate them both, you'd not miss them—they *can* only be a daily plague to your unnatural heart."

"I'm seeking a tenant for the Grange," he answered; "and I want my children about me, to be sure—besides that lass owes me her services for her bread; I'm not going to nurture her in luxury and idleness after Linton is gone. Make haste and get ready now. And don't oblige me to compel you."

"I shall," said Catherine, "Linton is all I have to love in the world, and, though you have done what you could to make him hateful to me, and me to him, you *cannot* make us hate each other! and I defy you to hurt him when I am by, and I defy you to frighten me."

"You are a boastful champion!" replied Heathcliff; "but I don't like you well enough to hurt him—you shall get the full benefit of the torment, as long as it lasts. It is not I who will make him hateful to you—it is his own sweet spirit. He's as bitter as gall at your desertion, and its consequences—don't expect thanks for this noble devotion. I heard him draw a pleasant picture to Zillah of what he would do, if he were as strong as I—the inclination is there, and his very weakness will sharpen his wits to find a substitute for strength."

"I know he has a bad nature," said Catherine; "he's your son. But I'm glad I've a better, to forgive it; and I know he loves me and for that reason I love him. Mr. Heathcliff, *you* have *nobody* to love you; and, however miserable you make us, we shall still have the revenge of thinking that your cruelty rises from your greater misery! You *are* miserable, are you not? Lonely, like the devil, and envious like him? *Nobody* loves you—*nobody* will cry for you, when you die! I wouldn't be you!"

Catherine spoke with a kind of dreary triumph: she seemed to have made up her mind to enter into the spirit of her future family, and draw pleasure from the griefs of her enemies.

"You shall be very sorry to be yourself presently," said her father-in-law. "If you stand there another minute. Begone, witch, and get your things."

She scornfully withdrew.

In her absence, I began to beg for Zillah's place at the Heights, offering to resign her mine; but he would suffer it on no account. He bid me be silent, and then, for the first time, allowed himself a glance round the room, and a look at the pictures. Having studied Mrs. Linton, he said—

"I shall have that at home. Not because I need it, but—"

He turned abruptly to the fire, and continued, with what, for lack of a better word, I must call a smile—

"I'll tell you what I did yesterday! I got the sexton, who was digging Linton's grave, to remove the earth off her coffin lid, and I opened it. I thought, once I would have stayed there, when I saw her face again—it is hers yet[1]—he had hard work to stir me; but he said it would change, if the air blew on it, and so I struck one side of the coffin loose—and covered it up—not Linton's side, damn him! I wish he'd been soldered in lead—and I bribed the sexton to pull it away, when I'm laid there, and slide mine out too, I'll have it made so, and then, by the time Linton gets to us, he'll not know which is which!"[2]

---

1   The features of George Clifford, 2nd Earl of Cumberland, were recognised by the Revd T.D. Whitaker when he opened the tomb, with permission: 'the face so entire (only turned to copper colour) as plainly to resemble his portraits', *Craven*, p. 314.

2   He arranges for the boards of their adjacent coffins to be open where they face each other, so that by the time Linton has decomposed, his remains will find that theirs have mingled. For this idea, see John Donne, 'The Funerall': 'Who ever comes to shroud me, do not harme...'. Notoriously, Haworth drinking water absorbed elements from the graveyard in the early 19th century.

"You were very wicked, Mr. Heathcliff!" I exclaimed; "were you not ashamed to disturb the dead?"

"I disturbed nobody, Nelly," he replied; "and I gave some ease to myself. I shall be a great deal more comfortable now; and you'll have a better chance of keeping me underground, when I get there. Disturbed her? No! she has disturbed me, night and day, through eighteen years—incessantly—remorselessly—till yesternight—and yesternight, I was tranquil. I dreamt I was sleeping the last sleep, by that sleeper, with my heart stopped, and my cheek frozen against hers."

"And if she had been dissolved into earth, or worse, what would you have dreamt of then?" I said.

"Of dissolving with her, and being more happy still!" he answered. "Do you suppose I dread any change of that sort? I expected such a transformation on raising the lid, but I'm better pleased that it should not commence till I share it. Besides, unless I had received a distinct impression of her passionless features, that strange feeling would hardly have been removed. It began oddly. You know, I was wild after she died, and eternally, from dawn to dawn, praying her to return to me—her spirit—I have a strong faith in ghosts; I have a conviction that they can, and do exist, among us!

"The day she was buried there came a fall of snow. In the evening I went to the churchyard. It blew bleak as winter—all round was solitary: I didn't fear that her fool of a husband would wander up the den[1] so late—and no one else had business to bring them there.

"Being alone, and conscious two yards of loose earth was the sole barrier between us, I said to myself—'I'll have her in my arms again! If she be cold, I'll think it is this north wind that chills *me*; and if she be motionless, it is sleep.'

"I got a spade from the toolhouse, and began to delve with all my might—it scraped the coffin; I fell to work with my hands; the wood commenced cracking about the screws. I was on the point of attaining my object, when it seemed that I heard a sigh from some one above, close at the edge of the grave, and bending

---

1 *den*: 'Dean, a valley' (Carr).

down—'If I can only get this off,' I muttered, 'I wish they may shovel in the earth over us both!' and I wrenched at it more desperately still. There was another sigh, close at my ear. I appeared to feel the warm breath of it displacing the sleet-laden wind. I knew no living thing in flesh and blood was by—but as certainly as you perceive the approach to some substantial body in the dark, though it cannot be discerned, so certainly I felt that Cathy was there, not under me, but on the earth.

"A sudden sense of relief flowed, from my heart, through every limb. I relinquished my labour of agony, and turned at once consoled, unspeakably consoled. Her presence was with me; it remained while I re-filled the grave, and led me home. You may laugh, if you will, but I was sure I should see her there. I was sure she was with me, and I could not help talking to her.

"Having reached the Heights, I rushed eagerly to the door. It was fastened; and, I remember, that accursed Earnshaw and my wife opposed my entrance. I remember stopping to kick the breath out of him, and then hurrying upstairs, to my room, and hers—I looked round impatiently—I felt her by me—I could *almost* see her, and yet I *could not*! I ought to have sweat blood then, from the anguish of my yearning, from the fervour of my supplications to have but one glimpse! I had not one. She showed herself, as she often was in life, a devil to me! And, since then, sometimes more, and sometimes less, I've been the sport of that intolerable torture! Infernal—keeping my nerves at such a stretch, that, if they had not resembled catgut, they would, long ago, have relaxed to the feebleness of Linton's.

"When I sat in the house with Hareton, it seemed that on going out, I should meet her; when I walked on the moors I should meet her coming in. When I went from home, I hastened to return, she *must* be somewhere at the Heights, I was certain! And when I slept in her chamber—I was beaten out of that—I couldn't lie there; for the moment I closed my eyes, she was either outside the window, or sliding back the panels, or entering the room, or even resting her darling head on the same pillow as she did when a child. And I must open my lids to see. And so I opened and closed them a hundred times a-night—to be always disappointed! It racked me! I've often groaned aloud, till that old rascal Joseph, no doubt believed that my conscience was playing the fiend inside of me.

"Now since I've seen her, I'm pacified—a little. It was a strange way of killing, not by inches, but by fractions of hair-breadths, to beguile me with the spectre of a hope, through eighteen years!"

Mr. Heathcliff paused and wiped his forehead—his hair clung to it, wet with perspiration; his eyes were fixed on the red embers of the fire; the brows not contracted, but raised next the temples, diminishing the grim aspect of his countenance, but imparting a peculiar look of trouble, and a painful appearance of mental tension towards an absorbing subject. He only half addressed me, and I maintained silence—I didn't like to hear him talk!

After a short period, he resumed his meditation on the picture,[1] took it down, and leant it against the sofa to contemplate it at better advantage; and while so occupied Catherine entered, announcing that she was ready, when her pony should be saddled.

"Send that over to-morrow," said Heathcliff to me, then turning to her he added, "You may do without your pony—it is a fine evening, and you'll need no ponies at Wuthering Heights; for what journeys you take, your own feet will serve you—Come along."

"Good-bye, Ellen!" whispered my dear little mistress. As she kissed me, her lips felt like ice. "Come and see me Ellen, don't forget."

"Take care you do no such thing, Mrs. Dean!" said her new father. "When I wish to speak to you I'll come here. I want none of your prying at my house!"

He signed her to precede him; and casting back a look that cut my heart, she obeyed.

I watched them from the window, walk down the garden. Heathcliff fixed Catherine's arm under his, though she disputed the act, at first, evidently, and with rapid strides, he hurried her into the alley, whose trees concealed them.

---

1   With the sex of the sitter reversed, Heathcliff's meditation resembles John Donne, 'His Picture' (Elegie 5), where the weather-beaten and ageing lover broods on the permanence of his love.

CHAPTER 30

I have paid a visit to the Heights, but I have not seen her since she left; Joseph held the door in his hand, when I called to ask after her, and wouldn't let me pass. He said Mrs. Linton was "thrang,"[1] and the master was not in. Zillah has told me something of the way they go on, otherwise I should hardly know who was dead, and who living.

She thinks Catherine, haughty, and does not like her, I can guess by her talk. My young lady asked some aid of her, when she first came, but Mr. Heathcliff told her to follow her own business, and let his daughter-in-law look after herself, and Zillah willingly acquiesced, being a narrow-minded selfish woman. Catherine evinced a child's annoyance at this neglect; repaid it with contempt, and thus enlisted my informant among her enemies, as securely as if she had done her some great wrong.

I had a long talk with Zillah, about six weeks ago, a little before you came, one day, when we foregathered on the moor; and this is what she told me.

"The first thing Mrs. Linton did," she said, "on her arrival at the Heights, was to run upstairs without even wishing good-evening to me and Joseph; she shut herself into Linton's room, and remained till morning—then, while the master and Earnshaw were at breakfast, she entered the house[2] and asked all in a quiver if the doctor might be sent for? Her cousin was very ill."

" 'We know that!' answered Heathcliff, 'but his life is not worth a farthing, and I won't spend a farthing on him.'

" 'But I cannot tell how to do,' she said, 'and if nobody will help me, he'll die!'

" 'Walk out of the room!' cried the master, 'and let me never hear a word more about him! None here care what becomes of

---

1   *thrang*: over-busy; usually, 'thrang as Throp's wife' (*throp*: village); also, 'thrang as three in a bed' (Carr); see 'Throp's Wife', in John Moorman, *Tales of the Ridings* (1920), pp. 36-46, a possible pointer to the status of Dent as a famous centre of hard work.
2   *house*: living room.

him; if you do, act the nurse; if you do not, lock him up and leave him.'

"Then she began to bother me, and I said I'd had enough plague with the tiresome thing; we each had our tasks, and hers was to wait on Linton: Mr. Heathcliff bid me leave that labour to her.

"How they managed together, I can't tell. I fancy he fretted a great deal, and moaned hisseln, night and day; and she had precious little rest, one could guess by her white face, and heavy eyes—she sometimes came into the kitchen all wildered like, and looked as if she would fain beg assistance: but I was not going to disobey the master—I never dare disobey him, Mrs. Dean, and though I thought it wrong that Kenneth should not be sent for, it was no concern of mine, either to advise or complain; and I always refused to meddle.

"Once or twice, after we had gone to bed, I've happened to open my door again, and seen her sitting crying, on the stairs' top; and then I've shut myself in, quick, for fear of being moved to interfere. I did pity her then, I'm sure; still I didn't wish to lose my place, you know!

"At last, one night she came boldly into my chamber, and frightened me out of my wits, by saying, 'Tell Mr. Heathcliff that his son is dying—'I'm sure he is, this time.—Get up instantly, and tell him!'

"Having uttered this speech, she vanished again. I lay a quarter of an hour listening and trembling. Nothing stirred—the house was quiet.

"She's mistaken," I said to myself. "He's got over it. I needn't disturb them." And I began to doze. But my sleep was marred a second time, by a sharp ringing of the bell—the only bell we have, put up on purpose for Linton, and the master called to me, to see what was the matter, and inform them that he wouldn't have that noise repeated.

"I delivered Catherine's message. He cursed to himself, and in a few minutes, came out with a lighted candle, and proceeded to their room. I followed—Mrs. Heathcliff was seated by the bedside, with her hands folded on her knees. Her father-in-law went up, held the light to Linton's face, looked at him, and touched him, afterwards he turned to her.

"'Now—Catherine,' he said, 'how do you feel?'

"She was dumb. 'How do you feel, Catherine?' he repeated. 'He's safe, and I'm free,' she answered, 'I should feel well—but,' she continued with a bitterness she couldn't conceal, 'You have left me so long to struggle against death,[1] alone, that I feel and see only death! I feel like death!'

"And she looked like it, too! I gave her a little wine. Hareton and Joseph who had been wakened by the ringing, and the sound of feet, and heard our talk from outside, now entered. Joseph was fain, I believe, of the lad's removal: Hareton seemed a thought bothered, though he was more taken up with staring at Catherine than thinking of Linton. But the master bid him get off to bed again—we didn't want his help. He afterwards made Joseph remove the body to his chamber, and told me to return to mine, and Mrs. Heathcliff remained by herself.

"In the morning, he sent me to tell her she must come down to breakfast—she had undressed, and appeared going to sleep; and said she was ill; at which I hardly wondered. I informed Mr. Heathcliff, and he replied, 'Well, let her be till after the funeral; and go up now and then to get her what is needful; and as soon as she seems better, tell me.'"

Cathy stayed upstairs a fortnight, according to Zillah, who visited her twice a-day, and would have been rather more friendly, but her attempts at increasing kindness were proudly and promptly repelled.

Heathcliff went up once, to show her Linton's will. He had bequeathed the whole of his, and what had been her moveable property to his father. The poor creature was threatened, or coaxed into that act, during her week's absence, when his uncle died. The lands, being a minor he could not meddle with. However, Mr. Heathcliff has claimed, and kept them in his wife's right, and his also—I suppose legally, at any rate, Catherine, destitute of cash and friends, cannot disturb his possession.

"Nobody," said Zillah, "ever approached her door, except that

---

1 The belief that children of mixed racial descent are weak and doomed is explored in M.-L. von Sneidern, '*Wuthering Heights* and the Liverpool Slave Trade', *ELH* 62 (1995), 171–96.

once, but I...and nobody asked anything about her. The first occasion of her coming down into the house, was on a Sunday afternoon.

"She had cried out, when I carried up her dinner that she couldn't bear any longer being in the cold; and I told her the master was going to Thrushcross Grange; and Earnshaw and I needn't hinder her from descending; so, as soon as she heard Heathcliff's horse trot off, she made her appearance, donned in black, and her yellow curls combed back behind her ears, as plain as a quaker, she couldn't comb them out.

"Joseph and I generally go to chapel on Sundays" (the Kirk, you know, has no minister, now, explained Mrs. Dean, and they call the Methodists' or Baptists' place, I can't say which it is, at Gimmerton, a chapel)[1]—"Joseph had gone," she continued, "but I thought proper to bide at home. Young folks are always the better for an elder's over-looking, and Hareton with all his bashfulness, isn't a model of nice behaviour. I let him know that his cousin would very likely sit with us, and she had been always used to see the Sabbath respected, so he had as good leave his guns, and bits of in-door work alone, while she stayed.

"He coloured up at the news; and cast his eyes over his hands and clothes. The train-oil,[2] and gunpowder were shoved out of sight in a minute. I saw he meant to give her his company; and I guessed, by his way, he wanted to be presentable; so, laughing, as I durst not laugh when the master is by, I offered to help him, if he would, and joked at his confusion. He grew sullen, and began to swear.

"Now, Mrs. Dean," she went on, seeing me not pleased by her manner, "you happen[3] think your young lady too fine for Mr. Hareton, and happen you're right—but, I own, I should love well

---

1 *chapel*: the West Lane Baptist Chapel and West Lane Methodist Chapel were founded at Haworth in 1752 and 1758 respectively; see W.D. Dixon and John Lock, *A Man of Sorrow* (1979), p. 218; also, John Petty, *The History of the Primitive Methodist Connexion*, new edn. (1880), chs. 9-11, pp. 85-137; and *Committees for Repeal of the Test and Corporation Acts: Minutes 1786-90 and 1827-8* (1978), ed. Thomas W. Davis (1978).

2 *train-oil*: whale oil, used for cleaning weapons (Dutch, *traan*).

3 *happen*: maybe.

to bring her pride a peg lower. And what will all her learning and her daintiness do for her, now? She's as poor as you, or I—poorer—I'll be bound, you're saving—and I'm doing my little all, that road."[1]

Hareton allowed Zillah to give him her aid; and she flattered him into a good humour; so, when Catherine came, half forgetting her former insults, he tried to make himself agreeable, by the house-keeper's account.

"Missis walked in," she said, "as chill as an icicle, and as high as a princess. I got up and offered her my seat in the arm-chair. No, she turned up her nose at my civility. Earnshaw rose too, and bid her come to the settle, and sit close by the fire; he was sure she was starved.[2]

"'I've been starved[3] a month and more,' she answered, resting on the word, as scornful as she could. And she got a chair for herself, and placed it at a distance from both of us.

"Having sat till she was warm, she began to look round, and discovered a number of books in the dresser; she was instantly upon her feet again, stretching to reach them, but they were too high up.

"Her cousin, after watching her endeavours a while, at last summoned courage to help her; she held her frock, and he filled it with the first that came to hand.

"That was a great advance for the lad—she didn't thank him; still, he felt gratified that she had accepted his assistance, and ventured to stand behind as she examined them, and even to stoop and point out what struck his fancy in certain old pictures which they contained—nor was he daunted by the saucy style in which she jerked the page from his finger; he contented himself with going a bit farther back, and looking at her, instead of the book.

"She continued reading, or seeking for something to read. His attention became, by degrees, quite centred in the study of her thick, silky curls—her face he couldn't see, and she couldn't see him. And, perhaps, not quite awake to what he did, but attracted

---

1   *that road*: in that way.
2   *starved*: frozen.
3   *starved*: deprived, in all senses.

like a child to a candle, at last, he proceeded from staring to touching; he put out his hand and stroked one curl, as gently as if it were a bird. He might have stuck a knife into her neck, she started round in such a taking.

"'Get away, this moment! How dare you touch me? Why are you stopping there?' she cried, in a tone of disgust. 'I can't endure you! I'll go upstairs again, if you come near me.'

"Mr. Hareton recoiled, looking as foolish as he could do; he sat down in the settle, very quiet, and she continued turning over her volumes, another half hour—finally, Earnshaw crossed over, and whispered to me.

"'Will you ask her to read to us, Zillah? I'm stalled of[1] doing naught—and I do like—I could like to hear her! dunnot say I wanted it, but ask of yourseln.'

"'Mr. Hareton wishes you would read to us, ma'am,' I said, immediately, 'He'd take it very kind—he'd be much obliged.' She frowned; and, looking up, answered,

"'Mr. Hareton, and the whole set of you will be good enough to understand that I reject any pretence at kindness you have the hypocrisy to offer! I despise you, and will have nothing to say to any of you! When I would have given my life for one kind word, even to see one of your faces, you all kept off. But I won't complain to you! I'm driven down here by the cold, not either to amuse you, or enjoy your society.'

"'What could I ha' done?' began Earnshaw. 'How was I to blame?'

"'Oh! you are an exception,' answered Mrs. Heathcliff. 'I never missed such a concern as you.'

"'But, I offered more than once, and asked,' he said, kindling up at her pertness, 'I asked Mr. Heathcliff to let me wake for you—'

"'Be silent! I'll go out of doors, or anywhere, rather than have your disagreeable voice in my ear!' said my lady.

"Hareton muttered, she might go to hell, for him! and unslinging his gun, restrained himself from his Sunday occupations, no longer.

"He talked now, freely enough, and she presently saw fit to

---

1   *stalled of*: bored with.

retreat to her solitude: but the frost had set in, and, in spite of her pride, she was forced to condescend to our company, more and more. However, I took care there should be no further scorning at my good nature—ever since, I've been as stiff as herself—and she has no lover, or liker among us—and she does not deserve one—for, let them say the least word to her, and she'll curl back without respect of any one! She'll snap at the master himself; and, as good as dares him to thrash her; and the more hurt she gets, the more venomous she grows."

At first, on hearing this account from Zillah, I determined to leave my situation, take a cottage, and get Catherine to come and live with me; but Mr. Heathcliff would as soon permit that, as he would set up Hareton in an independent house; and I can see no remedy, at present, unless she could marry again; and that scheme, it does not come within my province to arrange.

Thus ended Mrs. Dean's story. Notwithstanding the doctor's prophecy, I am rapidly recovering strength, and, though it be only the second week in January, I propose getting out on horse-back, in a day or two, and riding over to Wuthering Heights, to inform my landlord that I shall spend the next six months in London; and, if he likes, he may look out for another tenant to take the place, after October[1]—I would not pass another winter here, for much.

---

1   Lockwood's tenancy of the Grange runs from 1 November 1801-31 October 1802.

CHAPTER 31

Yesterday was bright, calm, and frosty. I went to the Heights as I proposed; my housekeeper entreated me to bear a little note from her to her young lady, and I did not refuse, for the worthy woman was not conscious of anything odd in her request.

The front door stood open, but the jealous gate was fastened, as at my last visit; I knocked and invoked Earnshaw from among the garden beds; he unchained it, and I entered. The fellow is as handsome a rustic as need be seen. I took particular notice of him this time; but then, he does his best, apparently, to make the least of his advantages.

I asked if Mr. Heathcliff were at home? He answered, no; but he would be in at dinner-time. It was eleven o'clock, and I announced my intention of going in, and waiting for him, at which he immediately flung down his tools and accompanied me, in the office of watchdog, not as a substitute for the host.

We entered together; Catherine was there, making herself useful in preparing some vegetables for the approaching meal; she looked more sulky, and less spirited than when I had seen her first. She hardly raised her eyes to notice me, and continued her employment with the same disregard to common forms of politeness, as before; never returning my bow and good morning, by the slightest acknowledgment.

"She does not seem so amiable," I thought, "as Mrs. Dean would persuade me to believe. She's a beauty, it is true; but not an angel."

Earnshaw surlily bid her remove her things to the kitchen.

"Remove them yourself," she said; pushing them from her, as soon as she had done; and retiring to a stool by the window, where she began to carve figures of birds and beasts, out of the turnip parings in her lap.

I approached her, pretending to desire a view of the garden; and, as I fancied, adroitly dropped Mrs. Dean's note onto her knee, unnoticed by Hareton—but she asked aloud—

"What is that?" and chucked it off.

"A letter from your old acquaintance, the housekeeper at the Grange," I answered, annoyed at her exposing my kind deed, and fearful lest it should be imagined a missive of my own.

She would gladly have gathered it up, at this information, but Hareton beat her; he seized, and put it in his waistcoat, saying Mr. Heathcliff should look at it first.

Thereat, Catherine silently turned her face from us, and, very stealthily, drew out her pocket-handkerchief and applied it to her eyes; and her cousin, after struggling a while to keep down his softer feelings, pulled out the letter and flung it on the floor beside her as ungraciously as he could.

Catherine caught, and perused it eagerly; then she put a few questions to me concerning the inmates, rational and irrational, of her former home; and gazing towards the hills, murmured in soliloquy,

"I should like to be riding Minny down there! I should like to be climbing up there—Oh! I'm tired—I'm *stalled*, Hareton!"

And she leant her pretty head back against the sill, with half a yawn and half a sigh, and lapsed into an aspect of abstracted sadness, neither caring, nor knowing whether we remarked her.

"Mrs. Heathcliff," I said, after sitting some time mute, "you are not aware that I am an acquaintance of yours? so intimate, that I think it strange you won't come and speak to me. My housekeeper never wearies of talking about and praising you; and she'll be greatly disappointed if I return with no news of, or from you, except that you received her letter, and said nothing!"

She appeared to wonder at this speech and asked,

"Does Ellen like you?"

"Yes, very well," I replied unhesitatingly.

"You must tell her," she continued, "that I would answer her letter, but I have no materials for writing, not even a book from which I might tear a leaf."

"No books!" I exclaimed. "How do you contrive to live here without them? If I may take the liberty to inquire—Though provided with a large library, I'm frequently very dull at the Grange—take my books away, and I should be desperate!"

"I was always reading, when I had them," said Catherine, "and Mr. Heathcliff never reads; so he took it into his head to destroy my books. I have not had a glimpse of one, for weeks. Only once, I searched through Joseph's store of theology; to his great irritation: and once, Hareton, I came upon a secret stock in your room...some Latin and Greek, and some tales and poetry; all old friends—I brought the last here—and you gathered them, as a magpie gathers silver spoons, for the mere love of stealing! They are of no use to you—or else you concealed them in the bad spirit, that as you cannot enjoy them, nobody else shall. Perhaps *your* envy counselled Mr. Heathcliff to rob me of my treasures? But, I've most of them written on my brain and printed in my heart, and you cannot deprive me of those!"

Earnshaw blushed crimson, when his cousin made this revelation of his private literary accumulations, and stammered an indignant denial of her accusations.

"Mr. Hareton is desirous of increasing his amount of knowledge," I said, coming to his rescue. "He is not *envious* but *emulous* of your attainments—He'll be a clever scholar in a few years!"

"And he wants *me* to sink into a dunce, meantime," answered Catherine. "Yes, I hear him trying to spell and read to himself, and pretty blunders he makes! I wish you would repeat Chevy Chase, as you did yesterday—It was extremely funny! I heard you...and I heard you turning over the dictionary, to seek out the hard words, and then cursing, because you couldn't read their explanations!"

The young man evidently thought it too bad that he should be laughed at for his ignorance, and then laughed at for trying to remove it. I had a similar notion, and, remembering Mrs. Dean's anecdote of his first attempt at enlightening the darkness in which he had been reared, I observed,

"But, Mrs. Heathcliff, we have each had a commencement, and each stumbled and tottered on the threshold, and had our teachers scorned, instead of aiding us, we should stumble and totter yet."

"Oh!" she replied, "I don't wish to limit his acquirements... still, he has no right to appropriate what is mine, and make it ridiculous to me with his vile mistakes and mispronunciations!

Those books, both prose and verse, were consecrated to me by other associations, and I hate to have them debased and profaned in his mouth! Besides, of all, he has selected my favourite pieces that I love the most to repeat, as if out of deliberate malice!"

Hareton's chest heaved in silence a minute; he laboured under a severe sense of mortification and wrath, which it was no easy task to suppress.

I rose, and from a gentlemanly idea of relieving his embarrassment, took up my station in the door-way, surveying the external prospect as I stood.

He followed my example, and left the room, but presently reappeared, bearing half-a-dozen volumes in his hands, which he threw into Catherine's lap, exclaiming,

"Take them! I never want to hear, or read, or think of them again!"

"I won't have them, now!" she answered. "I shall connect them with you, and hate them."

She opened one that had obviously been often turned over, and read a portion in the drawling tone of a beginner; then laughed, and threw it from her.

"And listen!" she continued provokingly, commencing a verse of an old ballad in the same fashion.

But his self-love would endure no further torment—I heard, and not altogether disapprovingly, a manual check given to her saucy tongue—The little wretch had done her utmost to hurt her cousin's sensitive though uncultivated feelings, and a physical argument was the only mode he had of balancing the account and repaying its effects on the inflicter.

He afterwards gathered the books and hurled them on the fire. I read in his countenance what anguish it was to offer that sacrifice to spleen—I fancied that as they consumed, he recalled the pleasure they had already imparted; and the triumph, and ever increasing pleasure he had anticipated from them—and I fancied, I guessed the incitement to his secret studies, also. He had been content with daily labour and rough animal enjoyments, till Catherine crossed his path—Shame at her scorn, and hope of her approval were his first prompters to higher pursuits; and instead of guarding him from one, and winning him the other, his endeavours to raise himself had produced just the contrary result.

"Yes, that's all the good that such a brute as you can get from them!" cried Catherine, sucking her damaged lip, and watching the conflagration with indignant eyes.

"You'd *better* hold your tongue, now!" he answered fiercely.

And his agitation precluding further speech; he advanced hastily to the entrance, where I made way for him to pass. But, ere he had crossed the door stones, Mr. Heathcliff, coming up the causeway, encountered him and laying hold of his shoulder, asked,

"What's to do now, my lad?"

"Naught, naught!" he said, and broke away, to enjoy his grief and anger in solitude.

Heathcliff gazed after him, and sighed.

"It will be odd, if I thwart myself!" he muttered, unconscious that I was behind him. "But, when I look for his father in his face, I find *her* every day more! How the devil is he so like? I can hardly bear to see him."

He bent his eyes to the ground, and walked moodily in. There was a restless, anxious expression in his countenance, I had never remarked there before, and he looked sparer in person.

His daughter-in-law on perceiving him through the window, immediately escaped to the kitchen, so that I remained alone.

"I'm glad to see you out of doors again, Mr. Lockwood," he said in reply to my greeting, "from selfish motives partly, I don't think I could readily supply your loss in this desolation. I've wondered, more than once, what brought you here."

"An idle whim, I fear, sir," was my answer, "or else an idle whim is going to spirit me away—I shall set out for London, next week, and I must give you warning, that I feel no disposition to retain Thrushcross Grange, beyond the twelvemonths I agreed to rent it. I believe I shall not live there any more."

"Oh, indeed! You're tired of being banished from the world, are you?" he said. "But, if you be coming to plead off paying for a place, you won't occupy, your journey is useless—I never relent in exacting my due, from anyone."

"I'm coming to plead off nothing about it!" I exclaimed, considerably irritated. "Should you wish it, I'll settle with you now," and I drew my notebook from my pocket.

"No, no," he replied coolly, "you'll leave sufficient behind, to cover your debts, if you fail to return...I'm not in such a hurry—sit down and take your dinner with us—a guest that is safe from repeating his visit, can generally be made welcome—Catherine! bring the things in—where are you?"

Catherine re-appeared, bearing a tray of knives and forks.

"You may get your dinner with Joseph," muttered Heathcliff aside, "and remain in the kitchen till he is gone."

She obeyed his directions very punctually—perhaps she had no temptation to transgress. Living among clowns¹ and misanthropists, she probably cannot appreciate a better class of people, when she meets them.

With Mr. Heathcliff, grim and saturnine, on one hand, and Hareton absolutely dumb, on the other, I made a somewhat cheerless meal, and bid adieu early—I would have departed by the back way to get a last glimpse of Catherine, and annoy old Joseph; but Hareton received orders to lead up my horse, and my host himself escorted me to the door, so I could not fulfil my wish.

"How dreary life gets over in that house!" I reflected, while riding down the road. "What a realization of something more romantic than a fairy tale it would have been for Mrs. Linton Heathcliff, had she and I struck up an attachment, as her good nurse desired, and migrated together, into the stirring atmosphere of the town!"

---

1   *clowns*: peasants.

CHAPTER 32

1802.—This September, I was invited to devastate the moors of a friend, in the North; and, on my journey to his abode, I unexpectedly came within fifteen miles of Gimmerton. The hostler, at a roadside public-house, was holding a pail of water to refresh my horses, when a cart of very green oats, newly reaped, passed by, and he remarked—

"Yon's frough Gimmerton, nah! They're allas three wick' after other folk wi' ther harvest."

"Gimmerton?" I repeated, my residence in that locality had already grown dim and dreamy. "Ah! I know! How far is it from this?"

"Happen fourteen mile o'er th' hills, and a rough road,"[1] he answered.

A sudden impulse seized me to visit Thrushcross Grange. It was scarcely noon, and I conceived that I might as well pass the night under my own roof, as in an inn. Besides, I could spare a day easily, to arrange matters with my landlord, and thus save myself the trouble of invading the neighbourhood again.

Having rested a while, I directed my servant to inquire the way to the village; and, with great fatigue to our beasts, we managed the distance in some three hours.[2]

I left him there, and proceeded down the valley alone. The grey church looked greyer, and the lonely churchyard lonelier. I distinguished a moor sheep cropping the short turf on the graves. It was sweet, warm weather—too warm for travelling; but the heat did not hinder me from enjoying the delightful scenery above and below; had I seen it nearer August, I'm sure it would have tempted me to waste a month among its solitudes. In win-

---

1   Settle appears twelve and a half miles south of Ingleton in *Paterson*, p. 247, and hence, 14 from Kingsdale; also, see above, Introduction, 'The Wuthering Heights Landscape', pp. 18-34.

2   He spares the horses; Baines, pp. 280, 620, notes the Royal Union coach's departure from Settle at 5 and arrival at Thornton in Lonsdale at 7.30 p.m.

ter, nothing more dreary, in summer, nothing more divine, than those glens shut in by hills, and those bluff, bold swells of heath.[1]

I reached the Grange before sunset, and knocked for admittance; but the family had retreated into the back premises, I judged by one thin, blue wreath curling from the kitchen chimney, and they did not hear.

I rode into the court. Under the porch, a girl of nine or ten, sat knitting, and an old woman reclined on the horse-steps, smoking a meditative pipe.

"Is Mrs. Dean within?" I demanded of the dame.

"Mistress Dean? Nay!" she answered, "shoo doesn't bide here; shoo's up at th' Heights."

"Are you the housekeeper, then?" I continued.

"Eea. Aw keep th' hause," she replied.

"Well, I'm Mr. Lockwood, the master—Are there any rooms to lodge me in, I wonder? I wish to stay here all night."

"T'maister!" she cried in astonishment, "Whet, whoiver knew yah wur coming! Yah sud ha' send word! They's nowt norther dry—nor mensful abaht t' place—nowt there isn't!"[2]

She threw down her pipe and bustled in, the girl followed, and I entered too; soon perceiving that her report was true, and, moreover, that I had almost upset her wits by my unwelcome apparition.

I bid her be composed—I would go out for a walk, and meantime, she must try to prepare a corner of a sitting-room for me to sup in, and a bed-room to sleep in—No sweeping and dusting, only good fires and dry sheets were necessary.

She seemed willing to do her best; though she thrust the hearth-brush into the grates in mistake for the poker; and mal-

---

1   The two West Riding landscapes, limestone and moorland, are sketched in the first and second phrases; at Bolton Bridge, seen by Emily in 1833, they occur together. After leaving his servant at Gimmerton, Lockwood proceeds two miles downstream, along the counterpart of the Greta, to find the Grange at a position matching that of 'Black Burton', the coal mining town.

2   *T' maister!*: 'The master! What, whoever knew you were coming! You should have sent word! There's nothing either dry or mannerly about the place, there isn't!'

appropriated several other articles of her craft; but I retired, confiding in her energy for a resting-place against my return.

Wuthering Heights was the goal of my proposed excursion. An after-thought brought me back, when I had quitted the court.

"All well at the Heights?" I enquired of the woman.

"Eea, f' owt Ec knaw!" she answered, skurrying away with a pan of hot cinders.

I would have asked why Mrs. Dean had deserted the Grange; but it was impossible to delay her at such a crisis, so, I turned away and made my exit, rambling leisurely along with the glow of a sinking sun behind, and the mild glory of a rising moon in front; one fading, and the other brightening,[1] as I quitted the park, and climbed the stony by-road branching off to Mr. Heathcliff's dwelling.

Before I arrived in sight of it, all that remained of the day was a beamless, amber light along the west; but I could see every pebble on the path, and every blade of grass by that splendid moon.

I had neither to climb the gate, nor to knock—it yielded to my hand.

That is an improvement! I thought. And I noticed another, by the aid of my nostrils; a fragrance of stocks and wall flowers, wafted on the air, from amongst the homely fruit trees.

Both doors and lattices were open; and, yet, as is usually the case in a coal district,[2] a fine, red fire illumined the chimney; the comfort which the eye derives from it, renders the extra heat endurable. But the house[3] of Wuthering Heights is so large, that the inmates have plenty of space for withdrawing out of its influence; and, accordingly, what inmates there were had stationed them-

---

1 William Howitt, *The Book of the Seasons* (1831) (1855 edn. at *P*) has a harvest moon in August: 'Scarcely has the sun departed in the West, when the moon in the east rises from beyond some solitary hill, and sails up into the still and transparent air in the full magnificence of a world'. A harvest moon in August would give May as the month for Heathcliff's death.

2 Hutton, p. 245, has: 'coals [...] from the pits at Ingleton, Black Burton, or properly Burton in Lonsdale'; also, Thomas Jefferys, *Map of the County of York* (1767) (Plate 1, above).

3 *house*: see above, p. 385, note 2.

selves not far from one of the windows. I could both see them and hear them talk before I entered; and, looked and listened in consequence, being moved thereto by a mingled sense of curiosity, and envy that grew as I lingered.

"Con-*trary*!"[1] said a voice, as sweet as a silver bell—"That for the third time, you dunce! I'm not going to tell you, again—Recollect, or I pull your hair!"

"Contrary, then," answered another, in deep but softened tones. "And now, kiss me, for minding so well."

"No, read it over first correctly, without a single mistake."

The male speaker began to read—he was a young man, respectably dressed, and seated at a table, having a book before him. His handsome features glowed with pleasure, and his eyes kept impatiently wandering from the page to a small white hand over his shoulder, which recalled him by a smart slap on the cheek, whenever its owner detected such signs of inattention.

Its owner stood behind; her light shining ringlets blending, at intervals, with his brown locks, as she bent to superintend his studies; and her face—it was lucky he could not see her face, or he would never have been so steady. I could, and I bit my lip, in spite, at having thrown away the chance I might have had, of doing something besides staring at its smiting beauty.

The task was done, not free from further blunders, but the pupil claimed a reward and received, at least five kisses, which, however, he generously returned. Then, they came to the door, and from their conversation, I judged they were about to issue out and have a walk on the moors. I supposed I should be condemned in Hareton Earnshaw's heart, if not by his mouth, to the lowest pit in the infernal regions if I showed my unfortunate person in his neighbourhood then, and feeling very mean and malignant, I skulked round to seek refuge in the kitchen.

There was unobstructed admittance on that side also; and, at the door, sat my old friend, Nelly Dean, sewing and singing a song, which was often interrupted from within, by harsh words of scorn and intolerance, uttered in far from musical accents.

---

1 *Contràry*: with similar accent mark, Carr, vol. 1, p. 85, has 'to contradict; to act in opposition'.

"Aw'd rayther, by th' haulf, hev 'em swearing i' my lugs frough morn tuh neeght, nur hearken yah, hahsiver!" said the tenant of the kitchen, in answer to an unheard speech of Nelly's. "It's a blazing shaime, ut Aw cannut oppen t' Blessed Book, bud yah set up them glories tuh sattan, un all t' flaysome wickednesses ut iver wer born intuh t' warld! Oh! yah're a raight nowt; un' shoo's another; un that poor lad 'ull be lost, atween ye. Poor lad!" he added, with a groan; "he's witched, Aw'm sartin on't! O, Lord, judge 'em, fur they's norther law nur justice amang wer rullers!"[1]

"No! or we should be sitting in flaming fagots, I suppose," retorted the singer. "But wisht, old man, and read your Bible, like a Christian, and never mind me. This is 'Fairy Annie's Wedding'[2]—a bonny tune—it goes to a dance."

Mrs. Dean was about to recommence, when I advanced, and recognising me directly, she jumped to her feet, crying—

"Why, bless you, Mr. Lockwood! How could you think of returning in this way? All's shut up at Thrushcross Grange. You should have given us notice!"

"I've arranged to be accommodated there, for as long as I shall stay," I answered. "I depart again to-morrow. And how are you transplanted here, Mrs. Dean? tell me that."

"Zillah left, and Mr. Heathcliff wished me to come, soon after you went to London, and stay till you returned. But, step in, pray! Have you walked from Gimmerton this evening?"

---

1   *Aw'd rayther*: 'I'd rather, half as much over again, have them swearing in my ears from morning till night, than listen to you, no matter what! It's a blazing shame that I cannot open the Blessed Book without you setting up those anthems to satan, and all the nasty wickedness that ever was born into the world! Oh! you're a proper nothing [Nelly], and she's another [Catherine], and between you, you'll bring the poor boy to ruin. Poor lad! he's bewitched, I'm certain of it! Oh! may the Lord judge them, for there's neither law nor justice among our rulers!'

2   A malapropism, it appears, for 'Fair Annie', in Walter Scott, *Minstrelsy of the Scottish Border* (K); see below, Appendix B. Emily may have been acquainted with a version of 'Fair Annie' appearing in Robert Jamieson, *Popular Ballads and Songs*, 2 vols. (1806), in which a wedding feast, prepared by the delinquent husband for his sister-in-law, is celebrated instead with his wife, amidst rejoicings, when the sisters expose his error. See above, Introduction, 'The marriage prohibition', pp. 39-49.

"From the Grange," I replied; "And, while they make me lodging room there, I want to finish my business with your master, because I don't think of having another opportunity in a hurry."

"What business, sir?" said Nelly, conducting me into the house. "He's gone out, at present, and won't return soon."

"About the rent," I answered.

"Oh, then it is with Mrs. Heathcliff you must settle," she observed, "or rather with me. She has not learnt to manage her affairs yet, and I act for her; there's nobody else."

I looked surprised.

"Ah! you have not heard of Heathcliff's death, I see!" she continued.

"Heathcliff dead?" I exclaimed, astonished. "How long ago?"

"Three months since[1]—but, sit down, and let me take your hat, and I'll tell you all about it. Stop, you have had nothing to eat, have you?"

"I want nothing. I have ordered supper at home. You sit down too. I never dreamt of his dying! Let me hear how it came to pass. You say you don't expect them back for some time—the young people?"

"No—I have to scold them every evening, for their late rambles—but they don't care for me. At least, have a drink of our old ale—it will do you good—you seem weary."

She hastened to fetch it, before I could refuse, and I heard Joseph asking, whether "it warn't a crying scandal that she should have fellies[2] at her time of life? And then, to get them jocks[3] out uh t' Maister's cellar! He fair shaamed to 'bide still and see it."

She did not stay to retaliate, but re-entered, in a minute, bearing a reaming, silver pint, whose contents I lauded with becoming earnestness. And afterwards she furnished me with the sequel of Heathcliff's history. He had a "queer" end, as she expressed it.

---

1   *since*: see below, Appendix A; a September harvest moon gives June as the month of Heathcliff's death, and thirty-eight as his age; a harvest moon in August (p. 400, note 1 above), gives May, nearer to Easter.
2   *fellies*: fellows, boyfriends.
3   *jocks*: jugs (of ale).

I was summoned to Wuthering Heights, within a fortnight of your leaving us, she said; and I obeyed joyfully, for Catherine's sake.

My first interview with her grieved and shocked me! she had altered so much since our separation. Mr. Heathcliff did not explain his reasons for taking a new mind about my coming here; he only told me he wanted me, and he was tired of seeing Catherine, I must make the little parlour my sitting room, and keep her with me. It was enough if he were obliged to see her once or twice a day.

She seemed pleased at this arrangement; and, by degrees, I smuggled over a great number of books, and other articles, that had formed her amusement at the Grange; and flattered myself we should get on in tolerable comfort.

The delusion did not last long. Catherine, contented at first, in a brief space grew irritable and restless. For one thing, she was forbidden to move out of the garden, and it fretted her sadly to be confined to its narrow bounds, as Spring drew on—for another, in following the house,[1] I was forced to quit her frequently, and she complained of loneliness; she preferred quarrelling with Joseph in the kitchen, to sitting at peace in her solitude.

I did not mind their skirmishes; but Hareton was often obliged to seek the kitchen also, when the master wanted to have the house to himself; and, though, in the beginning, she either left it at his approach, or quietly joined in my occupations, and shunned remarking, or addressing him—and though he was always as sullen and silent, as possible—after a while, she changed her behaviour, and became incapable of letting him alone. Talking at him; commenting on his stupidity and idleness; expressing her wonder how he could endure the life he lived—how he could sit a whole evening staring into the fire, and dozing.

"He's just like a dog, is he not, Ellen?" she once observed, "or a cart-horse? He does his work, eats his food, and sleeps, eternally! What a blank, dreary mind he must have! Do you ever dream, Hareton? And, if you do, what is it about? But, you can't speak to me!"

---

1   *following the house*: attending to the living room.

Then she looked at him; but he would neither open his mouth, nor look again.

"He's perhaps, dreaming now," she continued. "He twitched his shoulder as Juno twitches hers. Ask him, Ellen."

"Mr. Hareton will ask the master to send you upstairs, if you don't behave!" I said. He had not only twitched his shoulder, but clenched his fist, as if tempted to use it.

"I know why Hareton never speaks, when I am in the kitchen," she exclaimed, on another occasion. "He is afraid I shall laugh at him. Ellen, what do you think? He began to teach himself to read once; and, because I laughed, he burned his books, and dropped it—was he not a fool?"

"Were not you naughty?" I said; "answer me that."

"Perhaps I was," she went on, "but I did not expect him to be so silly. Hareton, if I gave you a book, would you take it now? I'll try!"

She placed one she had been perusing on his hand; he flung it off, and muttered, if she did not give over, he would break her neck.

"Well I shall put it here," she said, "in the table drawer, and I'm going to bed."

Then she whispered me to watch whether he touched it, and departed. But he would not come near it, and so I informed her in the morning, to her great disappointment. I saw she was sorry for his persevering sulkiness and indolence—her conscience reproved her for frightening him off improving himself—she had done it effectually.

But her ingenuity was at work to remedy the injury; while I ironed, or pursued other stationary employments I could not well do in the parlour—she would bring some pleasant volume and read it aloud to me. When Hareton was there, she generally paused in an interesting part, and left the book lying about—that she did repeatedly; but he was as obstinate as a mule, and, instead of snatching at her bait, in wet weather he took to smoking with Joseph, and they sat like automatons, one on each side of the fire, the elder happily too deaf to understand her wicked nonsense, as he would have called it, the younger doing his best to seem to disregard it. On fine evenings the latter followed his shooting expeditions, and Catherine yawned and sighed, and teased me to talk to her, and ran off into the court or garden, the moment I began; and, as a last resource, cried and said, she was tired of living, her life was useless.

Mr. Heathcliff, who grew more and more disinclined to society, had almost banished Earnshaw out of his apartment. Owing to an accident, at the commencement of March, he became for some days a fixture in the kitchen. His gun burst while out on the hills, by himself; a splinter cut his arm, and he lost a good deal of blood before he could reach home. The consequence was, that, perforce, he was condemned to the fire-side and tranquillity, till he made it up again.

It suited Catherine to have him there: at any rate, it made her hate her room upstairs, more than ever; and she would compel me to find out business below, that she might accompany me.

On Easter Monday, Joseph went to Gimmerton fair with some cattle; and, in the afternoon, I was busy getting up linen in the kitchen—Earnshaw sat, morose as usual, at the chimney corner, and my little mistress was beguiling an idle hour with drawing pictures on the window panes, varying her amusement by smothered bursts of songs, and whispered ejaculations, and quick glances of annoyance and impatience in the direction of her cousin, who steadfastly smoked, and looked into the grate.

At a notice that I could do with her no longer, intercepting my light, she removed to the hearthstone. I bestowed little attention on her proceedings, but, presently, I heard her begin—

"I've found out, Hareton, that I want—that I'm glad—that I should like you to be my cousin, now, if you had not grown so cross to me, and so rough."

Hareton returned no answer.

"Hareton, Hareton, Hareton! do you hear?" she continued.

"Get off wi' ye!" he growled, with uncompromising gruffness.

"Let me take that pipe," she said, cautiously advancing her hand, and abstracting it from his mouth.

Before he could attempt to recover it, it was broken, and behind the fire. He swore at her and seized another.

"Stop," she cried, "you must listen to me, first; and I can't speak while those clouds are floating in my face."

"Will you go to the devil!" he exclaimed, ferociously, "and let me be!"

"No," she persisted, "I won't—I can't tell what to do to make you talk to me, and you are determined not to understand. When I call you stupid, I don't mean anything—I don't mean that I despise you. Come you shall take notice of me, Hareton—you are my cousin, and you shall own me."

"I shall have naught to do wi' you, and your mucky pride, and your damned, mocking tricks!" he answered. "I'll go to hell, body and soul, before I look sideways after you again! Side out of t' gait,[1] now; this minute!"

Catherine frowned, and retreated to the window-seat, chewing her lip, and endeavouring, by humming an eccentric tune, to conceal a growing tendency to sob.

"You should be friends with your cousin, Mr. Hareton," I interrupted, "since she repents of her sauciness! it would do you a great deal of good—it would make you another man, to have her for a companion."

"A companion?" he cried; "when she hates me, and does not think me fit to wipe her shoon![2] Nay, if it made me a king, I'd not be scorned for seeking her good will any more."

"It is not I who hate you, it is you who hate me!" wept Cathy, no longer disguising her trouble. "You hate me as much as Mr. Heathcliff does, and more."

"You're a damned liar," began Earnshaw; "why have I made him angry, by taking your part then, a hundred times? and that, when you sneered at, and despised me, and—Go on plaguing me, and I'll step in yonder, and say you worried me out of the kitchen!"

"I didn't know you took my part," she answered, drying her eyes; "and I was miserable and bitter at every body; but, now I thank you, and beg you to forgive me, what can I do besides?"

She returned to the hearth, and frankly extended her hand.

He blackened, and scowled like a thunder-cloud, and kept his fists resolutely clenched, and his gaze fixed on the ground.

---

1   *side out of t' gait*: get out of the way; *side out*: tidy up (Carr).
2   *shoon*: shoes.

Catherine, by instinct, must have divined it was obdurate per-versity, and not dislike, that prompted this dogged conduct; for, after remaining an instant, undecided, she stopped, and impressed on his cheek a gentle kiss.

The little rogue thought I had not seen her, and, drawing back, she took her former station by the window, quite demurely.

I shook my head reprovingly; and then she blushed, and whis-pered—

"Well! what should I have done, Ellen? He wouldn't shake hands, and he wouldn't look—I must show him some way that I like him, that I want to be friends."

Whether the kiss convinced Hareton, I cannot tell; he was very careful, for some minutes, that his face should not be seen; and when he did raise it, he was sadly puzzled where to turn his eyes.

Catherine employed herself in wrapping a handsome book neatly in white paper; and having tied it with a bit of ribband, and addressed it to "Mr. Hareton Earnshaw," she desired me to be her ambassadress, and convey the present to its destined recipient.

"And tell him, if he'll take it, I'll come and teach him to read it right," she said, "and, if he refuse it, I'll go upstairs, and never tease him again."

I carried it, and repeated the message, anxiously watched by my employer. Hareton would not open his fingers, so I laid it on his knee. He did not strike it off either. I returned to my work: Catherine leaned her head and arms on the table, till she heard the slight rustle of the covering being removed, then she stole away, and quietly seated herself beside her cousin. He trembled, and his face glowed—all his rudeness, and all his surly harshness had deserted him—he could not summon courage, at first, to utter a syllable, in reply to her questioning look, and her mur-mured petition.

"Say you forgive me, Hareton, do! You can make me so happy, by speaking that little word."

He muttered something inaudible.

"And you'll be my friend?" added Catherine, interrogatively.

"Nay! you'll be ashamed of me every day of your life," he answered. "And the more, the more you know me, and I cannot bide it."

"So, you won't be my friend?" she said, smiling as sweet has honey, and creeping close up.

I overheard no further distinguishable talk; but, on looking round again, I perceived two such radiant countenances bent over the page of the accepted book, that I did not doubt the treaty had been ratified, on both sides, and the enemies were, thenceforth, sworn allies.

The work they studied was full of costly pictures; and those, and their position had charm enough to keep them unmoved, till Joseph came home. He, poor man, was perfectly aghast at the spectacle of Catherine seated on the same bench with Hareton Earnshaw, leaning her hand on his shoulder; and confounded at his favourite's endurance of her proximity. It affected him too deeply to allow an observation on the subject that night. His emotion was only revealed by the immense sighs he drew, as he solemnly spread his large Bible on the table, and overlaid it with dirty bank-notes from his pocket-book, the produce of the day's transactions. At length, he summoned Hareton from his seat.

"Tak' these in tuh t' maister, lad," he said, "un bide theare; Aw's gang up tuh my awn rahm. This hoile's norther mensful, nor seemly fur us—we mun side aht, and seearch another!"[1]

"Come, Catherine," I said, "we must 'side out,' too—I've done my ironing, are you ready to go?"

"It is not eight o'clock!" she answered, rising unwillingly, "Hareton, I'll leave this book upon the chimney-piece, and I'll bring some more to-morrow."

"Ony books ut yah leave, Aw sull tak intuh th' hahse," said Joseph, "un it ull be mitch if yah find 'em agean; soa, yah muh plase yourseln!"[2]

Cathy threatened that his library should pay for hers; and, smiling as she passed Hareton, went singing upstairs, lighter of heart,

---

1   *maister*: Heathcliff is still living; 'Take these in to the master, boy, and stay there; I'm going up to my own room. This hole's neither mannerly, nor seemly for us—we have to get out, and look for another!'

2   'Any books you leave, I'll take into the living room [...] and you'll be lucky [it will be much] if you can find them again; so, you can suit yourself!'

I venture to say, than ever she had been under that roof before; except, perhaps, during her earliest visits to Linton.

The intimacy, thus commenced, grew rapidly; though it encountered temporary interruptions; Earnshaw was not to be civilized with a wish; and my young lady was no philosopher, and no paragon of patience; but both their minds tending to the same point—one loving and desiring to esteem; and the other loving and desiring to be esteemed—they contrived in the end, to reach it.

You see, Mr. Lockwood, it was easy enough to win Mrs. Heathcliff's heart; but now, I'm glad you did not try—the crown of all my wishes will be the union of those two; I shall envy no one on their wedding-day—there won't be a happier woman than myself in England!

CHAPTER 33

On the morrow of that Monday, Earnshaw being still unable to follow his ordinary employments, and, therefore, remaining about the house, I speedily found it would be impracticable to retain my charge beside me, as heretofore.

She got downstairs before me, and out into the garden; where she had seen her cousin performing some easy work; and when I went to bid them come to breakfast, I saw she had persuaded him to clear a large space of ground from currant and gooseberry bushes,[1] and they were busy planning together an importation of plants from the Grange.

I was terrified at the devastation which had been accomplished in a brief half hour; the black currant trees were the apple of Joseph's eye, and she had just fixed her choice of a flower bed in the midst of them!

"There! That will be all shown to the master," I exclaimed, "the minute it is discovered. And what excuse have you to offer for taking such liberties with the garden? We shall have a fine explosion on the head of it: see if we don't! Mr. Hareton, I wonder you should have no more wit, than to go and make that mess at her bidding!"

"I'd forgotten they were Joseph's," answered Earnshaw, rather puzzled, "but I'll tell him I did it."

We always ate our meals with Mr. Heathcliff. I held the mistress's post in making tea and carving; so I was indispensable at table. Catherine usually sat by me; but today, she stole nearer to Hareton, and I presently saw she would have no more discretion in her friendship, than she had in her hostility.

"Now, mind you don't talk with and notice your cousin too much," were my whispered instructions as we entered the room; "It will certainly annoy Mr. Heathcliff, and he'll be mad at you both."

"I'm not going to," she answered.

---

1   Hutton, p. 255, notes: 'a ripe gooseberry was a natural curiosity in the summer season, in most parts of the district [around Ingleton]'.

The minute after, she had sidled to him, and was sticking primroses in his plate of porridge.

He dared not speak to her, there; he dared hardly look; and yet she went on teasing, till he was twice on the point of being provoked to laugh; and I frowned, and then, she glanced towards the master, whose mind was occupied on other subjects than his company, as his countenance evinced, and she grew serious for an instant, scrutinizing him with deep gravity. Afterwards she turned, and re-commenced her nonsense; at last, Hareton uttered a smothered laugh.

Mr. Heathcliff started; his eye rapidly surveyed our faces. Catherine met it with her accustomed look of nervousness, and yet defiance, which he abhorred.

"It is well you are out of my reach," he exclaimed. "What fiend possesses you to stare back at me, continually, with those infernal eyes? Down with them! and don't remind me of your existence again. I thought I had cured you of laughing!"

"It was me," muttered Hareton.

"What do you say?" demanded the master.

Hareton looked at his plate, and did not repeat the confession.

Mr. Heathcliff looked at him a bit, and then silently resumed his breakfast, and his interrupted musing.

We had nearly finished, and the two young people prudently shifted wider asunder, so I anticipated no further disturbance during that sitting; when Joseph appeared at the door, revealing by his quivering lip, and furious eyes, that the outrage committed on his precious shrubs was detected.

He must have seen Cathy, and her cousin about the spot before he examined it, for while his jaws worked like those of a cow chewing its cud, and rendered his speech difficult to understand, he began:

"Aw mun hev my wage, and Aw mun goa! Aw *hed* aimed tuh dee, wheare Aw'd sarved fur sixty year; un Aw thowt Aw'd lug my books up intuh t' garret, un all my bits uh stuff, un they sud hev t' kitchen tuh theirseln; fur t' sake uh quietness. It wur hard tuh gie up my awn hearthstun, bud Aw thowt Aw *could* do that! Bud, nah, shoo's taan my garden frough me, un by th' heart! Maister, Aw cannot stand it! Yah muh bend tuh th' yoak, an ye will—*Aw'* noan used to't and an owd man doesn't sooin get used tuh new barthens—Aw'd rayther arn my bite, un my sup, wi' a hammer in th' road!"[1]

"Now, now, idiot!" interrupted Heathcliff, "cut it short! What's your grievance? I'll interfere in no quarrels between you, and Nelly—She may thrust you into the coal-hole for anything I care."

"It's noan Nelly!" answered Joseph. "Aw sudn't shift fur Nelly —Nasty, ill nowt as shoo is; thank God! *shoo* cannot stale t' sowl uh nob'dy! Shoo wer niver soa handsome, bud whet a body mud look at her baht winking. It's yon flaysome, graceless quean, ut's witched ahr lad, wi' her bold een, un her forrard ways—till— Nay! It fair brusts my heart! He's forgetten all E done for him, un made on him, un goan un riven up a whole row uh t' grandest currant trees, i' t' garden!"[2] and here he lamented outright, unmanned by a sense of his bitter injuries, and Earnshaw's ingratitude and dangerous condition.

"Is the fool drunk?" asked Mr. Heathcliff. "Hareton is it you he's finding fault with?"

"I've pulled up two or three bushes," replied the young man, "but I'm going to set 'em again."

"And why have you pulled them up?" said the master.

Catherine wisely put in her tongue.

---

1 'I must have my wages, and I must go! I *had* meant to die, where I'd served for sixty years; and I thought I'd drag my books up into the garret, and all my bits of things, and they would have the kitchen to themselves, for the sake of quiet. It was hard to give up my own hearth-stone: I thought I could do that! But, now, she's taken my garden from me, and by the heart! Sir, I cannot stand it! *You* may bend to the yoke, if you must—*I'm* not used to it, and an old man doesn't soon get used to new burdens—I'd rather earn my bite and my sup, breaking stones with a hammer in the road!'

2 'It's not Nelly! I wouldn't move for Nelly—nasty, ugly nothing that she is; thank God! *she* can't steal anybody's soul! She never was so handsome as to make one unable to look at her without winking. It's that horrible, rude tart, that's bewitched our boy with her bold eyes and cheeky ways—till—no! it breaks my heart! He's forgotten all I've done for him, and helped him with, and gone and rooted up a whole row of the finest currant bushes in the garden!'

"We wanted to plant some flowers there," she cried. "I'm the only person to blame, for I wished him to do it."

"And who the devil gave *you* leave to touch a stick about the place?" demanded her father-in-law, much surprised. "And who ordered *you* to obey her?" he added turning to Hareton.

The latter was speechless; his cousin replied—"You shouldn't grudge a few yards of earth, for me to ornament, when you have taken all my land!"

"Your land, insolent slut? you never had any!" said Heathcliff.

"And my money," she continued, returning his angry glare, and meantime, biting a piece of crust, the remnant of her breakfast.

"Silence!" he exclaimed, "Get done, and begone!"

"And Hareton's land, and his money," pursued the reckless thing. "Hareton, and I are friends now; and I shall tell him all about you!"

The master seemed confounded a moment, he grew pale, and rose up, eyeing her all the while, with an expression of mortal hate.

"If you strike me, Hareton will strike you!" she said, "so you may as well sit down."

"If Hareton does not turn you out of the room, I'll strike him to Hell," thundered Heathcliff. "Damnable witch! dare you pretend to rouse him against me? Off with her! Do you hear? Fling her into the kitchen! I'll kill her, Ellen Dean, if you let her come into my sight again!"

Hareton tried under his breath to persuade her to go.

"Drag her away!" he cried savagely. "Are you staying to talk?" And he approached to execute his own command.

"He'll not obey you, wicked man, any more!" said Catherine, and he'll soon detest you, as much as I do!"

"Wisht! wisht!"[1] muttered the young man reproachfully, "I will not hear you speak so to him—Have done!"

"But you won't let him strike me?" she cried.

"Come then!" he whispered earnestly.

It was too late—Heathcliff had caught hold of her.

---

1   *wisht!*: be quiet!

"Now *you* go!" he said to Earnshaw. "Accursed witch! this time she has provoked me, when I could not bear it; and I'll make her repent it for ever!"

He had his hand in her hair; Hareton attempted to release the locks, entreating him not to hurt her that once. His black eyes flashed, he seemed ready to tear Catherine in pieces, and I was just worked up to risk coming to the rescue, when of a sudden, his fingers relaxed, he shifted his grasp from her head, to her arm, and gazed intently in her face—Then, he drew his hand over his eyes, stood a moment to collect himself apparently, and turning anew to Catherine, said with assumed calmness,

"You must learn to avoid putting me in a passion, or I shall really murder you, sometime! go with Mrs. Dean, and keep with her, and confine your insolence to her ears. As to Hareton Earnshaw, if I see him listen to you, I'll send him seeking his bread where he can get it! Your love will make him an outcast, and a beggar—Nelly, take her, and leave me, all of you! Leave me!"

I led my young lady out; she was too glad of her escape, to resist; the other followed, and Mr. Heathcliff had the room to himself, till dinner.

I had counselled Catherine to get hers upstairs; but, as soon as he perceived her vacant seat, he sent me to call her. He spoke to none of us, ate very little, and went out directly afterwards, intimating that he should not return before evening.

The two new friends established themselves in the house, during his absence, where I heard Hareton sternly check his cousin, on her offering a revelation of her father-in-law's conduct to his father.

He said he wouldn't suffer a word to be uttered to him, in his disparagement; if he were the devil, it didn't signify; he would stand by him; and he'd rather she would abuse himself, as she used to, than begin on Mr. Heathcliff.

Catherine was waxing cross at this; but he found means to make her hold her tongue, by asking, how she would like *him* to speak ill of her father? and then she comprehended that Earnshaw took the master's reputation home to himself: and was attached by ties stronger than reason could break—chains, forged by habit, which it would be cruel to attempt to loosen.

She showed a good heart, thenceforth, in avoiding both complaints and expressions of antipathy concerning Heathcliff; and confessed to me her sorrow that she had endeavoured to raise a bad spirit between him and Hareton—indeed, I don't believe she has ever breathed a syllable, in the latter's hearing, against her oppressor, since.

When this slight disagreement was over, they were thick again, and as busy as possible, in their several occupations, of pupil, and teacher. I came in to sit with them, after I had done my work, and I felt so soothed, and comforted to watch them, that I did not notice how time got on. You know, they both appeared in a measure, my children: I had long been proud of one, and now, I was sure, the other would be a source of equal satisfaction. His honest, warm, and intelligent nature shook off rapidly the clouds of ignorance, and degradation in which it had been bred; and Catherine's sincere commendations acted as a spur to his industry. His brightening mind brightened his features, and added spirit and nobility of their aspect—I could hardly fancy it the same individual I had beheld on the day I discovered my little lady at Wuthering Heights, after her expedition to the Crags.

While I admired, and they laboured, dusk drew on, and with it returned the master. He came upon us quite unexpectedly, entering by the front way, and had a full view of the whole three, ere we could raise our heads to glance at him.

Well, I reflected, there was never a pleasanter, or more harmless sight; and it will be a burning shame to scold them. The red firelight glowed on their two bonny heads, and revealed their faces, animated with the eager interest of children; for, though he was twenty-three, and she eighteen,[1] each had so much of novelty to feel, and learn, that neither experienced, nor evinced the sentiments of sober disenchanted maturity.

They lifted their eyes together, to encounter Mr. Heathcliff—perhaps, you have never remarked that their eyes are precisely similar, and they are those of Catherine Earnshaw. The present Catherine has no other likeness to her, except a breadth of forehead, and a certain arch of the nostril that makes her appear rather

---

1   See Appendix A: these ages are right for April.

haughty, whether she will, or not. With Hareton the resemblance is carried farther, it is singular, at all times—then it was particularly striking; because his senses were alert, and his mental faculties wakened to unwonted activity.

I suppose this resemblance disarmed Mr. Heathcliff: he walked to the hearth in evident agitation, but it quickly subsided, as he looked at the young man; or, I should say, altered its character, for it was there yet.

He took the book from his hand, and glanced at the open page, then returned it without any observation; merely signing Catherine away—her companion lingered very little behind her, and I was about to depart also, but he bid me sit still.

"It is a poor conclusion, is it not," he observed, having brooded a while on the scene he had just witnessed. "An absurd termination to my violent exertions? I get levers, and mattocks to demolish the two houses, and train myself to be capable of working like Hercules, and when everything is ready, and in my power, I find the will to lift a slate off either roof has vanished! My old enemies have not beaten me—now would be the precise time to revenge myself on their representatives—I could do it; and none could hinder me—But where is the use? I don't care for striking, I can't take the trouble to raise my hand! That sounds as if I had been labouring the whole time, only to exhibit a fine trait of magnanimity. It is far from being the case—I have lost the faculty of enjoying their destruction, and I am too idle to destroy for nothing.

"Nelly, there is a strange change approaching—I'm in its shadow at present—I take so little interest in my daily life, that I hardly remember to eat, and drink—Those two, who have left the room are the only objects which retain a distinct material appearance to me; and, that appearance causes me pain, amounting to agony. About *her* I won't speak; and I don't desire to think; but I earnestly wish she were invisible—her presence invokes only maddening sensations. *He* moves me differently; and yet if I could do it without seeming insane, I'd never see him again! You'll perhaps think me rather inclined to become so," he added making an effort to smile, "if I try to describe the thousand forms of past associations, and ideas he awakens, or embodies—But you'll not talk of what I tell you, and my mind is so eternally secluded in itself, it is tempting, at last, to turn it out to another.

"Five minutes ago, Hareton seemed a personification of my youth, not a human being—I felt to him in such a variety of ways, that it would have been impossible to have accosted him rationally.

"In the first place, his startling likeness to Catherine connected him fearfully with her—That however which you may suppose the most potent to arrest my imagination, is actually the least—for what is not connected with her to me? and what does not recall her? I cannot look down to this floor, but her features are shaped on the flags! In every cloud, in every tree—filling the air at night, and caught by glimpses in every object, by day I am surrounded with her image! The most ordinary faces of men, and women—my own features mock me with a resemblance. The entire world is a dreadful collection of memoranda that she did exist, and that I have lost her!

"Well, Hareton's aspect was the ghost of my immortal love, of my wild endeavours to hold my right, my degradation, my pride, my happiness, and my anguish—

"But if it is frenzy to repeat these thoughts to you; only it will let you know, why, with a reluctance to be always alone, his society is no benefit, rather an aggravation of the constant torment I suffer—and it partly contributes to render me regardless how he and his cousin go on together. I can give them no attention, any more."

"But what do you mean by a *change*, Mr. Heathcliff?" I said, alarmed at his manner; though he was neither in danger of losing his senses, nor dying, according to my judgment he was quite strong and healthy; and, as to his reason, from childhood, he had a delight in dwelling on dark things, and entertaining odd fancies—he might have had a monomania on the subject of his departed idol; but on every other point his wits were as sound as mine.

"I shall not know that, till it comes," he said, "I'm only half conscious of it now."

"You have no feeling of illness, have you?" I asked.

"No, Nelly, I have not," he answered.

"Then, you are not afraid of death?" I pursued.

"Afraid? No!" he replied. "I have neither a fear, nor a presentiment, nor a hope of death—Why should I? With my hard constitution, and temperate mode of living, and unperilous occupations, I ought to, and probably *shall* remain above ground, till there is scarcely a black hair on my head—And yet I cannot continue in this condition!—I have to remind myself to breathe—almost to remind my heart to beat! And it is like bending back a stiff spring...it is by compulsion, that I do the slightest act, not prompted by one thought, and by compulsion, that I notice anything alive, or dead, which is not associated with one universal idea...I have a single wish, and my whole being, and faculties are yearning to attain it. The have yearned towards it so long, and so unwaveringly, that I'm convinced it *will* be reached—and *soon*—because it has devoured my existence—I am swallowed in the anticipation of its fulfilment.

"My confessions have not relieved me—but, they may account for some, otherwise unaccountable phases of humour, which I show. O, God! It is a long fight, I wish it were over!"

He began to pace the room, muttering terrible things to himself; till I was inclined to believe, as he said Joseph did, that conscience had turned his heart to an earthly hell—I wondered greatly how it would end.

Though he seldom before had revealed this state of mind, even by looks, it was his habitual mood, I had no doubt: he asserted it himself—but, not a soul, from his general bearing would have conjectured the fact. You did not, when you saw him, Mr. Lockwood—and at the period of which I speak, he was just the same as then, only fonder of continued solitude, and perhaps still more laconic in company.

CHAPTER 34

For some days after that evening, Mr. Heathcliff shunned meeting us at meals; yet he would not consent, formally, to exclude Hareton and Cathy. He had an aversion to yielding so completely to his feelings, choosing, rather, to absent himself—And eating once in twenty-four hours seemed sufficient sustenance for him.

One night, after the family were in bed, I heard him go downstairs, and out at the front door: I did not hear him re-enter and, in the morning, I found he was still away.

We were in April then, the weather was sweet and warm, the grass as green as showers and sun could make it, and the two dwarf apple trees, near the southern wall, in full bloom.

After breakfast, Catherine insisted on my bringing a chair, and sitting, with my work, under the fir trees, at the end of the house; and she beguiled Hareton, who had perfectly recovered from his accident, to dig and arrange her little garden, which was shifted to that corner by the influence of Joseph's complaints.

I was comfortably revelling in the spring fragrance around, and the beautiful soft blue overhead, when my young lady, who had run down near the gate, to procure some primrose roots for a border, returned only half laden, and informed us that Mr. Heathcliff was coming in.

"And he spoke to me," she added with a perplexed countenance.

"What did he say?" asked Hareton.

"He told me to begone as fast as I could," she answered. "But he looked so different from his usual look that I stopped a moment to stare at him."

"How?" he enquired.

"Why, almost bright and cheerful—No, almost nothing—*very much* excited, and wild and glad!" she replied.

"Night-walking amuses him, then," I remarked, affecting a careless manner, in reality, as surprised as she was; and, anxious to ascertain the truth of her statement, for to see the master looking glad would not be an everyday spectacle. I framed an excuse to go in.

Heathcliff stood at the open door; he was pale, and he trembled; yet, certainly, he had a strange joyful glitter in his eyes, that altered the aspect of his whole face.

"Will you have some breakfast?" I said, "You must be hungry rambling about all night!"

I wanted to discover where he had been; but did not like to ask directly.

"No, I'm not hungry," he answered, averting his head, and speaking rather contemptuously, as if he guessed I was trying to divine the occasion of his good humour.

I felt perplexed—I didn't know whether it were not a proper opportunity to offer a bit of admonition.

"I don't think it right to wander out of doors," I observed, "instead of being in bed: it is not wise, at any rate, this moist season. I dare say you'll catch a bad cold, or a fever—you have something the matter with you now!"

"Nothing but what I can bear," he replied, "and with the greatest pleasure, provided you'll leave me alone—get in, and don't annoy me."

I obeyed; and, in passing, I noticed he breathed as fast as a cat.

"Yes!" I reflected to myself, "we shall have a fit of illness. I cannot conceive what he has been doing!"

That noon, he sat down to dinner with us, and received a heaped up plate from my hands, as if he intended to make amends for previous fasting.

"I've neither cold, nor fever, Nelly," he remarked, in allusion to my morning's speech. "And I'm ready to do justice to the food you give me."

He took his knife and fork, and was going to commence eating, when the inclination appeared to become suddenly extinct. He laid them on the table, looked eagerly towards the window, then rose and went out.

We saw him walking, to and fro, in the garden, while we concluded our meal; and Earnshaw said he'd go, and ask why he would not dine; he thought we had grieved him some way.

"Well, is he coming?" cried Catherine, when her cousin returned.

"Nay," he answered, "but he's not angry; he seemed rare and pleased indeed; only, I made him impatient by speaking to him twice; and then he bid me be off to you; he wondered how I could want the company of any body else."

I set the plate, to keep warm, on the fender: and after an hour or two, he re-entered, when the room was clear, in no degree calmer—the same unnatural—it was unnatural—appearance of joy under his black brows; the same bloodless hue: and his teeth visible, now and then, in a kind of smile; his frame shivering, not as one shivers with chill or weakness, but as a tight-stretched cord vibrates—a strong thrilling, rather than trembling.

"I will ask what is the matter," I thought, or who should? And I exclaimed—

"Have you heard any good news, Mr. Heathcliff? You look uncommonly animated."

"Where should good news come from, to me?" he said. "I'm animated with hunger; and, seemingly, I must not eat."

"Your dinner is here," I returned; "why won't you get it?"

"I don't want it now," he muttered, hastily. "I'll wait till supper. And, Nelly, once for all, let me beg you to warn Hareton and the other away from me. I wish to be troubled by nobody—I wish to have this place to myself."

"Is there some new reason for this banishment?" I inquired. "Tell me why you are so queer, Mr. Heathcliff? Where were you last night? I'm not putting the question through idle curiosity, but—"

"You are putting the question through very idle curiosity," he interrupted, with a laugh. "Yet, I'll answer it. Last night, I was on the threshold of hell. Today, I am within sight of my heaven—I have my eyes on it—hardly three feet to sever me! And now you'd better go—You'll neither see nor hear anything to frighten you, if you refrain from prying."

Having swept the hearth, and wiped the table, I departed more perplexed than ever.

He did not quit the house again that afternoon, and no one intruded on his solitude, till, at eight o'clock, I deemed it proper, though unsummoned, to carry a candle, and his supper to him.

He was leaning against the ledge of an open lattice, but not looking out; his face was turned to the interior gloom. The fire had smouldered to ashes; the room was filled with damp, mild air of the cloudy evening, and so still, that not only the murmur of the beck down Gimmerton was distinguishable, but its ripples and its gurgling over the pebbles, or through the large stones which it could not cover.

I uttered an ejaculation of discontent at seeing the dismal grate, and commenced shutting the casements, one after another, till I came to his.

"Must I close this?" I asked, in order to rouse him, for he would not stir.

The light flashed on his features, as I spoke. Oh, Mr. Lockwood, I cannot express what a terrible start I got, by the momentary view! Those deep black eyes! That smile, and ghastly paleness! It appeared to me, not Mr. Heathcliff, but a goblin; and, in my terror, I let the candle bend towards the wall, and it left me in darkness.

"Yes, close it," he replied, in his familiar voice. "There, that is pure awkwardness! Why did you hold the candle horizontally? Be quick, and bring another."

I hurried out in a foolish state of dread, and said to Joseph—"The master wishes you to take him a light, and rekindle the fire." For I dared not go in myself again just then.

Joseph rattled some fire into the shovel, and went; but he brought it back, immediately, with the supper tray in his other hand, explaining that Mr. Heathcliff was going to bed, and he wanted nothing to eat till morning.

We heard him mount the stairs directly; he did not proceed to his ordinary chamber, but turned into that with the panelled bed—its window, as I mentioned before, is wide enough for anybody to get through, and it struck me, that he plotted another midnight excursion, which he had rather we had no suspicion of.

"Is he a ghoul, or a vampire?" I mused. I had read of such hideous, incarnate demons. And then, I set myself to reflect, how I had tended him in infancy; and watched him grow to youth; and followed him almost through his whole course; and what absurd nonsense it was to yield to that sense of horror.

"But, where did he come from, the little dark thing, harboured by a good man to his bane?" muttered superstition, as I dozed into unconsciousness. And I began, half dreaming, to weary myself with imaging some fit parentage for him; and repeating my waking meditations, I tracked his existence over again, with grim variations; at last, picturing his death and funeral; of which, all I can remember is, being exceedingly vexed at having the task of dictating an inscription for his monument, and consulting the sexton about it; and, as he had no surname, and we could not tell his age, we were obliged to content ourselves with the single word, "Heathcliff." That came true; we were. If you enter the kirkyard, you'll read on his headstone, only that, and the date of his death.

Dawn restored me to common sense. I rose, and went into the garden, as soon as I could see, to ascertain if there were any footmarks under his window. There were none.

"He has stayed at home," I thought, "and he'll be all right, to-day!"

I prepared breakfast for the household, as was my usual custom, but told Hareton, and Catherine to get theirs, ere the master came down, for he lay late. They preferred taking it out of doors, under the trees, and I set a little table to accommodate them.

On my re-entrance, I found Mr. Heathcliff below. He and Joseph were conversing about some farming business; he gave clear, minute directions concerning the matter discussed, but he spoke rapidly, and turned his head continually aside, and had the same excited expression, even more exaggerated.

When Joseph quitted the room, he took his seat in the place he generally chose, and I put a basin of coffee before him. He drew it nearer, and then rested his arms on the table, and looked at the opposite wall, as I supposed, surveying one particular portion, up and down, with glittering restless eyes, and with such eager interest, that he stopped breathing, during half a minute together.

"Come now," I exclaimed, pushing some bread against his hand. "Eat and drink that, while it is hot. It has been waiting near an hour."

He didn't notice me, and yet he smiled. I'd rather have seen him gnash his teeth than smile so.

"Mr. Heathcliff! master!" I cried. "Don't for God's sake, stare as if you saw an unearthly vision."

"Don't, for God's sake, shout so loud," he replied. "Turn round, and tell me, are we by ourselves?"

"Of course," was my answer, "of course, we are!"

Still, I involuntarily obeyed him as if I were not quite sure.

With a sweep of his hand, he cleared a vacant space in front among the breakfast things, and leant forward to gaze more at his ease.

Now, I perceived he was not looking at the wall, for when I regarded him alone, it seemed, exactly, that he gazed at something within two yards distance. And, whatever it was, it communicated, apparently, both pleasure and pain, in exquisite extremes, at least, the anguished, yet raptured expression of his countenance suggested that idea.

The fancied object was not fixed, either; his eyes pursued it with unwearied vigilance; and, even in speaking to me, were never weaned away.

I vainly reminded him of his protracted abstinence from food; if he stirred to touch anything in compliance with my entreaties, if he stretched his hand out to get a piece of bread, his fingers clenched, before they reached it, and remained on the table, forgetful of their aim.

I sat a model of patience, trying to attract his absorbed attention from its engrossing speculation; till he grew irritable, and got up, asking, why I would not allow him to have his own time in taking his meals? and saying that, on the next occasion, I needn't wait, I might set the things down, and go.

Having uttered these words, he left the house; slowly sauntered down the garden path, and disappeared through the gate.

The hours crept anxiously by: another evening came. I did not retire to rest till late, and when I did, I could not sleep. He returned after midnight, and, instead of going to bed, shut himself into the room beneath. I listened, and tossed about; and, finally, dressed, and descended. It was too irksome to lie up there, harassing my brain with a hundred idle misgivings.

I distinguished Mr. Heathcliff's step, restlessly measuring the floor; and he frequently broke the silence, by a deep inspiration, resembling a groan. He muttered detached words, also; the only one, I could catch, was the name of Catherine, coupled with some wild term of endearment, or suffering; and spoken as one would speak to a person present—low and earnest, and wrung from the depth of his soul.

I had not courage to walk straight into the apartment; but I desired to divert him from his reverie, and, therefore, fell foul of the kitchen fire; stirred it, and began to scrape the cinders. It drew him forth sooner than I expected. He opened the door immediately, and said,

"Nelly, come here—is it morning? come in with your light."

"It is striking four," I answered; "You want a candle to take upstairs—you might have lit one at this fire."

"No, I don't wish to go upstairs," he said. "Come in, and kindle *me* a fire, and do anything there is to do about the room."

"I must blow the coals red first, before I can carry any," I replied, getting a chair and the bellows.

He roamed to and fro, meantime, in a state approaching distraction: his heavy sighs succeeding each other so thick as to leave no space for common breathing between.

"When day breaks, I'll send for Green," he said; "I wish to make some legal inquiries of him, while I can bestow a thought on those matters, and while I can act calmly. I have not written my will yet, and how to leave my property, I cannot determine! I wish I could annihilate it from the face of the earth."

"I would not talk so, Mr. Heathcliff," I interposed. "Let your will be, a while—you'll be spared to repent of your many injustices, yet! I never expected that your nerves would be disordered—they are, at present, marvellously so, however; and, almost entirely, through your own fault. The way you've passed these three last days might knock up a Titan. Do take some food, and some repose. You need only look at yourself, in a glass, to see how you require both. Your cheeks are hollow, and your eyes bloodshot, like a person starving with hunger, and going blind with loss of sleep."

"It is not my fault, that I cannot eat or rest," he replied. "I assure you it is through no settled designs. I'll do both, as soon as I possibly can. But you might as well bid a man struggling in the water, rest within arms-length of the shore! I must reach it first, and then I'll rest. Well, never mind Mr. Green; as to repenting of my injustices, I've done no injustice, and I repent of nothing— I'm too happy, and yet I'm not happy enough. My soul's bliss kills my body, but does not satisfy itself."

"Happy, master?" I cried. "Strange happiness! If you would hear me without being angry, I might offer some advice that would make you happier."

"What is that?" he asked. "Give it."

"You are aware, Mr. Heathcliff," I said, "that from the time you were thirteen years old, you have lived a selfish, unchristian life; and probably hardly had a Bible in your hands, during all that period. You must have forgotten the contents of the book, and you may have space to search it now. Could it be hurtful to send for some one—some minister of any denomination, it does not matter which, to explain it, and show you how very far you have erred from its precepts, and how unfit you will be for its heaven, unless a change takes place before you die?"

"I'm rather obliged than angry, Nelly," he said, "for you remind me of the manner that I desire to be buried in—It is to be carried to the churchyard, in the evening. You, and Hareton may, if you please accompany me—and mind, particularly, to notice that the sexton obeys my directions concerning the two coffins! No minister need come; nor need anything be said over me—I tell you, I have nearly attained *my* heaven; and that of others is altogether unvalued, and uncoveted by me!"

"And supposing you persevered in your obstinate fast, and died by that means,[1] and they refused to bury you in the precincts of the Kirk?" I said shocked at his godless indifference. "How would you like it?"

"They won't do that," he replied, "if they did, you must have me removed secretly; and if you neglect it, you shall prove, practically, that the dead are not annihilated!"[2]

---

1   She accuses him of contemplating suicide by self-starvation.

2   Heathcliff threatens to haunt Nelly if she does not fulfil his wishes; for the Epicurean belief that immortality exists for atoms and not souls or bodies, see Margaret Maison, 'Emily Brontë and Epictetus', *N&Q*, 223 (1978), 230-01.

As soon as he heard the other members of the family stirring he retired to his den, and I breathed freer—But in the afternoon, while Joseph and Hareton were at their work, he came into the kitchen again, and with a wild look, bid me come, and sit in the house—he wanted somebody with him.

I declined, telling him plainly, that his strange talk and manner, frightened me, and I had neither the nerve, nor the will to be his companion, alone.

"I believe you think me a fiend!" he said, with his dismal laugh, "something too horrible to live under a decent roof!"

Then turning to Catherine, who was there, and who drew behind me at his approach, he added, half sneeringly.

"Will *you* come, chuck? I'll not hurt you. No! to you, I've made myself worse than the devil. Well, there is *one* who won't shrink from my company! By God! She's relentless. Oh, damn it! It's unutterably too much for flesh and blood to bear, even mine."

He solicited the society of no one more. At dusk, he went into his chamber—through the whole night, and far into the morning, we heard him groaning, and murmuring to himself. Hareton was anxious to enter, but I bid him fetch Mr. Kenneth, and he should go in, and see him.

When he came and I requested admittance and tried to open the door, I found it locked; and Heathcliff bid us be damned. He was better, and would be left alone; so the doctor went away.

The following evening was very wet, indeed it poured down, till day-dawn; and, as I took my morning walk round the house, I observed the master's window swinging open, and the rain driving straight in.

He cannot be in bed, I thought, those showers would drench him through! He must either be up, or out. But, I'll make no more ado, I'll go boldly, and look!

Having succeeded in obtaining entrance with another key, I ran to unclose the panels, for the chamber was vacant—quickly pushing them aside, I peeped in. Mr. Heathcliff was there—laid on his back. His eyes met mine so keen, and fierce, I started; and then, he seemed to smile.

I could not think him dead—but his face, and throat were washed with rain; the bed-clothes dripped, and he was perfectly still. The lattice, flapping to and fro, had grazed one hand that rested on the sill—no blood trickled from the broken skin, and when I put my fingers to it, I could doubt no more—he was dead and stark!

I hasped the window; I combed his black long hair from his forehead; I tried to close his eyes—to extinguish, if possible, that frightful, life-like gaze of exultation, before any one else beheld it. They would not shut—they seemed to sneer at my attempts, and his parted lips, and sharp, white teeth sneered too! Taken with another fit of cowardice, I cried out for Joseph. Joseph shuffled up, and made a noise, but resolutely refused to meddle with him.

"Th' divil's harried off his soul" he cried, "and he muh hev his carcass intuh t' bargin, for ow't Aw care! Ech! what a wicked un he looks girnning at death!" and the old sinner grinned in mockery.

I though he intended to cut a caper round the bed; but suddenly composing himself, he fell on his knees, and raised his hands, and returned thanks that the lawful master and the ancient stock were restored to their rights.

I felt stunned by the awful event; and my memory unavoidably recurred to former times with a sort of oppressive sadness. But poor Hareton the most wronged, was the only one that really suffered much. He sat by the corpse all night, weeping in bitter earnest. He pressed its hand, and kissed the sarcastic, savage face that every one else shrank from contemplating; and bemoaned him with that strong grief which springs naturally from a generous heart, though it be tough as tempered steel.

Kenneth was perplexed to pronounce of what disorder the master died. I concealed the fact of his having swallowed nothing for four days, fearing it might lead to trouble, and then, I am persuaded he did not abstain on purpose; it was the consequence of his strange illness, not the cause.

We buried him, to the scandal of the whole neighbourhood, as he had wished. Earnshaw, and I, the sexton and six men to carry the coffin, comprehended the whole attendance.

The six men departed when they had let it down into the grave: we stayed to see it covered. Hareton, with a streaming face, dug green sods, and laid them over the brown mould himself, at present it is as smooth and verdant as its companion mounds—and I hope its tenant sleeps soundly. But the country folks, if you asked them, would swear on their Bible that he *walks*. There are those who speak to having met him near the church, and on the moor, and even within this house—Idle tales, you'll say, and so say I. Yet that old man by the kitchen fire affirms he has seen two on 'em looking out of his chamber window, on every rainy night, since his death—and an odd thing happened to me about a month ago.

I was going to the Grange one evening—a dark evening threatening thunder—and, just at the turn of the Heights,[1] I encountered a little boy with a sheep, and two lambs before him; he was crying terribly, and I supposed the lambs were skittish, and would not be guided.

"What is the matter, my little man?" I asked.

"They's Heathcliff, and a woman, yonder, under t' Nab," he blubbered, "un Aw darnut pass 'em."

I saw nothing; but neither the sheep nor he would go on, so I bid him take the road lower down.

He probably raised the phantoms from thinking, as he traversed the moors alone, on the nonsense he had heard his parents and companions repeat—yet still, I don't like being out in the dark, now—and I don't like being left by myself in this grim house—I cannot help it, I shall be glad when they leave it, and shift to the Grange!

"They are going to the Grange then?" I said.

"Yes," answered Mrs. Dean, "as soon as they are married; and that will be on New Year's day."

"And who will live here then?"

"Why, Joseph will take care of the house, and, perhaps, a lad to keep him company. They will live in the kitchen, and the rest will be shut up."

"For the use of such ghosts as choose to inhabit it," I observed.

"No, Mr. Lockwood," said Nelly, shaking her head. "I believe the dead are at peace, but it is not right to speak of them with levity."

---

1   *Heights*: a reference to Wuthering Heights hill; a 'Nab', or summit.

At that moment the garden gate swung to; the ramblers were returning.

"*They* are afraid of nothing," I grumbled, watching their approach through the window. "Together they would brave satan and all his legions."

As they stepped onto the door-stones, and halted to take a last look at the moon, or, more correctly, at each other, by her light, I felt irresistibly impelled to escape them again; and, pressing a remembrance[1] into the hand of Mrs. Dean, and disregarding her expostulations at my rudeness, I vanished through the kitchen, as they opened the house-door, and so, should have confirmed Joseph in his opinion of his fellow-servant's gay indiscretions, had he not, fortunately, recognised me for a respectable character, by the sweet ring of a sovereign at his feet.

My walk home was lengthened by a diversion in the direction of the kirk. When beneath its walls, I perceived decay had made progress, even in seven months—many a window showed black gaps deprived of glass; and slates jutted off, here and there, beyond the right line of the roof, to be gradually worked off in coming autumn storms.

I sought, and soon discovered, the three head-stones on the slope next the moor—the middle one, grey, and half buried in heath—Edgar Linton's only harmonized by the turf, and moss creeping up its foot—Heathcliff's still bare.

I lingered round them, under that benign sky;[2] watched the moths fluttering among the heath, and hare-bells; listened to the soft wind breathing through the grass; and wondered how any one could ever imagine unquiet slumbers, for the sleepers in that quiet earth.

---

1 *remembrance*: tip.
2 William Wordsworth ends *The White Doe of Rylstone* (1815) with Emily Norton, 'exalted Emily', the heroine of his tale, 'buried by her Mother's side' in Rylstone churchyard, in a 'Calm spectacle, by earth and sky / In their benignity approved'.

Appendix A: The Chronology of Wuthering Heights

Only the dates 1778, 1801 and 1802 appear in numerals; all others are defined through scattered clues, given in words which identify the years through seasons, birthdays, and ages. This enigmatic chronology was first unravelled by C.P. Sanger in his essay, *The Structure of Wuthering Heights* (1926).[1] Starting from Nelly's reference to Hareton's birth in 'the summer of 1778, that is, nearly twenty-three years ago' (ch. 7), however, he ignored the second half of Nelly Dean's phrase. Counted backwards from the forthcoming summer of 1802, the second half refers to 1779. Like others in *WH*, this riddle cannot be ignored.[2] The probable solution is consistent with her geometrical figures (Plate 4), and her enigmatic handling of landscape, symmetry, dreams, and slavery.

Two parallel chronologies, a 1778 series and a 1779 series, converge in the winter of the year 1801-1802, the dates written by Lockwood in numerals. Both chronologies appear to have been intended, since both are constructed as movable frameworks based on seasons, ages, and birthdays. Clues lead beyond the text into outside events dated along the lines of both series. As in the musical canon or fugue forms, the 1779 chronology is achieved by adding a year to the 1778 series. The two series follow these lines:

(a) **1779**: in this series, 1766 is the birth year of Catherine Earnshaw. Also, 1758 emerges as the birth date of Nelly Dean and Hindley Earnshaw. Together with the date set for the wedding of Hareton and Catherine, these are key dates, of the kind readily available among the West Riding Evangelical clergy who were Trustees of the K&K. They appear among K&K clients, in the historical Yorkshire story material which Emily used for the start of her story (Appendix C). The year 1803 marked the beginning of the end for the slaveholding estate of the Sills of Jamaica and Dent; 1766 was the birth year of Ann Sill of Dent, the architect of the transition for the estate from the feudal pretensions of the 1790s to its return to reality in the 1840s; and 1758 was marked by the Sills' advertisement for Thomas Anson, their runaway slave. A cutting of that locally notorious advertisement has been preserved among Dales families to the present.[3]

However, the 1779 series has a disadvantage, since it leads to the legally possible but improbable age of sixteen for the widowed younger Catherine at the time of Lockwood's arrival. Two Catherines, both aged seventeen at their weddings, are integral parts of a story designed to remove the marriage prohibition (see 'The marriage prohibition', Introduction, above). This number contributed, it appears, to Brontë's construction of her novel in two sets of 17 chapters. To achieve a credible age of seventeen at their first meeting, and eighteen at her forthcoming second wedding, she relinquished the 1779 series after the deaths of the elder Catherine and her brother, Hindley Earnshaw (chs. 16, 17). Slight blurring admits the presence of the 1778 series, which dominates the second half of *WH*, on Lockwood's first arrival at the farmhouse. Lockwood's otherwise inexplicable idea that Nelly Dean had left the farmhouse sixteen years before, and her correction: 'Eighteen, sir' (ch. 4), when nothing has been said on that topic, is accounted for by Brontë's brooding on this difficulty. Her mastery of the adjacent chronologies suggests that she was familiar with the Perpetual Calendar at the end of her Prayer Book.

(b) **1778**: through the chain of birthdays, this date sets the marriage year of the elder Catherine in 1783, the year of Hareton Earnshaw's fifth birthday. The dates of the elder Catherine's wedding, and the younger Catherine's conception and birth dates, are set as a frame around this date. The celebration of the younger Catherine's sixteenth birthday in the spring of 1800 (ch. 21) is confirmed by Nelly Dean's announcement about the events which bring that year to a close: 'These things happened last winter, sir' (ch. 25). The 1778 series assumes control from there onwards. In this series, Hindley and Nelly are born in 1757; the younger Catherine, born in 1784, will be eighteen by the date of her wedding on 1 January 1803; and Heathcliff dies at the age of thirty-eight. Evidently Emily constructed this series in memory of her mother, whose birth year, 1783, is also the crisis year in the affairs of the Lintons, the Earnshaws, and Heathcliff. This series gives Heathcliff's age at his death as thirty-eight, Maria Brontë senior's mother's age at her death in 1821.

As in geometrical and musical figuring, there is no room for chance coincidence in these structures: in these arts as in *WH*, coincidence means the intersection on the grand scale of lines and circles, numbers, chords, and keys. Since their results pervade the story from beginning to end, both numerical series would have been in Emily Brontë's mind from the start of writing. In this overriding riddle, the numbers associated with her life, her mother's life and death, and her knowledge of Yorkshire, are merged into a single set of numbers. They are 17, 18, 34, and 35. In the 1778 series, the elder Catherine is seventeen at her wedding; the younger Catherine is seventeen at her first and will be eighteen at her second wedding. Their combined ages are thirty-five, matching the age of Maria Brontë at Emily's birth in July 1818. Their combined ages at the seventeen-year old younger Catherine's first wedding add up to thirty-four, a match for the 34 chapters of *WH* and for the age of Maria Brontë at Emily Brontë's conception in 1817. These fixed numbers explain her preoccupation with the theme of mother and daughter in her story, her emphasis on dates of conception and birth, and the seemingly erratic chapter lengths which resulted from the priority she gave to her chapter numbering. Crowded chapters mark some of the endings of her divisions or parts, where loose ends are gathered up (chs. 9, 17). Others, which turn corners or mark time, are relatively short (chs. 5, 14). The seeming confusion in *WH*, it turns out, resulted from the use of a numerical scheme which symbolised Emily Brontë's life in relation to her mother and Yorkshire, and to her father's relationship with Wilberforce's Parliamentary and ecclesiastical cause. Possibly she finally framed her story, its chapter structure and double chronology around 1844-45, her twenty-seventh year and the age of Nelly Dean and Hindley Earnshaw at the time of his death.

The 1778 chronology is constructed in these steps:

(i) Hareton, born in the summer of 1778 (chs. 7, 8), turns five shortly after the marriage of the elder Catherine (ch. 9). All the remaining dates are fixed around this date. It gives the year 1783 for Heathcliff's return at the harvest moon in September and for the wedding of Edgar Linton and Catherine Earnshaw 'the space of half a year' (ch. 10) earlier, in March.

(ii) A seven months' child (ch. 21), the younger Catherine is born at the spring equinox, that is, six months after her conception at the time of the harvest moon (ch. 10). Her mother's delirium in the winter of 1784 (ch. 12) emerges as a cryptic sign of pregnancy at four to five months.

(iii) Hindley dies in the autumn following the younger Catherine's birth in March 1784. His twenty-seventh birthday, and Nelly Dean's, have happened by then (ch. 17). That gives 1757 as their birth year. At the time of the lovers' quarrel in the summer of 1780, Nelly notes her own age as twenty-two (ch. 9). This narrows the season of her birthday to the harvest weeks, between summer and autumn. That season explains the appearance of the harvest moon as her emblem at moments of crisis in the story (chs 4, 8, 10, 29, 34).

(iv) Hindley is fourteen when Heathcliff arrives in the harvest season (ch. 4). Since Hindley's birthday has taken place by the autumn (ch. 17), this gives 1771 as the year for Heathcliff's arrival, when Catherine is described as 'hardly six years old': in the 1778 series she has just turned six, and in the 1779 series she will soon do so. The year 1765 emerges as her birth year in the 1778 series. Under the loose-jointed term 'hardly', the 1779 and 1778 chronologies run parallel for the time being.

(v) Catherine is fifteen and Heathcliff has turned sixteen in the year of their summer quarrel (ch. 8). This sets that year in 1780, and gives 1764 as Heathcliff's birth year. Accordingly he is thirty-seven at his first appearance in 1801 (ch. 1), and he dies the following year in May or June, around the time of his next birthday: strictly, however, it can never be known. At this point Emily Brontë discloses her probable wish to match his age at his death to that of her mother, Maria Brontë, at her death in 1821.

(vi) The 1778 series assumes its dominant position at the younger Catherine's sixteenth birthday in the spring of the year 1800. The moorland excursion on that occasion (ch. 21) is in the spring of the year before Lockwood's arrival in the autumn of 1801. Her thwarted teenage love for her cousin Linton Heathcliff and his pining in the ensuing seasons of 1800 are assigned to that year when Nelly explains in 1801/2: 'these things happened last winter, sir' (ch. 25). That gives the younger Catherine the marginally credible age of seventeen and a half at her first meeting with Lockwood (ch. 2).

In this outline of the 1778 series, square brackets identify years found through birthdays, and the four divisions of *WH*:

ch.	action	year / season / clue
1 [I.1]	Lockwood arrives at the Grange, visits his landlord, Mr Heathcliff, at the farmhouse on the hill, and is attacked by dogs.	1801: November *Clue: Lockwood's diary begins in 1801; his lease on the Grange runs for a year from 1 November 1801 (chs. 1, 31).*
2 [I.2]	On a second visit to the farmhouse, Lockwood has difficulty in recognising the relationships between Heathcliff, Mrs Heathcliff, and the young Hareton Earnshaw.	the same *Clue: continued from ch. 1.*
3 [I.3]	Lockwood spends the night at the farmhouse and has two nightmares. Heathcliff appears and calls out to his lost childhood love.	the same *Clue: continued from above.*
4 [I.4]	Returning to the Grange, Lockwood falls ill and goes to bed. The housekeeper begins her narrative from thirty years earlier, when old Mr. Earnshaw brought home a dark-skinned orphan from Liverpool. Disruption ensues when Hindley turns against the newcomer, who	the same; then back to [1771] *Clue: Hareton is born in 1778; Hindley dies in 1784 (ch. 17), the year after Hareton's fifth birthday (ch. 10); Hindley is fourteen when Heathcliff arrives (ch. 4).*

is favoured by his father
and his sister.

5 [I.5]	Death of old Mr Earnshaw	[1777] *Clue: Hareton is born in the late summer of 1778 (ch. 7); Frances, Hindley's newly wedded wife, accompanies him to his father's funeral the year before (ch. 6).*
6 [I.6]	Hindley returns for the funeral after a 3 years' absence; he brings Frances, his wife, with him. Hard times ensue for Heathcliff, who runs down the valley with Catherine, his childhood sweetheart. They spy on the rich Lintons at Thrushcross Grange, where they are bitten by the dogs. Catherine stays at the Grange for 5 weeks to recuperate.	[1777] *Clue: as above; and Catherine's diary fragment (ch. 3). She is twelve.*
7 [I.7]	The Earnshaws entertain the Lintons on Christmas Day. A quarrel breaks out. Heathcliff is blamed, reduced to farm labour, and flogged. He vows revenge.	[1777]: December, five weeks later *Clue: continued from above.*
8 [I.8]	Hareton Earnshaw is born. Frances, his mother, dies soon afterwards of tuberculosis.	1778: harvest *Clue: Nelly gives the date in figures. (ch. 7), adding a second date, 1779. in the words 'nearly twenty-three years ago'.*
	Two years later, Heathcliff and Edgar embark on rivalry over Catherine.	[1780]: summer *Clue: Heathcliff is sixteen; Catherine is fifteen.*

9 [I.9]	Catherine promises to marry Edgar and defends her choice to Nelly Dean, who conceals the fact that Heathcliff had not heard her declaration of love for him. He runs away from the farm. Death of the elder Lintons.	[1780]: summer *Clue: as above.*
	Three years later, Edgar Linton is married to Catherine Earnshaw. Nelly Dean moves to Thrushcross Grange as Catherine's companion.	Spring [1783] *Clue: 'three years later' (ch. 9).*
10 [II.1]	Six months after the wedding Heathcliff returns, and urges his love for Catherine. He embarks on the seduction of Isabella and persecution of Hindley Earnshaw.	[1783]: September *Clue: 'half a year' after the wedding.*
11 [II.2]	Nelly Dean visits the farmhouse and is repulsed.	[1783/4]: winter *Clue: ten months after the move to the Grange (ch. 11).*
12 [II.3]	Catherine has a fit in the fifth month of her pregnancy; Heathcliff and Isabella elope around midnight.	[1784]: January *Clue: her 7 months' child is born in March 1784 (chs. 16, 21).*
13 [II.4]	In a letter, Isabella reports her unhappy marriage.	[1784] *Clue: continued from ch. 12.*
14 [II.5]	Tension between Edgar Linton and Heathcliff erupts in violence.	[1784] *Clue: as above.*
15 [II.6]	Heathcliff's impassioned visit to the pregnant Catherine during Edgar Linton's absence at church. Further violence.	[1784]: spring equinox *Clue: as above.*

16 [II.7]	Death of Catherine I and birth of Catherine II; Heathcliff's vigil and frenzy at her grave.	[1784]: spring equinox *Clue: as above; ch. 21 and ch. 29.*
17 [II.8]	Isabella flees from the farmhouse after a violent exchange between Heathcliff, herself, and Hindley. Death of Hindley after his 27th birthday; Nelly Dean is the same age. The farm is mortgaged to Heathcliff.	[1784]: autumn *Clue: continued from above;. Dr Kenneth refers to 'scarcely six months' between the deaths.*
18 [III.1]	12 years pass. Catherine II asks about the distant hills. On her 13th birthday, Catherine II makes a first excursion to the farmhouse on her pony. She meets Hareton, her cousin. Illness and death of Isabella Heathcliff.	[1796]: summer *Clue: 'twelve years' (ch. 18).* [1797]: spring equinox *Clue: stated here.*
19 [III.2]	Linton Heathcliff comes to the Grange and is claimed by Heathcliff.	[1797]: summer *Clue: continued from above.*
20 [III.3]	Linton Heathcliff goes to the farmhouse, arousing satirical remarks from Joseph and Heathcliff.	[1797]: summer *Clue: continued.*
21 [III.4]	Catherine II's moorland excursion to the farmhouse on her sixteenth birthday. She rediscovers her cousin Linton Heathcliff and spurns her cousin Hareton, who has shown her the Fairy Cave. Her love letters from Linton Heathcliff are found and destroyed by Nelly.	[1800]: spring and summer *Clue: sixteenth birthday stated.*

22 [III.5]	Illness of Linton Heathcliff; October: Heathcliff intervenes. Catherine II visits the farmhouse on several occasions.	[1800]: autumn *Clue: continued from above;*
23 [III.6]	Catherine's rediscovery of Linton Heathcliff. They quarrel. Nelly falls ill; Catherine embarks on a second clandestine courtship by visiting the farmhouse.	[1800]: autumn *Clue: continued from above;*
24 [III.7]	Catherine confesses her visits to the farmhouse. Nelly rebukes her for mocking Hareton's first interest in reading. The boys quarrel; Linton coughs blood; Catherine resumes visiting him. Nelly reports the affair to Edgar Linton, who forbids further visiting.	[1800-1801] *Clue: continued from above; and 'These things happened last winter, sir, hardly more than a year ago' (ch. 25).*
25 [III.8]	Edgar Linton forms a scheme to encourage the cousins to marry, so that his daughter can inherit the Earnshaw property. His health declines.	[1801]: summer *Clue: continued from above;*
26 [IV.1]	Catherine and Linton meet on the moor; his health is failing.	[1801]: late summer *Clue: continued from above.*
27 [IV.2]	Heathcliff conspires with his son Linton to imprison Catherine and Nelly in the farmhouse. Catherine is taken away for a clandestine tine, forced marriage to Linton Heathcliff. Nelly remains, locked upstairs. Five nights go by.	[1801]: a week later (Thursday) *Clue: given here.*

28 [IV.3]	Linton and Catherine are married. Catherine is imprisoned upstairs but is helped to escape by Linton. She reaches her father's deathbed shortly before his death.	[1801]: late summer *Clue: continued from above;*
29 [IV.4]	Linton Heathcliff dies. Heathcliff takes over the Grange. He confesses his vigil at the grave of the elder Catherine in 1784, when her ghost appears and leads him home 'unspeakably consoled'. He takes the younger Catherine with him to the farmhouse and leaves Nelly at the Grange.	[1801]: next evening (harvest moon) *Clue: continued from above;*
30 [IV.5]	At the farmhouse, Hareton's endearments to Catherine are repulsed: this story is told by Zillah to Nelly Dean, who ends her story for the time being.	[1801-2]: winter *Clue: the end joins the beginning.*
31 [IV.6]	Lockwood visits the farmhouse, where he finds Catherine lonely and sad. Hareton burns the last of her books. Lockwood leaves, reflecting that he could not have formed an attachment with Catherine.	1802: February *Clue: Lockwood's diary.*
32 [IV.7]	Lockwood returns to Gimmerton in September. Nelly has returned to the farmhouse, where she resumes her narrative. She tells Lockwood that Heathcliff died '3 months since'. Hareton and Catherine are reconciled and their wedding is planned.	1802: harvest *Clue: Lockwood's diary.* [1802: May-June]

33 [IV.8]	Hareton and Catherine re-design the garden. Joseph protests against the disturbance and they replant the fruit bushes. Heathcliff confesses his anxiety at the approach of death.	[1802]: after Easter *Clue: continued from above;*
34 [IV.9]	Heathcliff falls into depression and dies. Lockwood learns that the ghosts of Heathcliff and Catherine haunt the moor. He returns to the Grange via the churchyard, where he sees their graves by moonlight.	[1802]: the harvest moon *Clue: continued from above.*

Notes

1 See also, A. Stuart Daley, 'The Moons and Almanacs of *Wuthering Heights*', *Huntington Library Quarterly*, 37 (1974), 337-53.

2 This problem is regarded as an error by Edward Chitham in his book *The Birth of Wuthering Heights* (1998), p. 160; see below, Appendix B.

3 Personal information: with thanks to Kim Lyon and Margaret Sutton. See also, Gomer Williams, *Liverpool Privateers and Letters of Marque. With an Account of the Liverpool Slave Trade* (1897), pp. 475-76.

Appendix B: Literary Tradition

The critical response

The retreat from Charlotte Brontë 's Preface began soon after its appearance. In 'Haworth Churchyard' (1855), a poem ostensibly about Charlotte, whom he had met and whose death prompted his elegy, Matthew Arnold borrowed invocations of moorland scenery and the churchyard from *WH*, and endorsed Emily Brontë's exposition of the Epicurean theory of immortality in her poem 'No coward soul is mine'.[1] In *A Note on Charlotte Brontë* (1877), Algernon Swinburne placed Emily Brontë's writing in a category above that of Charlotte, the subject of his essay. He noted the forcefulness of her descriptions, her humour, her strength as 'a creature so admirably and terribly compounded of tragic genius and Stoic heroism', her 'dark unconscious instinct as of primitive nature-worship', and a 'genius [...] which found no corresponding quality in her sister's'.[2]

Charlote Brontë's image in the 1850 Preface of *WH* as 'moorish and wild, and knotty as the root of heath' did not survive the demonstration of coherence by C.P. Sanger in his essay *The Structure of Wuthering Heights* (1926) (McNees, pp. 71-82). He prefaced his proposal about property law in the story with a skilled unravelling of the chronology, a demonstration of the symmetry between the Earnshaw and Linton family trees, and indications that the landscape in *WH* was carefully mapped. In another pioneering essay, 'Emily Brontë and *Wuthering Heights*' (1934), David Cecil emphasized the brevity and naturalness of her writing, her 'power of visualization', the reliability of the narrators, and the symmetrical construction of her story around the antithetical ideas of storm and calm. He recognised her enigmatically presented moral scheme, proposing that the story is concerned 'not with moral standards, but with those conditioning forces of life on which the naïve erections of the human mind that we call moral standards are built up.' The text, he observed, is presented as a drama, 'in a series of set scenes linked together by the briefest possible passages of narrative', and he concluded that 'it is as well-constructed artistically as it is intellectually. [...] There is not a loose thread in it.'[3]

These essays transformed the discussion of *WH*. In the absence of documents, however, the Preface continued to exert pressure, for example, in the essay by Dorothy Van Ghent, who maintained that 'form, in short, is the book itself', and yet retained the Preface's judgments of, for example, the 'amoral love of Catherine and Heathcliff', Hareton's 'natural boorishness consequent on neglect', and 'the cannibal unregeneracy of Heathcliff'.[4] That vestige from the Preface faded before the recognition of irony as a structural component in *WH*, and by implication, of the author's supreme control over her story and its materials. That approach enabled John E. Jordan, in his landmark essay 'The Ironic Vision of Emily Brontë' (1965), to discount any assumption that there are topics or actions 'that the author is not aware of'.[5] Besides irony, the actions of characters sustained the drift against the Preface. A straightforward rebuttal of Charlotte's view appeared in the article 'The Villain in *Wuthering Heights*' (1958), by James Hafley, who saw Nelly Dean as 'one of the consummate villains in English literature'.[6] In another essay, John Fraser concluded that Emily Brontë revealed her message in Nelly's dictum: 'we *must* be for ourselves in the long run' (ch. 10).[7] Both these views are undermined, however, by the antithetical principle at work in this novel. In confessing how she maintained order by lying, concealment, and intrusion, Nelly Dean struggles towards truth and caring for others more than herself. An appraisal of the characters in their own light appeared in the essay '*Wuthering Heights*', by F.H. Langman. He recognised that Heathcliff had been 'at least as a child, more human than those around him, more sensitive, more responsive', that Heathcliff asserts a 'superior right' in his conflict with Hindley, that Hindley is Heathcliff's fellow conspirator in the defrauding of Hareton, and that the elder Catherine and Heathcliff 'recognise in each other their true humanity'.[8] In *Their Proper Sphere* (1966), a pioneering study of the position of female authors in a male world, Inga-Stina Ewbank proposed that the characters were presented, not as vehicles for ideas or objects of judgment, but 'symbolically, to explore the human condition'.[9] The stage was set for a reappraisal.

Further readings followed two courses, one into the *milieu intérieur* or structure of mind, and the other into its complement, the landscape or *milieu extérieur* in *WH*, and the society it portrayed.[10] Explorations of crises in mind and body emerged in *The Life and Private History of Emily Jane Brontë* (1928), by Romer Wilson, who observed about Emily Brontë's Gondal poems that 'The main sources of inspiration will be found in the private history of the dreamer'. She saw *WH* as an 'autobiography, the life of her soul on earth from that time when she was "barely six years old" to the time when her poems were discovered', and concluded: 'The real Emily was contrary to all that Charlotte struggled for'.[11] Enlarging the *milieu intérieur* to include the problem of family and blood line in *WH*, Eric Solomon proposed that tensions in the story grew out of a concealed case of incest. His proposition was adopted and broadened in a study of sibling jealousy among the younger Earnshaws by Q.D. Leavis (see above, Introduction (4) 'The marriage prohibition'). The related crises of self-discovery, body image, individuation, *alterity* or the other, and the rite of passage,[12] have been explored in two penetrating studies by Stevie Davies, *Emily Brontë. The Artist as a Free Woman* (1983) and *Emily Brontë: Heretic* (1994). Another contribution to this field is *Wuthering Heights. A Drama of Being* (1997) by David Holbrook. A medical and psychological problem of greater urgency than the symptoms of tuberculosis, if one were possible, is reconstructed by Catherine Frank in her book *Emily Brontë. A Chainless Soul* (1990). In a decisive article, Margaret Maison discerned a recognisable philosophy in Emily Brontë's writing, the Epicurean view of immortality in relation to the universe, which came from Epictetus, and showed the source advocating that frame of ideas in the 1840s.[13] The key poem, 'No coward soul is mine', had been hailed at the outset by Matthew Arnold. Though the poem is ostensibly in the voice of another speaker, its closely woven logic does not resemble a parody; the author's voice appears to have made a shy appearance there. It has an application to *WH*, since the Epicurean view of immortality appears under an ironic concealment at the end of the story. It is left for the reader to fill in the missing fragment: the dead achieve final rest not as blessed or damned souls, or walking ghosts, or sleeping bodies, but as indestructible atoms.

The breach with the Preface widened under pressure from the outside world, the *milieu extérieur* or social setting portrayed in the novel. In *An Introduction to the English Novel* (1951) (McNees, pp. 188-200), Arnold Kettle proposed that 'Heathcliff was born not in the pages of Byron, but in a Liverpool slum'.[14] This view was taken further in *Myths of Power. A Marxist Study of the Brontës* (1975), by Terry Eagleton, who explained Heathcliff as a case of 'the victory of capitalist property-dealing over the traditional yeoman economy of the Earnshaws'. However, he continued to read the text as 'an apparently timeless, highly integrated, mysteriously autonomous symbolic universe'.[15] The conflict remained unresolved in his recent essay, 'Heathcliff and the Great Hunger'.[16] A full recognition of the racial subject in *WH* appeared in a landmark essay by Andrea Dworkin, '*Wuthering Heights*'. Viewing mind and society, the *milieu intérieur* and the *milieu extérieur*, as a single interwoven process, Andrea Dworkin achieved the first explicit recognition of Heathcliff's moral vision. By viewing him as the text presents him, as a racial outcast, deformed by the prevailing social, mental, and moral system of ideas, yet burning through to the truth, she recognised Heathcliff's 'stunning lucidity, [...] a moral lucidity' (p. 82), and his tragic grandeur. Among critics she was the first to recognise and write out Emily Brontë's prophetic presentation of alienation and disruption, along lines defined a century later by Frantz Fanon in his book *The Wretched of the Earth* (1962). Recognising Brontë's control of her story and its psychological, social and racial material, Dworkin concluded that an enlightened reading had become possible: 'now it is time to read it fully awake'.[17] Another landmark essay took a further step. Still working within the text and the racial context, and viewing them in their own light, in her article 'Wuthering Heights and the Liverpool Slave Trade' (1995), Maja-Lisa von Sneidern showed the presence in the text of the character types and stereotypes from plantation society. Her conclusion defined Emily Brontë's intention: 'given the opportunity, all are capable of infinite brutality and falling victim to the addictive pleasure of possessing another human being'.[18] Her essay recognised the presence in WH of an issue handling of an issue which had for long been self-evident to Caribbean and black American writers, and which arose from early exposure to plantation society in the writings of John Woolman. Through these studies, recognition arrived for the position of WH in the main stream of literature.

Genesis

Further studies have reconstructed Brontë's development as a writer. A loosely articulated story about love, warfare and betrayal makes a shadowy appearance in her Gondal poems.[19] She began writing the poems in 1833 and continued them into her last years. Through them she articulated ideas which are ironically or obliquely present in her novel. Through pioneering studies, Fannie E. Ratchford[20] and Mary Visick[21] have reconstructed the story within the poems, and illumined the emergence of Brontë's art as a novelist. The Gondal story is set in two islands which are at war with each other, one in the north Pacific named Gondal, and the other, named Gaaldine, in the south Pacific. These localities match Japan and Australia, two Pacific territories which appear in J. Goldsmith, *A Grammar of General Geography* (1823), a book which the Brontës kept and used at home.[22]

The poems show Emily Brontë's familiarity with the impact of slavery on Africa. Among themselves, evidently, the Brontë children allotted the western seaboard of Africa to Charlotte and Branwell, and the eastern to Emily and Anne. The names Verdopolis, Angria, Northangerland, and Glasstown in Charlotte and Branwell's cycle are borrowed from Cap Verde, the regions north and south of Angra Pequeña (the modern Lüderitz), with Glass taken from the Ver[re] of Verdopolis and Cap Verde, and endings borrowed from Freetown and Capetown. At an early age, evidently, Emily Brontë recognised the central position of Ethiopia in African history. The 'Vocabulary of Proper Names' in the Brontës' copy of Goldsmith's *Geography* has manuscript entries, added between the lines, at or near their alphabetical positions, in a handwriting which appears to be Emily's, or, possibly, that of Anne. They read: 'Gaaldine a large Island newly discovered in the South Pacific', 'Elbe [...] kingdom in Gaaldine', and 'Gondal a large Island in the north Pacific'. The Gondal entry appears above Goldsmith's entry for Gondar, 'a capital city of Abyssinia' (pp. 168-70). Emily Brontë modelled her wars between Gondal and Gaaldine on the wars between Ethiopians and the Galla, their neighbours to the south.[23] The conflict included slave raiding, the cause and consequence of warfare in Africa until the later nineteenth century. The wars to the west are the subject of the Angria series by Charlotte and Branwell. However, Branwell's tendency to occupy both pitches appears in his 'Battle of Dongola', a reference to a town on the Nile, identified by Goldsmith as 'a province of Nubia'.

In contrasted ways which reappear in the novels, the Brontës' juvenile writings dramatised William Wilberforce's scheme in Parliament and beyond, to rid the globe of slavery. This subject is guardedly present through images of imprisonment and enslavement to love in Emily's cycle of poems. In their writings, however, the elder sisters dramatised opposed views about the causes and cures of slavery. The gulf between *WH* and its Preface reflects that conflict of ideas. In her novel, Emily Brontë simplified and tightened the loose articulation of her Gondal story into a closely woven web of concentric narratives. With skilled concealment she described the parts of the Dales which appear in *Jane Eyre* and which stood at the summit of northern English slaveholding and its Parliamentary patronage. She adopted the mode but not the manner of Sir Walter Scott, whose explicit renderings of history, legend and reality represented a landmark in the growth of the novel as a literary form. Features of *WH* which have no parallel in the Gondal series are the recognisable Yorkshire landscapes, with their sharply drawn distinction between the moorland south and the limestone north, the construction of Heathcliff as a child of slaveholding society, the use of three generations to remove the marriage prohibition which the elders had installed, the redemption of a blighted society in the second half of the story, the mixed attitudes, variously tender, violent, negligent, and possessive, towards children, the use of the diarist and other witnesses to verify every facet of the story, and the echoes and structural elements from ballads and folklore.

Emily Brontë's essays in the *Belgian Essays* (1996), edited by Sue Lonoff, mark a second phase in her literary development. Her grasp of history was deepened, it appears, by Chateaubriand and other writers she found in that middle year. Also, her style was toughened by her astonishing mastery of a variety of French prose which she made her own. In contrast to her sister's endeavours towards a correct and florid prose, Emily Brontë drove English constructions towards a certain French clarity with a sparkling compound of vigour and seeming absent-mindedness. In each exercise she brought a startling maturity to bear on her subject. She kept her teacher at a stretch, it appears, inspiring the compound of respect and exasperation which appeared in his letter to Patrick after her death. His phrase, 'she should have been a man', suggests a French sense, not that she lost her vocation but that she had the capabilities generally shown by men in science, conquest, and exploration, and that she infiltrated the curriculum in his school for boys across the road.

The manuscript and proofs of *WH*, and any correspondence in that connection, have never been found. This situation impedes any reading of the last phase of its author's writing career, since it has left the published text of her novel as the only reliable guide to itself and its context. In his book *The Birth of Wuthering Heights* (1998), a full-scale venture into this field, Edward Chitham has proposed that it was written in two phases, the second taking place in response to comments from a publisher who had seen a first draft. Inevitably, many questions remain unanswered.

Literary models

The combined resources of the Mechanics' Institute Library in Keighley (*K*), and at Ponden House near Haworth (*P*), totalled some 3,000 volumes.[24] With the exception of items collected by Henry Houston Bonnell (BPM), the extent of the collection at Haworth Parsonage can only be conjectured. The books at Keighley Rectory, the Pensionnat Heger in Brussels, and the Taylors' house in Gomersal, are not listed. From these fragments, none the less, Emily Brontë's reading can be traced at several points. It appears to have been omnivorous, retentive, and critical.

The literary models for *WH* fall into three groups:
(i) an outer structural edge of concentric stories built out of diaries, letters, and orally delivered narratives;
(ii) an inner core of ballads and traditional narratives from the north of England, Scotland and the Scottish border, and further afield; and
(iii) a repertoire of novels, plays, poems, and tracts on Emancipationist and Biblical themes, and from classical, Baroque, neo-classical, and Romantic literature. Echoes from these works are generally ironically used. Some outlines are:

(i) at its outer edge, *WH* was patterned on novels by Sir Walter Scott, for example *The Antiquary* (*K*), where a narrator discovers fragments of local history and traditional lore. Like Scott, Brontë used the resulting double focus to explore the conflict between past and present, and between the economic sections of society which had emerged in the eighteenth century. She built a tale resembling, at some points, Scott's stories of social displacement, economic oppression, and tragic love, *The Black Dwarf* (*K*) and *The Bride of Lammermoor* (*K*).[25] This narrative method improved on its precursor, the epistolary tradition, by forming a continuous story and interposing the character of a narrator who acts as an intermediary of greater or lesser reliability. Another example was *Frankenstein* (1818), by Mary Shelley, a novel with numerous points of resemblance to *Wuthering Heights*. Here, a tale of negative impulses is unfolded by a man-shaped creature, constructed out of pieces taken from graveyards by a misguided scientist named Franken-stein, the eponymous narrator, who tells the creature's sad tale, as the anonymous creature expounded it, to a memoirist, who re-tells it in the form of letters to his sister. In Mary Shelley's tale, the monster's destructive career is attributed to his exclusion from education and society. His moral downfall is occasioned by his creator's refusal to create a female partner for him.[26] The description of *WH* in Charlotte's Preface applies, indeed, more aptly to this tale of murder, violence, and destruction, than to the novel it purports to introduce.

The concentric narrative in *WH* is more tightly organised than Mary Shelley's. It includes the prophetic dreaming of her memoirist, and the interweaving of his male story with that of his female informant. She strengthened the narrator's use of the story as a confession of past errors, and replaced Mary Shelley's bleak ending with a redemptive second theme. Opposition to Mary Shelley's message appears in Brontë's references to magic, the alleged cause of the eponymous scientist's erring beliefs and practices in *Frankenstein*. This topic appears not to have posed any threat in Emily's thinking; she took it in her stride, in-corporating many literary features from the literary circle of the alleged necromancer John Dee, notably her modifications of Marlowe's Faust theme and her invocations of poems by Donne. Her moral outline, drawn from the main current of Emancipationist thinking in the age of Wilberforce, merges into that system of ideas.

Nearer home, Brontë evidently found a model for her memoirist in Frederic Montagu, author of *Gleanings in Craven* (1838). This book is writ-ten as a series of letters to a friend, describing the author's travels in the Craven highlands, and telling stories he finds there. His travels take him along the Brontës' coach route to Cowan Bridge, and to Bolton Bridge in Wharfedale, the site of their meeting with the Nusseys in 1833. Arriving at the foot of Ingleborough, he dreams about how he expects to be murdered for purposes of robbery at the New Inn in Clapham, where a dead body reposes in a coffin below, but he finds that the knocking on the door is merely the maid bringing his hot water (pp. 130-33). Montagu's compound of urbanity and curiosity about the Craven highlands evi-dently contributed to the formation of Lockwood's journal. Brontë re-used and improved Montagu's phrases to describe the limestone crags of the region around Gimmerton.[27] Her plan, evidently, was to construct a story around the gaps in his account of the landscapes she knew.

(ii) Following the example of Wordsworth in his poem *The White Doe of Rylstone* (1815), Brontë built her novel around an anthology of legends, ballads and family histories from the Dales. Like Wordsworth's poem, *WH* stands on a threshold between written and oral texts. Char-lotte's memory of Emily's presentation of her novel confirms its oral delivery and its moral intention:

If the auditor of her work when read in manuscript, shuddered under the grinding influence of natures so relentless and implacable, of spirits so lost and fallen; if it was complained that the mere hearing of certain vivid and fearful scenes banished sleep by night, and disturbed mental peace by day, Ellis Bell would wonder what was meant, and suspect the complainant of affectation.

Indirectly, Charlotte confirmed that the gruesome ballads and ancient tales in the background of *WH* were shared knowledge, and only hypocrisy or affectation would prompt a hollow complaint against a modern tale which incorporated their story material. The Brontë's acquaintance with ballads appears in Nelly Dean's singing ' 'Twas far in the night' to the infant Hareton a few minutes before his father's violent entry into the house and the child's narrow escape from death (ch. 9). This song is an adaptation of a translation made from a Danish ballad by Robert Jamieson, and published by Sir Walter Scott in the Notes to *The Lady of the Lake* (1810) (*K*). The ballad tells how a dead mother, ashen and unrecognisable, walks from her grave to warn that her children must be better looked after by their cruel stepmother. The warning is heeded. As in all Emily Brontë's handling of her literary models, her story cuts across the ballad it invokes. Until the arrival of Zillah, no stepmother or pseudo-stepmother cares for Hareton after Nelly Dean's departure to the Grange, yet Heathcliff recognises him as the gold in the Earnshaw heritage. Even when he wounds her by throwing a stone, he is admired by Nelly Dean, who sees in him the untarnished image of her childhood sweetheart and foster-brother, his father. Hareton's are the only tears shed for Heathcliff at his death.

Another ballad, 'Fair Annie', appeared in several versions in Scott's *Minstrelsy of the Scottish Border* (1807) (*K*) and in the collection *Illustrations of Northern Antiquities* (1814), by Henry Weber and Robert Jamieson. Less clearly identified than 'The Ghaist's Warning', this ballad appears through Nelly Dean's malapropism as 'Fairy Annie's Wedding' (ch. 32). The ballad obliquely dramatises the marriage prohibition which the Brontës knew in a modified form at first hand, but without transgression, since no offence appears to have taken place at the parsonage. The ballad tells how an erring husband goes in search of a new lady, but the bride he brings home finds that she is the sister of his wife, who is variously presented as compliant and rebellious. The sister withdraws. In Scott's version, rather than yield her children to another's rule, Annie is as willing to kill her children as the cat that devours a rat or dog that kills a hare. The image reappears in Emily Brontë's reference to the tail of a cat's half-eaten rat dangling from its mouth in her essay 'Le chat',[28] and in *WH* as the somewhat sweetened comparison of Edgar Linton to the cat which cannot leave 'a mouse half killed, or a bird half eaten' (ch. 8). In Weber and Jamieson's version, husband and wife celebrate the renewal of their marriage with the wedding banquet which he had ordered her to prepare.[29] No reconciliation was needed when Hindley Earnshaw brought home his lady; Nelly Dean silently underlines her position as foster sister by showing no resentment, and rejoicing when their son will marry his cousin.

A traditional tale, 'The Helks Lady', is similarly constructed around marriage prohibitions, in this instance, those restraining parents and their children before and after the Statute of 1540, and cousins in the years before Henry VIII. No parallel has emerged in the northern English repertoire, but it may tentatively be compared to the legendary death of Baldr, the favoured hero and seasonal god of Scandinavian oral tradition. No reason has emerged against adopting the account given by its first narrator, R. Balderston Cragg, who explains that he first heard this tale about Kingsdale and Thornton in Lonsdale from his mother during his childhood in Ingleton, in the early nineteenth century. The coach's pause at the Church Stile Inn, Thornton in Lonsdale (now the Marton Arms) would have been long enough for a re-telling to the Brontës by any of the few inhabitants of the hamlet, or by a passenger acquainted with the region. The manors of Thornton in Lonsdale and Harewood were linked by the ancient ownership of both by the Redmayne family (Redman; formerly D'Avranches).[30]

'The Helks Lady' is set in the decades leading to the Reformation, the Dissolution of monasteries, and the marriage statute of 1540. With the support of her mother and aunt, Lady Barbara Redmayne of Hallsteads, Thornton in Lonsdale, is secretly married to her cousin Sir Guy Middleton, of Middleton Hall, near Barbon. On discovering that she is pregnant, her father prepares an excursion to burn Middleton Hall, but falls dead when he is impulsively stabbed with a kitchen knife by his daughter. In grief she rushes to the Helks, the wild limestone terraces around Ingleborough and Gragareth, and is led by a voice to the nunnery at Twiselton. In due course, a similar voice leads the despondent Sir Guy through the forests to Hallsteads. He inherits that manor from Dame Redmayne, who tells him a secret on her deathbed. A page torn from a diary, found over a century later in a Bruges missal, reveals that the calling voice was Lady Barbara's. At the Dissolution, the nuns emerge from their priory, and a royal pardon is handed to the Prioress by Sir Guy, her husband. The couple are reunited, the nuns come to live with them at Hallsteads, and the reunited parents watch over the progress of their son towards the ministry in the seminary at Bruges. They die and are buried in the Redmayne vault at St Oswald's Church, Thornton in Lonsdale, but Lady Barbara walks as a ghost haunting the Helks in her grey costume from a bygone age. Some years later, Father Fawcett, the new vicar who has arrived at St Oswald's Church from Bruges, is visited by a lady dressed in grey. She tells him she has seen the Helks Lady, and that she would like to be laid to rest. At the exorcism at midnight on

Christmas Eve, an owl hoots, a gale springs up, the congregation's candles are extinguished, and the Helks Lady glides through the church, followed by Father Fawcett, whose candle stays alight. As she sinks into her tomb, he falls dead, taken to the other world by his mother. Readily recognisable elements from this story appear in *Jane Eyre* and *WH*. If the resemblances reflect literary knowledge by R. Balderstone Cragg, its first narrator in print,[31] he joins the small group of Dales writers who have recognised the Brontës' shared landscape and story material. None the less, his tale retains credibility among known fragments out of the Lunesdale legendary repertoire which he assembled in his book. The direction of movement appears to be from the tale into the novels, and not the other way around.

Legend, magic and history are bridged in *The White Doe of Rylstone* (1815), a narrative about the Dales by Wordsworth. His poem foreshadows Brontë's construction of her novel out of ballad themes, magic, Dales legends and Dales family histories. Wordsworth tells three tales from the Dales: the Boy of Egremont, the Shepherd Lord, and the white doe of the Nortons, who sits by the grave of Emily Norton during church services at Rylston, in Wharfedale. Suggestions for these stories appear in *The Deanery of Craven* (*K*), by T.D. Whitaker, who observed that Scott 'would have wrought [the white doe] into a beautiful story'.[32] The main story is about the Nortons, a Dales family whose males were exterminated when they resisted the Protestant dispensation at the Reformation. For this part of his poem, Wordsworth drew on the ballad 'The Rising in the North', in the *Reliques of Ancient English Poetry* (1765) (*K*), edited by Thomas Percy. Anticipating the last lines of *Wuthering Heights*, Wordsworth concluded his tale with the doe's sheltering by the graves of Emily Norton and her mother: 'Calm spectacle, by earth and sky / In their benignity aproved!'. Emily Brontë's oblique allusion to Wordsworth's poem at the end of her novel, it appears, indicates her love for her mother and readiness to follow her namesake to the tomb. Her link with her dead mother reappears in her echo from 'The Ghaist's Warning', and what appears to be her use of the orally transmitted 'Helks Lady' for the setting and theme of her novel. She improved on Wordsworth's example by weaving her Dales story material into a single narrative.

(iii) Brontë's direct literary models emerge as a voluminous assemblage of current and published works. Some of these can be outlined. A model for her reconstruction and adaptation of the story of Dent was *Hope On, Hope Ever!* (1840) (*K*), a novel about Dent by Mary Howitt (Appendix C). In this classic of Dales life,[33] the orphan Felix Law is fostered by the Swithenbanks of Dent, a chapelry in the parish of Sedbergh, neighbouring to Tunstall. He is drawn to Katie Swithenbank, their daughter, who becomes his childhood sweetheart. This attachment is cemented by his long search for her when she is thought to be lost. At a later stage he is fostered by another family during his five years of schooling in London. On his return to Kendal and Dent he is in a position to offer marriage to Katie. As with her other literary echoes and borrowings, Brontë appears to have intended a reply to Mary Howitt, whom she echoes at several points, notably in her natural descriptions, use of dialect, and warmth towards life in a Dales village. Her brief invocations of nature and the seasons are foreshadowed in Mary Howitt's chapter openings, for example: 'February wore on, and so did March and April, and it was now the beginning of May', and shortly after that: 'It was a pleasant thing indeed, to be driving abroad on such a fine morning, with the larks singing overhead, and the thrushes and blackbirds in the wayside plantations!'.[34] Brontë departed from her literary model by introducing sexual and social jealousy among the maturing teenage children (ch. 8), a feature with no parallel in *Hope On, Hope Ever!*. In Mary Howitt's novel, the search for the missing girl in her childhood lasts for days instead of the hours preceding Heathcliff's return from the escapade at Thrushcross Grange (ch. 6), or Nelly's search for the younger Catherine in her childhood (ch. 18). Emily darkened Mary Howitt's sugared picture of Dales life by transferring the foster relationship to Nelly Dean, who loses her childhood sweetheart when he finds someone else. Further darkening appears in the marriage prohibition which silently keeps the childhood sweethearts in *WH* apart for life. In *WH*, escape from the prohibition is possible only for the cousins in the third generation.

Novels, plays, poems and oral traditions which Emily Brontë evidently mastered gave her the command of Yorkshire topics which Professor Knoepflmacher has noted as her 'almost anthropological grounding of the novel in the region she knew best'.[35] Besides the Bible and Shakespeare, her resources included T.D. Whitaker's *The Deanery of Craven* (1805) (*K*), a rich fund of Dales tradition. His concluding study, *Richmondshire* (1823), on Lunesdale and the northern Dales, was too lavish for a public library, but was probably available at the Rectory of the library's Trustee, the Revd Theodore Dury. The Library was open only on weekday evenings, but as a Committee member with a commission to purchase books, Dury was in a position to set aside books, maps, and other sources for the Brontës to fetch or consult on Saturdays. For her infiltration of the Dales family histories behind and beyond the books, Emily Brontë evidently drew upon Dury's wife, Anne Greenwood, and Dury himself, who had known Byron at Cambridge. As a Trustee of the K&K and the Clergy Daughters' School, Dury was on a footing with the Dales landowners in the period down to 1840, the year of his departure for a parish in Hertfordshire (Appendix C).

Another northern classic was the *Worthies of Lancashire and Yorkshire* (1836) (*K*), by Hartley Coleridge. His essay on Lady Anne Clifford probably inspired Emily Brontë's use of that great Dales family history in the second half of her novel. Further insights into the literary possibilities of the Clifford family history appeared in *The Outlaw* (1839), a verse drama in the Spasmodic style by Robert Story, parish clerk of Gargrave and the leading literary figure in Branwell's Bradford circle. His play was serialised in *The Halifax Guardian*, a newspaper printed by Branwell's supporter and friend, Francis Leyland. In the 1830s, *Blackwood's* serialised Robert Southey's *The Doctor* (1838), a boisterous novel set in the Ingleborough region, and *Tom Cringle's Log*, a narrative of Caribbean travel, by Michael Scott. In the 1820s and 1830s, *Blackwood's* carried numerous essays by Mary Margaret Bush on literature in France and Germany, and one on ancient belief in Scandinavia. The presence in the Library at Keighley of the *Northern Antiquities* (1781) (*K*), by Henri Mallet, on ancient German and Scandinavian beliefs, reflects Theodore Dury's probable interest in this subject.

Another literary model which stood, like Wordsworth's poem, at the junction of oral tradition and printed stories, appears to have been *Le magasin des enfans* (1823). This teacher's manual for beginners in French carried the first telling of 'La belle et la bête' ('Beauty and the Beast'), a narrative originally written by Mme Le Prince de Beaumont, author of *Le magasin*. In this original form, the tale is told by Mlle La Bonne, a governess, and followed by a discussion of it with her pupils, Ladi Charlotte, Miss Molly, Ladi Spirituelle, and Ladi Mary. For the character of Nelly Dean, Emily Brontë appears to have drawn on Mlle La Bonne ('Miss Good', 'The Maid'), combined with elements from Mary Howitt in her tale of Dent, and from her own life as her father's housekeeper after 1842. At the first meeting, the Beast demands honesty from the merchant, rejecting flattery and insisting instead, 'qu'on dise ce qu'on pense' (p. 91), 'say what you think'. His daughter willingly accepts the Beast's bargain that she sacrifice herself to him for her father's sake: 'je me trouve fort heureuse, puisqu'en mourant j'aurai la joie de sauver mon père'—'in dying, I will rejoice in the happy fate of being my father's saviour' (p. 93). After the miraculous transformation of the Beast, Mlle La Bonne suggests that stories of this type are allegories to explain morality and history. On the grounds that she is about to turn twelve, Ladi Charlotte, the eldest, demands an explanation of the attraction between the sexes. Mlle La Bonne changes the subject by suggesting that they attend to their plants and insects, consider their metamorphoses, and take a walk. After tea, Miss Molly tells the Biblical tale of the flood.[36] The first excursion of the younger Catherine in *Wuthering Heights* takes place similarly at her thirteenth birthday, when she meets Hareton, her *bête noire* for the time being, and future prince. In a role borrowed from the *Arabian Nights* (*K*), she and her animals are an Arabian merchant and his camels. The excursion leads to the metamorphoses of character at the end of the story. The younger Catherine stands up to Heathcliff, and contributes to his metamorphosis by telling him that no one loves him: '*Nobody* loves you—*nobody* will cry for you, when you die!' (ch. 29). Stumbling over a truth, she is mistaken: Hareton weeps. Besides liberating Hareton, she precipitates Heathcliff's self-recognition, downfall, death and liberation, and reforms the estate. Other stories are woven into *WH* novel; this one, it seems, is its heart.

Similarly, the *Faust* plays by Goethe stood at the crossroads of the miraculous, the metamorphic, the traditional, the satirical, and the realistic. It is hard to imagine that a mature, quizzical and brilliant young woman's introduction to German with Constantin Heger would have lacked reference of some kind to *Faust I* (1808) and *Faust II* (1825-32). They are the advanced beginner's Pythagoras or Bach. Possibly Emily Brontë already knew *Faust: A Tragedy* (1839), by Wolfgang von Goethe, a translation of *Faust I* by J. Birch; and also, the *Characteristics of Goethe* (1833), by Sarah Austin. A defence of Goethe's sympathetic presentation of Faust, made by Edward Bulwer-Lytton in his book *Pilgrims of the Rhine* (1834) (*K*), was available to her. These works appear to have drawn her to Promethean characters in classical and modern mythology. They are suspected of being in league with Satan, yet they create the human species out of clay, steal fire for its benefit, and are chained and punished. Transformations of the traditionally damned Faust began with Christopher Marlowe's ironic presentation of a Mephistopheles who carries hell with him, and a Faustus who sees but cannot find the perpetually available grace, or salvation. In that story, Faustus' death is caused by despair, not words on paper. Goethe metamorphosed hell into the hero's state of remorse. Faust's cry, 'How darkness closes in, as fades the light.—/ Even so it is with me! in my breast all is night',[37] ('Und Finsternis Drängt ringsum bei! / So siehts in meinem Busen nächtig') reappears in Nelly's reference to Heathcliff's last days: 'I was inclined to believe, as he said Joseph did, that conscience had turned his heart to an earthly hell' (ch. 33). The redeemed Faust appears in Sarah Austin's *Characteristics*: 'we must be completely in error if Faust is not finally saved— if Heaven is not victorious over Hell. *Faust* is a philosophico-, or, if people will, a religious-didactic poem'.[38] As Heathcliff approaches his end, he says: 'Last night, I was on the threshold of hell. Today, I am within sight of my heaven—I have my eyes on it—hardly three feet to sever me!' (ch. 34). In his study of the tradition, J.W. Smeed found an 'epidemic of *Faust* versions in the nineteenth and twentieth centuries'.[39] It seems to have reached the author of a work which is frequently referred to, not without reason, as the greatest of English novels.[40]

Another literary model appears to have been *Poems on Several Occasions* (1719) (*P*), by John Donne ('*Poems*'). The rapidity, contradictoriness, and eloquence of Donne's style, and his fusion of religious and secular imagery in poems at the summit of wit in English, appear to have contributed to the frequently observed and similar features in Brontë's prose. With Browning, Coleridge, and others, it seems, she joined the pioneers of Donne's restoration to the eminence he held in

Shakespeare's day. As though he were a pair of compasses, Lockwood doubles the distance across the park at the start of the story: 'the distance from the gate to the Grange is two miles: I believe I managed to make it four' (ch. 3). In Donne's poem 'Valediction: Forbidding Mourning' (*Poems*, pp. 35-6), compasses enact the lovers' peaceful separation, which Donne envisages as a version of tranquil death: 'As virtuous men pass mildly away / And whisper to their soules, to goe, / Whilst some of their sad friends doe say, / The breath goes now, and some say, no'. That image of tranquillity is echoed at the death of Edgar Linton, whose words to his daughter are reported by Nelly Dean:

> "I am going to her, and you darling child shall come to us;" and never stirred or spoke again, but continued that rapt, radiant gaze, till his pulse imperceptibly stopped, and his soul departed. None could have noticed the exact minute of his death, it was so entirely without a struggle (ch. 28).[41]

As with the ballads, *WH* cuts across the *Poems*, yet maintains their literary mode. Brontë followed Donne in her construction of scenes, her abrupt chapter openings, her terse, elliptical style, and her sparkling images: 'the gunpowder lay as harmless as sand, because no fire came near to explode it' (ch. 10); or: 'I've dreamt in my life dreams that have stayed with me ever after, and changed my ideas; they've gone through and through me, like wine through water, and altered the colour of my mind' (ch. 9). She followed the Donne tradition which Abraham Cowley defined from the viewpoint of the new scientific style: 'the old fashion[ed] way was like *disputing* [...] where half is left out to be supply'd by the hearer; ours is like Syllogisms, where all that is meant is exprest'.[42] Like Donne's poems, Emily's novel celebrates the oneness of nature, the species man, and mind, with their storms, horrors, and paradisal moments. It is constructed as a hieroglyph or emblem out of intersecting parts, conceived as circles, around a crossroads which has two houses on the circumference at a radius of two miles.

The echoes proliferate in the chapter following the death of Edgar Linton. Preparing to rejoin the dead Catherine, Heathcliff relates how he arranged for the boards on the facing sides of the adjacent coffins to be opened, so that by the time Linton's remains spread about, he will find that Heathcliff's and the elder Catherine's have merged. His brooding combines a Baroque trope with the notorious pre-Victorian tendency for the village drinking water to absorb the contents of Haworth churchyard. Brontë re-states Donne's meditation on death in 'The Funeral' (*Poems*, p. 42). Heathcliff says:

> 'I'll tell you what I did yesterday! I got the sexton, who was digging Linton's grave, to remove the earth off her coffin lid, and I

opened it. I thought, once I would have stayed there, when I saw her face again—it is hers yet—he had hard work to stir me; but he said it would change, if the air blew on it, and so I struck one side of the coffin loose—and covered it up—not Linton's side, damn him! I wish he'd been soldered in lead' (ch. 29).

In 'The Funeral', a poem opening with 'Who ever comes to shroud me, do not harm', John Donne urges the attendants at his burial not to damage the image of his soul, which is present in the hair at the head of his coat of arms, or the hair on the upper part of his body: 'That subtile wreath of haire, which crowns my arme'. His soul has gone to heaven, leaving that lesser hair, the nerves which run down from his head, to bind together the parts of his body which his nerves once controlled. Sliding in the Donne manner from the soul as 'she' to 'she' as a lady, the poem runs on to say that she, his beloved, would not have him, yet she manacled him. Whatever she meant by the imperious control which imprisoned him, he continues, he asks for that imperiousness to be buried with him, so that he can keep some of her, and preserve it from debasement into a holy relic. She would not have him when he was alive, he laments, but he can take some of her, her imperiousness, with him to the grave: 'I bury some of you'. This difficult poem seems not to have puzzled Emily for long, if at all. Its substance reappears in Heathcliff's wish to merge after death with the beloved who rejected him. In the breathless manner of Donne, he continues:

'and I bribed the sexton to pull it [her neighbouring board] away, when I'm laid there, and slide mine out too, I'll have it made so, and then, by the time Linton gets to us, he'll not know which is which!' (ch. 29).

None the less, the vengeful element in Donne's poem is absent from Heathcliff's thoughts. He wishes only to share the space occupied by his loved one; not to punish her for dominating him.

The proliferating echoes include Donne's Elegie V, 'His Picture' (*Poems*, p. 66). Nelly Dean reports Heathcliff's obsessive gazing at the portrait of the elder Catherine: 'he resumed his meditation on the picture, took it down, and leant it against the sofa to contemplate it at better advantage; and while so occupied Catherine entered, announcing that she was ready, when her pony should be saddled' (ch. 29). All indications point to Brontë's left-handedness and mirroring of the world with ease. As though in a fractured mirror image, with the sex of the sitter, the direction of the gift, and the position of the lovers in relation to death and each other reversed, Heathcliff's meditation restates Donne's poem. In Elegie V, Donne imagines that he will return from a voyage, dead, rough, and coarse, but the picture he gives his beloved, who rejects him, will remind her of what he was. She, though faded, will be strong enough to rejoice that they have outgrown their childish love, and no longer need 'the milke, which in loves childish state / Did nurse it'. Emily proposes instead that childhood is never outgrown, and that the dead cannot punish the living. In her seemingly endless flow of extraordinary improvisation, the child breaks in with her pony, a happening of the kind which is lacking in Donne's poems.

In Heathcliff's jealous intrusion into the married love of Edgar Linton and the elder Catherine, and his outraged protestations that she has murdered him, Brontë parodied Donne's sanctification of his vengeful jealousy, and the idea that the betrayal of love is a form of murder, in his poem 'The Apparition' (*Poems*, p. 34). As in everything else, her touch remains sweet in the midst of terror. Like Donne, Heathcliff accuses the elder Catherine of murdering him; he can love her, but he cannot love her murderer, whom he construes as herself, as though her choice of Edgar Linton had been a suicide:

'It is hard to forgive, and to look at those eyes, and feel those wasted hands,' he answered. 'Kiss me again; and don't let me see your eyes! I forgive what you have done to me. I love *my* murderer—but *yours*! how can I?' (ch. 15).

He repeats the figure at their last meeting, when his animal embrace precipitates the premature birth of her child, and her death:

'And I pray one prayer—I repeat it till my tongue stiffens—Catherine Earnshaw, may you not rest, as long as I am living! You said I killed you—haunt me then! The murdered *do* haunt their murderers. I believe—I know that ghosts *have* wandered on earth. Be with me always—take any form—drive me mad! only *do* not leave me in this abyss, where I cannot find you! Oh, God! it is unutterable! I *cannot* live without my life! I *cannot* live without my soul!' (ch. 16).

Here, Heathcliff acts out Donne's idea that the lover is murdered by the treacherous object of his jealous love. In 'The Apparition' (*Poems*, p. 34), Donne, the rejected lover, accuses his loved one of murdering him, and lying with another man. He will haunt her, and on seeing his ghost, in an icy sweat she will turn to that man, who will turn away from her, thinking (Donne more tactfully explains) she is demanding more sex when he is exhausted. The ghost will then say something, but what that may be, the poet declines to reveal, since it may cause her to avoid that horror: he would rather torture her by letting her learn by experience. She will be more ghostly than her jealous lover: 'a verier ghost than I'. Brontë expanded and reversed the idea: if the lovers' ghosts find each other, it is their renewed search for bliss, and remorse for the past. Brontë adopted Donne's rhetoric of love, murder, and haunting, reversing it by excluding murder from her story. She restricted haunting to dreaming (ch. 3), reflections in a cupboard door (ch. 12), a visitation at the grave (ch. 29) and the experiences of a shepherd boy and his dog (ch. 34). The jealous drama in Donne's poem is reversed in her story. Heathcliff's return precipitates a quarrel between the Lintons, their reconciliation (ch. 10), followed by the pregnancy of the elder Catherine (ch. 12), and the birth of their child (ch. 16). Nelly Dean's horror is mistaken: that child lives to redeem the greater horrors of the marriage prohibition and plantation morality.

Through invocations of Donne and the ballads, as well as Shakespeare and the Bible, it appears, Brontë sought to restore an English tradition which had wilted under the impact of concealment and hypocrisy about sex, slavery, and the industrial blight. She found models, it appears, pointing towards a prose narrative which would bridge the gulf between lyrics and ballads on the one hand, and history and legend on the other. Suggestions appear among novels on the blighting effects of slaveholding society by Honoré de Balzac, George Sand, and Frederika Bremer. Probably she found and knew them. The French founders of romantic realism are praised for their clarity by G.W.M. Reynolds in his book *The Modern Literature of France* (1839) (*K*). Reynolds observed about French writing after 1830:

> A sudden impulse was given to the minds of men by the successful struggle for freedom which hurled the imprudent Charles from his regal seat. [...] Thus regenerated, and suddenly raised from a state of slavery to a position of comparative freedom, the people felt their ideas expand (pp. xii–xiv).

He praised Balzac's *Eugénie Grandet* (1834) as a work exemplifying the new spirit in literature:

> The literature of France, previous to the Revolution of 1830, resembled that of England at the present day; in as much as moral lessons were taught through the medium of impossible fictions. Now the French author paints the truth in all its nudity; and the development of the secrets of Nature shocks the English reader, because he is not just yet accustomed to so novel a style (p. xvii).

Reynolds classified *Eugénie Grandet* as 'a history of mankind, seen through the mirror which reflects the life and destinies of two or three individuals', and 'a volume, each word of which falls upon the memory with as indelible a trace as molten lead on the sensitive flesh' (pp. 26, 34). In a review in *The Quarterly Review* (*K*), J.W. Croker classified Balzac's novel as an exception to the general view that French novels were indecent.[43]

Since both studies were available in Keighley, there is a fair chance that by the time she planned and wrote *WH*, Brontë had found and absorbed *Eugénie Grandet*, together with comparable novels by George Sand and Frederika Bremer. Balzac relates how Charles Grandet, a cousin fallen from riches through his father's bankruptcy, arrives from Paris to stay with his relations in Saumur. He falls in love with his cousin Eugénie. Their shared love is thwarted by parental opposition. He enters the Caribbean plantation world, and ignores his cousin's love letters. On returning with a frozen heart, he marries a wealthy partner. She does the same in an unconsummated marriage, and devotes herself to charitable works. The brutalising effect of slave society in Balzac's handling of Charles Grandet reappears in Heathcliff's hostile mood on his return from what can only be the Caribbean. However, Brontë avoided the smothered love in Balzac's story, restored warmth and feeling to Donne's negative handling of jealousy and death, and constructed a ballad-like tale of childhood love beyond the bed and the grave.

A less abrupt presentation of Balzac's idea appeared in *Indiana* (1834), George Sand's handling of a five-sided crisis of love and death in plantation society. In this novel, Mme Delmare, nicknamed Indiana, a pale Creole who grew up on Réunion (l'Île Bourbon) in the Indian Ocean, divides her life between France and Réunion. She appears in the dreary company of three persons: her phlegmatic cousin and admirer since childhood, Sir Ralph or Rodolphe Brown, a baronet whose only passion is hunting foxes; her retired military husband, the tedious and endlessly suspicious M. Delmare; and Noun, her dark Creole lady's maid and foster-sister, who was born around the same day as herself. A fifth person arrives. An affair between Noun and Raymon de Ramiére, a neighbouring visitor, leads to Noun's pregnancy and suicide when she realises the hopelessness of her position, since the false Raymon has in the meantime developed an infatuation for Indiana. A frenzied relationship ensues, threatening compromise and ruin. After an attempted suicide, from which she is rescued by her cousin, she returns to Réunion with her husband, from whom she flees again, unaware that he is about to die. On returning to France in the midst of the 1830 revolution, she finds with horror that the house which was formerly hers is occupied by a wealthy orphan whose father has bought the house for her, so that she and the idle cuckoo Raymon, who has married her, can live there. Sick at heart she is accompanied by her indefatigable cousin Ralph to Réunion, where she plans a double suicide with him, but that attempt is thwarted by the island's rock formation. They live on in poverty, using their wealth to free the slaves.

Brontë's hawk-like reapportioning of the components in George Sand's story can be seen at a glance. She appears to have trimmed, simplified, and re-set George Sand's story by divesting it of its trappings, notably the lurid ending, which is preceded by a lengthy autobiographical extravaganza by Sir Ralph, the suicide, and the florid intrigues in Paris which lead to Indiana's first attempted suicide. Oceanic shuttling, she evidently felt, could be omitted. None the less, the stylishness, density, satire and classical unity of George Sand's plot evidently exercised a hypnotic appeal. The thirty-one chapters of *Indiana* are numbered continuously in four parts of nearly equal length, eight chapters each for the first three and seven for the fourth. A scarcely different form governed the numerical layout of *WH*. George Sand's first eight chapters outline the tale of jealousy which Emily appears to have absorbed and recast in the chapters between the return of Heathcliff and the death of Hindley Earnshaw. In his confession at the end, Sir Ralph welters in a phantasmal bath of consanguinity by proclaiming himself brother, father, lover and intending partner in suicide of Indiana.[44] In *WH*, that aspect of the story is trimmed to the dimensions of reality and spread across two generations. The anonymous narrator of George Sand's story is a patronising and invasive male who burdens his narrative with a stream of jocular, anti-female, anti-Creole and world-weary platitudes: he and his type are opposed, worn down and rejected by the story he tells. In Emily's hands, too, this dialectical contradiction is trimmed and incorporated within a story which provides, instead, a moral education for Lockwood. *WH* reflects Emily's sympathy for the servant and farming classes, hostility towards George Sand's garrulous and intrusive male narrator, sympathy rather than his pitying contempt for the central female figures, and a constructive view of the cousin relationship.

In the course of a proliferating literary search, Emily Brontë appears to have read *The Bondmaid* (1844), a tale written in the form of a two-part symbolic drama by Frederika Bremer. This is one among eleven translations of Frederika Bremer's novels, published in 1844 and bringing into an English focus her domestic scenes, crystalline dialogues, mythological insights, and natural descriptions. A literary flow from Scandinavia to the English writers is signposted by the dates. Evidently, Frederika Bremer bridged the gap between the assertive manner of Scott and the domestic and symbolic style of the Brontës.[45] Bremer appears to have shared Brontë's feeling that *Indiana* invited a reply. For certain aspects of her servant's tale about the northern landscape, orphanhood, slavery, mythology, and love beyond death, set in the period before the demise of the Liverpool slave trade, and written from the viewpoint of the post-Emancipation decade, Brontë appears to have followed the example of *The Bondmaid*. This novel portrays death, emancipation from slavery, the Nordic traditional belief about death, the levelling of the slave, servant and employing classes, and a union of souls after death. The story is presented as a dramatic narrative in two parts of nine and eight scenes. Emily mirrored those numbers in her two sets of seventeen chapters, each with nine and eight chapters. Several outlines of *WH* are prefigured in Bremer's tale of Kumba, the orphan child of a white freeman and a black slave. Her mother had been flung on the flames when queen Gunilda died. Kumba discusses her fate with Feima, her fellow slave in the court of Princess Frid, who is betrothed to King Dag: 'See you over the dreary swamp, the mist-wreath borne hither and thither by the wind? There see you the slave's after-life', she says (p. 8). In the harvest season, Princess Frid approaches death, and Kumba follows her to the mountains, where she dies, holding hands with her oppressor, whom she has poisoned. Princess Frid concludes: 'It may be, that in the after-life, princess and slave shall be but empty names.—Come, join thy soul with mine'.

The mountains, swamps and mists in *The Bondmaid* resemble the region described in *Wuthering Heights*. Autumn storms are explained in a note by Frederika Bremer as signs of the approaching death at Christmas of the god Baldr, the favoured god of greenness, fertility, and alcohol, whose annual rebirth falls in the month of May. He is killed at Christmas by his blind brother with a mistletoe arrow which is directed by the god of lies, chance, and mischief. He is welcomed in the underworld by Hela, custodian of the elysian and non-punitive domain for the dead in ancient northern belief, which was named hell. As one who never lied he is exempted from punishment in the perpetual fog and ice of Niflheim, but as a civilian lacking front wounds, he is denied the comforts of Valhalla. The name of Baldr's castle, Breidablik, identified in Bremer's notes to her Act I Scene 8, echoes Braeda Garth, the Kingsdale model for Brontë's farmhouse named Wuthering Heights.[46] The notes explain Baldr's position in Scandinavian mythology and the calendar. Further explanations were available to Emily in the *Northern Antiquities* (1781) (*K*), by Henri Mallet, and the article 'Scandinavian Mythology' by Mary Margaret Bush in *Blackwood's Magazine* (*K*).[47] Probably guided by these expositions of the northern seasons, Brontë constructed her story around the harvest moon (chs. 4, 10, 28, 34), as well as the spring equinox and other seasonal festivals. Their order is mirrored and reversed in her hands, but the traditional points of emphasis remain. Christmas, the season of Baldr's death, is the season of Heathcliff's humiliation and imprisonment by his adoptive brother and the boy from the neighbouring Thrushcross Grange (ch. 7). May, Baldr's month of rebirth, marks Heathcliff's death, shortly after the replanting of the garden at Easter (ch. 34). In the year of his death in 1802, that festival fell unusually late in April.[48] As in her handling of other literary antecedents, Brontë preserved an ironic distance from *The Bondmaid*, her probable literary model, avoiding explicit borrowing while retaining its outlines and directions, inverting its values, and avoiding suicide and murder. If an origin were sought for the depth, clarity, simplicity, and unified tone of *Wuthering Heights*, it would be in the critical use which Brontë made of this and other novels from the new literary movement in Germany, France, and Scandinavia.

Literary following

Contrary to many suppositions about the isolation of her novel, Brontë pioneered modern fiction about Atlantic social relationships. Her role as leader, pointing towards novels such as Olive Schreiner's *The Story of an African Farm* (1883), Henry James's *The Turn of the Screw* (1898), and Joseph Conrad's *Heart of Darkness* (1902), acquires depth in that setting. Emily's literary strength was first recognised at home. In childhood the Brontës apportioned Africa among themselves, and repeated the process, it appears, in handling English settings in maturity. Probably Emily Brontë took the lead in reconstructing Lunesdale, its slaveholding society and related family histories in the period before the Abolition of the Slave Trade Act (1807). In what appears to have been a roughly outlined trilogy, the sequels to *WH* would have been: first, *Jane Eyre* (1847), which took the Dales landscape and its society into the period of the Restoration in France and England in the decade before the Abolition of the Slave Trade Act (1833); and next, *Shirley* (1849), Charlotte's reconstruction of the Luddite years around 1811, through the perspective of the decades after the Reform Act. In this novel, Charlotte revived Emily's presence as her model for the principal figure,[49] and dramatised the Emancipationist campaign for the replacement of the plantation economy abroad by industrial output and exports from the British Isles. In the obscurity attending the writing of the mature Brontës' first series of novels, their order of composition and the relationships between the texts can only be surmised. The blurred account in Charlotte's 'Biographical Notice of Acton and Ellis Bell', appended to the Preface, sheds little or no light on how or in what order the authors planned their publication. Possibly *Jane Eyre* was conceived at first as a sequel to *Wuthering Heights*, and was laid aside when both became too long to form the first two of three volumes about Yorkshire, on the model of the *Poems* (1846) by Ellis, Acton and Currer Bell. The short novel *The Professor* turned out to be unrelated and unusable as a first or third volume in the original submission to Newby. A four-volume novel would not fit into any publishing scheme, and one-volume novels lay ahead in the future. Whatever confusion surrounded it, the compact manuscript of *Agnes Grey* survived as a third volume, with *WH* as Volumes One and Two. None the less, if they are set out along the lines of their historical and topographical story material, *WH*, *Jane Eyre* and *Shirley* adopt the form of a trilogy or triptych. On Emancipationist lines they define three stages of social change in the course of the half-century leading to the Reform Act (1832) and the Emancipation of Slaves Act (1833).[50]

As with other aspects of literary life in Haworth, it is hard to imagine that this dovetailing of the subject matter of the most celebrated novels in English took place without some discussion, before or after Patrick's bedtime at 9 p.m. Some such collaboration evidently lay behind Charlotte's veiled reference to her sister's mastery of family histories in the Dales, the region described in their two novels about the setting of their first school: 'she knew them, knew their ways, their language, and their family histories; she could hear of them with interest, and speak of them with detail, minute, graphic, and accurate'. The two novels handle the same landscape under different aspects, and in apportioning the patron families of the region and their clients, avoid crossing each other's lines. Whatever the relationships between the Haworth writers may have been, and contrary to the expectations raised in the Preface, it appears, Emily Brontë and her first following within her family circle, including her uncle Hugh (Appendix D), made a main contribution to the rise of social awareness in the ensuing century of English fiction.

The outlines of *WH* reappeared in many novels of the nineteenth and early twentieth centuries. Many of these have been identified and discussed by Patsy Stoneman in her illuminating book, *Brontë Transformations* (1996). Another sample may show the range and depth of Brontë's example. A simplified version of her narrative method reappears in *Heart of Darkness* (1902), Joseph Conrad's nightmare journey into colonial aggression. This novel restates her theme, that through the cruelties of slavery and its successor, colonization, the Atlantic colonising nations and the colonised societies were plunged equally into violence and moral corruption. Goethe's version of Faust, the underlying model for Heathcliff, reappears in Conrad's presentation of Kurtz, whose story is told in the narrative framework which Emily had developed from earlier, less skilled examples. Within that framework, Conrad recast Goethe's Helen as Kurtz's doomed forest companion, and replaced Goethe's betrayed village maiden with the saintly Intended, who never finds out what happened. Marlowe, the appropriately named narrator, finds a modern, ironically presented Faust. Conrad's versions of Gretchen and Helen are drawn from the age of imperial expansion by England and Belgium, under the protective umbrella of the Berlin conference of 1885.[51] By common literary practice, Conrad invoked and cross-cut the Faust tradition along lines which Goethe and Emily Brontë had made familiar. Through this channel and others, *WH* contributed dynamically to the main stream of literature in the century after 1850.

Notes

1 See C. Heywood, 'Yorkshire Landscapes in *Wuthering Heights*', *EIC* 48 (1998), 13-34. Also, note 13 below.
2 A.C. Swinburne, *A Note on Charlotte Brontë* (1877), p. 73-85.
3 David Cecil, 'Emily Brontë and *Wuthering Heights*', in his book *Early Victorian Novelists* (1934) (McNees, pp. 102-26).
4 Dorothy Van Ghent, *The English Novel. Form and Function* (1953), pp. 153-70.
5 John E. Jordan, 'The Ironic Vision of Emily Brontë', *NCF* 20 (1965), 1-18.
6 James Haflcy, 'The Villain in *Wuthering Heights*', *NCF* 13 (1958), 199-215 (p. 199).
7 John Fraser, 'The Name of Action: Nelly Dean and *Wuthering Heights*', *NCF* (1984), p. 79.
8 F.H. Langman, '*Wuthering Heights*', *EIC* 15 (1965), 295-312.
9 Inga-Stina Ewbank, 'Emily Brontë: The Woman Writer as Poet', in her book *Their Proper Sphere* (1966), pp. 86-155 (p. 96).
10 For the origin and early use of the term 'stream of consciousness', see my essay, C. Heywood, 'D.H. Lawrence's "Blood-Consciousness" and the Researches of Xavier Bichat and Marshall Hall', *Études Anglaises*, (1979), 397-413, revised as '"Blood-Consciousness" and the Pioneers of the Reflex and Ganglionic Systems', in *DH Lawrence. New Studies*, ed. C. Heywood (1987), pp. 104-23.
11 Romer Wilson, *The Life and Private History of Emily Jane Brontë* (1928), pp. 155, 261, 243.
12 For the origin of the phrase, see Arnold Van Gennep, *The Rite of Passage* (1960), throughout.
13 For the ideas, see Margaret Maison, 'Emily Brontë and Epictetus', *N&Q*, 223 (1978), 230-31.
14 Arnold Kettle, 'Emily Brontë: *Wuthering Heights* (1847)', in his *An Introduction to the English Novel*, 2 vols. (1951); see also Raymond Williams, *The English Novel from Dickens to Lawrence* (1970), pp. 64-5, and throughout.
15 Terry Eagleton, *Myths of Power. A Marxist Study of the Brontës* (1975), p. 97, and throughout.
16 Terry Eagleton, *Heathcliff and the Great Hunger. Studies in Irish Culture* (1995); see Appendix D below, 'Alice Brontë's interview'.
17 Andrea Dworkin, *Letters from a War Zone* (1988), pp. 68-86.
18 Maja-Lisa von Sneidern, '*Wuthering Heights* and the Liverpool Slave Trade', *ELH* 62 (1995),171-96 (pp. 195-96).
19 Emily Brontë, 'Gondal Poems', BL. Add. MS. 43, 483.
20 Fanny Elizabeth Ratchford, *The Brontës' Web of Childhood* (New York, 1941); and *Gondal's Queen. A Novel in Verse by Emily Jane Brontë*, arranged, with an Introduction and Notes, by Fannie E. Ratchford

(Austin, 1955).

Mary Visick, *The Genesis of Wuthering Heights*, 3rd edn. (1980); see also, Derek Roper and Edward Chitham, *The Poems of Emily Brontë* (1995), pp. 9–11.

Catalogue of the Bonnell Collection in the Brontë Parsonage Museum (1932), ed. C.W. Hatfield, p. 19, item 45.

See C. Heywood, 'Africa and Slavery in the Brontë Children's Novels', *Hitotsubashi Journal of Arts and Sciences*, 30 (1989), 75–87; also: Christine Alexander, 'Imagining Africa: The Brontës' Creations of Glass Town and Angria', in *Africa Today*, edited by Peter F. Alexander, Ruth Hutchinson, and Deryck Schreuder (Canberra: 1996), pp. 201–19; and Mordechai Abir, *Ethiopia: the Era of the Princes* (1968), pp. 112–13, 148–49, and throughout.

See T. Winnifrith, *The Brontës. Facts and Problems* (1973), ch. 6, 'The Brontës and their Books', pp. 84–109.

See F.B. Pinion, 'Scott and *Wuthering Heights*', *BST* 21 (1996), pp. 313–22; Q.D. Leavis, 'A Fresh Look at *Wuthering Heights*', in F.R. Leavis and Q.D. Leavis, *Essays in America* (1969).

See Mary Shelley, *Frankenstein*, ed. Marilyn Butler (1993); also, Chris Baldick, *In Frankenstein's Shadow* (1996), p. 43.

See above, p. 284, note 1.

Charlotte and Emily Brontë, *Belgian Essays*, ed. Sue Lonoff (1997), pp. 56–59.

'Fair Annie', in H. Weber and R. Jamieson, *Illustrations of Northern Antiquities from the Teutonic and Scandinavian Romancies* (1814).

See W. Greenwood, *The Redmans of Levens and Harewood* (1905), pp. 157–85 and throughout.

See R. Balderston Cragg, *Legendary Rambles. Ingleton and Lonsdale* (Bingley, undated; around 1900); also, C. Heywood, '"The Helks Lady" and other Legends Surrounding *Wuthering Heights*', *Lore and Language* 11 (1992–93), 127–42.

T.D. Whitaker, *Deanery of Craven* (1805), p. 383.

Mary Howitt, *Hope On, Hope Ever!* (1840); reprint, ed. David Boulton (Sedbergh: Hollett, 1989).

Hope On, Hope Ever! (reprint), pp. 109–10.

U.C. Knoepflmacher, *Emily Brontë. Wuthering Heights* (1989), p. 28.

Mme Le Prince de Beaumont, *Le magasin des enfans, ou Dialogues d'une sage gouvernante avec ses élèves*, 4 vols. (Paris, 1823), vol. 1, pp. 80–125.

J. Wolfgang von Goethe, *Faust. A Tragedy*, trs. J. Birch (1839), p. 190.

Sarah Austin, *Characteristics of Goethe*, 3 vols (1833), vol. 3, p. 235; reviewed in *Leeds Mercury*, 10 Aug. 1834, p. 4.

J.W. Smeed, *Faust in Literature* (1975), p. 133; see also E.M. Butler, *The Fortunes of Faust* (1979), throughout; also, C.H. Herford, *Goethe* (1913); Eugene Oswald, 'Goethe in England and America', *Publications of the English Goethe Society*, 11 (1909); and M. Montgomery,

'The First English Versions of Faust' and 'Dichtung und Warhheit', ibid. (1926).

40 Further works in German are noted as possible literary models in John Hewish, *Emily Brontë. A Critical and Biographical Study* (1969), and in the introduction by Mary Ward (Mrs Humphry Ward) to *WH* (1900) (McNees, pp. 41-56).

41 For another version of Donne's image, see Robert Browning, 'Childe Roland to the Dark Tower Came', stanza 5; see also Joesph E. Duncan, *The Revival of Metaphysical Poetry* (1959), p. 57, and throughout.

42 From Abraham Cowley, *Poems*, ed. A.R.Waller (1905), p. 214, cited by Joesph E. Duncan in *The Revival of Metaphysical Poetry* (1959), p. 11.

43 J.W. Croker, 'French Novels', *Quarterly Review*, 56 (1836), 65-131.

44 George Sand, *Indiana*, trs. Sylvia Raphael, with Introduction by Naomi Schor (1994), p. 259. For another possible link, see Patricia Thomson, *George Sand and the Victorians* (1977), ch. 5, '*Wuthering Heights* and *Mauprat*', pp. 80-89.

45 Charlotte's disclaimer against plagiarism in the case of Bremer's *The Neighbours* (1842), noted by Elizabeth Gaskell in her *Life of Charlotte Brontë* (1985, pp. 509, 622) spices a literary relationship which reached beyond plagiarism, evidently traversing several of the remaining ten translations. See also, Carol Hanbery MacKay, 'Lines of Confluence in Fredrika Bremer and Charlotte Bronte', *NORA: Nordic Journal of Women's Studies* 2.2 (1994), 119-29.

46 Scandinavian settlement and naming in the region of Braeda Garth, Kingsdale and Dent is noted in Bertil Hedevind, *The Dialect of Dent-dale* (Uppsala, 1967).

47 Mary Margaret Bush, 'Scandinavian Mythology', *Blackwood's Magazine*, 38 (1835), 25-36.

48 Perpetual Calendar, in Emily Brontë's copy of the *Book of Common Prayer* (BPM)

49 See Kathleen Tillotson, *Novels of the 1840s* (1954).

50 See C. Heywood, 'Yorkshire Slavery in *Wuthering Heights*', *RES* 38 (1987), 184-97.

51 See Patsy Stoneman, *Brontë Transformations*, (London: Prentice Hall, 1996) pp. 236-38.

Appendix C: Family Histories

Forming the story

Proof of Brontë's ability to master the speech habits of her own region appeared in another pioneering study, *Wuthering Heights and the Haworth Dialect* (1970), by K.M. Petyt. In relation to the transcription of Haworth English in *WH*, he noted: 'it is hard to imagine that Emily did not realise what she was doing'. The value of his passing remark is the inverse of its brevity. His exhaustive study defined Brontë's mastery of Haworth spoken English. The pattern reappears in her mastery of the family histories behind Charlotte's reference to 'their language, their ways, their family histories'. The family histories which Charlotte evidently had in mind came from three Dales regions: from Skipton and upper Wharfedale, the long history of the Cliffords; from lower Lunesdale, Tudor and modern fragments about the Stanleys, Haringtons, Marsdens and Wrights of Wennington, Tatham and Hornby; and from upper Lunesdale, the interwoven Sills, Suttons and Masons of Dent and Thornton in Lonsdale. Family histories from nearer home at Haworth and Halifax, notably the Heatons of Ponden and the Walkers and Jack Sharp of Halifax, though differing from the story in the novel, evidently contributed to Emily's expertise in infiltrating family histories from the Dales around Skipton and Cowan Bridge.

Brontë's starting point in devising her two-part story can only be surmised. It would not wrench any surviving document to suggest that she constructed her story by working outwards from a central knot surrounding the death and burial of the younger Catherine's father, her opposition to Heathcliff, and her relationships with her two cousins. That set of chapters takes place at the harvest moon of 1801, shortly before Lockwood's first visit. These chapters, the last in the series before Lockwood's departure from the Grange, contain the heart of the story: the rise to maturity through a first forced marriage of the younger Catherine, Heathcliff's confession of consolation at the graveside of her mother, and the imminent transformation of Hareton the Beast into the yeoman Prince. They also contain the strongest traces of Brontë's probable attachment to the poetry of Donne, Goethe's play, and the novels of 'George Sand' (Aurore Dupin) and Frederika Bremer. The steps leading to Heathcliff's position in the family, the marriage prohibition, and the steps leading to its resolution, lead up to that crisis. These steps can be worked backwards from there across the two bridges which mark the death and birth of the two Catherines (chs. 16-18) at the middle of the book, and the flight and return of Heathcliff (chs. 9-10) at the middle of the first half. Like a geometrical theorem or exercise in musical composition, these outlines of *WH* can be assumed to have been in Emily's mind before she set pen to paper. Parts of the writing, especially at the first and second bridges, appear to have run away with her pen, taking more pages to work through than she anticipated. These were necessary parts of her effort to leave no loose ends untied. Certainly the concluding sequence (chs. 26-34) could not have been improvised as a solution to problems raised in the first nine or seventeen chapters of the novel. The reverse seems to have happened: the first half of the novel functions, rather, as a prologue to that ending.

The journey to school at Cowan Bridge took the Brontës along middle and upper Airedale, across Ribblesdale to the foothills of upper Lunesdale, along the westwards-facing rock formation known as the Craven Fault. Wharfedale, which faces east, was the site of her day tour in 1833. These Dales are the partly hidden landscape in the view of the Craven highlands from Withins Height, the model for the title of *WH*. The relationship between Hareton and the younger Catherine grew, it appears, out of her interest in a celebrated Yorkshire family, the Cliffords of Airedale and Wharfedale. With persistent alterations, but the yet with the main points of emphasis intact, the two groups of chapters in the first half of her story are patterned on the Lunesdale family histories associated with Hornby and Dent, both near Cowan Bridge.

The Cliffords of Skipton

Brontë created the younger Catherine as a child of heather-clad moors which exactly match her own at Haworth. Despite the accurate delineation of the limestone landscape, the moorland remains the moral, aesthetic and natural centre of gravity in *Wuthering Heights*. Except in the colour of the hair, the appearance of the younger Catherine in maturity, 'donned in black, and her yellow curls combed back behind her ears, as plain as a quaker, she couldn't comb them out' (ch. 30), matches the appearance of Anne Clifford in the picture titled 'Anne Clifford' (Plate 7) which illustrates the essay (pp. 241-92) in Hartley Coleridge's book *Worthies of Yorkshire and Lancashire* (1836) (*K*).[1] Emily Brontë's lifelong adherence to *gigot* sleeves evidently owed something to what appears to have been an enthusiasm for that picture.

The background of the Great Picture at Appleby Castle, a triptych portraying the Clifford family and commissioned by Lady Anne, shows Lady Anne Clifford as a young lady to the left, and as a mature lady in a festive version of a dress of Puritan or Quaker style, with her ropes of pearls, to the right.[2] The engraving in the edition of Whitaker's *Deanery of Craven* in the 1812 does little to improve the poor engraving of that picture in the 1805 edition, from a weak version of the painting at Skipton Castle. Though the Brontës cannot have had access to either of the original paintings, Emily Brontë appears to have inquired about them. Behind the figures in the picture are family portraits, a portrait of the poet Samuel Daniel, who had been Lady Anne's tutor, various coats of arms, and shelves decked with Lady Anne's books. The legible titles include poetry by Donne and Herbert, and philosophical works by Boethius and Epictetus.[3] Lady Anne's stock of books, it appears, resembled that of the Heatons of Ponden House. Given the extent of Brontë's knowledge about the Dales, and her apparent admiration for this lady, no surprise need arise over the possibility of her having acquired information about her own literary and philosophical kinship with this patron of the arts in Yorkshire. Information about the titles of the books could have come to her through Theodore Dury, the Sidgwicks of Skipton, and the Birkbecks of Settle. Hartley Coleridge observed in his essay on Anne Clifford (p. 288) that '[s]he was a patroness of poets and a lover of poetry', and cited from the funeral oration by the Bishop of Carlisle, who recounted 'that a prime and elegant wit, well seen in all human learning (Dr. Donne) is reported to have said of her, that she knew well how to discourse of all things, from predestination down to slea-silk' (p. 291). In the second half of *WH*, it appears, Emily Brontë modelled the younger Catherine on her moorland childhood and her later work as her father's housekeeper, merged into the life story of Lady Anne Clifford, whose work lay in rebuilding her father's ruined estate.

Lady Anne's powers appear in a dedication of a literary work by Anthony Stafford to Lady Anne, probably suppressed, and of extreme rarity but circulating somehow, and a cause of her displeasure, which opens with his confession of 'actually admiring a woman' and concludes: 'I am afraide that (ere long) you will disable my sex, falsifie the Scriptures, and make Woman the stronger vessel'.[4] A less back-handed admiration pervades Hartley Coleridge's essay, who echoes Whitaker's unreserved admiration for Lady Anne: 'She was one of the most illustrious women of her own or of any age [...] She had all the courage and liberality of the other sex, united to all the devotion, order, and economy (perhaps not all the softness) of her own'.[5] Apart from the march of economic events, the ruin of the Clifford estates in the first half of the seventeenth century had three main causes: the extravagances and infidelities of George Clifford, third Earl of Cumberland and father of Lady Anne; the long dispute over Lady Anne's title to the estate after the deaths of her two brothers, settled only after the deaths of two male cousins, whose rival claims were felt to have been stronger; and the civil war in England. For several decades following the death in 1605 of George Clifford, his widow, Margaret, Countess of Cumberland (Lady Margaret Clifford, *née* Russell) fought a legal battle 'against the male line of the family',[6] and against the legal system which favoured male succession.

On gaining the titles, Lady Anne organised the rebuilding of her family's ruined manors in the third quarter of the seventeenth century. *WH* lends support to victims of Valois ('Salic') law, the source of discrimination against female inheritance. In an abbreviated echo from that problem in the Clifford estate, *WH* culminates in a series of male deaths. The early death of Heathcliff's son ensures that his widow will inherit her mother's estate at her father's, husband's, and husband's father's deaths. In a seemingly farcical race to the grave, the men die in that order. This puzzle behind appearances, which is halfway to a resolution, bewilders Lockwood on his first visit to the farmhouse. Nelly Dean's story explains it. The reader finds gradually that the seemingly servile Mrs Heathcliff, who is denied authority to offer the visitor a cup of tea, is a domestic version of Lady Anne Clifford. In the frozen northern hell which greets him, Lockwood is gripped instead by hounds and the fairy mythology, but at the end it has become the elysian haunt of the non-military class.

George Clifford's extravagances and money losses included his pioneering patronage of the English slave trade. In his history of the family, T.D. Whitaker cites from the log book of a captain on a voyage sponsored by George Clifford, second Earl of Cumberland. The captain's notes include the following:

> Nov. 5, our men went on shor and fet rys abord, and burnt the rest of the housys in the negers towne; and our bot went doune to the outermoste pointe of the river, and burnt a toune, and brout away all the rys that was in the toune.[7]

The passage reappears in Hartley Coleridge's essay (p. 264). The treatment in *WH* of the Dales as a site for liberation from enslavement has one of its roots there. The two cousins who stood between Lady Anne and her inheritance, and the two marriages which took her to Kent first, and then Wiltshire, are melted down in the novel to the marriages of the elder and younger Catherine, and the younger Catherine's inheritance of the estate through marriage to two cousins. In the novel, Nelly Dean insists that the children sleep together in innocence: 'no parson in the world ever pictured Heaven so beautifully as they did, in their innocent talk' (ch. 5). Perhaps an irony is intended: it seems a little too good to be true. However, it metamorphoses the state of society which Hartley Coleridge resisted in his essay, which relates how the bygone feudal estate owners caused their children to marry in infancy in order to secure the property. On the marriage of Lady Anne Clifford's father to Lady Margaret Russell in their childhood, he observed: 'The poor children, when they attained puberty, were obliged to stand by the impious and unnatural bargain' (p. 256). Expanding the point, he cites the marriage of Elizabeth Clifford to Robert Plumpton in early Tudor times at the age of six, 'and the said Sir William [Plumpton, father of Robert] promised the said Lord Clifford that they should not ligg togedder till she came to the age of sixteen yeres' (p. 256). That situation is parodied twice in *WH*, amiably in the relationship of Heathcliff and the elder Catherine, and harshly in the marriage of Linton Heathcliff and the younger Catherine.

Another Clifford story, the early Tudor tale of the Shepherd Lord, appears to have provided suggestions for the character of Hareton. 'Who has not heard of the *good* Lord Clifford, the *Shepherd Lord*?', Hartley Coleridge asked (p. 249). The strained relations between Henry, 10th Lord Clifford, nicknamed the Shepherd, and his reprobate son Harry, 1st Earl of Cumberland and great-grandfather of Lady Anne,[8] form the subject of *The Outlaw* (1839), by Robert Story, the poet of Gargrave and principal in Branwell's Bradford literary circle. The Shepherd Lord gained his nickname through a Shakespearean childhood, when he was smuggled out and brought up among shepherds at the time of the ascendancy of the house of York, which appropriated his father's estates. On being restored he learned to read as an adult beginner, but he remained reclusive and attached to poetry, magic and mathematics. Robert Story's verse drama about his forgiveness towards his son was serialised in the *Halifax Guardian* in 1835. It appears to have contributed to Brontë's grasp of the Cliffords' family history, and to have inspired her use of it for the central argument in her story.

The Cliffords' vast estates and contribution to the rise of English power are screened off behind Charlotte's equivocating reference in the Preface to 'the secret annals of every rude vicinage'. On the contrary, the Cliffords have unmatched prominence in the annals of the old West Riding, and no one is 'compelled to listen to' (in Charlotte's phrase), their history; it stares the Dales traveller in the face. In Robert Story's play, the Tudor outlaw Harry Clifford meets Margaret Percy in the wild Dales landscape around Malham and Gordale Scar. They shelter in Janet's Cave nearby, named the Fairy Cave in the play. Margaret Percy is accompanied by Fenwick, a rival to Harry Clifford for her affection, and by Roddam, who yearns for his lost childhood love, Cathleen. Simplified by a consummate feat of literary recasting, many features in *The Outlaw* reappear in *WH*, persistently warmed by the author's humour and sympathy, and by her ironic distance from ancient horrors. The rivalry between the rough Harry Clifford and the courtly Fenwick reappears in the rivalry between Heathcliff and Edgar Linton, and in the tussle in the younger Catherine's mind between her smooth cousin Linton and her hairy cousin Hareton. The female protagonist's choice in Robert Story's play is twice reversed in *WH*, but followed at the third attempt: the elder Catherine chooses the smooth Edgar Linton; next, the younger Catherine favours the smooth Linton, but at the last trial she follows Margaret Percy's example by choosing the rough but golden Hareton. In *WH*, Robert Story's romantic theme about Roddam's love for Cathleen, his boyhood sweetheart, reappears in Heathcliff's thwarted love for the elder Catherine. Robert Story's tale of Fanny Ashton, who is killed when she takes a stab which had been aimed at her father, reappears in softened form in the brawl at the farmhouse, where Isabella is gashed when she tries to separate the contestants.

Brontë recast Story's four love stories into the set of five marriages leading to the resolution of the marriage prohibition and the usurpation of the estates. She retained many of his themes, settings, and symbols. Her story shares his invocations of hell and wickedness, the benign effects of the Fairy Cave, the restoration of order in a divided estate through female intervention, and Roddam's cry, 'O Cathleen!' and 'Oh! —CATH' during a scrimmage in a storm (p. 121), when he imagines he has been killed. For the character of Hareton Earnshaw, Brontë appears to have drawn on the outlaw Harry and his forgiving father, the Shepherd Lord. He follows the depredations of the outlaw Harry by throwing a stone at Nelly Dean, and cursing (ch. 11). Like Harry, he begins his moorland courtship in the Fairy Cave (ch. 18). He resembles the Shepherd Lord when he learns to read late in life, and forgives his persecutors. He forgives Heathcliff, and weeps at his death: he expiates and replaces his grandfather's mistaken charity with the boundless affection of the heart, for which his name is an anagram. Like Harry, who marries into the vast Percy estate in Northumberland, Hareton will inherit the Earnshaw estate as well as the Lintons' through his marriage to Catherine Heathcliff. All this points to *WH* having been rooted at its first conception in the tale of the younger Catherine's redemption of a society blighted by its violent past, modelled on high points in the vast history of the Cliffords in Yorkshire.

The Masons, Sills, and Suttons of Dent

Writing independently and without naming the Brontës, in her article 'Whernside Manor' (1979), Kim Lyon identified beyond reasonable doubt the historical figures who provided the Dales story material in the first part of *WH*.[9] Her article opened the door for a retrieval of the Yorkshire topography, legend and history which lay concealed behind the Preface. By identifying the extensive links between the Sills of Dent, their Caribbean estates, and the practice of plantation slavery in Yorkshire, Kim Lyon pioneered the insights which were found later, through independent reading of the text, by Andrea Dworkin and Maja-Lisa von Sneidern (see above, Appendix B). Evidently yielding to intervention, Kim Lyon veiled her account in her article by omitting the Brontë names; this working procedure, a residue of the extraordinary reticence created in England by the black presence, combined with a general reluctance to associate it with Adam Sedgwick of Dent, was clarified in her later publication.[10] This was followed by my article,[11] which sought to expand and consolidate the argument which had been inaugurated by Kim Lyon.

Unknown to all these writers, the Dent story material and its Caribbean links had been transparently unravelled and lightly veiled in *Wooers and Winners* (1880), a novel by Isabella Banks. The veil which Charlotte cast over Emily's novel, and maintained in her contacts with Elizabeth Gaskell, was not easily shed. Taken together, the writers on slavery and the Dales have entered and elucidated the substance of *WH*. The first act or Part of the four-part story took its outlines from the story of the Sills of Dent. It serves as a prologue to the second part, the usurpation on Heathcliff's return. These first two parts of the story lead to the second half of the novel, which was modelled, as we have seen, on the Clifford family history and its literary heritage. The story of Dent appeared in the wake of a visit made by the Howitts in 1837. In that year the history of the Sill estate in Jamaica and Dent was still circulating. William Howitt termed it, 'a most extraordinary story', adding: 'we found one of these quiet dales ringing with it from end to end, and this was the account given by most trustworthy people, who knew the parties well, and one of them was the lady's confidential servant'.[12] It turns out that Howitt consulted a retired and undoubtedly embittered housekeeper, probably Ann Mason, one of the family whom the Sills had bought out with their purchase of West House in Dent, in 1792. As a result he found a garbled, fragmentary and one-sided account of the Sill estate, with no mention of its inheritance and later history, and no reference to the yeoman Sills' rapid rise to a semblance of 'statesman' (estate owning) standing through purchase of the Mason property. A heavily sweetened version of the story of Richard Sutton appeared in his the novel by his wife, Mary Howitt, *Hope On, Hope Ever!*.

Like Isabella Banks, Brontë evidently drew on confidential sources for information which was withheld from the Howitts. In patterning her novel on *Hope On, Hope Ever!*, she pointed to the historical and topographical source material she had mastered. In his account, which veils the participants in anonymity, William Howitt exaggerated the number and reliability of his informants, took at face value their defamatory remarks about the executors of Ann Sill's will, missed its main provisions, doubled the cash value of the Sill estate, and missed the relationship between the Sills and the Masons, whose old farmhouse, West House, stood at the foot of Deepdale in the vale of Dent. If the Howitts had made their visit a few years earlier, and if one had been offered, they would have gained a more reliable account from Nelly Middleton. Until her death in 1830,[13] this lady was an impoverished cousin and lifelong domestic companion of Ann Sill of Dent. *WH* emerges as a blend of Emily's thinking about slaveholding society in the Dales, and details in the story which Nelly Middleton would have told. Notable instances of Brontë's fidelity to Dales social history include the Liverpool link which led to the wealth and extinction of the Sills, her handling of the drift towards mortgaging in the rural economy, the alleged brutality of the adoptive brother towards the orphan in their midst, and the rivalry of the old 'statesman' Masons and the yeoman farming Sills of Dent. Among numerous suggestions that she had penetrated the family secrets of Dent, she appears to have included in her portrayal of Heathcliff (ch. 7) a family trait found among the male Suttons, their bushy dark hair and dark, joined eyebrows.[14]

The story of Dent can be reconstructed in outline through the records, from the parts of Howitt's story which have a ring of truth, and from oral testimony collected in Dent by Kim Lyon. At the death in 1796 of Richard Sutton the elder, a migrant from Thornton in Lonsdale, some eight miles off at the southern foot of Whernside, his son, the younger Richard Sutton, was taken into the family by the Sills of Dent at the age of thirteen. He was, it appears, bullied by her three brothers, Edmund, James, and John Sill, and sheltered by the daughter of the house, Ann Sill (1766-1835). The abrupt rise and fall of the Sill estate in Jamaica and Dent was precipitated by the brothers' early deaths, the last dying in 1803.[15] Veiled, recast in the form of a bargain on the lines of Beauty and the Beast, moved over the hill from its setting in Dent to the landscape which the Brontës had seen, and allegorised to replace the boy from across the hill with a black orphan from Liverpool, the outlines of this story reappear in the first six chapters of Nelly Dean's narrative. Links with Liverpool are ingrained in her landscape, since Thornton in Lonsdale stood then as now at the junction of two roads, one from Liverpool to Dent, the other from Kendal to London. The date of birth of Ann Sill, who was baptised in St Andrew's Church, Dent, on 24 March 1766,[16] is divided in *WH* between the date of birth of the elder Catherine Earnshaw in that year, according to the 1799 chronology (Appendix A above), and the birth of her namesake daughter at the spring equinox eighteen years later. Both chronologies in *WH* converge on the year 1803 as the year of the younger Catherine's forthcoming second marriage.

These dates would be readily found among the West Riding clergy and sponsors of the K&K and the Mechanics' Institutes. With substantial cash at the bank and eleven farms mortgaged to their estate, the Sills were sturdy users of the K&K. Ann Sill might have been expected to contribute to the funding of the Clergy Daughters' School, since two generations of the Carus family had stood as bondsmen at the purchase and mortgaging of seven out of the eleven farms in their estate.[17] The arrival in the Dales of Martin Pickersgill under the care of his guardian at the age of thirteen, in the novel *Wooers and Winners* (1880) by Isabella Banks, who evidently recognised Brontë's use of Dent story material in *WH*, confirms the close watch which the Mechanics' Institute circle maintained over the Sills and the Suttons: three months after the death of his father, the orphan Richard Sutton turned fourteen. In her novel, too, Banks re-used the story material of *Hope On, Hope Ever!*, thereby pointing conclusively to her mastery of Brontë's literary model as well as her use of story material from Dent.

Ann Sill, the unmarried daughter of the house, appears in William Howitt's account as 'a very wealthy widow lady, who seemed to have been of weak intellect'. This hardly matches the known story of her unmarried life. The wealth of the Sills appears in her will, drafted in 1807 and passed through probate in 1835, which left £40,000 in cash and assets, including thirteen properties in Dent and two estates in Jamaica. The Executors were James Davis, a Sedbergh lawyer who died in 1837 and who handled the affairs of over seventy estates with every sign of thoroughness, and Adam Sedgwick (1785-1873), a native of Dent who later became Professor of Geology at Cambridge. These men appear in a hostile light in Howitt's account: 'this lawyer twenty years ago made her will, in which he had appointed himself one of the executors, and a gentleman of high character, living at a great distance, the other'. Together with Richard Sutton, who had been taken into the Sill family when Ann Sill was thirty, the executors were ten per cent legatees. Ann Sill bequeathed Rigg End, the Sills' family farm on the shoulder of the hill above West House, to Richard Sutton, who rented out West House for a while after purchasing it in 1836. Substantial sugar revenues from Jamaica in the early 1790s had enabled the Sills to buy out their neighbours, the Masons, in 1792, and to build West House, their ungainly house of manorial type, over one of the Masons' old farmhouses. The revenues came from Providence, the sugar plantation near Montego Bay, founded around 1765 by John Sill, the uncle of Ann Sill and her three brothers. The inheritance was held in trust for the niece and nephews during their minority by their uncle William Sill, who appears in Yorkshire records as an exciseman at Rochester in Kent.[18]

As with the story material from the Cliffords, the Sill family's links with slaveholding appears to have attracted Brontë's notice. It appeared publicly in *Williamson's Liverpool Advertiser*, where the Sills published a runaway slave notice on 8 September 1758:

> Run away from Dent, Yorkshire, on Monday 28 last, Thomas Anson, a negro man, about 5 ft 6 ins high, aged 20 years and upwards, and broad set. Whoever will bring the said man back to Dent, or give any information that he may be had again shall receive a handsome reward from Edmund Sill of Dent, or Mr. David Kenyon, of Liverpool.

The advertisement is remembered to the present. The Caribbean link, and the presence of an orphan in the family, reappeared in *Wooers and Winners*, by Isabella Banks. This Manchester novelist was strategically placed to supplement Charlotte and Elizabeth Gaskell. A skilled writer on the history of the northern region, with supplementary information found through her marriage to George Linnaeus Banks, Secretary of the North-West Sub-Union of Mechanics' Institutes, Isabella Banks, who wrote under the name Mrs G. Linnaeus Banks, had roots in the Dales: 'my father's family came from Craven', she wrote in a letter to William Andrews, her correspondent in Hull.[19] Her recasting of *WH* foreshadows her re-use in *Bond Slaves* (1893), a novel about the Luddite rising of 1811-12, of the historical material in Charlotte Brontë's *Shirley* (1849). In another letter to William Andrews she observed about this novel: 'Mr Horsley was a Mr Horsfall of Marsden. Wainwright was Cartwright of Rawfolds. Wm. Hartland, was a Wm. Hartley, tailor of Warley. I think those are the only Yorkshire names I have disguised'.[20]

Mary Howitt's themes reappear in *Wooers and Winners*, where they are combined with numerous touches from *WH* and an exposition *à clef*, under a thin disguise, of the historical originals in the first part of *WH*. Isabella Banks tells the story of Martin Pickersgill, a dark-skinned orphan from Jamaica who is fostered at the age of thirteen by Archibald Thorpe, the guardian of the Earnshaw orphans, Edith and Allan. The Earnshaws live at Settle, in Ribblesdale, the Dale adjacent to Lunesdale, among the southern foothills of Ingleborough and Penyghent. After a long estrangement, which includes Edith Earnshaw's engagement to Jasper Ellis, who turns out to be an unprincipled villain, Martin is able to marry his childhood sweetheart. He achieves reconciliation with Allan, her brother, who had befriended Jasper Ellis. Archibald Thorpe encourages Martin in his geological studies and in the development of a mining interest which he inherits in the south Yorkshire coalfield near Barnsley. When he is killed in a rock fall, his body is guarded by his faithful dog named Keeper. The exposure of Jasper Ellis as a cheat resulted from his failed attempt to defraud his employer, the lawyer named Proctor who drafted the will (vol. 3, p. 117).

In this novel, Banks wrote a thinly veiled fictional guide to the literary and historical sources from lower and upper Lunesdale which Brontë used in the first half of her novel. The name of the geologist Archibald Thorpe is taken from the geologists Archibald Geikie and William Thorp, followers of Adam Sedgwick (1785-1873), Professor of Geology at Cambridge University, and a son of Richard Sedgwick, Perpetual Curate of St Andrew's Church, Dent.[21] Beyond these thinly veiled references, the novel is thronged with Yorkshire personalities who appear under their own names, for example, the Birkbecks, George Hudson, railway entrepreneur of York, Robert Story, poet of Gargrave, and others. Banks linked her story to *WH* through the names Earnshaw, Jasper, Ellis, and Keeper, named after Brontë's characters, her pheasant named Jasper, her pen name Ellis, and Keeper, her dog. These names signal her knowledge that Brontë founded *WH* on a mastery of Dales family histories. Brontë appears to have founded her story of Catherine and Heathcliff along lines drawn partly from Mary Howitt's novel and partly from the historical relationship between Ann Sill and Richard Sutton, who appears in Howitt's story as 'a man brought in the house of the lady'. Hints of the tension between Heathcliff and Catherine appear in Howitt's account: 'the man had for years lost the good opinion of the lady, by his misconduct, and had not been permitted to come into her presence for two years'. Brontë introduced the tragic theme in her story by developing that hint. Her adaptation of Howitt's narrative appears in her departure from his account of Richard Sutton's early life among the Sills: 'This man, who first came into the lady's house as a shoe-black, or some such thing, and had on one occasion for his misconduct, the alternative offered him either to quit her service, or be carried up to the top of the neighbouring fell, on the back of one man and down again, while he was flogged by another, and was of so base a nature that he had chosen the flagellation, and continuance in a family where he was regarded with contempt'. Brontë's hints about the rumoured wealth of Heathcliff and his renting of the manor house, while living on the farm on the hill, reflect her insight into Dent realities which Howitt did not discover. At the time of the Howitts' visit, Richard Sutton was living in the farmhouse above West House, the latter being rented out at the time.

Further details in Howitt's story relate to unfounded allegations of 'cruelty and wickedness' in the conduct of James Davis, Ann Sill's lawyer in Sedbergh, and of irresponsibility on the part of his co-executor, who remains similarly anonymous. This was Adam Sedgwick.[22] These accusations rebound on Howitt's source, probably a person who had entertained hopes of a legacy. As executor to the will of Ann Sill of Dent, Adam Sedgwick knew the histories of the families concerned. The will bequeathed West House, the Sills' newly built house of manorial type at the foot of Deepdale, to her cousin Ann Sill of Rochester in Kent. The property had been bought from the Mason family, the long established 'statesmen' (estate owners) of Dent, whose declining fortunes had led to their being mortgaged to Miss Crump. The absence of Ann Sill of Rochester, probably deceased at the time of her cousin's death, caused West House to be put on the market. It was purchased at a valuation by Richard Sutton out of the ten per cent legacy of £4,000 bequeathed him in Ann Sill's will, plus a mortgage of £3,500. Richard Sutton's relative poverty at his death appears in the £1,500 cash assets in his will, to be shared among his children and his wife, Nelly Constantine.[23] A sidesman or elder of Dent parish church, in the 1851 census Richard Sutton appears as a 'landowner' living at West House. By the 1840s, the Sills' bid for manorial status in the Dales, and all their wealth from sugar and slaveholding, had disappeared. A motive for correcting and dramatising William Howitt's account appears indirectly in his book *A Popular History of Priestcraft in all Ages and Nations* (1833), which imputed the ills of the world to ecclesiastical authority. This widely known view would have prompted a counter-attack from Patrick's Evangelical circle. His daughter's contribution to the conflict appears to be her novel based on dates and information available to the West Riding Evangelical clergy.

Stanley, Marsden, and Wright of Hornby

The change of mood in the chapters following the return of Heathcliff from abroad reflects Brontë's use of another estate and family history as a source and model. A celebrated lawsuit, published verbatim as *Tatham v. Wright* (1834) and widely reported in various newspapers as the Great Will Cause, drew attention to the notorious attempted usurpation of the Marsden estate at Hornby in lower Lunesdale. As with her penetration of the Sill and Sutton family histories, Brontë appears to have mastered its intricacies, both those appearing in print and those which can only have been available to her through confidential sources. In addition, echoes from the Plantagenet past of Hornby appear in the legendary story of Edward Stanley, Lord Monteagle, which appears to have contributed to the formation of *WH*. As with the story of the Sills and Suttons of Dent, Brontë's use of Hornby story material in *WH* was exposed by Banks in *Wooers and Winners*.

The Hornby story related to the will of John Marsden of Hornby, whose death in 1826 precipitated the lawsuit *Tatham v. Wright*. The case lasted twelve years, running through eight trials which culminated in the Lord Chancellor's casting vote in the decision by the House of Lords. The final outcome was the repossession of Hornby Castle by Admiral Sandford Tatham, Marsden's cousin and intended heir, in 1838. The defeated usurper was George Wright, who had been brought into the Marsden family in childhood as a servant, followed by promotion to estate manager. Brontë appears to have taken up the challenge offered by George Wright's defence lawyer in *Tatham v. Wright*, who maintained that the implied conspiracy was too far-fetched to be credible: 'a more strange romance never emanated from the most fertile brain of any poet or novelist'.[24] Social reality and fiction are merged in *Wuthering Heights*, rather, along the lines given at a later date by James T. Hammick: 'In real life cases [...] the circumstances are sometimes as strange as any presented in fictitious narratives'.[25]

It was finally found that the will of John Marsden could not stand, and he had died intestate. Though it could not easily be proved at the Assizes, the will had been dictated to a mentally retarded man who was competently diagnosed as a victim of 'connate imbecility' by a medically qualified witness at the trial. The reconstruction of the case by Emmeline Garnett shows the extent of Brontë's penetration behind the scenes in this case.[26] The legatee, George Wright, the fraudulent estate manager, was ejected on generous terms, and the estate returned to Admiral Tatham, the plaintiff in the case and Marsden's next of kin. Wright's accomplice in the usurpation attempt was Sarah Cookson, the house-keeper and manager of her imbecile cousin. The liaison which led to the conspiracy between the housekeeper and the usurper, who was twenty-three years her junior, though generally known, could not be intro-duced at the trial without risk of libel. As at the Assizes trial and in Isabella Banks's novel, the affair between the housekeeper and the usurper is excised with ostentatious care in *WH*. Nelly Dean's inexplic-able unease on Heathcliff's return reflects, it appears, Emily's skilled excision of that element from her source story.

Emily signalled her penetration behind the scenes of *Tatham v. Wright* in more than one instance. These can be reconstructed from *John Marsden's Will* (1998), an illuminating study of the case by Emmeline Garnett, who has shown that George Wright's temporarily successful usurpation depended on a Bradford lawyer for the suppression in 1780 of the will of Henry Marsden, the elder brother who died young, and on a Lancaster lawyer for the fraudulent drafting of John Marsden's will shortly before his death in 1826.[27] Certainty about that event, which could not be introduced at the trial, depends on the deposition of Robert Humber, the confidential gardener at Hornby, another witness whose inside knowledge did not appear at the trial and who has been iden-tified by Emmeline Garnett in her study of the case. The role of Joseph in *WH* is exactly foreshadowed at Hornby in the position of Robert Humber, who kept the garden as an outside worker, yet slept in the house and knew all its secrets. Robert Humber recalled an occasion when he was sent into the house to call Wright for a discussion outside: 'he came out of Mrs Cookson's room, with his clothes upon his arm; I told him who wanted him, and I went away; he had his clothes over his arm; I saw nothing but his shirt that he had on'. Emmeline Garnett observes: 'the delicious scandal grew and spread and lost nothing in the telling—a servant lad of twenty-two and a widowed lady almost old enough to be his grandmother'.[28] Sarah Cookson, who was fifty-three at the start of the affair, was caught in a downward spiral: as an aunt of the Marsden brothers she stood no chance of inheriting the Marsden estate, but by securing it for Wright, and keeping her retarded nephew in cir-culation as a dummy for her partner's machinations, she earned a dubi-ous pension as a threadbare lady of the manor, and opened the way for its inheritance by Wright's children through marriage to a younger woman. By the time of her death, the relationship had collapsed in acrimony over his interest in the woman whom he eventually married and whom he used to visit on walks through the woods.[29]

Brontë's excision of the Hornby sex motive left the jealous and sub-versive actions of her fictional counterpart, Nelly Dean, unexplained. She incites Heathcliff to overthrow the owners of the farmhouse and the Grange when she remarks: 'you could knock him down in a twin-kling; don't you feel that you could?' (ch. 7). For no apparent reason, she resists the childhood romance between Heathcliff and Catherine (ch. 7), and wrecks Heathcliff's relationship with Catherine, first by concealing his presence, and next by falsifying the moment of his departure from behind the sofa (ch. 9). She never explains the marriage prohibition; turns violently against Heathcliff on his return, when she feels, inexplicably, that she is trapped in a false position in the household (ch. 10); and blocks the teenage love between the younger Catherine and her cousin. Deprivation of sex ensured her mature power as an impartial narrator, but at a price: she acts out the natural dilemmas of Sarah Cookson, but with the motives removed. Compared with her historical original, Nelly Dean is a mewing mother cat whose kittens have been drowned. Not unaccountably, her irrational actions have earned her a difficult reputation in the critical repertoire.[30] The shadows of sex at the farmhouse have been reconstructed in *Catherine, Her Book* (1985), by John Wheatcroft, but the reconstruction misses the historical mark and reappears transformed into a florid affair between Nelly and Hindley. This recaptures the atmosphere but misses the grand sweep of the historical story material behind *WH*.

Brontë signalled her penetration into the hidden parts of the Hornby case at one point only, by using the name Green for Heathcliff's corrupted lawyer. This could be done without over-strong risk of libel, since Thomas Greene of Gray's Inn, the uncorrupted lawyer who served the London branch of the Marsden estate for a time, was long since dead.[31] This part of the 'secret annals' of the Hornby case, as Charlotte termed them in her Preface, appeared not in 'every rude vicinage', as she maintained, but in a unique case from a major region of rural England, its outlines reported in most newspapers and brought finally to the House of Lords. Nor, indeed, can Emily Brontë be accused fairly of having brooded only on 'tragic traits' in the morbid manner claimed by Charlotte. Among various details tending to prove the mental incapacity of John Marsden, the published testimony includes tales of his being whipped by Wright in their indoor horseplay, his love of music, expressed through incompetent violin playing, his fondness for drinking and card games, his dread of geese and fondness for checked aprons. The mirth raised by these fragments of evidence, which proved nothing, caused the Judge at the Lancaster Assizes, Lord Gurney, to offer on more than one occasion to clear the court if the laughter did not cease. Some of these features reappear in *WH*, shorn of the comic aspect they presented in *Tatham v. Wright*, and shaded with the dark colouring which Emily borrowed from Wilberforce and other Emancipationists. Her acquaintance with the trial appears in the whip and the violin which were requested by the Earnshaw children in *WH* (ch. 4), and the gambling and drinking which bring Hindley to ruin and death (ch. 17).

Through securely aimed touches, Banks signalled that she had recognised Brontë's penetration into the hidden as well as the published parts of the Hornby lawsuit. Mr Proctor, the lawyer in *Wooers and Winners*, takes his name from the Revd Robert Procter, vicar of Hornby, one of three witnesses with inside knowledge who did not testify in *Tatham v. Wright* and whose attestations have been found by Emmeline Garnett in her study of the case.[32] Banks's reference to a will which is written 'in the last stage of imbecility' by James Vasey of Hornby, as a consequence of his being 'tyrannised over by a despotic and designing housekeeper' (vol. 3, p. 64), refers unambiguously to the central issue in that celebrated case. This was the secret history behind Isabella Banks' cryptic references to this notorious lawsuit.

Despite the dark picture of life at the farmhouse in *WH*, Brontë humanised Hornby history and legend. An allegedly satanic legend about Hornby does exist, but in *WH* this motif, too, adopts a humane form. A Tudor legend relates that Edward Stanley, Lord Monteagle of Hornby, married his neighbour, Anne Harington, whose family estate lay in the neighbouring parish of Tatham. All traditions maintain that he secured her estate for himself by murdering her brother, Sir John Harington. His liaison with a witch, one version maintains, led to the birth of their son, whom he later installed as vicar of Hornby. This legendary history was felt by T.D. Whitaker to be 'a combination of treachery and cruelty not often exceeded even in the stories of ancient tragedy'.[33] The purpose of the marriage prohibition in *WH* becomes apparent at this stage: it shelters Catherine Earnshaw from exploitation through marriage for her property. By the same token, it shields Hindley Earnshaw, who occupies a position similar to that of Sir John Harington, from any threat of assassination. Fundamentally, it directed her story and its numerous literary successors away from the domain of crime and into the modern novel's psychological domain of dreaming, sensation, mental experience, mythology, and conscience.

The marriage prohibition explains Heathcliff's fairytale-like impulse to lie next to Catherine in the grave, as they had done as children in the box bed. As children, until social and sexual jealousy drives them apart, they are innocent. Marriage is forbidden in their maturity, but in the grave their bodies will dissolve and merge, and their ghosts walk as they did in childhood. The Monteagle murder motif is temporarily reinstated, but only as a pattern of thought which arises when Nelly Dean suspects that Heathcliff murdered Hindley (ch. 17). Her suspicion is thwarted by the witnessed alibi which is supplied by the hostile Joseph. Against the grain, his humane honesty overrides his wish to destroy his new master (ch. 17).[34] The murder motive is similarly warded off by the relatively average affair of jealousy and the marriage prohibition. Heathcliff marries Isabella Linton to further his usurpation plot. However, any motive to murder Edgar Linton, her brother, to secure the Linton property on the Monteagle model, is doubly blocked by the entail of the estate in the female line, and by the prohibition against marrying Edgar's widow if he were removed. Shadows of the Monteagle murder pattern survive in the dangerous encounters between Heathcliff and Edgar Linton at the Grange (chs. 14, 15), but they come to nothing.

Haworth, Halifax, the Dales, and the Brontës

Silence greeted an inquiry made to Ellen Nussey by T. Wemyss Reid about the family histories referred to by Charlotte in the 1850 Preface. Reid asked: 'Do you know anything about the originals of the characters in *Wuthering Heights*? or were there any?'[35] No reply was forthcoming. Either Ellen Nussey concealed what she knew, or more probably, Charlotte had maintained silence towards her friend, over the fragments of social history which appeared in her sister's novel. The Preface was written under the same constraints which led Charlotte to deny her authorship of *Jane Eyre* in a letter to Ellen Nussey.[36] Only surmise can reconstruct the channels bringing a mass of Dales information from behind the scenes, and beyond the books and newspapers, to the Brontës' ears.

As in the rest of Yorkshire, a relatively thin population encourages the spread of information about neighbouring and distant families. Brontë appears to have known two stories from Haworth and Halifax, and to have borrowed vignettes from them. These tales from her neighbourhood undoubtedly sharpened her interest in family histories from the Dales she had seen: Lunesdale, Airedale, and Wharfedale. A tale from Haworth, about the seduction by the opportunist John Bakes of Elizabeth Heaton, of Ponden House, and her early death, has been suggested by Mary Butterfield as an element in *WH*. This probably stood as a part model for the story of Isabella, except that she flings herself at Heathcliff despite warnings against her fate. In addition, Mary Butterfield has convincingly proposed the interior and exterior of Ponden House, near Haworth, as models for the architectural and domestic details at the farmhouse in *WH*.[37] Similarly, architectural details at High Sunderland Hall, Halifax, now demolished, yield hints for the farmhouse exterior in *WH*.[38] Law Hill, in Halifax, where Emily Brontë worked as a teacher, yields the story of Jack Sharpe, an adopted but more exactly, a fostered orphan, it appears, in the Walker family's woollen manufacturing business in Halifax. Though it lacks the links with Liverpool slavery and manorial society in *WH*, this story, first collected by Winifred Gérin, probably drew Emily's attention to the theme of usurpation in West Riding society. The further suggestion has been made by Winifred Gérin, that Jack Sharpe's degradation of a young boy, Sam Stead, stood as a model for Heathcliff's degradation of Hareton Earnshaw.[39] These vignettes supplement the main outlines of Brontë story material from the Yorkshire Dales.

As with the landscape, the family histories appear along the K&K, the Brontës' route to school. Probably the principal providers of inside information about Dent were the Birkbecks of Settle, among whom John Birkbeck of Anley in Settle stood as Executor to the Will of Adam Sedgwick.⁴⁰ Through this channel, the inside information which reached Isabella Banks and, it appears, the Brontës, would have found a short chain of reliable raconteurs. The Brontës' links with the Dales began with the Durys, and beyond these, the Greenwoods, the Birkbecks, and the Sedgwicks and the Sidgwicks of Dent and Lothersdale. The Birkbecks' link with Dent appears among the Trustees of the K&K, to whom they stood as bankers. The list included Theodore Dury and the Revd John Sedgwick, Adam Sedgwick's brother and Perpetual Curate of Dent. Another Trustee was the Revd Anthony Lister, Vicar of Gargrave and a cousin of John Marsden of Hornby, another prominent figure who stood near the centre of Brontë's labyrinthine story material from the Dales.⁴¹ Though seemingly inaccessible, any reasonable inquiry within Evangelical circles would readily supply the details she collected.

Discretion was called for when Charlotte wrote her Preface was written within this influential network. Richard Sutton, a sidesman of St Andrew's Parish Church, Dent, and one of several Dales persons who stood as models for Heathcliff, was at the time still living in the Sedgwicks' parish. Many West Riding parishes, and Haworth not least among them, viewed with alarm the decline of Evangelical tradition, the rise of Puseyism, and the various followings found by the Catholic revival, Positivism, and the atomic theory of the universe, in mid century. Three currents converge at this point: the hostile Preface and its objects, motives and methods; the novel which it veiled and overshadowed for over a century; and the origins of *Shirley*.

Notes

1 For the likelihood that the sitter for the portrait was Lady Anne Clifford's daughter and not herself, see C. Heywood, 'Portraits of a Lady: Lady Anne Clifford and *Wuthering Heights*', *Quarto* (Kendal), 30 (1993), 10–14.

2 See Hugh Clifford, *The House of Clifford* (1987) p. 108 and throughout.

3 With thanks to the Curators of Appleby Castle, Appleby-in-West-morland.

4 George C. Williamson, *Lady Anne Clifford. Countess of Dorset, Pembroke & Montgomery 1590-1676* (1922), p. 331.

5 *Craven*, p. 277, and pp. 224-35, 277-82.

6 *Craven*, p. 290.

7 *Craven*, p. 271.

8 Hugh Clifford, *The House of Clifford* (Chichester: Phillamore, 1987), pp. 81 and following.

9 Kim Lyon, 'Whernside Manor', *Dalesman Annual 1979* (1979), pp. 76-82.

10 Kim Lyon, *The Dentdale Brontë Trail* (Dent: privately published, 1985).
11 C. Heywood, 'Yorkshire Slavery'.
12 William Howitt, *The Rural Life of England*, 2 vols. (1838), vol. 1, pp. 316-20.
13 CRO/K: Dent Church Register, burial of Nelly Middleton, aged 76, 24 October 1830; and personal information.
14 Personal information, with thanks to Bert and Margaret Sutton.
15 CRO/K: Dent Church Register, burials 1803; LRO: WRW/Sill 1803, will of John Sill.
16 CRO/K: Dent Church Register, baptisms 1766, Ann Sill.
17 WYA/W: CO.428.602; FK.592.730; AY.300.405; BA.640.861; BE.163.196; BQ.464.622; DT.726.925
18 C. Heywood, 'Yorkshire Slavery'.
19 Isabella Banks, MS letter, 20 April 1895, John Rylands Eng. MS 1202.30. Also, William Andrews, *North Country Poets* (1888), pp. 1-7, 48-56, on Isabella Banks and her husband, George Linnaeus Banks.
20 Isabella Banks, MS letter of 20 April 1893, John Rylands Eng. MS 1202.15. Also: Robert Lee Wolff, *Nineteenth Century Fiction*, 2 vols. (1981), vol. 1, pp. 48-50, where *Wooers and Winners* is omitted.
21 See Archibald Geikie, *The Founders of Geology* (1897), pp. 256-69 (on Adam Sedgwick); and William Thorp, *Map of the Yorkshire Coalfield*, (1840), West Yorkshire County Library, Wakefield; also, *Leeds Mercury*, 10 Oct. 1840, p. 7 (Yorkshire Geological and Polytechnic Society meeting, with Adam Sedgwick as guest speaker and Lord Fitzwilliam in the chair).
22 C. Heywood, 'Yorkshire Slavery in *Wuthering Heights*'.
23 LRO, WRW/DL, Sutton, 1851 (will of Richard Sutton); Dent census, 1841, 1851; WYA/W, MD.517.508, 'Sutton to Davis' (purchase of West House); CRO/K: Dent Parish Register, 1851 burials.
24 *Tatham v. Wright*, vol. 1, p. 121, cited in Emmeline Garnett, *John Marsden's Will* (1998), p. 61.
25 James T. Hammick, *The Marriage Law of England*, 2nd edn. (1887), p. 49.
26 See *John Marsden's Will* (1998), throughout; also *Tatham v. Wright*, 2 vols. (Lancaster, 1834), throughout.
27 Garnett, p. 28.
28 Garnett, pp. 21, 33.
29 Garnett, pp. 60-61.
30 See James Hafley, 'The Villain in *Wuthering Heights*', NCF 13 (1958), 199-215.
31 Garnett, p. 66.
32 Garnett, pp. 86-87, 100.
33 T.D. Whitaker, *An History of Richmondshire*, 2 vols. (1823), vol. 2, pp. 255-59; also, R. Balderston Cragg, *Legendary Rambles. Ingleton and Lonsdale* (undated: around 1900), pp. 86-96; and Ian Grimble, *The Harington Family* (1957), p. 57.

34 A murder is postulated by John Sutherland in his short essay, 'Is Heathcliff a Murderer', in his book *Is Heathcliff a Murderer?* (1996), pp. 53-58.
35 T. Wemyss Reid, Letter of 23 Nov. 1876 to Ellen Nussey (Leeds: Brotherton Collection, Nussey papers).
36 Elizabeth Gaskell, *The Life of Charlotte Brontë* (1985), p. 343.
37 Mary Butterfield, *The Heatons of Ponden Hall* (Privately printed: undated, around 1955), pp. 16-17 and throughout.
38 Emily Brontë, *Wuthering Heights*, ed. Ian Jack and Hilda Marsden (1976), pp. 414-15.
39 Winifred Gérin, *Emily Brontë* (1979), pp. 75-79.
40 London, Somerset House: National Register of Wills, Adam Sedgwick, 3 April 1873; John Birkbeck of Anley, Settle, as Executor.
41 WYA/W: RT.50: K&K Minutes, 1821-25.

Appendix D: Documents

1. Landscape

i. John Hutton, *Tour to the Caves* (1781)

[Hutton's *Tour* appeared as an Addendum to Thomas West, *A Guide to the Lakes in Cumberland, Westmorland, and Lancashire* (1781), which was among books available to the Brontës at Ponden House. At numerous points, Brontë borrowed and improved Hutton's phrases describing the region around Cowan Bridge. Hutton's text runs:]

A Tour to the Caves in the West-Riding of Yorkshire, *in a letter to a Friend*

> Of antres vast, and deserts idle,
> Rough quarries, rocks, and hills whose heads touch heav'n,
> It was my hint to speak.

Sir,

According to promise, I sit down to give you an account of our summer excursions.—After having made the tour of the lakes, we were induced to proceed from Kendal by Kirkby-Lonsdale, Ingleton, Chapel in the Dale, Horton, and Settle, in order to see the caves and other natural curiosities in Craven, in the West-Riding of Yorkshire. [...] The strong and nervous sensations require objects proper for their gratification, no less than the most nice and delicate tastes.—If elegant prospects and the refinements of art are suited to *these*, the rough, irregular, and stupendous works of nature, are no less adapted to the enjoyments of the former. Objects accommodated to the genius of a hardihood truly sublime, are only to be met with, in this island, among the wild and irregular mountains of the north, among the roaring cataracts that roll foaming down precipitate from those lofty summits, and the huge and dreary caverns or profound and yawning chasms they contain within their sides. It is here that Nature delights, as it were, to perform her magnificent works in secret, silently satisfied with self-approbation.

[Proceeding down Lunesdale and towards Leckbeck, which is crossed at Cowan Bridge...] During our excursion through the gardens and pleasure grounds adjoining [Overborough, between Cowan Bridge and

Tunstall], we were presented with views of a different sort to any we had hitherto enjoyed: sometimes we were embowered with woods and lofty trees—nothing of the adjacent country to be seen, save here and there the blue peak of Ingleborough, or some neighbouring mountain; till we crossed a broad vista, which suddenly exhibited a new and unexpected scene of the winding vale beneath. A stranger, in going from the hall to the gardens, must be struck with a surprise bordering on terror, on viewing the profound and gloomy glen by the side of his way. The trees which guard this steep bank prevent the eye from seeing the river Leck, which flows through a chasm amongst rocks at the bottom: imagination is left to conceive the cause of the deep and solemn murmurs beneath.

[…] The number of small carts laden with coals, and each dragged by one sorry horse, that we met, was surprising to a stranger. Many of the smaller farmers, betwixt Kirkby-Lonsdale and Kendal, earn their bread with carrying coals, during most part of the year, from the pits at Ingleton, Black-Burton, or properly Burton in Lonsdale, to Kendal and the neighbouring places, for fuel, and burning lime, in order to manure their land. These beds of coal, we were informed, are six or seven feet in thickness. A steam-engine was erected at Black-Burton, more commodiously to work their best collieries.

[Then through Thornton in Lonsdale to Ingleton, and up the glen to Thornton Force and beyond] […] This little river [the Twiss] is worthy the company of the curious tourist for about a mile along its course through a deep grotesque glen, fortified on each side by steep or impending high rocks. About a mile higher we came to the head of the river, which issues from one fountain called Keld's head, to all appearance more copious than St Winifred's Well, in Flintshire; though there is a broken, serpentine, irregular channel, extending to the top of the vale, down which a large stream is poured from the mountains in rainy weather. We now found ourselves in the midst of a small valley [Kingsdale], about three miles long, and somewhat more than half a mile broad, the most extraordinary of any we had yet seen. It was surrounded on all sides by high mountains, some of them the loftiest of any in England—Whernside to the south-east, and Gragareth to the north. There was no descent from this vale, except the deep chasm where we saw the cascade. It seemed opened in some distant age, either by the gradual effect of the washing of the river, or some violent and extraordinary flood bursting open the rugged barrier that pent it up. The vale above has all the appearance of having been once a lake, from the flatness of its surface, and its rich soil, like a sediment subsided on the bottom of a stagnant water. We were informed, that the subterranean cascade beneath, just now mentioned, has but lately made its appearance, and is every day more and more enlarging. We were quite secluded from the world, not an habitation for a man in view, but a lonely shepherd's house, with a little wood, and a few inclosures near it, called Breada-

Garth: it is on the north side of a high mountain, seldom visited by man, and never by the sun for near half a year. The shepherd, its solitary inhabitant, with longing eyes looks for returning verdure, when the sun begins to throw his benign rays on the solitary abode. No monk or anchoret could desire a more retired situation for his cell, to moralise on the vanity of the world, or disappointed lover to bewail the inconstancy of his nymph. The soil seemed the deepest and richest, in some parts of this vale, of any we had ever observed, and no doubt is capable of great improvement. We could not but lament, that instead of peopling the wilds and deserts of North America, our fellow-subjects had not peopled the fertile wastes of the north of England. [...]

While we were musing on the many bad effects of peopling distant countries, and neglecting our own, we arrived at the objects of this excursion, Yordas Cave: it is almost at the top of the vale, on the north-west side of it, under the high mountain Gragareth. We discovered it by some sheep-folds, at the mouth of a rugged gill or glen, in which we safely pent up our horses. In rainy seasons, we were told, a copious stream is poured down this gill, and a cascade falls over the very entrance into the cave, so as to prevent any further approach. We were, however, favoured by the weather, and met with no obstacle of that nature to stop our ingress, but boldly entered a large aperture to the left, into the side of the mountain, like the great door of some cathedral. Having never been in the cave before, a thousand ideas, which had been for many years dormant, were excited in my imagination on my entrance into this gloomy cavern. Several passages out of Ovid's Metamorphoses, Virgil, and other classics, crowded into my mind together. At one time I thought it like the den where Cadmus met the huge serpent. [...]

As we advanced within this *antre vast*, and the gloom and horror increased, the den of Cacus, and the cave of Poliphemus, came into my mind. I wanted nothing but a Sybil conductress with a golden rod, to imagine myself, like Eneas, going into the infernal regions. [...] While we were regaling ourselves with the provisions we had brought, we enquired of our guide, if he could furnish us with any curious anecdotes relative to this cave. After informing us that it had been alternately the habitation of giants and fairies, as the different mythology prevailed in the country, he mentioned two circumstances we paid some attention to.—About fifty or sixty years ago, a madman escaped from his friends at or near Ingleton, and lived here a week in the winter season, having had the precaution to take off a cheese, and some other provisions, to his subterranean hermitage. [...] Since that time, he told us, a poor woman, big with child, travelling alone up this inhospitable vale to that of Dent, was taken in labour, and found dead in this cave. [...]

[At Gingling Cave, further up Gragareth, they experience an earth tremor:]

[...] this cave is on the edge of that flat base of the mountain [...] Ingleborough appearing a little to the left, or north-east of Breada-Garth, which was almost opposite. [...] Two dogs that were with us, and a small horse brought up by one of the party, seemed violently agitated, and under fearful trepidations, under horrors resembling those we are told the animal creation are seized with preceding or during an earthquake. Though our reason convinced us of the impossibility of the ground falling in beneath us, we could not but feel many apprehensions, accompanied with sensations hitherto unknown. [...]

[Returning to Ingleton:]

Ingleton is a pretty village, pleasantly situated on a natural mount, yet at the bottom of a vale, near the conflux of two rivers, over which are thrown two handsome arches. If the streams are sometimes small, the huge stones and fragments of rocks which have rolled down the beds of these rivers, will serve to show that at other times they are remarkably full and impetuous. [...] The murmurs of the streams below sooth the ear, while the eye is selecting a variety of objects for its entertainment. On the back-ground are the lofty mountains of Gragareth, Whernside, and Ingleborough, the summits of which, when they are not enveloped in the clouds, can scarcely be seen for their high intervening bases. When the top of Ingleborough is covered with a thick white mist (or, as the country people say, when he puts on his night-cap) there are often strong gusts, called helm winds, blowing from thence to that part of the country which adjoins to its base. [...]

[Then up Chapel le Dale on the east side of Whernside, northwards from Ingleton:]

[...] the chapelry produces neither wheat, oats, barley, pease, nor any other sort of grain; nor apples, pears, plums, cherries, nor any kind of fruit—a ripe gooseberry was a natural curiosity in the summer season, in most parts of the district; even their potatoes they have from other places. [...] They abound with excellent hay ground and pastures, and were rich in large flocks, and herds of cattle, which enabled them to purchase every conveniency of life. Having little intercourse with the luxurious, vicious, and designing part of mankind, they were temperate, substantial, sincere, and hospitable. We found an intelligent, agreeable, and entertaining companion and guide, in the curate, who served them also as school-master. [...] [At Hurtlepot, another cave, Hutton reflects:] The descent of Eneas into the infernal regions came again fresh into my imagination [...] but alas! how fatal would be the consequence, if any adventurer should attempt to wade across the abyss on this *shadow* of a foundation! [...] On our return from the margin of this Avernian lake, we found the observation of the poet Virgil very applicable,— [...] 'The gates of hell are open night and day; / Smooth the descent, and easy is the way' (*Dryden*)

[On climbing Ingleborough:[1]]

The fineness and clearness of the day, however, induced us to ascend its side, and gain its summit. Though we had many a weary and slippery step, we thought ourselves amply repaid, when we got to the top, with the amusement we received in viewing the several extensive and diversified prospects, and in making our observation [...] All the country betwixt us and the sea, to the extent of forty, fifty, and sixty miles, from the north-west, by the west, to the south-west, lay stretched out beneath us, like a large map, with the roads, rivers, villages, towns, seats, hills and vales, capes and bays, in succession. Elevation is a great leveller; all the hills and little mountains in the country before us, appeared sunk in our eyes, and in the same plain with the adjacent meadows. To the north-west, the prospect was terminated, at the distance of forty or fifty miles, by a chain of rugged mountains in Westmorland, Lancashire, and Cumberland, which appeared as barriers against the fury of the ocean. To the west, the Irish Sea extends as far as the eye can penetrate [...]

2. Emancipation

i. John Woolman, *Journal* (1776)

[Brontë appears to have had access to the *Journal* and *Essays* of John Woolman, the Quaker from Philadelphia whose journey to London and York in 1772 sowed the seeds of the Emancipationist movement in England. The 1840 edition of his *Journal* and essays (1776) probably brought his thinking to the notice of the Taylors of Gomersal, and others of Emily Brontë's literary circle. Along the K&K he foreshadows *WH*: he dreams of being among angels in heaven, coughs blood, rejects luxury, searches for the moral rock beneath the social surface, and expresses concern over the corrupting influence of poverty and in his essay *Considerations on the Keeping of Negroes* he foreshadows Brontë's creation of a borderline character, between white and black.[2] Parts of the 1840 edition of the *Journal* run thus:]

I have felt great distress of mind, since I came on this island, on account of the members of our Society [of Friends] being mixed with the world in various sorts of business and traffick, carried on in impure channels. Great is the trade to *Africa* for slaves! And in loading these ships, abundance of people are employed in their factories; amongst whom are many of our Society. Friends [Quakers], in early times, refused on a religious principle, to make or trade in superfluities [luxury items]; of which we have many testimonies on record: but for want of faithfulness, some, whose examples were of note in our society, gave way; from which others took more liberty. Members of our Society worked in superfluities, and bought and sold them; and thus dimness of sight came over many: at length, Friends got into the use of some superfluities in dress, and in the furniture of their houses; which has spread from less to more, till superfluity of some kinds is common among us.

In this declining state, many look at the example of others and too much neglect the pure feeling of truth. Of late years, a deep exercise hath attended my mind, that friends may dig deep, may carefully cast forth the loose matter, and get down to the Rock, the sure foundation, and there hearken to that Divine voice which gives a clear and certain sound; and I have felt in that which doth not deceive, that if friends who have known the truth, keep in that tenderness of heart, where all views of outward gain are given up, and their trust is only in the Lord, he will graciously lead some to be patterns of deep self-denial in things relating to trade and handicraft labour: and others who have plenty of the treasures of this world, will be examples of a plain frugal life, and pay wages to such as they may hire, more liberally than is now customary in some places.

23rd of 8 mo. I was this day at Preston-Patrick [near Kendal], and had a comfortable meeting. I have several times been entertained at the houses of friends, who had sundry things about them which had the appearance of outward greatness; and as I have kept inward, way hath opened for conversation with such in private, in which divine goodness hath favoured us together, with heart-tendering times.

26th of 8 mo.—Being now […] in the county of Westmoreland, I feel a concern to commit to writing, that which to me hath been a case uncommon.

In a time of sickness with the pleurisy, a little upward of two years and a half ago, I was brought so near the gates of death that I forgot my name. Being then desirous to know who I was, I saw a mass of matter of a dull gloomy colour, between the south and the east; and was informed, that this mass was human beings in as great misery as they could be, and live; and that I was mixed with them, and that henceforth I might not consider myself as a distinct or separate being. In this state I remained several hours. I then heard a soft melodious voice, more pure and harmonious than any I had heard with my ears before; I believed it was the voice of an angel, who spake to the other angels: The words were —"John Woolman is dead." I soon remembered that I was once John Woolman; and being assured that I was alive in the body, I greatly wondered what that heavenly voice could mean. I believed beyond doubting it was the voice of an holy angel; but as yet, it was a mystery to me.

I was then carried in spirit to the mines, where poor oppressed people were digging rich treasures for those called Christians; and heard them blaspheme the name of Christ; at which I was grieved; for his name to me was precious.

Then I was informed, that these heathens were told, that those who oppressed them were the followers of Christ; and they said amongst themselves, "if Christ directed them to use us in this sort, then Christ is a cruel tyrant."

All this time the song of the angel remained a mystery; and in the morning, my dear wife and some others coming to my bedside, I asked them if they knew who I was: and they telling me that I was John Woolman, thought I was light-headed: for I told them not what the angel said, nor was I disposed to talk much to any one; but was very desirous to get so deep, that I might understand this mystery.

My tongue was often so dry, that I could not speak till I had moved it about and gathered some moisture, and as I lay still for a time, at length I felt Divine power prepare my mouth that I could speak; and then I said, "I am crucified with Christ, nevertheless I live; yet not I, but Christ that liveth in me. And the life I now live in the flesh, I live by faith in the Son of God, who loved me, and gave himself for me." Then the mystery was opened, and I perceived there was joy in heaven over a sinner who had repented; and that the language "John Woolman is dead" meant no more than the death of my own will.

Soon after I coughed, and raised much bloody matter, which I had not done during this vision. My natural understanding returned as before—Here I saw, that people's getting silver vessels to set of their tables at entertainments, was often stained with worldly glory; and that in the present state of things, I should take heed how I fed myself from out of silver vessels. Going to our monthly meeting soon after my recovery, I dined at a friend's house where drink was brought in silver vessels, not in any other. Wanting something to drink, I told him my case with weeping, and he ordered some drink for me in another vessel. I afterwards went through the same exercise in several friends' houses in America, as well as in England, and I have cause to acknowledge with humble reverence, the loving kindness of my heavenly Father, who hath preserved me in such a tender frame of mind, that none, I believe, have ever been offended at what I have said on that subject.

After this sickness, I spake not in public meetings for worship for near one year; but my mind was very often in company with the oppressed slaves, as I sat in meetings and though, under this dispensation, I was shut up from speaking, yet the spring of the gospel ministry was, many times, livingly opened in me; and the Divine gift operated by abundance of weeping, in feeling the oppression of the people. It being so long since I passed through this dispensation, and the matter remaining fresh and livingly in my mind, I believe it safest for me to commit it to writing. [...] (pp. 162-65).

[In the same edition (pp. 180-83), the *Testimony of Friends in Yorkshire at their quarterly meeting held at York on 24th and 25 of March 1773* includes the following:]

[...] He was deeply concerned on account of that inhuman and iniquitous practice of making slaves of the people of Africa, or holding them in that state; and, on that account, we understand he had not only written some books, but travelled much on the continent of America in order to make the negro-masters (especially those in profession with us) sensible of the evil of such a practice; and though in this journey to England, he was far removed from the outward sight of their sufferings, yet his deep exercise of mind, and frequent concern to open the miserable state of this deeply injured people, remained; as appears by a short treatise he wrote in this journey. His testimony in the last meeting he attended was on this subject, wherein he remarked, that as we, as a society, when under outward sufferings, had often found it our concern to lay them before those in authority, and thereby, in the Lord's time, had obtained relief, so he recommended this oppressed part of the creation to our notice; that we may, as way may open, represent their sufferings in an individual, if not in a society capacity to those in authority (p. 182).

ii. John Woolman, *Some Considerations on the Keeping of Negroes* (1754)

[In the two-part essay *Some Considerations on the Keeping of Negroes. Recommended to the Professors of Christianity of every Denomination* (first printed in Philadelphia in 1754 and 1762) (1840 edn., pp. 191-239), Woolman foreshadowed *WH*, and the arguments in William Wilberforce's *A Practical View of [...] Real Christianity* (1797) (*H*) at several points. Parts of the essay run thus:]

Placing on men the ignominious title SLAVE, dressing them in uncomely garments, keeping them to servile and dirty labour, tends gradually to fix a notion in the mind, that they are a sort of people below us by nature. If a person who in our esteem is mean and contemptible, should use language or behaviour towards us which is unseemly or disrespectful, it excites wrath more powerfully than the like conduct in one, whom we account our equal or superior; and when this happens to be the case, it disqualifies for candid judgment; for it is unfit for a person to sit as judge in a case in which his own personal resentments are stirred up. [...] The English government hath been commended by candid foreigners for the disuse of racks and tortures, so much practised in some states; but this multiplying of slaves now leads to it; for when people exact hard labour of others, without a suitable reward, and are resolved to continue in that way, severity to such as oppose them becomes the consequence; and several negro criminals, among the English in America, have been executed in a lingering, painful way, very terrifying to others.

[...] Through the force of long custom, it appears needful to speak in relation to colour. Suppose a white child, born of parents of the meanest sort, who died and left him an infant, should fall into the hands of a person who should endeavour to keep him a slave; some men would account the man unjust in doing so, who themselves appear easy [unconcerned] while many black people of honest lives and good abilities, are enslaved in a more shocking manner than the case here supposed. This is owing chiefly to the idea of slavery being connected with the black colour, and liberty with the white; and when false ideas are insinuated into our minds, it is with difficulty they get fairly disentangled.

[...] How is it that men, who believe in a righteous omnipotent Being, to whom all nations stand equally related, and are equally accountable, remain so easy about enslaving their fellow creatures? Is it not that the idea of a negro and slave is so interwoven in the mind, that they do not discuss this matter with that candour and freedom of thought which the case justly calls for? To come at a right feeling of their condition, requires humble, serious thinking; for in their present situation, they have but little to engage our natural affection in their favour. Had we a son or a daughter involved in a case similar to what many of them are, it would alarm us, and make us feel their condition without seeking for it. [...]

The blacks seem far from being our kinsfolks; and did we find an agreeable disposition and sound understanding in some of them which appeared as a good foundation for a true friendship between us, the disgrace arising from an open friendship with a person of so vile a stock, in the common esteem, would naturally tend to hinder it. They have neither honours, riches, outward magnificence, nor power; their dress being coarse, and often ragged; their employment drudgery, and much in the dirt [earth], they have little or nothing at command, but must wait upon the work of others, to obtain the necessaries of life; so that in their present situation, there is not much to engage the friendship or move the affection of selfish men; but it is a thing familiar to such as live in the spirit of true charity, to sympathize with the afflicted in the lowest stations of life (pp. 223-29).

3. Slavery

i. 'The Sorrows of Yamba'

[This 18th-century Emancipationist classic was republished in the Keighley magazine for children, *The Monthly Teacher* (March, 1830, pp. 32-36), edited by Theodore Dury:]

THE SORROWS OF YAMBA

In St Lucia's distant isle,
  Still with Afric's love I burn;
Parted many a thousand mile,
  Never, never to return.

Come, kind death! and give me rest;
  Yamba has no friend but thee;
Thou canst ease my throbbing breast;
  Thou canst set the Prisoner free.

Down my cheeks the tears are dripping,
  Broken is my heart with grief;
Mangled my poor flesh with whipping,
  Come, kind death! and bring relief.

Born on Afric's golden coast,
  Once I was as blest as you;
Parents tender I could boast,
  Husband dear, and children too.

With a baby at my breast
  (Other two were sleeping by)
In my hut I sat at rest,
  With no thought of danger nigh.

From the bush at even-tide,
  Rush'd the fierce man-stealing crew;
Seiz'd the children by my side,
  Seiz'd the wretched Yamba too.

Then for love of filthy gold,
  Strait they bore me to the sea,
Cramm'd me down a Slave ship's hold,
  Where were hundreds stow'd like me,

Naked on the platform lying,
  Now we cross the tumbling wave;
Shrieking, sick'ning, fainting, dying;
  Deed of shame for Britons brave!

At the savage Captain's beck,
  Now, like brutes, they make us prance;
Smack the whip about the deck,
  And in scorn they bid us dance.

Nauseous horse-beans they bring nigh,
  Sick and sad we cannot eat,
Whip must cure the sulks, they cry,
  Down their throats we'll force the meat.

I, in groaning, pass'd the night,
  And did roll my aching head;
At the break of morning light,
  My poor child was cold and dead,

Happy, happy, there she lies;
  Thou shalt feel the lash no more;
Thus full many a Negro dies,
  Ere they reach the destin'd shore.

Thee, sweet infant, none shall sell;
  Thou hast gain'd a wat'ry grave;
Clean escap'd the tyrants fell,
  While thy mother lives a slave.

Driven like cattle to a fair,
  See, they sell us, young and old;
Child from mother too they tear,
  All for love of filthy gold.

I was sold to Massa hard,
  Some have massas kind and good:
And again my back was scarr'd,
  Bad and stinted was my food.

Poor and wounded, faint and sick,
  All expos'd to burning sky,
Massa bids me grass to pick,
  And I now am near to die.

What, and if to death he send me,
  Savage murder tho' it be,
British laws shall ne'er befriend me,
  They protect not slaves like me.

Mourning thus my wretched state
  (Ne'er may I forget the day)
Once in dusk of evening late,
  Far from home I dar'd to stray.

Dar'd alas! with impious haste,
   Tow'rds the roaring sea to fly;
Death itself I long'd to taste,
   Long'd to cast me in and die.

There I met upon the strand,
   English Missionary good;
He had the Bible-book in hand,
   Which poor me no understood.

Led by pity from afar,
   He had left his native ground;
Thus, if some inflict a scar,
   Others fly to cure the wound.

Strait he pull'd me from the shore,
   Bid me no self-murder do;
Talk'd of state when life is o'er,
   All from Bible good and true.

Then he led me to his cot,
   Sooth'd and pity'd all my woe;
Told me 'twas the Christian's lot
   Much to suffer here below.

Told me then of God's dear Son,
   (Strange and wond'rous is the story)
What sad wrong to him was done,
   Tho' he was the Lord of Glory.

Told me, too, like one who knew him,
   (Can such love as this be true?)
How he died for them that slew him,
   Died for wretched Yamba too.

Freely he his mercy proffer'd,
   And to Sinners he was sent;
E'en to Massa pardon's offered:
   O, if Massa would repent!

Wicked deed full many a time,
   Sinful Yamba too hath done;
But she wails to God her crime,
   But she trusts his only Son.

O, ye slaves whom Massas beat,
  Ye are stain'd with guilt within;
As ye hope for Mercy sweet,
  So forgive your Massa's sin.

And with grief when sinking low,
  Mark the road that Yamba trod;
Think how all her pain and woe
  Brought the Captive home to God.

Now let Yamba, too, adore
  Gracious Heaven's mysterious plan;
Now I'll count my mercies o'er,
  Flowing through the guilt of man.

Now I'll bless my cruel capture,
  (Hence I've known a Saviour's name)
Till my grief is turn'd to rapture,
  And I half forget the blame.

But tho' here a convert rare,
  Thanks her God for Grace divine;
Let not man the glory share,
  Sinner, still the guilt is thine.

Here an injur'd Slave forgives,
  There a host for vengeance cry;
Here a single Yamba lives,
  There a thousand droop and die.

Duly now baptiz'd am I,
  By good Missionary man;
Lord, my nature purify,
  As no outward water can!

All my former thoughts abhorr'd
  Teach me now to pray and praise;
Joy and glory in my Lord,
  Trust and serve him all my days.

But tho' death this hour may find me,
  Still with Afric's love I burn;
(There I've left a spouse behind me)
  Still to native land I turn.

And when Yamba sinks in death,
  This my latest prayer shall be,
While I yield my parting breath,
  O, that Afric might be free.

Cease, ye British sons of murder!
  Cease from forging Afric's chain,
Mock your Saviour's name no further,
  Cease your savage lust of gain.

Ye that boast '*Ye rule the waves*,'
  Bid no Slave-ship soil the sea;[3]
Ye, that '*never will be slaves*',
  Bid poor Afric's land be free.

Where ye gave to war its birth,
  Where our traders fix'd their den,
There go publish '*Peace on Earth*,'
  Go, proclaim, '*good-will to men*.'

Where you once have carried slaughter,
  Vice, and slavery, and sin;
Seiz'd on Husband, Wife, and Daughter,
  Let the Gospel enter in.

Thus, to Yamba's native home,
  Where her hut of rushes stood;
Oh, if there should chance to roam,
  Missionary kind and good;

Then in Afric's distant land,
  He might meet the man I love;
Join him to the Christian band,
  Guide his soul to realms above.

There no fiend again shall sever
  Those whom God hath join'd and blest;
There they dwell with him for ever,
  There '*the weary are at rest*.'[4]

ii. Robert Brougham (1778–1868): '*On the Immediate Emancipation of Negro Apprentices*'

[This speech to the House of Lords on 20 February 1838 was reported in the *Leeds Intelligencer* and the *Leeds Mercury*, two newspapers which were read by the Brontës. It was flanked by Brougham's essays on slavery and Emancipation in *The Edinburgh Review* (K). In *WH* Brontë bridged the gulf between slave and slaveholder by portraying Heathcliff first as slave and then as slave-driver. The suffering and tyranny he endured and imposed are equal and opposite. Embattled in a political arena with power held by whites, Brougham emphasized the legal inequalities, and argued from a virtually unbridgeable gulf between whites and blacks. After graphic details on the legalised horrors of the past, and reference to the efficacy of the reform which removed them, Brougham proceeded:]

[…] I have demonstrated […] that a more quiet, peaceful, inoffensive, innocent race, is not to be found on the face of this earth than the Africans—not while dwelling in their own happy country, and enjoying freedom in their natural state […]—but after they have been torn away from it, enslaved, and their nature perverted in your Christian land—barbarized by the policy of civilized states—their whole character disfigured, if it were possible to disfigure it—all their feelings corrupted if you could have corrupted them. Every effort has been made to spoil the poor African—every resource of wicked ingenuity exhausted to deprave his nature—all the incentives to misconduct placed around him by the fiend-like artifice of Christian civilized men—and his excellent nature has triumphed over all your arts—its unnatural culture has failed to make it bear the poisonous fruit that might well have been expected from such abominable husbandry. Though enslaved and tormented, degraded and debased, as far as human industry could effect its purpose of making him blood-thirsty and savage, his gentle spirit has prevailed, and preserved, in spite of all your prophecies, aye, and of all your efforts, unbroken tranquillity over the whole Caribbean sea! Have I not then proved my case? I show you that the whole grounds of the arrangement of 1833, the very pretext for withholding complete emancipation, alleged incapacity and risk of insurrection, utterly fail. […]

[…] Once more I call upon your lordships to look at Antigua and Bermuda. There is no getting over that; no answering it; no repelling the force with which our reason is assailed by the example of thirty thousand negroes liberated in one night—liberated without a single instance of disturbance ensuing, and with the immediate substitution of voluntary work for hire in the stead of compulsory labour under the whip. There is no getting over that—no answering it—no repelling the force with which it assails the ordinary reason of ordinary men. But it is said that those islands differ from Jamaica and Barbadoes, because they contain no tract of waste or woody ground to which negroes may flee away from their masters, conceal themselves, and subsist in a Maroon state. I meet the objection at once in front, and I pledge myself to annihilate it in one minute by the clock. Why should free negroes run away and seek refuge in the woods, if slaves, or half slaves like apprentices, never think of escaping? That the slave should run away, that the apprentice should fly, is intelligible; but if they do not, why should a bettering of their condition increase their inclination to fly? They who do not flee from bondage and the lash; why should they from freedom, wages, independence, and comfort? But that is not all. If you dread their escape and marooning now, what the better will you be in 1840? Why are they to be less disposed then than now to fly from you? Is there any thing in the training of the present system to make two years more of it disarm all dislike of white severity, all inclination for the state of the Maroon? The minute is not yet out, and I think I have disposed of the objection. Surely, surely, we are here upon ground often trodden before by the advocates of human improvement, the friends of extended rights. This is the kind of topic we have so often been fated to meet on other questions of deep and exciting interest. The argument is like that against the repeal of the Penal Law respecting Catholics; if it proves any thing, it proves far too much; if there be any substance in it, the conclusion is that we have gone too far already, and must retrace our steps; either complete the emancipation of the Catholics, or re-enact the penal code. The enemies of freedom, be it civil or religious, be it political or personal; are all of the same sect, and deal in the same kind of logic. [...] [...] [A]n immense benefit has been conferred by the cart-whip being utterly abolished. Even if the lash were ever so harshly or unsparingly or indiscriminately applied in execution of sentences pronounced by the magistrate, still the difference between using it in obedience to judicial command, and using it as the stimulus to labour is very great. The negro is no longer treated as a brute, because the motive to his exertions is no longer placed without himself in the driver's hand. This is, I admit, is a very considerable change for the better in his condition, and it is the only one upon which he has to congratulate himself since the Act of Emancipation was passed. In no one other respect whatever is his condition improved—in many it is very much worse.

[...] Let freedom then be once established, place the negroes on the same footing with other men, give them the uncontrolled power over their time and labour, and it will become the interest of the planter, as well as the rest of the community, to treat the negro well, for their comfort and happiness depend on his industry and good behaviour. The African, placed on the same footing with other men, becomes in reality our fellow-citizen,—to our feelings, as well as in his own nature, our equal, our brother. No difference of origin or of colour can now prevail to keep the two castes apart. The negro, master of his own labour, only induced to lend his assistance, if you make it his interest to help you, yet that aid being absolutely necessary to preserve your existence, becomes an essential portion of the community, nay, the very portion upon which the whole must lean for support. This ensures him all his rights; this makes it not only no longer possible to keep him in thraldom, but places him in a complete and intimate union with the whole mass of Colonial society. Where the driver and the gaoler once bore sway, the lash resounds no more; nor does the clank of the chain any more fall upon the troubled ear; the fetter has ceased to gall the vexed limb, and the very mark disappears, which for a while it had left. All races and colours run together the same glorious race of improvement. Peace unbroken, harmony uninterrupted, calm unruffled, reigns in mansion and in field—in the busy street and the fertile valley, where nature, with the lavish hand she extends under the tropical sun, pour forth all her bounty profusely, because received in the lap of cheerful industry, not extorted by hands cramped with bonds. [...][5]

4. Blacks in England

i. *Sambo's Tomb*

[The essay 'Samboo's Tomb' in *The Lonsdale Magazine* (vol. 3, 1822, 188–192), signed 'J.T.', Kendal, invokes the monument to a slave who had been found dead shortly after arrival at Sunderland Point, across the Lune estuary, Lancaster, in 1836. The monument was created in 1796, consecrating the ground in which the black man, following custom of the time, had been buried unconsecrated. Heathcliff's burial at the edge of the churchyard in *WH* refers obliquely to that custom and the erroneous belief which buttressed it. Against the grain of the piety professed in the article and the elegy, 'Samboo's Tomb' exposes the captain's negligence, his cruelty in separating Sambo from his family in the West Indies, Sambo's incarceration and difficulty in speaking English, and the practice of clandestine burial for blacks in unconsecrated ground. The introduction concludes:]

About the year 1736, Samboo, the subject of the following epitaph and elegy, arrived at Sunderland [Point] from the West Indies in the capacity of servant to the captain of the ship. After she had discharged her cargo, he was placed at the inn now kept by James Birkett, with the intention of remaining there upon board wages till the vessel was ready to sail; but supposing himself to be deserted by his master, without being able, probably from his ignorance of the language, to ascertain the cause, he fell into a complete state of stupefaction, even to such a degree that he secreted himself in the loft of the brewhouse and stretching himself out at full length on the bare boards, refused all kinds of sustenance. He continued in this state only a few days, when death terminated the sufferings of poor Samboo. As soon as Samboo's exit was known to the sailors who happened to be there, they excavated him a grave in a lonely dell in a rabbit warren behind the village, within twenty yards of the sea shore, whether they conveyed his remains without either coffin or bier, being covered only with the clothes in which he died. [...] the Rev James Watson, formerly master of the grammar school of Lancaster and chaplain to Lancaster Castle, [...] walked frequently about sunset in the warren before mentioned; and being shown the site of Samboo's grave by old George Jackson, who then kept the inn, and who also acquainted him with every circumstance relative to his death and interment, he was induced to write the elegy alluded to; and in the course of the summer he collected of the visitors to Sunderland at the rate of one shilling per head, so much as enabled him to erect a monument to the memory of Samboo. [...]

[The elegy follows, written in the style of Gray's 'Elegy written in a Country Churchyard'. The concluding Epitaph runs:]

> "Full sixty years the angry winter wave
>   Has thundering, dash'd this bleak and barren shore,
> Since Samboo's head, laid in this lonely grave,
>   Lies still and ne'er will hear their turmoil more.
>
> "Full many a sand bird chirps upon the sod,
>   And many a moon-light Elfin round him trips;
> Full many a Summer's sunbeam warms the clod,
>   and many a teeming cloud upon him drips.
>
> "But still he sleeps,—till the awak'ning sounds
>   Of the Archangel's Trump new life impart;
> Then the Great Judge his approbation founds,
>   Not on Man's colour but his worth of heart."

5. Slavery in Yorkshire

i. *The Leeds Mercury*, 1831

[In a leading article, 'Slavery in Yorkshire' (19 March 1831), the *Leeds Mercury* summarised a communication from Richard Oastler, manager of an estate near Huddersfield, on the plight of factory workers in the new industrial economy. The article runs:]

We have received a letter, under this head, from Mr. Richard Oastler, on the subject of Mr. Hobhouse's Bill, and of the resolutions of the Halifax Worsted Spinners [...]. The letter is of such unmerciful length that it is impossible for us to insert it in full; and it is at the same time written with such extreme violence of language, that on that account alone we should decline to publish the greater part of it. Mr Oastler is, we doubt not, actuated by the most humane motives, but his humanity seems to be connected with infirmity, and to transport him beyond the bounds of reason and justice. He applies to the worsted spinners [woollen factory owners] every epithet in the language connected with the bottomless pit—"fiendish," "diabolical," "infernal," "hellish," &c., besides the milder and more soothing appellatives of "tyrants," "monsters," "freebooters," &c. &c. Really this brimstone rhetoric is not to be endured. We are confident that he would attain his own ends much more effectually by temperate statements and by appeals which would move the heart without outraging the judgment. We present several extracts from Mr. Oastler's letter:—

'TO THE EDITOR OF THE LEEDS MERCURY.

GENTLEMEN,—I had hoped, after the long controversy which has already taken place on this subject, it would have been unnecessary that I should have troubled you with any more remarks. It appears, however, that after all that has been said, *Avarice and Self-Interest* (having yet to learn that the "treasures of wickedness profit nothing," and that "whoso mocketh the poor reproacheth his Maker;" and "whoso stoppeth his ear at *their cry*, he shall also cry himself and not be heard), are determined to perpetuate that hateful system of cruelty which every humane mind anticipated was about to receive its death-blow.—A bill has been brought into Parliament by Mr. Hobhouse, supported by Lord Morpeth, to curtail the hours of labour in all mills, and to limit the ages of children employed therein.

This bill, with one of two alterations, must have the sanction of every friend of humanity; but a certain portion of the Mill-owners, who are determined not to be "frightened out of their propriety," (as Mr Crossley has it) are about to use all their powers to prevent this truly charitable and humane measure taking effect. May the Almighty strengthen the hands of the Honourable Mover and Noble Seconder of this bill, and if needful, may he put it into the hearts of the people to support them out of the house, by numerous petitions, so that the evil designs of its opposers may be triumphantly frustrated. Surely Britons, who hate oppression and love their children, will not be backward to support a measure in favour of those who have too long been exposed to all the horrors which cruelty and avarice could inflict, *and who have not the power even to petition Parliament that they may be free.* Will not every minister of religion, every patriot, feel it to be his duty to support a measure which has mercy and liberty for its object?—Mercy and liberty to those the least deserving of oppression—and most justly claiming the highest place to our affection and regard, *Mercy towards our Children!*'

Mr. Oastler then gives a commentary on each of the long series of resolutions passed by the Worsted-Spinners of Halifax and the neighbourhood, and advertised in our last. We select a passage which contains two important attestations from medical men of the injurious effects of over-working young children, together with a little of Mr. O.'s mild seasoning:

'Resolution 5 is certainly the "ne plus ultra" of falsehood and impertinence. Falsehood it must be—no human being can, or even did, believe that infants just turned seven years of age "are *more* capable of undergoing long-continued labour" than adults just arriving at the age of twenty-one years! But what unblushing effrontery must the men possess who absolutely publish this and append to it the following remark: "For confirmation of this opinion we would appeal to all the medical men of the district!" Is it possible?

Well, I have conversed with many very highly respectable men in the medical profession, who have given a decidedly contrary opinion as far as I have been able to gather; they all agree with Mr. C. Turner Thackrah, who in treating on this subject in his excellent work on the Effects of Trades, &c. on Health and Longevity, says at page 45, "The employment of young children in *any* labour is wrong. The term of physical growth ought not to be a term of physical exertion. Light and varied motions should be the only effort; motions excited by the will, not by the task-master,—the run and the leap of a buoyant and *unshackled* spirit. How different the scene in a manufacturing district! No man of humanity can reflect without distress on the state of thousands of children, many from six to seven years of age, roused from their beds at an early hour, hurried to the mills, and kept there, with the interval of only forty minutes, till a late hour at night; kept moreover in an atmosphere impure, not only as the air of a town, not only as defective in ventilation, but as loaded also with noxious dust. Health! cleanliness! mental improvement! How are they regarded? Recreation is out of the question—there is scarcely time for meals. The very period of sleep, so necessary for the young, is too often abridged. Nay, children are sometimes worked even in the night." Now here you have the recorded opinion of one medical man, and I sincerely thank him for having written so fully on this subject, and recommend every spinner and every legislator, before they oppose this bill, to read this book. On the same page Mr. Thackrah gives the following extract from the Report of the Manchester Board of Health, 1805:—"We have still to lament the untimely and protracted Labour of the Children employed in some of the Mills, which tends to diminish future expectations, as to the general sum of lives and industry, by impairing the strength, and destroying the vital stamina of the rising generation; at the same time in too many instances it gives encouragement to idleness, extravagance, and profligacy in the parents, who, *preventing the order of nature, subsist on the oppression of their offspring.*" It was to remove this evil in Cotton mills that an act of parliament was passed to shorten the hours, &c. Let me seriously request every man who attended this Halifax meeting to read these two extracts at least three times a day for three days together, and then ask himself if, as a Christian, a Briton, a Father, he can any longer dare to frustrate any attempt to put down such an accursed evil?'

Mr Oastler sums up the principles, which he says are contained in the resolutions of the Halifax Worsted Spinners, as follows:—

'1st. God's laws must bend and break at the call of avarice and self-interest!

2d. Money is of more value than principle, morality, and religion!

3d. Government is no longer of any use, because it is unable to protect the innocent and weak against the rapacity of the guilty and strong!

4th. The state of the trade of this country is really such, that its very existence depends upon excessive and over-working on the part of the operatives!

5th. It is better that the labouring classes should live by the excessive and overpowering toil of their infants, than that the parents should labour for the support of their offspring!

6th. The exorbitant taxes which we are obliged to pay, the loss we sustain by the East India monopoly, the corn-bill, and every other abuse, as a matter of clear right and justice must and ought to be paid and borne out of the blood, bones, and sinews of our infantile population!'

The letter concludes as follows:—

'Such must have been the dreadful synopsis of the individuals who formed these notable resolutions. Unhappy those who "heartily concur" in such a system.—Fortunate mishap—that some of them were already "committed and pledged" on the side of mercy and truth! I shall not for one moment mock your readers by attempting to destroy the argument founded on such diabolical principles. If they are true, all I ever yet have learnt is false. If they were proved to be true—they prove that death is better than life!!!

That this Bill will cause some temporary inconvenience no one will deny (even the parting with a sinecure is not a very "convenient" sensation—ere long, however, I fancy it will be tried; they will be obliged to put up with the "inconvenience" for the public good). But the good effects of the Bill will incalculably overbalance every inconvenience it may produce. The destruction of night working and long hours will increase the number of mills—employ more labourers—and prevent that destructive plan of compelling kind and feeling masters, in their own protection, to work long hours, because others who are covetous or in need pursue that plan. The Bill will, in fact, give both the capitalist and the labourer a fair chance, and prevent those excessive "gluts," which are, at intervals, found to be so destructive to the property of the former and the employment of the latter. It will be a triumph of principle over avarice—of mercy over cruelty—of the law of God over the powers of darkness. I am truly obliged by your kindness in giving insertion to my former letters on this subject, and hope you will excuse my troubling you with this. I am ready to meet any opponent on one condition—that he appears with a proper name—anonymous epistles I cannot notice.

I remain most respectfully, Gentlemen,
Your obliged servant,
RICHARD OASTLER'

6. Image of the rocks

i. Adam Sedgwick (1785-1873)

[In his Letters to Wordsworth, appended to the 1842 edition of Wordsworth's *Guide to the Lakes* (1810), Adam Sedgwick outlined the new geology in readily understood terms. His account of the northern rock formation anticipates Brontë's division of the Earnshaw family history into three main phases. She appears to have noticed that the gap he proposes between social history and geology can be bridged in a metaphor. Her story material is patterned partly on Adam Sedgwick's account of the earth's formation and partly on his work in Dent, where he officated as an ordained clergyman in his father's and brother's parish during the vacations. Sedgwick's igneous or volcanic phases, then termed 'plutonic', appear below as his phases III, IV, and VII, and X. These correspond approximately to the phases of disruption among the Earnshaws and the Lintons in the four parts of *WH*. Sedgwick explains:]

[...] Let me now endeavour, in imagination, to re-construct the great frame-work of the Cumbrian mountains:

I. Beds of mud and sand were deposited in an ancient sea apparently without the calcarious matter necessary to the life of shells and corals, and without any traces of organic forms.—These were the elements of the Skiddaw slate.

II. Plutonic rocks were then, for many ages, poured out among the aqueous sediments—beds were broken up and re-cemented—plutonic silt and other materials in the finest comminution were deposited along with the igneous rocks—the effects were again and again repeated, till a deep sea was filled with a formation many thousand feet in thickness.— These were the materials of the middle division of the Cumbrian slates..

III. A period of comparative repose followed. Beds of shells and bands of corals formed upon the more ancient rocks; they were interrupted by beds of sand and mud, and these processes were many times repeated; and thus, in a long succession of ages, were the deposits of the upper slates completed.

IV. Towards the end of the preceding period, mountain masses of plutonic rock were pushed through the older deposits—and after many revolutions, all the divisions of the slate series were elevated and contorted by movements not affecting the newer formations.

V. The conglomerates of the old red sandstone were then spread out, by the beating of an ancient surf, continued for many ages, upon the upheaved and broken edges of the slates.

VI. Again occurred a period of comparative repose; the coral reefs of the mountain limestone, and the whole carboniferous series, were formed; but not without many great oscillations between the levels of land and sea.

VII. An age of disruption and violence succeeded, marked by the discordant position of the rocks, and by the conglomerates under the new red sandstone. At the beginning of that time was formed the great north and south 'Craven fault,' which rent off the eastern calcarious mountains from the older slates; and soon afterwards, the great 'Pennine fault,' ranging from the foot of Stainmoor to the coast of Northumberland, and lifting up the terrace of Cross Fell above the plain of the Eden. Some of the north and south fissures (shown by the directions of the valleys leading into Morecambe Bay) may have been formed about the same time;—others must have taken place at later periods.

VIII. Afterwards ensued the more tranquil period of the new red sandstone; but here our records, on the skirts of the lake mountains, fail us, and we have to seek them in other countries.

IX. Thousands of ages rolled away during the secondary and tertiary epochs. Of those times we have no monuments in Cumberland. But the powers of nature are never in respose; her work never stands still. Many a fissure may in those days have started into an open chasm, and many a valley been scooped out upon the lines of 'fault.'

X. Close to the historic time, we have proofs of new disruption and violence, and of vast changes of level between land and sea. Ancient valleys may have been opened out anew, and fresh valleys formed by such great movements in the oceanic level. Whatever strain there may have been in the more solid parts of our island at this time, their greatest power must have been exerted upon ancient valleys, where the continuity of the beds was already broken. Cracks among the strata may, during this period, have passed into open fissures—vertical escarpments have been formed by unequal elevations on the sides of the lines of fault—and subsidences have given rise to many tarns and lakes. The face of nature may there have been greatly changed while the land was settling to its present level.

But let me not be misunderstood; this last period may have been of very long duration. I am only attempting to give an outline of a long series of physical facts, proved by physical evidence. I wish to pause before I reach the modern period; and do not profess to link geology to the traditions of the human race. By some rash and premature attempts of this kind, much harm has been already done to the cause of truth and Christian clarity. [...][6]

7. The Brontës in Ireland

i. Alice Brontë's interview

[The tale of 'Welsh' was narrated at a date which can be assigned to the early 1850s by the Revd David McKee, a teacher of Classics in County Down. His auditor and pupil, William Wright (1837-99), then a schoolboy aged about sixteen, who was preparing for the entrance examinations to Queen's College (now University), Belfast, later became Co-Ordinator of Translations for the Bible Society (British & Foreign Bible Society). In the early 1890s, at the zenith of his life's work, Wright wrote out from memory the tales about the Brontës which he had heard from David McKee, and published them in his book *The Brontës in Ireland* (1893). Referring to the tale of Welsh, the showpiece in his book, Wright claimed that he had found the historical originals of the Brontë sisters' novels. However, the tale of Welsh was recognised by Angus MacKay in his book *The Brontës. Fact and Fiction* (1897) as an oral borrowing from *WH*, and not its source. This insight is justified by the interview with Alice Brontë, Emily's aunt, with the Revd J.B. Lusk, who jotted down her words more or less verbatim. His text has survived. It supports the view, explained with fuller documentation elsewhere,[7] that the tale of Welsh was not part of the Brontë family history in Ireland, but was, rather, an oral improvisation, based on the probable presence at Emily's reading from her manuscript at Haworth, of her uncle, Hugh Brontë III. Her nickname 'The sphinx of literature'[8] resulted from the seeming intractability of this fragment of literary history.

Alice Brontë's words run thus:]

Miss Brontë

Her father from Drogheda. Stout, not very tall. Welsh and Hugh great
fighters. Neighbours drew them into quarrels.

Her father slave, followed making ditches. Hugh built all the house.

Patrick born in Emdale. The rest in Lisnacreevy. Alice born in Ballynaskeagh. One sister died [after] a day's sickness.

Father very fond of family. Mad about his "own childer". Wrought to
the last for them. Mother died after father. Counted very purty. Minister of Magnally said when they were going out [that they were the]
Prettiest couple [he had] ever married.

Father had but one girl.

Father sandy haired. Mother fair haired. At her best before her father died.

Patrick kept school at Glasker Hill. In Meeting House she thinks.
(Alice at a wee sod school house. School master has to get meat & lodgings in the houses.)

In very young days went to Drumballyroney Church. All christened &
all buried there.

Patrick taught school in old John Rogers time. Andy Harshaw taught in
Ballynafern. Jamie saw Charlotte said she was terrible sharp and inquisitive. 'That she was for nothing but ornamenting a parlour.' Charlotte
asked about the Knock Hill & Lough Neagh. (Patrick tallest. Hughy &
Welsh nearly the same height.)

Ann[e Brontë] the youngest wanted to come with Jamie. Jamie thought
it queer that she called Ireland home. Charlotte fainted in the theatre.
Terrible troubled with a sore head.

Alice lived in Ballynaskeagh till they were all dead & left her (marching
Lisnacreevy: only river between her house & Lisna).

Mother's maiden name Alice McClory born about Ballynaskeagh. An
uncle (of her father) took her father [Hugh II] when he was 8 years old
to make him his heir. But after he went his wife had a child then her
father [Hugh II] 'left' and never saw either them or his mother again.
His sister however came to see him. "Tarrible purty she was". Shop
keeper in Rathfriland courted her but she would not have him.

Miss Gregg from Lisburn (a gentlewoman) came to see Miss Alice Bronte & wanted to push on her nephew Nelus. "Wanted him for a man."

Brothers had great fight with the bully of Warrenpoint; Bab Wilson raised fight. Welsh took his part. Hughey away & when he came he vauntered any man (Barney Ker the bully. Mother's name Ker in Warrenpoint.)

Hughey very stout hearted. Rose up at 12 or 1 o'clock at night to haunted place. Took gun or sword in one hand & the Bible.[9]

The salient feature of Alice's history of her family is that it does not include the disputed tale of Welsh. Wright's embarrassment over the point emerges through his attempt to omit that main feature by blurring the value of her testimony in his book and in subsequent correspondence. Against the Yorkshire background of *WH*, the tale of Welsh emerges as a repository of fragments from Brontë's historical and legendary sources, her novel itself, and improvisations on the Brontë family's notion of their social status in Ireland. The resemblances between the tale of Welsh and *WH* are accounted for by admiration for his niece on the part of Emily Brontë's uncle, Hugh III, a humorous *raconteur* and occasional visitor to his brother's Parsonage at Haworth. He would have heard her reading from her manuscript, memorised the story and its historical background, and woven it into a fanciful rendering of his family's history, for the amusement of his clergy friends in County Down.

Notes

1   Hutton proposes: 'The word *Ingleborough* seemed to be derived from the Saxon word *ingle*, which signifies *a lighted fire*, and *borough*, or *burgh*, which comes originally from the Greek word *purgos*, and signifies *a watch tower*'; however, Smith, 6, p. 242, notes: 'The original form of the first element in Ingleton and Ingleborough [...] could be an Old English compound *ing-hyll* "peak hill".'

2   See *The Journal and Major Essays of John Woolman*, ed. Phillips P. Moulton (1971), throughout.

3   Dury adds a footnote: 'England has abolished the Slave Trade many years ago, and is attempting to induce other nations to do so likewise.' For Dury's Emancipationist editorial essays on slavery, see *The Monthly Teacher*: 'The Death of a Slave', 2 (1830), 37-9; 'Slavery', 2 (1830), 142-43; 'Ethiopia Stretching out her Hands to God', 4 (1832), 109-10.

4   *Job*, 3:17; also, Branwell Brontë, *And the Weary are at Rest* (MS, Berg Collection, New York Public Library; privately printed, 1924), a

fragment of a novel satirising the slaveholding economy in Yorkshire, and its support among the clergy.

5   'Speech on the Immediate Emancipation of the Negro Apprentices', *Speeches of Henry Lord Brougham*, 4 vols. (Edinburgh, 1838), vol. 2, pp. 184-224.

6   W. Wordsworth, *Guide to the Lakes* (1842), published as *A Complete Guide to the Lakes, comprising Minute Directions for the Tourist with Mr Wordsworth's Description of the Scenery of the Country, etc, and Five Letters on the Geology of the Lake District, by the Rev. Professor Sedgwick* (Kendal, 1853), pp. 214-15.

7   See C. Heywood, 'Hugh Brontë's Tale of Welsh: A Brontë Narrative', *Durham University Journal* (1995), 279-88; also, Angus MacKay, *The Brontës. Fact and Fiction* (1897), p. 137; Angus MacKay, 'A Crop of Brontë Myths', *Westminster Review*, 144 (1895), 120-60; Mildred G. Christian, 'The Brontës', in *Victorian Fiction. A Guide to Research*, ed. Lionel Stevenson (1964), pp. 214-44 (226-27); R.W. Crump, *Charlotte and Emily Brontë, 1846-1915. A Reference Guide* (1982), pp. 98, 111.

8   Clement Shorter, *Charlotte Brontë and her Circle* (1896), p. 158.

9   Lusk MSS (private collection): photographic copy of MS notes by Rev. J.B. Lusk; punctuation added.

Select Bibliography

Editions of Wuthering Heights

'Ellis Bell' [Emily Brontë] *Wuthering Heights.* London: T.C. Newby, 1847
Emily Brontë, *Wuthering Heights.* New Edition, with Preface and Bio-
graphical Notice of Ellis and Acton Bell, by Currer Bell [Charlotte
Brontë]. London: Smith, Elder, 1850
Emily Brontë, *Wuthering Heights.* Ed. Ian Jack and Hilda Marsden. Ox-
ford: Clarendon Press, 1971
Emily Brontë, *Wuthering Heights.* Ed. William M. Sale, Jr., and Richard J.
Dunn. New York & London: Norton, 1990
Emily Brontë, *Wuthering Heights.* Ed. Linda H. Peterson. Boston: Bedford
Books, 1992

Other works by Emily Brontë

Charlotte and Emily Brontë, *The Belgian Essays,* ed. Sue Lonoff, New
Haven & London: Yale University Press, 1996
The Poems of Emily Brontë, ed. Derek Roper and Edward Chitham, Ox-
ford: Clarendon Press, 1996

Anthologies of critical essays

Allott, Miriam, ed., *Emily Brontë. Wuthering Heights.* London: Macmillan
(Casebook), 1970
Allott, Miriam, ed., *The Brontës.* London: Routledge (Critical Heritage),
1974
McNees, Eleanor, ed., *The Brontë Sisters. Critical Assessments.* 4 vols.,
Robertsbridge: Helm Information (Emily Brontë, vol. 2), 1996
O'Neill, Judith, ed., *Critics on Charlotte and Emily Brontë.* London: Allen
& Unwin, 1968
Sale, William M., Jr. and Richard J. Dunn, eds., *Wuthering Heights.* New
York & London: Norton, 1990
Smith, Anne, ed., *The Art of Emily Brontë.* London: Vision Press, 1976
Stoneman, Patsy, ed., *Wuthering Heights. Contemporary Critical Essays.*
London: Macmillan (New Casebook), 1993
Vogler, Thomas A., ed., *Twentieth Century Interpretations of Wuthering
Heights.* Englewood Cliffs, NJ: Prentice-Hall, 1968

Winnifrith, Thomas John, ed., *Critical Essays on Emily Brontë*. New York: G.K. Hall/Prentice-Hall, 1997

Studies of Emily Brontë and Wuthering Heights

Berg, Maggie, *Wuthering Heights. The Writing in the Margin*. New York: Twayne, 1996

Chitham, Edward, and T. Winnifrith, *The Brontës. Facts and Problems*. London: Macmillan, 1973

Chitham, Edward, *A Life of Emily Brontë*. Oxford: Basil Blackwell, 1987

Chitham, Edward, *The Birth of Wuthering Heights. Emily Brontë at Work*. London: Macmillan, 1998

Crump, R.W., *Charlotte and Emily Brontë, 1846-1915. A Reference Guide*. Boston: G.K. Hall, 1982

Davies, Stevie, *Emily Brontë. The Artist as a Free Woman*. Manchester: Carcanet, 1983

Davies, Stevie, *Emily Brontë: Heretic*. London: The Women's Press, 1994 (reprint 1999)

Eagleton, Terry, *Myths of Power. A Marxist Study of the Brontës*. London: Macmillan, 1975

Ewbank, Inga-Stina, 'Emily Brontë: The Writer as Poet', in Inga-Stina Ewbank, *Their Proper Sphere*. Cambridge, MA: Harvard University Press, 1966 (pp. 86-155)

Figes, Eva, *Sex and Subterfuge. Women Writers to 1850*. London: Macmillan, 1982

Gérin, Winifred, *Emily Brontë*. Oxford: Oxford University Press, 1979

Harrison, G. Elsie, *The Clue to the Brontës*. London: Methuen, 1948

Hewish, John, *Emily Brontë*. London: Macmillan, 1969

Heywood, C., 'Yorkshire Slavery in *Wuthering Heights*', *Review of English Studies* 38 (1987), 184-97

Heywood, C., 'A Yorkshire Background for *Wuthering Heights*', *Modern Language Review* 88 (1993), 817-30

Heywood, C., 'Yorkshire Landscapes in *Wuthering Heights*', *EIC* 48 (1998), 13-34

Knoepflmacher, U.C., *Emily Brontë. Wuthering Heights*. Cambridge: Cambridge University Press, 1989

Moore, Virginia, *The Life and Eager Death of Emily Brontë. A Biography*. London: Rich and Cowan, 1936

Petyt, K.M., *Wuthering Heights and the Haworth Dialect*. Menston: Yorkshire Dialect Society, 1970

Pinion, F.B., 'Scott and *Wuthering Heights*', *BST* 21 (1996), 313-22

Sneidern, Maja-Lisa von, '*Wuthering Heights* and the Liverpool Slave Trade', *ELH* 62 (1995), 171-96

Stoneman, Patsy, *Brontë Transformations. The Cultural Dissemination of Jane Eyre and Wuthering Heights*. London: Prentice Hall/Harvester Wheatsheaf, 1996

Thompson, Patricia, *George Sand and the Victorians* (pp. 80-89, '*Wuthering Heights* and *Mauprat*') London: Macmillan, 1977

Van Ghent, Dorothy, *The English Novel. Form and Function*. New York: Rinehart, 1953

Visick, Mary, *The Genesis of Wuthering Heights*. Stroud: Ian Hodgkins, 3rd edition, 1980

Williams, Meg Harris, *A Strange Way of Killing*. Strathtay: Clunie Press, 1987

Yablon, G. Anthony, and John R. Turner, *A Brontë Bibliography*, (1978)

Northern Studies

Banks, Isabella (Mrs G. Linnaeus Banks), *Wooers and Winners*. 3 vols., 1880

Clifford, Hugh, *The House of Clifford*. Chichester: Phillimore, 1987

Clifford, D.J.H., *The Diaries of Lady Anne Clifford*. Stroud: Alan Sutton, 1990

Coleridge, Hartley, *The Worthies of Yorkshire and Lancashire*. London: Frederick Warne, 1836

Garnett, Emmeline, *John Marsden's Will. The Hornby Estate Case 1780-1840*. London: Hambledon, 1998

Howitt, Mary, *Hope On, Hope Ever!* (1840), republished with Introduction by David Boulton. Dent: Dales Historical Monographs, 1988

Howitt, William, *The Rural Life of England*. 2 vols., London: Longman, 1838

Hughes, E, *North Country Life in the Eighteenth Century*. 2 vols. (Cumberland and Westmorland, vol. 2), London: Oxford University Press, 1965

Jefferys, Thomas, *Map of the County of York*. (no place; no publisher), 1771

Ingle, George, *Yorkshire Cotton. The Yorkshire Cotton Industry, 1780-1835*. Preston: Carnegie Publishing, 1997

Lock, John, and W. T. Dixon, *A Man of Sorrow. The Life, Letters and Times of the Rev. Patrick Brontë*. London: Nelson, 1965 (reprint, Stroud: Ian Hodgkins, 1979)

Lyon, Kim, 'Whernside Manor', *Dalesman Annual 1979*. Clapham: Dalesman (1979), 76-82

Mallet, Paul Henri, *Northern Antiquities*, introd. by Thomas Percy. 2 vols. (1770)

Oastler, Richard, *Yorkshire Slavery. The 'Devil-to-do' Amongst the Dissenters in Huddersfield*. Leeds, 1835

Sedgwick, Adam, 'Letters to Wordsworth', in *A Complete Guide to the Lakes [...] with Mr Wordsworth's Description of the Scenery of the Country* (1842). London: Longman, 1853

Sedgwick, Adam, *Memorial of the Trustees of Cowgill Chapel* (1868), with *Supplement* (1870); republished with Introduction by David Boulton, Sedbergh: Hollett, 1984

Smith, A.H., *The Place-Names of Yorkshire*, Parts 1-8. (English Place-Name Society, vols 30-37). Cambridge: Cambridge University Press, 1961-63

Speight, H., *The Craven and North-West Yorkshire Highlands*. London: Elliot Stock, 1892

Story, Robert, *The Outlaw. A Drama in Five Acts.* London: Simpkin, Marshall, 1839

Victorian Bradford. Essays in Honour of Jack Reynolds, ed. D.G. Wright and J.A. Jowitt. Bradford: City of Bradford Libraries, 1982

Whitaker, T.D., *The History and Antiquities of the Deanery of Craven*. London: Nichols & Son, 1805

Whitaker, T.D., *An History of Richmondshire*. 2 vols., London: Longman, 1823

Williamson, George, *Lady Anne Clifford*. Kendal: Titus Wilson, 1922

Atlantic communities and literature

Anstey, Roger, and P.E.N. Hair, *Liverpool, the African Slave Trade, and Abolition.* Warrington: Historic Society of Lancashire and Cheshire, 1976

Banton, Michael, *White and Coloured. The Behaviour of British People Towards Coloured Immigrants*. New Brunswick, NJ: Rutgers University Press, 1960

Barker, J., *The Africa Link. British Attitudes to the Negro in the 17th and 18th Centuries*. London, 1978

Behn, Aphra, *The Royal Slave* (around 1688), edited by Ernest A. Baker. London: Routledge, 1913 (adapted for the stage as *Oroonoko*, 1695, by Thomas Southern; and others)

Bolt, Christine, *Victorian Attitudes to Race*. London: Routledge & Kegan Paul, 1971

Cadbury, Henry J., *John Woolman in England*. London: Friends Historical Society, 1971

Coleridge, Henry Nelson, *Six Months in the West Indies in 1825*. London: John Murray, 1826

Craton, M., James Walvin, and David Wright, eds., *Slavery, Abolition and Emancipation*. London: Longman, 1976

Dabydeen, David, ed., *The Black Presence in English Literature*. Manchester: Manchester University Press, 1985

Davis, Charles T., and Henry Louis Gates, Jr., *The Slave's Narrative*. Oxford: Oxford University Press, 1985

Davis, David Bryon, *The Problem of Slavery in Western Culture*. London: Penguin, 1970

Debrunner, M.W., *Presence and Prestige. Africans in Europe before 1918.* Basel: Basler Afrika Bibliographien, 1979

Equiano, Olaudah, *Equiano's Travels* (1789), selected and edited by Paul Edwards. London: Heinemann, 1967

Fanon, Frantz, *Black Skin, White Masks.* New York: Grove Press, 1967 (*Peau noire, masques blancs*, Paris: Seuil, 1952)

Fryer, Peter, *Staying Power. The History of Black People in Britain.* London: Pluto Press, 1984

Genovese, E., *Race & Slavery.* Princeton: Princeton University Press, 1979

Hanke, Lewis, *Aristotle and the American Indians: A Study in Race Prejudice in the Modern World.* London: Hollis and Carter, 1959

Honour, Hugh, *The Image of the Black in Western Art* (4 vols.), vol. 4, parts 1 & 2. Cambridge, MA, & London: Harvard University Press, 1989

Horn, Pamela, *The Rise and Fall of the Victorian Servant.* Dublin: Gill & Macmillan, 1975

Jones, Eldred, *Othello's Countrymen.* Oxford: Oxford University Press, 1964

Lewis, M.G., *Journal of a West India Proprietor Kept during a Residence among the Negroes in the West Indies* (1835), edited with an Introduction and Notes by Judith Terry. Oxford: Oxford University Press, 1999

Scobie, E., *Black Britannia. A History of Blacks in Britain.* Chicago: Johnson, 1972

Sheridan, Richard B., *Sugar and Slavery. An Economic History of the British West Indies 1623-1775.* Baltimore: Johns Hopkins University Press, 1974

Shyllon, Folarin, *Black People in Britain 1555-1833.* London: Oxford University Press, 1977

Soderlund, Jean R., *Quakers and Slavery. A Divided Spirit.* Princeton, NJ: Princeton University Press, 1988

Stephen, James, *England Enslaved by her Own Slave Colonies.* London: Hatchard, 1826

Vizram, Rozina, *Ayahs, Lascars and Princes. Indians in Britain 1700-1947.* London: Pluto Press, 1986

Walvin, James, *Black and White. The Negro in English Society 1551-1945.* London: Macmillan, 1973

Walvin, James, *England, Slaves and Freedom 1776-1838.* London: Macmillan, 1986

Woolman, John, *The Journal and Major Essays of John Woolman*, ed. Phillips P. Moulton. New York: Oxford University Press, 1971

General

Bursell, Rupert D.H., *Liturgy, Order and the Law.* Oxford: Oxford University Press, 1996

Butler, E.M., *The Fortunes of Faust.* Cambridge: Cambridge University Press, 1979

Goethe, J. Wolfgang von, *Faust. A Tragedy*, translated into English verse by J. Birch. London: Black and Armstrong, 1839

Jackson, Rosemary, *Fantasy: the Literature of Subversion*. London: Methuen, 1981

Kenyon, Howard N., *American Kenyons and English Connections*. Rutland, Vermont: Tuttle, 1935

Marlowe, Christopher, *Dr Faustus*, edited by David Bevington and Eric Rasmussen. 1993

[Naipaul, V.S.] 'A Symposium on V.S. Naipaul's *Guerrillas*', *Journal of Commonwealth Literature*, 14 (1979), 87-132

'Sand, George' [Aurore Dupin], *Indiana* (1832), trs. Sylvia Raphael. Oxford: Oxford University Press, 1974

Sherrard, R.H., *The White Slaves of England*. London: James Bowden, 1897

Wolfram, Sybil, *In-Laws and Outlaws*. London: Croom Helm, 1987

Wollstonecraft, Mary, *Vindication of the Rights of Woman* (1792), ed. with Introduction by Miriam Brody Krammick. London: Penguin, 1985

broadview literary texts

"This is a series in which the editing is something of an art form."
The Washington Post

"Broadview's format is inviting. Clearly printed on good paper, with distinctive photographs on the covers, the books provide the physical pleasure that is so often a component of enticing one to pick up a book in the first place .... And, by providing a broad context, the editors have done us a great service."
Eighteenth Century Fiction

"These editions [*Frankenstein, Hard Times, Heart of Darkness*] are top-notch – far better than anything else in the market today."
Craig Keating, Langara College

The Broadview Literary Texts series represents an important effort to see the ever-changing canon of English literature from new angles. The series brings together texts that have long been regarded as classics with lesser-known texts that offer a fresh light – and that in many cases may also claim to be of real importance in our literary tradition.

Each volume in the series presents that text together with a variety of documents from the period, enabling readers to get a fuller, richer sense of the world out of which it emerged. Samples of the science available for Mary Shelley to draw on in writing *Frankenstein*, stark reports from the Congo in the late nineteenth century that help to illuminate Conrad's *Heart of Darkness*; late eighteenth-century statements on the proper roles for women and men that help contextualize the feminist themes of the late eighteenth-century novels *Millenium Hall* and *Something New* – these are the sorts of fascinating background materials that round out each Broadview Literary Texts edition.

Each volume also includes a full introduction, chronology, bibliography, and explanatory notes. Newly typeset and produced on high-quality paper in an attractive Trade paperback format, Broadview Literary Texts are a delight to handle as well as to read.

The distinctive cover images for the series are also designed (like the duotone process itself) to combine two slightly different perspectives. Early photographs inevitably evoke a sense of pastness, yet the images for most volumes in the series involve a conscious use of anachronism. The covers are thus designed to draw attention to social and temporal context, while suggesting that the works themselves may also relate to periods other than that from which they emerged — including our own era.